i

Marching With Caesar-
Conquest of Gaul

R.W. Peake

For Bri

My Touchstone

Foreword

Like all such works, this is a labor of love, but I won't go into all the sacrifices I made during the four year odyssey to get this done. Nor will I talk about the fact that I bought the complete kit of a Roman Legionary and tromped around the wastelands of Big Bend National Park in order to get a feel for what it might have been like to be one of those men that Caesar used to change not just his world, but the world we live in today. (I will mention that I used Big Bend not as much for its rugged terrain but for its remoteness, and because the likelihood that one of the drug runners I might encounter was carrying a camera was very small. There are some things better left unseen.)

What I will say is that, again like all such works, this would not have been possible without the unwavering support of my family, consisting as it does of my mother and daughter, and although small in number, they are mighty in the power of their love. To them, particularly to my Mom, I owe a debt of gratitude that I can only hope this effort of mine goes a small way to pay. Also, I would like to thank Dr. Frank Holt of the University of Houston, for his unwitting role in introducing me to ancient Rome, and by expressing his passion for the subject he was teaching, imbuing in me a sense of curiosity that drove me to delve more deeply into that world myself. Finally, thanks to Dr. Janet Lucas of Peninsula College for her help with editing and encouragement at a time when it was really needed.

I have endeavored to make this work historically accurate, and to portray the lives of the men in this novel in as authentic a manner as possible. When I began my exploration of Ancient Rome, starting with the classics before going on to the excellent series by Colleen McCullough, I noticed something that bothered me a great deal. As I expanded my reading of the fiction genre covering Ancient Rome, what I discovered was that, while there were a number of authors who portrayed the lives of common Legionaries (Simon Scarrow's Macro and Cato series most notably), they all focus on the time period after the reforms of Augustus. However, all of the works of historical fiction that cover the Late Republic are all focused on the "movers and shakers" of the day, and not on the lives of the men in the ranks. This is not surprising, when one thinks about it, simply because of the amount of material detailing the lives of the people, particularly those men in the Legions, is so much more abundant when compared to the time period known as the Late Republic. But I think that this does a grave injustice to the memories of those men who marched with the original Caesar, particularly because his actions, and by extension theirs as well, had the most impact on what Rome would become than any other figure from Roman history. Without Caesar, there is no Octavian, and there are no Caesars.

That is the motivation behind this work. One day, as I was reading about Caesar, the thought struck me; what was it like for his men? What was it like to be standing in the ranks, facing the Gauls of Vercingetorix, or looking over your shield on the dusty plains of Pharsalus? What were their lives like when they weren't fighting? What did they talk about as they sat around the fire at night? It was from this idea that Marching With Caesar was born. But what was more important to me than the story itself was the accuracy of the research behind it. This is probably due to my training as a History major and the rigorous belief in the use of primary sources drilled into me by my professors. Of course, there is a dearth of sources when it comes to documenting the everyday life of a Roman Legionary in the 10th Legion, of the enlistment raised by Gaius Julius Caesar in 61 BC. This is, pun slightly intended, a sword that cuts both ways. While it gives me as an author some freedom and flexibility to create a world that fits my narrative goals, it also requires me to strike a very fine balance if I want to adhere to my number one goal, authenticity. Fortunately for my research purposes, but not necessarily my pocketbook, there was a revival of interest in the exploits of Caesar in the late 18th and 19th centuries, spawning a number of excellent works on the period. Much of that scholarship was based on the work of the tireless Col. Stoffel, under the auspices of Napoleon III for his own work on Caesar. Out of this body of work from the 19th century, I relied most heavily on the work of T. Rice Holmes, and in fact, the maps that are available on my website are from his works "Caesar's Conquest of Gaul" and "Ancient Britain and The Invasions of Julius Caesar". Thanks to the wonders of modern technology, I was able to "walk" about the battlefields of Gaul, most notably the site of Caesar's second battle with the Helvetii outside Toulon sur Arroux, his desperate fight with the Nervii on the Sambre River, and of course, Alesia, all of this done using Google Earth's 3D view.

But perhaps the most valuable part of my research was not found in the written material, but in my experience as a career Infantry Marine. Because although the technology might change, the essence of the fighting man and those things that are important to him never do. One only has to read the first-person accounts from any war through the ages to know that life for a "grunt", no matter what era they come from, is boiled down to its most basic essence. Food, sports, women, the stupidity of officers, women, the harshness of NCO's, women, the brutal work, women, and what surprises most civilians, humor. A lot of humor, although it is almost all tinged with cruelty, but even in the harshest conditions, under the most trying of circumstances, fighting men find ways to laugh, mostly at each other, but at themselves as well. If this is true for the men who fought at Antietam, Waterloo, or even Agincourt, I don't think the conversations would be all that different sitting outside a tent in a Roman military camp. Whether it's about the chances of the USC Trojans being in the BCS Championship game or which chariot team is the best, the Greens or Blues, the essence remains the same; anything but the pervasive fear that tinges the inner thoughts and nightmares of men in combat. I do think that one slight difference between today's warriors and their Roman counterparts lies in their attitude towards the politics of the day. The average Roman citizen was much more involved politically than their modern counterparts, but I think this has more to do with the idea that Roman politics, particularly of the era covered in Marching With Caesar was just as much of a bloodsport than any contest in the arena.

I have also chosen something of a hybrid approach between two extremes. Anyone who has read the McCullough series will probably recall that whenever possible, she used the proper Latin terms and colloquialisms, while most other authors in the genre have Anglicized everything, including the curse words. I have chosen to use a sprinkling of expressions and words in Latin that I found particularly evocative, but for the most part have chosen the latter route in everything else. The other exception is in my use of the proper Latin terms for ranks, which I do for a number of reasons. Probably the most important one is that, perhaps counter-intuitively, I believe using the Latin ranks is less confusing. For example, most semi-serious students of Roman history know that the Primus Pilus is the Senior Centurion of a Legion, and that has been Anglicized as First Spear. But where it gets confusing, at least for me, is how to characterize, for example, the Centurion in command of the Fourth

Century, Fifth Cohort. Characterizing it as such seems very awkward to me, and I think the Latin rank of Quintus Princeps Posterior is actually easier on the eye, once one learns the rank structure. To make that easier, I have included a Glossary, with these ranks and some of the other terms with which casual readers may be unfamiliar.

For serious Romanophiles who might spot what they see as inaccuracies or inconsistencies, for the most part these are intentional. While I will not go into detail about my reasons for doing so here, what I will say is that most of these differences between the account of battles that can be found in Caesar's Commentaries, for example, and what my characters experience is my way of illustrating how different a battle can look, depending on one's perspective. For a man in the ranks, fighting for his life and the life of his comrades, what his commander might see as a complete victory can easily look like a resounding defeat to the blood-spattered and weary men of the Legions. Also, while the rules and regulations of the Roman army are fairly well-known, that knowledge primarily covers two distinct and separate eras. First is what is known as the Polybian Legion, followed by the Legions of the Empire, particularly the Late Empire. While there are many similarities between the two, there are also key differences, most of them coming about as part of the Augustan reforms. Smack dab in between these two extremes are those Legions of the Late Republic, and for which very little documentary evidence exists. Again, this is both an opportunity and a challenge, and anyone interested in a more in-depth explanation and analysis of some of these differences, a complete bibliography of my sources, along with maps that show all of Gaul, the tribal territories, and the various battles please visit http://www.marchingwithcaesar.com.

Finally, I hope you enjoy reading about Titus Pullus, Vibius Domitius, Sextus Scribonius, and all of the other men of the tent section that comprised part of the First Century, Second Cohort of Caesar's 10th Legion as much as I did bringing them to life.

Semper Fidelis,

R. W. Peake
June, 2012

Marching With Caesar- Gaul

Prologue

When you are old, you dream a great deal. Some of these dreams are pleasant, but for an old man who marched with Caesar and spent forty years under the standard, just as many of them are the type that leaves you screaming awake, your nightclothes drenched in sweat. And there is one in particular that haunts me the most.

I am once again a young *Gregarius*, standing in the ranks of the First Century, Second Cohort of the 10th Legion, Caesar's Legion. Because of my size I am standing on the right end of the last rank, while Sextus Scribonius is in his usual place to my left. Farther down the line is my childhood friend and close comrade Vibius Domitius. We are formed up, standing silently in the growing light of a dawn morning, staring at the smoldering fires of a large camp, filled with the forms of sleeping men, women and children. These are the Usipetes and Tencteri, two tribes from across the Rhenus (Rhine) who have openly defied Caesar's orders, and they are about to be punished for that defiance. I stand, shifting nervously from one foot to the other, and even in my dream I can feel the twisting of my stomach that always happens before we are about to see action. A line of cold sweat is trickling down between my shoulder blades, despite the chill in the early September air; we are farther north and east than we have ever been to this point, and winter comes early in those parts. In other words, in most ways it is the normal sensations one experiences before battle, but this time will be very, very different.

We have drawn up in a line of Cohorts side by side, in order to surround the camp, spending most of the night moving into position, as quietly as possible for an army of our size. We are now just 300 paces away, all of the enemy sentries placed around the camp having been silenced by men selected for their stealth and skill in the silent kill. Caesar, in his red *paludamentum*, the scarlet

1

general's cloak, is barely visible astride his horse Toes, who is now almost as famous as his rider is. He is positioned in front of the 10th, as we are his favorite Legion, a fact that we take great pride in and the other Legions resent a great deal, which pleases all of us to no end. All of our eyes are on Caesar, waiting for him to raise his sword and unleash the Furies down onto the unsuspecting heads of these Germans. Because of my height, I have an unobstructed view of our general, so I see him as he draws his sword and I feel my hands tightening their grip, one on my shield, and one on my javelin. He raises his weapon into the air, while turning to address his *cornicen*, the man carrying the great curved horn that will send the blast of notes that signals those men who cannot see Caesar in the pre-dawn from where they are ringed around the camp. The sounds of those notes will be the first idea these Germans get that the moment of their death has arrived, Caesar giving very strict and explicit orders that no man, woman or child is to be left alive. The thought strikes me, as I stand waiting, what a queer feeling it must be to go from sound sleep to the realization that your life can be measured in a finite fashion, that you only have a certain number of breaths to take, a certain number of heartbeats left. Of course, all of our lives are finite but when that number is down to a veritable handful, what a strange feeling that must be.

My rumination is interrupted by the sight of Caesar's sword swinging downward in a silver blur, to end pointing at the camp, as almost simultaneously the *cornicen* fills his lungs and blows the horn on his shoulder. The heavy bass notes blast through the air, but only for a moment are they audible, instantly replaced by the roaring of thousands of men, all of us shouting at the top of our lungs as our Centurions give the order to begin the assault. Normally, we would approach at a steady march, in complete silence until the last moment, but as usual Caesar has been very thorough, being ordered to make as much noise as possible and to start at the dead run. All of this is done in order to maximize the surprise and confusion on the part of the Usipetes and Tencteri, in the hope that they are disoriented to the point where they are slow to react. We will arrive at the camp a bit winded, it is true, but for what we are about to do it should not be a problem. It does not take all that much effort to plunge a sword or javelin into the bodies of sleeping or just-roused people.

As expected, the surprise is total, as we come pounding into the camp itself, our roar now being met by the cries of surprise and shock from the Germans lying at our feet, clustered in small family

2

groups around a fire. Unlike we Romans, the tribes of Gaul and Germany disdain the use of defenses like a ditch and rampart, preferring instead to draw their wagons together to form a makeshift barrier, but curiously, they do not sleep within its protection. Instead they choose to sleep in the aforementioned family circles, just outside the meager protection of the wagons. I suppose their idea is that their sentries will give them enough warning to allow them to rise and make their way behind the wagons, which is true enough, if their sentries had still been alive. Now these wagons are little more than minor obstacles around which we must navigate, with the front ranks of each Century and Cohort leading the way deeper into the camp. We all know that the key is to penetrate as deeply into the camp as quickly as possible, so our comrades in the front ranks of each Century bypass the first groups of sleeping people, counting on us in the rear to deal with them. My rank comes across our first small bunch of people, most of them just beginning to sit up, their looks of surprise and fear etched in my memory as we fall upon them. I begin using my javelin, my first victim a man of indeterminate age, bearded and heavyset, who is fumbling for his spear next to him. Using an overhand grip, I plunge my javelin directly into his throat, feeling the hardened point scrape against the bone of his neck as I watch his eyes widen in shock, and I remember to twist the javelin as I withdraw it, both to cause more damage and to free it in the event it has lodged in the bone itself, as the man falls away. I am barely conscious of the sound of the woman lying across the fire from the man screaming, but it registers enough that I now turn on her, and using the javelin in the same manner, plunge it deeply into her breast. This time, the softer metal shaft of the javelin, on meeting the stronger resistance of her breastbone, bends a little, though the point still penetrates as it plunges directly into her heart. Letting out a shriek the woman, who I can now see is actually young and very pretty, grabs at the shaft of the javelin, clawing at it in a vain attempt to pull it from her body while her eyes lock with mine. I expect to see hatred and fear there, but instead I see only a great sadness as she looks up at me, dying on the end of my javelin. Although our javelins are specifically designed to do what has just happened and bend, so that once they strike a target after being thrown they are useless to throw back, it means that I must discard it and now draw my sword. Releasing the javelin, I leave it protruding from the chest of the young woman to draw my sword, called the Spanish sword because the Legions of Rome adopted it after facing the tribes in Hispania many, many years ago. It feels good in my hand as I turn my attention away from this fire, looking for other

3

targets, my comrades having taken care of the other people around it.

The air is now filled with the screams of the Usipetes and Tencteri, the full horror of what is happening to them becoming apparent. This also means that some of their men have managed to rise and grab weapons, except instead of banding together, they do the natural thing and stand to defend their own small group. It is a normal instinct to defend one's own family first, but in truth it just makes our job easier. It is much less of a challenge to defeat one or two men at a time than dozens or hundreds.

We are now moving through the camp from fire to fire and it is not long before my sword is wet almost to the hilt from the blood of the people I have slaughtered. So far I have been lucky because I have yet to come across any children; I take no pleasure in the slaughter of young ones. I do not enjoy killing women for that matter, but there is something less disturbing about killing an adult than a child, at least to me. Many of my comrades have no such problems with that distinction, and I can see them killing everything in their path without mercy or distress. The German men can now be seen standing with their weapons at their fires, sometimes just one, but most of the time two, three and sometimes four men standing to protect their families who are huddled behind them. Surprisingly, most people seem content to stay put, counting on the protection of their warriors, but it is still early in the assault and I am sure that once they see their men being cut down, they will begin to try to run and escape, or hide. Heading for the nearest group bypassed by the front ranks, I am thankful at least that these men did not have the wit to turn on my comrades who had moved past them to fall onto their unprotected backs, instead choosing to stand and fight.

Calling to Scribonius, Vibius and the rest of the men in my rank for help, we head for the group of men. There are three of them, all warriors, one older man and two about my age or a little older. The older man has a long sword, the other two spears, and all three have thought to pick up their shields. I wait for a moment for my own comrades to catch up, then form a single line, shield to shield, with me in my usual spot on the far right. This means I do not have the protection of a shield to my right, but my placement here is no accident; I am not boasting when I say that I am far and away the best man with a sword out of my rank, or my Century and Cohort for that matter. So it is with confidence that I walk side by side with my comrades towards the waiting men. By this point,

4

some of the wagons have been set alight, and despite it now being sunup, the forest in this part of the world is so thick that the light from the flaming wagons is still strong and lurid, making shadows dance and adding to the atmosphere of menace and destruction. The men await us, their faces set and determined and I can see over their shoulders that there are at least a dozen other people, huddled together, their arms around each other as they call out to their men in their tongue. I have no doubt they are exhorting their warriors to protect them, but their men do not answer, each of them completely concentrating on us. Stopping a few paces away, for a strange moment, nothing happens. All around us there is chaos, mayhem, blood and destruction, yet we are locked in our own little world, almost like we are encased in some sort of bubble. Despite the noises of the slaughter taking place, I can somehow hear my breathing, each side seemingly waiting for some signal. Our eyes are locked on each other; I am staring at the older man with the sword, while he does the same, probably drawn to me because of my size. Then, surprising even myself I am moving forward and I can hear a roar, realizing that it is coming from my lips as I lead with my shield. Moving quickly for a big man, this is both a blessing and a curse, because it catches not only my foe but my friends off balance, so it takes an instant for my comrades to realize that the fight has begun. The older man also hesitates, but that at least was my goal; moving first, striking the first blow in battle cannot be overestimated in its importance, and he has barely enough time to bring his own shield up as I smash into him, relying on my size and strength to push him off balance. However, he somehow stands his ground but thankfully before either of the younger warriors can react and turn on me, my comrades are on them. Outnumbering them more than two to one, I nonetheless call to my friends to leave the older man to me; in those days, I was always anxious to prove myself as the best. For a moment, we stand shield boss to shield boss, glaring at each other over the rim of our shields, he trying to strike me with an overhand blow, using his long sword, as I come underneath with my shorter Spanish sword. Because of the length of his sword, he is trying to end me with a slash, but we Romans have long since learned that the point always beats the edge. I hear his blade whistle past my ear as I move my head to the side, wincing as it strikes a glancing blow off of my shoulder. My mail, which is reinforced in that area, absorbs the blow, so that a few links break but otherwise I am unharmed. Meanwhile, the point of my own sword flickers upward from beneath my shield and I feel the point strike into the flesh of his thigh. We are close enough that I

5

hear the hiss of pain escape his lips, eyes narrowing in agony and hatred, but he does not yield an inch. I realize he is fighting for his family, that this gives him the courage of the doomed, so rather than try to continue pressing him, I suddenly step backward, hoping to draw him off balance. He is too experienced to fall for that, instead choosing to recover himself. Meanwhile, his two comrades, who I assume to be his sons, are still desperately standing back to back, surrounded by my friends, who are alternating in their attacks on the pair. No matter what is happening with them I cannot pay any attention to their battle, and I renew my attack, not wanting to give the older warrior any respite. His left leg is now soaked in blood, and he is clearly favoring it, but is still refusing to yield an inch as I thrust my shield out, using the boss in an attempt to smash his nose flat. We are to use the shield in a manner that makes it as much an offensive weapon as a defensive one, so that my move takes him by surprise, but he manages to bring his own shield up to meet my attack, and I smile grimly, because that is exactly the reaction for which I am hoping. Bending my knees while maintaining the pressure of my shield against his, I whip my blade around parallel to the ground, in a wide sweeping arc so that the edge is now traveling back toward me, except that his left knee is between me and the blade. This is one of our most effective attacks, known as the third position, and is the only time where we favor the edge over the point. It is also why we do go to the trouble to sharpen both edges of our swords. Normally, it is enough to cut the two tendons at the base of the hamstring, but as I said, I am a very strong man and my blade is very sharp, so I can feel the shock travel up my arm as the blade cuts through his leg all the way to his kneecap. My blade continues through so that I sever his leg completely, and I can feel the spray of blood splash on my arm as he lets out a shriek of unbearable agony, collapsing immediately to the ground. The sight of their father defeated stuns both of the other warriors so completely that they suddenly drop their shields to just stand there defenseless as my comrades cut them down. Standing over my foe as he stares up at me, his face a picture of despair and agony, one hand clutching the stump of his ruined leg, I can read in his face the knowledge that he has failed to protect his family. All I feel is a savage exultation that I have bested another man, giving him a smile that holds nothing but cruelty as I plunge my sword into his throat.

All around us, similar scenes are being played out as the Legions of Rome go about their business of slaughter. With the three warriors dispatched, I turn to face the remaining group of

6

people. There are four women, one older with iron gray hair and a seamed face, probably the woman of the man that I dispatched, and from the way she is gazing down at the bodies of the two young men, their mother. She stands protectively in front of the rest of her family, arms outstretched despite the fact she has no weapon. Even as I move toward her, before I can get to her another of my comrades, Spurius Didius, steps close enough to run his sword into her stomach before twisting the blade savagely, disemboweling her in one practiced motion. His move is met with disgust and contempt by the rest of us; we may be under orders to kill everyone, orders that we would readily obey, but that did not mean that we had to make defenseless people suffer needlessly. However, that is in his character; he is the cruelest among us, and renowned for some of the actions he has taken, mostly against defenseless or helpless people. The woman lets out a blood-curdling scream as she collapses to the ground, her intestines slowly oozing out to lie in a glistening pool next to her.

"You stupid bastard, you punctured her bowels. Now we have to smell her shit," Vellusius, another member of our tent section complains, but Didius just grins. The sight of the matriarch of this group savagely cut down finally spurs the others to action, and they turn to run away, scattering in every direction.

"See what you made them do?" I hear Scribonius shout as each of us start off in pursuit of one of the fleeing Germans.

Without thinking, I choose one of the other women, a younger one who I had noticed snatching up a bundle lying near the fire. She was wrapped in a cloak, but quickly shrugged it off since it slowed her down, and I can see she has fiery red hair that streams behind her as she runs, still clutching the bundle. I chase after her, and despite being much faster, she is damnably quick, changing direction whenever she senses that I am within reach, so that in moments I am not only out of breath, I am getting very angry. The pursuit continues in this manner for some time, with her darting around and through the small knots of Romans and Germans who are still trying to put up a fight. By this time, others like her have realized that it is pointless to fight, and begin their own headlong flight, each of them seeming to choose a different direction in which to escape. Wagons are ablaze, the air growing hot and close from the flames, making my lungs burn even more. The girl is making me look the fool, and I can just imagine that the others are getting a great laugh from the sight of my large frame chasing this slight girl about like a dog chasing a chicken. She is now heading for the river bordering one side of the camp, along with what now appears to be several hundred other Usipetes and Tencteri. Some of them are much closer and much slower than this girl, meaning I could easily stop chasing her to concentrate on an easier target, but I refuse to be drawn off. Finally she starts to tire, her sudden changes in direction becoming less frequent, until I have now closed with her so that I can reach out and give her a shove that sends her sprawling. The bundle she has been carrying goes flying from her hands to land a few feet away from her, but before I can pin her down to finish her, she scrambles up, leaving me to curse bitterly, as much as I can with my lungs on fire. Gasping for air, I am prepared to resume the pursuit, but for reasons I cannot understand at first, instead of trying to get away, she runs straight to the bundle, picking it up.

"That's a foolish thing to do, girl," I gasp. "No amount of money or whatever you have in there is worth dying for."

I know she cannot understand me, so instead she just stands there looking at me, with an expression on her face that I need no translator to interpret for me. My heart is pounding, and I realize that it is not just from the exertion; she is really very beautiful, her cheeks flushed from our chase, her red hair spread around her face like fire. I feel a stirring in my loins that I do not expect, and I take a step toward her, our eyes locked together. Just as I am about to reach her, she says something in her tongue, then thrusts the bundle out in front of her. That is when I see a pair of the deepest blue eyes I have ever seen, staring at me from within the bundle. A round face, with a wisp of the same color red hair on its head, the babe does not seem frightened at all, just stares at me with an intense curiosity. I feel like I have been dashed with a bucket of cold water, my member going limp immediately from the shame of what I was about to do, followed immediately by the return of the anger. Anger at this woman for trying to use her child as a shield to spare her life, counting on whatever it is in the human heart that wants to protect a helpless infant; anger at being put in this position in the first place, knowing that my orders are very clear and very strict. Most of all, I am angry at myself for this feeling that is in me, a sense of shame at what I am about to do that I interpret as weakness. Looking over the head of the babe into the mother's eyes, I can see in that instant she knows that there is no mercy to be had. Not from me. Not from Caesar. And not from Rome. For I am a Legionary of Rome, and I do as I am commanded. At least, that is what I tell myself as I plunge my sword, through the baby and into her mother.

8

That is when I always wake up, soaked in sweat with a pounding heart, despite it being almost forty years since that day that we destroyed the Usipetes and Tencteri tribes as we were conquering Gaul, while marching with Caesar.

Chapter 1- Who Is Titus Pullus?

These are the words of Titus Pullus, formerly Legionary, Optio, Pilus Prior and Primus Pilus of Caesar's 10th Legion Equestris, now known as 10th Gemina, Primus Pilus of the 6th Ferrata, and Camp Prefect, as dictated to his faithful former slave, scribe and friend Diocles.

This is being written in my 61st year, three years after my retirement as Camp Prefect, in the tenth year of the reign of Augustus, and 489 years after the founding of the Roman Republic. I have more than 40 military decorations, including three gold torqs, three set of phalarae, two coronae *civica*, three coronae *murales*, and a *corona* vallaris. I have more than 20 battle scars on my body, all of them in the front, and my back is clean, never having been flogged in my 42 years in the Legions, nor turning my back to the enemy. Although my record is not as great as the revered Dentatus, I am well known in the Legions, and I have given the bulk of my life and blood to Rome.

My goal is straightforward; with these words I plan on recording all of the momentous events that I participated in as a member of Rome's Legions, during a period that changed the very foundations of Rome itself.

When I was young, Rome was ruled by the Senatus et Populus Que Romanum, the Senate and People of Rome. Every year two Consuls were elected from the Senate to run Rome for that year; now, only one man rules, the members of the Senate are his pets, and Rome has never been stronger or mightier than it is right now. The letters SPQR are now famous throughout all of the world, known and unknown.

Although it is no longer in my nature to express excessive pride that some have called hubris in the same way as I did in my youth, it is with some justification that I lay claim to playing a small role in expanding Rome's fortunes. However, I do so in the name of my fellow Legionaries, those still living and those long or recently dead. For it was with our strong right arms and our sharp blades that such titanic changes were made possible, our legs that carried us as the agent of change to be used by a great man, a man who saw what needed to be done in order to ensure the future prosperity of the city and country he loved more than life itself. His work was unfinished when he was struck down, and it is the very same man known now as Augustus, whom under a different name, that of his adopted father, picked up the ivory baton of imperium and carried it forward to complete what the great man started.

If, dear reader, you are looking for elegant and witty prose, know this now; I am a simple soldier, and have a simple soldier's story to tell. Despite being literate and possessing a fair hand for simple letters and documents, I have no training or experience in these matters. This is why I am dictating this account to my former slave, scribe and friend Diocles, who is trying his best to keep up with me as I talk. My purpose is to offer an account of these great events, and a viewpoint of the great men of our day, as I saw them and lived through them. I make no claim to be intimates of all of the First Men of Rome, yet I can say that most of them of whom I speak in this account knew me by name. I saw them at their finest, and some I saw at their lowest point, but most importantly I saw them as they appeared to the eyes of their Legions.

Also in this account, I will endeavor to recall conversations and events as exactly as possible, and I must beg the reader's forgiveness because of the coarseness and crudity of some of the conversations, because they are the words of soldiers and are not the manner of speech one would normally use in polite company. However, I have made a vow to Jupiter Optimus Maximus that I will recount as faithfully as I can all that transpired in those days. One might ask, how is it possible that I will be able to remember conversations that occurred thirty or forty years earlier? First, I have been blessed with the type of memory that seems to retain more than others, and second, even as events were transpiring, I had an idea that they were noteworthy. Perhaps I even had it in the back of my mind that I would one day want to record the events of the day, although I had no idea how I could accomplish this. When I enlisted in the Legions, I was barely literate, able to write my name, and to read very simple instructions and the like, meaning the idea of writing this down would have been nonsense. However I somehow always knew that one day I would be in the position where I either had the ability myself, or I would be able to use someone to create this record. In fact, that was the great, burning ambition of my life, to elevate not only myself but those who follow bearing my name into the equestrian class, an ambition that has been fulfilled.

Now, as I look back on my life, I know that I am nearer to the end than to the beginning, and despite being in good health, only the gods know how much longer I will live. Therefore, I have decided to start this last mission of mine, and will devote almost all of my time to it. In truth, I have nothing much else to do; I am a wealthy man, and while I hold office here in Arelate it is mainly a ceremonial post, leaving me free to come and go as I please, just as long as I am present to march at the head of the procession on festival days. Truth be told, I am bored. I know that I no longer have the strength of body to continue in the Legions, but my spirit is still as if I were a 16 year old lad, on the lookout for adventure and a way to improve my station in life. Such is the cruel humor of the gods; ability may wane, but desire never does.

And I am lonely; I miss my comrades, I miss the Legions and the life of the Legions. I will find myself staring at my armor, my helmet, shield and sword, and thinking, if only I could stop time. But I can't, so there is no use in dwelling on it. Perhaps that is why those few comrades of mine who managed to survive as long as I have drink as much as they do. In particular, I miss my friends Vibius and Scribonius, but Vibius is dead more than ten years now, and while Scribonius is alive, he is far, far away and with his nose buried in a book, I am sure. Thinking of Vibius in particular only makes me more melancholy, both for his death and for all that transpired between us. When all is said and done, I am a warrior without a war to march to, and I fear that this fact alone, not any sickness of the body or just plain old age will finally send me to the afterlife.

Before I go, however, I have one last job to do, not dissimilar to some of the jobs I had to do in the Legions. It will take patience and endurance, but most importantly it will require me to relive certain memories that I have not thought of in many, many years. Nevertheless, now I must turn my mind's eye to the past, moving back over the years, and the miles, and the battles, to find the young man that I was, the young man who was looking for adventure and a way out of his life, along with his best friend.

12

Chapter 2: Joining the Legion

I joined the Legions as part of the *dilectus* authorized by the Senate in the year of the Consulships of Marcus Piso Frugi and Marcus Mesalla Niger, journeying to the provincial capital of Scallabis where the new Legion was gathering. I came to the capital accompanied by my best friend Vibius Domitius and his father, along with my own father and our slaves Phocas and Gaia. Growing up on a small farm outside the town of Astigi, a two day's journey south of Corduba, it was a farm in name only. My father was completely indifferent towards making the farm anything more than a source of subsistence, and a poor one at that, preferring instead to lavish his love and time on endless amphorae of wine. In short, he was a drunkard, and he hated me with a passion, claiming that I was the source of all of his sorrows, insisting that I had killed my mother. I was, and am very large in both height and breadth, and I was such a large baby that the strain of delivering me into the world was too much for her. The result was that she died shortly after I was born, and it was for this reason my father bore me such hatred that rarely a day went by that he did not remind me of the circumstances of my birth. The one fortunate outcome his feelings for me had, however, was that he was persuaded to swear that I was of a legal age to join the Legions in this *dilectus* when in fact I was still only sixteen, a year short of the minimum age at that time, albeit with a little prodding on my part. I took this risk because it was the only way that Vibius and I could join together, since he was a year older than I was, and we had been friends for ten years. We met by virtue of my rescuing him from having his head being dumped into a bucket of *cac* by some older boys one day when I went to town to buy some nails. Vibius was small, both as a boy and now as a man, but he was exceptionally strong, was quick as lightning, and possessed that ferocity that comes from being small one's whole life and having to fight for everything. We made an odd pair to look at, yet from the day we met we were inseparable, and both of us shared the dream of joining the Legions since either one could remember, making it unthinkable for one of us to join the army without the other, even if it meant that I had to lie to get in. Both of us were so fixated on being the best Legionaries possible that we badgered one of Pompey's veterans who lived nearby, a man who lost an eye fighting Sertorius and who we called Cyclops, into training us in the exact manner of the Legions. He had been drilling us for two years, several times a week, making us confident that we would acquit ourselves well when we began our real training. In fact, on the day when we bade Cyclops farewell, he took me aside to tell me that he thought I had the makings of a superb Legionary, the highest praise I had ever been given, by anyone.

I was leaving behind my two sisters, Livia and Valeria, and despite the fact I loved both my sisters, it was Valeria I was closest to, because she had essentially been my mother in everything but name. Now they were both married and I was left alone to fend for myself with our father. Our slave Phocas, and his woman Gaia, the names given to them by my father, did their best to protect me from Lucius, but they were slaves and there is only so much a slave can do to a master. Fortunately, my father's beatings were long since ceased, once I became much larger and stronger than he was, yet that did not stop him from constantly reminding me how worthless I was, and how I would never amount to anything. Deep down I knew that if I did not leave the farm soon, there would come a point where I would strike my father down. When I was young, I possessed a fearsome temper, and had not developed the sufficient amount of self-control to that point to be sure that I would be able to stop myself if my father went too far one day, and no matter what the provocation, any son who kills the *paterfamilias* faces the harshest punishment under Roman law. Therefore, it was better for everyone that I took this step in joining the Legions, and to that end I made a deal with my father that if he would swear that I was the legal age to join, he would never have to gaze on my face again, a pact that was mutually satisfactory. Of course, nothing is ever that simple; in order to finally persuade him it was in both of our best interests, I swore that if he did not enter into this agreement that he would never be able to sleep soundly again, for I would find a way to kill him.

For Vibius it was more straightforward. He was the youngest of several sons, with no hope of inheriting his father's business, so his options were limited. He could have been apprenticed to another craftsman, but the dream of joining the Legions burned so brightly in both of us that in truth there was little question which path he would take. Dreams of glory and the riches that waited were too strong a lure to keep Vibius in Astigi, despite his feelings for Juno, a friend from our childhood and to whom he had pledged his eternal love, a promise that she returned. The fact that I was in love with Juno as well was something that I kept hidden for the whole length of our friendship.

14

Two days after I first donned the *toga virilis* on my sixteenth birthday in April, about a third of a watch before first light, Phocas and I hitched the mule to the wagon, with Gaia packing the food we would eat on the way, along with various other essentials. All my belongings, or at least those that I planned on taking with me, were in a bundle as part of the load, along with obligatory amphorae of wine to keep my father Lucius properly lubricated along the way. He was much more pliable and cooperative with a skin full of wine at hand, and both Phocas and I were nervous that somehow things would fall apart and my father would try to sabotage the deal we made. He had been more sullen than usual since our agreement, yet to that point did or said nothing to indicate he was having a change of heart. To remind him of the threat I made, I had taken to wearing a dagger, given to me as a gift by our tutor Cyclops. The point, so to speak, was not lost on Lucius, as I saw him eying it continuously, no doubt imagining the feeling of it plunging into him should he try to betray me. Once the wagon was loaded, Phocas went to inform my father Lucius that all was ready. He walked out, wrapped in his cloak, already staggering a bit, since he had not slept but been drinking all night. Without a word, he climbed into the back of the wagon, onto the makeshift pallet that Gaia had prepared, and within moments was snoring loudly. Phocas and I exchanged a glance, then he mounted the wagon and with Gaia beside him and with me walking beside the wagon, we left the only home I had ever known. I wondered as I stopped for a moment to gaze back at the modest farm, its main house not much better than some of the hovels I would come across in Gaul, if I would ever see it again, and if I did, under what circumstances. Then I turned and trotted to catch up with the wagon.

Just after dawn, we met with Vibius and his father, both of them astride mules. Vibius' father stank of lime and rawhide, marks of his trade as a tanner, but he was pleasant enough. His good spirits I suspected came from the relief he felt at having solved a dilemma without lifting a finger, increasing his family fortunes by subtraction since Vibius was one less mouth to feed. I also believe our choice absolved his conscience of having to make a decision about Vibius' future since he was not going to inherit the business. Despite that, I could also sense some genuine affection on the part of Vibius' father towards his youngest son, a feeling only strengthened by what I witnessed on our journey to Corduba. At least I could see a resemblance between the two; Vibius was the image of his father, the same short but powerful frame and bandy legs, as if they had been born astride a mule, with pigeon chests and muscular forearms. And they had more similarities than physical, as I was to learn on the journey. Juno was standing there, her eyes red-rimmed and puffy, signs that she had spent the last night with Vibius in a state other than connubial bliss. Despite the fact that they were as yet unmarried, their love for each other, and the ardor that young men and women all suffer from combined to make any idea of Juno's maidenhead remaining intact, as by rights it should have, an impossible burden for the both of them to bear. Normally, this might have caused Juno's father to exercise his rights as *paterfamilias* and kill Juno while demanding some sort of punishment from Vibius and his family, except their love for each other and the affection that Juno's father had not just for his daughter but for Vibius as well, all worked to cause him to turn a blind eye to their passion. I knew that Vibius and Juno were having sexual relations, but Vibius was kind enough and cared enough about Juno to avoid the normal boasting a man does to his best friend about his conquests. Although we never spoke of it, I believe that Vibius knew I loved Juno as he did, and it was a mark of his friendship that he did whatever he could to avoid rubbing what was in effect a failure in my face. Regardless, it hurt; nevertheless, I smiled as I went to Juno to give her a farewell hug. Putting my arms around her, I could feel my heart racing, the unbidden and unwelcome thought coming of what it would be like if there were no clothes between us, if we were alone and........I shook my head, trying to banish the thoughts that were bound to make my feelings known if I allowed them to continue.

Juno, for her part seemed oblivious to my struggle, stood on her tiptoes to whisper in my ear, "Titus, please take care of Vibius. Make sure he comes home to me."

"I will," I promised, and I meant it sincerely.

Despite my feelings for her, they were still overridden by my love for Vibius. Suddenly grabbing both of my arms, in a grip that was surprisingly strong for a girl her size, she whispered urgently, "Swear it on Jupiter's stone, Titus. Swear that you'll bring him back to me alive."

Flattered that she put that kind of faith in my ability, and somewhat unnerved by her passion, I made the oath, which calmed her down. While I was making my farewells to Juno, Vibius' father had ridden his mule over to our wagon, where he saw Lucius sprawled in the back of it, snoring away.

16

Glancing over at me, I could feel the heat in my face rising, but before I could speak, Phocas said smoothly, "My master has been suffering from ague and flux, and it's weakened him considerably. But despite his illness, he didn't want to deprive his only son of his greatest wish to join the Legions."

Vibius' father nodded gravely, clearly not convinced in the slightest but not wishing to make a fuss about it either. Farewells done, we turned our little caravan towards the road out of town leading towards Scallabis.

The trip was pleasant enough; the weather cooperated, and Vibius' father turned out to be a veritable fount of chatter, telling awful jokes and fantastic tales of the exciting life in the tanning business. He was not that bad, truth be known, and as we talked, I could see where Vibius got his sense of humor and buoyant nature. Lucius regained consciousness a watch or so into the journey, leaning over the side of the wagon to retch violently. Phocas handed the reins to Gaia in order to aid Lucius, his help being in the form of handing him an amphora of wine.

Seeing Vibius and his father watching and unable to ignore what was taking place, Phocas announced, "This is a potion that's served to ease my master's suffering in the past. We paid a Greek doctor for a large quantity since it's proven so effective."

I silently thanked the gods for Phocas and his quick thinking; despite the transparency of the fiction, neither Vibius nor his father seemed inclined to dispute it, and given that Lucius' sickness seemed to pass as soon as he drank of the "potion", there was no unpleasantness. In fact, once Lucius was fully conscious, he began a conversation with Vibius' father, who rode beside our wagon as they talked. They began discussing the current political situation, with the aftermath of the Catiline conspiracy still fresh on every citizen's mind. While they talked, it gave Vibius and I the opportunity to drop back a way, he riding and I walking as we talked. The only topic of interest was our immediate future, and we both speculated on what was facing us. As much as Cyclops had told us, there was as much and more that we did not know, of which we both were all too aware.

Arriving in Scallabis after almost two weeks of hard travel, it was the first time I had been to the provincial capital. To my country-boy eyes, it was the height of glamour and excitement, a bustling metropolis that always seemed to be buzzing with activity as farmers, muleteers, merchants, whores and all sorts of shady characters flocked to the city. Of course, it was not a metropolis, but I had yet to see Rome or Alexandria, another point about which Lucius was only too happy to remind me, seeing it as one more sign of my inadequacy. Just as our party entered the city through the main gate, my father made a loud declamation how this pile of *cac* was nothing when compared to Rome, going on to relate how his father, who loved him well, took he and his brothers to the eternal city to see none other than Pompey Magnus. His words immediately drew hostile stares from the others around us, and I felt my face turn red from embarrassment, with Phocas turning to give Lucius a warning look as he sat in the back of the wagon, swilling wine and running his mouth, completely ignoring the both of us.

Vibius and his father looked equally embarrassed at this display, and finally I dropped back to the wagon to hiss, "By the Furies, if you don't shut your mouth, I'll kill you on the spot!"

He opened his mouth to say something back to me, but evidently the look on my face stopped him, because he snapped his mouth shut and remained quiet, sullenly sucking on his wine skin.

Making our way to the Praetor's residence, this was the site of the *dilectus*, the *dilectus* being the official recruiting effort for the Legion. Because it was just after mid-day, there was a line of young men, accompanied by the men who would vouch for them, waiting for their turn in front of the *conquisitores*, the group of officials charged with finding qualified enlistees to enroll in the name of the Praetor. It was in this line that I first heard the name of the Praetor, a name that every citizen of Rome and probably every human being in the known world has heard of by now. It was by way of overhearing a couple of the older men, obviously the fathers of other boys.

"So do you know anything of the new Praetor, since you're recently arrived from Campania?" asked one of the men, some sort of artisan by the look of him. The man he was asking was dressed as a member of the equestrian class, although it was clear that his toga had seen better days.

The equestrian nodded, and said, "I know of him. Gaius Julius Caesar is his name, of the Julii."

18

The artisan shrugged, responding, "Never heard of him. What do you know?"

The equestrian gave a snort of derision. "He's ambitious, I'll give him that. He's so ambitious," he said with a sly grin, "that he supposedly became Nicomede's 'woman' when he was serving under Marcus Thermus in Bithynia."

This caused the other man to hoot with laughter; it has always been the case that the lower classes love any hint of scandal attached to their social betters.

The equestrian became serious, "Whether or not that's true, that's what's said. But what I do know is that Caesar is well-loved by the people of your class."

He did not say this as a compliment, yet if the other man took offense, he gave no sign,

"Well," the artisan grunted, "what I care about most is whether or not he can properly lead a Legion. The gods know in my day it was hit or miss."

The equestrian looked at the other man in some surprise, "You were in the Legions, citizen?"

"One of Marius' mules," the other replied with quiet pride, as well he should have.

The men of Marius' head count Legions were the first of their kind, and showed their supposed betters that they could fight just as well as anyone in the higher classes, better perhaps. In fact, it was the reforms of Marius that opened the door for those of my class to enter the Legions and perhaps advance their own fortunes. For the rest of the time we stood in line, the equestrian was completely respectful of the artisan, and indeed began plying him with questions about Gaius Marius.

Such was the nature of the conversations all along the line as we shuffled slowly towards the entrance to the building, which even I could see was not much more than a large villa. It served as the headquarters and the living space for the Praetor sent by Rome to govern the province, and as I was to learn, carries the same name as the headquarters tent of a Roman military camp, the *Praetorium*. While we waited, we saw much bustling about, with couriers coming and going, jumping from their horses to walk quickly into the building, then reappearing in a matter of moments, their dispatch bag full, either of answers to the original dispatch they had delivered, or some sort of counter-orders or further questions, or at least so I imagined. Phocas was monitoring Lucius carefully, to ensure that while he was sated enough to be lucid and appear to have all of his faculties, my father was not allowed to render himself insensible. With the day passing and the sun sinking lower, I began to worry that we would be out of luck since my father had not remained this sober for this long in some time, and despite my threats I was worried that he would bring ruin to all Vibius and I had planned because of his thirst. Finally, it became our turn; Vibius and his father would follow us, and I took my father by the elbow, applying extra pressure just before the impatient guard made a comment, giving him a look that was meant to convey exactly what awaited him if he failed. His fear was palpable, but he nodded his head and we entered the building.

There were a series of tables, where not one but three *conquisitores* were actually standing, each behind a slave who was working as a scribe, writing down the necessary information dictated to them by the *conquisitores*. The third table to the farthest side of the room was empty, and the *conquisitore* behind it waved to us impatiently.

"You're here to enlist no doubt," he said briskly, but I could only nod dumbly. Turning to my father, the official spoke just as briskly, "And you're here to swear to his citizenship and age, aren't you?"

For a moment, my father did not speak, and my heart began to hammer even harder. Glancing out of the corner of my eye, I could see his lips working but nothing came out.

Finally, his words came in a hoarse whisper, "Yes your Excellency."

Obviously unimpressed with my father's oratory skills, the *conquisitore*, a middle-aged man wearing a toga with the badge of his office worn around his neck, snapped, "Out with it, citizen. Who are you?"

Finally given a question he could answer, my father replied, with just a hint of pride, "I am Lucius Pomponius Pullus, citizen of

Rome and a member of the tribe Pupinia, of the gens of the Pomponii."

Nodding, the *conquisitore* pointed at me, and asked, "This is your son? Is he the one joining the Legion?"

I spoke up with the rehearsed answer that we were told to give by Cyclops when he explained the process to us.

"Yes, I am Titus Pomponius Pullus, also a citizen of Rome by virtue of my father and his father and grandfathers before him. I am also of the gens of the Pomponii, and my mother was a citizen as well, of the tribe Galeria, and of the gens of the Asinia."

The *conquisitore* indicated to his scribe to write down the appropriate information.

Once completed, the *conquisitore* looked at Lucius and asked, "And his age?"

Here was the moment of truth; we had rehearsed this many times. As you know, gentle reader, the years of the birth of Roman citizens are recorded by the number of years from the founding of Rome and the Consuls for that year. It had been drilled into me that I was born in the year of the Consulship of Publius Servilius Vatia and Appius Claudius Pulcher but now in order to perpetrate this fiction, we were forced to consult the annals to determine the Consuls for the year before. I could feel the sweat beginning to trickle down my back as I waited for what seemed to be the week that it took my father to answer.

However, it must not have been long because I detected no change in the expression of the *conquisitore* or the scribe when my father finally said, "My son Titus Pomponius Pullus was born in the year of 430, as reckoned from the founding of Rome, under the Consulship of the dictator Lucius Cornelius Sulla and Quintus Caecilia Metellus Pius, may the gods favor both of their memories, on the date of April Twentieth."

This raised an eyebrow from the *conquisitore*, though not in a suspicious manner.

"Just a few weeks ago, eh boy? Couldn't wait to join the Legions, could you?"

Finally, an answer that I could give honestly!

"No Your Excellency, I couldn't. It's been my dream since I was a boy to serve."

"Good," the *conquisitore* replied. "Would that all of your fellow citizens had your patriotism. But it's auspicious, your birth date, because you'll be assigned to the 10th Legion, and its symbol has already been established."

Looking at me, smiling, he added, "It's the sign of the bull, the symbol under which you were born. It must be that the Fates have brought you here."

And with that, my father's part was essentially done. The scribe used his stylus to write down the relevant information on a beeswax tablet then handed it to me, instructing me to go through a door on the left to be examined by a fellow who would determine that I was fit enough to join the Legion. Lucius was told by the scribe to wait, pointing him to the back of the room where other fathers were standing, while I went into the other room for my physical examination. There, another man waited, quickly identified as a doctor and with his own scribe standing next to him, to whom I handed the tablet. I was told to disrobe for the doctor to examine me, if that is what one could call it, asking me a few questions about my overall health, telling the scribe to write that I was physically fit and had no identifying marks. In particular, they apparently were looking for any marks to indicate that I was once a slave. Passing the examination, I was told to dress, then handed the tablet and told to go back into the original room, where Lucius was still waiting. The process took no more than a few moments. My father was presented with a document, written on vellum, containing the information that we gave concerning my birth, with the extra information provided by my physical examination, which he signed, his hand barely shaking at all. It was done. The *conquisitore* told us what would happen next.

"Lucius Pullus, your part is done. Titus Pullus, you're now a *probatio*, and as such will take an oath before you're sent to the camp of the 10th Legion. It's not the full oath that all Legionaries must take; that will only be administered once you're considered to be worthy to be a soldier of Rome."

I bristled a bit at that; if he only knew who he was dealing with! However, he either missed my irritation or ignored it and continued with, "You're to report at first light at the camp of the 10th Legion. Until then, you may spend your last evening as you wish. The scribe will give you the directions to the camp. It's just outside of the city walls."

Whereupon he had me swear an oath to Mars, Jupiter and Roma, then once completed he motioned to the door, indicating that our business was finished. By this time, Vibius and his father had entered and were in the same process I had just endured, and we grinned at each other as I walked out the door.

Phocas was waiting for us; when I told him that our ruse worked, he whooped with joy, ignoring decorum as he hugged me with all his might. While he did so, I was reminded that this was a moment I should be sharing with my father, except he had made a straight line for the wagon and the amphora, ignoring the celebration. For a moment, just one, I experienced a terrible sadness as I watched my father make his supplication to the only god he truly worshiped, or for whom he had any feeling for that matter. Then I shook it off, enjoying the moment Phocas and I were having. Presently, Vibius and his father emerged from the villa, Vibius' face plastered with what must have been the same grin that was on my face, and we embraced. We had done it! We had joined the Legions together. The thought that this was merely a first step never entered our minds; as far as we were concerned, we were both as good as Legionaries. Fortunately, the gods did not disagree with our assessment.

Spending the night at an inn, it turned out to be the last night either Vibius or I would spend under a roof for some time to come, although we did not yet know it. There was a tavern attached to the inn, and Vibius' father at least was determined to give us a proper send-off, which my father was only too happy to participate in, since it meant that the wine would be flowing. I was ashamed at Lucius' obviously naked desire to suck up all the wine that Vibius' father was willing to pay for, but thankfully Vibius' father was gracious, despite his modest means. By this point, enough time had passed for me to witness that, despite Vibius' lowly status in their family, there was real affection between father and son, and I mused about what that must feel like. Despite the convivial atmosphere, I drank just enough wine, watering it at that, to keep from appearing ungracious. I was not much of a drinker of wine in those days, and although I am not much of one now, I certainly have experienced moments of which Bacchus would be proud. The evening progressed, and Vibius, his father and my father got drunker, even as I grew more impatient.

At some point, one of the whores that can always be found in such establishments made their way to our table, and Vibius' father poked his son in the ribs and winked, "Well son? How about your father giving you a real going-away present, huh?"

Vibius' face flushed immediately, a combination of embarrassment and anger.

"Father, I'm sworn to Juno, and she's the only woman I want."

"Just wait, that'll change," his father laughed, which Lucius found equally amusing.

"No it won't," Vibius snapped, and I could see he was very angry now. So could his father, who made a placating gesture.

"*Pax*, son. I was only joking. Forgive a father for trying to give his son something to remember," he said.

Vibius softened immediately. "No, Father. I should be begging your forgiveness. I know you meant well; it's just that I already miss Juno."

Vibius' father put his arm around his son, and nodded. "I understand Vibius. You're just like me. I've been with your mother going on twenty-four years, and she's still the only woman for me."

He paused. "Most of the time."

He said this last with a roar of laughter, and even Vibius could not remain upset.

The evening passed by quickly enough but once it was time to retire I found I could not sleep, being much too excited and for a moment I envied Vibius, who lay across the room, snoring peacefully, making me think that perhaps more wine would not have been a bad idea. Lying on my cloak that I threw over the pallet of straw, I stared at the sky through the small window placed high on the wall, wondering how different my life would be one short day

24

from now. It was with this thought in my head that somehow I finally fell asleep.

Chapter 3: *Tirones*

A
ny regret from the night before about not partaking of wine was immediately dismissed when I saw poor Vibius, who looked slightly green, his eyes rimmed red and his breath smelling like my father's in the morning. We had paid the slave maintaining the watch to wake us two parts of a watch before dawn, despite it being only a short walk to the camp. Neither of us could rouse our respective fathers, which was fine with me, but I felt a pang about not going to the slave quarters to wake Phocas and Gaia. Making our way down to the main room of the inn, we rummaged around until we found a loaf of bread and some oil that was close to turning rancid, and split the loaf, soaking it in the oil. Carrying our portions out the door, we began to make our way in the dark, the few belongings we were bringing with us slung over our shoulders, along with the appropriate token that we were to hand to the soldier at the gate to show that we were now part of the Legion. Walking slowly, neither of us said much. Despite our eagerness, we also knew that we were embarking on something momentous. After all, we were still boys to a large degree, and I would be lying if I said we did not have any fear of what we were headed into.

Arriving at the gate, we stopped a short distance away, not wanting to just walk up on some guard who might be half-asleep and would kill us before our career even started, so we sat on the ground, waiting for the light to become strong enough so that we could approach without fear. While sitting there, we made out other shapes of men approaching, then heard them talking quietly, as the others who enlisted the day before began to show up. Vibius and I smugly but quietly congratulated ourselves for being the first to arrive, making no sound to alert the others to our presence, though I do not know why. Instead, we sat listening, learning about our fellow *tiros* as they talked among themselves.

"So what do you think it'll be like?"

This from a high-pitched, nervous sounding voice.

"It'll be the hardest thing we've ever done," came the response from a grim-sounding deeper voice.

"By the gods," came another, "I can't wait to kill some barbarian scum! I bet I have the most kills of anyone in this Legion!"

Both Vibius and I glanced at each other, and despite barely seeing the other in the gloom, I could tell we were both making a mental note of that voice. We wanted to see this mighty warrior for ourselves as soon as it was light.

"*Gerrae*! That's awfully big talk," replied the grim-sounding voice, which I could just begin to make out as a shape against the slowly lightening sky.

It was hard to tell from my vantage point sitting on the ground, but he seemed to be nearly as tall as I was.

"You'll probably be the first one to piss yourself the instant one of those barbarians looks at you cross-eyed."

"Watch your tone, you! I've beaten better than you, I swear by Hercules I have!"

This from the great warrior, although I sensed a note of uncertainty, despite the brave words.

"That's easy to say," said the other coolly.

"Easy boys," this came from a previously unheard voice. "There'll be plenty of time enough for everyone to get as much fighting in as any man could want."

This voice sounded older, more confident. The others seemed to sense it as well, and consequently there was no more bickering. Besides, the light was growing, so that what were indistinct shapes before took on more definite form, and the areas of the camp that were not illuminated by torchlight earlier could now be made out. At that, Vibius and I stood from where we were sitting completely silent, causing our new companions to yelp in alarm and jump away. I could not help noticing that the one who yelped the loudest was also the one bragging, but I held my peace. No need to make enemies so early, I thought. One day I might be fighting beside that man. Stepping forward, I called to the other men; I could now see that there were a total of six other men standing there.

"*Salve*, citizens," I called with what I hoped was a tone of friendliness.

They returned the greeting in a ragged chorus.

As I got closer, one of the other men exclaimed, "Gods, you ARE a big one, aren't you? Remind me to stand next to you Ajax."

This brought laughter from the others, and I joined in since I had been teased about my size my whole life. The man I thought might be my height was tall, though nowhere near as tall as I was; I had a good two to three inches on him. Standing for a moment, we surveyed each other now that the light was strong enough, but before we could speak, we heard the sound of a call inside the camp, then the gates opened, each half pushed open by a man dressed in armor and full kit.

"Well," I said, "I guess that means they're ready to receive us."

And without waiting, I began walking towards the gate, where a third man appeared, standing in the middle of the gateway, hands on his hips. As we drew closer, I could see that while he was in basically the same uniform as the other two, his helmet was different. He wore a crest of horsehair, transverse across the helmet, going from ear to ear. His face looked like wrinkled leather, the kind one sees after wearing a set of shoes for a long time in all types of weather. In one hand was clutched a stick of some sort, which he was slowly twitching against his leg as he watched us approach. He was short, but very stocky, and once I got close enough I could see that on one arm a livid scar ran from his elbow all the way down his forearm, slowly twisting until it stopped just above his wrist. I had trouble taking my eyes off of it, but when I did and looked the man in the eye, I saw no welcome in his expression. In fact, if I were to characterize the look on his face, the best I can conjure is to ask you to imagine that a *numen* or other invisible shade is hovering just in front of him, holding a huge, steaming pile of *cac* under his nose, *cac* that only he can smell. That was how he looked at us, and I was soon to find out that my description was not far off from the truth, except that the pile of *cac* was actually us.

28

"All of you fall in, in a single line starting right here, with the tallest first to my left," he pointed to a spot with his stick, and I headed that way, knowing already that this would be my spot.

His voice sounded like he had eaten gravel for breakfast, with his tone matching the look on his face, and he obviously was not pleased with what he saw. We struggled to get into the proper order; my part was easy but the others had to gauge each other to determine exactly where they were supposed to be. After a couple of moments, we were more or less settled into a line, and I looked over to my left to see where Vibius ended up. Suddenly, I was slammed in the stomach by something that felt very much like a dagger, except it was blunt and the wind rushed out of my lungs as I dropped immediately to my knees, gasping for breath and clutching my stomach expecting to feel blood, so sure I was that I had been stabbed. Seeing a pair of boots in front of me, much like the pair that Cyclops wore, I looked up to see the Legionary with the stick in one hand, tapping the other end of it into the palm of his other hand as he looked down at me with a sneer on his face.

"Nobody told you to look around, did they you *cunnus*?" he snarled, his voice even more gravelly than before because he pitched it loudly enough for all to hear.

Not sure what to say, I shook my head. Instantly, the stick lashed out, catching me just above my ear, causing stars to explode in my head.

"I asked you a question, boy," he roared, and now more afraid than any time I could remember in my life, I answered quickly, "No, sir.....I mean, Your Excellency."

WHAM! Another blow, this time on the top of my head, and now I felt something more than fear, as I began to get angry. Was there no pleasing this man?

"I work for a living, you *cunnus*," he bellowed at an even louder level, which I had not thought possible if I had not heard it. "I'm no Excellency! You'll address me by my proper title."

Suddenly, his voice dropped back to normal, and he continued talking, as if there was nothing untoward taking place an instant before.

29

"On your feet boy. And look straight ahead, you got that?"

I pulled myself to my feet, a little unsteadily, but before I could answer, he continued.

"Of course, none of you know what my proper title or my name is, because you haven't been taught such things. So we'll begin with that. My name is Lucius Favonius, and I'm the Primus Pilus of the Tenth Legion. I know that the title means nothing to you now, but you'll learn what it means in time. Right now, all you need to know is that as far as you're concerned, I and anyone who wears this," he pointed to his helmet, "are to be considered on the same level as the gods you worship, because like the gods, we exercise the power of life and death over each of you."

I gulped; this was not going exactly as I had seen it in my mind's eye, and I wondered how Vibius was taking this. My gut was still throbbing, and my head still ringing, so it was hard to pay attention, but I knew that what I was being told was important.

"I'll escort you to the *Praetorium*," he turned and pointed at a huge tent, dead in the middle of the camp, several hundred feet away.

Without waiting for an answer, he turned to stride away, with all of us following quickly behind him. When we drew close, he stopped us several paces away from the entrance. Standing in front of it were two Legionaries, obviously on guard duty, and similarly to the Praetor's residence, the area around the tent was a bustle of activity as soldiers and civilians came and went into it. As I was to learn, anywhere our commanding general, the Praetor Julius Caesar, was located, it was always like a beehive.

"You'll hand in those tokens, and you'll then return to that spot outside the *Praetorium*, where you'll get into the exact same line you're in now, facing the tent, and you'll wait for me. Is that clear?"

"Yes, Primus Pilus," I answered quickly, before anyone else had a chance to answer, catching him a bit by surprise.

He looked at me for a moment before giving a harsh chuckle.

"Maybe you're not as stupid as you look, boy."

30

You have no idea, I thought grimly, but I am going to take your job, old man.

Turning in our tokens to a clerk, we gave our name, which was matched up to the documents that were created as part of our records and sent from the Praetor's residence the day before. On turning in our tokens, we were informed that we were now no longer *probatios*, but had achieved the lofty status of *tirones*, or *tiros* as we were more commonly called, when of course we were not called all manner of other names. None of us had any idea what the distinction was, or why it mattered, although we would learn, and the difference was actually quite important. As *probatios*, while subject to some of the rules and regulations governing the army, it was not the complete set, so that if we ran afoul of one of those rules during our brief time in that status, the range of our punishment was limited. The status of *probatio* usually lasted longer because normally the *conquisitores* were out in the countryside and would march groups of new recruits to the training camp, but it was not necessary in our case. However, as *tirones*, we were now under the full authority of the Roman Legion, meaning that we could be flogged, or worse, executed for a breach of the rules, if deemed serious enough. We were then presented with another document that we were told to sign, something I found impossible to read because it seemed to be in some sort of language that I did not understand. I would come to master it and read it as easily as I read any document written in the normal fashion, but it would take some time. Back then, I just signed like everyone else and was informed that this involved our pay.

"So when do we get our pay?" piped up the one I had marked as being the loudmouthed great warrior.

His name was Spurius Didius, and he was also on the tall side, standing third from the end where I stood. He had a sly look about him, always peering about like he was searching for something to steal, which as it turned out, was exactly what he was doing, but that is for later. The clerk looked up in surprise at the question, then burst out laughing.

"Why don't you ask the Primus Pilus about that?" he replied, and I sensed that this would not be a good idea, something that Didius obviously did not pick up on, as he exclaimed loudly, "I'll do just that."

Once we turned in our tokens and signed our documents, we went outside and fell into our positions in line more quickly than the first time. There was just enough time for Vibius to whisper a quick question about how I was doing, and I reassured him that I was fine, if still hurting a bit. However, I was determined that I learned my lesson and would let someone else make the mistakes from here on in. Standing in line again, we waited for what seemed like a full watch and I sensed, as did some of the others, that this was some sort of test, so I made sure to stand as still as I could and not look around.

The waiting turned out to be too much for some, and I heard someone whisper loudly, "Pluto's cock, what are they waiting for?"

Instantly I heard quick footsteps, followed by the sound of what had to be a stick smashing into someone's body, then a thud as the man fall to the ground, the unfortunate gasping for air much like I had.

"Did anyone tell you to speak, *cunnus*?" it was the voice of the Primus Pilus.

"N-no, Primus Pilus," the man managed to gasp.

"Then on your feet, you pathetic piece of *cac*", the Primus Pilus spoke scornfully. "I didn't hit you near as hard as I did the oaf on the end, so get up and quit sniveling like a woman."

The Primus Pilus reappeared in front of us, but instead of turning my head to look again, I watched him out of the corner of my eye. He wore the same expression on his face, except this time he was not alone. Standing next to him, in identical uniform, though without quite as many phalarae, torqs and arm rings, was a slightly taller, slender man, who also looked a bit younger. He bore a scar down the right side of his face, from the middle of his ear to midway down his jaw, giving him a look of wickedness, and he too was carrying the same kind of stick as Primus Pilus Favonius, although he stood slightly behind the Primus Pilus.

Indicating the second Centurion, Primus Pilus Favonius announced, "This is Secundus Pilus Prior Gaius Crastinus. He's the commander of the Second Cohort of the Tenth Legion. You'll accompany him to the quartermaster, where you'll be issued your

32

equipment. You'll obey him in the same manner you obey me, or you'll wish you had never been born. Is that understood?"

This time, we responded in a more unified manner, although it still did not impress the Primus Pilus, or the Pilus Prior for that matter. The two Centurions exchanged a quiet word before the Primus Pilus disappeared into the *Praetorium*, leaving us to the tender mercy of Pilus Prior Crastinus.

"Right," he called out, "the first thing we're going to learn is how to go from one point to another without looking like a mob. Understood?"

"Yes, Pilus Prior," we answered.

"The first thing you *cunni* need to know is how to stand correctly," he continued.

I was somewhat surprised; I did not know until that moment that there was a right and wrong way to stand!

As if reading my mind, he said, "As you'll learn, there are only two ways of doing things in the Legions. The Legion way and the wrong way. When you hear the command *Intente*, you'll come to the position that I'm about to show you."

He demonstrated; pulling himself erect, he looked straight ahead, pulling his chin in, with his chest out, his feet together and his arms straight down by his sides.

Holding that position for a moment so that we could see it, he broke the position then immediately snapped, "*Intente!*"

Instantly we tried to emulate the position he had just shown us, as he walked up and down, inspecting us, correcting my comrades with a quick smack to the part of the body that was not in the proper position. His progress was punctuated by grunts and groans as he made his way to me, and I prayed to every god I knew that I had done it correctly because I was still sore from my earlier lesson. Once he reached me, I concentrated on looking straight ahead, despite my natural inclination to look at him. This was one time where my height actually helped, since I could look directly at his horsehair device and not in his eyes. Luckily, he just rapped my knuckles to make me put my hands into the correctly curled position before he returned to the front of our group.

"That is pathetic, truly pathetic," he sighed, with what sounded like genuine sadness, "but since we have so much to do today, we'll have to work on this another time. Now, I'm going to give another command, to tell you to turn to the right. When this command is given, you'll all immediately pivot, like so," he demonstrated by pivoting on the ball of his left foot, while simultaneously turning on his right heel, then after turning, bringing his left foot back to its original position next to his right foot. "You will not move until you hear the last word of the command," he commanded next, which confused me.

How would we know which was the last word?

However, it became clear that this was yet another trick, when he called out, "*Ad GLADIUM*," putting the emphasis on the second word, causing at least three of the others to turn in the manner he had demonstrated. For some reason I did not move; I think I was already beginning to understand how things worked, or so I thought at the time.

Immediately, the Pilus Prior screamed, "Do not move!" Then he ran over to the unfortunates and roared at one of them, "You miserable bag of *cac*! I said to wait for the FINAL word of the command."

"But Pilus Prior," the man replied, in a whining, wheedling voice that I recognized immediately as belonging to Didius.

Before he could get another word out, however, the thud of the stick smashing into his gut sounded, and I heard him fall, choking.

"But what? There is no but, you *cunnus*, you piece of filth! You'll wait for the command!"

Before Didius could give any response, Pilus Prior Crastinus leaped to the other two, administering the same type of punishment to them that he had doled out to Didius. It turned out that one of them was Vibius, although I did not find out until later, because he was at the farther end of the line, towards what would become known as the "little end."

Once the three recovered and were at the original position of *Intente*, the Pilus Prior again commanded, "*Ad Gladium......Clina*!"

Immediately, we all turned in the manner we had been taught, except that now, one of our group, while he had indeed turned in the exact manner that was specified, turned to the left instead of the right. This sent Pilus Prior Crastinus into an ecstasy of rage.

"By the gods, what has been sent to me?" he asked rhetorically.

Running over to the man standing facing the one to his left, instead of staring at the back of the man to his right as he should have, I could hear by the tone of voice that this had taken the anger of the Pilus Prior to a new level.

"Are you daring to tell me that you don't know your left from your right?"

"N-n-no, Pilus Prior," came the answer, almost forcing me to look down the line to see who could possibly not know their left from their right.

The response obviously caught the Pilus Prior by surprise as well, because there was silence for a moment, then he asked in a deceptively calm voice, "What's your name, boy?"

"Q-Q-Quintus Artorius, Pilus Prior," came the answer, in a quaking voice.

"Well, Quintus Artorius, seeing as your whore of a mother and slave of a father never bothered to teach you your left from right, let me show you."

SMACK!

"That's the left side of your face."

SMACK!

"That's the right side of your face. Which hand do you eat with?"

"Th-this hand, Pilus Prior," came the answer.

SMACK!

"That's your right hand! That's the hand you'll hold a sword in, do you understand? So when I give you the command, *Ad Gladium, Clina*, which direction do you suppose you'll turn towards? No, don't tell me, point."

A silence, where Artorius obviously pointed in the right direction.

"Very good, Artorius. Now, turn around and face the way everyone else is facing. And remember, if you obey an order and find yourself as you just were, you were wrong. Got it?"

"Yes, Pilus Prior."

Once we were faced the correct way, he taught us the command to march, starting on the left foot first, which made sense because it automatically put our shield side first, and would be how we would fight. After a few fits and starts, and more beatings, we finally got it right, then marched to the section of the camp, behind the *Praetorium* but still part of the headquarters area, where the quartermasters were housed in their own tent, almost as large as the *Praetorium*. Inevitably, we bungled the halting when the order came, which was of course by design of the Pilus Prior, to whom we were taking a healthy dislike at this point. After more beatings, and practice of starting and stopping, we were then told to go into the tent, where we would be issued our basic necessities as a Legionary. I was first in line, and immediately ran into trouble because of my size, when I was handed a tunic, the soldier's tunic, plus a spare and told to try it on. Instead of hanging loosely in the proper manner, it was fairly tight, particularly across the shoulders. The first pair of boots I was handed were too small as well, as were the next few pairs. Finally, after rummaging around, the Legionary assigned as *immunes* for the quartermaster found a pair that almost fit.

"You'll have to have one of the cobblers outside of camp make you a pair, special."

"How much will that cost?" I asked, dismayed.

The Legionary shrugged, "No more than a few sesterces, I expect. I wouldn't know."

He immediately moved on to the others, passing out their own set of boots, all of which fit, I noted dismally. This was not shaping up to be a great day for me. While the armor I was handed fit, it was also a little snug. Fortunately it was not enough to restrict my movement, and I gave a quiet thanks to the gods for that small favor. Some of the other lads looked lost, and more than one staggered when they were handed the armor and told to put it on over the tunic. We were told by the *immune* to invest in a padded undershirt that was not issued, but could be made by one of the merchants dealing in such items who were a permanent fixture outside the camp. Handing us our belt and harness next, he showed us how to bunch the mail of our armor above the belt so that it would distribute the weight better. Next came the helmet, and once again I presented a problem, although this was more my problem than for the *immunes*. The helmet fit, except that it fit more tightly than it did on the others, so that the felt padded cap that the others wore was useless to me, at least with its normal thickness. I was sure that this too would require a trip outside camp at the first opportunity. In the meantime, the helmet was riding on my head with nothing in between it but my hair, which kept catching on some of the internal fittings. Because of that discomfort, I resolved that I would cut my hair as short as I could, a style that I wear to this day. Hair may be the pride of a woman, but it is the shame of a warrior, at least that is what I told the others when they teased me about being practically bald. A hidden benefit of shaving my head was that it gave the normal cap just enough room to fit, saving me a few sesterces. Even so, it was still a snug fit but I learned fairly quickly that this was an advantage; it kept the helmet from slipping down over my eyes or turning sideways which was a constant problem for a lot of my comrades. Once the helmets were passed out, we were given our shield, not the real one but the one made of wicker with which Cyclops had trained Vibius and me. Having held a shield many times by this point, Vibius and I had no trouble, something that did not go unnoticed by the *immune*, who narrowed his eyes though he did not say anything. The others had some trouble, handling it awkwardly, not sure how to grasp it correctly. One of the others even dropped his, causing a string of curses to be launched by the *immune*, yet thankfully there was no beating, the Pilus Prior not being nearby at the time.

There were a number of other pieces of equipment; a spade, which was handed to us by the *immune* with a smirk and a comment, "You're going to get to know that piece of equipment very well."

We stared at him blankly, not knowing exactly what he meant, but he was right. Along with the spade came the turf cutter, our *patera* from which we would prepare and eat our meals, a basket to put the smaller items in, the pack and a grinding mill that was to be shared by our tent section, along with spare thongs and other odds and ends. Finally, we were left with just two pieces of gear to be handed to us, and again Vibius and I thanked the gods that we knew what to expect. Alone out of our group we knew that we would not be getting the real sword or javelins that day, just the wooden sword and practice javelins. Therefore, when we were handed our wooden weapons, we made not a sound, which was fortunate, because the Pilus Prior had just entered the tent behind us, although we did not yet know it.

"What's this?" demanded none other than Didius. "Are we children that we don't get a real sword?"

"Exactly," exclaimed one of the others, someone in the middle of the line, a somewhat swarthy lad standing next to someone who looked remarkably similar to him, although not close enough to be twins. "Aren't we good enough to rate having a real weapon?"

For the second time that day, Didius was struck down by the Pilus Prior, followed closely by his fellow complainant, and then was joined by the man that had to be his brother, who out of reflex I suppose had reached down to help him.

"Nobody told you to touch him," the Pilus Prior snarled.

It was beginning to become clear to us that nobody was going to do anything unless they were specifically told to do so, and I made a mental note of it.

"Sorry, Pilus Prior. He's my broth..." he did not get a chance to finish his sentence, struck again by that infernal stick.

"And nobody asked you for an explanation you *cunnus*," the Pilus Prior snapped. "On your feet, the lot of you."

Once they climbed back to their feet and came to the correct position of *Intente*, which the rest of us had immediately assumed, the Pilus Prior spoke to the rest of us.

"So, is there anyone else who feels like complaining about not being handed a real sword?" he asked in a deceptively pleasant
38

voice. Fortunately this did not fool anyone, even Artorius, into answering. "You *cunni* can barely walk in a straight line, so you don't really expect that we'd hand you a real weapon, do you? You have a LONG way to go before you reach that point."

Seeing that we had received our basic allotment of gear, he indicated that we should leave the tent, carrying the gear that we were not wearing in our basket or stacked on top of it, along with the possessions we had brought with us and gave the order to *ad signa*, to get back into our assigned places in line. It did not take us as long fortunately, or perhaps the Pilus Prior had just resigned himself to our ineptitude, so we only had to do it once. Giving us the order to turn to the right again, he started us marching towards the far side of the camp. As we marched we passed by other men, apparently in different stages of training, which I watched only out of the corner of my eye, not daring to turn my head. After a few moments, we reached the far corner of the camp, near the *Porta Praetoria*, the main gate. There were several rows of tents arranged in a square, all of the outermost tents facing the walls of the camp. Immediately behind each tent facing the walls was the back of another tent, whose opening faced in the opposite direction, away from the wall. Across a wide pathway from those tents was another line of tents, whose openings faced in the direction of the tents closest towards the wall. The effect was that there was a series of streets, with rows of tents acting as the houses, although it was much more neatly arranged than most cities. Such is the camp of the Roman army, even to this day. The camp we were at housed a total of four Legions, the 7th, 8th 9th and 10th. Normally the most experienced Legions are placed closest to the walls, but since we were in friendly territory and had no fear of attack, placing was not as important. This was to be our new home for most of the time we were in the Legions.

Indicating a tent, the Pilus Prior told us, "This is where all of you will be living. There are eight of you here; your Sergeant has already been selected, and one man will be joining you shortly. This is your tent section; look around at each of these men, because they'll be the ones you're living with from here until your time in the Legion is up. Or until you die, whichever happens first."

He gave a short, barking laugh at this, which none of us found particularly amusing. Before he dismissed us to arrange ourselves he gave us one last instruction.

"Before you go in, each of you needs to select one other man from your tent section. This'll be your companion, your closest companion and friend for the time you're in the Legion. He'll be the holder of your will, he'll be the man who watches your back wherever you go. Whenever possible, you'll go together, even when you go out into town, so choose wisely. I'll give you a few moments to do that, then you're to go into your tent, and with your choice in mind, you'll select the spot where you'll be sleeping. The cot that your Sergeant occupies is the one closest to the entrance; you'll be able to tell because it's already occupied with his gear. Now, I'll return in a sixth part of the watch. Or maybe sooner," he said this last with quiet menace, "just to make sure that you're doing what you're supposed to be doing and not already fucking off."

Turning and stalking off, he left us standing there a bit bewildered, if I am to be honest.

The man next to me, the second tallest man who I had judged to have some intelligence, nodded to me, "My name's Sextus Scribonius. You seem to have your wits about you, like me," he grinned as he said this. "What do you say we pair up?"

Somewhat regretfully, I told him that I could not because I already had someone, and since my hands were full I nodded in the direction of Vibius, already walking towards me with a smile on his face. Scribonius was clearly disappointed, but he took it well, especially when I explained that we had been best friends for so many years. Immediately he turned to his left, but that was Didius, with whom he clearly had no intention of pairing.

Vibius whispered, "Well, at least this part is easy. Why don't we duck in now and claim our spots while the rest of them are arguing?"

Which we immediately did, to the protests of some of the others, Didius most notably and unsurprisingly. However, the two brothers, seeing us, quickly followed. I selected the spot across from the Sergeant nearest to the door, with Vibius taking the spot next to me, the second man to the left. The brothers headed for the two cots directly across the doorway from Vibius and placed their gear on them, claiming the space as theirs. They were followed by two others, who claimed the spots at the back, next to the brothers, and it was then I began to notice something that did not make sense. There were a total of eight cots, but there were eight of us already, plus the

40

unnamed Sergeant, and the Pilus Prior had told us that one more would be joining us. That made ten men, but only eight spots. Vibius caught on as well, and we were looking at each other in a puzzled manner when we heard a new voice at the entrance to the tent. We both turned to see another Legionary, wearing a uniform identical to us, with the exception that his helmet had a flowing black horse tail on top of it, the tail spilling down near his shoulders.

"So, apparently someone can count," he said laconically as he stood in the doorway.

He was a well-built man, in his mid-twenties it appeared, with even features and cool grey eyes that appraised each of us. His gaze lingered on me, taking in my size and he pursed his lips in a silent whistle, but did not say anything to me. Instead, he turned to the whole group and announced, "In case you haven't guessed, my name is Lucius Calienus, and I'm the Sergeant of this tent section. I was a member of Pompey's 1st Legion, and was promoted to help fill this Legion out with some men who knew their ass from their elbows. And judging from what I'm seeing in this lot, I might as well kiss my ass goodbye because I'm as good as dead the moment we go into battle."

This did not set well with me, but I kept my mouth shut.

Calienus walked into the tent, standing in the narrow area between the cots and said, "So I see that you, or at least some of you" he turned to nod in the direction of Vibius and myself, "were catching on that there seems to be a problem with the numbers in this tent."

Not sure how to address him at this point, we contented ourselves with just nodding.

"Well, you'll be happy to know that you're correct in your assumption, so there may be hope for some of you yet."

Turning to the outside to the remaining man, he motioned him to come inside. Having seen that Scribonius had grabbed Artorius, despite the early signs that Artorius might be a weakling, I assumed that Scribonius must have decided that Artorius was the lesser of two evils. Didius walked in, and I have to say that he looked a little upset that he was not picked, although he did not say anything about it.

Calienus said to Didius, "So you're the odd man out, neh?"

Didius nodded, and Calienus laughed, but while it was not necessarily a cruel laugh, it still obviously rankled Didius.

"Maybe you're just slow to make friends. Or," he became serious, "it means that you're someone I have to keep an eye on. Either way, you're out of luck, neh?" Without waiting for an answer, Calienus turned to the rest of us, and explained the mystery of the two missing cots.

They were not missing at all. Instead it meant that at any given time, there would be two men on some sort of duty, at least once we finished training. Even during training, there would be at least one man on watch on our assigned sector of wall, so that at some point, someone was sleeping in your cot while you were out on duty. During training only one would be missing, requiring that someone slept on the ground, but in order to be fair, it was rotated evenly, even Calienus participating. Also, while the sleeping arrangements would change, the area where we stored our gear, under our cots, would remain the same. Didius and the unknown tenth man were given two corners of the tent as their area, making it somewhat inconvenient for them, but was designed to stop gear from being "accidentally" mixed up, a practice that turned out to be a very good precaution with Didius in our tent, although we did not know that then.

Once that was explained to us, Calienus showed us the proper way to stow our gear underneath our cots, taking the remainder of the time allotted to us by the Pilus Prior. I imagine it was a sixth part to the instant when we heard a shrill whistle sound outside. Vibius and I knew what the whistle meant, even if we had never actually heard one, thanks to Cyclops, so we immediately grabbed our shield, put our helmets back on, picked up our wooden sword and hurried outside. Falling into our places at the opposite ends of the line, we were followed in a matter of moments by the rest of the group, who seemed to follow our lead and came out carrying their weapons and shields. They got in line quickly, but none of us were sure how to stand at *Intente* holding our shields or wooden sword. That we assembled in this fashion clearly surprised the Pilus Prior, but he made no comment about it and fortunately, we were not penalized, for whatever reason. Instead, the Pilus Prior showed us how to hold the wooden sword vertically; normally our sword would be sheathed, but since we had not been issued them yet, and the wooden sword would not fit in the scabbard anyway, we were taught this method. Then he told us to go stow the gear in our tents and come back outside.

Once we did so, he marched us over to the forum, which in an army camp is the large clear area next to the *Praetorium* where the Legions are mustered when they are to be issued orders en masse, or some other event occurs that requires everyone's presence. The rest of the time, at least in the early days of the Legion, it was being used by us *tiros* as we were taught how to march and perform close order drill. There were other small groups, along with a couple of large ones, composed of a full Century, normally eighty men. However, in the case of our Legions, and in every Legion raised by Caesar from that point forward, he made a change by commanding that a Century would consist of a hundred men, which was changed back to eighty men by the man now known as Augustus. This was why we had the unusual sleeping arrangements in our tent; normally eight cots were sufficient, since the Century of traditional size consisted of ten sections of men, one section to each tent. Of course, we did not know this was unusual, and would not learn otherwise until much later in our careers. Now, these Centuries were all marching about under the order of their respective Centurions. Assisting them was the Centurion's Optio, the second in command of each Century; we had yet to meet ours because he was working with the rest of the Century. As it turned out, we were the last of the First Century of the Second Cohort to be added, explaining why we were getting the undivided attention of the Pilus Prior and not the Optio. The Pilus Prior had us watch the other groups marching for a moment, and even to our untrained eye, we could see that they were in different stages of training. Smaller groups like ours still displayed a tendency to look like they were shambling along, and they were being "encouraged" with the Centurion's stick more often than the others. It was also plain to see that being smacked with that stick was going to be a regular part of our lives for some time to come.

After a few moments, the Pilus Prior said, "You can see that you'll be spending a great deal of your time just learning how to march in the proper manner, and obey the commands given you while you march. And know this you *cunni*," he finished, "my Cohort will be the tightest, best drilled Cohort in this Legion, or you'll all die trying."

He laughed at his own joke, if indeed it was. For ourselves, we were not sure. The rest of the day was spent marching about, with a liberal amount of bashing with the stick, which we learned was called the *vitus* and is a symbol of the Centurion rank. Up and down we marched, learning the basic commands, and I never suspected one could become so tired from just walking around, yet by the time we were through, I was exhausted. So were the others if the looks of them were any indication. We marched through at least two watches; the watch is divided into increments of three hours each, and the end of each watch is signaled by the sounding of a horn. I could not tell which horn it was, but as I learned later the change of the watch is sounded by the *bucina*. Either the Pilus Prior thought we had been through enough, or we were at a point where we would not have improved, but either way we were thankful for the break.

We were marched back to our tent and put in the charge of Sergeant Calienus, who informed us that it was almost time for the evening meal, so he spent the time waiting showing us the proper way to stow our gear under our cots. As one might surmise, everything had to be arranged just so, and although he did not have to do so, Sergeant Calienus explained why.

"Let's say it's the middle of the night, and you're all sound asleep, thinking of the women you're missing back home," he said, drawing a chuckle from us, which he did not seem to mind. "Then out of nowhere, the horns are blasting and men are shouting because an attack on the walls has started. It's pitch black, and you have to fall to your defensive station, which" he added, "I'll show you where it is on the wall on the way to draw our meal. Anyway, everyone's screaming and shouting, there's a horrible racket coming from the barbarian horde outside the walls, and it's utter chaos and confusion."

While he was talking, he was seated on his cot facing us, except he was demonstrating as he spoke, pulling out first his armor and putting it on as he continued explaining, "So you've got just a moment to get your gear on and stand to on the wall, or there'll be Hades to pay, or worse. What if the breach to the wall happens in your area, because you couldn't get armed and ready in the proper amount of time?"

By the time he was finished, he had put on his helmet, donned his armor, strapped on his baldric, grabbed his shield and was ready to go, all without looking for any piece of his gear. We were all suitably impressed, and I at least saw the immediate sense of what he had said. As we were to learn, this was the way of Sergeant Calienus; while the Pilus Prior used his *vitus* and the most inventive cursing I had ever heard in my life to that point, Sergeant Calienus talked to us like we were already Legionaries. I supposed it was because he was not as far removed from having been like us as Pilus Prior Crastinus, although I was hard pressed to imagine that Crastinus was ever a *tiro*. In fact, I imagined that he had been born in his armor, fully formed and ready for battle from the day he was born, an image that I was to learn was carefully cultivated by him, and one that I would come to use myself.

Sergeant Calienus marched us back to the *quaestorium*, the tent that is located next to the *Praetorium* and serves the quartermaster, where we were given our flat loaf of *panis castrenis*, had the small stoppered bottle for our olive oil filled, and watered wine put into our flask. Some of the boys looked at what they were being handed with a combination of puzzlement and distaste; for me, it was nothing since I had always been indifferent to food as far as what it tasted like. I did miss my meat, although I did not say anything since that would have exposed my poverty to the others. Over the years I have developed a belief that one reason I was so large was due in part to my father's lack of success as a farmer. Because we did not have much grain with which to make our bread, we ate more meat than was normal for most Romans, and I have since seen people like the Germans who are my size and whose diet is composed mostly of meat, which seems to support my idea. Still, it was not something I liked to talk about with the others, so I pretended that I liked the diet of bread and chickpeas just as much as everyone else.

"We get bacon every other day, a nice salted chunk of it, but today's not the day. And you're lucky that we're in camp and only training, or it would be straight water, no wine," Calienus explained.

Once we were given our ration, we marched back to our tent, where Calienus had us sit on the ground outside, and we began eating our evening meal. While we ate, Calienus gave us more information.

"If I were you, boys, I'd save a bit of the bread and oil for the morning, because we only get our one ration a day."

Granted, the loaf, which was round and flat and about four inches high by about one foot in diameter was a good size, but I still wondered how we were to survive on this alone, even with the bacon as supplement.

"Once we begin marching, our rations will increase," explained Calienus, who obviously was a mind reader.

Or, he had once been a *tiro* and wondered the same thing.

"But while all we're doing right now is drill and weapons training, the general doesn't want us getting fat and lazy."

I did not see how that could happen, but I was content to take him at his word. Calienus then went around the group, asking questions of each of us in order to learn more about them. It was in this manner that I learned the names and basic information of the men I would spend the next several years with, some of them at least. Along with Vibius and myself, there was Sextus Scribonius, the man who stood next to me when we were arranged by height. Scribonius said he came from Corduba, yet he was vague about what his father did or anything else about his family, for that matter. It was a subject that he rarely discussed, and it would not be until many years later that I would learn that he was lying about where he was from, but that is for later.

Then there was Quintus Artorius, and his story was a fairly common one, not unlike mine. His father was a blacksmith and they could not get along, so after a particularly bitter argument, Artorius threatened that he would go join the Legion, whereupon his father called his bluff. It was clear to all of us that he seemed to be having second thoughts, an impression that was only reinforced as time went by. His was the nervous voice I heard in the pre-dawn of that day when we all reported. He was also the smallest member of our group, which I do not imagine helped his outlook.

The two who looked alike were indeed brothers, Marcus and Quintus Mallius, and it was a common occurrence for all of us to mix them up. Before long they both earned nicknames, but until they did, it was a source of exasperation for all of us. They were sons of a farmer in the province, outside the town of Illurco and were quick to point out that there was a pretty good chance that the olive oil we were dipping our bread in came from their farm, since they had accompanied their father making a delivery to the army.

The brothers decided to enlist because there was a multitude of brothers Mallius. Marcus was the oldest by a year, although they could have almost passed for twins. Both had a cheerful disposition generally, though Quintus possessed a fearsome temper, which got him in trouble more than once during our time together.

Next was Publius Vellusius, who stood to the right of Vibius in our line, and up to that point from who I had barely heard a word. His story was similar to Marcus and Quintus, and Vibius for that matter; an excess of sons, with Vellusius being the excess. His father had a farm in the far north-west of the province in Nertobriga; it took him a week to arrive at Corduba and he had gotten a later start like we had, accounting for his relatively late arrival along with the rest of us. He was about as tall as Vibius, but built much more slightly, with a bristle of black hair that seemed to stick straight up, no matter how much oil he used to keep it flat. To me, he looked a bit like a bird, with the same kind of nervous movement and constant peering at his surroundings, as if waiting for a cat to come along, but he turned out to be a good soldier, though, one of the best in our Century.

Finally, there was Didius, who had calmed his mouth somewhat, just not enough to suit me or the others. Despite being shorter than I was, he was built similarly to me, and indeed he turned out to be quite strong, perhaps as strong as I was, something I had not encountered before. Perhaps, if I am being honest, that is one of the reasons that I disliked him as much as I did, although if that is true it does not adequately explain the hatred the others held for him before much time would pass from this first day. Still, at that moment, we were willing to give him a chance, despite his bragging and generally unpleasant attitude. Didius told us that he was born to be in the Legions, like his father and father before him, who were great heroes in their own right, although he would outshine them, and the rest of us. I took care to hide my feelings, munching on my bread with what I hoped was a bland expression.

Calienus just gave a slight grin, as if he had heard it all before, which he had. Once we were done, he told us about himself. He was 28, and had been in the Legion for ten years, but re-enlisted for the full 16 year term that Caesar set as the length for this enlistment of the 10th Legion, all for the chance of promotion to Sergeant. He was also *immune*, having skill as an armourer, his father being one before him and teaching him his craft. That meant that he was exempt from most of the other duties, with the exception of standing watch during the night hours, when he would not have been working anyway. Calienus was in Pompey's 1st Legion, a fact that gave him instant respect, and had been with Pompey during his short but sharp campaign against the pirates, recently returning from the war against Mithridates, which was the talk of the Roman world ever since. He fought in over 30 engagements, and was wounded four times, once so seriously that he almost died from the infection. Calienus was a hardcore Pompeian, and I sometimes wonder if things had worked out differently what road he would have traveled.

But I am ahead of myself again; forgive me, gentle reader, it is the prerogative of the elderly to sometimes meander. Introductions done, with the light beginning to fade, we continued talking and asking questions of Calienus, all of which he answered with great patience. Finally, the horn blew that signaled it was time to retire, and we entered the tent to make preparations for sleep. Because it was our first night, we were not entered as part of the duty rotation, though that would change the next day when the last member of the tent section joined us. It was just as well; we were all exhausted and I think even if Hannibal himself had risen from the dead to mount an attack on the camp, it would have been impossible to rouse us from our slumber. I do not even remember lying on my cot, and in the morning I awoke in the exact same position in which I had fallen asleep, something that would become a common occurrence over the next few weeks.

The next morning we were roused, again before daylight, to start our day, being given just a few moments to eat what we saved from the night before, then forming up outside the tent. Pilus Prior Crastinus came striding up, with the same invisible *numen* waving the same invisible turd under his nose.

"Well, you *cunni*," he snarled by way of greeting, "I was expecting half of you to be gone like the sorry specimens you replaced."

This was a shock; it was the first we heard that we were not just original drafts but instead had replaced others. As we learned the story over the next few days, we were added to the Legion to replace *tiros* in the Second Cohort that failed to measure up, for one reason or another. Rather than sprinkling us into the Centuries of the Cohort that lost men, they instead consolidated by moving the men who were in our Century out to the ones that had missing men. The logic was obvious; at least, once it was explained to us. The other

48

Centuries were all at more advanced stages of training, and dropping in a brand new *tiro* into one of them would have been a hardship that compromised the training of the other Centuries. Instead our Century, the First Century, was selected to be the one to dole out men to make a hole to fill, with members of the First Century serving as replacements for those who had fallen out. Like with most things in the army, once explained it made perfect sense. It was just relatively rare that things were clarified for us, especially as time passed. The more experienced we were, the less it was considered important to at least give us an idea of what was going on or why we were doing something; we were just expected to obey as if the order came from Jupiter's mouth directly to our ears. Again, if one thinks about it, it makes some sense. By that time, you are indoctrinated in the ways of the Legion. In your first days, you are still more citizen than Legionary, and as part of the process, there is a certain amount of explanation that is given to you. Not much, but a little, which is more than more experienced Legionaries got.

This also explained why we were in the First Century, so we could have the undivided attention of the Pilus Prior, not that we were very appreciative. He marched us over to the forum, and we picked up where we left off the day before, learning the basic drill movements and commands. Over and over, with the word "*Repitate*" ringing in our ears, along with the sting of his *vitus* to help remind us, we marched up and down, up and down. The only break in the monotony was in mid-morning, when the last member of our tent section joined us, having drawn his gear and been escorted by either Sergeant Calienus or the Optio to our tent. He was introduced to us as Marcus Atilius, and he slotted into our line between Scribonius and Didius, much to the relief of Scribonius. Atilius appeared to be somewhat older than the rest of us, with the exception of Calienus, though it turned out to be more a case of hard living. When he joined us, he wore the same look as Vibius the morning before, somewhat pale and a little unsteady on his feet, the result of a particularly festive farewell party, or so we thought at the time. However, we would learn that every day was an occasion for a festival as far as Atilius was concerned. Because he was also behind in learning the basic movements, we were told to run around the camp along the *Via Sagularis*, the road that runs around the inside perimeter of the camp along the walls, while he received personal instruction.

When we all hesitated for a moment, confused, the Pilus Prior snapped, "Well? What are you waiting for?"

"How many times, Pilus Prior?"

This came from Scribonius, which is exactly what I wanted to know, but thank the gods he beat me to it, because it earned nothing more than a smack with the *vitus* and a snarled, "Until I tell you to stop, you idiot."

With that pleasant admonition, we began to run. Being in the lead, I set what I thought would be a pace that everyone could keep up with, yet would be sufficiently quick enough not to earn a beating from the Pilus Prior. However, I miscalculated, badly. While Cyclops made Vibius and I do plenty of exercises that helped our dexterity and overall endurance wearing helmet and armor, he never had us do any running, so very quickly I found that what I thought would be a comfortable pace was putting me into difficulty. However, I was also too proud to slow down, and I continued on, trying to ignore the pain in my side and the feeling that I was breathing pure fire. Leading the way for one circuit, then two, I never looked back, now afraid that since nobody behind me asked to slow down, I was running slower than they would have had they been leading.

It was not until I was halfway through the second lap of the camp that I heard a gasping shout, "*Eho* Pullus! By the gods man, are you trying to kill us all?"

Startled I looked around to see Scribonius, his face as red as our new *sagum*, the soldier's cloak, staggering as he caught up to me now that I had slowed down. Looking over my shoulder, I saw to my dismay that the others were far, far behind, barely visible just turning the second corner of the second circuit of the camp. Scribonius, hands on his knees as he sucked in air, began to gag, making me feel horrible, and good all at the same time.

In between retches, he gasped, "Didn't you hear us shouting for you to slow down? I swear that all of us were begging you to slow your pace, but you just ran along like you were Mercury himself."

Despite the fact that I was breathing as hard as he was, and was fighting the urge to vomit as well, I tried to sound nonchalant as I

50

replied, "Really? No, Scribonius, I'm truly sorry. I didn't hear a thing. I just thought I was running at a pace that wouldn't get us in trouble with Pilus Prior Crastinus."

He looked up at me to see if I was joking, but in that at least I was telling the truth; by this time the others had joined us, and all assumed the same position as Scribonius, each of them cursing my name, my father and my ancestors. Even Vibius was angry with me, and I wavered between embarrassment and anger at the invective they were using against me.

Defensively I protested, "I already told Scribonius I was sorry. I didn't realize I was running so fast."

"Well, clean your ears out, damn you," spat Didius, pushing my mood immediately to anger.

"If you can't keep up, that's not my problem," I retorted, and he stood up straight, making a move towards me as if he had more to say, but before he could, Vibius stepped in between us and grabbed my arm. "None of us could keep up Titus," he spoke sharply, "because you forget that you have these great long legs."

That it was Vibius talking so immediately deflated me and I apologized again, this time more humbly, which seemed to satisfy everyone except for Didius, who continued to glare at me. That is when I knew that he and I were destined for trouble at some point. To make matters worse, the Pilus Prior happened to look up and saw us standing in a group, and we could hear his booming voice, over all the other noise of camp, and we jumped a little in panic.

"I don't believe I told you *cunni* to stop," he roared. "The next time I look around, you had better be running, ladies."

We looked at each other, and then Scribonius said, "The Pilus Prior didn't tell us what order to run in, did he?" Shaking our heads, he continued quickly, "Well then, let's run with the little end at the front, that way we won't have to worry about Pullus galloping off on us."

This was immediately accepted, even by me, not wanting to draw the ire of the others any more than I already had, although I now knew that I could run more slowly without being afraid of being seen as weak. Quickly reversing our order, we started up again with Artorius leading us off. Almost immediately we could all see that while this was a good idea in theory, Artorius was so weak and slow the chances of evading the wrath of the Pilus Prior was practically non-existent. Fairly quickly we rearranged yet again, putting Vibius in front, who set a pace that most of us could follow with a moderate effort, except for Artorius. I assumed that the reason he was so far behind was that he was at the little end of our line, but it turned out that not only was he the smallest physically he was the weakest, in more ways than one. We made a couple more circuits before we heard the Pilus Prior yell at us to stop, which we did, heading back to where he and Atilius were standing. Poor Atilius, being the only focus of the Pilus Prior, already had several large red welts on his arms and legs but his face showed no emotion as he stood there at *intente*. It became apparent that Atilius had taken his personal lessons to heart, because he immediately matched us in terms of our skill level. Once more, the rest of the day was spent in drill, and it was a weary group that trooped to the tent. Sergeant Calienus joined us shortly, and informed us that we were going to be put into the rotation for guard duty, starting that night. During our *tiro* period, we would only be standing watch at night so that we could get all the training in possible. The brothers drew the first watch, followed by Scribonius and Artorius, then Vibius and myself. In this manner, everyone would be able to sleep through the night on a cot, although there would have to be some shifting around.

"But as soon as we finish our meal, I'm taking you boys to the bath house," Calienus told us, wrinkling his nose, "because you stink. And I'm not going to share a tent with a bunch of animals."

This was my first experience with regular bathing; on the farm we bathed at most once a week, usually on the market day, using a large wooden tub for the purpose, after which Phocas or Gaia would oil us down. Actually, I stopped allowing Gaia to bathe me when I was perhaps ten or eleven, but I certainly had never heard of bathing in the middle of the week; it was at least three more days to market day! Nevertheless, I quickly grew accustomed to it and to this day I bathe every day, at least whenever possible. Back then though, I was just a country boy who thought such refinements a waste of time. After the meal, Calienus took us to a large tent near the *quaestorium*, where a line of men stood, all waiting for their turn. This was our first time actually mingling with the other Legionaries, and we obviously looked as green as grass because almost immediately we were jeered and teased. When I heard those

52

mocking words, I felt the heat in my face and my anger starting to rise, when a gentle but firm hand on my elbow stopped me; I was not aware, but I had begun moving towards one particularly mouthy man who looked about the same age as Calienus, just softer. Turning, I saw that was in fact who was grabbing my elbow, giving me a stern look as he shook his head.

"Hold, Pullus. You can't go getting upset when someone runs their mouth at you. Besides," he grinned, "you are fresh meat, and the boys are just having some fun. Soon enough, you'll be doing the same to poor *tiros* like you are now."

I listened and obeyed, except I did not believe him, promising myself that when I was in their shoes, I would not be so callous. It was just one more promise broken in a life full of them. The interior of the tent was lit by oil lamps, and there was a buzz of laughter and conversation, ribald jokes and the kind of complaining that only soldiers can do. There were a couple of dozen slaves who rubbed down each man with oil, then scraped him clean.

Seeing that there were no bath tubs, I looked to our Sergeant and Calienus explained. "No, we don't have proper baths in camp; that only happens in winter quarters when we build more permanent facilities. Here we just have the oil and scraping."

Like other things I had been told, it made perfect sense to me. Not only was it time spent, it was a matter of resources; we should not be wasting water on luxuries like baths. Even so, it was refreshing, and I left feeling like a new man, invigorated by the skilled hands of the slave who rubbed down my tired and sore muscles. It may seem like a small thing, yet I firmly believe that one reason we are invincible is because not only are we well-trained, we are well-cared-for and well-fed. There is no doubt in my mind that the rubdowns that we receive help us recover from our exertions more quickly and thoroughly, so that we are revitalized and able to do more work than our enemies, in every phase and facet of warfare.

Just like the night before, I was asleep before I finished lying down, and it seemed but a moment before I was being shaken awake by Scribonius, while Artorius did the same for Vibius.

"Your turn," Scribonius whispered, and I came awake immediately, something that I somehow managed to teach myself and it has served me well throughout my career. I can be sound asleep, but at a word I am instantly awake. This night, I sat up and copying what Calienus showed us, tried to do the same thing, pulling my gear from underneath my cot from memory. Instead, I immediately dropped my helmet, making a horrible racket and earning me a round of curses from my comrades. Finally stumbling out, I waited for Vibius who managed to equip himself without making a sound, then we headed to the wall that was our sector. I could see in the darkness the same thing happening up and down the wall as the guard changed. Stifling a yawn I climbed the rampart, feeling somewhat ridiculous not properly armed. I had not yet seen the view from the wall and despite it being dark, there was enough light from the moon and the nearby torches that remained lit throughout the night hours to see the disposition of the outside of the camp. About 30 feet away was a ditch, although from the gloom I could not tell its depth. It was in fact 12 feet deep, different than the standard nine feet, but with Caesar as our general, he favored ditches that were 12 feet deep by 15 feet wide, versus the nine foot by twelve foot wide standard. This in turn allows for a higher wall, therefore the camp of a Caesar-led Legion was always harder to storm than those of other generals.

We stood behind a crenellated palisade made of wood; as I was to learn, two of those stakes belonged to me, and I would carry them everywhere we went, or more accurately our section mule did, along with those of every other Legionary, giving them up to form the wall that protected us. The earthen rampart that I stood on was the product of the dirt that came from the ditch, making the rampart six feet wide. It was tamped down to give us a solid footing and wide enough to allow men to move behind others manning the walls in the event they had to run to a trouble spot. The rest of the dirt formed a ramp leading to the rampart, allowing us to run up to the wall without having to worry about climbing ladders. The Roman camp is second to none of its kind and for as long as anyone could remember, this was how a camp was built, almost every single night on the march, with very few exceptions and only slight variations depending on the threat level. In our long-ago past, some unfortunate army did not go to the trouble and was massacred, so from that time on this was the standard. While Vibius and I stood there, shivering in the damp despite our *sagum* wrapped around our shoulders, we could hear the low buzz of voices from the other Legionaries on the wall. Vibius and I glanced at each other; the Pilus Prior had been very specific about the prohibition on talking on guard duty, but it seemed that there were others who did not get that warning from him, or were ignoring it. However, we were still too new to even consider disregarding the rules at this point, so we just shrugged and turned back to stare out into the blackness.

All I can say about my first turn on guard duty is that I wish the hundreds and hundreds of times that I have done since then had passed as quickly as that one. I think it must have been the novelty, because before I could believe that the proper amount of time had passed the horn was blowing, and I could see a very faint lightening in the sky. Since we stood the last watch, we at least had the advantage of being fully dressed and returned to our tent as the more experienced Legionaries who had the day watch relieved us, giving us the proper password. There is a new password and countersign issued every full day, and our shift would be the last to use the old one. Now, the commander of the guard Cohort would go to each station and issue the new password and countersign. Like the camps, this was done without exception, no matter where the Legion was located; as I would learn, even on the Campus Martius just outside Rome, we would have to learn and remember the password and countersign. I would also learn that the method of relief that we used the night before was not the norm; the relief of the guard, especially when on campaign, is much more formalized and is done by the commander of the guard that shift, who marches the men of the relief to their specific spot on the rampart. Those being relieved then fall into the marching formation, taking the place of the men who relieved them, continuing in formation to the next post, where the process is repeated. Only after a complete circuit of the camp is made do those that were relieved get dismissed to go back to sleep, or resume their other duties. That morning, the others were just getting dressed and while we waited, Vibius and I gnawed on the small piece of bacon and bread left over from the night before. By this time, our third day, we knew enough to immediately form up outside the tent, and before long the Pilus Prior showed up, snarling his usual cheery morning greeting. Then we went marching off to begin another day.

Thus set the pattern for the next week, where every day seemed to blur together into one long continuous day of marching and the command *Repitate* ringing in our ears over and over and over. Of course, the command was almost always accompanied with the smack of the *vitus*, and although I was a bit farther ahead than the others, as was Vibius, I received my fair share of blows. Our days became measured by the sounds of the tromping of our feet and the blowing of the *bucina* marking the change of watch, yet slowly, we began to at least look like Legionaries, even if the Pilus Prior kept insisting that we were the worst collection of *tiros* that he had ever seen. Finally, the day arrived for which all of us, particularly Vibius and I, had been waiting. The morning started in the usual manner, but we were told to carry our wooden sword, and instead of being marched to the forum, we marched past it, took a right turn and headed out the *Porta Principalis Sinistra*, the side gate on the left hand side of every camp, exiting it and stopping on the other side of the ditches. Arrayed before us were a huge number of stakes, the same type that Cyclops had trained Vibius and me on, and despite Vibius being a few men down from me, I was sure that he was fighting the urge to smile as well. Finally! We would get our chance to show that we were not as raw as the others, and I could feel my stomach twist in excitement at the thought of finally doing something with which I was familiar.

Of course, it was not going to be so easy. They were not going to just turn us loose to start whacking away, and for this task, we were formally introduced for the first time to our Optio, who acted as our Cohort's weapons instructor. He was a bit taller than average and at first glance looked rather pudgy, but as I would learn that was extremely misleading. Although I did not yet know it, he was the only man in the Legion clearly stronger than I was by a good margin. That was not the only deceptive thing about the man; the other impression that one came away with just by looking at him is that he might have been a bit on the slow side. He wore a somewhat slack expression on his round face, with a tendency for his mouth to hang open slightly when he was not engaged. However, once he took up a weapon, he became something entirely different, a blur of motion and controlled savagery the likes of which none of us had ever seen before. Unlike most of the more experienced men he bore no visible marks or scars, which I supposed was a testament to his fighting prowess. Still, I would be lying if I said that the first day we met I was particularly impressed and I wondered if this man would actually have anything that he could possibly teach me after my tutelage with Cyclops.

"This is Optio Aulus Vinicius," the Pilus Prior announced.

Vinicius gave the slightest nod in our direction as we stood examining him.

56

"He's the second in command of this Century, and he's also our Cohort's weapons instructor. Today he'll begin to show you *cunni* what it truly means to be in the Legions."

Turning to Optio Vinicius, he said loudly enough so that we could hear, "Good luck Vinicius. You're going to need it with this lot." Returning his attention to us, Crastinus finished, "You'll spend the day with the Optio. I'll be by to check on you, so don't think I won't know if any of you are slacking off! All the marching and drill is fine, but this is what your real purpose is, to fight and kill for Rome. And die, if that's the will of the gods," he added, superfluously in my opinion.

With that ominous warning he left us to the Optio, who was still standing there, not having said a word. It was almost as if he were in a trance, though when the Pilus Prior left the area, he snapped out of whatever fog he had been in.

"All right," he announced, "first thing is for you to gather round that stake right there," he pointed to one a little distance off.

We assembled around it as he took my wooden sword from me, then had us maneuver so that our backs were turned to the other men who were training on the stakes around us. My first thought was that was smart because we were a little distracted watching other men working on the stakes, but as I came to find out, Optio Vinicius also did not want us infected by what he considered the bad habits that the other Cohort's weapons instructors were instilling in their pupils. He held a very high opinion of his abilities, and all I can say is that I am still alive after more than 40 years in the Legions because of what I learned from him, in addition to what Cyclops taught me. There must have been truth to his opinion. Once he had us arrayed like he wanted, he showed us the basic positions that we would use in training. These were exactly the same positions that Cyclops had shown us, making it a struggle to appear interested. Inwardly, I was chafing to get started, yet Vinicius had his own pace and was not going to be rushed by a bunch of *tiros*, particularly a couple who thought they knew what they were doing. He also took time to show us how he wanted us to grip our wooden sword and as I looked at it, I saw that it was not the way that Cyclops had taught us, so I dismissed it as unimportant, confident that once I demonstrated my skill that some quibbling thing like the way I held it would not be an issue.

Finally, after what seemed like a full watch, he had us each stand in front of a stake and he returned my wooden sword to me. Then he walked from one of us to the other, checking our stance, kicking a foot wider here, turning a set of hips there. Finally, he returned to me, and I felt a flush of pride when he looked at my position and found it satisfactory.

Then he saw the way that I was holding the wooden sword but instead of hitting me, he just said quietly, "You're not holding the weapon the way I demonstrated."

"No Optio," I answered, yet I made no move to change, instead just waiting for the chance to show off to him, sure that he would desist from this lunacy.

"And why aren't you holding it the way I showed you?" he asked, as if he were truly interested.

"I...I've had training, Optio, from a man who was in the Legions, and this is the way I was taught to hold it."

I winced in anticipation of a smack of some sort but instead, Vinicius merely nodded.

"You're right, that's the way the majority of the Legions are taught to hold the weapon, but that's not the way I teach it," he explained.

Unsure what to do, I stood there but still did not change the grip.

Sighing, he simply said, "All right, I can see you need some convincing. So, turn and face me and assume the first position."

This was the position that makes us ready to strike, with the blade held parallel to the ground, the arm pulled back, ready to strike and with the hips twisted slightly. That was the position he had told us to get in originally, so I dropped back into it, facing him.

"Now, strike me. As hard as you can. Give me a killing blow."

I was confused and very apprehensive. Confident as I was in my strength and ability, I was sure that even with the wooden sword I would impale the man, or at the very least break his ribs when I struck. If he was worried, he certainly did not seem to be, and he

58

repeated, a little impatiently, "I said, strike me. Give me all that you've got."

As if sensing my concern, he added, "And don't worry, if you land the blow, I'll absolve you with my dying breath."

He said this last with enough sarcasm that it made me angry, so I immediately struck my blow, punching the wooden sword forward hard as I twisted my hips with as much force and speed as I could. To this day, I am sure that if he were any other man, I would have killed him, wooden blade or no. Instead, with a speed that I had never seen before he lashed out with his bare left hand, using a sweeping motion across his body to make contact with the wooden blade before it touched him, sending the wooden sword flying from my hand. Even as my eyes tried to comprehend what was happening, he made his own move, stepping forward to strike me hard in the stomach with the end of his *vitus*, which he held in his right hand. Now I was the one who was sure that I was going to die, despite wearing my armor, and I dropped to the ground as if I had been ordered to fling myself down, so violently did I hit the ground. I am not sure how long I was out; it could not have been that long because everyone was still clustered around me, leaning over with a combination of worry and malicious glee. Vibius looked worried, while Didius grinned like it was the happiest day of his life. Optio Vinicius was the only one not bent over. Instead, he stared down at me impassively, hands behind his back, watching as I slowly crawled to my feet.

"I thought for sure you were dead," Vibius exclaimed, thumping me on the back in relief.

"So did I," I answered honestly, slowly pulling myself erect, my pride fighting to overcome the searing pain in the pit of my stomach where he had hit me. That night, when I removed my armor and pulled up my tunic, I sported a huge bruise as big around as my fist on my stomach, which stayed with me for several weeks, turning all sorts of interesting colors.

"Do you know why I was able to do that?" Optio Vinicius asked politely.

I considered the question. To me the answer was obvious; he was simply quicker than I had been, yet I knew that was not the answer he was looking for, so I thought carefully. Slowly, the answer came to me, and as the look of understanding came to my face, he smiled slightly.

"Because my thumb was exposed," I answered, and he rewarded me with a nod.

And therein lay the secret. The thumb is the weakest part of the hand. The normal method of holding the sword is by wrapping the hand around the hilt, with the thumb on the outside of the fingers. When pressure is applied in the right direction by a sudden violent force, against the base of the thumb, it is too weak to maintain its position. By wrapping the fingers over the thumb, the thumb is supported and protected. While it is true that if one were to fight barehanded in this manner it would break your thumb, the pommel and guard of the sword provide enough protection to prevent this from happening on those occasions you use that end of the sword in a fight. Despite the obvious evidence I was still not convinced, because there was one disadvantage that I could see. I debated opening my mouth, yet to this point he was almost gentle with us, despite the ache in my stomach, which I had asked for, after all.

"But…" I started, unsure of how to continue, and again I was rewarded with that slight smile.

"But," he finished for me, "the problem with that grip is that it restricts your blade from moving laterally, so that you don't have the same freedom of movement. Is that what you were about to say?"

"Yes, Optio," I answered excitedly, although to be honest I was not sure that was what I was going to say until he did it for me.

He nodded again, and replied, "You're correct, *tiro*…..?"

"Pullus, Optio. Titus Pullus."

"You're correct, *tiro* Pullus that at first your movement is more restricted. But," he said this with the quiet confidence of a man who knew what he was about, "you'll regain that with practice. By the time I'm finished with you, nobody will be able to tell how you grip your weapon."

He turned to the others and finished, "Except that you'll be alive, and your enemy dead."

Of course he was right. And it did not take nearly as long as I thought it would. By the end of the second day, I felt almost as comfortable using the new grip as I had the old. The only men who experienced difficulty with it were the men with smaller hands who did not have as much length in their fingers to wrap around their thumb sufficiently. To compensate for this, Optio Vinicius prescribed special exercises for them to strengthen their hands, exercises that once I saw them performing, I began as well. Vinicius had them thrust their hands into a bucket of sand, with their fingers splayed out. Once their hand was buried in the sand, they drew their fingers in as if they were grabbing a handful of sand. It is an extremely effective exercise, and my hands are still strong because of those exercises. Once we became accustomed to the new grip, Vibius and I started demonstrating that we were indeed more skilled than our comrades, a fact that did not escape the notice of Pilus Prior Crastinus. It was toward the end of the third day working on the stakes that I became aware of the Pilus Prior standing nearby, watching me with narrowed eyes. Unnerved, I struggled to concentrate on my work, the sweat running freely off of me while my arms, having been hardened and conditioned to such labor, still contained a great deal of energy, reflected in my thrusts.

"This isn't the first time you've held a wooden sword is it Pullus?"

The question, posed in what passed for a conversational tone by the Pilus Prior, completely flustered me. Unsure what to do, I stopped, snapped to *intente* and replied, "No, Pilus Prior."

"Who trained you?" he asked with some interest.

"Quintus Ausonius, Pilus Prior," I answered, which was immediately met with a roar of laughter.

"*Edepol*! You were trained by old Cyclops himself? He swore that he'd never pick up a weapon for the rest of his life, the bastard."

I was so shocked that you could have knocked me over with the lightest touch, although I should not have been. Back then, the Legions were still relatively few and small; men such as Cyclops who gained renown were known throughout the Legions. The fact that he was my brother-in-law meant that it never occurred to me to think of him in this manner.

"And how by Pluto's cock do you know Cyclops?" Pilus Prior Crastinus demanded.

"He's married to my sister," which drew another roar of laughter.

"By the gods, he's married too! Well, maybe there's hope for an old bastard like me yet," he chuckled.

And then he did something that amazed me even more. Stepping up to me, he slapped me on the back as if I were a comrade and finished, "Well Pullus. You couldn't have had a better teacher. I'm going to keep an eye on you."

And with that, he turned and walked over to Optio Vinicius, who was standing there looking as bemused as I felt. The Pilus Prior whispered something in his ear that I could not catch, but Vibius did. Later that night, Vibius relayed to me excitedly, "You know what that old knob Crastinus said to Vinicius?" Without waiting for me to answer, he continued, "'Watch out for Pullus, Vinicius', he said, 'he may take your job.'"

I felt like I was ten feet tall. Those words, however, had the opposite effect than I expected, though looking back, perhaps the Pilus Prior understood me better than I thought. From that day, I was pushed much harder by Optio Vinicius than any of the other *tiros*, and was subject to scathing critique of everything I did. The night of the incident, Vibius and I discussed the idea that Vibius should point out that he too was trained by the legendary Cyclops but luckily, for him anyway, before he got a chance to open his mouth the next day he saw the lay of the land. Indeed, not only did he keep his mouth shut, he also endeavored to hold back a bit so that he would not be singled out for special attention in the same manner that I was. It seemed I could not do anything right; my thrusts were sloppy, my slashes were weak, my recoveries were atrocious. Indeed, if Vinicius were to be believed, I would be lucky to survive the first contact of the first battle I was in. If the goal were to take me down a peg, it had the opposite effect. Instead, it just spurred me to work harder and prove him wrong, and I looked forward to the day where we would be finally allowed to pair off.

After a week, we began working with the shield as well, and we were beginning to pick up on the rhythm of training. Everything appeared to work in cycles of a week, with a new skill being added

62

to the training each cycle. That did not hold for everyone, however. It was after the first week of work on the stakes that Artorius was held back a couple of extra days because he was not considered adept enough with just the wooden sword to move forward with the more advanced work. This was when Vibius first started showing signs of being more than just the average Legionary, because he stepped in and offered to work with Artorius in the evenings, after our meal. It would have been perfect if Artorius showed any enthusiasm, but after the first few days, it became apparent to all of us that Artorius' heart was not in learning to become a Legionary. The fight with his father seemed a long-past event; he even admitted to us one night that he could no longer remember what it was about. It is not that he was necessarily a bad Legionary; I just believe that some of us are born to be one thing, others are born to be another, and Artorius was clearly not born to be a Legionary. He did make an effort, so that he was not quite bad enough to be one of the *tiros* dismissed as unfit for duty, yet not only was he clearly the weakest in our tent section, he was the weakest in our Century and may have been the weakest in the Cohort. However, that discovery was still in the future, so Vibius spent his spare time with Artorius, working with him tirelessly. I marveled that Vibius had the energy, because I was still exhausted at the end of every day, but my friend had always been blessed with more vitality, much to my dismay at times.

While the rest of us would sit and take care of the myriad little things that occupy a Legionary's free time while watching Vibius and Artorius, it was during those periods that we got to know each other. For some reason I found that I spent more time with Scribonius than the others, at least during those times I was not with Vibius. He was somewhat quiet, with a thoughtful manner about him, yet I discovered that his placid exterior masked a razor-sharp wit and a sense of the absurd that I enjoyed immensely. Meanwhile, Didius introduced the other boys to dice, and he had to be the luckiest man I have ever seen, or he was an extremely good cheater. Either way, most of the others, with the exception of Scribonius, Vibius and I ended up owing him things like their next day's rations, something that was expressly forbidden for Legionaries to wager. It is also one of the more flouted rules in the Legions my entire time in the ranks. However, Didius was smart, I will give him that. He did not actually take the others' rations; instead, he traded them back for favors, things like mending his gear or standing watches for him. I do not know that the three of us were smarter than the others. I think it was more our mutual dislike of Didius than anything, which meant that of our tent section we were the only ones who never owed Didius anything. Something that he did not like at all.

Also by this point, we had been integrated into our Century in terms of marching and drill, on which we still spent a portion of the day working. Since we were the last to join the Century, we were the very back rank, a fact that bothered me to no end. That meant that the battles would all be over before I got to have my turn, I fumed to myself, and where would the glory be for me? Being the tallest and the biggest in my Century, and one of the largest in the Cohort, I was sure that I would be placed in the front rank. However, the system that has operated in the Roman army for hundreds of years by that point did not allow for the vanity of a young man. That is how I thought of myself, a young man, despite easily being the youngest in the Legion because of my deception. Later I was to learn that there were several others who were sixteen; they were just older than me by months and in a couple of cases weeks. Even so, I was still sure that I was bound for glory, and I was eager to show what I was made of.

It was not until a full month passed that we began working together as a whole Legion, with every Cohort, and we were full strength for the first time and one of the last Centuries to be so. I am not sure, but I would guess that we started losing men within the first three to four months of our existence, by virtue of illness or desertion, and it is only just now becoming standard practice, 40 years later, that replacements are placed within a particular Legion. However, back then, once we attained our full complement of men, every one lost from that point was one less in the Legion. Even so, it was an amazing sight to see upwards of 6,000 men standing in formation, rank after rank, Century after Century, the Cohorts lined up in their order. We, being the First Century of the Second Cohort were privileged to be fairly close to the front of the formation, giving us a better view of the proceedings when the Tribunes and the other officers gathered together. My height also helped with the view, except when we were in full dress uniform with everyone wearing their horsehair plumes, which was nothing but a damn nuisance. I am as proud of being a Legionary as any man who has ever served Rome, but I was never much for the pomp and polish, and I always hated those formations where some prig of a Tribune or Legate decided to flex his muscle and call for a dress inspection for no other reason than he could. Luckily for us, once Caesar took command and we began fighting, that sort of nonsense was kept to a minimum. Ironically, the times we wore our full dress uniform the most often was going into battle under Caesar, because he believed it help the men fight harder. This I did not mind as much because it had a point to it.

Speaking of Caesar, the occasion of our first full formation as a Legion, carrying all of our gear no less, was also where I first laid eyes on the man. I must say that I was somewhat disappointed. He was shorter than I was by a few inches and somewhat slight, with very fair complexion and features. I did not know it at the time, but no matter how much time in the sun he spent, and he was in the elements as much as we were, he never turned brown the way we did. Some of the boys said it was proof of his noble birth; there were others who were not so gracious, saying it proved that he was womanish and that the rumors of his liaison with the king of Bithynia were true as well. I was not yet confident enough in those days, but before long any man who uttered such nonsense in my presence would have trouble on their hands of a sort that they did not want.

However, that day, I was not impressed to say the least. Caesar mounted the rostra, giving a speech of welcome to us, noting that although we had been here for varying lengths of time, we gathered as a Legion just that day, making welcoming us appropriate. Despite my lack of awe at his appearance, I will say that he gave very good speeches. He was not like some of the patricians that took a turn at leading us, who would talk to us like we were children or spoke to us of high-flown principles and ideals, for which none of us gave a rotten fig. No, Caesar spoke plainly, and I could see that I was not the only one who appreciated it. He did spend some time telling us how we were upholding the finest traditions of Rome, and how under his command we would make our ancestors proud, yet it was not overdone. Such rhetoric is like adding spice to a stew; the right amount, and it makes for a memorable meal, one that you will tell others about for days to come. Too much, however, ruins it, and while it still is memorable, it is for the wrong reasons. So we stood and listened while he told us that he would always lead from the front, indeed starting that day, then when he was finished he stepped down from the rostra, turning over command to the Tribune in nominal command of the Legion. Such was my first physical contact with the man who would lead us down the path to our destiny.

After he stepped down he strode to the *Porta Praetorium*, the main gate of the camp, and leading us, took us on our first long march. To that point, once we were integrated with our Century and our Century with our Cohort, we had started forced marches, but they were all out a certain distance then back to the camp. All this was done with the goal of building us up to this moment when we were going to put in a full day's march, then make a marching camp for the first time. None of my tent section had been present for the building of the camp that we were staying in at that time, with the exception of Sergeant Calienus; because it was a semi-permanent camp, we had only been involved in work details making improvements. Although we had never stayed outside of the camp at the end of a march, we always carried all of our gear, some of it put in the wicker basket that is then attached to the pack, which we carried over our shoulder using a stick with a crossbar called a *furca*, to which we attached everything. Our shield, in its leather cover, was strapped to our back, our helmet attached to that. We wore our arms and armor, carrying a javelin in our left hand to serve as a staff, while our second javelin we held in the same hand as our *furca*. For the *tiros* it meant carrying the wooden sword, which was attached to our belt with a leather thong instead of a scabbard, and practice pilum, and it was only when we were arrayed in such a manner that we could finally tell exactly how many veterans were among our comrades. It turned out that all of the leaders of each Century were veterans, along with the Sergeants of each tent section and a few *Gregarii* in each Century, so almost a quarter of the Legion appeared to be veterans.

Taking our spot in the column, we were marching in the lead spot just behind the command group, with the First Cohort serving as the vanguard, meaning that we did not have to worry about eating as much dust. This was something that we would learn to treasure, although on this first march we were more worried about how we would bear up, this being our first real test. The fact that just in front of us marched our commanding general, along with his bodyguard, all of whom rode while he walked, did not help with the pressure that we felt. And he set a cracking pace, quite a bit quicker than what we were accustomed to on our other marches, and for once I was thankful for my long legs. Normally, in standard close order drill I had to pay particular attention to avoid stepping on the back of the man in front of me, but with this type of route march we could stretch our legs a bit more. The weather was pleasant; it was still late spring, but my country is warmer than most places, and what felt pleasant to me I have learned is unbearably hot for others, mostly Gauls or people who come from those areas farther north.

66

The first few miles passed easily enough, yet I could see others were struggling to varying degrees, the worst of them being Artorius. Both Pilus Prior Crastinus, and Optio Vinicius roamed up and down the length of the Century, using their *vitus* to encourage laggards. Between them, they must have easily covered twice the distance of our march. My admiration was tempered by the knowledge that they did not carry the same loads that we did, their gear being carried on one of the pack mules attached to our Century. Our tent section not only had its own pack mule but its own slave, a miserable little creature we called Lucco, who was responsible for guiding the mule to our final destination, wherever that was, among a variety of other duties. We stopped every two parts of a watch for a short break, during which we were allowed to ground our gear yet not allowed to sit down.

"Once you sit down we'll never be able to get you up," Sergeant Calienus explained, whose spot when we were in full formation was actually right in the middle of our rank. We were allowed to place our hands on our knees and bend over a bit in order to relieve some of the strain on our back brought on by the weight of our shield and helmet, but that was all. As we would find out later, once sufficiently conditioned we would be allowed to sprawl out in any position we chose, although someone would always be on guard, but until we reached that point we had to content ourselves with standing there. Despite being only slightly fatigued at this point, I could feel the strain of the load I was carrying and wondered how I would feel after more miles. During our rest, most of us talked quietly; Scribonius and I discussed our new general.

"What did you think?" He eyed me curiously as he asked me, yet all I could think to say was, "He gives a good speech. Why, what did you think?"

He frowned, something I noticed that he did a lot, then shook his head. "I don't know, really. All I do know is that I've seen him somewhere before, but I can't remember where."

The *bucina* cut our conversation short, and I thought no more about it.

By the time we made our second stop, I was beginning to feel true fatigue, and the weaker men like Artorius were clearly at the end of their tether, barely managing to make it to this point because their fear of the wrath of the Centurions was greater than their fatigue, yet I could not help wondering how much longer that would last. As we rested again I looked over at the general, standing talking to the Primus Pilus of our Legion, who had fallen back to talk to him, I supposed, from his place up in the vanguard. Neither of them seemed to be in the slightest bit fatigued, something that angered me more than anything else. How could they appear as if they were just out for a daily stroll, without a care in the world? Well, I was determined that I would not falter in front of them, no matter what! When we set out for the final leg of our march, I was grimly determined to appear just as fresh as they did now, no matter how much of a sham it might have been. The idea that they would even notice a lowly *tiro* in his private struggle never occurred to me; like all youngsters, I was still of the opinion that somehow the world revolved around me.

It was with a great amount of relief to the *tiros* when we arrived at the site of the evening camp, which the advance party had already marked and staked out. That feeling was short-lived, however, when after just a few moments' respite we were told to ground our gear, and the real work began. The Centurions and Optios began running about as each Century of each Cohort was assigned with a task. To our inexperienced eyes it was chaos, yet as we were to learn, that was deceiving; everyone had a role to play, and once assigned their tasks, the seeming chaos would disappear.

The Pilus Prior, after a brief conference with the command group, came to us and said without any ceremony, "Right, we've been assigned the ditch," which was greeted by groans from the experienced men, to which the Pilus Prior snarled, "Shut your mouths, you lazy bastards! Now, I expect the Sergeants to take their tent section and give these fresh young things a quick lesson on what they're to do. I'll give you some time to explain and then," he pointed with his *vitus* to a point a distance away where some stakes were placed, "get to work. That's our section. I'll be around to make sure that you don't make a complete mess of things."

And with that he strode off to do whatever it was that Centurions do while the rest of us worked, which as I was to learn, was to walk about keeping a sharp eye out for the inevitable lagging. Sergeant Calienus stood in front of us. "You'll need your turf cutter and your spades," he said simply, waiting while we pulled them from our baskets. "Follow me," he called over his shoulder once we produced them, as he headed over to the area that the Pilus Prior had

68

pointed out. "All right, what we're going to do is to dig our section of the ditch."

As he talked, each tent section was receiving its instructions all around us, so it was somewhat difficult to understand him over the babble of other voices, but it soon became clear what was expected of us. Our section was going to be one of the ones digging; another tent section was tasked with carrying the dirt that we produced in their wicker basket to create the rampart that formed the internal boundary of the camp. Another group was tasked with collecting our two stakes apiece, which were loaded on our pack mule, to form the palisade. While this was all new to us, this is the manner in which Roman camps have been constructed for as long as anyone could remember, and soon enough it would become second nature for us.

Turning to our task, we first used the turf cutter to cut out squares of sod. These would be used as foundations for some of the structures in the camp, along with serving as the surface of the rampart. Once that was done, we began to dig. Despite my fatigue, this was work that I was used to, but some of the others began having trouble, the most surprising to me being Vibius. However, as he explained later, working as a tanner did not involve the use of a spade or turf cutter. There was one piece of luck, although we would not understand it for some time to come. As I explained earlier, Caesar required the ditches to be deeper and wider across than any other general; fortunately for us, we did not know any better, so the work we were doing did not seem to be any more onerous than what any other Legion endured. It took us the better part of two parts of a watch to make our section of ditch, no more than ten feet of the total, the proper depth and width and we were utterly exhausted, but as I turned around, what I saw amazed me. The wall, made of the combination of our stakes and the spoil from the ditch, was almost completely up in our sector, with the men in that area putting the finishing touches on the rampart. Other parties who went out into the surrounding area came back with enough timber to create the guard towers that are placed on each corner of the camp, and although not finished, their form was plainly visible. Despite the dust, noise and bustling activity, it was clear that we knew what we were about, or at least our leaders did. At this point we were no more than just brute labor, although after a few more of these camps, as we rotated in our duties, we would all learn our parts and by the end of a year, each of us would be able to build one of these camps in our sleep.

Finally finished, we staggered back to our area, at least knowing where we were located in the camp because it was the same as back at our home base. The slaves of each tent section in the Century, working together, had erected our tents and dragged our equipment into them, placing our gear in our accustomed place, knowing where to put it by the names inscribed on the leather covers of our shields. They had also started a fire, and Sergeant Calienus proceeded to show us how to turn our rations of grain into bread, this being the first time it was not baked for us. Each of us took our ration and ground it in our section's grinder before contributing it to the community pot, where Sergeant Calienus showed us how to make bread, using the *panera* that we had been issued. I know I was looking forward to falling into a deep sleep as soon as we were finished eating, but my hopes were dashed by the Pilus Prior, who came and announced that we were the guard Cohort for the night. We all groaned, prompting the Pilus Prior to walk among us, lashing out with his *vitus* and snarling at us to keep quiet. His progress was marked by the same sounds as he relayed the word to the rest of the Cohort, something that gave us a little solace that we were not the only whiners.

I was never more thankful for Vibius than that evening on watch, because without him I would surely have fallen asleep on guard duty, though I think he was as thankful for the same reason. Even so, a decent number of *tiros* were caught asleep, and if it had happened in enemy territory it would have meant death, but since it was in training it still called for a flogging. Luckily, only one poor soul was selected for that punishment, which was administered when we returned to base camp, only because he had been caught not once but twice. Since it was our first such march, I guessed, the Centurions were content with administering a particularly severe session with their *vitus* to the men caught asleep. In our case, Pilus Prior Crastinus, Optio Vinicius, and even the Tesseraurius, a man named Titus Cordius who was our designated man to receive the challenge and password every day, came to check on us at regular intervals. Somehow even Artorius managed to stay awake, by virtue of being paired with Scribonius I expect, so that we were one of the few tent sections who did not have anyone fall asleep.

The next morning, if that is what it could be called, it being at least two parts of a watch before first light, I was as sore as I had ever been during my training with Cyclops, and judging from the slow movements and groans of my comrades, I was not alone. I had used muscles previously unstrained, at least to this extent, and I was

70

hard pressed to determine where the soreness came from, the marching or the digging. Either way, we were awakened by the call of the *bucina*, whereupon we got up and packed the gear that we would be carrying, leaving the striking of the tents to the slaves, who performed this task while we ate our morning meal. We were now going to march back to the base camp, except this time we would not be in the lead. It was our turn in fact to take up the rear; it is in this manner that no Cohort can complain that they are mistreated. Everyone shares equally in all the unpleasant duties in the army, which is one of the things that makes us stronger and bonds us together as much, if not more than, combat itself. There is no glue like shared misery.

The march back was going to be an ordeal, since we were still sore from the day before, the only slightly cheerful thought being that because the camp back home already existed, at least we would not have to dig. At least, so we thought, until we were informed that before we began the march back we were going to go to the spot where we had dug the ditch the day before, and fill it back in. This was not a punishment, because every other Century involved in digging the ditch was doing the same thing. Fortunately it did not take nearly as long to fill it in as it did to dig it. As we marched away, the early morning sky was lit by fire as the guard towers and the wooden structures that were not part of the palisade made by our carried stakes was put to the torch. It was on the occasion of this first march that we were introduced to this practice, one that if the truth be known, bothered us probably more than anything. On the march during a campaign, we never left a camp intact, and despite the fact we could all see the sense in doing so, it still pained us to see the fruits of our sweat and labor destroyed, every day. Speaking only for myself, it was something I never became accustomed to, despite the hundreds, maybe thousands of times I have done so.

It was on the way back that Artorius fell out of the ranks and despite the curses of the Pilus Prior, could not be induced to keep his place in the march. Finally, he was abandoned, to the disgust of the Pilus Prior, Optio and, truth be known, the rest of us. Weakness is not tolerated in the Legion, and no matter how we might have sympathized to a degree, none of us were doing any more or any less than Artorius. The fact that he was weak physically was not his crime, at least in my mind. It was his mental weakness that I found most damning. I know now that I was being unkind; I tended, and still tend, to view others as if they were me, that they were born as big and strong as I was, and that is not usually the case. It is a failing, the gods know, and I hope that I have mellowed with age. It also did not help that we were the tail end of the column, eating the dust of the rest of the Legion, yet I suspect that he would have fallen out even if we were in our place of the day before. He finally came staggering into camp a full third of a watch after we arrived, and he was warned that two more such failures would result in his dismissal from the Legion, a fate that he did not seem to be entirely unhappy about. Our general, meanwhile, had marched at the head of the Legion both days, never showing any sign of fatigue, and as we were to learn, this was not just a case of Caesar showing off. He would always walk when we walked, and lived as we live, as much as it was possible for him to do so; being a general there are certain requirements when dealing with others that elevate him above the rest of us. However, he ate what we ate, drank what we drank, and in his actions began to form a bond with us that is famous to this day. Never before, even in the days of Pompey Magnus or the great Scipio Africanus, has a general been loved in the way we in the 10th loved Caesar, and the foundation for that love was formed on that first march, and strengthened in the months to come. Although as it would turn out, not all of us shared the same feelings about our general.

Our training continued; we learned the battle formations, the *acies triplex*, the *acies duplex*, down to the formations that only Centuries used, such as the famous *testudo*, which is known and feared throughout the world. Our weapons training continued as well, now with the shield, and we also began work throwing the javelins. Once we got over the slight bump in the beginning of our relationship, Optio Vinicius and I seemed to form a bond. Perhaps he recognized in me someone as devoted to the learning of the skills of arms as he was, yet whatever the reason, I became his star pupil, something that did not please Didius. I was still constantly scrutinized and criticized, but not only had I become accustomed to it, I recognized what it meant. However, along with the status came the responsibility. I was always the subject for the new lessons to be learned so that I took the bumps and bruises first, something that was lost on Didius. He began muttering choice names for me under his breath, loud enough for the others to hear but not me, some of them finding what he was saying witty enough to laugh. Growing more and more in my dislike for Didius, I consoled myself with the idea that soon enough, we would be squaring off one on one with the wooden sword. Then we would see who was laughing.

Proving that the Optio was not oblivious to what was going on, the very first day that we finally had progressed enough that we could begin beating on each other, he pitted me against Didius. Of course, the way it was expressed to us was not that we had progressed, but that Rome could not afford to wait the ten years it would take us to know the sharp end of a sword before we continued in the pursuit of our enemies.

Still, when the Optio beckoned to me and Didius and told us to square off, he whispered in my ear, "I'm not deaf. The only thing I'll tell you is that you're forbidden to kill him. Understand?"

I nodded, but I had to swallow down the lump that suddenly formed in my throat. Despite my confidence, any time you face an adversary that you have never faced before, there is some trepidation. I cursed myself that I had not paid any attention to Didius' work on the stakes so that I would have an idea of his weaknesses, but that vessel was already broken and could not be mended now. For his part, Didius did not appear to be his usual, blustery confident self, for which I was grimly satisfied. Approaching each other, both of us in the first position, I instantly saw that Didius showed a weakness in his grip of the shield, holding it in a slightly tilted manner and not in the direct vertical way that we were taught. I tucked that away, because I had decided that I did not want a quick kill. No, my goal that day was to completely dominate him, embarrass him and leave no doubt who was the master.

Looking back on that decision now, with the blessing of hindsight and age, I wonder if I had been satisfied with just a straightforward end to our bout whether things would have been different. Somehow I think that Didius and I were destined to clash, but the truth is that this might be the wishful thinking of an old man; only the gods truly know. In the moment, however, I slowly circled Didius, taking the role of the attacker, and observing him I could see he was actually afraid.

Grinning, I called out to him loud enough for the others to hear, "*Ave* Didius. How long will it take me to make you my whore?"

This taunt brought a chorus of gasps and chuckles, and I saw Didius' eyes narrow in anger.

"Why don't you come and find out, you *cunnus*?" he snarled, to which I laughed and replied, "Be careful what you ask for, Didius."

And before I finished saying his name, I struck. Despite the fact I am not as quick as Vibius, I am very fast, deceptively so, probably because of my size. Using the shield I banged into Didius hard enough to send him stumbling back a few feet, while I pressed the attack, slashing with the wooden sword instead of thrusting in the manner we were taught, smacking him hard on the arms and shoulders, causing him to roar in pain and anger. Lashing out wildly, he attempted to restore his equilibrium as I parried his blows contemptuously with my wooden sword, not even bothering to use my shield.

This drew a comment from the Optio, "Careful about showing off, Pullus," he said evenly, "It's sloppy and it can become a habit."

Nodding that I heard him, I relented enough to allow Didius to regain his position, happy to hear that the cheering from the others was clearly in my favor. I decided to use that to my advantage.

"Hear that, Didius?" I asked, while I continued to circle him, "it sounds like your comrades don't care for you too much."

"What do I care about those *cunni* for?" he growled, which was met with the howls of derision that I expected it would invoke.

"Oh, I don't know," I kept my tone casual, "maybe because one day you'll have to rely on them to save your life."

Again, as I finished speaking I attacked, but this time Didius was prepared, managing to bring his shield up to meet mine and we crashed into each other, shield to shield, neither of us giving an inch. He was strong, I had to give him that, and I resolved that I would go ahead and show him that I was indeed stronger. Dropping my hips a bit before uncoiling my whole body, I let out a roar as I did so, and once again Didius went backwards, except this time instead of stumbling he fell flat. Immediately I leaped astride him, putting the point of the wooden sword under his throat.

"You make this too easy," I told him contemptuously, then stepped away to turn to my comrades, raising my arms as if I were a victorious gladiator.

74

The blow was completely unexpected, and I dropped to my knees, my lower back on fire from where Didius had hit me hard along the kidneys. I would piss blood for a week from the blow, but he made a fatal mistake in not following it up, allowing me to get to my feet. Spinning around, I was angrier than I think I had ever been to that point, and there was complete silence as we faced each other.

"Who's the whore now?" Didius taunted with an evil grin on his face.

Looking over at the Optio, he gazed back at me with an impassive face, but almost imperceptibly, I saw him nod. Taking this as permission to continue the fight, I did not bother to talk. Instead, I launched a massive attack, using both shield and wooden sword as offensive weapons, completely disdaining the defense and relying on the fury of my attack to protect me. Didius desperately parried my blows, backing up and giving ground, the only sound the thuds of wood hitting against wicker and wood and our harsh breathing. I was inhaling heavily, yet Didius was positively panting from the exertion of trying to meet my blows and keeping them from landing. Finally relenting, I waited for the moment I had planned when I first saw his telltale tilting of the shield. Now, because of his fatigue, it was tipped outward even more, for which he tried to compensate by pulling the top of the shield even closer to his face. Using a move that I learned from Cyclops and had once used on Vibius, I smashed down on the bottom edge of his shield with my own, pushing the top of his shield even farther out and down to expose Didius' head, then once again I lashed out, smashing Didius' nose with a backward slash to the face. And just like Vibius, his nose exploded blood as it was smashed flat against his face, whereupon he dropped his shield and wooden sword, falling to his knees and screaming in pain. At least, I thought to myself with satisfaction, Vibius had not acted like a little girl. Turning and walking back to my comrades, still panting with exertion and blood lust, this time I knew that he would not be getting back up. Our friends were still quiet; half of them seemed to be entranced by the sight of Didius, who was on his knees with his hands to his face, trying to stanch the flow of blood with little success. The others were looking at me, with expressions that were hard for me to place, a mixture of respect and....something else. Vibius was the only one who approached me, gently taking my weapons from me then patting me on the back.

"As much as I hate him, I do sympathize," he said wryly. "I know what it's like to be hit like that by you."

"I hit him harder," I replied simply, and he nodded his understanding.

"Thank the gods that you did that to him and not me."

Scribonius came up to us with a grin. "Remind me never to make you angry."

The Optio had gone to Didius, trying to help him to his feet, which Didius angrily refused, getting to his feet on his own. Despite his voice being muffled by his hands, we could hear him clearly when he asked the Optio, "Well, are you going to do something? Isn't there some sort of charge you can write against him?"

I was shocked, and apparently so was everyone else. The Optio asked with mild amazement in his voice, "And what, pray tell, would I write him up for?"

"What for?" Didius retorted, "You saw what he did to me. There are rules against striking the face and head in training."

He was right; we had been briefed about the penalties for striking blows to the head and face of a fellow Legionary in training. For a moment, my stomach began to twist.

"There are also rules against striking a fellow Legionary when he's not prepared," replied the Optio calmly. "You had been knocked down, *tiro* Pullus bested you and the bout was over."

"I didn't capitulate," Didius protested angrily, and now I could see that the Optio was beginning to get irritated himself.

"More fool you," Vinicius retorted, "because Pullus had finished you. The fact that you're too stupid to know it isn't his or my fault. Now, follow me to the *medici*."

He turned to lead Didius away, and as Didius was passing he stared at me with undisguised hatred. "This isn't over," he hissed, although it was hard to understand him because he was still clutching his face.

I merely smiled and replied, "Any time you want another beating I'm more than happy to oblige."

He did not say anything else, instead following the Optio to the *quaestorium* where the doctors and *medici* were constantly busy patching men up. Our training is supposed to be bloodless combat, and our battle bloody drills, but sometimes, at least with the former, accidents happened and blood did flow.

As we watched them leave, Scribonius said quietly, "I'd watch your back if I were you."

I nodded, and Vibius answered for me, "I'll be there to do it, don't worry about that."

The pace of training picked up; we began doing a march three times a week, both to condition us and also to teach us how to make a camp, rotating the various jobs of building so that we learned everything we needed to about building one. We also began battle drills, Century against Century, which we all enjoyed the most, despite it also giving us the most bumps and bruises. Slowly but surely we were beginning to look more like a real Legion and not a great gaggle of fools who happened to be wearing the uniform of a Legionary. That was not the message that was being relayed to us by our Centurion, yet even so we could detect the slightest change in his tone with us. We were not raw *tiros* anymore, but not quite full *Gregarii* either, yet for most of us, the idea had become solidified that we would make it to the final swearing in ceremony. Most of us, anyway.

Artorius was still struggling mightily, and while he seemed to willingly put in the extra work to correct his deficiencies, of which there were many, I for one suspected that he was going through the motions rather than putting any real effort into his training. However, when I asked Vibius this question he bristled at the suggestion; apparently he had taken his tutoring of Artorius to heart.

"I believe he's putting everything he has into his extra work," Vibius snapped, his swarthy face flushing darker. "He can't help it if he's not as strong as you Titus. Not everyone is; in fact, few people are, yet you seem to think everything should come as easily to them as it does to you."

That surprised me quite a bit. In my mind I was struggling just as much as anyone else, and this was the first I learned that there was a perception that the opposite was true. I could not hide my surprise when I answered, "*Edepol*! Who says that things come easily to me? I have to work just as hard as anyone else."

Vibius looked at me steadily for a moment before replying quietly, "I know you think you do, but I don't think you have the slightest idea just how much stronger and better you are than the rest of us. Haven't you seen not just us, but the other men in the Century stop to watch you when you're going through the drills?"

I shrugged. "What of it? I'm sure that they're just watching me because I stick out, being so large."

And that is truly what I thought at the time; I had been stared at most of my life because of my size, and it was simply something to which I had become accustomed. Vibius shook his head vigorously, and using his finger for emphasis, pointed to my chest and replied, "That's not why at all, Titus. You make these drills look easy. I know; I hear the other men talking. There are even men betting on how many barbarians you'll kill in our first battle."

Now I was shocked. It is true that men in the Legions will bet on absolutely anything, but I had no idea that the others, including the veterans apparently, saw me in this light. My chest constricted as the thought settled into my mind and I realized the implications of it. Suddenly, I had a reputation to uphold, and I had yet to fight my first battle!

This revelation from Vibius rocked me, so I began surreptitiously watching others when they looked in my direction, trying to discern what their true thoughts were. I began feeling an enormous amount of pressure, whether it was warranted or not and soon found myself fretting about what might happen when we actually did go into battle. There had been rumblings for some time that the Legions were about to move out and begin campaigning. It was already late May, and the campaigning season was open for some time now, meaning a late start for us, but Caesar was forced to spend that time training us because we were a new Legion. Despite that, the word around the fires was that we would be moving soon, and it would be north, into the wilds of Hispania north of the Tanis River, to pacify the remaining tribe in the area, the Lusitani, who had revolted again. To that end, we were finally equipped with our real weapons, the sword that most of us would carry for as long as it lasted, and our two javelins, along with our shield, emblazoned with the symbol of the 10th Legion, the bull. My first thought was how ridiculously light the weapons were compared to the training weapons we had been using, but that is the point of our training. As I examined my blade, still unmarked from where I would work it with the sharpening stone to put as fine an edge on it as I could, I hefted its balance, trying to imagine thrusting it into the body of another man, rather than a stake. Glancing about, I could see all of my tentmates doing the same thing, and I wondered if I wore the same grin on my face.

It was about that time that Artorius fell out of his third march, despite Vibius' almost frantic efforts to help him keep up, even as it caused the Pilus Prior to give Vibius a good thrashing for doing so. It did not help; less than halfway along our march back to our base camp Artorius fell out. We had suspected this as a likely event, it becoming clear to all of us that the effort of the extra training, along with the burden of our normal regimen was steadily wearing him down. He was barely able to eat the evening meal, sitting listlessly and chewing his bread with the same vigor as a cow chewing its cud. The next morning as we broke camp and made ready to begin the march back, he moved like a man sleepwalking, and it was so noticeable that the Pilus Prior came over to him to smack him in the face. That seemed to stir him a bit, and he was responsive when we formed up to begin the march back, then at some point after the first break he dropped from the ranks. Vibius did not notice straight away, but when he did he immediately fell out himself, trotting back to find Artorius, despite the cursed warning directed at him by the Pilus Prior. Optio Vinicius then went back to retrieve both of them and he returned shortly, along with Vibius carrying his own pack and Artorius' as well, trying to balance both *furcae*, one on each shoulder, his face shining with perspiration from the exertion and strain. Artorius was being dragged by the arm by the Optio, who was trying to use encouragement instead of the threats that the Pilus Prior favored. All of this was taking place amid the normal noise and chaos of a march; the dust swirling all around from the tramping of thousands of feet, the clinking and clanking of gear as it bounced against each other, the steady underlying hum of the men talking to each other in snatched conversations, trying to pass the time. I will say that even for me it was hard to breathe and I was higher up than Artorius, so I could imagine how choking it was in his spot, which could not have helped. Looking over at him, I could see that his face was white as chalk, with a clammy look about it that we had learned indicated someone who was having trouble coping with the heat. His mouth hung open as he gasped for air, while his eyes would seem to focus for a moment, as if he was conscious of his surroundings, then begin wavering before rolling back in his head, whereupon he started stumbling again. The Optio would shake his arm, he would snap back to the present, then after a moment would drift off again. It was almost like he was falling asleep as he walked, something I had never seen before. Over the years, I would be on marches where all of us looked like that, but to that point he was the first to exhibit these signs, and I was morbidly fascinated.

By the time we made it to the second break, Artorius was nowhere to be seen, even when the *bucina* sounded the signal to begin the start of the last leg of the march. Vibius stood to the side until the last moment, looking to the rear of the column before getting another whack from the Pilus Prior and a snarled order to get into the ranks. Vibius was obviously hoping that Artorius would somehow come staggering up, but he did not. Continuing on, we finished the march, almost all of us not very fatigued from the effort except for Vibius, who had carried Artorius' gear most of the way back. The last few miles Romulus and Remus, the nicknames we gave to the Mallius brothers, tried to relieve Vibius of his load, but he would have none of it and in fact got downright nasty about it.

"I don't need any of you *cunni* helping me," he snarled at Marcus, who we called Romulus, and I swear that if Vibius did not have his hands full he would have punched Romulus in the face. For his part, Romulus did not appreciate having his offer spurned in such a manner.

"Prick! I'm sorry I asked," he snapped back, "and see if I ever offer to help you again."

He turned away to complain to Remus about Vibius' brutish behavior, the whole exchange drawing the jeers and catcalls of the men around us, prompting the Pilus Prior to suddenly appear in our midst and lash out with his *vitus*. There were times I really wanted to take that thing away from him and break it over his head.

Artorius was brought in on one of the wagons of the baggage train, a Centurion in the Cohort marching behind it having thrown him in the back. By this time we were already finished with our evening routine, having our bath and meal, and were in fact just a few moments away from the call to retire. I began to treasure these quiet moments around the fire, listening to the wild tales of the veterans and watching the inevitable dice game which was a feature at almost every tent. I always thought it somewhat interesting that men would almost always gamble with other tent sections but not with their own tentmates, unless there was no other choice. The only exception to this was Didius, but he was already starting to be shunned by our section and was therefore forced to look elsewhere. I believe that for most of the men, besides Didius, it had something to do with the idea of not wanting to cause any bad blood between such close comrades. Whatever the reason, the idea seemed to be that fleecing men from other Legions was always best; if not other Legions, then other Cohorts, and if not other Cohorts at least other Centuries. However, many times not even this was possible, and nothing stops a Legionary from gambling, so it was inevitable that there would be disagreements among the closest of friends. Personally, I was never much for gambling. It is not that I had anything against it; I could take it or leave it, not to mention I had big dreams that only a large amount of money would fulfill so it was not a fever with me the way it was with other men like Vibius, who I swear would wager on anything, no matter how ridiculous. For a while, he was trying to make wagers on which of the men in the tent would break wind next, yet soon enough he found out that there was cheating going on, because in the dark one cannot tell whether the sound was true or made by using our mouth and he was terribly put out that we ruined such an exciting game for him. However, there was nothing exotic this evening; it was dice, and as usual the next day's wine ration was up for wager, something that was strictly forbidden but always ignored, when Artorius came stumbling up. He was not wearing his helmet or armor, carrying them instead, and his head was down as he approached, refusing to meet our eyes. There was an awkward silence as he approached, because we had already been told that since this was his third failure he was being dismissed from the Legion. He came to get all of his gear and return it to the Legion quartermaster, where he would be issued a civilian's tunic and shoes, then given a small amount of money along with a document that he was to carry with him that detailed his disgrace. Because he had committed no crime, unless one considered failing to make it as a Legionary a crime, as I did, he was not punished in any way other than having to carry the shame of his failure back to his family, if he did indeed go back to his family. Many young men were too ashamed to do so, making their way to the nearest big city to try and seek some sort of life there. Despite feeling badly for him, there was also a sense of relief that we would not have to worry any longer about whether or not he would hold up in the trials of combat. It also created some relief to the problem of space in our tent, now having one less body to shift around. Still, it was difficult; we did not know what to say to him, only offering a sympathetic pat on the back instead. While he looked relieved, there was also a new look of fear in his eyes, undoubtedly caused by the dread of what was facing him, the uncertainty of a life that no longer held any particular value to the rest of the world. His only hope lay in his father forgiving him and both of them patching up their differences; otherwise he was all alone in the world, with no real skills. Knowing what I know now, I should have realized that he would most likely turn to a life of crime. He was not cut out to be a highwayman, the type of hard man that lays in wait for unsuspecting travelers. Because of his temperament and his slight build, he probably went into a life of petty crime, stealing what he needed to survive, at least until he got caught. Most of those types eventually do, and ours is not a forgiving society like some of the others I have encountered in my travels. Once he gathered up his gear, Optio Vinicius escorted him to the *quaestorium*, our last view of him struggling to carry all his equipment, with the Optio walking beside him.

Before we went into the final phase of our training, we held the lustration ceremony, a sacred rite that calls for the gods' favor onto the standards of the Legion and the Legion itself. Because of its sacred nature, I cannot speak of it. I will say that it is a rite that is usually performed at the beginning of the new campaign season. However, since we were new *tiros* it was not seen as fitting for us to participate until we were deemed worthy of being called Legionaries. After the ceremony for the rest of the army, we *tiros* were ordered to remain in our places in formation, where we were faced by the Praetor who was standing on the rostra, dressed in his armor and his general's *paludamentum*, the scarlet cloak of general rank. Arrayed in front of him, also facing us, was all 60 of our Centurions, all wearing their dress uniforms, with their phalarae, torqs, and other badges of office and decoration gleaming with the strength of a hundred suns.

"Soldiers," Caesar addressed us, causing a stir in our ranks because this was the first time we were spoken to in this manner, and it took a moment for the meaning to sink in. We had done it! We were being addressed as soldiers by Caesar because that is what we were. All of the pain and sweat of the last almost four months

82

was as if it never happened, just like the last mist of a bad dream dissolving when you awake because of the brilliance of the new day.

"Today is a great day for you, and for Rome," he continued, using what I would learn was his oratorical voice, which he pitched higher when addressing large crowds so that it would carry farther.

"You are about to be entered into the rolls of the brave men who have served Rome so well in the past, covering both our eternal city and themselves in glory."

He indicated the Centurions standing in front of him.

"Perhaps some of you will elevate yourself to the glory and rank of the men you see standing before you. Perhaps not."

He paused for a moment before continuing in a way that sounded as if he was speaking quietly, yet somehow still pitching his voice loud enough for all to hear, at least in the first few ranks.

"What is certain is that some of you will die, if that is the will of the gods."

This had our complete attention.

"But if it is the will of the gods that you die, it is still up to each of you to choose how to die. And in dying well, you add even more glory and fame to Rome, to your tribe, to your family, and to yourselves."

It is a curious characteristic of young men, at least in my lifetime, so I suppose that it has always been so and always will be. As Caesar talked of the possibility of death, while I was at the position of *intente* I still looked at the others out of the corners of my eyes, and I remember thinking to myself, poor bastards, I wonder which of them will die? As I was to learn later when we talked about the speech, every one of my comrades claimed that they had the exact same thought, for it never occurs to the young that they might be one of those unlucky souls who fall before they live to a ripe old age. It is not until one of us actually falls that it becomes real, and from that moment nothing in one's life is the same. But at that moment we were still young, full of bright hopes and brash courage, and it was the greatest sense of pride I had ever known in my short life when we finished the oath to finally become *Miles Gregarii,* the common Legionary in the service of Rome. We were dismissed for the rest of the day, as those of the Legion who were veterans came to congratulate us. Perhaps the biggest shock was the change in the demeanor of Pilus Prior Crastinus, who was the first man to stand us to a round of drinks at one of the shabby, ramshackle inns that had been thrown up outside the camp.

"Welcome home, boys," he roared, the color of his face showing a hint to us that he may have started the celebrations ahead of us.

Passing among us, he shook each of our hands, gave us a slap on the back and made some sort of comment about something we did in training that had either amused him or angered him, although he still relayed the latter with a laugh.

When he got to me, he looked up at me and shouted, "Well! Here's the hero! Hasn't seen a battle yet but he already has those Lusitani *cunni* shaking in their tracks!"

I could feel the blush moving up my neck to my face, and I quickly glanced around. Of course, I was the center of attention but I could not determine what the looks I was receiving meant. Some of the men were grinning at me, apparently delighted at my discomfort; some were not smiling yet still looked friendly. There was only one whose countenance I could not mistake; Didius glowered at me, the bruises under his eyes still slightly visible, making him look like he badly needed a night of sleep. Seeing his displeasure made me feel somewhat better and I grinned, first in his direction then back down to the Pilus Prior.

"I certainly hope that I can live up to your belief in me Pilus Prior," I said honestly.

He laughed and replied, "You will, boy. You will. I have no doubt of that. Once I saw you working the wooden sword, I knew that you'd be one to watch. Just save some for the rest of the boys, eh?"

With another slap on the shoulder, he moved on to the next man, leaving me to stare bemusedly into my wine cup. I was glad that he possessed no doubts; that made one of us. Vibius saw my thoughtful expression and came over to me, leaning against the wall of the rude hut that served to shelter all of the carousers who found their way there every night.

84

"Aaah," he cried cheerfully, "quit moping about, you big ox. You'll be fine and you know it. He's right, you'll probably kill so many of those barbarians that there won't be enough left for the rest of us."

Despite his jovial tone, I was still not willing to give up my contemplative mood.

Shrugging, I could only reply, "I hope it works out like that. But the truth is, none of us really know, do we? I mean," I continued, lowering my voice, "nobody truly knows how they'll react until it happens, neh? So for all I know, I may find that my knees turn to water, and I piss myself like a girl."

Having gotten it out at last, I hurriedly took a swallow of my wine so I could hide my face and shame at having made such an admission.

"That much is true," a quiet voice sounded next to me, and I swiveled my head to see Calienus standing there.

Obviously he had heard what I said, so I saw no point in pretending otherwise. He examined me with a kindly expression, one that I imagined a big brother would use when his little brother came to confide in him some wrong done to him. Without waiting for me to answer, he continued, "Nobody really knows what they'll do the first time they face the enemy, unless they're a liar or fool like him," he jerked his head in the direction of Didius, who had managed to draw a crowd around him, no doubt boasting of the glory he was going to earn. "All you can do is this; rely on your training, and put your trust in the man next to you." Grabbing me by the shoulder, he turned me about so that he could look me in the eye as he spoke. "The rest will come much easier than you think. When the moment comes, trust me, you'll know what to do." Turning to Vibius then, he finished, "And both of you need to watch each other's back at all times."

"All right, Sergeant, but we haven't started the fighting yet," protested Vibius with a laugh, which died in his throat when he saw that Calienus was not joining him. "I wasn't talking about the Lusitani," he replied in a voice pitched just loudly enough to be heard over the din but not any farther than where we were standing. "I'm talking about with him."

He nodded his head, again in the direction of Didius. Perhaps it was a coincidence, perhaps not, but when we looked over in the direction that Calienus had indicated, we both saw Didius drinking from his cup, staring straight at us.

I had never drunk so much in my young life as I did that night, and truthfully, I do not remember much of what transpired. However, I vividly remember the next day, when we were roused by the Pilus Prior, who amazingly seemed none the worse for wear, and was in his normally loud state.

"On your feet you *cunni*," he roared when he shoved his face into our tent, his customary morning greeting. If we were expecting that the goodwill that he had shown to us the night before would be present this morning we were disappointed. Indeed, as the day progressed it was as if the day before never happened, which we found not only puzzling, but a little disturbing.

Going to Calienus for guidance, he explained to us, "It's going to be like this a little while longer, at least until we're blooded. The Pilus Prior is going to keep pushing us until he knows exactly what we can do in battle. If we do well, then you'll see more of what you saw last night, though not as much."

I for one, despite understanding what he was saying, still did not like it. We were *Gregarii* now after all; that is what the whole ceremony had been about the day before, and I expressed this to Calienus, who shook his head.

"What happened yesterday was unusual. Normally you'd have completed your four months of training before swearing in, but Caesar's anxious to move because it's already late. So he had you sworn in earlier than usual. It didn't sit well with some of the Centurions, I'll tell you that." Before we could ask the question, Calienus added, "The Pilus Prior wasn't one of them though. I heard him telling the Optio he thinks our Century is ready to go right now. Second Century," he rolled his eyes and we laughed, "is another story."

The conclusion of our training was a forced march of all the Legions, the 7th, 8th 9th and 10th, culminating in the creation of two marching camps, followed by a mock battle the next day with two Legions against two Legions, along with the cavalry and auxiliaries, now numbering about another 5,000 men, split evenly

86

between the two sides. Particular emphasis was placed on the changing of formations; from column into line, then moving as quickly back into column as we could, simulating the march to contact, with a battle, then a pursuit of a withdrawing force. The last thing that we practiced was how to stage a fighting withdrawal, and much was made by the Centurions that although we would never likely use this, it was still good to know. We wholeheartedly agreed, taking their word for it that we would never use it, the veterans among us openly scoffing at the idea.

"I haven't taken a backward step on the battlefield yet," barked the Pilus Prior, "and with you bastards with me, I don't plan on it ever happening."

This brought a roar of approval from us, and it was clear to all of us that we were ready to march, for real this time, against a real enemy.

Chapter 4- Campaign in Lusitania

We were given two days in which to arrange our affairs, deposit excess baggage into stores, and put finishing touches on our weapons and uniforms. All last-moment items like the replacement of thongs that tied pieces of gear to us that had broken, or javelins that had become unserviceable were taken care of, in anticipation of leaving the camp for good, or at least for the rest of the season. Spirits were running high, as were tempers, and there were a number of minor skirmishes among Legionaries from different Legions, Cohorts and Centuries, yet that was to be expected. At least that is what Calienus told us.

"I don't know about you," he remarked as we were waterproofing our shield covers, "but I've had enough of training. It's time for some real work."

Every one of us barked our approval at this, yet even as I joined in, I felt my stomach do a twist at the thought. Supposedly, at least according to the other men, I was the most ready of all of us and the most likely to attain glory, so why did I feel so apprehensive? If I was as good as they said I was should I not truly be looking forward to this without any doubts or fears, which is certainly not how I felt now? These were the thoughts crammed into my head as I busied myself packing, making sure that varnish was properly applied to straps, buckles were polished, all the myriad things that occupy an army before it moves. The camp was a swarm of activity, with men running this way and that; scribes and Tribunes were marching about carrying scrolls and wax tablets, all of them trying to look like the message or order they carried involved the fate of the Republic itself. Up to this point, we had little to do with the Tribunes, but they were slowly becoming more visible as they gained a little confidence and we advanced in our training. The smart ones and being honest, there are precious few of those in the army at any given point, let the Centurions run the Legions and mostly stayed out of the way. However, there were an officious and arrogant few who, having read a manual thought themselves the experts in all manners relating to the military arts. Not surprisingly, their attitude was met with barely disguised contempt by the Centurions but fortunately for us, Caesar was the type of general who made sure that his Tribunes knew their place. Nonetheless, high and noble birth apparently makes some men a bit thickheaded, as a few, thank the gods a precious few, still sought to establish their authority over us.

There was one in particular, and being honest I do not remember his true name; there have been so many Tribunes pass through my Legions in the last 40 years that they all seem to blend together. Relatively few ever stick out in my memory, and those that do are because they are either spectacularly good at their job or spectacularly bad, and unfortunately the latter outnumbered the former by a huge margin. While I do not remember his true name, I do remember what we called him however; Doughboy. He was named that by Scribonius I believe, and it was an apt name for many reasons. For one, he had the pasty complexion of the kind of dough that graces the finest tables, while his body betrayed a fondness for sweets and pastries. It was more than just his physical attributes that led to his nickname, because he was about as useful as a lump of dough, and when heat of any sort was applied he would puff up, just like a loaf of leavened bread, falling back on his status as a patrician of one of the old families of Rome. He was an Appius, I believe, yet for the life of me I cannot remember his name; it is funny how the memory works sometimes as one grows older. On that day, he was the acting commander of the Legion, because in those times it rotated daily among each of the six Tribunes assigned to our Legion, and since it was his day this meant that there would be more than the usual silliness. He was constantly stalking among us, snapping at us about things like not coming to *intente* as he walked by, forcing us to constantly stop packing or working on our gear since he seemed to do nothing but walk in circles around and around our part of the camp. Compounding matters, he would insist on stopping to inspect our gear then berate us for not having everything ready, polished and packed, apparently simply because he thought we should have been finished by that point.

"Doesn't he have anything better to do?" Vibius muttered in his wake, after Doughboy chastised him for not having his leathers properly varnished. Despite still being new, we had been in long enough to know that doing something stupid, like pointing out that we could only do one thing at a time, would have gotten us in more trouble than the momentary satisfaction was worth, so Vibius simply responded in his best parade ground manner, "Absolutely correct, sir. No excuse sir. Won't happen again sir."

Apparently expecting something else, Doughboy stood there nonplussed for a moment, his mouth hanging open, causing his second chin to quiver slightly, a sight that threatened to make me laugh so much that I was forced to bite the inside of my mouth until it bled. Finally snapping it shut, Doughboy replied in a tone I am sure that he thought was very officer-like, but to us reeked of his uncertainty, saying, "Very well then. Just make sure that it doesn't happen again."

Then he stood there for what seemed like a full watch, though was just a few heartbeats, as if unsure what he was supposed to do next. Finally he said, "Right. Well then. I must go, there are many duties to attend to."

Doughboy then went wandering off, leaving us staring at his retreating back.

"Apparently no, he doesn't have anything better to do," I spat a bloody gob on the ground. "But just make sure it doesn't happen again," I finished, in my best attempt to mimic Doughboy, which set us both to laughing as we turned back to our work,

At last, all was ready, giving us the opportunity to lie where we were to catch some sleep before we started out on the march, a real march heading towards a real enemy, making the energy definitely different than our training jaunts. One other thing that made it different was that we were all required to wear our dress uniforms. For we *Gregarii* that was not much more than the horsehair plume, which I hated because if the wind was coming in the wrong direction it would whip around and hit me in the face. It was the Centurions and the officers that had the most to worry about; rather, their slaves did. Still, it was a sight! The glittering array of the eagles and standards, the panoply and pomp as we were led out of the gate by Caesar himself for that first time, followed by the officers of the Legions, was a sight that will be with me until the day I die.

Wondering that Caesar would be at the very front, without a vanguard of any type, I asked Calienus who replied, "That's only for the first mile or so. Then he and the others will pull to the side, and let the 7th lead the way."

For that is how it was that first day; we marched in the order of our numbers, so that we walked drag, ahead of only the baggage train and the rearguard. When an army of that size is on the march, it does not make any sense for the trailing Legions to even start forming up for the first watch or so, which is why once the initial formation was dismissed and the march began we were allowed to break ranks to go stand by the gate to watch the procession. None of the veterans bothered; they lay down and immediately fell asleep again, using their packed gear as a pillow, but for those of us for whom this was the first campaign, we could not be drawn away from the spectacle. When you are young, things like sleeping or eating can be made up later, but it would not be long before we learned one of the most valuable lessons of being a soldier, that when you have the chance, you sleep, and eat. However, we did not know that yet, so I stood with the rest of my tentmates watching the first Legions go marching by.

There was the usual banter and jeering among us, the men of the 7th calling out to us, "That's right 10th. In the rear with the gear where there is no fear!"

"They're just saving the best for last," someone shot back, which of course we cheered as the wittiest retort ever made, while the men of the 7th did the opposite.

I cannot help but think back to that day, when despite our bickering we were all comrades, none of us knowing the great struggle that lay ahead, where we would be looking over our shield across at some of these same men, preparing to kill or be killed. Such is the fickle nature of the gods and the Fates I suppose, yet despite knowing that we are subject to their whim, it is still hard to understand how we came to that place. However, that was far in the future, and on that day, even the gods seemed pleased. The sacrifices had been made, the auspices taken, and there were eagles sighted flying over the camp in the direction of our march, so for everyone, it was seen as a sign that the gods were with us. That day the weather was glorious, at least to me. Consequently, I reveled in the feeling of the sun on my face as I watched men just like me go marching by, and when I looked at Vibius, my grin could have split my head wide open.

"This is what we've been waiting for Vibius," I crowed, "since we were boys. We're on the march with the Legions. Can there be anything more glorious?"

Vibius shook his head in agreement, replying "I don't think so Titus. I don't think so."

It was almost two parts of a watch before it was our turn to set out, and when we marched the few men who were remaining behind, those too sick to march and a few of the marginal men who it was felt would be better suited to keep the camp open and running, were all that remained as our audience when we exited the gates. The worst part now was the horrible dust that hung in a pall over us, making the sun appear as just a hazy orb in the sky that you could actually look at without hurting your eyes, it was so heavily obscured. This meant that the choking, coughing and cursing began at almost the same time, and despite the Centurions telling us to shut up and quit whining, soon enough they were choking, coughing, and cursing along with us, especially the cursing. Another thing that makes walking drag so unpleasant is that marching behind first the cavalry, then the officers means that no matter how careful you are, before a couple of miles go by, your feet are covered in the deposits of dung left behind by the thousands of animals. The combination of the freshness and the heat also did not help with the smell, so it was not long before some of the more delicate stomachs were heaving, beginning a chain reaction of sorts. All in all, it was a miserable experience.

Because we could only march as fast as the baggage train, with the drag Legion being charged with guarding it and the train being slower than the rest of the Legions, the one small blessing was that this meant that the other Legions got to do the work of making the marching camp. The camp outline, the ditch walls and palisade were already finished when we arrived, with the streets and tent areas all staked out and ready for the pitching of the tents. Filing in, we were followed by the wagons, entering through the *Porta Decumana*, the rear gate of the camp, then marching to our area to erect our tents.

Since there was not a bath like at our permanent camp, we had to make do the best we could to clean off the filth of the march by just oiling down and being scraped clean where we stood, performed on our section by Lucco. The one piece of good news was that we would be the vanguard the next day, so we would not have to go through the same ordeal that we endured that day. Such is the way of the Roman army, and one of the many small reasons we are so great. Everyone shares equally in both the easy duties and the onerous tasks; it is all a matter of time before it's your turn for both. The only exception is latrine duty, which is reserved for Legionaries on punishment, and I thanked the gods that there were enough men who fell afoul of the rules and regulations that it never became a regular duty, although at one point or another we all took turns mucking out the stables. For some reason, the idea of cleaning up the *cac* of an animal is not nearly as loathsome as that of a human's and although I have no idea why this is so, I just know that it is.

Falling asleep easily that night, the talk was held to a minimum by our fatigue, and this began the pattern of the next several days as we moved northwest to confront the Lusitani. Drawing closer to the enemy, the terrain became more difficult, consisting of rolling hills that were not particularly high, yet whose slopes were steep, so that we felt the effort even if it did not take particularly long to crest each hill. Crossing the Anas (Guadiana) River, we were told this marked the southern border of the Lusitani territory, and was the home of the Turdetani and Lusitani branches. While they were reputed to be the more civilized of the tribes; it was the Celtici and particularly the Vettones who were the most savage back then, the Lusitani and Turdetani were still supposed to be formidable warriors. Crossing the river took the better part of a day, there being only one narrow ford and the river bottom was sandy, meaning that the lucky lads immediately in front of the baggage train got to push and pull the wagons when they inevitably got stuck. While we were happy to march as the vanguard that second day, it also meant that we would have the most work to do constructing the camp. Now that we were officially in enemy territory, we were ordered to be even more vigilant, and part of that vigilance included making our camp more secure. The depth of the ditch was deepened a foot more, and widened another foot, making the rampart that much higher. Also, the guard was doubled, and it was also our turn for that duty, so that we made up for the easy day we had as far as eating dust and not stepping in *cac* by getting less sleep. As I said, it all evens out.

Since this was our first night in what was considered to be enemy territory, there was little trouble staying awake during our turn on the walls. The fact that there had been a sighting of the enemy as the camp was being completed just made it all the easier, not that it amounted to much. It was Rufio, one of the veterans in our Century who spotted them first and raised the alarm. There was a bit of a hubbub as his shout got all of us scrambling for our shields and javelins; we were already wearing our helmet, though this was not standard when we made camp but we were ordered to do so because we were in enemy territory. Normally we wore our sword and dagger at all times, on pain of punishment ranging from a flogging to execution. As it turned out, the sighting was a huge army of three men, sitting their horses on the nearby ridge as they watched us work. They were some distance away, so it was impossible to make out details, yet I for one felt my pulse race. It did not matter that there were only three of them, there they were! The enemy, the barbarian horde, the feared Lusitani, the scourge of Hispania! I could tell that my friends were just as excited and even Calienus seemed to be a little more than his usual placid self. It was enough of an occasion that the Pilus Prior did not immediately start thrashing us when we stopped working to stand watching the men observing us. After a moment, we heard him yelling something about our sorry asses getting back to work, so we returned to our respective labors. This day it was my turn to carry dirt, a job that I detested until, that is, I realized that it was a good way to keep working on my strength by trying to carry more than the others. Also, it was a chance to show off a little, I must admit. I could not help being born bigger and stronger, but I saw no reason why I should not demonstrate it from time to time, for which my tentmates would roundly jeer me. However, I could tell that they were secretly proud of the fact that I was already considered one of the strong men of the Legion. Just before we set out, we had held games, including wrestling bouts with men picked by their comrades from each Legion facing each other. Naturally I was picked, despite never having wrestled a day in my life, and it was only due to brute strength that I won my first two matches, advancing to the penultimate round, where I was thrashed soundly by a man much smaller than I but who was an experienced wrestler. While I had not shamed myself or my Legion, I was still determined that I would avenge that loss, deciding that when the campaigning season was over I would learn to wrestle. If I lived at least.

As we were breaking camp the next morning, the alarm went up once again. This time, however, it was not just three men, but several hundred, all of them mounted and who watched us from the same spot as the first three. Again there was a stir among all of us, since this was obviously not just a scouting party, even though there was no way that they could match us in strength and were extremely unlikely to attack us. Because of the presence of these men, who one of the scouts confirmed were Lusitani, we marched out in a column of squares called an *agmentum quadratum*, which is an extremely difficult formation to control on the march, except I think it was more just to show the Lusitani that we had seen them and were prepared for anything they cared to throw at us than from a fear of being attacked. We were told to continue carrying our shields on our back but to remove the covers so that they were instantly ready should we need them. It turned out that we did not; instead, the horsemen were content to shadow us as we marched, always staying just out of reach of a sudden attack by our cavalry screen. After about two parts of a watch, the column was halted, and we were shaken out into our standard marching formation, with our Legion in the middle this time. Again, because of my normal marching place on the outside of the column, I was able to pass the time watching the men on the horses, who were split into two groups, with one group on each side of the column. Even with my lack of experience then, I could at least tell that these men were born to ride a horse; indeed, it was hard to tell where the man stopped and the horse started. Perhaps, I thought, they are really centaurs, and I let this thought occupy my mind as we marched; it is in such ways that one learns to pass the monotonous watches of marching, staring at the back of the man in front of you.

It was shortly before we were to stop for the day when it happened. Suddenly, from behind us came the blaring of *bucina*, and then the *cornicen*, the curved round horn with a deep bass voice that carries a great distance and is used to relay orders in battle, instantly telling us that something important was going on. Craning our necks to look to the rear, it was still impossible to see, and indeed, as we learned later the sounding of the horns that we heard were merely the relayed signals sent up to the front. Whatever happened had occurred far to the rear, although we did not know that then.

"Eyes front you *cunni*," the Pilus Prior snarled as he strode by us down the side of the column, heading towards the rear to see what was going on. "Let me find out what all this racket's about."

The column had halted, and just a few heartbeats later Caesar and what looked like his entire staff came galloping past, heading in the same direction. Shortly after, one of the cavalry *ala* that was up front came back as well.

"What do you think it is?" Scribonius asked me, as if I would have any better idea than he would. "The gods only know," I answered, trying to hide my irritation at being asked a question to which I obviously did not know the answer.

"My guess is that those bastards who've been following us picked off some stragglers," this came from Calienus, and we instantly accepted this as truth since Calienus was a veteran.

There was a buzz of conversation from all the men speculating about what happened, with the consensus seeming to be what Calienus had predicted, so now it was just a matter of waiting to see what the truth was.

Vinicius came to us and ordered, "Keep alert. Don't keep your attention to the back of the column. This may be a trick to draw our attention away from some other point."

The reality of this hit me immediately, and I snapped my head to look around. My heart leaped a little when I saw that the horsemen who had been on my side of the column the whole day were gone.

"Where did those horsemen go?" I asked Vinicius, hoping that one of us was paying attention. He had been.

"They peeled off a mile or so back, a little while before the alarm sounded," he replied. Inexperienced I may have been, but I knew that this was not a good sign. Had they rejoined their comrades to launch an attack on the rear?

In fact, Calienus was right. One of the wagons had a mule go lame and was forced to drop from the column. A Century had been assigned to guard it while the rest of the wagons continued, a spare animal being drawn from the pool of spares and the lame beast slaughtered, meaning someone would get mule for supper. When that happened, the Lusitani obviously decided that this was the moment for which they were waiting. Apparently sending a rider to the group that had been on my side of the column, they raced back to join forces to support the attack launched by their comrades in the second group. It was a short but bitter fight, the aftermath of which we saw once the Century was escorted into the camp with the cavalry. Several men wore bandages on various parts of their body, but the most sobering sight was the wagon, its driver seat soaked in blood, with a number of spear shafts protruding from the wooden sides. However, it was the extra cargo that riveted our attention, and silenced all of us immediately. The men of the Century gently unloaded the bodies of two of their comrades, their corpses in that shapelessly limp form that only the dead possess once their spirits have fled their body and the spark is gone. The camp, for all the usual hustle, bustle and noise of thousands of men talking and going about their business, stopped completely as every single eye turned towards the *Praetorium*, where the wagon had stopped. These were the first deaths in combat that these Legions had suffered; while the 7th, 8th and 9th were veterans in the sense of the amount of time served, they had not seen any combat to that point. As we learned later it was our comrades in the 8th Legion, 3rd Cohort that were hit, and it suddenly made what we were doing very real. Instinctively I moved towards Vibius, to stand closer to him, sharing in silence the burden of lost innocence. This was no longer a game, and we glanced at each other, both of us giving a look that communicated that fact.

The one consolation for all of us was that the Century inflicted several casualties on the Lusitani, well in excess of what they suffered. Still, the camp was the quietest any of us ever heard it that night as we all sat at our fires, choosing this night to stay with our closest companions. Normally, the men would wander from one area to the other to spend time with other friends outside their Century, yet this night, as if by unspoken agreement, everyone chose to spend that time with their tentmates. Even Didius was silent that night, although I was not sure whether it was due to his own thoughts or because there were no takers for his inevitable attempts to fleece others. Whatever the cause I was thankful for it, being in no mood to hear him prattling on that night.

Finally breaking the silence, Remus said, "Well, at least they took a few of the bastards with them."

"I was talking to a friend in the 8th," Calienus spoke up, "and they said that there were more than twenty bodies around the wagon. Now that," he finished quietly, "is how a Roman dies. Taking as many of the *cunni* with him as he can."

We all nodded our agreement at this, although to be truthful we had no idea what we were talking about. The Pilus Prior came up to us and squatted by the fire. We all braced for some sort of cursing for paying too much attention to what was going on in the rear of the column, but none of were prepared for his true purpose.

"Evening boys."

We all replied automatically, still worried about what was to come.

"How's everyone holding up?"

Whatever we were expecting, this was not it. Without waiting for an answer, he continued, "It's always a shock when you see men killed the first time, I don't care who you are. And that's the one thing that we can't train you for, that moment when you see your first dead comrade."

We all nodded, mystified at this new apparition we saw before us. After the night of our swearing in ceremony he immediately reverted back to the Pilus Prior that we all knew, hated, and feared, so this human being was something very strange to our sight.

"But if you're being honest, while you're sad, you're also a little bit relieved that it's not you, or one of your friends. Am I right?"

Despite agreeing with this, this time it was a bit more reluctantly.

"And that's normal. Don't think there's something wrong with you for feeling this way. It doesn't mean that you're not sorry to see good men die when you're happy that it's not someone you know. If they were alive now, and you were the dead ones, they'd be feeling the exact same way." He stood to leave, but before he did, he finished with, "That's why we train so hard, so we have as few of these moments as we can. If I do my job right, none of you will have to feel how the men in that Century are feeling tonight."

Bidding us good night, he left to go to the next tent and talk to them, leaving us even deeper in our thoughts than before.

The next two days were spent in that camp before marching again, it being the custom to take one day off after a few days of

98

continuous marching, although Caesar regularly ignored this later on. Another thing that Caesar ignored was the customary distance and stopping time for the day, preferring to push on for at least two more parts of a watch, so that we often ended up working in the dark to finish the camp, yet this was one of the things that made Caesar as feared as he was, because of the rapidity of his movements. Coupled with his famous lack of hesitation, it meant that his army could appear somewhere long before they were expected, and was a key factor in keeping our enemy off balance. However, I think that the extra day was not just because of the rest, but also because we had suffered our first casualties, and were a largely unblooded army. Caesar wanted the veterans to have time to talk to those of us who had yet to see battle and try to help us understand what it all meant, as well as prepare proper funeral rites for our first dead without having to rush. I for one was eager to get back on the march, because the sooner we reached the barbarians, the sooner we could engage and avenge the deaths of our comrades. Despite not knowing them, they were men who suffered through the same things I had; the forced marches, the feeling of the *vitus* across our backs, the fatigue of trying to stay awake standing on a wall where you knew nobody was going to attack or make any other kind of mischief. They were brothers to all of us, even if the best I could say was that I had seen them around the camp during our training. Such is the feeling that we have for each other, and that feeling is fostered and encouraged by our officers. It is yet another reason why the Legions are so rightly feared; to hurt one of us is to hurt our brother, and we will have vengeance if that happens.

The mood as we set out on the march again was subdued, yet underlying that was a sense of anticipation. Despite remaining stationary those two days, our scouts had been extremely active, and came back with news that there was a town a day's march away, and judging from the tracks, it served as the source of the mounted men who attacked the Century and the wagon. The news of this find ran up and down the army like a bolt of lightning, with the idea of vengeance putting a sudden urgency into our step. No longer did our Centurions have to curse at us to keep the pace up; indeed they found themselves in the unusual position of trying to slow us down so that we did not leave the baggage train and the rear Cohorts too far behind.

"Do you think we're going to attack the town tomorrow, or will we assault it as soon as we get there?" Romulus asked this of Calienus, who shook his head.

"There's no telling," the Sergeant replied. "It all depends on whether or not it looks like they're ready for us I would guess."

This made sense to us, except that he was wrong, but only because we were marching with Caesar. Any other general would have done the prudent thing as Calienus suggested, a thorough reconnaissance before making any decisions, yet other generals were not Caesar. However, we were blissfully unaware of this as we marched towards the village.

I do not know the name of the town, but it was easy to see. It sat perched on a hill that commanded the surrounding plain so the barbarians could see us coming just like we could see them sitting there. At first it was just a dark spot on the horizon, a speck sitting on a bump that ever so slowly got larger as we marched. All of our eyes were fixated on that spot, knowing that for most of us, we would be facing battle for the first time in our lives. This was not training, this was going to be the real thing, and none of us who had yet to be blooded could imagine what we were about to face. Perhaps Vibius and I, and some of the others with kin that served, had a better idea, yet even we knew that no matter how descriptive veterans were with us, it was going to pale in comparison with what we were about to experience. With the sun moving across the sky, while it did not seem to be any hotter than any other day up to that point, I found that my sweat poured more freely than during any previous day's march. Glancing over at Scribonius, I could see that his face glistened with moisture as well, so I at least knew that if it was not the heat but nerves I was not alone. The chattering that was normal as we marched was also less than other days, kept to a few muttered comments between men who marched next to each other, the customary banter and catcalls that men in one Century or Cohort would call out across the ranks almost completely missing, so that the sounds of the clinking and clanking of our gear along with the rhythmic thudding of our feet dominated the air. Slowly, ever so slowly, the village became more distinct and started to take shape.

It was just about two thirds of a watch before sundown when we were halted a little more than a mile from the town, which we could plainly see now. It had a wooden wall around it, but did not appear to have any kind of ditch or other defensive measures, relying on its position on the hill and the slope that would have to be climbed first to get to the base of the wall before any assault of the town could begin. The wall itself appeared to be about ten feet tall, and while made of wood, the parapet was crenellated, with men

100

clearly seen in the gaps watching us as we slowly spread out before them. The 8th was given the vanguard that day, in honor of the fallen men, so they were arrayed first, in the *triplex acies* formation. We were third in line, just ahead of the baggage train, making it almost sunset by the time we arrived to take a place to the left of the 8th and the 7th , occupying the far left of the line. The *cornicen* sounded the signal for the Legion officers to join the command group, with the Primus Pilus and Tribunes for each Legion moving to where Caesar's standard was displayed, the red pennant that denotes the presence of the commanding general. Being in the First Century of the Second Cohort meant that we were in the front line, although I was in the last row of the Century, with the Fifth Century immediately behind us, and I could hear them talking behind me, the topic the same thing that occupied all of us. Were we going to attack, this late in the day? We were standing easy, with our gear grounded, the only order given to that point indicating we might be going into battle being the order to unsling our shields, which we rested on the ground in front of us. Staring at the walls, I examined the men watching us as they moved about, gesturing at us to their comrades, saying the gods only knew what. I remember wondering if what they were thinking was similar to what I was thinking, which was wondering what they were thinking. Still, no matter what was in their minds they were certainly active, bustling about and starting fires behind the walls, their locations identified by the trails of smoke. That got me wondering what the fires were for, but none of the ideas that I could come up with gave me any comfort.

As if reading my mind, I heard Romulus say, "Maybe they're cooking us dinner."

This was met with a laugh by all of us; I think it was probably more hearty than the joke actually deserved, yet it served to relieve some of the tension as we waited to hear what we were about to do.

I do not know how much time passed, but finally the Primus Pilus came back then ordered our *cornicen* to sound the assembly for the Centurions of our Legion, who quickly moved to gather around him to get instructions. Craning my neck, once again I was thankful for my height as I peered at the group of Centurions, watching them nod in acknowledgement of what the Primus Pilus was telling them. After just a moment, the group of men broke up, and all 59 Centurions came striding back to their respective Centuries. The Pilus Prior came to us and bellowed in his command voice, "Listen up ladies, we're going to be making a marching camp, but it's going to be a little different than usual. We're going to create two camps, with two Legions in each camp. We're pairing up with the 9th, which is just coming up now."

Pointing to an area some distance away, when we looked over to where he was indicating, we saw a group of men that are part of the advance party. Their job is not only scouting for campsites, but also to provide any engineering and pioneer work to clear the way for the Legions should the terrain require it. To this point in our march the terrain, despite being hilly in places, consisted of low scrub vegetation, with only occasional patches of woods that we could easily bypass. It was not until we were in Gaul that I saw the real value these men provided, when we would advance through forests that lasted for days, but here in Lusitania it was not necessary for them to clear the way. Instead, they would usually have our camp boundaries already staked out and ready for us to start entrenching and building, except on this day they were held back from their normal task until the army had arrived and Caesar decided what to do. Now, they were using their instruments to survey and mark out our camp.

Continuing, Pilus Prior Crastinus said, "The way it's going to work is that we're going to stay here in formation, while the 9th makes the camp. Same for the other two Legions; one works, the other watches. The one thing that we're going to change is that we're changing to single line to extend our coverage of the ground here."

What this required was the Legion to counter march, in this case to the left, and extend the spaces between each Century so that the second Century of each line could then move forward and to the oblique to fill in the space created. Consequently, instead of three lines of double Centuries, we would have three longer lines of single Centuries. Although it did not provide the depth, it would extend the coverage, making it harder for the barbarians to sally forth and move around our flank. As far as we were concerned, the news could not have been better; no digging, no carrying, no chopping for us! It was hard for us to contain our grins, but the Pilus Prior saw some of our expressions and snapped, "Go ahead and laugh now, because sooner or later, Fortuna is going to piss all over us."

That killed the mood of joy immediately, because we knew he was right. Not for the first time I cursed the Pilus Prior and his talent for taking the fun out of any occasion.

It was more than a full watch past dark before we were given the order to fall back and into the camp, and while nothing exciting happened, we still learned a valuable lesson that day. Even when one is standing still, when it is a requirement to stay vigilant and ready to go into action at a moment's notice, it can be just as tiring as making a camp. I for one was surprised to find how fatigued I was, but the others confirmed that they were in the same state, making me feel somewhat better. Additionally, we were ordered to have no fires either, confined instead to chewing our fat bacon and gnawing at whatever bread we managed to keep to the side. That night the guard was doubled, so the prospect for sleep was not auspicious either. All in all, our first sighting of the enemy was proving to be more boring and troublesome than anything else. While we sat in a circle outside the tent finishing what passed for our meal, the Pilus Prior came by, accompanied by Optio Vinicius. He had just been to the command group briefing, and was spreading the word about what we could expect the next morning, and he called all of the men in our Century to gather in the Century street, then motioned for us to sit down while he talked. Squatting in front of us, we could just make out his bulk by the light of the half moon and the glow of the few torches that were allowed to be lit along the walls.

"We attack at first light," he announced, causing all of us to stop chewing our food to listen intently. "The engineers are going to be busy tonight making scaling ladders, and we're going to assault the town from two sides. The artillery will begin a barrage a third of a watch before first light, and soften up the defenses. I doubt that what we have with us will be big enough to knock down any of that wall because it looks pretty strong, so it'll probably be the ladders that'll get us over the quickest. The 8th is going to use the ram," he was referring to the mobile ram that was broken down and carried as part of the baggage train, "to assault the main gate, which is the most heavily defended. The other two Legions will be support, which is why we're in the camp together."

Suddenly, I understood why two camps were made, and in the darkness I could just make out Vibius' face and saw that he recognized it as well. Thinking about it more, I realized that the 7th and 8th's camp was directly in front of the main gate of the town, while our camp was arrayed opposite the side of the town where we would be assaulting. Maybe this Caesar did know what he was doing after all.

The Pilus Prior paused a moment to let all this sink in before finishing, "You'll receive more detailed orders in the morning, but I just wanted all of you to know now what was going to be happening. In the morning we'll assign the sectors of the wall and who'll be the first over it. So get some sleep, because tomorrow is a big day."

With that, he stood and strode off, leaving us to talk excitedly to each other. Looking over at Vibius, he gave me a tight smile, his teeth shining dully in the moonlight.

"I bet we're one of the first over the walls," he said, his voice quavering just enough so that only I, his closest friend who had known him for all these years, would recognize the fear in his voice. I felt my throat constrict, so instead of answering, I just nodded.

"That just means my first *Corona* Muralis", Didius' voice cut the air between us; neither of us had realized that he was within earshot or even listening.

Feeling the familiar tickle of my anger rising, instead of lashing out, I replied as coolly as I could, "Or you'll be the first man dead."

I could see the whites of his eyes as he glared at me angrily and snapped, "As you could be Pullus. Don't forget that."

Then he turned heel to stalk away, but despite feeling a little sense of triumph for having rattled him, his words and the warning of Optio Vinicius collided in my mind, sending a shiver up my spine. Was I going to have to watch both my front and my back, as the Optio had warned me?

There was little sleep that night, I suspect by any of us in the army, with the possible exception of the veterans. The Centurions certainly did not sleep; they were prowling around the camp, checking on the men in their Century, conferring with each other about the coming day. In our tent only Calienus lay snoring softly, oblivious to our whispered conversations. Vibius tossed and turned for a while, and I could hear him mumbling to himself, while I lay just staring at the roof of the tent, trying to think of other things that had nothing to do with what was happening in just a couple of watches.

Finally giving up his attempt to sleep, Vibius rolled over to face me and whispered, "Do you have it in a safe place?"

Inwardly I cursed; this was probably the fourth or fifth time he had asked me that question this night. Biting back a sharp retort, instead I sighed, "Yes Vibius. I have it in a safe place. It's wrapped in the greased leather bag in the bottom of my pack. The same place it's been the last four times you asked me about it."

I could not resist this last gibe, but fortunately for both of us, and for the rest of the tent section, he was too agitated to take offense.

"I know, I know. I'm sorry I keep asking. It's just that......"

"I understand," I whispered.

And I did; if the truth were known, I had found myself wanting to ask him the same question about my will. As my designated comrade, one of the primary responsibilities we had concerning the other was keeping each other's will in a safe place. Each of us was also responsible for carrying out the bequests made in the will, ensuring that we carried out the last wishes of our closest comrade and friend. We were ordered to draw up the wills in the days prior to starting our campaign, just another somber reminder that this was indeed serious business, and we did so with the guidance and help of our Sergeant, along with the Tesseraurius Cordius who had experience in these matters. One of the duties of the Tesseraurius, besides keeping the watchword, is to act as the Century's banker, and also in the case where a man lost his comrade, hold the will of the lone man until he found another comrade to do so. Cordius was well liked and trusted by all of us, a critical trait for that position, almost as important as the ability to calculate sums. Both Vibius and I knew our letters, but neither of us had much practice at actually writing a document, a very common fact in the Legions. Some were even illiterate, so instead they dictated the terms of their will to their Tesseraurius who wrote it for them. Didius was one of those illiterates, a fact that brought on him much derision and jeers from the tent section, especially since each of us had been subject to his bullying or boasting. Consequently, this piece of information was filed away by all of us to bring up at opportune moments, much to Didius' rage and consternation.

"And you remember what to do?" Vibius pressed and this time I could not keep a groan from escaping.

"By the gods, yes Vibius I remember!"

But he would not be satisfied just with that. "Tell me," he insisted. "What are you supposed to do?"

Sitting up, I glared at him, although it was pitch black.

Since he obviously was just not going to let this go, through gritted teeth, I replied, "I'm to take your ashes not to your family, but to Juno and give them to her. Then I'm to tell her that she's no longer bound to you, and has your blessings and prayers for her happiness."

"And what else?"

Sighing, my anger deflated; it was hard to stay that way when you were talking about your best friend's possible death, especially when it was that same friend who brought it up.

"I'm to tell her you died well, facing the enemy. Even if........." I did not finish, because I did not want to.

"Even if it's a lie," he finished quietly. "I want her to always remember me in a good light, Titus. Surely you can understand that."

I nodded, although he could not see me and responded, "Yes, Vibius I do understand that. It's just that neither of those is going to happen. I won't have to lie because you're not going to die, and even if you do, you're not going to die with your back to the enemy. It's just not in you."

"I hope you're right," was all he said to that and I dropped back down on my cot, willing the time to pass more quickly.

Somehow I managed to doze off, because when the *bucina* sounded the signal for waking, I about jumped out of my skin. Sitting up, I heard the others rustling about, along with the cries and calls of the Centurions greeting their men that signaled the start of the day. Looking through the flap, I saw that it was still dark, which was not unusual. It was the shade of darkness that told me that we had been roused even earlier than normal. The one change from the

106

night before was that now we were allowed to start fires and actually cook our breakfast. Immediately the men designated to cooking duty that day began gathering the ingredients from their comrades that would make breakfast. It would be the standard porridge, with salt bacon thrown in, and as many spices and flavorings as could be scrounged up. Soon enough, the smells of simmering porridge sent the signal to my stomach via my nose and despite my anxiety, I found I was famished. Since our officers evidently wanted us fortified with a good hot meal before battle, I felt obligated to eat, despite my misgivings. My comrades all seemed to feel the same way and more quickly than normal the porridge pot was emptied. Once we were finished, the Pilus Prior again summoned us in the darkness, although this time Optio Vinicius carried a torch, the light from it dancing on the rugged features of Pilus Prior Crastinus, the shadows accentuating even more the hook of his nose. One difference I noted immediately in his demeanor is that it seemed as if the invisible man waving the turd was given the day off, and he looked at all of us with an expression that we had not yet seen on his face. Could it be pride, I wondered? Might this man actually be proud of his Century and the men we were becoming? While the Pilus Prior was in direct command of our Century, he was also the senior Centurion for the entire Cohort, so he called for the entire Cohort to be assembled to ensure that he only had to relay orders one time.

"As I told all of you last night," his voice rang out, "we've been selected by General Caesar to be the assault element on the walls of the town, while the 8th Legion will be conducting a simultaneous assault on their front gate. Our assault is going to work like this. First, Second, Third and Fourth Cohort will be first over the walls. The First and Second Maniple of our Cohort, commanded by me will scale the walls, while the Third Maniple will provide covering fire at the base of the hill. Once we're over the Third Maniple will follow suit. We'll be followed by the other Cohorts, in numerical order. An artillery barrage will precede the assault, and all the Scorpions for both the 9th and 10th are being assigned for our use. They'll station themselves on a small rise a couple of hundred paces away, and they'll be providing close support, only lifting their fire when we begin climbing the ladders. That should make those bastards keep their heads down while we take care of business."

He paused for a moment to let all of this sink in. I cannot say I was surprised that we would be the first over the wall but it was still a frightening prospect. Continuing, "There's also been a slight change from what I described to you last night. Instead of acting as our reserve, the 9th is going to march to the far side of the hill, in order to ensure that there's not a sortie by the enemy from the rear gate, or any escape when we take the town."

This last piece of news caused some heads to turn as we looked at each other, aware of the import of what he had just said. It did not appear that we were going to let anyone escape if we could help it. Sometimes defenders are allowed to flee, in order to avoid facing an enemy that will fight that much harder knowing that certain death or slavery awaited them. Giving them an open escape route meant that there was an alternative for them, and would encourage them to give up the fight more easily. However, because these people were technically in rebellion, Rome declaring this region pacified some years ago, these people were not going to be given that option. In such ways are examples made that discourage those people foolish enough to think that they can escape Rome's dominion.

"So tonight, when we're victorious," his eyes narrowed and his voice took on a hard quality, even more than his norm, "and we will be victorious, we'll be spending the night under a roof, in a nice bed, and maybe there'll be a woman beside you. Willing or not," he finished with a wolfish smile. The Cohort burst out into a cheer, then we were dismissed to go don our armor and gather ourselves for the coming trial.

Once we were prepared, we assembled in the forum, both the 9th and 10th Legion, where the Legates for both Legions were standing on the rostra. Legates are the nominal commanding officer of the Legion; while the sub-command is rotated by the six military Tribunes, the position of Legate is more permanent and is appointed by the Praetor, although in Caesar's army Legates were moved about as well. Both of them gave short speeches, but I honestly do not have any idea what they said. In fact, I have been trying as I dictate this to remember the name of our Legate back then, but for the life of me I cannot, he was that unremarkable, though I believe that was due more to Caesar's presence than any real shortcoming of his own. Once they were done inspiring us, we marched out of the camp to array ourselves, shortly before first light, where Caesar's design became clear. He wanted these Lusitani to wake up, rub their eyes and look out to see the might of Rome arrayed before them, ready to strike and wreak a type of havoc they could not possibly imagine. The artillery had been rolled out of the camp earlier and

108

was already in their position, with the ballistae arrayed so that they focused on the front gateway. The scorpions had just finished being pushed up a small hill to the southeast of the town, about two hundred paces away. They were accompanied by a Century to serve as a guard in the event the Lusitani made a sortie to try and destroy the artillery. Back then each Legion only carried four scorpions apiece, but Caesar put great store in artillery, so when we began the campaign in Gaul the number of both scorpions and ballistae were doubled. Each of the scorpions has a two man crew drawn from their respective Legions, and while each of us had practice fired both the scorpion and ballistae in training, those who showed the greatest aptitude were designated as artillerymen, working almost exclusively with the weapons until such time that artillery was no longer called for, whereupon they took their place back in the ranks. As the sun rose, another facet of Caesar's genius became clear to us. The town's gates were arranged along the customary north/south axis, with the front gate facing north and the rear to the south. In terms of terrain, other than the small hill previously mentioned, there was not much variation, which was what made the establishment of this town on this hill so sensible. Since there was no real advantage offered by terrain; the area immediately surrounding the town out to at least a quarter mile was cleared of vegetation that might hide an advance of a large body of men, Caesar used something else to our advantage. By choosing to assault the east wall, he not only took advantage of the only other high ground in the area, where he placed his scorpions, but arrayed as we were, we had an even more powerful ally in the sun rising behind our backs, forcing the Lusitani to stare straight at it in order to watch our advance. Another advantage, and one that I did not appreciate at the time but learned to as I gained a better understanding of how men thought, was in the symbolic gesture made by this approach. Caesar chose to ride over to join our side of the assault, partly I am sure because he had already spoken to the other element while they were still in the camp, which explained their roaring earlier. The other reason became plain when we saw him sitting on his horse, motionless, his *paludamentum* in all its splendor resting on his shoulders, rippling gently in the soft breeze that was blowing, facing the fort bareheaded but dressed in his ceremonial armor, a glittering cuirass made of silver and chased with gold with matching greaves. It was as if he was a god, which I now know was precisely the effect he was hoping for, so that as the Lusitani rose that morning and saw before them this glittering army, headed by a man whose very essence seemed to be framed by the sun, it had to be a devastating blow to their morale. Rome had come, led by a part man, part god, and all who stood before him quaked in fear.

Apparently, however, their morale was not damaged enough to see reason. Before launching the assault Caesar sent a Tribune, under a white flag, to parley with the occupants of the town. We watched him approach warily, stopping about a hundred feet short of the gate, on the rutted road leading into it. Even though the Tribune tried his best to sit stock still, his horse was obviously very nervous, hopping and skipping about and acting very skittish. As I learned later, he had been sent by Caesar with one last offer to submit to Rome, showing their good faith by the payment of a tribute and giving of hostages, the customary measures with such matters. The Tribune sat on his horse, obviously listening as a man stood on the wall above the gate, actually climbing onto the crenellation so he was standing in plain view, pointing down at the Tribune and then gesticulating back towards the town. This man was obviously of some importance, wearing what appeared to be armor made of some sort of golden scales, and a high, conical helmet. He looked to be a fairly large man, although that may have been because he was standing on the wall.

"Come on, let's get on with it," muttered Scribonius, and I wholeheartedly agreed.

Despite being scared out of my wits, the waiting was even harder, and I could only imagine the tension the next time if this parley was successful and the Lusitani in the town gave up without a fight. We would march on, something like this would happen again, and we would again find ourselves arrayed and ready to do battle. As far as I was concerned, it was just time to get it over with.

Luckily for us, unluckily for the Tribune, the parley was unsuccessful. Our first inkling that our terms were rejected came when suddenly, without any warning whatsoever, we saw what looked like a sliver come slicing down to strike the Tribune in the chest, almost knocking him from his horse as he reeled with the impact. Obviously, it was not a sliver but a spear, and from the combination of the height and the obvious strength of whoever threw it, the spear transfixed the Tribune and we could clearly see the bladed end protruding from his back. Almost before this could register, a number of other such darts struck him down from his horse, leaving it to gallop away in a panic, a short spear lodged in its flank, streaming blood. Despite our discipline, seeing the death of

110

the Tribune brought a collective gasp from all of us, and I am sure across all the ranks of men who saw what happened. Shock was immediately followed, at least in my case, with a terrible anger. The flag of truce was clearly on display; there could be no mistake in what they had seen, but they still murdered one of our Tribunes in cold blood. Even as we were absorbing that act, the gate was flung open, two men came dashing out and before we could do anything more than shout a protest, they dragged the bloody body of the Tribune, now looking like a pincushion with multiple shafts sticking from his body, back into the town, shutting the gates. Then, a moment later the man on the wall reappeared, except this time in his hand he was waving as a trophy the head of the Tribune, dripping blood and gore from the severed neck. His call of defiance was drowned out by the roar of more than 20,000 men, all of them screaming with rage. It was absolutely deafening; I felt more than heard myself screaming out in inarticulate fury and I could feel the ground vibrate under my feet from the sound. I had reached yet another new level of anger in my life to that point, and it was clear I was not alone.

Caesar remained motionless, his only visible sign of distress in the clenched fist that he struck against his thigh over and over. It was when he turned to face us, riding in our direction, that we could see his lips thinned in rage, but once he got close enough it was his eyes that arrested all of us. They were like glittering points of ice, and it was with a start I realized that this was the first time I had been close enough to see the color of his eyes, a bluish-grey that looked like an angry sea. Drawing his sword then waving it over his head to get our attention, slowly we stopped our invective to listen to his words. In the brief silence before he began speaking, we could hear the Lusitani, chanting on their own, working up their own courage since they could have held no illusion what was facing them now. They had cast their die, and were trusting their skill to avert the righteous vengeance that they deserved. I for one vowed to myself that they would need more than skill this day.

"Soldiers," Caesar's voice rang out clearly, and even using his oratorical voice, his outrage was plain to hear, and we could tell that it was unfeigned, "you have just witnessed one of the most abominable acts any supposedly civilized nation can perform, the slaughter of a defenseless emissary under a flag of truce." Suddenly dropping his sword and pointing directly at the 10th Legion, he roared, "What do you propose to do about it?"

111

Our answering cry once again shook the ground, except this time we replied not just with voice, but with pounding our javelin against our shields in a rhythmic manner that lasted for a couple of moments before he motioned us back to silence.

"Very well," he called, "I have your answer. Now," he pointed to the wall "show me your answer in deeds. I will give" with his left hand he pulled a leather purse that looked as if it were bursting with coin, "one hundred sesterces to the first man over the wall, along with the reward of a *corona murales*."

One hundred sesterces! That was a fortune! How could one man possibly spend that much money, I wondered? I laugh now at my naiveté; I have wasted a hundred sesterces in a single night's debauchery since, but for the country boy from Baetica I was back then, I could not comprehend such riches. Finished with us, he raced off to the 8th to make the same offer, while his command staff distributed themselves among the Legions to take nominal command. My heart sank when I saw none other than Doughboy approaching, and my sentiments were echoed by the muttered curses of the men around me.

"Gods, why us?" I heard Calienus groan.

Trying to remain optimistic, I ventured, "Maybe he'll be smart enough to let the Primus Pilus give the orders."

"*Gerrae*! You know better than that Pullus."

I shrugged. He was right, but one could always hope. Doughboy marched up to where the Primus Pilus, Pilus Prior Crastinus and some of the other Centurions were gathered. Even from a distance we could see the barely disguised contempt on the face of the Centurions, something Doughboy either ignored or was too stupid to see.

"Well, men," he called out in a loud voice, thinking, I guessed, to inspire us with his words of wisdom. "Are we ready to go over the wall and spill some Lusitani guts and get our hands wet, eh?"

"Of course sir," answered the Primus Pilus smoothly, without a hint of mockery in his voice, "as long as we know that you'll be the one leading us over the wall."

112

Doughboy's face blanched, before he realized he was letting his feelings show.

"Pardon me, Centurion?" he started but got no further.

"That's Primus Pilus, if you please sir," the Primus Pilus responded, his voice a mask of formal politeness. "It's just that I worked hard to get here, sir, and well, it's my proper title."

Doughboy's eyes narrowed in suspicion as he glared at the Primus Pilus, trying to decide if he was being toyed with, but the Primus Pilus was cowing young Tribunes since before Doughboy had been expelled from his mother's womb, and was the picture of rectitude and respect. Obviously deciding to drop the matter, Doughboy started again.

"Forgive me, Primus Pilus. You're correct, of course. Anyway," he cleared his throat, "back to what you were saying earlier."

"Yes sir," the Primus Pilus replied cheerfully, "as I was saying, we'll follow you anywhere you choose to lead us. Isn't that right sir?"

Now Doughboy looked nonplussed; how could he answer this in a way that let it be known he had no intention of being the first to anything other than the food line, and not expose his cowardice? Therefore, he apparently decided that silence, accompanied by a thoughtful nod of the head and stroking of his chin, as if seriously considering the remarks, was the best course.

The silence dragged on for a few heartbeats, before the Primus Pilus continued helpfully, "It's just that you're a young man on the rise sir. Nothing makes a young patrician's career like being the first over the wall. Besides," for this he turned to his companions, "that sort of thing is a young man's game, isn't it boys?"

This was greeted by a chorus of agreement, each of the Centurions looking at Doughboy with wide eyed innocence.

Clearing his throat yet again, Doughboy looked at the ground as he murmured, "It's just that, if I'm first over the wall, I won't be able to assess the overall situation, you see? I thought it would be better for me to remain in a place," he looked up at the Primus Pilus earnestly, "close to the wall of course, not completely out of danger, but far enough back so I can have an idea of what's going on."

The Primus Pilus pursed his lips, slowly nodding his head in thought.

"I do see your point sir. Indeed, I'm not sure of these things, so you're no doubt correct. I'm sure that you've read many more manuals than I have on the subject," despite what I guessed was his best effort, the Primus Pilus could not entirely conceal the scorn with this last remark and just barely remembered to finish with, "sir."

Doughboy's ears turned a roasting red yet there was really nothing he could do because there was nothing objectionable in the Primus Pilus' words, despite knowing that it was an insult.

Cutting his losses, he muttered, "Right. Well then, carry on."

Whereupon he stalked off down the line to station himself in the proper place to avoid the appearance of cowardice, while not exposing himself to much danger. The other Centurions, during this last exchange, were all feverishly studying the ground but we could see their shoulders shaking with silent laughter, threatening our own composure. When the Primus Pilus turned and saw that we had witnessed and heard the whole thing, his only response was to grin and give us all a wink, destroying all remnants of our façade and we laughed heartily.

Our barrage started immediately after that exchange, the sound of the ballista snapping against the cross bar causing a crash, followed by a whirring sound as if a flight of birds was taking off, and we all looked up to watch the stone arc through the air. The first shot landed short, the stone thudding into the ground with a spray of dirt before its momentum took it skipping to where it smacked into the base of the wall just next to the main gate on the north side, which we could see from our spot on the far right of the line. This was immediately followed by a stone that actually hit the wall, and even from where we stood, we could see the dust fly as the timbers vibrated. One after the other, the stones hit the area around the front gate, and in the pause as the ballistae were reloaded, we could hear the cries of the Lusitani raising the alarm that the assault had begun. It was just about a third of a watch past dawn, and now we would wait while the artillery either did its work, or did nothing more than raise some dust. While we were told to remain in formation, we were allowed to stand at *otiose*, meaning that we could turn, talk to the men around us and bend our legs and so forth, but not leave our position in ranks. The customary way it is observed is that as long as your left foot stays in position, you can pivot around to talk to the others. I turned to face down my rank and Vibius immediately caught my eye.

With a completely straight face he asked, "Do you have it in a safe place?"

Reaching down, I grabbed a clod of dirt and threw it at him then we both laughed. Grabbing my crotch to make an obscene gesture, I answered, "Oh yes, it's in a safe place all right. It's right here. I used it to wipe my ass this morning."

"You mean you're smart enough to wipe your own ass now?" he shot back. "I guess it's true that the Legions can teach ANYONE if they can finally teach you."

I promised that I would make him regret his words, to which he answered with an obscene gesture of his own.

"All right you bunch of women. Shut your mouths," this came from Optio Vinicius, who was standing next to me, and I turned in time to watch him yawn then scratch himself as if we were standing around camp. "I've heard you two going back and forth about that damn will for too long now. Can't you talk about something else?"

Indignantly I pointed to Vibius and protested, "Don't yell at me, yell at him. He's the one who keeps asking."

"Yes, and you keep answering him, so who's the bigger fool? The fool who asks or the fool who answers?"

I really was not sure what to say, because with Vinicius it was always very hard to tell whether he was being serious or not, especially since he looked like the messenger of death all the time. As I was starting to form an answer, I saw just the corner of his mouth twitch in a gesture that I had learned was his version of a smile. Rolling my eyes, I looked back to the front and kept my mouth shut.

The front gate was completely obscured by dust, and while we saw splotches of a lighter color that indicated the wood of the walls were scored, we had no idea if it meant a substantial weakening or just a spot where the bark was knocked off. Meanwhile, we saw the trails of smoke again, at various spots along the walls, and now I could not resist the temptation.

Looking over to Vinicius, I asked, "What's the meaning of the smoke, Optio?"

He looked at me with his deadpan eyes and seemed to consider something before he shrugged, then answered, "I imagine they're heating up some pitch to pour down on us, or maybe some sort of oil."

Shuddering at that, he saw me do so and asked quietly, "Would you rather have me lie to you?"

I shook my head, "No Optio. But still......" I did not finish, and he merely nodded.

"I know, boy."

The order of *intente* was sounded, and we immediately snapped to, with our shields up and a javelin in our other hand, the second javelin held along with the shield in our left hand, which is awkward to say the least.

Our Primus Pilus strode out to where he could be seen, and called out, "Before we start out, I want everyone in the assault elements pass their javelins down to your supporting Maniple. You won't be able to throw them from a range where they'll do any good, and they're going to be useless once you get on the ladders. Give 'em to the boys who'll be supporting you, and they can deliver 'em to those bastards for you."

As weak a joke as it was, we still smiled. Passing mine off, while it felt strange to have my right hand empty, I was grateful to be able to hold my shield cleanly. I could feel my heart thudding heavily and when I looked down, I was surprised to see my armor jumping slightly with every beat of my heart. As we were passing the javelins a wagon rumbled up, and in the back there were a few dozen ladders the engineers had lashed together. Each Century in the assault elements were given two ladders with the order to place them at least three shields' width apart to deny the defenders massed targets.

The Pilus Prior stood in front of us and called out, "Right, I want my veterans up front to pick up the ladders." As those men like Calienus did so, he continued. "They're going to be the ones carrying the ladders and will be between files so that the rest of you boys can hold your shields up to cover them since they'll have their hands full."

Then the Pilus Prior designated between which files he wanted the men, and those files moved out a little to widen the gaps while still having enough spacing so that they could provide protection. This forced all of us over a couple of steps and we quickly adjusted.

"Now, listen and listen carefully," Crastinus continued, oblivious to the fire of the scorpions that were just starting in preparation for our move to the walls. They make a deep twanging sound when the bolts are launched, and it was hard not to watch as they worked, but I managed to stay focused on the Pilus Prior. "I'm going first up the ladder. Normally I wouldn't, but since this is you boys' first engagement, you just follow me and everything will be fine. The Optio," he motioned to Vinicius, "will be the first up the other ladder. We'll need one man, one very strong man to brace each ladder against the wall while the others ascend."

Immediately the men in my vicinity turned to me, and I could feel my face burn. The Pilus Prior looked over at me thoughtfully before shaking his head.

"Not Pullus. I want him up early after me. He's been the best in training, and besides," he grinned, "the very size of him is going to scare half of those bastards to death before he lifts a finger."

I was in an agony; part of me glowed at the distinction I was being given while the other was petrified because it was clearly expected that I would perform valiantly. That feeling of pressure that was almost non-existent once we started the march came flooding back, and I struggled to maintain my composure. For a fleeting instant, the thought of screaming out the fact that I was still underage crossed my mind, sure that if I did so, I would not have to go up the ladder. Just as quickly the shame of that idea washed over me, and I recognized that, if I were to do such a thing, while it might get me out of being killed in battle, it might not necessarily save my life. Enlisting under fraudulent circumstances is a serious crime; we had been forced to witness the execution of two men, from different Legions, whose identity as slaves were uncovered. First they were scourged, then executed, and the sense of shame that such a death brought was more overpowering than my fear. Consequently, I just stood there as if mute, hoping my face did not betray the stark terror that I was feeling. Instead of me, Crastinus picked Didius to hold our ladder, who responded with a "Yes, Pilus Prior" that was as close to insolent as one could get and still escape the *vitus*. That was not lost on Crastinus, who glared at Didius before choosing the man for the second ladder, another recruit named Macro. He was shorter than I was, but built very thickly with rippling muscles. As I was turning back to face my immediate fate, Scribonius tapped me on the shoulder.

With a tight smile, he murmured, "Good luck, you lucky bastard. Try not to kill all of them before the rest of us get there."

The smile I returned felt more like a grimace. At that moment, the *cornicen* from the command group sounded his call, followed by the *bucina* from each Cohort, with the standards dipping in acknowledgement of our order to begin the advance. Stepping off, for a moment I was struck by a sense of panic because I was still in my accustomed place at the back of the Century; how was I supposed to follow Crastinus up the ladder from the back? Glancing over to my right, I saw the Optio was next to me, also in his accustomed place, confusing me further. Despite the fact that talking was forbidden when we were advancing, I felt there was enough urgency to risk breaking the rules.

"Optio," I hissed.

My call seemed to snap the Optio out of some sort of trance, because his head jerked around in surprise. Or maybe he was taken aback that I dare talk at a time like this. He did not rebuke me however, just asking, "What is it Pullus?"

"How am I supposed to get from back here," I motioned to our location while trying to maintain my alignment with the rest of the rank and the cover of my file, "to up there?" I indicated the spot with a jerk of my head.

"You follow the file of men with the ladder, idiot," was his response. "The Pilus Prior'll be there at the base of the ladder while the ladder is being lifted. Then you follow him."

"Oh."

Chagrined that the answer was that simple, when I looked over, I was suddenly not so sure it was indeed that easy because they were three files over, putting men between me and them. I was in too much of a state for me to think it through, so I shrugged my shoulders and turned my attention back to the front. The town was looming larger, but the snapping of the bolts being fired over our heads was an oddly comforting sound. I could clearly see men on the ramparts of the wall now, only in glimpses though, as they were forced to keep their heads down because of the scorpions. Every so often, one of them would risk a quick peek around one of the crenellations to see when we would be in range. Even as I watched, apparently either one of them was a little too regular in deciding when to peek his head out and one of our gunners noticed, or he was just the unluckiest man in the world, because the timing of when he poked his head out and the bolt arriving in the spot his head now occupied, however briefly, could not have been better. In front of my very eyes, I saw the blur of the bolt, then saw the man's head explode, the top half of his skull shooting off to the right while the continuing blur of the bolt, now with what looked like a fine red mist trailing it, went hurtling further into the town. My eyes were riveted to the sight, and I heard the exclamations of the men around me who saw it happen as well, all of us watching as the torso, with the lower half of the man's head still attached, totter there for a moment before collapsing back behind the wall.

"Remind me not to ever get in front of one of those things," Scribonius muttered, and all I could do was nod.

Our front ranks hit an unseen line marking the spot where we now came in range of their slingers. While not of the same renown as the slingers from the Balearic Islands, they were highly skilled nonetheless, and in the space of just a few moments we would learn to respect and fear these weapons almost more than any other that the Lusitani wielded. Dozens of men appeared, whirling their slings above their head, preparing to launch them despite weathering the bolts from a partial volley of scorpions that knocked a couple of the men off the wall.

"*TESTUDO!*"

That command was roared simultaneously all along the leading line and it was in this first moment that it became apparent to every new *Gregarii* that all of the training and the beatings that came with it possessed a value that could not be overestimated. Even before I consciously thought about it, I crouched down and lifted my shield above my head, since the threat was coming from ahead and above us. If we were exposed to enfilading fire from the side, I would have held my shield across my body, while sheltering under Scribonius' shield. A bare instant later, there was a sound like a sudden hailstorm as the stone shot that the Lusitani used bounced off the surface of our shields, mostly inflicting no damage. Scattered among the rattling sounds indicating no damage done however, there was another, a sickening thud either followed by a grunt, or worse, by a scream of pain that made the hairs on the back of my neck stand up. Although we kept advancing, we could not move as quickly as we normally would in standard formation, so there is a tradeoff of sorts. Despite being more protected, the amount of time we were exposed to the slings was longer. The first volley did not inflict any casualties on our Century, but after the second rattling of shot, and more shouts and screams, there was a ripple in the formation as someone fell to the ground and we automatically compensated, closing up the spot where the man fell. While I could see a prone figure out of the corner of my eye, I could not see who it was, and I realized with a shock that we were now blooded. We had suffered our first casualty, but judging from the ferocity of the volleys that we were absorbing, it was not likely to be our last.

"Jupiter Optimus Maximus, protect this Legion, soldiers all," someone cried out the Legionary's prayer, and while appreciating the sentiment, I wondered whether or not Jupiter really cared.

Our advance hampered by the use of the *testudo*, the distance closed agonizingly slowly, and for the first time I began noticing that my arm was getting a little tired from holding my shield above my head. Glancing over at Scribonius, the sweat was pouring from him as if he were standing in a rainstorm, his face red from the exertion. Meanwhile, the smacking and thuds of the shot continued, and more times we had to adjust the formation. Then, a man two ranks ahead of me, his arm obviously tiring from holding the shield, let it slip just a bit, enough so that I noticed the crack of daylight that allowed a beam of pure light to shine through as if shot down from the heavens. A sharp-eyed slinger saw that crack too because just a heartbeat later there was a thwanging sound, slightly different than those I had quickly become accustomed to, and the Legionary dropped to the ground without a sound, not moving. The man in front of me, Papiria was his name, almost stumbled over the body, which would have left several men exposed, but with a curse he managed to maintain his balance and I resolved not to make the

120

same mistake, forcing myself to look down as I came on the body. I wish I had not; he was lying face up, with one eye hanging partially from its socket, a gaping hole showing between the orb and where the bridge of his nose had been, while his heart still pumped blood in a spray, the bone of his nose apparently carried by the shot into his brain. I felt the bile rise as the ghastly sight was burned into my memory forever and even today, I can close my eyes and still see him, alive but not, his heart not yet receiving the message that it was no longer needed. Dragging my eyes away now that I had stepped clear of him, one detail tugged at my mind. The rim of his helmet had a huge dent in it, and for some reason that image occupied my thoughts. Even as we were still moving forward, in formation, I thought about it and finally understood the thwanging sound I heard must have been the shot hitting the rim of the helmet, which in turn deflected it down, into his eye and through his brain. The helmet was not penetrated and when thinking about it later, I realized that if we were facing an enemy on the same level, and not occupying higher ground, the chances were very good that he would have been struck a glancing blow, except the projectile would angle up instead of down, and all he would suffer from it is a headache and ringing ears. Such are the whims of the Fates.

Making it to the base of the hill we started up, with one thing becoming clear immediately. The distance from the bottom of the hill to the base of the wall was deceptive; the Third Maniple would be forced to move higher up the hill to launch their javelins than originally planned. Our Century had shrunk even more, and when I anxiously glanced over to my left my heart sank as I saw that my rank was at least four people narrower than before. Meanwhile, the slingers continued their assault on us, the racket of missiles hitting the shields or occasionally striking something else and scoring a hit almost continuous. I tried to determine how many of the men in my tent section were missing from the back rank simply because they moved up to replace a gap, and how many had gone down themselves. From what I could remember, at least two men in files ahead to my left had fallen, and I thought there might be a third as well, yet that still left one of my tentmates unaccounted for, and my greatest fear was that it was Vibius. What if he were right after all? Trying to shut that out of my mind, I turned my attention back to the task at hand, and in a panic I saw that I had dropped my shield a fraction while thinking about something else. Quickly I readjusted, just in time to feel my arm shudder, hearing the unmistakable strike of a shot as I cursed myself for my inattention and vowed that I would not falter again. We were beyond the base of the hill now, reaching a point where the angle between our *testudo* and the slingers was such that the only way for a slinger to launch a missile at us was by leaning out over the edge of the wall. A couple of them tried and almost immediately were scoured from the wall by the scorpions. That is when they turned their attention to the Third Maniple, and it was like the hailstorm suddenly stopped now that it was their turn to come under fire. From our spot, the predominant sound was now the whirring sound of the slings circling around the men's heads, followed by the whistle of the projectiles slicing into men behind us. Reaching the base of the wall, the Legionaries carrying the ladders immediately moved into action as we moved our shields to the side to allow them room.

Half the men got on each side, grasping the ladder, while the Pilus Prior commanded, "Didius, get your sorry ass up here."

Didius was one of the men who had moved up, putting him a little closer to the front of the formation, but he still had to push his way past the other men of the Century, drawing curses as he jostled them and forced their shields over, exposing them for an instant. Fortunately, nobody was struck down and it became apparent that we were relatively safe from fire, so Crastinus ordered us out of the *testudo* and I dropped my arm, thankful for the brief respite. The ladder team planted the feet of the ladder on the ground, while Didius was moved into position by the Pilus Prior, who grabbed him by his harness and faced him in the opposite direction from the rest of us, with the ladder between him and the Century. Then pushing him down, he forced Didius to sit, while simultaneously the ladder team walked forward with the ladder and it started to rise. The Pilus Prior then made his way to the base of the ladder once it was raised to a sufficient height.

"Pullus, you big oaf. Get behind the Pilus Prior!"

This came from Vinicius as he made his way past me over to the other ladder team, which was doing the same thing as ours. Startled out of my observation of what was going on, I moved quickly behind the Pilus Prior, just in time for him to look behind him to see if I was there, as I gave a brief thanks to the gods that he apparently had not missed me before this, shuffling in behind him as the ladder was raised.

"Good luck," I heard a man mutter, but I found my throat was too dry to respond, so instead I just nodded. My heart was pounding harder than if I sprinted the whole way to the wall, and I was sure that if things continued, it would explode right then and there. A different kind of sound added to the cacophony of noise, and I sensed the rapid movement of objects heading towards the walls, looking up to see the javelins thrown by the Third Maniple slice through the air and into the wall, some striking the Lusitani. Immediately after this were screams of pain, followed by dull thuds of men falling down to the ground off the rampart. Very quickly, another volley landed, with much the same effect. The Lusitani were now huddled behind their walls, unwilling to expose themselves to any more of the javelins, telling us this was our moment. Didius reached out to grab the sides of the ladder, pulling it taut against the wall so that it would not slip. While watching him do this, the Pilus Prior was already halfway up the ladder before I realized it.

"Get up there, you stupid bastard. We're right behind you," I could not see who it was, though it sounded like Calienus' voice.

Gulping down the huge lump in my throat I began climbing, taking two rungs at a time in an attempt to catch up while trying to hold my shield above my head. There was still no sign that the Lusitani felt safe enough to peek their heads up to see what was happening, and again I offered a prayer that our luck would hold a few more moments.

It was at this moment that there sounded a horrible scream, something so inhuman that it caused all of us, Roman and Lusitani alike, to freeze. For just a moment all activity stopped, and I looked in the direction of the noise, which was just dying out, seeing that it came from a man on the other ladder. I say it was a man, but it would be more accurate to say that what I was viewing was merely a large lump of scorched meat. What had been his face was blackened, along with every inch of his exposed skin, which was issuing a thick smoke, like when the fat in meat catches fire, and I suppose that is exactly what was happening. The part of his tunic not covered by his armor was burning brightly, the flames licking up around his head, and covering him from head to feet appeared to be a substance that to my inexperienced eye looked like boiling honey. Immediately I realized that it was the pitch that they were heating in preparation for just such a moment. However, as much as the scream, it was what the man was doing that I think arrested everyone's attention, for he was still ascending the ladder, very slowly but definitely noticeably, and despite my horror at the sight I also felt a fierce sense of exultation. This was how a Roman died, I thought! Even dead on his feet he still advanced, and I imagined that this sight must strike fear and despair into the heart of the Lusitani. We could not be stopped, and as if in answer to that thought, I felt the ladder begin shaking again as the Pilus Prior continued his climb, even Crastinus stopping like everyone else. As Crastinus did so, the other man slowly toppled off the ladder, still in flames and smoking, and I saw the men below scatter out of the way in order to avoid being hit and burned by his body, which in a sense had become a weapon of the enemy's on its own since anyone touched by it would be horribly burned as well. I started climbing again too, when I was struck by the sudden thought that the man on the ladder had nobody above him. That meant that he was first, so it must have been Vinicius who I just saw incinerated. Just moments ago, I was talking to him about the very thing that killed him, and I wondered when we would next talk again in the afterlife. Maybe sooner than I think, I thought grimly as I peered up to see the Pilus Prior almost at the top. Just then, a Lusitani appeared in a gap in the wall just next to the Pilus Prior; letting out a cry in his language, he used a long spear to try and skewer the Pilus Prior. However, his war cry alerted Crastinus, who dodged out of the way, almost losing his grip on the ladder, which he now clung to with only his right hand. Without waiting for another blow and displaying a speed that astonished me, he jumped up and over the wall, disappearing from sight, then I heard the thud of his borrowed shield as he smashed the boss against the Lusitani, followed by a wild yelp of pain. Even as Crastinus did this, I scrambled the last couple of rungs then pulled myself up onto the wall, where for the first time I could see into the town. The parapet of the wall was also made of wood, about ten feet across and crowded with men. All of them were armed, although there was a wide variety of weapons, some of the men brandishing nothing more than hoes and sticks with sharpened points. Nevertheless, there was also a fair amount of men in armor, and these were the men crowded around the area where we were assaulting the walls, the more poorly armed men obviously in reserve.

All of this I took in over a matter of no more than a couple of normal heartbeats as I jumped down onto the parapet before turning to my right, barely in time to meet a wild swing of a Celtic sword with my shield. Feeling the shock of the blow move all the way down my arm, making it go numb instantly, it was only because of my size that I did not stagger backward. For the first time my opponent seemed to notice my bulk, his eyes going a bit wider. Dumbly I stood there, allowing him to recover before I did and strike once again, this time in an overhead swing, I guess to try to split me down the middle. Once more, as if of its own volition, my arm went up to block the blow, my body again vibrating from the shock.

"Pullus you stupid bastard, draw your sword and kill that *cunnus*. Quit messing about," I instantly recognized the voice of the Pilus Prior, and only then did I realize with a great amount of chagrin that he was right; I had yet to draw my sword.

I was ashamed of myself; here I was supposed to be the star pupil and I could not even remember to draw my weapon! Grasping the handle while holding it in the manner Vinicius taught me, I unsheathed the sword and immediately dropped into the first position, my sword pulled back and parallel to the ground. Instantly, I felt a surge of confidence as my body reacted to the familiar, and my opponent must have sensed the change because he assumed a wary expression as I advanced toward him, grimly determined to retrieve my dignity, also remembering that I needed to make room for the men coming up behind me. So far no more than a dozen normal heartbeats had elapsed, and I heard other men landing behind me as I moved towards him. Suddenly, I lashed out with the shield, catching him by surprise because he was obviously expecting me to make a move with what he considered my offensive weapon, not realizing that to Romans, the shield is as much of one as the sword. He staggered back but in his attempt to regain his balance used his own shield, much smaller and round compared to our larger oval, moving it backward in an automatic movement to try and recover by counter-balance. Both of us knew in that instant that he just made a fatal mistake, because I saw the despair in his eyes as I lunged, thrusting the blade while twisting forward with my hips in a perfect, training ground thrust. My blade pierced him in the left side, in the ribcage, and he let out a short, sharp shriek before collapsing as I made a perfect recovery. Rather I tried to, yet I had not been quite as training manual perfect as I thought. One of the first things we are taught is to strike with the plane of the blade parallel to the ground, so that if we do strike in the rib area, it is more likely to slide between the ribs and not get caught in the bone. I obviously did the opposite, holding the sword with the plane perpendicular to the ground so that when I went to recover, the sword stuck in his body, causing me to almost lose my grip. At the same instant, another man, this one carrying a long spear and with the same type of shield, came charging at me, again forcing me to parry the blow with my shield, but unable to counter because I could not get the damn blade out of the other man's body. This Lusitani lunged at me again, and again, but despite being able to block, I was having a hard time maintaining my focus on him while trying to twist the sword free. After his third strike, my blade finally came free just in time to use it to parry his lunge by knocking his spear down while stepping forward and using the boss of the shield to smash him hard in the face. I heard the bone crunch, and he made a choking cry as his mouth and nose filled with blood. I hit him once, twice then three more times, until his face was pulverized and he fell to the ground twitching. Within the first moments on the wall I made my first two kills, and I could feel the confidence surging through me as my training took over.

By this time I was joined by another man, who stood by my side shoulder to shoulder, there being only room for two of us to stand this way on the parapet at this moment with a bit of room to maneuver. There were still a sizable number of Lusitani in our vicinity of the parapet, but they had seen the fate of their two companions and now were not quite as bold. The two of us moved slowly forward, our shields locked together, then I felt someone grasp my harness behind me to brace me in the way we were trained.

"Let's go get these bastards," I heard Calienus say, and realizing that he was the one behind me made me feel even more confident. For the first time since I was on the wall, I became aware of the sounds of battle going on around me; the clashing of metal on metal, the roars of men trying to slaughter each other, the cries of the wounded and shrieks of the dying. I was too inexperienced to know how the fight was going by the sound; that would only come after several engagements, so I had no idea how the assault was progressing. Moving forward, we stepped over the bodies of the two men I had slain, taking care not to trip as we tried to close the distance between us and the remaining Lusitani. At first they were content to keep backing up, making half-hearted jabs with their weapons, then one of them looked behind him and saw what we had seen already; they were running out of room. Immediately behind them was a series of large log columns protruding above the parapet, effectively blocking it off from the parapet on the other side. There was a ladder next to the columns but they knew as we did that the moment they tried to climb down we would be on them, and while the wall was only ten feet high on the outside, the actual level of the town was lower by a few feet where they had dug down to create streets and such. This was not a height that would kill them if they jumped, but it would definitely stun or knock the wind out of them, which was just as dangerous. However, this was actually a bad spot for us as well, because now that they knew there was no escape, their only choice was to attack or die. Not that it mattered much in the larger picture; the murder of the Tribune sealed the fate of the defenders of this town, along with the citizens, but first we had to finish what we started. One of the men, a decent-sized warrior a bit older than us, was the first to attack and in doing so, showed us a characteristic of the Lusitani that I have since seen in other Gallic tribes, with whom the Lusitani are distant cousins. Unleashing a war cry, he lunged forward, a whirlwind of ferocious movement as he slashed at us with his long sword. Both the man next to me and I raised our shields as we were buffeted by blow after blow, each of them sending shocks traveling down our arms that were clearly transferred backwards as we recoiled. Keeping our guard up while watching through the crack between the shields, we waited for an opening, and it soon presented itself. For a moment the Lusitani dropped his guard as he panted for breath, both his sword and his shield moving just a bit. Like a snake striking, my comrade, who I recognized as a veteran from my Century that was salted into our ranks, thrust his blade through the gap between us, plunging it into the gut of the Lusitani who let out a gasp of air as if he was punched. Before my mind even registered it happening, the blade was back behind the shield and I looked down to see that fully half of its length was covered in blood. The Lusitani took a step back, began to turn around, then toppled off the parapet, whereupon another man took his place, and it was then that I noticed this strange custom. The Lusitani, much in the same way as the Gallic tribes, have this notion of single combat and whenever possible prefer to attack one at a time. At least, that is how they start out; usually, by the third or fourth time we faced them they learned the folly of their ways, but since this was our first battle with the Lusitani, they still were determined to fight in the manner in which they were accustomed. The next man apparently did not learn anything from watching his comrade, instead coming and swinging wildly at us, making it a matter of a few heartbeats before he was dispatched. It was in this manner that we slowly moved forward, eliminating all of the men on that section of the parapet.

Once our section of the parapet was cleared of the enemy, we turned our attention to the fighting around us. The immediate area was now crowded with Legionaries, yet none of us had made sufficient headway against the Lusitani to enable us to get off the parapet and down onto the ground. While our Century was clearly holding its own, I thought that they would welcome the help of the rest of us in our small group, but I was not sure what to do, so I turned to Calienus for direction and he seemed to weigh the options in his mind. Narrowing his eyes in thought, oblivious to the mayhem that was taking place just feet away from us, he announced, "We've cleared our section, so we could go down the ladder and come back up behind them farther down the wall," and I looked down at the area immediately surrounding us.

It was full of the Lusitani in reserve, and although they obviously did not have the weapons and probably did not have the training of the Lusitani on the wall, they made up for it in numbers, at least as I saw it. However, I would obey my Sergeant no matter what he said.

"But I think that while we could take most of those bastards, there's just too many to make it a sure thing," and I heaved a sigh of relief at the decision, "so let's go help the boys over there," he pointed to where Crastinus was fighting.

Running along the parapet, we were forced to hop over the bodies heaped there, it surprised me how quickly I was becoming inured to the feeling of wanting to throw up whenever I saw a corpse. Less than a full watch ago, I felt like I wanted to vomit when the Tribune was decapitated, but now I hopped over mangled bodies like they were no more than a log. I have always found it interesting how the human mind works that way. Making our way to the rear of the group of men from our Century who were in the assault team with the Pilus Prior, I grabbed the back of the harness of the man in front of me who twisted in surprise, in turn giving me a shock, albeit a happy one. It was Vibius!

He grinned when he saw me and I returned it as he asked, "Well, how many have you done for so far?"

"Three, and helped with a couple of others. You?"

He looked a little embarrassed as he shook his head, then nodded towards the front and replied, "Those bastards up there won't give me a chance. They won't rotate through like they're supposed to."

128

Standing on tiptoe I could see that, indeed, the Pilus Prior was still up front, thrusting away with short, brutal strokes and I could see men toppling over in front of him, most of them either falling or being pushed off the parapet to land on the ground. Next to him was one of the veterans of the Century, a Legionary named Figulus, who was doing the same. Looking down at the growing pile of bodies heaped below the parapet, I saw some of them moving and trying to crawl away, with others being completely still. Trying to estimate how many there were, I thought maybe twenty or thirty, but there appeared to be at least that many men left between us and the rest of the Century that had been led by the unfortunate Vinicius, so that pressure was being applied on both sides as the two parts of the Century moved towards each other, making the results inevitable.

After another few moments of fighting, we cleared the area of rampart that we were assigned, whereupon Crastinus pointed down with his sword at the mass of men standing in what passed for a street in towns like this, though was nothing more than a wide expanse of rutted dirt with puddles of mud.

"Let's sort those bastards out," he yelled so that he could be heard over the noise.

Despite our immediate area being clear, we could see down the length of the parapet to see very fierce fighting still going on, extending all the way to where the wall curved out of sight, following the contour of the hill. There were a couple of spots that looked like the Legionaries were getting the worst of it; whether it was that the Lusitani in command of that local area was made of better stuff, or the men themselves were more organized I could not tell. I wondered briefly if we would go to their aid, except it became clear very quickly that the Pilus Prior was not concerned with them. Turning to us, he scanned our faces, found someone and pointed at him, beckoning him to stand next to the Pilus Prior.

"Rufio, you're the acting Optio. If you don't completely fuck things up in the next little while, maybe you'll be Optio for real," he said this matter-of-factly, and I was troubled that he did not make any mention of Vinicius. He was the whole reason for Rufio being promoted after all, yet as I was to learn, those emotions that one feels at the loss of a close comrade are to be put away for later, after the battle, and Crastinus was more concerned with keeping the rest of us alive. Rufio joined him then Crastinus turned to the rest of us to give us our orders.

"Half the Century is going to go down that ladder," he pointed at the one nearest us, "and the other half is going down that ladder."

He indicated back behind us to the ladder that we were closest to earlier.

"So, Sections One through Five on me, the rest on Rufio. We go when I give the signal. Look around to see if there are any javelins that can be used lying around here. We'll use them to keep these savages away from the foot of the ladders while the rest of us go down. I go first down my ladder, and Rufio goes first down his. Just make sure you don't end up like Vinicius."

The mention of Vinicius affected us, and Crastinus saw it. "Mourn him later, boys. We still have work to do," he ordered.

Then he sent us on our way, and as we went back the way we came, we looked around the parapet for any javelin whose pin had not sheared. One of the things that make our javelin so fearsome is its design. It has two pins affixing the iron shaft to the wooden one, with one pin made of iron, while the one closest to the head is made of wood, and is designed to shear off on impact. Also, although the tip of the javelin is tempered and hardened, the metal shaft is not, making it bend easily. Combined with the wooden pin, it makes the javelin a weapon such that once it strikes something substantial, like flesh, bone or even the wood of a shield, the iron shaft bends and partially detaches from the wooden shaft at the spot where the wooden pin shears off at impact, making the weapon unusable to throw back at us. The other advantage is that if it strikes the enemy's shield, once again it will bend, the weight of the javelin making the shield basically useless after that. Managing to scrounge up about two dozen that were sufficiently undamaged to use to keep the Lusitani at bay while we descended the ladder, it also did not appear that they were overly anxious to meet us. Perhaps it was the nature of the men held in reserve that they were not as aggressive as the warriors who occupied the walls. I think it was just as much that they had experienced a taste of Roman fighting and found it not to their liking. Whatever the case, we gathered quickly as Rufio, still unaccustomed to his new status, tried to decide how we would descend the ladder. Looking around, his eyes caught mine, and with a sinking feeling, I realized what he was thinking.

"Pullus, you were second up, you may as well be second down," he commanded.

130

At first I felt inclined to argue but felt the eyes of my comrades on me, so instead I simply nodded, not willing to trust myself to say anything. Rufio turned his attention to the others, quickly counting out the order that we would line up and designating six men to remain behind to provide support with their javelins while we established a presence on the ground, men who had proven to be accurate with the javelins in training. The Lusitani, guessing our intentions, started to surge forward but even to my inexperienced eye I could see that it was more for show than anything. Even so, there were still a couple hundred of them. They stayed just out of range of our javelins, except there was no way to be sure that they would not charge us when we started down the ladder, and there was only one way to find out.

Rufio took a breath before calling to the men providing support, "Watch our backs on our way down."

Immediately he began descending, back to the Lusitani who, seeing us start down started their chanting and bashing of their shields all over again. Then on a signal by a man who apparently was their leader, the enemy began rushing towards us. I was not about to repeat the mistake I made on the way up the wall, so the instant Rufio cleared the first couple of rungs, I started following him down. There is no real way to describe what it is like turning your back on a large group of men who want to kill you, and I tried to ignore the shaking of my knees as I made my way down. Rufio made it to the bottom, as did I an instant later, then the man behind me, followed by another, whereupon we took a few steps forward to make room for the rest of our group, standing shoulder to shoulder as the horde approached. Hearing Calienus give the command to ready the javelins, followed immediately after that by the order to release, we sensed them flying towards the men, now not more than 20 paces away. There were only six of us throwing, so it did not come close to stopping their charge, yet every one hit its mark and the men who went down caused others to stumble, checking their wild advance for just a moment. Then, just as they started their charge again, the command to release was repeated, with more men going down. In the intervening time, another half-dozen of us made it down and I glanced over to see Vibius step into place to my left, where we had just enough time to grin at each other before the mob closed the remaining distance to slam into us. The collision was terrific, and I recoiled backwards from the mass of men who were the first to meet our fragile wall of shields. Feeling my feet skidding backwards, I strained forward, putting all of my weight against the

131

Lusitani screaming just inches from us, so close I could smell their stinking breath. Peeking over the edge of the shield I locked eyes with a man who appeared to be several years older, with his hair worn long in their manner, pulled back into a knot at the back of his head. His face was decorated with some sort of patterns made with what looked like paint, which combined with his wild eyes and shouting chilled my blood. Desperately I looked for an opening for a thrust to his face or body because it was impossible to use my shield in any offensive manner, then I felt a hand grab my harness to start pushing against me, least stopping my backward slide. There was one small advantage in the sudden and surprising fervor of the enemy; in their haste to destroy us they ran headlong into our shield wall, the back ranks pushing their leading warriors up against our line, crushing them against us so tightly they could not wield their weapons with any effectiveness. However neither could we strike back, forcing something of a stalemate, yet it was one that we would inevitably lose because of the numbers we faced, unless something happened in our favor. Glancing at Vibius, his face contorted with the effort of maintaining the integrity of the formation, and I could tell that he was rapidly weakening. Something had to be done or we would be overwhelmed, even with the rest of our group now on the ground with us, and it had to be done quickly.

The answer came with probably no more than a few normal heartbeats' of time left before one of us in the front line failed and caused a breach. Instead of disaster, it was one of those accidental events which, now with my experience in hundreds of battles and skirmishes, has as much to do with deciding the outcome as the tactics and strategy of the generals. The man pushing against Vibius, who looked no older than we were, had been trying to poke Vibius with what appeared to be nothing more than a sharpened stick, thrusting it over the top of Vibius' shield as Vibius hunched behind it, dodging every jab. Finally in frustration, the man dropped the stick to grab the top of Vibius' shield with both hands, giving a mighty yank, and succeeded in pulling it almost out of Vibius' grasp, exposing my best friend to the warriors surrounding him. Feeling a roar of rage burst from my throat as I saw Vibius about to die and finding a strength I did not know I had, I threw the man facing me off with a huge push, staggering him backwards into his comrades, causing a ripple as the men pushing him from behind were knocked backwards as well. Turning my body, I brought my sword up to strike out at the men threatening Vibius, yet before I could there was a blur of movement as the man to Vibius' left also

132

saw him in trouble and used the opening created to strike a blow on his own. His blade entered the neck of the man who dropped the stick and was still holding onto Vibius' shield, blood spraying us as the blade was withdrawn just as quickly as it struck. I could not see who was next to Vibius; I reminded myself to find out and thank him later, but Vibius was not out of danger yet as another warrior, this one better armed than the first man, moved his arm forward in a sweeping arc in an attempt to take advantage of the gap that was still there. It is hard to describe events that take place in a matter of heartbeats accurately, yet when in battle, something strange happens, and time seems to stand still. Your mind can track things that are taking place literally in the blink of an eye like they are happening in slow motion, and one at a time instead of simultaneously. All that I am describing here took perhaps five or six normal heartbeats at the most, and still, more than 40 years later I see them as clearly as I see poor Diocles straining to keep up with me! Perhaps even more clearly, since my eyes do not seem to be as sharp as they have been in the past, even a year ago. Continuing, I saw that Vibius was still in danger, as one of the few men armed with one of the long Gallic swords that the Lusitani favored was swinging it down to cleave him in two. Instead of thrusting at the man, I instinctively swung my sword up in a backhand sweep that started at my waist, with my blade meeting the man's arm just before his own weapon crunched into Vibius' head, who had closed his eyes in anticipation of the blow. My blade severed the man's arm as it moved upward through his limb just below the elbow, the reward being another shower as the severed portion of his arm tumbled end over end, splattering blood and flying just above Vibius' head to smack the man behind him. It turned out to be Scribonius, the arm hitting him dead in the face while the long sword clattered harmlessly to the ground as our friend bellowed out a roar of disgust, and despite the gravity of the situation I felt a grin on my face. Vibius had recovered at this point, his shield back up in the first position, and he struck a blow of his own, gutting the man whose arm I had removed as he stood there staring dumbly at the stump pulsing blood in rhythm with every beat of his heart.

Once he went down, between his and the man with the stick's deaths, we had formed a small pocket of space, and I heard Rufio roar, "Move forward, Pullus. Use your fat ass for something useful."

Nodding that I heard him, I stepped forward to meet the man who had originally been opposing me, by now having regained his balance to come back at me. I saw that he held a spear, a wicked looking thing with a large head that appeared to have barbs on it, in his other hand the small round shield they favored, and he advanced warily. Feeling Vibius move forward back to my side, it made me feel secure and allowed me to concentrate on the man who wanted to kill me. Even as my foe moved forward, another Lusitani apparently thought to help him and moved next to him but my opponent snapped something, causing the second man to look angry and make a gesture before turning his attention to Vibius. Now that my opponent was not screaming and acting like he was possessed by a demon, I could see that there was something different about him than the others; he was better dressed for one, and there was an intelligent, almost humorous look in his eyes. When our eyes locked he gave me a grim smile before making a short, mocking bow, then attacked. He was weaving the spear back and forth, and despite myself I followed it with my eyes, exactly what he wanted. Lunging suddenly, he forced me to move my shield in the direction of the lunge to deflect it, also what he wanted me to do. Realizing my mistake at once, it was nevertheless too late, the head of the spear punching at me as he made a backhand, slashing thrust, causing me to twist my upper body in desperation. My countermove saved my life because instead of striking square, the point struck a glancing blow along my ribs, sliding off my armor but still knocking the breath out of me. Even with the protection of the chain mail, I felt a searing pain, making me wonder if he had drawn blood as he instantly recovered to launch another attack, which I managed to block with my shield this time instead of my body. The Lusitani struck at me again and again, yet despite regaining enough of my composure to defend against him, I was still rattled and did not try to strike back. Being truthful, my pride and confidence were hurt more than my side, as I realized that I had been taken in by the constant praise and the belief in me that my comrades displayed, and had convinced myself that I was invincible. Now, this Lusitani had almost proven me and everyone else wrong. Gripping my sword more tightly, I resolved to make up for my mistake and not do it again, waiting for his next attack. He began the weaving again and I smiled grimly, determined not to make the same error. This time when he lunged my shield remained still, not moving to meet his supposed target, instead I took a step forward to make a thrust of my own in the instant where the momentum of his lunge created a gap between his own shield and the shaft of his spear. The point of my blade shot through that small gap, punching into his body just below his breastbone. This time I remembered to keep the blade parallel to the ground then twist it to cause more damage before withdrawing.

134

His eyes widened in shock as his knees collapsed, staring up at me, and I thought, you're not smiling now are you, you bastard? Vibius in the meantime had dispatched his adversary, enabling us to move forward just a bit more, slowly but inexorably giving our section more room to form into a proper formation. Rufio did not have a whistle, so he was forced to bark out verbal orders for us to rotate through, which he did at that point. Vibius and I each gave a heave to the Lusitani we were engaged with before taking the step to the side, allowing Calienus and Scribonius to take our respective places. Backing up, I kept my shield up since I was on the outside of the formation, then fell behind the last man in the group.

I had not realized how fatigued I was, but when I turned to speak to Vibius I found that no words came because I did not have the breath yet. Finally, I gasped, "That was a close one, neh?"

Vibius was holding onto the harness of the man in front of him and did not answer, keeping his eyes straight ahead, his face flushed with what I guessed was more than effort. He seemed to be embarrassed and I tried to tell him it was of no matter, yet he refused to speak so, irritated, I turned my attention back to what was going on. Advancing across the clearing to the edge of where the first round huts that comprised the beginnings of the town were located, we rejoined the rest of the Century as the Pilus Prior took charge again. We took a moment to collect ourselves and look around; the wall was now breached, and we could see the other Centuries moving down the dirt streets, heading towards the center of the town.

"All right, boys," called the Pilus Prior, "we head down that street," he indicated a dirt track winding in between the rows of cottages that seemed to head in the direction we needed to go. "Keep tight, stay sharp, and by the gods, watch the alleys and spaces between these *cac*heaps. These bastards are regrouping somewhere, but they probably left some men behind to hold us up."

With that admonition ringing in our ears, we began moving down the track, pushing our way into the town. Moving past the first of the native huts like we were ordered, we kept our eyes open for any stragglers or ambushes. Instead of a threat, we saw the women and children of the warriors fighting us and whose fate was being decided as they sat, huddled in abject terror and fear. The sobbing and cries of them as we moved down the muddy street could clearly be heard, and despite knowing that they brought this fate on themselves, I felt my heart lurch at the sights and sounds. We did not run into any resistance, the remnants of the defenders apparently deciding to form up for a last stand somewhere ahead. Although the town was not yet taken, we could already hear the sounds of a city that falls by the sword. It has been a custom since the gods only know when that a town that resists leaves themselves open to the complete destruction and sacking of it. Nothing is safe; no property and no person, and we could already hear some of the Legionaries in the other Cohorts begin taking what was now theirs before the fight was finished.

Pilus Prior Crastinus heard it too, and commanded, "If one of you *cunni* take so much as a crust of bread until you're told, I'll personally flog you until there's nothing left but a bunch of bloody meat, understand?" We responded, and he finished, "Just because those bastards don't have any discipline it doesn't mean that we're going to be like them. The Second Cohort isn't a bunch of fucking rabble, got it?"

Again we answered, except I could plainly hear the bitterness and disappointment in some of the men's voices. Since I never participated in the sacking of a town before, I had no idea what to expect, and therefore did not know that I was missing anything, nor did any of my comrades who were *tiros*. Approaching the town center, we heard the clash of arms from other Cohorts running into resistance before reaching the large clear spot that served as their market and assembly area. It was not dissimilar to my town of Astigi, despite the fact it had not been Romanized, making it more native in appearance than Roman. Smoke was beginning to curl up from different parts of the town where the Legionaries had started putting things to the torch. Forming up just at the edge of the town center, we waited for the rest of the Cohort to join up, and they came streaming out behind us, spreading out in a single line. Facing us, about 150 paces away, were the remnants of the defense, perhaps 500 men all told, many of them clearly already wounded. This time there was not a lot of their screeching and jumping about, just a grim silence as they awaited their fate, except we were just as silent, from our training and discipline, but also from the deep seated belief that the end was inevitable and Rome's army would be victorious once again. While we waited, the Pilus Prior ordered each of the section leaders to do a head count of their tent section, which was quickly done.

136

"Anyone seen what happened to Didius and Vellusius?" Calienus asked us.

"I saw Vellusius go down before we got to the wall," Remus replied. Glancing back at Scribonius from my place in the rank ahead, he responded with a shake of the head. "I didn't see it," he said quietly.

"What about Didius?"

Atilius spoke up from his spot two ranks ahead of his normal spot, "I saw him fall off the ladder when we were coming down, but then I got busy."

This drew a laugh from us, the sound carrying over to our enemies, and I clearly saw the anger and humiliation on their faces, since I am sure they thought we were laughing at them. That we were doing so at all, no matter what the reason, clearly rattled them a great deal and I have seen such things many times since. It is part of the Roman mystique, if you will; the fact that we can laugh when death is all around is no small feat, and is yet another reason why we are so feared. What kind of man is it who laughs in death's face instead of shrinking back when it looks at him? I was worried about Vellusius, though it is probably not surprising that I did not have the same feelings for Didius. His death would remove a source of worry on my part, but I was not to be that lucky.

Once the butcher's bill was tallied, we were ordered forward once more, and this time we possessed no javelins to launch. No more than a third of a watch had passed since we assaulted the walls, and I hoped that we would be finished soon, looking forward as I was to what was about to happen once we were turned loose on this town. First though, we had to take care of this business and I turned my attention back to the problem at hand. Once we were about 50 paces away, we were halted to have our lines dressed. To our right, arrayed in the same manner were four Cohorts of the 8th Legion, compared to our five Cohorts, a total of about 2,500 men to maybe 500, and of those 500 many of them were already wounded. Primus Pilus Favonius moved to the front of the line where he could be seen, not only by us but by the Primus Pilus of the 8th. Next to him was his *cornicen*, who blasted the signal to prepare for assault, causing a ripple of movement as we crouched down and got ready. Glancing over, I saw that the 8th's Primus Pilus was holding his sword in the air in the same manner as Primus Pilus Favonius, both of them watching each other. The moments passed, then the 8th's Primus Pilus, obviously deciding that the tension was raised to the sufficient level, swept his arm down, followed an instant later by Favonius. Even as the *cornicen* blew the signal for the attack as well, the sound was almost drowned out by our roar as we began the charge. Adding my voice, I ran forward, following my comrades as the distance closed rapidly. The Lusitani apparently had decided to stand and meet the charge, rather than try to countercharge to create their own momentum, always a mistake. So much of what happens in a battle hangs on that first collision and standing still is a foolish, or desperate, thing to do. Slamming into the Lusitani, the clash by now a familiar sound to me, it was still difficult to listen to the cries and screams of wounded and dying men. Ignoring those feelings, I held on to the back of the harness of the man in front of me as we settled into the rhythm of battle. Now that we were reunited and working as a Century again, we listened for the Pilus Prior's whistle, so I moved up at each blast, until I was next to go. When the whistle sounded for my turn I waited for the Legionary in front to push off, then stepped in to see that there were perhaps 300 men left, with a number of bodies lying at my feet and along our front. The man I relieved did a good job because the Lusitani he was facing still had not recovered his balance, so I finished him with a quick thrust. There seemed to be a renewed energy in the Lusitani, except it was that of desperation, the courage of men for who all hope is gone and all that is left for them is to die well. When the next warrior I faced came screaming at me, I noticed that he was one of the few I had seen to that point who was fully armed and armored. On his head was a high conical bronze helmet, and he wore the same kind of armor that I saw on the man who slew the Tribune, a series of scales made of bronze overlapping each other, but unlike the leader, his armor was tarnished and had some scales missing. Carrying the long sword and customary shield, he was somewhat darker than the men around him, his face smeared with blood, and I wondered whose it was as he came at me, immediately trying to take my head from my shoulders in a single blow. I took it on the shield instead, but the impact was fierce; this man was the strongest I had faced to this point. It did at least answer whose blood it probably was on his face, that idea fueling my desire to end him and wreak vengeance. As he recovered, I smashed him with my shield, expecting the same reaction that I experienced before, except this man met me boss to boss, blocking the blow, although it sent him back a step. This surprised me, and I told myself not to take this man lightly because he possessed the most skill and strength of anyone I had met in this

138

first battle. For the next few moments we both bashed at each other, desperately seeking an opening, me for a thrust, him for a slash, but neither of us finding one. Finally we stopped, glaring at each other, panting like dogs on a hot summer day and cursing each other in our own tongue. Because I was younger I recovered more quickly, but just as I moved towards him, the whistle blew again and I cursed my luck. One more time that day, my pride was stung and I worried that he would not be around to finish our battle, so I pretended that I had not heard the whistle and kept moving forward. Instead of meeting me, he took a step back and I felt some grim satisfaction as I closed the distance; obviously he had learned that I was not one to be trifled with.

"Pullus, you idiot. You're too far out in front," I recognized the roar of Pilus Prior Crastinus.

Immediately looking around in surprise, I gasped in shock at the sight. I was several feet in front of the rest of the line; my opponent was not scared, he had taken my measure. He saw I was a young, prideful fool and had drawn me out. Instantly after this recognition, I was attacked by a man to my left, who fortunately for me was armed only with a short spear instead of their usual long one. The point of his spear embedded in my shield and it was only because of my strength that I was able to wrench the spear out of his hand while keeping my shield up, despite the awkwardness of having the shaft sticking out of it. My original opponent then saw his chance, leaping at me to slash in a great, sweeping arc, trying once again to separate my head from my shoulders. Desperately parrying with my own blade, the grip that Vinicius taught us saved my life, because the momentum of his heavier blade would have knocked it from my hand if I was holding it in the standard fashion. Even so, my arm instantly went numb and I almost dropped the sword anyway. At that instant, there was a roar of rage and I sensed a blur to my right launching at the man, getting inside his guard before he could recover. There was a flash of a blade, the point punching the man in the throat to go through his neck and out the other side for an instant before being withdrawn. Even before the man wielding the sword hit the ground, I dispatched the owner of the short spear, then stepped back past the front of the line and moved to the back, wrenching the spear out of my shield as I did so.

When I passed the Pilus Prior, he caught my eye and growled, "You and I'll talk about this later."

I gulped and answered him, continuing to the rear. There to greet me was Vibius, who said "Now we're even."

I looked at him in surprise. "That was you? You moved so fast I couldn't tell who it was."

"I've always been faster than you," he shot back, then smiled at me.

Grinning back, I saluted him. "You're right. Now we're even." Then we turned back to the fighting.

It took two more rotations before we finished off the last stand of the Lusitani in the town, but that did not mean the fighting was over, as hundreds of warriors melted into the town, most of them hurrying to their families. That is where they were found; in their huts, weapon in hand, determined to protect their families to the death, which is what they did. While we rested in the town square, Caesar and his command group rode up and we were called to *intente*, the Primi Pili giving their report to him. Once they were finished, he addressed us, sitting astride his horse.

"Comrades," he called us, the first time that he ever did so, explaining why with his next breath, "for that is what you have become today. We have shed blood and had our own shed. Undoubtedly you will have comrades who have been killed, or may Fortuna smile, been wounded, and that is a bond that can never be broken. Today we become comrades in arms, the most precious connection any man can share, even more precious than the bonds of family. As a salute to your bravery and as a gift, I give you this town and all that is in it, to do with it as you will!"

Finishing with a sweeping flourish of his arm to indicate the expanse of the town around us, we cheered him lustily before he rode away to address the other men scattered about the town.

The Pilus Prior stepped up to bellow in his command voice, "All right boys, you heard Caesar. The town's yours."

Cheering that again, some did so more loudly than others, for truly, we new *Gregarii* had no idea what that meant. Oh, we had been told stories around the fires by the veterans, but just like battle, describing it and living it are two different things.

140

"Here's how it will work," he continued, "you new veterans," we cheered his acknowledgement, however faint, that we were no longer mere *tirones*, "will follow the older men's lead. Do what they do. And you're going to do it," he indicated the path we followed into the town, "in that area we just came through. You take what you can carry and that's it. And don't forget," he added in warning, "that you have to clear the houses before you can take anything. You can hear that the fighting's not over; it looks like a fair number of their warriors are still about and in the houses, so be careful. And remember, the more you leave alive, the more slaves there'll be for sale."

With that, we were dismissed and Calienus called us together, pointing to an area, "Let's get going before these selfish bastards take everything worth taking."

Then he started trotting towards the huts, with the rest of us tagging behind. Vibius and I exchanged a glance, to which I shrugged. I had no idea what to expect; Cylops never talked about this aspect of war to us. I soon found out why. As often as I have done it since, the first time I participated in the sacking and destruction of a town was an experience that will never be forgotten, as much as I try. I also wish I could tell you that the troubling feelings I experienced struck me while we were doing it, yet in the heat of the moment, after facing death and dealing it out, I felt nothing but a wild exultation as I did my share of all that comes with the taking of a town and putting the inhabitants to the sword. As much as I learned of combat that day, I learned as much and more about the darkness that we all carry in our hearts, being tutored in the finer points of pillage and rape. Following Calienus into the first hut we found a family of four, with nobody to defend them, just an older woman and her three children, all of whom we killed, leaving their bodies where they fell. He showed us where people were likely to hide their valuables; under a loose stone in the hearth seems to be the most common, and how to leave no possibility, however unlikely, unexamined. As we left each hut we marked it with a symbol, etched into the doorway that designated it as being searched by our Century. It was not until the third hut that we met resistance; a warrior came screaming at Calienus as soon as he kicked in the flimsy door, but Scribonius and Romulus were standing on either side, cutting him down immediately with thrusts to the body. He collapsed yet did not die immediately, and as I stepped over him, I saw the absolute despair and anguish on his face.

"Well, well, I can see why he was so keen to fight us," Calienus laughed, pointing to a figure huddled in the corner of the one room.

It was a young woman, obviously the man's wife, and Calienus was right. She was a rare beauty and instantly the mood in the room changed as we all looked at her hungrily. She had raven colored hair, offsetting her smooth white skin, but even with the dirt on her face, it could not disguise the fine nose and high cheekbones, and while her eyes held fear, there was a hint of pride and disdain there that only served to inflame us further. Nobody said a word; nobody had to say what was on their mind because we were all thinking the same thing.

Finally, Scribonius spoke up, saying nervously, "Maybe we should leave her be. She'll fetch a good price as a slave, won't she?"

Calienus laughed again.

"That may be, but that doesn't mean we can't have a taste first. It's not like she's a virgin, right? That was obviously her man we just did for, so there's no harm in taking a sample."

As he said this he was unbuckling his belt and harness, dropping it to the floor. The woman tried to shrink even further into the corner, it being clear to her what Calienus was about to do. Looking over his shoulder at us, he grinned, "This is one time I'm pulling rank boys. You can have a go after me, but don't mark her up because that'll hurt her price. Got it?"

Nobody said anything, just nodded in agreement, whereupon Calienus turned back to the woman, who began whimpering in fear. Our Sergeant approached her and she made a desperate lunge to get past him, but he was more experienced at this game than we were. Laughing, he stuck a leg out as she ran past so that she fell to the dirt floor with a thud. I could not seem to tear my eyes away, despite feeling a sense of shame at what was going on, but it was not strong enough for me to try and stop what was happening. Calienus fell on the woman, his weight pinning her down, and I sensed a movement behind me, turning around in time to see Vibius leave the hut.

I followed him, while Romulus and Remus jeered and laughed at me, Romulus saying, "You lose your place in line if you leave Pullus."

142

I did not answer, feeling a flush rise to my face. Leaving the hut, I stood by Vibius, who was looking down the street watching other Legionaries as they carried loot out of the huts, some of it in the form of screaming women tossed over their shoulders. The smoke was intensifying as more and more of the town was put to the torch, and over it all we could hear the sounds of fighting, women screaming, the harsh laughter and shouts of men sating their lusts.

For a short time neither of us spoke, then Vibius said, without looking at me, "I can't do something like that Titus. I swore to be true to Juno, but it's not just that. When I looked at that woman, I saw Juno. How would I feel if that happened to her?"

I did not know what to say, yet I tried anyway. "But that would never happen to Juno. She's a Roman, Vibius. Nobody will ever beat us."

He looked at me with a sad smile, and replied simply, "And that bothers me too."

Resuming our silence, it was only broken when Romulus came out, a huge grin on his face as he buckled his harness back up. "Your turn Pullus," he called out cheerfully. "We left enough for your share."

I could not look Vibius in the eye as I turned and went back into the hut.

By the time the sun was going down, the town that we assaulted no longer existed, nor do I remember its name. The surviving Lusitani were bound in chains, destined for the slave markets that would send them to Rome and the Republic. Seeing the bound prisoners as they were led away, I was troubled by a thought; was this how Phocas and Gaia had come into my life? It had never occurred to me to ask how they came to be slaves, and I found that thought troubling. All of us were filthy; for the first time I noticed that my hands were caked with blood, and I remembered thinking that they were sticky at some point during the attack, but it never occurred to me to look down to see why since I was too busy. Now when I looked down it surprised me to see that not just my hands were covered, but almost every inch of me was spattered with other men's blood, and I dully wondered how long it would take to get it out between the links of my armor. It was only then that I became aware that my side still hurt, so I struggled out of my armor, the effort making me gasp in pain as the dull ache increased to a sharp stabbing pain. Feeling something warm starting to seep down my side, soaking my tunic even more, I did not want to look. Instead I used my fingers to explore, touching the area gingerly then feeling around the edges of what was a gash perhaps two or three inches long along my right side. Needless to say, it was extremely tender to the touch, made even more so because the blood had dried my tunic to and around the wound.

Bracing myself, I was just about to yank it free when I heard Calienus call out sharply, "Don't do that. It'll make it bleed even more."

Turning to see him behind me, he was already shed of his armor and headed for the baths when he obviously saw me poking at myself.

Walking up to me, he smiled, "I guess I have to show you new boys everything, including how to take care of yourself."

Looking at the gash, he pursed his lips. "This is more serious than I thought. You're going to need to get it cleaned up and stitched. I can do the cleaning part all right, but you'll have to go to the *medici* to get it stitched up."

I was dubious, to say the least, since I had never been injured to the point where I needed to have anything stitched up, and I was none too keen on the idea. However, Calienus ordered me to go, so I went to the *quaestorium* where the medical section was located.

I wish I had not. This had been a day of firsts, and this was one I wished I had never seen, not just because I did not like to see my fellow Legionaries suffer. The knowledge that it had only been a matter of luck that I was not one of them, moaning in pain while trying to will it away was sobering, to say the least. Or I could have ended up worse; of all the things I learned that day, it was that I was not nearly as skilled and invincible as I thought, and I vowed that I would never take my skills lightly, nor would I ever stop training with dedication and focus. Of all the vows I have made in my life, this is the one that I can say I abided by more closely than any others. The interior of the large tent was lit with numerous lamps, the heat from them making the atmosphere stifling, not helping the stench, and I was forced to fight back a gag. The aftermath of a battle, whether one wins or loses, is horrible. Some men's wounds

144

are too horrific to describe, so the *medici* are just as busy putting men who cannot be saved out of their misery as they are stitching up wounds and setting bones. Some wounds have to be cauterized, and this more than any other smell made my stomach lurch. Because I was one of the walking wounded, I was not a priority; once I was assessed, I was told to go sit on the ground and wait with others in similar condition. There were almost a hundred men like me, and with a staff of maybe 20 *medici ordinarii*, some of them physicians though most were orderlies, it meant I was in for a long wait. Finding a spot, I made myself as comfortable as possible, trying to avoid eye contact with the other men around me, not being much in the mood for talking, especially to strangers. Luckily, they all seemed to be of the same mind, so we contented ourselves with trying to shut out the screams of men as their wounds were cauterized or their bones set. Almost as frequently, two orderlies would carry a man out who had not survived, and all of us scanned the faces of the men on the stretchers to see if we knew them. Some of them it was impossible to tell, as their wounds were to their head and facial area.

At one point I heard a man gasp as the orderlies carried a body out, then heard him mutter, "Well, that makes our tent roomier. Poor bastard."

Finally, I was seen and my wound cleaned, albeit a bit roughly for my taste, except I was determined not to give the orderly a hint of the pain I was feeling as he pulled the tunic from the wound, starting a fresh bout of bleeding. Once cleaned, my wound was stitched up, the orderly obviously proud of his handiwork, but I was an indifferent audience. Just as I was leaving the tent I heard someone call my name and I looked at the rows of men lying on cots who had been treated, finally seeing someone wave to me. Walking over, once I recognized him I smiled in genuine pleasure at the figure of Vellusius, lying on a cot with a grin equally as broad.

"Vellusius, I thought we had lost you, old son."

He gestured to the bandage that was awkwardly wrapped around his right shoulder and across his chest diagonally. I noticed that his arm was immobilized as well, and he explained. "I got hit by one of those cursed missiles, right on my collarbone," he grimaced even as he said this. "It broke it, but it also slowed the damn thing down so it just lodged in my shoulder."

"Did they get it out?"

He nodded, making a face. "And that hurt like Dis I can tell you, but I'm feeling all right now. They gave me some wine and some sort of herb mixed in that tasted like the butt end of a mule, but I'm feeling pretty good right now. Wait, I said that already."

He laughed, and I could not help but join in, partly out of relief at seeing him alive, yet also because of the woozy smile he was giving me. Turning serious, I asked him, "What about your wound? It's not going to put you on disability is it?"

He shook his head."No, they said I should be good as new in a few weeks, as soon as the bone knits."

Vellusius smiled the smile of a man who has beaten the system, even if it is temporary.

"You know that that means, right Pullus? No digging, no guard duty, no marching about." He smacked his lips. "Yes, I could definitely get used to that."

I laughed again, and bade him goodnight, promising to tell the others the good news.

"Be sure you tell those thieving bastards to stay out of my stuff. Especially Didius," he called to my retreating back, which I acknowledged with a wave.

Making my way back to the tent, I stopped just long enough to get some porridge dished up from the section pot, then went to the baths to get clean, taking a fresh tunic and loincloth. Despite feeling clean physically afterwards, in some ways I still felt dirty, in a manner that is hard to define. By the time I returned, I was completely exhausted and thankful that we had been given the next two days off from normal duties. The fires from the town still cast a glow that gave the camp an orange pall, which would be intensified shortly when our dead were cremated. I was curious about whether we would be required to attend the funerary rites since it appeared that Didius was dead, given that I had not seen him at the aid tent. I also wondered if the fact that I would not grieve meant that I was a bad person. Getting back to the tent, the others were gathered around, with a pile of loot that was being divided out evenly.

"Pullus," my comrades cried out.

Smiling, I took my normal place next to Vibius, where we exchanged a long look at each other, not saying a word yet communicating our mutual relief that we were both alive. I told them that I had seen Vellusius, which was greeted by cheers all around and they all laughed when I passed on his last message, except I left out the part about Didius, thinking him dead. Calienus was in charge of dividing up the spoils, such as they were, there being just a small pile of coin. However, most of the valuables were in the form of jewelry of one sort of another, and there was some bickering about the value that Calienus assigned each piece as he distributed it out. I saw the pile for Vellusius, which was going to be watched by his newly designated mate Scribonius. Scribonius had originally been the close comrade of Artorius, but to both Vellusius and Scribonius' relief, Artorius' dismissal from the Legion meant that Scribonius needed a new one, and Vellusius was originally forced to partner with Didius. Immediately after Artorius left, Scribonius and Vellusius approached our Sergeant, who was as aware as all of us the loathing in which we held Didius and vice versa. Didius did not take the rejection well, making his usual dire threats to Vellusius, which so far were unfulfilled. Thinking of that event, it in turn led me to the fate of Didius, and I was unsure how to broach the subject. While the rest of my tentmates knew how I felt about him, I still did not want to make my feelings for him too obvious, especially if he were dead. I noticed that there was a pile for him as well as Vellusius, except that did not necessarily mean anything. It is the custom that in the event of death, the spoils taken would be sent to the slain man's family, if he had one, or put into the funeral fund that is kept to pay for the proper sacrifices and rituals that are observed when a Roman Legionary dies, along with paying for an appropriate monument.

Finally, my curiosity could not be quelled any longer, so I cleared my throat then asked, "So, what about Didius?"

I was not sure what reaction I expected, but it was certainly not the one I got. Nobody said anything; instead there was a silence where the prevailing attitude, if I am any judge of facial expressions, was one of disgust.

"I'm in here. Why Pullus, did you miss me?"

Though muffled, it was still clearly the voice of Spurius Didius, who apparently was in our tent. This puzzled me, but when I looked to the others for the story they steadfastly refused to speak, in turn looking at Calienus, who tried to ignore them. Finally sighing in exasperation, he said in as neutral a tone as he could manage, "Didius was injured on the way down the ladder. He took a serious fall."

This news was followed by what sounded like a cough, and I glanced over to see Remus staring at the ground with what I thought was a grimace, except that his cough seemed to ignite a fit of sounds. Finally he could not contain himself any longer and began openly laughing, which as it tends to do, started a conflagration of the same behavior, soon becoming a riot of guffawing hilarity that I was swept up in despite having no idea why.

"Quiet, by the gods, or I'll come out there and gut every one of you," I heard Didius roar, just making things worse as far as the laughter.

Our refusal, or inability, to subside prompted him to appear, but it was the way he did so that ignited a fresh round of laughter. He was hopping on one foot, his other leg dangling off the ground.

"I told you to be quiet or all of you will pay," I know he meant this to be a threat that we would take seriously, except it came out as a petulant whine. "I bet that if any of you had happen to you what happened to me, you'd have been doing the same thing."

I was still unclear on why it was so funny that he was hobbling around, until Calienus finally explained. "It seems that our dear Didius, when he jumped off the ladder, landed on a nail that went into his foot."

Amid the continuing hooting, I asked, "Why didn't he pull it out?"

This triggered even more mirth, as now some of the boys were literally rolling on the ground, tears streaming from their eyes. "Because he couldn't; he was too squeamish," this came from Romulus, eliciting a roar from Didius who hopped closer to the fire to shake his fist at all of us. "It was in too deep, I tell you! None of you would have been able to pull it out if it had been in your foot."

Remus got up to reenact what Didius had done. He jumped up to begin miming going down a ladder but when he landed, he immediately fell to the ground, screeching, "By the gods, I've been shot! I'm dying! Oh gods, the pain... the pain...." Remus was now rolling around on the ground, clutching his foot, whimpering and carrying on, so that quickly I was laughing as hard as the rest of them.

"I tell you, it was all the way into the bone," Didius made one last attempt at restoring what was left of his shredded dignity. "By the gods, you'll all pay for your insults....."

Before he could finish, Calienus shot back, "Oh do be quiet, Achilles. Go rest your foot."

And this was how Didius earned the nickname he was to carry for the rest of his time in the Legions.

The next three days were spent resting, cleaning our gear, and mourning our fallen. In our Century, we had lost three men dead, including Optio Vinicius. Vinicius' replacement Rufio had been judged to have avoided messing things up enough to warrant him losing the title, so Rufio became our new Optio. However, there was a surprise for all of us, when the Pilus Prior came to find me lying on my cot in our tent, dozing. I was awakened by a kick to my feet, opening my eyes to see the Pilus Prior standing there, with his *vitus* and the invisible man with the turd back on duty as well. Jumping to *intente*, I tried not to wince at the pain in my side from the sharp movement, but the Pilus Prior had been around too long to be fooled.

"Side still bother you?" he asked gruffly.

"Not much, Pilus Prior. Only when I move suddenly."

That prompted a bark that passed for his laugh. "Well, you'll be doing plenty of that. I've decided to make you our weapons instructor in place of Vinicius. Rufio agreed that you're the best choice."

Stunned, I opened my mouth to protest, then thought better for a moment and shut it. There was a silence as he watched me, and mentally cursing myself, I plunged in anyway.

"That's a great honor, Pilus Prior," I began but he cut me off.

"I don't give a fucking brass obol if you think it's an honor. It's an order, and the only response I expect is 'Yes, Pilus Prior' or 'Yes sir'."

I should have shut up then, yet I couldn't, I just had to keep going. "But sir, why me? I thought after what happened on the wall when I forgot to draw my sword you'd realize that I'm not ready for this. Maybe someday......"

I got no further; now the Pilus Prior was truly angry, and he stepped close enough that I could smell the *posca* he had consumed for breakfast on his breath.

"Are you doubting my judgment, *Gregarius*?"

Despite saying this in a deceptively quiet voice, I had learned this was the sign that I had truly angered him, along with addressing me by my rank and not my name. Trying to remain solidly at *intente*, I could nevertheless feel myself leaning backwards as he thrust his face up at mine, although it was even with my chest. It was the disconcerting feeling that must come from a wolf leaping up at your throat, and I could not have been more terrified.

"N-n-no, Pilus Prior," I cursed myself again for stammering like Artorius. "I just....I just.....nothing, Pilus Prior. I'll do my absolute best, sir."

Just as quickly, he changed back to his normal hard-ass self and clapped me on the shoulder. "Good, it's settled then. You won't be expected to start training the others until you're completely healed."

Turning to leave, he then stopped to face me once again and said quietly, "I know you can do this, Pullus. I have faith in you, which is why I picked you. I know you won't let me down."

Whereupon he turned heel and walked out, leaving me a mass of confusion. How was it possible to want to kill a man and die for him, all in the same instant? Such is the nature of a great leader that he can inspire those feelings; it was a lesson I never forgot and did my best to emulate when my turn came, however poorly I may have done so.

After our recovery period, we broke camp to continue heading north, and once we were deep into Lusitani lands, Caesar gave the order to start laying waste to the countryside. It was not harvest time, so the crops were still young and green, making them somewhat harder to burn, and we were forced to get inventive. One method was to line us up, with each man standing on a row, armed with their shovel. When we were given the signal, we walked forward, using the shovel to pull out the young shoots by the roots, as we were followed by slaves who gathered them up to use as forage for the livestock. It was somewhat time consuming, but in our Century, the Pilus Prior made a contest of it, offering an extra ration of wine to the first five finishers.

"I joined the Legions to get away from the farm," Romulus grumbled one day as we worked side by side.

"Look at the bright side," I told him, "at least you're not planting crops, you're pulling them up."

"Like that's a big difference."

I laughed as he kept mumbling to himself. The livestock were kept to feed all of us; it is amazing how much an army eats, and I think another secret to the success of the Roman army is that a large part of the effort and organization to sustain the army in the field revolves around feeding us, and truth be known, we ate much better than a lot of us ever had before, myself included. For the first time in my life, bread was as plentiful as meat, although I still found it funny that for most of the men, if you gave them a choice between a nicely roasted haunch of beef or pork, or a loaf of bread with some olive oil, most of them would take the bread. My tentmates always gave me grief about my taste for meat, yet I did not mind, because it meant that there was more for me. However, I do not want to give the impression that our activities in spoiling the countryside went unopposed or unmolested. The Lusitani were experts in hit and run tactics, suddenly appearing out of nearby woods to attack small groups of men, or slow-moving targets like wagons that were sent out to round up supplies of one sort or another. Our losses were small, but it was aggravating and nerve-wracking nonetheless, and it meant that none of us ever really felt we could relax, except when we were in our marching camp. Regardless of this harassment, we continued to march northward, torching every single farm or small village that we found, rounding up the inhabitants to be sold into slavery. As far as loot went, the pickings were slim to say the least, and we began to look forward to another sizable town to take and hoped that the Lusitani would be as stubborn as before.

A little more than a week later, we approached the city known as Conimbriga, which is a Roman colony built on the site of a Lusitani village. The city is near the Muna (Mondego) River, and is about a day's march from the ocean, sitting on a plain at the foot of the hills that ring the city from the south. The scouts reported that this town had gone over to the Lusitani, but without any shedding of blood of the Romans who were living there, which was a bit unusual. Calienus thought that it was a sign that their hearts were not really in it, and the citizens of the town did not want to do anything to provoke Caesar. The word of what we had done to the first town and of our scorching of the land that we passed through naturally preceded us. Thus, when we arrived, the townspeople immediately sent a deputation of the Lusitani who were involved in the rebellion to surrender the city immediately. Caesar accepted the surrender, demanding that hostages be given by the noble Lusitani families, and a fine be paid for rebelling, even if it was one in name only, since it went directly into Caesar's chest instead of being sent to Rome. Thus satisfied, we continued to march northward.

This set the pattern for the next few weeks; we would march through territory, destroying everything that we could not carry or consume, and whenever we approached a town, the example set by our first attack was sufficient to convince the Lusitani to quickly capitulate and offer up whatever Caesar demanded. Initially, this was fine with us, but the monotony of marching and digging, followed only by more marching and digging was beginning to get to us. We began to grumble among ourselves when we were sure the Centurions could not hear us.

"How are we supposed to make any money on this campaign?" was how Calienus put it. "When I marched with Pompey, we took a pirate town or city a week almost, and they were all taken by storm, so we had a share of the spoils. And those pirates were rich!"

It might be appropriate to relate how Calienus' remark pertained to our situation. For as long as anyone could remember, and is still certainly the accepted practice, there is a method by which the average *Gregarius* can expect to enrich himself and begin a climb to higher status, which as I have already related, was very important to men like me. The custom is that if a town falls by assault, the spoils of what is taken from the town in the form of loot and slaves is divided equally among the men who participate in the sacking. However, if a town capitulates on its own, then whatever payment the general demands, whether it be in gold or other forms,

152

particularly in confiscated slaves, goes directly to the general himself. I imagine the logic behind it, although nobody ever bothered to explain it to us, was that it is usually due to the general in command's persuasive powers that convinces a city to surrender without bloodshed, and therefore he deserves all that comes with that. Since by this time we had subdued at least a half-dozen such towns in this manner, Caesar had made a tidy sum of money. The gossip at the time was that he had accrued enormous debts, which was one reason why he was so keen to convince the towns to surrender.

"He's the only one getting rich," Vibius grumbled, and I must admit I was surprised, at least at first, that Vibius spoke in this manner. Before this moment, he had uttered nothing but good things about Caesar as a general and as a man. This was the first time I could remember where he said something critical, though it was not going to be the last, something I would find out much to my dismay.

"He uses his skills as an orator to talk them out of putting up a fight, just so he can keep all the money," Vibius continued, and just when I was prepared to argue the point I could see that most of my tentmates agreed with him, or at least seemed to since they were all nodding their heads. Accordingly, I kept my mouth shut and held my own counsel, except the way I saw it, he was keeping us alive. What was the sense in wearing us down when we all knew that the further north we went, the worse the terrain and the more vicious the enemy? Still, I have to admit that I was beginning to get a little itchy myself for something to break the monotony of what we had been doing. Despite there being numerous skirmishes, and even a couple of engagements that involved more than one Cohort, we had not seen any of that action since the taking of the town. And like any young man, the horrors that one swears they would never want to endure again fade quickly as the days go by, so that by this point, it was not only my scar that needed scratching.

Continuing north, it turned out that Caesar was not blind and deaf to the rumblings of his army, and he took steps to mollify the men. Leaving the 8th Legion behind in Conimbriga to patrol the surrounding area and remind the inhabitants of their promise to him, this left him with the 7th, 9th, and us. After a three day march we arrived at the walls of another town and once again, a deputation ran out to greet him, falling all over themselves to do so. However, they were in for a rude surprise, because Caesar gave them terms that were so exorbitant that it would have bankrupted every person in town. He further insulted them by demanding that whatever slaves they owned were to be handed over to him to dispose with as he saw fit, and if the number of slaves did not meet with his satisfaction, he would demand that the leaders of the town turn over some of their citizens to make up the supposed shortfall. The Lusitani could not agree to this, something Caesar knew very well, and to add further insult to injury, when the deputation made to return to the town, Caesar had them seized and held as prisoners. Consequently, the Lusitani were left with no choice but to fight. Because the 10th was the assault element in our first town, this time we acted as reserves while the 7th and 9th got their chance to attack. The same stratagem was used on this town, with the 7th using the ram on the main gate, and the 9th going over the wall. One difference was that, unlike the first town this one did not have a natural defense like being on a hilltop, forcing the inhabitants to go to greater lengths to fortify their town, starting with a ditch several feet wide and several feet deep. Implanted in the ditch, on the bank nearest the town wall, were rows of sharpened stakes pointing outwards, while the ditch was half-filled with water that had gone stagnant, and was covered in a green slime. As in the first town, all brush and other matter that could provide even the most modest form of cover was removed, leaving a killing field of at least 200 paces in a swath around the town wall. The wall itself was again made of wood, but was even taller than the first town's since it did not have the advantage of a hill, and was about 15 feet high. What I found curious is that there were no trees visible in the surrounding area that would have qualified to be included as part of the wall, making me wonder where the ones that made up the wall came from, and in such number. I would have understood if I had at least seen stumps that indicated that this place was forested at one time, but there was nothing like that. I asked Calienus, who shrugged, obviously never having thought of such a thing before.

"I guess they dragged them here from someplace else."

Acting in our capacity as the reserve we were split into two, five Cohorts each, acting as support for the assaulting Legions. Our section supported the 7th assaulting the gate, giving us a front row seat to watch what the 8th had done from a different view. Positioned where we were, on a small rise perhaps a furlong from the walls and slightly to one side of the gate, it also meant that we could act as judges on how the other Legions did their business, and it would probably not surprise anyone to know that we found them seriously wanting. We were allowed to sit on the ground, still in formation of course, and watch the artillery go to work. This time the scorpions were evenly divided between the two sides because there was a significant enemy presence on the parapet above the gate and immediately surrounding it. The 7th formed up, with a Century pushing the ram, once again covered in green hides, which we could easily smell from our positions. As further protection, the hides were liberally doused with water so that the ram was dripping as it was pushed forward. Two tent sections, eight to ten men on each side, pushed the ram forward, with the rest of the Century following in *testudo* creeping along behind it, waiting for a man to fall. Whenever that happened, one of the men in the *testudo* would leave the formation, run to the vacated spot, yank out the fallen man's shield to lay his own on the rack provided on the ram, then start pushing. In this manner, the ram never slowed down for any length of time. To further protect the men, the ram was constructed so that the roof jutted out above them, with the hides working as cover from the missile fire as they approached the walls. On the parapet, there was the usual array of men, dressed in their usual array of armor, or lack thereof, some of them armed with slings and a few even with bows, something that we had not run into before. Our scorpions kept up a steady rain of bolts, occasionally hitting something besides the wood of the wall, thereby consistently forcing the men on the wall to keep their heads down for more than a brief instant.

"They're taking nowhere near the kind of beating we took," sniffed Remus, and we all nodded our heads in sage agreement, accepting as fact something we did not have the experience at that point to truly judge. Meanwhile, the rest of the 7th came forward behind the ram, formed in *testudo*s by Century just as we had done attacking the wall, their form drawing further commentary from the men around me. Consequently, the slingers on the front wall had more of a concentrated target than those along the walls around the town, knowing as they did that the Legion was headed for the main gate. Casualties mounted as the 7th advanced, with men beginning to fall out of their respective Centuries, some of them dead, while most howled in pain. Some of the stricken writhed on the ground, calling for help, but others just lay quietly waiting for the slaves and scribes that worked in the headquarters and who acted as stretcher bearers to come get them. One could sense that these men had been wounded before, and knew that there was no sense flopping about, yelling like a cat set on fire. Once the first men fell, all the joking among us ceased; there was nothing funny about seeing one of our own suffer.

The ram made it to the gate to begin its work, while the rest of the 7th sat absorbing the punishment, waiting for their chance to assault the gate. The air was thick with missiles and arrows, most of the arrows having been set alight and targeted at the ram, inevitably meaning that some of the men at the ram fell to them. A few men suffered the further misfortune of catching on fire, causing them to shriek even more horrifically than the other fallen, and we averted our eyes at the sight as those unfortunates staggered about, a couple of them lucky enough or with enough of their wits about them to run the short distance to throw themselves into the ditch and the slimy water to douse the flames. Even as this was happening, the ram began to do its work, with the men heaving it back and forth on its sling, and we could see the dust fly with each impact. Naturally, some of the men began to bet on when the massive oaken gate would give way; there is nothing that a *Gregarius* will not wager on, and nothing that he will not wager. Wine rations were the most common, since few of us had any coin with us, even after our spoils from the first town; this bounty was promptly deposited with Cordius, our Tesseraurius, who refused to give any of it back, despite the most urgent pleading, the loudest whining, or the vilest threats. That lack of cash meant that anything else of value was used instead. Besides wine and food rations, turns on duties that were considered easy were wagered the most often. Where the line was drawn was with pieces of equipment, since losing anything because of a bet guaranteed a flogging while the rest of the Century watched. Once the gate finally burst open, one who was unaware might have been taken aback that along with the lusty cheers there were scattered howls of protest and disappointment, as the men who picked the wrong number saw something precious to them go to one of their comrades. Almost immediately, a new line of betting was arranged, this one on the amount of time it would take before the town was declared taken. It turned out that nobody won the bet, because it took well into the night before the last Lusitani warrior was subdued. For a period of time we were called to *intente* and there was some debate about whether or not we would be thrown in to help finish the job, with both Tribunes of the assaulting Legions arguing with Caesar against it, claiming that it would dishonor their Legions since they had not been called to assist us. Or so that was the word that spread around, which we took with smug self-satisfaction, nodding to each other as if it merely confirmed what we

156

had known all along, that nothing could be accomplished without the good old 10th Legion coming in and saving the day. Therefore, we were turned away to sit back down and watch the flames grow higher around the town, the yells and cries of men fighting and dying soon accompanied by the chorus of screams of the women who were unfortunate enough to live there.

Once more we found ourselves staying in one place for a couple of days when it was the turn of the other Legions to nurse their wounds and regroup. Even so, we were being sent out in Century and Cohort-sized patrols while they rested, ranging the countryside looking for both Lusitani and anything worth eating or destroying. Late in the day of our second day in place, our Century and the Second Century was finishing the burning of a farm and surrounding buildings when we were attacked by a mixed force of mounted warriors and infantry. It was only because of the Pilus Prior that, despite being surprised, we were not unprepared, since he had drilled us over and over for just such an eventuality. There is no way to overstate the value of the type of drill that the Roman army does, because it prepares us for just such emergencies, making our reactions as close to second nature as I believe it is possible to get. In this case, the enemy waited until we were finished torching the farm, so that some of the men were occupied with driving the half-dozen cattle while others were carrying freshly killed chickens. Perhaps a third of one Century was thus occupied, while a section scouted ahead on foot and another section acted as rearguard. Caesar's army during this campaign was hampered by a lack of cavalry and it was because of this deficiency that a body of men more than three times the size of our two Centuries could get close enough to try and ambush us. They waited until we were passing through a heavily wooded section, which the Pilus Prior had pointed out to us as a good spot for an ambush as we passed through, something I believe was a factor in our quick reaction as well. Despite this, it was not enough to save some of us, with the attack signaled by a volley of spears that flew out from either side, a half-dozen of them finding their mark among us. The hissing sounds were instantly followed by thuds as they struck the bodies of our comrades, two or three of them screaming in pain as they were impaled, but the others perhaps were luckier, falling immediately without a sound and I caught a glimpse of a man in the front of the formation transfixed through the chest, his eyes staring vacantly at the sky, his spirit already having fled before he hit the ground.

"Form square!"

The Pilus Prior roared this command and we instantly obeyed, even as the Lusitani descended on us from the surrounding woods, their war cries suffused with joy that they had already struck some of us down. Because of the surprise, we had no time to form in our normal manner, with each section arranged in its usual line of march side by side, so I found myself for a change in the middle of the line instead of on the end, and at the rear of the formation which was not exposed to immediate attack, though soon enough the warriors flowed like water around us on all sides. Risking a quick glance, I saw that once again Vibius was by my side, this time to my right, with a man named Plautius from the third section on my left. That was all the time I had because the Lusitani came throwing themselves at us, using their bodies as just as much of a weapon as any of their spears or swords. They had learned that their best chance to defeat us was to break our formation, and one thing I cannot take away from them is their bravery. There never seemed to be a limit to the number of men willing to sacrifice themselves on our wall so that their comrades would have a space in which to strike at us. Again the continuous drill proved priceless, when the Lusitani managed to knock a man down a short distance away from me, whereupon he was immediately hacked to death by the howling mob. This was their mistake, because during the time they turned their attention onto the unfortunate Legionary, it gave the man behind him the opportunity to step into his spot. One of our many problems was that we only had a double line, formed in a square twenty-odd men across and two deep, and even in the second line there were a couple of empty spots. It was when we were arrayed in this manner that it was brought home to me that we had lost men in battle already, and any more that we lost would make us that much weaker. Perhaps one of the most difficult things about fighting in square, at least as far as I was concerned, is that you are quickly surrounded and despite the fact you are facing your part of the enemy, you are still constantly aware that there is fighting going on behind you and to the sides, outside of your peripheral vision. Simply put, if there is a breakthrough in those parts, you are very likely to be slaughtered. But one has to have faith in one's fellow Legionaries, just like they have to have faith in you, and for me at least it was this knowledge that drove me in striving never to be the one who subjected my comrades to death. This group of Lusitani, while brave, was not particularly skilled and dressed in a slightly different fashion than what we faced before, a sign that they were from another branch. In quick succession, I dispatched three men facing me, so that it was only a matter of moments before the

158

Lusitani who kept coming had to slow down to scramble over the bodies of their fallen, something that worked to our advantage. My arm began to grow weary, but this is where our training serves us best, because there is no waste motion; unlike our opponents there is no flailing about, screaming and gnashing of teeth, all of which consume energy. That is why the nature of battle is a series of ebbs and flows; at the beginning it is all sound and fury, with each side doing its best to kill each other. Inevitably, the energy levels fall, and then both sides will spend a few moments doing little more than stand several feet apart, glare and curse at each other before recovering enough to do it again. However, the only time that the fury of battle is equal to the opening clash is when one side or another begins to smell that the end is near, with one great effort tipping the scale in their favor. It is during this period where the conditioning of the Roman Legionary is most evident; we are generally the ones with the reserves of energy left to make that final push and finish off our enemy.

This day, the battle unfolded in a similar manner. Once we sustained the initial assault the Lusitani settled into their usual series of rushes of small groups of men, trying first one side of the square then the other, which were easily repulsed. In fact, it seemed to be much easier than it should have been, and it was Calienus who first brought it to our attention.

"Something's not right," he muttered from his place in the second rank.

Calienus turned to the Pilus Prior, commanding from a spot in the middle of the square. Lying at his feet were four men who had been wounded thus far, one of them looking as if he would not last the day, which he did not.

"Pilus Prior," he called out.

"What is it Calienus?"

"Does this seem right to you? I mean, do these bastards seem like they're just trying to hold us in place more than they're trying to kill every one of us?"

The Pilus Prior looked around, taking in each side of the square, his eyes narrowed in thought. Nodding his head, he replied, "You're right. They're trying to keep us pinned here while they wait. I don't know what they're waiting for, but I don't want to find out."

Then he leaned down to examine the wounded men, speaking softly so that what he said could not be heard over the din. One of the men shook his head, while the others grimaced as they pulled themselves to their feet. Turning my attention back to the front, I saw that it was my turn to step forward while Romulus, who had originally been directly behind me, pushed the Lusitani away before stepping to the side so that I could take his place.

"Right," the Pilus Prior's voice rang out clearly above the din, "we're not going to wait around for whatever these bastards have planned for us, so everyone stand ready. When I give the command, we're going to march out of these woods and try to find some better ground."

As we exchanged nervous glances, I felt a shiver of dread; we had practiced marching in square a great deal, but this would be the first time that we would be trying to do it while in combat. As if reading our minds, the Pilus Prior called out, "Remember your training boys. This is no different than on the drill field except we have these little bastards as a nuisance. Think of them as you would a rock or a log in the way."

This brought a nervous chuckle, one in which I did not share. I have been blessed, or cursed depending on how one looks at it, with an overly vivid imagination, but there was no stretch of it that I could make that turned these sweating, howling madmen waving spears in our faces into logs that just happened to be strewn in our path. Thinking about this evidently showed on my face, because I heard a laugh and glanced back to see Vibius smiling at me.

"By the gods Titus, did you just swallow a bug or something?"

"No, I just don't like logs that are waving a sword at me," I growled in irritation, which was compounded when he merely laughed again.

"You're not turning into an old woman are you, Titus?"

I shot him a murderous glance but said nothing. We got ambushed shortly after we entered the wooded area, making the fastest way to clear and higher ground back the way we came. The

160

problem was that the relative safety of that high ground lay in the opposite direction of our camp. However, the Pilus Prior decided this was the lesser of two evils, so we began moving toward our refuge. Vibius and the rest of us on what had been the rear of the square now became the front, so for us it was a straightforward march ahead, pushing those Lusitani who tried to stop us out of the way, or cutting them down if they tried to fight. It was straightforward in that sense only; the front rank has to make sure they are not moving too fast for the two sides of the square, who are sidestepping as they move, which is obviously more difficult than just walking forward. The biggest risk was that we would open up a gap at the junction of where our lines met, which could be exploited by the Lusitani. At this point they were still making a token resistance, losing a few men before contenting themselves with screaming imprecations at us that we could not understand though we could guess the intent because of the gestures involved. They also hurled the occasional rock, not often, just frequently enough to keep us on our toes. However, as hard as the side files had it, it was even worse for the back ranks, forced to back up the whole way. These Legionaries at the rear of the formation were put under the most pressure by the Lusitani, who were darting in and out trying to make one of the men take a careless step backwards and fall. All of these factors meant that we could not move very quickly. Meanwhile, the Pilus Prior and Pilus Posterior of the Second Century, a man named Vetruvius, along with the Optios, Signiferi and *cornici* of both Centuries all walked within the square, helping the wounded keep up. Pilus Prior Crastinus was calling out the count, with the rest of the officers exhorting us to keep our cohesion, warning men whose alignment was getting too far off and generally trying to make sure we stayed together. The worst part was that if a man went down and was unable to get up, he was left behind, a fate that all of us feared more than a quick death. There had been Legionaries who fell into the hands of the Lusitani during the campaign, and if the tales told about their fates were true, it was not a fitting end for a beast, let alone a man. However, I also know that these tales may have been made up, because if there is one thing that competes with gambling in the heart of a Legionary, it is gossip and lurid tales, the bloodier the better. Finally making it to the edge of the woods, we could see in the distance a large plume of dust hanging in the still air, there generally being no breeze at that time of day. Despite having perhaps a watch and two thirds of one of daylight left, it now being the height of the summer, we all knew that we were in dire straits indeed if we were forced to stay out overnight without the opportunity of making some sort of camp. Yet at that point it did not look like we were going to be given the opportunity to do anything of the sort. Once we entered the clearing, another source of misery came into our lives; while there was no breeze, when we were under the cover of the trees of the woods we at least had shade, but now there was neither. Almost instantly I felt the sweat start to form, and before we went more than a furlong it was running down my face and into my eyes, which I had trouble keeping open because of the sting of the salt in my perspiration. I could not use my arms to wipe the sweat away either; if I moved my shield I would expose Plautius, still on my left, but if I used my sword arm, the time it took to wipe my brow would obscure my vision. This was just the kind of thing the Lusitani were waiting for in order to make some sort of move or to throw a rock while I was not in a position to duck or dodge. Making matters worse, I was not the only one in this condition, as the curses I heard all around me attested to, but despite this hardship we continued to trudge along. The Pilus Prior had pointed to the small, low hill that would be where we tried to make some sort of stand about a half mile away. This may not seem like much, but when you are under constant pressure in the way we were, it is the same as making it back to Rome. It was this small hill I was completely focused on, thinking of nothing else when finally someone made a mistake. Unable to see any more, one of the men in the rear rank walking backwards took the risk of trying to wipe the moisture from his eyes, or at least so I was told later by the man next to him. I do not know why, but for some reason he stumbled and fell, but before he could scramble to his feet a rock sailed from the mass of Lusitani, hitting him square in the face.

The man next to him started to move towards him to drag him to safety, now that the rear had taken another step or two backward, but the Pilus Prior's voice cut through all of us like a dagger as he roared, "You take one step towards him I'll cut you down myself. He's a dead man! Leave him to his fate!"

I was appalled and from the look of it so were Vibius and Plautius who both muttered curses under their breath.

"*Silete!*"

This came like the crack of a whip from Calienus, adding to our shock and confusion. Meanwhile, once the man on the ground, who was in the fifth section of the Second Century and one of the

162

new men like us, was left behind far enough out of range that we could not protect him with either sword or javelin, the Lusitani descended on him. While I could not see, I could plainly hear their cries of triumph as they surrounded him the way a pack of wolves do when they close for the kill, and I said a silent prayer to the gods that he was still unconscious. Unfortunately, the gods were not listening because I was not even finished when I heard him shriek with the kind of pain that comes from the most agonizing of mortal wounds. Despite my attempts to shut it out of my mind, I began speculating on exactly what they were doing to him, his screams continuing for a few moments before, as abruptly as they began, they stopped just as suddenly. We moved just a few more paces when there was a flurry of activity in the surrounding hordes, and after a moment it became clear that one or a group of them was doing something that aroused the rage and frustration of both Centuries, as behind us we could hear the others cursing the Lusitani with a venom missing to that point. I got my answer why when a Lusitani came sprinting within our line of sight, out of range of a javelin but certainly close enough to see and hear him. He was brandishing a spear, on the point of which sat the head of the man they had just slain, and I felt my stomach roil as I fought the urge to unman myself by vomiting at the sight, the blood still dripping from the severed neck, the source of his agony made apparent by the clear visual evidence that he was not decapitated in one clean blow, but in three or four. Still wearing the look of shock and horror that I imagined was his last, his eyes were open, staring at us. They had even left on his helmet and this barbaric display was met with roars of approval from the surrounding Lusitani. Finding myself joining in the cursing, I hurled every vile imprecation I could think of, and as I was doing so, I locked eyes with one of them. This Lusitani was a medium-sized man a few years older than I, with long hair pulled into the knot that was their custom, bare-chested and armed with a long spear and a small shield made of painted wood. Looking me in the eyes, he grinned and with his spear made a gesture across his throat, then pointed and laughed at me. Staring grimly at him, I marked him as a man for whom I would be on the lookout if I was given the opportunity.

Just a hundred paces short of the hill, it was only then that our front rank took a casualty. It was the man behind Plautius, and he was hit by a rock that skipped off the ground to smash into his shin, shattering the bone, forcing him to fall to the ground clutching his leg. As we marched past him he reached out, grabbing Calienus by the leg, forcing him to alter his stride.

"Don't leave me," he begged, "for the sake of all the gods, don't leave me with those savages!"

Calienus refused to answer, but the wounded man would not relinquish his grasp, and now Calienus was falling behind in a way that endangered the line, which in turn endangered the Century. From the corner of my eye I saw a flash of silver; Calienus dispatched the man with a quick and merciful thrust, saying loudly for all of us to hear, "If we break ranks we'll all die. I'll do the same to you, and I expect you to do the same to me if it's needed."

I did not need any more encouragement to keep my place, trying to shut out what I had just seen. Despite knowing it had to be done to ensure the survival of all of us, seeing Calienus kill one of our own was hard to take. Finally, we made it to the base of the hill, even as the cloud of dust had grown closer, and it now looked like there was a sizable force of Lusitani no more than two miles away. The punishment was not all one way; as we made our way up the hill, the warriors opposite us were now walking backwards up the hill when one of them lunged at us to try striking at what he thought was a weak spot in our line with his long sword, but the blow was deflected easily. As he backed up, however, he tripped over his own feet just a couple of paces away from us but before he could regain his feet he was done in with a quick thrust, his death met with a howl of outrage from the Lusitani. Reaching the top of the hill, we underwent a brief struggle with a few of the more stubborn warriors who realized the advantage we would have if allowed to stay on the crest. My chest was heaving from the effort and I recognized this as a good sign; the hill was much steeper than it looked, and any advantage we could wreak from the situation helped. Even so, things looked bleak until the gods smiled on us, in the form of the Lusitani themselves.

Once it was clear that we would make the crest, the warriors that had steadily harassed us now withdrew to the base of the hill, seemingly content to watch us while they waited for reinforcements. The Pilus Prior did not waste any time; since we were out on a patrol that included destroying crops and chopping down vines and trees, we had a semi-complete set of tools with us, lacking only a turf cutter. Crastinus ordered our Century to dig a defensive ditch, using the spoil for a makeshift rampart, while the other Century

164

remained on guard. We were told to keep our armor and helmet on while leaning our shield and javelins close to hand as we worked, so if I thought I was hot and sweating profusely before, I was mistaken. As I dug, I watched the water pouring off the end of my nose in a steady stream whenever I bent over, and I wondered dully how long it would be before I ran out. There was no time to even drink, let alone rest, so that before long I was desperately thirsty. Meanwhile, the Lusitani leaders huddled up in a discussion once they saw what we were doing, with a lot of arguing back and forth, men gesturing first to us and then to the dust cloud, which seemed to remain stationary, although we knew that was impossible. Very quickly the reason for the debate became fairly clear; there was a sizable contingent in the group that considered it vital to attack us immediately to keep us from erecting a defense, no matter how flimsy. This discussion quickly became an argument that grew increasingly heated, a fact that was not lost on us.

"Maybe they'll kill each other first," I heard someone on guard say and I thought, one can only hope. However, while they bickered we kept digging, and I at least was thankful for the delay. Crastinus kept exhorting us, calling out so that we could all hear, "Keep it up boys. The digger you deep, the safer we'll be."

The trick was to dig a ditch wide enough where they could not leap across it and deep enough so that they could not just simply step down into it without slowing down. Additionally, the deeper and wider the ditch, the higher the rampart, which half our tent section was erecting as the other half dug. For once, even Didius was not shirking, clearly seeing the danger we were in as much as the rest of us. I was digging, while Vibius was packing the spoil to form a rampart and it was brutal work, the hardest I had performed at that point during my short time in the Legions. Our shovels and pickaxes were flying as we worked frantically, yet the gods were smiling on us because the Lusitani debate quickly degenerated into a physical confrontation, with warriors clearly dividing into two camps, both sides shaking their fists and doing a lot of yelling at each other. Then, someone pushed someone else and all of us, despite our predicament, stopped to watch as a brawl developed among our enemies, so astounding was the sight.

Even the Pilus Prior stood there, mouth open in amazement for a moment, before snapping out of it and snarling at us, "All right, that's enough of the show. Put your backs into it you *cunni* or I'll stripe you good."

165

We immediately turned to again, smiling in spite of the threat.

By the time their reinforcements arrived, assessed the situation, then arrayed themselves to attack us, it was late in the afternoon and I had never been as tired as I was at that moment. Even with the tension and imminent danger, I was fighting a losing battle against falling asleep on my feet. More than once I would feel myself pitching forward, only opening my eyes and averting an unforgivable lapse of discipline less than a heartbeat before I reached the point of no return and fell flat on my face. No matter what I told myself, how horribly I cursed my weakness, I could feel the tendrils of sleep curling around my brain. I was struck by the thought that perhaps dying in one's sleep would not be such a bad way to go, and looking at my comrades, I saw they were much in the same condition. Having finished what preparations we could make, we were now standing behind a parapet that stood chest high for most of the men yet was only just above my waist. The only saving grace, at least as far as I was concerned, was that it was fairly thick and despite being low for our tastes, we could still kneel down and be covered from most missile weapons, especially if we set our shields on top of the parapet. Not for the first time we thanked the gods that the Lusitani did not use the bow very often, and we could see there were only a few scattered in the mass of men who surrounded us now. Calienus, being the most experienced, estimated that the new arrivals numbered between 400 and 500 armed men, adding to the 300 or so that ambushed us, although we had whittled that last group down by 50 or thereabouts. Regardless, they were long odds, of which we were all too keenly aware. Lusitani were milling about at the base of the hill, flowing around it like a flood encircling us, and once again beginning their pre-battle rituals, the sound rolling up to us, steadily growing as they worked themselves into a frenzy. Speaking for myself and I imagine a lot, if not all of the other newer men, I was almost beside myself with fright. Looking around to see that we were completely surrounded by a vastly larger force, I could not see any way to get out of this alive, and I was positive our Centuries were about to be wiped out to the last man. Then, I heard someone laugh.

Turning to see Optio Rufio and Calienus walking towards us, I saw that it was Calienus laughing. He and the other section leaders had been called over by the Pilus Prior to be given their orders, and he was returning to relay to us what we were supposed to do. Yet here they were, acting like they were back in camp, strolling along and having a good laugh, just moments or at the most a matter of a couple watches before their death. It astonished me, and I could not even begin to fathom how one could be so lighthearted knowing they were about to perish.

Calienus came to us, with Rufio going to talk to another group, and our Sergeant called us closer, but before he could speak I blurted out, "What in the name of the gods could be so funny at a time like this?"

Calienus looked at me, eyebrow raised in surprise. "Time like this? What do you mean?"

Then, waving towards the Lusitani, he laughed again. "Oh, you mean this bunch? Do you really think we're in that much danger, Pullus?"

Feeling my face flush, I knew that I was being ridiculed for some reason, but I was not about to just roll over. "We're outnumbered five or six to one, Calienus. Are you saying that's not cause for worry?"

Nodding, he replied, "You're right Pullus. We are outnumbered, but numbers don't tell the tale." Without being obvious, he indicated the men below us encircling the hillside with a nod of his head. "Do you notice anything Pullus?"

I was still not seeing what he was, and told him so. "What I see are a lot of men down there who want to kill us."

"Yes, but look carefully. They've encircled us, correct?"

Biting back a sharp retort, instead I merely nodded.

"You want to know why I'm not worried? Because they have us surrounded." Thankfully, I could see that I was not the only one who was puzzled. Sighing, he squatted down, indicating that we were to follow suit. Continuing, he explained, "Now, if they were in one big bunch, I'd be very, very worried. See, I know that each one of us can handle five or six of those bastards each, right? I mean, how many kills did you have on the attack on the town Pullus?"

"More than that," I admitted grudgingly.

"See, their problem is that they're thinking like warriors, not like an army. I promise you that each one of them has picked one of us out that he's sworn to his gods he's going to kill personally."

This made sense and I was beginning to get a glimmer of where he might be going.

"And like I said, each of us can handle a half-dozen of these bastards. Now," he shook his head and smiled, "what would scare me out of my wits is if they were down there, in a formation like we use, and focusing their attack on just one part of the defenses. And if they had a leader half as smart as the Pilus Prior, that's exactly what they'd be doing right now, so thank the gods that they don't. Because if they hit one area, they'd take a lot of casualties, but it'd be a matter of moments before they'd overwhelm that point in the defenses, and that's when our lack of numbers would really show. No," he finished, "this isn't going to be all that difficult to handle."

Calienus started to rise, then Scribonius asked him quietly, "But how long are we going to have to hold this hill? I see that you're right about the way they're going to attack, but I have to believe that it's a good chance that there'll be other Lusitani showing up before too long."

Calienus nodded. "You're right, and I forgot, that's what I was supposed to tell you before I got off course patting Pullus' ass for him," this brought a round of laughter, and despite being the butt of the joke I found myself joining in. "The Pilus Prior wanted us to pass the word that we'll probably have to hold this hill through the night and the first couple of watches tomorrow, but since we weren't sent on an overnight patrol, Caesar will know that we're in trouble. The command group also knows where we were assigned, so they'll immediately send aid, probably the rest of the Cohort."

This cheered us up immensely; at least having some sort of finite time where we could expect help was a tremendous boost to our morale. Once Calienus was done, we stood and took our places, ready to face the Lusitani.

Pilus Prior Crastinus had ordered us to construct our defense tightly enough that roughly only half of us stood at the parapet at any one time. Although this lowered the number of swords we could bring to bear, it meant that we were able to be relieved, and would have someone else to step in should we fall. Provided that we did not lose more men than we could replace, I remember thinking. In the center of the ring we piled all of our excess equipment, forming a last-ditch set of breastworks in the event the parapet was breached and became untenable. Naturally, we were forced to lose the cattle and forage when we marched to the hill, but that just gave us one less thing to worry about as far as we were concerned; their numbers could always be made up. Our breastworks were not much, yet perhaps they would serve, but I prayed that we would not have to find out. Once again, I had chosen to be next to Vibius, who gazed out over the waving, threatening mob with an expressionless face.

Sensing that I was looking at him, he turned to me and asked, "Is it in a safe place?"

We both burst out laughing, causing looks of disbelief and snorts of derision to be thrown our way, but we were oblivious to it, quickly finding ourselves laughing hysterically, neither of us able to stop. Finally, we heard the voice of the Pilus Prior growling behind us.

"I wonder if you two laughing boys would find it funny if I pitched both of you on the other side of the ditch?"

That immediately shut us up, so we turned back to our foe, who were just sending forth their slingers, appearing to number about 80 men.

"Slingers!"

Someone shouted the warning and we automatically lifted our shields, resting them side by side on the parapet, creating an impenetrable wall. At least as long as nobody got anxious to have a peek like last time, I thought, though hopefully everyone had learned their lesson. Recalling the pulverized face of the man I walked over during our assault on the town, I knew that I had at least. Because the slingers were intent on trying to hit all of us, they too were spread around the base of the hill, making the fire much less concentrated than what we faced attacking the wall of that first town. Still, the sound of the lead and rock missiles cracking against the faces of our shields was loud and constant enough to dominate any attempt at conversation. Instead, we were forced to content ourselves with affecting profound boredom, conspicuously yawning to show our comrades that this was now old news for us, and was nothing to give much thought or worry about. Even so, someone had to peek, except this time it was someone I knew. Didius decided to try being sly by peeking around the edge of his shield, but his effort was rewarded by a sharp crack, instantly followed by the hollow ring of something striking metal, whereupon he collapsed in a heap. Immediately, the man behind him, kneeling just a few feet away, crawled over to him, looked into his face and frowned. Despite my loathing of him, I felt a pang of sympathy, remembering that I had seen a missile do exactly the same thing as what appeared to have happened to Didius.

As all this was happening Romulus, standing next to Didius, called out, "Achilles is down!" This elicited a sharp reaction from everyone around us, since we were the only ones at that point to use the nickname.

"Who in Hades is Achilles?" snapped the Pilus Prior as he crouched over to us.

"Er.......I meant Didius, sir. Sorry."

"You will be, trust me you little *cunnus*. I don't care if you call him Aphrodite, next time use his proper name so I know who it is. I don't have the time to learn all your pet lover's names." Turning to the man checking on him, he asked, "Is he dead?"

Even I was somewhat relieved when the man shook his head. "No sir. It looks like it deflected off his shield first, then his helmet and hit him in the forehead. He's out cold, but he's breathing, and it doesn't look like his skull is broken. In fact, there's not much of a bump here at all."

I, along with all my tentmates twisted our heads sharply, exchanging glances, and I know we were all thinking the same thing. However, the Pilus Prior at this point was unaware of Didius' history and merely ordered, "Then drag him over to the middle behind the breastworks. Maybe he'll come to and be of some use."

The man complied, taking care not to rise above the level of the parapet since the missiles were still whizzing around. Grabbing Didius by the harness, he began dragging him, prompting me to look over at my tentmate once he was at a point where I could clearly see his face. He did have a mark on his forehead, a red bump, but there was no bleeding and it did not look terribly damaging. Just as the man pulled him over the breastworks and I continued watching, my

170

heart leapt when I swore, for just a heartbeat, that I saw Didius open his eyes before quickly shutting them again. Immediately I told Vibius what I thought I had seen, and he looked back at Didius who was still lying unconscious, or pretending to, his lips compressed into a thin line of contempt.

"It wouldn't surprise me at all, the bastard," he said quietly.

"Do you think I should tell the Pilus Prior?"

He considered, then shook his head. "The Pilus Prior doesn't know about the ladder, but what he does know is that you two hate each other, so he's unlikely to take what you say seriously."

I nodded; he was right. Besides, there were more important things to worry about at that moment besides one coward, and it was coming up the hill towards us. After waiting a few moments for the slingers to try inflicting damage, with only Didius being brought to the breastworks, heartening as it was, the Lusitani began marching up the hill. Speaking frankly, I can use the word marching only in the loosest sense, since it was more of a shambling half-trot, replete with the usual complement of screaming and hopping. The slingers, because of their position downhill, were forced to lift their barrage almost immediately to avoid hitting their own men, and the Lusitani were rapidly approaching the range of our javelins.

"Prepare Javelins!"

At the command, we assumed the position, our right foot back, right arm pulled all the way back with the shaft of the javelin laying on the length of the arm, the hardened point aimed skyward to create the arc that helped it pick up momentum. My arm trembled a bit as I readied my body for the effort, choosing not so much a target but a spot where I wanted it to land, confident that there would be a man occupying that space when it arrived.

"Release!"

The air filled with the black lines that signaled the javelins in flight, and as I followed through, it brought me to a crouched position where I could look directly at the Lusitani. To a man, they all looked up, trying to catch the flight of our rain of death, hoping that they could isolate and focus on the one that posed the most danger to them personally. Some of them were lucky, yet most in

171

the front rank were not, with almost every javelin finding something in which to bury itself. The thuds of our missiles hitting flesh and wood of shields were punctuated by the screams of the men hit, and in turn they caused a slight pause in the uphill climb as the wounded men crashed into one of their comrades, knocking him down or staggering him, with the dead men becoming obstacles to step over. It did not slow them long, however.

"First line kneel, second line prepare javelins!"

I immediately knelt as did the rest of the men on the parapet.

"Release!"

The javelins went whizzing just over our heads as we watched them arc and again slice into the advancing Lusitani. Another shudder of more men going down, then we in the front rank stood to fire our last salvo.

"Prepare!"

"Release!"

One of the advantages in being on the hill was that it increased the effective range of the javelin. Normally, both lines would not have been able to launch two salvos before we had to go to the sword, but we used all of the javelins we carried, to maximum effect.

Immediately after we finished throwing our second, the Pilus Prior commanded, "Front rank kneel and draw swords!" The metal made a comforting rasping sound as the blades left the scabbard, even as the second rank discharged their last volley. Quickly estimating that more than two-thirds of our javelins had hit a target and put it out of action, whether it was a warrior or a shield, it still meant perhaps 150 men were either out of action or severely hampered with no protection. This might have been enough to stop the attack, except the Lusitani by this time had learned that we only carried two javelins apiece, and if they absorbed the punishment they would be able to close the distance to fight us hand to hand. That is exactly what happened; after they took a moment to recover from the last volley, a large man wearing one of the high conical helmets and dressed in the fish scale armor that was common of their nobles, waved his sword in the air, moving it in a circle while

172

bellowing a command in their language, before dropping his arm to point at us, the signal for them to stop their steady advance and throw themselves at us at a run.

"Here they come," someone yelled.

"Oh, really? Thank you for alerting us Hannibal," Calienus muttered, causing us to stifle a nervous laugh as we braced for impact.

Part of the reason for their delay in the attack was that they had gathered together bundles of wood, or were even using our sacks of forage to throw into the bottom of the ditch, allowing them to cross over without having to climb out of it. Hurling everything they gathered into the ditch delayed their charge, as the thought flashed through my mind that we would have been better served waiting to launch our javelins until that moment, and I had to grudgingly acknowledge that the Lusitani might be smarter than we thought. Crossing over their makeshift bridges, they came at us with the usual crash of shields and swords, roaring their rage at us, smashing against what was nothing more than a wall of thin wood and loosely packed dirt. The wall held, but only just as the Lusitani tried to pull our shields down, clawing at the rims to gain a purchase. A grubby hand appeared in front of my face, curling around the top as I felt the man behind it begin to pull and I suppressed a smug smile, knowing that I was stronger than he was and not worried that he would succeed. Very quickly the smugness disappeared when just a heartbeat after his hand started pulling another hand, quickly followed by another, began tugging as well, and I could feel my grip rapidly weakening under the added pressure. Gritting my teeth, I brought my sword up to hack at the hands, but even with the awkward angle, I was able to lop off several fingers, their screams of agony accompanied by my cry of disgust as the fingers went flying, one of them striking me in the face while another found its way into the gap between my tunic and armor, where I could feel it sliding down to rest above my belt. Bile rose in my throat but I could not indulge myself in vomiting since I had bought only a temporary reprieve. Immediately a spear came thrusting over the top of my shield, which I barely ducked, followed by a second thrust aimed at a different point. This one caught me a glancing blow on the helmet, causing a burst of stars to explode in my head, and for a moment I felt like I was losing my balance and falling backwards, but the man behind me braced me, shoving me back forward.

"Go on Pullus, have at 'em."

Shaking my head to clear it, I saw the spear come at me for yet a third time, except instead of ducking, this time I grabbed the shaft, thankful that my hand was big enough to maintain the grasp on my sword at the same time even with the Vinicius grip, then gave a mighty yank. Even above the din I could hear a yelp of surprise as I relieved the Lusitani of his weapon, dropping it on the ground next to me. Their initial assault was starting to ebb a bit; we could tell both by the sound and the fact that the hammering against our defenses was slowing as the Lusitani's energy began to flag. So far nothing had penetrated, yet even as they fell back a little way down the hill to regroup, we knew that another charge was imminent. During the interval, I debated whether I had time to get that damn finger out from under the armor and took a peek, but I saw that they were about to come back. This time they chose not to work themselves into a lather; on some signal that we did not hear or see, they simply launched themselves at us again. Once more there was the smash of bodies and metal, this time accompanied by a couple of grunts of surprise from some of the men not paying close enough attention.

"This would have been a good time to warn us boy," griped Calienus. I suppressed a smile, turning my attention to bracing myself as someone tried their best to kill me.

We managed to stop the second attack. By this time the sun was disappearing over the horizon, apparently prompting the Lusitani to decide that their best course was to withdraw and rest for the night. Having the advantage of numbers, they could afford to actually build fires and eat, while keeping a small portion of their men on guard at any given time. Unfortunately, we did not have that luxury, instead being forced to keep half the men on watch, with the rest of us chewing our cold rations then trying to get some sleep before relieving the men on guard. The Pilus Prior ordered no fires, both because there was little enough wood and any light could silhouette one of us who might fall prey to an opportunistic slinger. By this time Didius, his new nickname Achilles now an open joke in the Century, helped along by Remus' spirited retelling of the event that earned it for him, regained consciousness, if he had truly ever been out. Scribonius came to sit next to Vibius and I while we chewed on some salt bacon, quietly discussing our predicament, and we glanced at him curiously; it was not like Scribonius to horn in on others' conversation unless he had something to say, but when he did he was not usually shy to say it, yet this time he seemed to struggle to find the right words.

Finally, he whispered, "Did either of you happen to look at Achilles at all while we were fighting?"

We both shook our head; the last time I remembered glancing his way was right after they dragged him to the breastworks.

"Why do you ask?" At first Scribonius did not answer Vibius' question, instead staring intently at the ground, his face faintly illuminated by the half moon and the usual cloudless sky. Finally, he shrugged and replied, "It's just that I could have sworn that I looked his way and he was watching us fighting, just like he was lying in his bunk."

This caused me to straighten up; so I was not mistaken. Excitedly, I whispered back, "I saw it too. I thought I must have been seeing something, but I swore I saw him peeking at us."

Sitting there for a moment, all three of us were clearly unable to speak. The implications were enormous; if Didius was accused by us and was found guilty, he would be crucified in front of the entire army, but not before he was scourged first as an example to all of what happened to cowards. As much as I despised him, I was not sure that I wanted the burden of such a horrible death on my conscience.

With that in my mind, I looked at Scribonius and asked, "What do you think we should do?"

He thought for a moment, then shook his head. "I don't think there's anything we can do."

This did not sit well with me, or Vibius for that matter and we both spoke up in protest, which Scribonius silenced with a wave of his hand.

"Think about it Pullus. It's well known that you hate him, and he you. And it's well known that he threatened you. I went and got Vellusius to split with him as close comrade, so there'll be suspicions about me as well."

He paused to let this sink in, and I realized he was right.

175

However, I still did not feel right about it. "There has to be something we can do."

Vibius spoke. "There is. But we can't do it now. We'll have to wait until we get back to the main camp."

Searching his face in the gloom, it bore no hint of what he had in mind, so I accepted this idea with a shrug, as did Scribonius. With that matter temporarily settled we lay down, pulling our cloaks from our packs to keep out the evening chill, aware that getting as much rest as possible under the circumstances was vital. It was not until I lay down that I was struck by a thought, sitting bolt upright with a curse, startling Vibius and the other men around me.

"What in the name of Dis has gotten into you?" Vibius demanded.

Ignoring him, I quickly undid my harness instead, then climbed to my knees, shaking my armor until something dropped out. Vibius obviously heard something plop on the ground, and asked curiously, "What was that?"

I did not answer; instead, I picked up the finger then held it close enough for him to see what it was. He squinted as I moved it almost under his nose, then his eyes shot open in shock and he recoiled.

"You bastard!"

He said this loudly enough for others to drown him out with orders to shut his mouth, and I don't think I had ever laughed that hard in my life. Throwing the finger out over the parapet and still chuckling, I lay back down, falling asleep immediately.

Suddenly awakened by the call "To arms!" I opened my eyes to chaos. Men on relief were scrambling to their feet, fumbling for their weapons in the dark, while all around us was the crashing din and cries of men fighting.

"What's happening?" Vibius called out as we tried to make sense of the situation.

Out of the dark, the answer made our hearts drop.

"The wall's been breached!"

Whirling around, I tried to determine where the danger was coming from, but doing so was extremely difficult because of the gloom. Consequently, it took a moment before I could determine where the sounds of battle seemed to be emanating from, and I turned to Vibius who had just finished pulling on his helmet. Indicating he was ready, we began making our way to the sounds of the battle, but the bulk of the Pilus Prior suddenly appeared from the dark, and I felt his rough hand grab my arm.

"Where do you think you're going you big oaf?" he growled.

"To the fighting Pilus Prior."

I could barely make out the crest on his helmet moving as he sneered, "And what if this is just a diversion? That's just what the *cunni* want us to do."

"But I thought the wall was breached."

He laughed. "That's just some woman posing as a Legionary saying that. They attacked all right, but they haven't breached anything yet and aren't going to, unless you fall for a trap like that."

Chastened, I turned back in the direction of where I thought my position was, with him giving me a helping shove to get back to my post. Stumbling back over to our designated area, where those comrades already on watch were still standing, Vibius and I joined them to peer into the dark. A short distance away, we could see the winking lights of the enemy campfires, the Lusitani camping far enough away where it was impossible to determine whether there were men gathered around it.

"Figures those bastards would pull a stunt like this and put us on full alert so we won't get a wink of sleep. Or a bite to eat."

Vaguely I recognized the voice of a man in the second section, since the first five had drawn first duty, and I sympathized, but sleep was now out of the question, at least for me so I spoke up, "How about we take over and you boys go get your rations, as long as you promise to come back here quick so we all don't get on the punishment list for deserting our posts?"

I sensed a movement as someone turned to peer in my direction in the gloom, trying to make out who their benefactor was.

"Pullus, is that you? That's a splendid idea. May Fortuna smile on you for thinking of us and grant you long life."

I flushed with pleasure as they hurried by, proud of myself for what I had done.

"You do realize that when he's wishing you a long life, it just means that he's wishing the same for himself, since if you live the chances are good he will too," this came from Vibius, who always had a knack for finding the rat turd in the honey.

"You don't know that," I responded indignantly, "because I may die a week from now, and he might die tomorrow."

"True, but first we have to get through tonight."

Pilus Prior Crastinus had been right; the attack was a diversion. Apparently during their council of war, they decided on a different approach than what they used during their daylight attack, instead setting out to do the worst thing that they could under our circumstances, what we had feared since we climbed the hill, or at least since Calienus made us aware of it. As they were making a demonstration on one side, the bulk of the remaining Lusitani, using their skills as hunters, climbed stealthily up to within a few paces of the wall before leaping up with a great cry. It was as if apparitions from the underworld just materialized from the ground, the kind of *numen* that mothers tell young children about to make them behave. Faint moonlight glinted silver on their brandished weapons as they closed the distance to the wall in a matter of a few heartbeats, with the main impact several paces away from me. Even though the Lusitani focused their attack across a narrow area, we could not afford to move to help the others trying to hold them back since the Lusitani in the rear ranks would immediately shift from their spot to flow over the deserted wall like a raging flood sweeps away an earthen barrier. Consequently, we were forced to endure the sounds of fighting, more furious than ever before, and for the first time we heard the cries of our own men dying, crying out in our tongue as they fell. Gripping my sword tightly, as if it would help me to shut out the sounds, I kept my eye on the area in front of me and I am sure that my comrades were trying to do the same thing. I heard the bellows of the Pilus Prior, along with Pilus Posterior Vetruvius, exhorting the men around them to hold, using a combination of threats and promises as a means to motivate our men to fight ever harder. For the second time that night, we heard the cry that the wall was breached, and I peered hard in that direction, trying to determine whether this was another false alarm. It did seem that this time there was more of a tumult, an impression of a flurry of movement, while the noise changed, sounding nearer than ever before. Gritting my teeth, I turned to head over in that direction, but a hand pushed at my chest.

"You can't leave Pullus," this was Calienus, and I knew that I should turn back to my post, yet I had made up my mind.

"I have to Sergeant, they need our help."

"Maybe, but we haven't been given orders to move yet."

"I think that it's too dark for anyone to fully know what's going on," I replied desperately, pushing against his hand.

"So you know better than the Pilus Prior?" This provoked a laugh from Calienus, and I could tell that he was not going to bend. But neither was I, so I used my size once again to bear over him.

"Sergeant, I'm going over there. If you want to have me flogged for it, fine. But I know they need our help."

Pushing past him, I was torn that he did not try stopping me since a large part of me was screaming at myself to stay put, and I walked perhaps only ten paces when something came rolling out of the gloom to bounce into my legs. Almost tripping and falling, I just managed to catch myself then moved to kick whatever it was away, but when my foot touched something wet, warm and yielding, I peered down and again had to fight the urge to vomit. It was a head, and even in the gloom I could see that there was a Roman helmet on top of it.

I walked into the jaws of Cerberus. It was not a false alarm; the wall in fact was breached and the struggle to contain the incursion created an inward bulge as the Lusitani pushed across the barrier. They were now feeding men into this pocket that their warriors created, trying desperately to exploit the crack in our defenses. Even as I drew closer it was hard to tell exactly what was going on as men slashed and hacked at our thin line, now reduced to a single line of Legionaries desperately holding them back. The Pilus Prior was bellowing out; locating him from the sound of his voice, I rushed to a spot in the line as far away from him as I could get. I knew I was taking a huge risk defying the latest order I was given, but I reasoned that if things were as bad as they appeared, we were all dead men anyway, and if we turned them back it would take all of us to do so.

Picking a man, I braced him from behind, causing him to glance back. "Thanks, I was about done in," I heard him gasp.

"When you get a chance, I'll relieve you," I answered and instantly a small voice inside me began cursing myself. What was I volunteering for? Certain death? I could do my part right where I was, the voice said. You're already in enough trouble Titus old boy, without compounding it by putting yourself in a position where you will certainly be killed. Such is the nature of that voice, one I have learned is in every Legionary, and I suspect in all of us. There seems to be a part of you whose only goal is to keep you alive, at all costs, yet what makes man different from the rest of all the animals is that we can choose not to listen to that voice. Ignoring that voice is what defines us, at least in the Legions. So when I felt the man in front of me make a huge effort, tensing up just before thrusting his shield into the body of a Lusitani to send him staggering back, I took my cue, moving quickly into his place. Panting his thanks, I felt him holding me an instant later as the man he threw off came back, sending a shock up my arm when he smashed his blade into my shield, turning my arm numb. In the darkness I could not tell much about the man except for his size, which was average despite packing quite a punch for his stature. He came at me again, his second blow as strong as the first, and I could feel my grip slipping as the numbness spread to my hand and fingers, knowing that another blow like that might knock the shield from my hand. Instead of waiting for it I took a half step forward, lashing out with the shield, using my boss as the weapon and I was gratified to hear a crunching sound accompanied by a muffled scream as I smashed his face. Stunned by the pain, he was standing there stationary, making a perfect target for the thrust of the sword that I followed up with and he toppled over, falling on top of what appeared to be a Legionary. My first kill was immediately replaced by another man, his outline in the dark telling me he was slightly larger, except he used his body as a weapon, smashing into me and thinking to knock me back, but I was braced by my comrade behind me so when he reached out to grab hold of the rim of the shield, with a grim smile I struck, this time taking the whole hand instead of just fingers. This was the pattern for the next few moments; truthfully I have no idea how much time went by, but judging from the fatigue I felt when

180

there was a brief respite it was a substantial period. I was satisfied that there was now a small pile of dead and dying in front of me, the wounded still trying to crawl to safety, making the tangle of limbs and torsos shift eerily in front of me in the moonlight, and if I had not known the cause, I might have thought there was something otherworldly about it. Someone tapped me on the shoulder, the man behind me asking if I wanted to be relieved. Just as I was about to say yes, I thought better of it and shook my head. Thinking back, I believe this was the first appearance of a trait and belief that I developed over the years, which was my reluctance to trust my fate to others if I was able to have any say in it. Part of it was the hubris of youth, to be sure; however, it was also based in a belief I have in myself that I am the best arbiter of my destiny and whenever possible, I should take control of the situation. I will say that he did not argue too hard about it.

The respite lasted perhaps a span of 50 normal heartbeats, certainly no longer, before the assault was renewed and finally our wall of men protecting the pocket from expansion broke when a Legionary fell from a wound and there was nobody to step into his place. Hearing the roar of triumph from the Lusitani, I immediately sensed a flurry of movement as their men rushed to exploit the gap, accompanied by the shout of our two Centurions as they met the enemy from their spot behind us. The clash of metal and the thuds of blows to the wood of our shield wall increased as well, the growth of the pocket meaning that more men could fill it.

"All those on relief on me, at the double!"

This came from the Pilus Prior and the message was unmistakable; the enemy was within our thin dirt wall. Turning to my relief I gasped out, between exchanging blows with a man who stank of onions, "Here, you take my place and I'll go."

He had already turned to leave, but came back readily enough, patting me on the back to let me know he was there. The onion man, wielding a huge club, swung it over his head in an obvious attempt to inflict a devastating downward blow that would split my shield and dash my brains out at one stroke but I was ready, launching a simple thrust over the top of my shield before he could bring the club down, hitting him in the throat. Feeling the grating of bone that told me the blade had exited the back of his head, I withdrew as quickly as I struck. In the time it took for him to collapse, I moved aside, breathlessly thanking my relief as I hurried to the Pilus Prior's

181

voice. Tripping a couple of times as I stumbled on bodies at my feet, one of them uttered a short cry before hurling curses at me as I stepped over him, while I mumbled an apology. Reaching a spot where I could make out the Pilus Prior, who was now as engaged as the rest of the men around him, I could not help admiring his form and economy, seeing his blade glint in the moonlight, making a silvery streak in the air as it struck, each blow being rewarded with a scream or gasp of pain and surprise. Then I saw another one of our men go down, alive but wounded, before attempting to pull his body under his shield, dragging it on top of himself as the victor stepped over him while drawing his arm back to drive his spear into the back of the Pilus Prior, who was engaged with another Lusitani. Letting out the loudest bellow of rage that I had ever uttered, it startled the Lusitani just enough that it stayed his hand for the fraction of the heartbeat that I needed to jump across the space between us. Crastinus was just starting to turn at the sound of my shout as, while still in mid-air, I violated the elementary rule that the point beats the edge, swinging my arm while twisting my body to add to the force, and in one smooth motion my blade sliced through the tissue and bone that composed the Lusitani's neck. His head flew up in the air as I landed, tumbling crazily and spurting blood in all directions as the torso, the heart still sending a fountain of blood spraying several inches in the air above the stump of his neck, stood for a second as if trying to decide what to do before crumpling in a heap to the ground. When I landed, it was with one foot striking another body, so that for a sickening moment, I found my arms whirling as I tried to maintain my balance, knowing that if I went to the ground I was dead. Finally managing to restore my footing, I saw the Pilus Prior peering at me in the gloom, trying to determine who had just saved him, and I gave him a wave and a smile.

"Is that you Pullus?" he asked, his surprise obvious.

"Yes Pilus Prior, and you're welcome." I don't know what I was expecting him to say, but it certainly was not what came out of his mouth.

"Welcome, am I? We'll see how welcome I am once I've striped your back you *cunnus*. I seem to remember telling you specifically to remain at your post."

"But…" I was cut off before I could finish my protest.

182

"But nothing. Those were your orders and you disobeyed them. Your ass is mine." Without another word, he turned back to face another Lusitani, parrying a blow as easily as if he were waving his *vitus* around. I was stunned, but I was also angry, so I turned it on the Lusitani. With another roar, I waded into a small knot of men engaged in a desperate struggle, knocking both Lusitani and Roman aside to begin thrusting, hacking, and swinging my sword about, barely registering when I scored any kind of hit except by the shouts or screams of men I wounded or killed. Disdaining the use of my shield for any kind of defense, instead I began swinging it about, smashing into both friend and foe that stood in my way. I felt myself giving way to the anger and rage I felt inside, that instead of gratitude I faced a flogging from the Pilus Prior for saving his life. It also angered me that these men were trying to kill me, that men like Didius could shirk their duties of defending Rome, it angered me that Juno picked Vibius over me, that Vibius beat me at dice just the night before, and it angered me that my father hated me because in my birth I had killed the only thing he ever loved. In that moment, I felt the rage surge through me, washing over me in a warm flood, giving me more energy than I had ever experienced in my life. Feeling the blood spattering my face, instead of my normal revulsion, I reveled in it, loving the warm sticky fluid as it started to dry on my skin. Becoming dimly aware that the roars of triumph coming from the Lusitani were turning into cries of alarm, it only fueled me to keep killing and maiming. It was in that moment that I knew I had found my purpose in life; I was a killer, a machine, and there was nothing that could stand in my way and live if I did not wish it to be so.

My next conscious memory is standing alone, panting, my legs trembling and feeling the fatigue so greatly that I could not lift my arms, even if it meant my life to do so. I also became gradually aware that the noise of battle was gone; not totally, but certainly the furious sounds of frantic combat had disappeared. The wider world around me slowly came into focus, and it surprised me when I noticed that I seemed to be standing by myself, so I peered around in the dark until I saw several Roman helmets profiled against a lightening sky. It appeared that all heads were turned towards me as I continued my return by noting that the ground around me seemed to be piled much higher with bodies than anywhere else. With my breathing slowing, I felt a slight surge of energy coming back, so I began to move towards my original position on the wall, and was annoyed to find that I had to lift my leg like I was climbing a low fence, except this one was made of flesh and bone, some of which was still moving and emitting low moans. I was unbelievably weary, to the point that all I wanted to do was to sit down somewhere and rest, especially once the memory of the words I had exchanged with the Pilus Prior came back to me. If I was going to be flogged, I wanted to be as fresh as I could get. By this point, the fighting had almost completely ceased; I heard the clash of metal on metal and shouts over where the diversion started, except there was none of the urgency in the voices of the section leaders and the men in that spot. Very quickly I was surrounded by my comrades, two of them stepping aside to let me through without saying a word, for which I was thankful, because I was barely able to move; adding talking to the burden I felt sure would cause me to collapse. Steering myself in the direction of where my gear was lying on the ground just behind where I had been posted on the wall, I focused on just putting one foot in front of the other. A slight breeze blew except instead of being refreshed I felt clammy and was surprised to realize that every part of my body where open skin showed was wet, and as the breeze did its work to dry the moisture, I could feel my skin tighten as whatever covered me cooled. It must be blood, I thought. That did not stop me from finding my gear, feeling in the dark to count from the end of the pile to where mine would be, before collapsing more than sitting down. Not even bothering to shed my armor, I laid down my shield then arranged my sword so it was not in the way, removed my helmet and fell backwards, asleep before my head hit the ground. The fact that I was violating all sorts of regulations and had not been given leave to rest did not even cross my mind.

I was awakened by a kick to my feet, opening my eyes to a blinding sun shining right in my eyes. Jerking alert, I sat up immediately, trying to clear my head a bit as I strained to see who it was standing above me, outlined like a god coming down from the heavens with the sun behind him. It was no god, just the Optio, and his face was expressionless when he spoke.

"Get up, Pullus. The Pilus Prior wants to see you now."

Groaning, partly from the soreness I felt as I got up but more because of the dread of facing Pilus Prior Crastinus' wrath, I got to my feet, swaying a little, and the Optio put out a quick hand to steady me.

"Easy Pullus. Well," he shook his head after looking me up and down, "you're quite a sight but it'll have to do. You all right now?"

Without waiting for an answer, he turned and led me to where the Pilus Prior was standing with the section leaders. I estimated that it was at least two parts of a watch past sunrise, and I was surprised that I was not roused earlier. All of the carnage from the night before was now clear to see, causing my step to falter as I looked around at the mangled bodies and the huge dark spots on the ground where men's lifeblood had left their body to return to the earth. Work parties were carrying corpses and throwing them into a pile of enemy dead, but I was more concerned with the bodies wearing our uniform and I looked around for a spot where they might be laid. Surveying the surroundings, I saw there was one spot with a concentration of bodies much higher than what was strewn around the rest of our makeshift walls, identifiable as well by the fact that they were on the inside of the dirt barrier. I was almost to the Pilus Prior when I frowned; while everyone was still wearing their gear, and there were Legionaries on the wall facing where the Lusitani camp was, there were still a significant number of men who were busy with other tasks. From where I was, I could not see over the wall to their camp to see what the Lusitani were doing, and I was unable to pay any more attention because I was now standing in front of the Pilus Prior.

Coming to *intente*, I saluted in my best parade ground fashion and barked out, "*Gregarius* Titus Pullus reporting as ordered, sir."

Crastinus continued directing the section leaders as I stood there. He was clearly ignoring me, only fueling my sense of anxiety, and I tried not to fidget as I waited for him to turn his attention to me. Once finished with them, the section leaders dispersed, among them Calienus, who was sporting a bandage on his upper arm and a slash along his jaw. Meeting my eyes as he passed me, he did not say anything; the shake of his head was eloquent enough. Once they were away I continued standing there, trying to tell myself that the shaking in my legs was because I was still tired, but Crastinus continued to ignore me, barking out orders to some of the nearby Legionaries. Finally, after what seemed like a third of a watch but was probably no more than a hundred heartbeats, he turned his full attention to me, looking me up and down, his face expressionless, the invisible man with the turd again taking the day off. Staring at a spot above him, out of the corner of my eye I could see the fatigue

185

in his face, the lines etched by the countless days of weather and sun even deeper now than before, with the rings under his eyes making it look like he had been punched in the face. It was the first time I saw Gaius Crastinus as just a man, like me and the rest of my comrades, and not some demigod sent by Mars to torment young Legionaries. When he spoke, it was not in his command voice, but with a tone I had never heard from him before, even the one night when we were sworn in.

"You know if I were to abide by the regulations, I should have you scourged at the very least, and scourged and crucified at the very worst."

My jaw clenched as the fear caused by his words struck deep into my heart. Besides the pain, the shame and humiliation would be unbearable, and I was already regretting my rashness. Then, a miracle happened.

"But," my heart did another skip, "it wouldn't be very gracious to kill a man who saved my life. Besides," he continued, "it wouldn't help morale, seeing as how you also probably saved the lives of the rest of the Century, not to mention the Second's as well."

Shaking his head, he tried to suppress a smile; his words had already unburdened my soul and I could feel my chest beginning to swell with pride.

"What you did last night, boy, was one of the stupidest things I've seen in all my years under the standards, but it was also the bravest. I told you once that I thought you might have a future in the Legions, and last night didn't change my mind."

Fighting the urge to smile, that urge was blown away like smoke in a strong breeze with his next words. Stepping close to whisper in my ear so only I could hear, there was no mistaking his tone, even at a whisper.

"But if you ever disobey me again, I don't care how decorated or famous you are, I'll gut you myself, and I'll make it look like you were killed in battle and nobody will ever know. Do you understand me?"

"Yes sir."

186

It seemed crystal clear to me that this was the only answer I could give, especially since I held no doubt whatsoever that he was completely serious, and capable of doing what he promised. I could handle myself and more with the barbarian tribes, but I harbored no illusions how long I would last with a man like Crastinus. Just as quickly, he switched back to a human being and clapped me on the shoulder.

"Good. And we'll speak no more about it. I know I won't have to."

Making my way back to my section's gear, I passed the area where the bodies of our dead were laid out, and I am somewhat ashamed to record the relief that I felt when I saw faces I recognized, but none from my own Century. There were nine men on the ground, and as I moved on, I saw an even larger group, all of them in varying degrees of distress from their wounds. One man was moaning while the *medici* who was assigned to us did what he could to make him as comfortable as one can be when the only thing keeping one's guts inside their body is a linen bandage. It will be ten dead at least, I thought as I walked past, then I spotted Romulus sitting on the ground, a bandage on his head obscuring one eye. It struck me with dread at the thought that he might be maimed and unable to continue in the Legions, except I was too timid to ask him, so I decided I would ask Remus when I saw him since he would undoubtedly know. I found my tentmates seated by their gear eating their morning meal. Vibius, looking up and seeing me, smiled and rose to his feet, then the others saw me, whereupon they too stood. I slowed as I got near; this was not how I was usually greeted.

Vibius stepped forward and ignoring the gore that was still caked on me and my gear, embraced me, and whispered, "You crazy bastard. If the Lusitani hadn't killed you, I swore I was going to for scaring me so badly. But now when I see you I'm just happy that you're still alive."

"Me too."

There was nothing more said before the rest of my comrades were on me, pounding me on the back and congratulating me. Only two men hung back; Didius, which did not surprise me, but Calienus was the other, which did, and I was mystified by the reception.

"Everyone in the Century is talking about it," Scribonius explained. "You single-handedly saved both Centuries last night. Those bastards had broken through and it was you who stopped them and saved all of us."

I did not know what to say, but in truth, I was not of a mind to dispute what was said. When you are young and dream of glory, how hard are you going to argue when such honors are laid at your feet?

The Lusitani had withdrawn; they approached under a flag of truce while I was asleep early in the morning asking to retrieve their wounded, which the Pilus Prior granted. They left behind almost 300 dead, out of an original force estimated to be between 500 and 600 strong. My tentmates claimed that there were less than a hundred unscathed, the rest being wounded to various degrees. Our butcher's bill ended up with ten dead, twelve wounded that would return at some point to full duty, and another nine whose wounds were disabling to the point where they would be put out of the Legion on permanent disability. Added to that were the four men we lost when we moved to the hill. It did not matter whether they were killed outright, or had been too seriously wounded like the man who grabbed at Calienus' ankle; once they fell they were dead men. I was just happy that Romulus was not one of those too badly wounded to continue under the standard, sustaining a serious wound just above his eye, while the eye itself was spared. The scar he carried gave him the look of a pirate or brigand of some sort, except much to our surprise and chagrin, we discovered that it seemed to be a point of attraction to the ladies, who would coo and flutter about him, asking him how he got it. It was not long before some of us were hoping that we could someday be mutilated in the face to enable us to become the object of the same kind of attention. Even as the Lusitani were finishing up the gathering of their wounded and making preparations to retreat, a column of dust started drifting towards us, the sign that Crastinus had been correct; help was indeed on the way. While we waited for the relief column to arrive, the Pilus Prior sent small groups of men out foraging for wood to build funeral pyres, and some sort of animal, preferably a white goat or sheep, to sacrifice during the funeral rites. Although the latter group came back empty handed, it turned out that it did not matter. As usual, Caesar thought of everything so that when he dispatched the column in relief, he sent along the proper animals for sacrifice, knowing that we would have had casualties. It was also a subtle message to all of us that said he knew the only reason we could possibly be delayed was because we were locked in desperate battle. The remaining men were detailed to dig a pit to throw the bodies of the Lusitani in, with a small number of men standing guard. Between the beating we had just given them, and the sight of the column, Crastinus was convinced that the Lusitani would not do anything foolish and just be content instead to limp off with their tail between their legs. I was exempted from duties as a reward for my antics the night before, yet after a few moments, I could not watch my friends digging without getting up to help, so I pitched in. It also helped pass the time, and gave us a chance to recount the events of the day before. In between shovelfuls, Atilius gave a running commentary on everything that happened as he saw it, with the others adding in their own obol's worth.

"Yeah, I thought we were well and truly fucked," he said as he threw another spade's worth of dirt out of the hole, "because I couldn't see a damn thing and all I could hear was that abominable screeching they do when they attack."

"I was pissed because I'd just gotten off light duty," added Vellusius, still working at a disadvantage because although the bone was healed, he had lost some range of motion in his arm, making activities like shoveling painful. "I thought, by the gods, if I get wounded again and put back in the hospital, I'll go mad." His face was red and he was dripping sweat at a much faster rate than the rest of us, and despite doing his best to hide it, we all saw how much strain this was putting on him. However, when we suggested that he could stand down to let the rest of us dig, he refused. "I've been lying about long enough. I need to pull my weight just like everyone else."

I do not know if it was meant in the way it was taken; all I do know is that immediately after Vellusius spoke those words, every eye shifted to Didius, who as usual was doing more leaning on his shovel than actually working with it. Of course he noticed immediately and scowled at us collectively, with extra malice towards Vellusius. However, he was wise enough this time to keep his mouth shut. The bump on his head was still noticeable, but only just, and was certainly not enough of a justification to put himself on the sick list, although I was a bit surprised that he did not try.

Atilius was sporting a massive bruise on his thigh just above his knee, courtesy of a bouncing rock from a sling and so was hobbling a bit, added, "I got knocked down, and I knew I had had it.

'Atilius old son,' I said to myself, 'if you get out of this one it'll be because of the divine intervention of Fortuna herself. You better show her how grateful you are if she sees fit to spare you.'"

"Well, she obviously did, so what kind of sacrifice are you going to make?" Vibius asked.

"You know, I've been thinking about that," Atilius stopped digging for a moment. "I don't know what's appropriate. What do you boys think?"

This engendered a debate on what would be a proper measure of gratitude, before we finally decided on a white kid goat.

"How much do those cost I wonder?"

Scribonius supplied a guess, "I shouldn't think more than twenty sesterces."

Atilius almost choked. "Twenty sesterces! By Dis, I'm not THAT grateful. She'll have to do with something less than that then."

We laughed at that, prompting a visit by the Pilus Prior to bark at us, saying that if we had breath to laugh we were not working hard enough. The section all stood at *intente*, faces made of stone and with hearts as pure as the Vestal Virgins until he stalked off, whereupon we picked up where we left off, just more quietly this time.

The grave was dug, with the grisly task of pulling bodies over and throwing them in the pit falling to us as well, and we paired up. Vibius and I worked out a system whereby we alternated grabbing the legs or the arms, because holding the legs in most cases is the least unpleasant since you are farther away from the gore of the wounds that killed them. Sometimes though, the bodies were in pieces and we would find ourselves carrying some limbs, or just a torso, which was the worst. The sun beating down ensured that it did not take long for the stench to get to a point where it was not only noticeable but was becoming hard to bear, spurring us on to finish as fast as we could. Once all the bodies and parts were collected and thrown into the ground, we covered them up with dirt. It is a strange sensation when one looks down into a hole and sees a face staring back up at you, with open eyes and a mouth still set in the expression they were wearing when death claimed them. For some, it was a look of surprise; for others it was a look of terror, and still others a look of pure anger and hatred. It was these last that I did not mind throwing dirt over to hide their visage, while for the others, I felt a sort of sadness as I interred them, and I remember wondering what sights their eyes would be missing from that point on. They would never see their women again, or their children grow up. They would not revel in another sunrise or sunset, or stare into a fire and think the private thoughts that all men have at some point in their lives. But they had chosen their path, I thought, and this is where it led them. Pity is not an emotion in which a Legionary can indulge, and I resolved to myself that I would banish such unseemly feelings from me, no matter how hard it might be.

While we were busy digging the grave and filling it up, the Second Century, now being aided by the Second and Third Cohort that had been dispatched to come to our aid, built funeral pyres for our dead, using the scented oils for such ceremonies that were sent along with our rescuers. The fact that we actually needed no rescue was a source of great pride to all of us, and it gave us a bit of a swagger from that day onwards. The news of our stand spread throughout the army and I would be remiss if I did not add that it was at this point my name first became known to more than just the men in my Legion. Our dead were laid on the pyre, their bodies and uniforms cleaned up then wrapped in linen as is our custom. One of the priests attached to the Legion was sent along with the Cohorts to perform the ceremony, and we stood in formation as the pyres were lit and our comrades consumed by the cleansing flames. We had been so busy that none of us had time to clean up our own gear, but that could not be helped and once the fire died down, their ashes were collected, the ashes from each put into ten urns that would be sent to their families. With that duty performed, we formed up to march back to the main camp. Our Century was given the place of honor, just behind the vanguard, while our wounded were loaded on the wagons brought by the relieving force. As we marched away, none of us could stop ourselves from giving a last glance back at the little hill where we had made our stand. The dirt wall was still there, the breached part of the wall clearly visible, and there was still the normal debris strewn around that signifies a battle has taken place; only the bodies were missing, but one could still clearly see the darkened splotches where men had fallen. It was on that hill that we truly became veterans, and from that day forward, the First Century of the Second Cohort of the 10th Legion was no longer treated as if we were still new *Gregarii*. We had been in the Legions a total of four months and two weeks.

Our return to camp was also the occasion of my first face to face conversation with Caesar. Since Caesar ordered that we would stay in the same camp for an extra day, we were given time to clean and mend our gear, which in my case meant a lot of vigorous scrubbing, using a stiff horsehair brush to get the caked blood and gore from between the links of my armor, a process that took the better part of an afternoon by the time I felt presentable. The next morning, after our morning meal and formation that is held whenever we were not packing up to march and where the orders of the day are passed along, the Pilus Prior held me back while dismissing the others.

He looked at me critically, eying me up and down, reaching out to make an adjustment here and wipe off some speck of something there, before he said curtly, "Follow me."

Then he turned to head toward the *Praetorium*, slowing enough for me to catch up and walk beside him, unusual in itself and increasing my anxiety. The thought that perhaps my transgression was not forgiven flitted through my mind, but I instantly dismissed it. I was sure that I would have sensed that the Pilus Prior experienced a change of heart at some point before this, yet that only lessened my anxiety a fraction. For such is the nature of the ordinary *Gregarii* that any type of summons to headquarters is enough to send the stomach down to one's feet and one's heart up into the throat. Even for someone like myself, who had decided that they did not want to be just one of the faceless masses of men who were in the Legions, it was still a cause for concern.

"Right, now listen up," the Pilus Prior spoke quietly so that only I could hear. "I turned in my report to the Legate, who forwarded it on to Caesar, who interviewed me himself. He wants to meet you."

It is hard to describe which emotion I felt first or the strongest between exhilaration and fear. The best way to put it is that it was not dissimilar to the feeling one gets before going into battle, and I swallowed down the lump in my throat.

"So what should I do?"

He looked at me sharply. "Do? You don't do a damn thing. You answer his questions with a Yes, Sir or No, Sir and otherwise keep your mouth shut. Got it?"

I nodded, except I was still troubled. "What if he asks me a question that doesn't have a yes or no answer?"

The Pilus Prior puffed out his cheeks impatiently, and snapped, "Then you answer the damn question, but use as few words as you possibly can."

Nodding again, I was about to say something else but knowing the look that the Pilus Prior had on his face, I kept my mouth shut. Approaching the guards, we were stopped and the Pilus Prior stated our business. One of them entered the headquarters tent, returning a moment later to motion us in. The Pilus Prior removed his helmet, placing it under his left arm, and I followed suit, then he took a breath, squared his shoulders and marched inside, with me following behind him. The tent was brightly lit with many lamps, and there were a number of scribes, all of them with their own desk, copying out orders of one sort or another. Tribunes were hurrying about carrying wax tablets, looking their normal officious selves, and out of the corner of my eye I caught sight of Doughboy engaged in conversation with another Tribune slightly younger than he was. I had seen him before but did not know his name, and made a mental note to ask the Pilus Prior about him. He was a little unusual for a Tribune in that he had an air about him that betrayed a sense of competence, and the few times I was around him, I also noticed that he did not speak to us *Gregarii* as if he thought his *cac* did not stink. Crastinus and I made our way across the outer room and into the section that acted as Caesar's office, separated by a doorway made from a leather flap that could be pulled aside. I am not sure what I was expecting, but it was not what I saw. Knowing that Caesar was a patrician from an old family, I expected his office to reflect his status and be filled with all sorts of luxury items and ornate decorations. Instead, there was a simple desk directly across from the flap, noticeable only because it was larger than the other two in the room, those against each wall of the tent, and each with its own scribe. Caesar was standing behind his desk, reading from a scroll while simultaneously dictating to the scribes and it was here that I got my first glimpse of one of the things that most people know about him today and made him the greatest man of our age, or any other for that matter. He would dictate a sentence to the scribe on his left, who would begin writing rapidly, and while waiting for him

193

to finish, he turned to the scribe on his right, dictating yet another sentence on a totally different topic, all the while his eyes never leaving the scroll that he was reading. He only stopped when the Pilus Prior and I approached, with the both of us halting the prescribed distance from his desk to give him our best parade ground salute.

"Secundus Pilus Prior Gaius Crastinus, of the 10th Legion, reporting with Legionary *Gregarius* Titus Pullus as ordered sir."

Caesar laid the scroll on the desk to acknowledge our salute with the same solemnity and gravity that it was given. For a moment he said nothing, just inspecting the two of us, spending more of his attention on me as I kept my eyes locked at a point above his head, yet even so, knowing that I was being inspected by the general commanding the entire army ignited in me the queerest feeling I had ever experienced in my life to that point. It was a mixture of pride, apprehension, exhilaration and not a little bit of anxiety, all while I tried to remember the Pilus Prior's instructions. His inspection done, Caesar smiled then walked around the desk to face me, doing something that I will never forget.

Extending his hand, he said with a smile, "*Salve, Gregarius* Titus Pullus. The Pilus Prior has told me of your valor in your engagement, and I wanted to offer you my hand in thanks."

I did not know what to do; this was so far out of anything I had contemplated that I was flummoxed, but the habits of a lifetime saved me and more importantly Caesar any real embarrassment, as before I could even think about it I extended my hand and we shook hands in the Roman manner, clasping each other's forearms. His hand was warm, and I could feel the calluses formed by many hours practice with the sword. Most importantly, his hand was not like a wet and clammy fish, his grip instead strong and dry. Before I could stop myself I looked down at him, meeting his eyes, yet despite my horror at this slip in discipline, he did not seem to take any umbrage whatsoever. His eyes carried a measure of warmth that I was not expecting, with none of the disdain I saw in those of men like Doughboy when talking to their social inferiors. It was the appreciation of one fighting man to another, and I am not ashamed to say that in that moment, I became Caesar's man forever.

Withdrawing his hand, he continued, "It's good to know that Rome will be served by young men such as you in the coming years.

194

I fear that she will have more need of your services than either of us would like."

I was confused as to the proper response; this was not a question. Did he want me to comment? The best I could do was to say, "And I'll be ready sir, whenever Rome needs me and wherever I'm needed."

He smiled again, nodding his head as if I had passed some sort of test. "This is what I wanted to hear. I must confess, when I was told that a young *Gregarius* was being selected as the weapons instructor for their Century, I was a little hesitant to approve. But the judgment of the Pilus Prior has been confirmed in a way that leaves no doubt in my mind."

My chest swelled, and for a brief instant I wished that by some miracle my family could be there to hear his words, even my accursed father. Perhaps then he would relent in his hatred of me, I thought. Concluding the meeting, Caesar finished, "Well, I just wanted to meet the young *Gregarius* I had heard so much about in the last couple of days. I will be keeping an eye on you, Pullus. I expect great things from you in the coming years."

I did not even try to hide my pleasure. We were dismissed, and I felt I was a foot taller than when I had walked in. As we walked back to our area, the Pilus Prior grumbled, "Don't go getting a big head now, boy. I'll still knock the *cac* out of you if you mess up."

Despite the harshness of his words, I could tell by his tone that he was as pleased and proud as I was, so all I said was, "Yes Pilus Prior."

Continuing our northward push, the army entered the lands of a tribe known to be particularly warlike and never fully accepting of the Romanization of Hispania to that point. They were called the Gallaeci, and were supposedly a branch of the Lusitani, yet to the *Gregarii* like me, it did not really matter much. They were enemies to be defeated because that was what Caesar, and by extension Rome, wished, so it would be done. There was one material difference between the rest of the Lusitani and the Gallaeci, and it was in their use of horses. While we had seen and been harassed by Lusitani cavalry before, the Gallaeci took it to another level, specializing in using missiles, either throwing something similar to our javelin or using bows. Although this was not unique, what made them different was in the way they would employ their cavalry, their warriors having learned the art of galloping around in a large circle, providing them with the security of constant motion and making them extremely hard to hit. When they were in part of the loop nearest to us, they would launch their missile attack, then keep riding in the loop to repeat it over and over again, until they either ran out of missiles or we found some way to drive them off. By this point in our campaign, Caesar had partially rectified the dearth of cavalry on our side by having cavalry auxiliaries sent to him. There was an *ala* of auxiliary cavalry, consisting of ten *turmae* attached to each Legion, so the *ala* consisted of a total of about 300 men at full strength. The trick was to use our cavalry properly as a screening force and as *exploratores*, but not send them out so far that they could not be recalled quickly to repel attack by the Gallaeci horsemen. The closer we approached the Durius (Douro) River, with the last Roman colony at the time being Portus Cale, the more lurid the tales became of the skill and devastating accuracy of these mythical horsemen. I believe that in every Legion there is a group of men determined to paint the grimmest picture that they can, and they foretell our defeat and slaughter in every upcoming battle. Why they do so I have no idea, but they are always given more credence than I think they deserve, and as I was to find out a few years later, their dire outlook could infect a whole Legion if the Centurions did not put an end to it.

It was near the Ides of Sextilis, meaning the campaign season was drawing to a close and in consequence, Caesar picked up the pace of the operations. Portus Cale had been taken by a confederation of the Gallaeci Bracari and the Gallaeci Lucenses, who normally warred on each other but were now united in their common hatred of Rome, and slaughtered all the Roman citizens who did not flee. By the time we arrived at the walls, Caesar's practice with the last few towns and cities was well known, so there was never any question as far as the enemy was concerned whether or not he would offer terms. To delay the inevitable, they burned the bridge across the Douro, which at that time was made of wood, and it was here that Caesar made a demonstration of his abilities as an engineer. To be fair, it was a demonstration of his ability at design, since it was the *praefecti fabrorum* who had to actually put his design into use. It was not as large or ambitious as his later bridge over the Rhenus (Rhine); still it clearly awed the Gallaeci, who stood watching helplessly from a distance as in the space of a day, a pontoon bridge was built over the river using confiscated boats. On

196

top of the boats, planking was laid of a sufficient strength that a Legion and an *ala* of cavalry could march across to set up a defensive camp protecting the selected site. The main problem of building a more permanent bridge, besides the Gallaeci trying to destroy it, stemmed from the banks of the Douro rising up steeply from the river, with very little flat and stable riverbank on which to build. Much later a bridge of stone was erected, but at the time our orders were to erect one that was sufficient to allow the Legions, along with their baggage trains and artillery to pass over, just not one that would take more than a few days to build. One challenge was finding timber suitable for using as the piers to hold the bridge up, but within a half day of our arrival, Caesar had seen what needed to be done. Simultaneously ordering the construction of the pontoon bridge, he also sent several Cohorts and wagons out to scour the area for wood of sufficient size for a more permanent structure. It was found a half-day's march from our location, and it was a good thing that Caesar did not tarry, because fairly quickly the Gallaeci succeeded in destroying the pontoon bridge, sending several fire rafts downstream to run into the boats holding the bridge up. This effectively cut the 9th off on the far bank, not as much of a military threat as it meant that the three day's rations they marched over with would have to suffice. The 7th and 10th were left on the south side of the river as a labor force, while the artillery was set up on the high bank of the Douro to provide covering fire and to keep the Gallaeci from getting any more ideas. By dawn on the fourth day, the bridge was finished, and even from a distance it was easy to read the despair of the mounted men who were our constant shadows while we worked and the 9th watched. They made no attempt to attack the 9th in its camp, which was probably a mistake, though it was one that suited us perfectly fine. It was clear to us that they thought that they had earned enough of a reprieve that it would allow time for the Gallaeci Lucenses to send fresh reinforcements down from the north to help them stop us, but the problem for them was that Caesar knew it as well. However slight the delay was, we still had to be quick about taking the town, and it was here that Caesar made another one of his decisions that is a demonstration of his tactical brilliance. Leaving the 7th to besiege the town, he continued the march north with the 9th and 10th to confront the Lucenses separately, trusting the 7th to take care of the Bracari. This was totally unexpected by both parts of the enemy force, and it was no more than two days after we crossed the Douro that our scouts came galloping back to the main column to report that they had spotted the advance scouts of the Lucenses column. Approaching to within sight of their own advance party, for the better part of a third of a watch the two sides sat on opposing hills no more than two miles away while the Lucenses scouts and what we presumed were their leaders talked over what to do. Not that we were idle; the *cornu* and *bucina* were blaring out orders that told us to array along the top of the hill in a *triplex acies*, although we still were waiting for the 9th to arrive in full since they were marching drag. But as usual, Caesar knew what he was doing. Just the sight of our one Legion making preparation for battle was enough to convince the Lucenses that they needed to fight another day, and even before we finished shaking out into battle formation, the dust cloud that signaled the location of their column began to rise in the air again as they reversed march to head back north. Resuming our own progress, as soon as we approached the hill from which they had observed us, we saw in the distance beyond that there was yet another formation a short distance behind the original column, traveling on a parallel track that was more to the east than the one that we had been observing. Seeing this other force, Caesar decided to wait and see what they would do, deciding that we had gone far enough that day and ordering us to make a marching camp on top of the hill. It was while we were in the process of making camp that a courier from the first column obviously made it to the second, because they also turned around to head back north, deciding to find better ground, which we expected. What we did not expect was that they would pick an island, or rather, a number of islands.

Over the next two days, we were never able to catch the Lucenses, although I am not altogether sure that Caesar wanted to, given the length of our marching column, strung-out as it was because of the terrain. Coming to the Minus (Guadiana) River, it was here that we ran into a challenge bigger than the one that we faced at the Douro. This river empties into the great ocean, and is guarded on both sides by high hills. On the opposite bank, there was a good sized fortified town, right at the mouth of the river and with a commanding view of the area. Compounding the problem, this was the best area for miles to build a bridge, but was out of the question because of the position of the town. There was no bridge in place; instead, the Lucenses were using a large number of flat-bottomed boats to ferry their army across, and we were greeted by a frustrating sight. Climbing the last hill of the opposite bank just in time to see the last boatloads cross, we could only stand helplessly and curse as of course they did not send the boats back. The Minus was too wide and deep to cross by fording; even a pontoon bridge at that location was out of the question because of the vulnerability to the Gallaeci army and the swift current as the river emptied into the ocean. Consequently, we would have to march upriver and Caesar wasted no time in giving that order. We were in the vanguard that day, so Caesar diverted the 9th to send them east up the river, while we now became the rearguard. A cavalry *ala* was left behind to keep watch on the Gallaeci in case they thought to go back across the river and follow behind us. To further forestall that, once we moved up the riverbank and crossed over another hill out of sight from the town, Caesar dropped the 8th, 9th, and 10th Cohort of our Legion off on the reverse slope, directing them to build a camp. By climbing the short distance up the hill to the summit, sentries could keep an eye on the Gallaeci to make sure that they did not come after us. If they did there would be a blocking force that could intercept them if they came onto our side of the river, or at the least warn us if they followed on the other side. We knew that we could not keep them from observing our actions, yet that did not mean we had to make it easy on them.

Another ten miles had to be covered before we found a suitable site on which to build, and the one blessing was that the surrounding hills possessed enough timber that we did not have to travel much farther in order to supply the building materials. This bridge took longer than the one at the Douro because we had less manpower. The 8th had been left behind more than a month ago; the 7th was besieging Portus Cale, and my Legion was reduced by the three Cohorts we left to guard the route behind us. Meanwhile, Caesar kept all of the *ala* still with us busy scouting the area in order to provide us with enough warning in the event of any surprise the Lucenses might care to come up with. Once our camp was prepared, and the artillery that came with us was arrayed to provide covering fire against the opposite bank, we immediately set to work on building the bridge. For five days we labored, with our artillery driving off those Gallaeci who came too close. We could not keep what we were doing secret, but we could keep them from doing anything to stop our progress. Some of the auxiliary cavalry had forded the river and stood by to drive off any of the enemy who got too close, or delay an enemy sortie if it came in force. However, for whatever reason, the Gallaeci seemed to be resigned that we would not be denied from crossing the river, an accurate judgment. Once the bridge was completed we marched across, heading back towards the coast and the fortified town. Along the way, we ran into an attempted ambush but brushed it aside with few casualties on our side and heavy losses to the Gallaeci. Nevertheless, it was enough to delay us so that we could not begin an assault on the town until the next day. For what seemed like the hundredth time we found ourselves digging and building a marching camp within sight of a town's walls. Unlike the other towns, this one was more of a fortress than anything we had seen before, with walls made of stone, as were most of the buildings. It was also on the shelf of an extremely large hill, almost at the top, forcing us to climb up in the face of heavy fire. The truth is that nobody, especially the veterans looked forward to assaulting this place, and the mood was grim as we gathered around our fire that night.

"That's going to be a real bastard to take," Calienus announced quietly.

Even with the ramparts in the way, we could look past them and see the town spread out on the slope rising toward the crest, perched there as if daring us to attack it. We newer men took a cue from the mood of the veterans, knowing that if they were not enthused about the prospects, we certainly should not be ourselves. Nobody answered him; there was not much to say about it. The town was there, meaning it had to be taken because it had not surrendered and we could not leave its inhabitants in our rear as we marched further north.

We should have had more faith in Caesar, because he immediately saw that the very feature that the Gallaeci were counting on, their position on the side of the hill, was also their biggest weakness. The shelf on which the town was built was perhaps two-thirds up the side of the hill, leaving higher ground above them. The opposite slope of the hill was extremely steep, a feature that the Gallaeci were undoubtedly counting on as being precipitous enough so that nobody would try to climb it in order to take a position above the town. They did not account for Caesar's determination and imagination, because that is exactly what he did, or we did. Word was sent out among us asking for those men with experience in scaling such slopes, and from our two Legions was assembled an *ad hoc* group about two Cohorts strong. They were assigned the task of sneaking out of the camp at night, carrying not just extra javelins, but a number of the scorpions and one of the smaller ballistae that was broken down, then stealthily making their way to the back side of the hill. Using the darkness as cover, they scaled the steep slope of the back side, despite losing almost a dozen men who lost their footing and fell to their deaths, dragging the

200

artillery behind them and using ropes to pull the pieces up. About two thirds of the watch before dawn, the rest of us were given the order to assemble in battle array outside our camp, located less than a mile from the town and in clear sight of the Gallaeci standing on the walls looking down on us as the sun rose. They were greeted by the sight of two Legions arrayed for an assault on the town, minus the two mixed Cohorts who were at that moment just getting into position and reassembling the artillery. Meanwhile, the rest of our artillery deployed and were ready to begin the bombardment of the walls to create a breach. The veterans had assured us that, despite the apparent greater strength of a stone wall, it is actually easier to knock it down with artillery than a wooden wall is, because there is no give in the rock, making it more brittle. Despite finding this hard to believe, we had learned to trust their judgment on these matters since they were seldom wrong. From our formation, Caesar sent another Tribune under a flag of truce, except this time with an armed escort, none of us forgetting what happened at the first town. That group approached the walls and began to parley with the Gallaeci in the town. We were ordered to keep our eyes turned on the exchange at the gate; Caesar did not want anything to betray the surprise being prepared above and behind them, since some observant Gallaeci who noticed that our heads were turned to the top of the hill might get suspicious. Still, most of us, myself included, kept our heads turned to the parley, but nevertheless watched the top of the hill out of the corner of our eye.

"There they are," someone called out, and although it took me a few heartbeats, I saw a group of men, barely more than dots, appear on the crest of the hill followed moments later by larger shapes as they assembled the artillery pieces. Finally one of the men on top of the hill waved what appeared to be a flag as some sort of signal, which the Tribune negotiating with the Gallaeci had obviously been waiting for, because he immediately pointed up to our force on the hill.

The battle for the town was over before it really began. Once the Gallaeci saw our men on top of the hill, with our artillery pointing down at them, they did not even need a couple of projectiles thrown their way to convince them that they were finished. They accepted the terms that the Tribune was offering almost immediately, except they still had one trick to play, as we were about to find out. Regardless of what lay in the immediate future, all of us who were going to be assaulting that town heaved a huge sigh of relief; for once, the idea of survival outweighed the lure of plunder and when the surrender was announced, we all cheered heartily. Meanwhile, the Gallaeci continued haggling with the Tribune about minor details, something the Tribune was too inexperienced to recognize as a ploy. Finally, Caesar grew impatient when none of the enemy came out of the town to surrender, prompting he and his command group to ride over to the Tribune, whereupon Caesar began pointing and gesturing at both the Tribune and the Gallaeci who were still standing on the wall above the gate.

"Something's wrong," Scribonius mused, "or else Caesar wouldn't be so worked up."

As we watched, Caesar jerked his horse around and came galloping back to the formation, giving orders for the artillery to open fire and focus on the gate. This sudden reversal swept through the ranks and we began to talk amongst ourselves, speculating on what could have happened.

"Silete!"

The Pilus Prior seemed more irritable than usual, and I wondered if even he was beginning to get nervous about what was going on. With the artillery all concentrating their fire on the gate, it did not take long before it crashed open, one of the doors hanging by what appeared to be a thread from a distance. Immediately afterwards, the *bucina* and *cornu* sounded the advance at the double and the First Cohort peeled away, jogging towards the gates, followed by us, then the rest of the Legion.

"Keep your intervals you bastards," roared the Pilus Prior as we drew closer, our eyes fastened on the parapets, waiting for men to suddenly pop up and start bombarding us with missiles. Fortunately it never happened; the First Cohort went sweeping through, followed by us immediately behind them, they fanning out to the left as planned, us fanning out to the right. Immediately we noticed that the area of the town surrounding the gate seemed to be deserted, except for a few old men and women, along with some people who looked infirm and weak. This town was arranged in such a manner that it was laid out in two levels; the original part of the town was built on the shelf of the hill and was fairly level, then as it grew, a second level had gotten added that was built further up the slopes of the hill. After a quick search of the lower town, we huffed and puffed up the narrow streets to the second level, finding only more old and sick people. All of these we put to the sword since they held no value as slaves.

It turned out that the only able-bodied men left were the few men on the parapet above the gate negotiating with first the Tribune, then with Caesar. As we descended back down, we saw them by the gate, bound and on their knees, surrounded by the officers and some of the senior Centurions. Despite their state, they looked up at the men surrounding them with defiant expressions, a couple of them even smiling, like they had won some sort of victory, which in a sense they had. It was only after one of them was summarily executed that the others began to talk, finally explaining how the inhabitants of a town, not only combatants but all of the citizens who lived there that could walk, had vanished. One of the men indicated a street that was very hard to spot, branching off the larger street on the side of the town nearest the ocean that led up to the upper town. Because of the stone construction, it blended in as part of the wall that the street followed and was not really visible until you were almost on top of it. Sending a Cohort down the road, they came to a sheltered cove, where the boats that had hauled the people across the river had been moored. With the upper part of the hill above this spot dropping off into a sheer face more than a hundred feet above the water, the approach to the drop was so steep that the men on top of the hill had no way to get close enough to look down and see the harbor. It turned out that even before the sun came up to shine on our army ready to assault the town, the Gallaeci had determined that there was no real way to stop us from taking it. Our reputation preceded us and they knew that we would not just go away until the town fell and once it did, all the people in it would suffer a terrible fate. Therefore, as soon as the sun went down, they began evacuating the place and the only reason the men on the parapet seemed to have a change of heart and ceded the town was because the last of the boats had just pulled away. By the time the last boat that left after the sun came up reached a point where they might have been seen by our men on the hill, their attention was turned completely on the town, this being when Caesar gave the order to make ready to fire on the town with their artillery. Despite ourselves, we held a grudging admiration for the guile and skill of the Gallaeci, even if it meant that we would have to face these same men again.

The town was sacked, except there was little of value left behind, and we were immediately given orders to break camp to resume our pursuit of the Gallaeci. Those Gallaeci who remained behind to stall us were tortured, but it became clear that they did not know where their compatriots were headed. Since they were under no illusion that they would escape their situation alive, there was no need for them to know where the rest of the tribe was headed. This was not good news, because it meant that we were forced to march along the coast, which in this part of Hispania is extremely hilly. While giving us a commanding view of the ocean and the area ahead, it also meant that our pace was considerably slowed, no matter how hard Caesar pushed us. The end of the campaign season was rapidly approaching, betrayed by the cooler nights and shorter days, and it was our baggage train that slowed us the most. At some point every man found himself, his shoulder hard up against the back of a wagon, pushing with all their might as the mules and oxen struggled to pull their load up each hill. In many ways, however, going down the hill presented more risk, since there was a danger of a wagon being too heavy for the beasts to control, so we would use ropes attached to the back of the wagon and act as a multi-man brake to keep the wagon from careening out of control down the hill and smashing into other wagons or our comrades. Despite it being a little more than 30 miles from the town to the spot where we finally caught sight of the Gallaeci, it still took the better part of four days to cover the distance.

When we finally found them, there was a collective groan from the entire army. Our scouts had come rushing back with some sort of news, but it was not until we crested a hill and looked down on what lay before us that we in the ranks saw what we were facing. There was a bay, with a deep inlet that crossed in front of us, cutting some few miles deep into the land, the bulk of Hispania being to our right. Out in the bay were a number of islands, three small ones arranged in a row, crossing to our front perpendicular to our line of march, all clearly deserted. Farther out past that were a pair of islands, arranged parallel to our direction, and much larger. One of them appeared to be deserted as well but even from a distance, the second island, even farther away, was clearly inhabited because of the smoke rising above it that signaled the presence of people. We had to make a sharp right turn in order to follow the inlet around to a point where we were opposite the larger islands and as we drew closer, more details appeared. The larger of the two islands is shaped like a crescent, with the open end facing away from us and on the low hills of the island we could see fortifications. There were a large number of boats of varying sizes pulled up onto the beach opposite where we stood and it did not take a military expert to know that this is where the Gallaeci had fled from the town. To make matters worse, soon after we arrived opposite the first island the scouts came back to inform us that further north, perhaps ten miles ahead, was another island that was fortified in a similar manner. We stood watching the low hills of the first island as the command group conferred and the mood was apprehensive, to put it mildly. Very few of us had any experience on the water, making the idea of getting in boats to be ferried over to either of these islands unappealing in the extreme. However, Caesar was not to be denied, and in truth, it did not make sense for us not to finish the job so we resigned ourselves to our fate and waited to see what we were supposed to do.

Our mounted scouts scoured the area of the inlet, along with another inlet opposite the second island, yet could not find any craft large or seaworthy enough to ferry us across the water to either island.

"Maybe he'll call off an attack," Vibius said hopefully, a sentiment that I answered with a snort of dismissal.

"Not very likely. We've just marched across the entire length of Hispania; do you really think Caesar is going to be denied now?"

Despite not liking what I said, neither could he argue and he knew it, just answering with a shake of his head as he viewed the expanse of water with trepidation. Caesar's answer to the lack of boats was simple; we would make them. Once again we found ourselves finding, felling and dragging back trees that the engineers deemed suitable for our purposes. There were men with experience in shipbuilding who were put in charge of the work, with the rest of the Legions supplying the manual labor. It took a full week, and was done far enough up the inlet that results of our labor was not visible to the Gallaeci on the islands. While we were involved in this work, those Gallaeci that for whatever reason had not joined their comrades on the island did whatever they could to delay us, most commonly attempting to fire the boats at night. They managed to burn one, so after that raid we kept a constant vigil, forcing a lot of us who worked all day to go without much sleep at night as we stood guard. Despite the Gallaeci's attempts, the work progressed until we had a dozen flat-bottomed barges, each of them able to hold two Centuries and an artillery piece. Meanwhile, the command group worked out the plan for the assault, deciding that our best chance was to cross at night, something that became a symbol of

Caesar's, the sudden movement that the enemy did not expect. However, a night attack requires a huge amount of coordination and not a little luck but as we were to learn, almost as much as his skill, Caesar was renowned for his good fortune and he never hesitated putting his faith in it during tough times. The 10th was chosen to lead the assault, with the First through Fourth Cohorts designated as the first group the boats would take across, and the decision was made to attack in three days' time, there being no moon starting that night, a sword that cut both ways. It would make our approach harder to detect, but it also meant that the chances of a mistake were much greater. To help guide us a small group of men, using a boat commandeered from somewhere that was small enough to be harder to detect, would row over to the island the night before the assault, then remain hidden during the day. On the next night, at a pre-appointed time, they would light a shielded lantern on the beach only detectable from our spot out on the water to help guide us in. To further the subterfuge, the boats would not be brought down the inlet until after dark, requiring us to hurry to load up then row across to the island, using the lamp as our guide. It would require a minimum of foul-ups in order to be successful, and the fact that Caesar put his faith in us made us all the more determined.

When the night of the assault arrived, helping our cause was a heavy cloud cover, or at least so we thought. However, shortly before the boats were supposed to arrive it also began to rain, with the wind picking up, blowing off the ocean and directly into our faces. That made the trip down the inlet more difficult for the men selected to row the boats, so they arrived later than planned. By the time they pulled up onto the beach, the wind had increased so that the falling rain was almost horizontal and the waves had become increasingly choppy. Peering through the rainy dark at Vibius, I saw an expression of real apprehension that not even the gloom could conceal, bringing me a bit of comfort now that I knew he was as worried as I was. Both of us were country boys, our first glimpse of the ocean occurring on a training march from our camp at Scallabis several months earlier, while neither of us had been in so much as a rowboat, let alone a flat-bottomed troop transport. Calienus and the other veterans who had participated in amphibious operations with Pompey did their best to put us at ease, but their own looks of concern did nothing to assuage our fears. Being the First Century of the Second, we were one of the first to load up, bringing on board with us two artillery pieces, both scorpions, whereupon we rowed out a short distance then dropped anchor to wait for the other units to load up. Before much time passed, the violent bobbing made most of us sick, so the gunwales of the boat were lined with Legionaries puking their guts out. I am not ashamed to say that I was one of them; it was not until much later that I got my sea legs but even then, I did not, nor do I now like sea voyages of any duration. It took perhaps a third of a watch to load the rest of the Centuries of our four Cohorts into the boats, then we ran into another problem. With the rain getting steadily worse, it became so heavy that we could not see the beacon that was supposed to be guiding us to the island.

"If we can't see the damn light, how can we know which way we're going?" this was Didius' voice, and for one of the few times I was in complete agreement. "For all we know, we may end up 20 miles out to sea, then what'll happen?"

"We'll all drown, you idiot, what do you think will happen?" Even Calienus' voice sound strained when he replied to Didius.

Vibius and I, as usual, were standing together and Vibius whispered to me, "Titus, I'm not going to lie. I'm scared to death."

"Me too," was all I could manage, before retching again, despite having lost everything in my stomach.

Ignoring the lack of a guiding light, the men at the oars began to heave when the order was given and once more, someone called out, "Jupiter Optimus Maximus, protect this Legion, soldiers all," as we began making our way towards what we hoped was the island.

It took the better part of a third of a watch, with the men at the oars straining all the way, before we got close enough to the island for someone to see the lantern.

"There it is, off to the right," I heard an excited voice call out.

"By the gods, we almost missed the damn island," another voice exclaimed, and there was a chorus of agreement. If we had passed by with the island off to our right, we would have headed out to open sea and certain death by drowning.

"Well, at least we found the damn thing." That was the Pilus Prior, who for once seemed as apprehensive as we were, not bothering to tell us to shut up once. Continuing, he told us, "Listen up, boys. You just saw how long it took us to get to this island. It

207

won't take them half as long to get back because the wind is at their back, but it'll take them just as long, if not longer to bring up the next four Cohorts. In fact, we'll probably be on this island for at least a full watch by ourselves, so keep that in mind. No heroes; make sure we stay together because it's darker than Pluto's bunghole out here. Hopefully the boys on the island'll be able to point us in the right direction."

"Pilus Prior, wouldn't it make more sense to wait until the whole Legion is on the beach?"

I do not know who asked that but I believe that only the total darkness emboldened him to question our orders. What was even more surprising was that the Pilus Prior did not take offense. In fact, he agreed.

"Yes, it would make more sense, but that's not our orders. Caesar has commanded that we begin the assault immediately, and that's what we're going to do. The thing that worries me is that the artillery won't be able to use the combustibles to start a fire in their defenses to give us light, so we're going to have to be very careful and stay in formation. Make sure that nobody gets separated by keeping close enough to each other so that you're touching. If you lose contact with someone on either side, call out immediately so they'll know to close back in and get in contact, but by the gods keep your voices down when you do it."

Answering him, it was just as we felt the bottom of the boat scraping the beach. Without waiting, Pilus Prior Crastinus called out, "All right boys, let's go give these bastards some Roman iron. They escaped their fate once; we're not going to let 'em get away a second time."

With that, we heard a splash above the sound of the waves lapping at the beach as he jumped over the side, and immediately we began moving forward as we disembarked. Landing in thigh-deep water, I was thankful for my height because it was shockingly cold; if I was shorter the water would have hit a part of my body that never reacts well to anything cold touching it. I was assigned to help carry some of the pieces of the artillery ashore, so I grabbed what was handed to me before turning to wade the few paces to the shore. Immediately I bumped into someone, my bigger size knocking them down, and my heart sank when I heard the voice of the Pilus Prior cursing me, my mother, my father, and all my ancestors. Muttering

208

an apology in a voice that I hoped he would not recognize, I skirted past him to get as far away as I could. It was impossible to see anything and the only way that we got organized was by calling out to each other, then following the sounds of voices. Doing this was only possible because of the rain and howling of the wind; if it had been quieter I do not know what we would have done. The rest of the men carrying the artillery pieces stumbled over and we began assembling them by feel. Hearing a curse, I recognized the voice as one of the men assigned as an artilleryman and asked him what the problem was.

"The torsion rope is completely soaked. That means that it's useless."

This was not good news; not only would we be assaulting in the dark, without reinforcements, now we did not even have the help of at least one artillery piece. Immediately, a quick inventory discovered that all of the pieces had the same problem, leaving us without anything heavier than our javelins to assault the fortifications. Our Pilus Prior made his way over to Primus Pilus Favonius while we all stood there, shivering and miserable, having been ordered to leave our cloaks behind and take only our weapons. One thing that we had to be thankful for is that we were told to leave our leather covers on our shields; there is nothing quite as heavy or as useless as a water-soaked shield.

The Pilus Prior came back a bit later and called out, "Change of plans. We're going to wait until the next Cohorts arrive to see if they had any better luck with their artillery. We're not going to release all of the boats until we find out, so that we can send one back and tell the command group the situation and see what they want to do."

While this made sense, and was something of a relief, it also meant that we had to sit huddled up as close to each other to keep warm and wait. When one is truly, thoroughly miserable, the hardest thing to do is to accurately gauge the time. You are sure that at least two full watches have gone by, only to learn that it is less than a quarter of that, and as we sat there, soaking wet and getting colder by the moment, we occupied ourselves with trying to guess how much time had passed. Of course, it was not long before there was betting going on, which I ignored, preferring instead to sit there trying to tell myself that this was making me stronger and would come in handy someday. It would turn out I was right, though it was a small comfort to be sure. With the arrival of the next boatloads and more men piling ashore, our officers informed the Centurions joining us of the situation. A quick check revealed that the artillery in this wave was in the same shape as ours, so the word was passed to the returning boats of the situation, with a request for further orders. More time passed and despite my discomfort, I dozed off somehow, because when the third wave arrived, I almost jumped out of my skin, prompting a laugh from Vibius. Just a few moments later, the Pilus Prior returned to inform us that the assault was going to be postponed until first light, and that the next wave would be bringing assault ladders with them so that we could scale the walls of the fortifications. Trying to make light of this news, we told each other that this was old stuff for us; we had done this before and it had turned out fine, except that my stomach, just beginning to recover from the boat trip, began twisting again. However, there was nothing that could be done and at least we would be doing it with some light to help us. Of course, it also meant that the Gallaeci would see us coming.

By the time the Legion was assembled on the beach, with assault ladders, the rain that continued pouring down had caused us to get so cold that we were shaking uncontrollably and were unable to keep our teeth from chattering. When one man's teeth are knocking about the sound is negligible, but when it is a complete Legion, it is impossible to describe the din. Our only comfort was that the wind was not abated, and it served to keep the noise we were making from reaching the ears of the enemy, or at least so we hoped. Huddled together, we tried to stay close enough to create a little more warmth, which was negligible. In the meantime we stared towards the east, in the direction of the mainland and the hills beyond, willing the appearance of the dawn so that we could get started. Nobody really talked much, there not being much to say, each of us retreating into our own thoughts, a characteristic common to all fighting men I have known as they wait to go into battle. Finally, Vibius nudged me and when I looked up, I saw the sky beginning to lighten and the Legion beginning to stir, whispers passed along alerting all of us that dawn was approaching. Not more than a few moments later, the order was quietly passed for us to stand up and get back into our formations, with the men designated to carry the assault ladders making their way over to the pile of them to grab one then returning to fall back in formation. Once more, I was selected to be one of the first over the wall, although I would not be second but fourth of the first section. For the hundredth time I

210

checked that my sword was ready to slide out of the scabbard easily, then fiddled with the cords that kept my helmet firmly on my head. I tried to ignore the numbness in my extremities brought on by the cold and wet, stamping my feet to try getting some feeling back in them, as were most of the men around me. Straining my eyes, after a few moments I finally made out the outline of the wall in front of us, barely visible but unmistakable.

"Get ready boys," the Pilus Prior whispered to us. "We'll be going in shortly."

Once the time passed we were motioned ahead, doing our best to move as silently as possible. There was one hidden blessing about the rain because it packed the sand of the beach and the area beyond it down so that we could walk on it without sinking down or stumbling, something that might have caused us to make enough noise that our presence was detected, even with the wind. Moving quickly into position a few paces away from the walls of the fortification, I saw that we were partway up a low hill. As we crouched, waiting for the command to move, I noticed that I was no longer cold; in fact, a warm trickle of sweat began moving down my back, mingling with the cold rain soaking my skin. Then there was a blast of a *cornu*, followed immediately by an explosion of sound as we all jumped up, roaring out the signal that death was approaching the Gallaeci. As one man, the Legion began running towards the wall. The light had increased sufficiently that we could see the dark forms of the few men standing on the ramparts, and even above our own cries we heard the shouts of alarm from them as they realized they were under attack. Reaching the wall, I ran to stand behind the ladder group I was assigned to, taking my place behind the men I was assigned to follow over the wall, thankful that I remembered the lessons I learned from the first time I had done this. Once the ladders touched the walls we scrambled up, still yelling at the top of our lungs, and in a matter of moments the parapet was cleared of any enemy. Jumping down into the fort, we swept past the crude shelters made of skins and wooden frames that housed not only the warriors but their women and children, while I could hear the screams and sobs of the women as we cut their men down without any mercy. They were caught completely by surprise; the weather had helped mask our plans and it also contributed to their sense of security, sure that we would not be crazy or stupid enough to brave crossing in such weather. The fight for the fort took less than a third of a watch, although it took longer for us to stop killing anyone and anything in our path. Our Centurions did their best to restore order, but as usual we had our blood up, and the fact that we had been subjected to the cold and rain, coupled with the rough crossing, did not help their cause.

"The more of these bastards you kill, the less slaves there'll be, and the less money for your own purses, you idiots." Pilus Prior Crastinus was repeating this over and over as he trotted around, bashing us with his *vitus* to emphasize his point, but it still took quite some time before the slaughter and rape stopped. The surviving Gallaeci were rounded up and put under guard, where they sat on the ground, watched by a Cohort, the women wailing, the children crying and the men who survived staring at us with undisguised hatred. None of them held any illusions about their fate; they were headed to the slave markets around the Republic, where children would be separated from their parents, husbands from their wives, and families split asunder to feed our insatiable need for slaves. The "lucky" ones would be sent to some household somewhere, and in all likelihood actually live a better life than they had now, although I could understand how they would not see it that way. However, they chose to revolt against Rome, and by doing so, sealed their fate. I was finding that the more I was exposed to this type of misery, the less I was affected by it.

There was now just one island left, north of the fort we had just taken. It was a much larger island and less hilly, so the fortifications on it were more elaborate, with the garrison and people sheltering within its walls in much larger numbers than the first fort. In fact, their works gave every appearance of having been in place for some time, and that the Gallaeci had made even more improvements to the fortifications after their arrival. For example, there was a double wall now instead of a single one, with a defensive ditch in between, sown with a number of obstacles. The outer wall had wooden towers at intervals along it, with sloping roofs and firing slits, making knocking them out difficult, while the inner wall surrounded a low hill that was the dominant feature of the island, and it was within the second wall that all of the defenders and their families were located. The rumor was that there were more than 5,000 warriors, along with another 15,000 people within the fortification, and these numbers did not make us feel any better. Add to that the fact that this was their last bastion and would be the site of their last stand meant that all the signs added up to a very bloody fight indeed. Our casualties during the assault on the first island were extraordinarily light, but we harbored no illusions that we would be that lucky this time. Both Legions still with Caesar would take part in the assault, attacking in two prongs. The 10th would approach from the south, from the general direction of the first island, with the 9th coming from the east, directly across the bay. The news that we would be attacking from the direction of the first island was met with a lot of muttered complaints since it meant that we had a good distance to go. Distance between the two islands was around ten miles, but even cutting at an angle between the two islands before turning north, we would still be in the water for almost two full watches, a prospect that none of us viewed with any enthusiasm. One blessing was that the weather had broken, with clear skies and calm seas; we could only pray to the gods to make sure that it stayed that way. Another difficulty was that we needed more boats, since this was going to be a two Legion assault and one of the original boats had gotten too damaged by the rough water. Although we avoided losing any men, the boat itself had to be scrapped, so one more week would be spent building more boats, during which the weather could change again. Every morning we woke up scanning the skies with a worried eye, hoping that our luck would not run out, also knowing that Caesar was not likely to delay even if it did. After all, we took the first fort in horrible conditions with minimal loss, so why would he delay a second time? So we cut down trees and dragged them back to the beach, not bothering to hide our intentions this time, sawing, hammering and sweating so that after another week, we had a second fleet of flat-bottomed boats. Instead of using Legionaries to row this time, the Gallaeci men captured in the first assault were pressed into service and forced to row us to kill their comrades and kin. Despite myself, I found I had some sympathy for these men; it must be a terrible fate indeed to be forced to help in the destruction of your people.

The day of the assault dawned with much rejoicing and prayers of thanks that the weather dawned sunny, clear and calm. In fact, the surface of the water was barely rippled, looking almost as placid as the surface of a small lake. For reasons known only to Caesar, he had decided not to use the same tactic of a night assault; Calienus guessed that it had something to do with the distance that the 10th was going to have to cover, which made sense to us. Even with clear weather, several miles of water is a long distance, and much could go wrong. The Gallaeci had not helped; at night, they restricted their fires to the lower parts of the fort, not up on the hill, so it was almost impossible to see the lights from any distance. Therefore at dawn we piled aboard the boats, once again cursing our fate and grumbling about how we were not made to spend time on water. Setting out, despite the calm waters I found my stomach rebelling, so that before long I was again standing at the gunwales with some of my other comrades, launching my breakfast into the ocean. Those men with stronger constitutions jeered at us but we were too miserable to take offense. With the island just a black line barely visible on the horizon, we soon grew bored watching it and willing it to grow larger with every stroke, so instead we began our normal routines of gambling, gossiping and complaining. Sitting with my back against the side of the boat, I watched my comrades, and despite the seasickness and apprehension of the coming battle, I felt my heart swell with a kind of pride that comes when one has a sense of truly belonging to something greater than oneself. I smiled as Romulus and Remus bickered about something that had happened months before; Scribonius and Vellusius were playing their own game of dice; Calienus and Rufio were having a contest trying to see who could balance their dagger on the tip of their finger the longest. Vibius had found a spot where he could stretch out and was laying with his face up to the sun, smiling contentedly as he soaked up the warmth and nourishment of the sun's rays. Despite the fact that we were about to throw ourselves into another type of contest, where the stakes were much, much higher, I realized that there was no place on earth that I would rather be than in this boat, with these men. And there is no amount of money that a man can possess that is worth that feeling.

Finally, after what was a little less than a full watch, we got close enough that the signal was given to the 9th to begin their crossing, since they were required to wait for some time before starting. The plan was that we would arrive at the fort at the same time, although we were going to land at the southern end of the island, about a mile away from the fort. In order for this to work, we had to be almost to our landing point before the signal was given to the 9th to proceed. Once more I was assigned to help carry the artillery, except this time I would actually have to lug it across the sand. There was only one problem; there was no sand. Rowing closer to the southern end of the island, we passed by a smaller island that was deserted and had blocked our view of the larger island.

Once past it, I heard one of the men with some experience as a sailor call out in a worried voice, "This isn't good."

The words and tone immediately got us all scrambling to our feet, and we peered ahead. At first, I could not see anything that to

214

my inexperienced eye would cause any concern. There was a strip of white at the base of the island where it met the ocean, and I assumed that it must be the beach that we were to land on. After a few moments, I began to look again, puzzled by something that did not seem right, so I tapped Calienus on the shoulder, pointed and asked, "Sergeant, have you ever seen sand that white before?"

He looked closely, then shook his head. Before he could say anything, the sailor, having heard my question answered for him. "That's because it's not sand, *Gregarius*. That's foam."

"Foam? What exactly does that mean?"

"It means that that's not a beach; it's rocks, and the foam is from the water striking the rocks. There's no way we can land there."

Before we could react, he turned quickly to his assistant to snap some orders, who in turn began giving directions to the men rowing, and for the first time it occurred to me that we were in some danger. Once we cleared the small island, we were less than a half mile from the large one, and in the space between the two land masses, some forces were at work that created a current that was propelling us with alarming speed straight for the rocky shore. In the same moment I recognized that danger, the thought struck me that the men rowing held our fate in their hands; they could exact their revenge by refusing to obey the orders of the men commanding the ship, and let us go dashing onto the rocks. They were chained to their benches, so they would undoubtedly die, but they would at least do so with the satisfaction that they were taking a lot of us with them. We were one of the two lead ships, and if we did not correct our course, there was no reason that the other ships following us would not be led to their destruction as well.

Those next few moments reinforced my loathing of being at sea, at the mercy of forces much greater than ourselves and outside of our control. However, the gods smiled on us in the sense that the Gallaeci, who also held the power of life and death over us, were in love with living as much as we were, because they frantically began reversing our course. Slowly we turned away from the jagged rocks waiting to turn our boats into tinder, managing instead to move up the eastern side of the island. It took us closer to the fort, yet that was another blessing in disguise, at least for me and the others who were supposed to carry the artillery. Finding an area that, while not a sandy beach, was smooth enough that it was deemed to be safe for landing without damaging the boats excessively, we immediately began unloading then moving onto the beach, and as we fell into formation to begin the march to the fort, we could see the boats of the 9th disappearing behind a headland that jutted out to our east.

"We're going to have to hurry if we want to be in place when we're supposed to be," Vibius commented, and I nodded in agreement. It had apparently not taken the 9th nearly the amount of time to cross that they had thought it would, so despite our landing closer to the fort, it was evident that we could not tarry if we wanted this assault to have the coordination that Caesar expected. To that end, the Centurions bawled out the order to begin the march and we immediately set out, with a couple of Centuries sent ahead of us to scout out any possible ambush. The ground was fairly level but was extremely rough, causing a bit of stumbling and a lot of cursing as we moved along, the higher part of the fort clearly visible above a line of trees just ahead. At our approach, we heard shouts and the clash of arms as the advance Centuries ran into something ahead.

"First Cohort, on line!"

The Primus Pilus sounded the order, and the First immediately spread out in a line of Centuries, the sounds of fighting growing in intensity and volume as now the cries of men being struck down was added to the din.

"Advance at the double!"

The First started trotting ahead, with the rest of us following, hearing more than seeing the fighting in the trees. A few moments later, the First slammed into the Gallaeci lying in wait, and in short order the fighting was over. Entering the tree line we saw several dozen dead Gallaeci, with our own dead and wounded interspersed among them. The *medici* that had come with us moved up through our ranks, examining our men, assessing the casualties and administering treatment in less severe cases, or a quick slash across the throat for those who were too severely wounded to survive. No matter how often we saw this happen we could never get used to it, and to a man we always averted our eyes from the unfortunates whose lives were being ended as we walked by.

Exiting the trees, we were some 200 paces away when we saw the first wall, manned now by what looked like a few hundred

216

Gallaeci. Orders were given to assemble the artillery and I moved with the section of men I was working with to help put together the piece. In short order, everything was assembled and made ready to fire but we did not begin a barrage, being under orders to wait for the signal from the 9th, consisting of horns and fire arrows shot into the air. Watching to the right where the 9th was supposed to be, we waited to start while the Gallaeci stood behind their walls, taunting us and shaking their weapons in our direction, telling us in no uncertain terms what they were going to do to us. The fact that we reduced their first fort with such ease did not seem to have any impact on them and we stared across the expanse of ground, silent and grim, as they continued to harangue us. Moving back to my place in formation once I had discharged my duties with the artillery, I stood there with my friends trying to keep from fidgeting as we waited. After a few moments, we finally heard the blasts of the *bucina*, followed by a streak of light as a fire arrow shot into the sky to our right.

"Open fire!"

The command to begin the barrage rang out, and immediately we heard the twang of the torsion arms snapping forward as the missiles hurtled towards the fort, some of them striking the wall while others either fell short or sailed high to land beyond the first wall. While we brought ladders, the plan was to open breaches in the outer wall and save the ladders for the inner wall. However, the first few volleys were a disappointment since it did not seem that the barrage was having the desired effect. There was a lot of dust and as we had seen before, the missiles tore the outer bark off the wooden walls, but that was about all that was happening. After several moments of this, the Primus Pilus signaled a halt to the barrage then called for a conference of the Pili Priores, while we had to endure the jeers and taunts of the Gallaeci who celebrated the lack of success. After conferring, the decision was made to concentrate the fire of the artillery on just two points on the wall, instead of the half-dozen that were originally planned. This was not good news for those of us who were going to be charging in through the gap, since it allowed the Gallaeci to concentrate their forces, but there was no real alternative. Immediately our intentions became clear to them, as in a matter of perhaps a half dozen volleys the two points on the wall started to fail, with huge chunks of wood and splinters flying from every strike. Our scorpions were holding their fire, since they would be more useful in keeping the Gallaeci's heads down as we approached the walls. Then the work was done, two good-sized gaps torn in the walls, just the jagged stumps of the wood protruding from the ground, with enough room for a section to enter the breach abreast. Through the dust we could see the bodies of some of the men who were in the wrong place at the wrong time, yet to this point the casualties had been minimal, on both sides. That was about to change.

The *cornicen* sounded the advance, this time the Fifth and Eighth Cohorts being selected to be the first into the breach, another example of how the dirty end of the stick is grasped by all of us at one time or another. Second Cohort was consigned to watch as the others began the advance, the scorpions opening fire once the Cohorts were within range of the Gallaeci bows and slings. Despite the barrage, we saw gaps open in the Centuries, quickly filled by other Legionaries moving up to take the spot of the fallen man, their bodies left behind in the wake of the advancing Cohorts. Missiles issued from the wall in a thick flurry, as it appeared that almost all of the men on the wall carried some sort of sling or bow. Our men started to fall more frequently, some of them with more than one shaft protruding from their bodies, obviously making some sort of mistake in exposing themselves, or even worse, one of their comrades made the error and they had to pay for it. Ignoring the punishment, the Cohorts moved forward, the scorpions continuing their suppressive fire, making me wonder how much worse it would be for us if they had not been there at all. By the time the assaulting Cohorts were within 50 paces of the breaches, it appeared that they had lost more than a third of their numbers, the ground behind them now littered with our dead and wounded. On some unseen signal, the Gallaeci launched one last massive volley, and at that range it was impossible for any missile to miss its mark, while in fact the arrows had enough velocity at that range to pass through one man's body to penetrate the man behind him. It looked like an invisible hand swept through the ranks of the Fifth and Eighth, and despite ourselves, we let out a collective gasp of shock and grief.

"They're getting slaughtered," I muttered, without thinking the words came out.

"Shut your mouth, Pullus."

This came from Optio Rufio, who looked at me as if he wanted to strike me down for uttering the words that I was sure all of us was thinking. Knowing better than to protest when an officer had that look on his face, I bit my tongue, bitterly cursing him in my mind instead. Both the Fifth and Eighth came to a shuddering stop, their men trying to regain some semblance of order, stepping over the bodies of their friends and comrades to fill the gaps made by their loss. For a sickening moment, they both looked like they could go no further, except in doing so that essentially spelled their doom because they would be picked apart. Even worse than standing there was the option of retreating; they would be even more vulnerable trying to back up while tripping over all the bodies lying between them and safety. As brutal as it was, their only chance for survival was to move forward.

"Second Cohort, prepare to advance!"

This caught us all by surprise, especially since we had not been selected to be in the second wave.

"Boys, I know we're not slated to go next, but we can't let our brothers take that kind of beating. We're going to double time over there, stop when I give the signal to redress the lines and catch our breath, then we're going to show those *cunni* what happens when you mess with the 10th!"

I honestly do not know if our hearts were in the cheer that we raised with those words, or we were sufficiently conditioned to know when it was expected of us, but we let out a cheer nonetheless.

"*Procedite Ite Aciem, Move!*"

Beginning the advance, the sudden movement drew the stares of the other Cohorts, along with a thankful wave from the men of the Cohort who were supposed to be next. The Primus Pilus, along with the Tribune assigned to "command" the Legion that day came sprinting over to the Pilus Prior, who stepped to the side but ordered us to continue advancing. By virtue of my place on the outside of the column, I could hear the heated exchange between the Centurions and I worried that we were witnessing the end of the Pilus Prior's career. Although we still hated him in some ways, our regard and affection for him had grown strong enough to outweigh any residual negative feelings that lingered from our training. As hard as he was on us, the Second had already garnered a reputation as being the best Cohort in the Legion, a fact that looking back, now that I have been in his shoes, I am sure he was counting on saving him. That and his utmost confidence in us that we would be victorious and save what was turning into a disaster. As I passed by, I caught the last of their words.

"All I can say is that this better work, Crastinus, or you know what's going to happen."

The Primus Pilus' words were menacing enough, but his tone emphasized the seriousness of the situation.

"It'll work," the Pilus Prior responded simply.

"But what about the second wall? Your Cohort was supposed to assault the second wall, not the first. Who's supposed to do it now?"

"We'll do both," Crastinus answered calmly, before saluting and trotting past me to rejoin the head of the formation.

My heart sank; we were going to have to clear both the breach and then scale the wall?

I was about to say something to Scribonius, but before I could, he muttered bitterly, "I heard the bastard. Well, Titus, it was nice knowing you."

Immediately after the Pilus Prior resumed his position, the command to begin the advance double time was given and we broke into a trot, the sound of our gear clanking and bouncing about mixing with the tramp of our hobnailed boots slapping the ground. Up ahead we saw that the Fifth and the Eighth had entered the breach, with it looking like the Fifth was having a rougher go than the Eighth, so the Pilus Prior veered us in that direction. Behind us I heard a roar, so I chanced a look back to see that another Cohort was starting the advance as well. I wondered briefly if it were the Cohort originally slated to support the Fifth, and if so whether or not their Centurion possessed the presence of mind to move to the other breach. If not, then it was going to be a major mess as our two Cohorts tried to jam ourselves into one hole that already had the remnants of a Cohort in there.

Crossing the ground swiftly, just before we got to the point where the first bodies of our fallen were laying, the Pilus Prior halted us to dress the lines. We were going in as a column of Centuries, so that once again being the First Century had its disadvantages. Nevertheless, I cheered myself with the thought that

220

at least I was in the rear rank, the comfort of which lasted just a few more heartbeats before I heard my name called.

"Pullus, get your fat ass up here!"

Moving out of my spot, I trotted up while the Pilus Prior called the names of the other large men of the Century, where he arranged us at the front, intent on using our bigger bodies to increase the impact when we went smashing through the breach. Up ahead we could see the Fifth fighting for its life, having made a small pocket just inside the first wall, where they were surrounded by what looked like several times their numbers, and even in the short time we watched we saw our men falling to the ground. Some of them got up again, but others just lay there or tried to crawl away. Once we were set, we were given the command to start out again, and for perhaps the first time in my life I cursed the fact that I had been born bigger and stronger than most everyone else. I was on the front rank, on the outside right, with the Pilus Prior running next to me as we advanced. One tiny blessing was that the Gallaeci had stopped with the bows and slings and were now down on the ground fighting it out with the Fifth and the Eighth. The closer we got, the more treacherous the footing as we had to pick our way over the bodies of our comrades, most of whom were still alive and trying to continue crawling away from the fighting. When a man is seriously wounded, it seems to be the overriding urge to move however one can away from the fighting that served to hurt them, and we had to call out to the men to lie still as we pounded around and over them, trying to leap their writhing bodies. We were not always successful; behind me I could hear a scream, followed by a curse as someone stepped on one of the wounded, yet we had no time to stop and help. With the distance rapidly closing to the breach, we could clearly see the faces of the Gallaeci facing us as they looked over the shoulders of the Fifth and saw us coming. Once again, the Pilus Prior knew how to maximize our advantage; I could see the eyes of the enemy widen in shock and terror, seeing what to them must have looked like giants from the underworld come to seek their deaths.

"Kill 'em all, boys!"

The Pilus Prior shouted, and when I glanced over I saw him grin, his lips pulled back over his teeth and his eyes shining with bloodlust as he circled his sword in the air just before dropping it down to point at the Gallaeci.

"Porro!"

This time our roar was wholehearted and I was sure that the gods in the heavens and down below sat up to take notice. Dis was going to have his hands full, I thought as I went smashing into the breach, shouting at the men of the Fifth that the Second was here to save them.

Hearing our cries, the men of the Fifth engaged with the enemy gave the last of their energy to bash the Gallaeci backwards before stepping aside to let us come charging through their lines. Even as we went hurtling past, I glimpsed the fatigue and relief on the faces of the Fifth before I barreled into a warrior, knocking him head over heels. Flying backwards, he struck two other Gallaeci, who in turn fell down in a heap and before any of them could recover, I stepped up to make three quick thrusts, ending each of them. Our Century came pouring into the breach and in the space of a few heartbeats what was a slight bulge no more than a few feet across by a few feet deep now expanded out until our whole Century was inside the first wall. Spreading outwards along the base of the first wall, we kept it to either our left or right as we moved parallel to it, rapidly expanding our position in order to allow the other Centuries to come piling in. The men of the Fifth withdrew, giving us room to add more men, and within moments the first wall was effectively taken in our sector. Pausing a moment to assess the situation, a quick inventory was taken by the Pilus Prior. There were a couple of wounded in our Century, yet no deaths, a great start but it was not over by a long shot because we still had to cross the open ground to the second wall. Some of the more alert of the Gallaeci arrayed further down the wall saw us bursting through and realized that they were in real danger of being cut off, so they began streaming off the first wall, heading back to the second where more of their comrades waited. As we watched, ladders made of both wood and rope were dropped over the side to allow the defenders on the first wall to climb to safety, and the Pilus Prior dispatched two Centuries to hurry over to try to cut them off, but they were driven back by heavy fire from the slingers and bowmen on the second wall. Despite making a good start, we were about to be exposed to another danger; as long as there was a fight going on for the first wall, the missile troops on the second wall dared not fire for fear of hitting their own men, but once we killed or drove off those defenders, the way was clear now for them to open fire.

"Testudo by Centuries!"

222

Despite moving quickly, some of us fell before we could get into the proper formation. Meanwhile, the Pilus Prior of the Cohort immediately behind us did indeed have the presence of mind to shift his attack to the second breach, and shortly after we were finished they had secured that one as well. Now we had to cross the open ground, maneuvering across under fire, while also negotiating a ditch laced with sharpened stakes and caltrops, nasty devices that consist of two spikes twisted around each other so that no matter how you throw them to the ground, there is a sharpened point sticking up. And we had to do it under fire, while carrying ladders. In other words, a right bastard of a job.

"There's no use just standing here giving them targets to hit," the Pilus Prior said this in a manner that suggested he was talking to himself more than he was to us, while we huddled underneath our shields, waiting for the word to advance.

By this point, I was back in my normal spot in the formation, as were the other large men, our Century moving a way out from the wall to allow for the others of our Cohort to form up inside the wall.

"Pilus Prior," this was the Optio's voice, and we strained to hear what he had to say over the din of the lead missiles from the slings skipping off our shields. "Did you notice anything strange about when those bastards left the first wall?"

"What do you mean, Optio? Spit it out man, we don't have time for riddles."

"What I mean is that they had to negotiate the ditch and obstacles just like we will, right? But did you see how quickly they scampered across? It was almost as if........."

Cutting him off, Pilus Prior Crastinus finished excitedly, "As if they had a path across the ground that allowed them to move like the obstacles weren't there in the first place."

The pride in the Optio's voice was clear for all of us to hear. "Exactly. There has to be a way across where we won't have to worry about that damn ditch. It's further down that way."

And despite our situation, we grinned at each other. We all liked Rufio a great deal, making any success of his good news for us as well as far as we were concerned. The command was given and

223

we began walking slowly, still in *testudo*, along the inside of the first wall. Both the Optio and Pilus Prior, using the shields picked up from fallen men to protect them, as is the habit of the officers in battle, searched for the signs of the path across. It soon became clear to the Gallaeci what we were up to, so they began concentrating their fire on our officers, who were then forced to integrate with our formation for better protection, making finding the path even more difficult. Further compounding the difficulty was the fact that we were also carrying the ladders inside the *testudo*, which is a trick I can promise you. There was a steady hail of missiles by now, creating such a racket that even as we shouted at each other, it was almost impossible to hear. It was only because the years of drilling made his lungs as powerful as leather bellows that we heard the Pilus Prior cry out in triumph when he found the path, marked by a series of stakes. If the Gallaeci had been smart, they would have pulled them up as they crossed over, but I gave a promise to Fortuna that I would make a sacrifice in thanks that they had not. The Pilus Prior sent Rufio to tell the other Cohort at the second breach what we found and what to look for, while we turned to head across the ground towards the second wall. Despite the hail of fire, we all had learned our lessons well about not giving into the temptation of taking a peek by shifting our shield even an inch, so we did not lose anyone crossing the ditch. Despite the stakes, we still had to be careful, the path being barely wide enough to accommodate the width of our Century; I grazed several of the stakes with my hip as we passed them. Climbing out of the ditch with our *testudo* still intact, within another couple of moments we made it directly underneath the second wall. Now it was our turn to inflict some punishment, as some of us waited with our javelins for one of the Gallaeci to take a chance of leaning out over the wall to try hitting us with a sling or arrow. It only took a few of them getting a javelin through the face to discourage the rest sufficiently that we could break out of the *testudo* and begin the process of placing the ladders while some of our comrades covered us with javelins. Looking back over my shoulder, I saw a line of Centuries, all in *testudo*, following the exact path we had taken, with what looked like the boys of the Sixth Century immediately behind us just climbing out of the ditch. They would move further down along the wall, and we would wait while the ladders were in place at several points before we all went up them at the same time. This gave us a bit of a chance to regain our breath, which we took advantage of, pulling out our canteens and sucking down as much water as we could, knowing that it would be some time before we could do so again.

224

It took almost a sixth part of a watch for all of the Centuries of both Cohorts to get across the ditch and into place for the assault up the wall. The remaining Cohorts had made it to the first wall and were sheltered just on the other side, safe from the missiles of the men on the second wall. One disadvantage of their position was that the supporting Cohorts could not see us up against the second wall, and therefore would have to rely on the sounds of the horns to know when it was time for them to come across to make their own ascent once we had cleared the wall. While we waited, we could hear the sounds of battle going on over where the 9th was assaulting, although it was impossible to tell what was happening exactly or how it was going for them.

"They're probably fouling it up," Vibius sneered with the disdain one Legionary holds for a Legion not his own. "You know those *cunni* couldn't find their ass with both hands."

I wholeheartedly agreed with him, as did the others.

"Get ready boys," the Pilus Prior called out to us as he returned from the other Centuries. What makes the job of the senior Centurion of a Cohort so challenging is that he not only has to run his own Century, but he has to ensure that the others are doing what they are supposed to be doing as well, requiring him to be in several places at once, a feat that Crastinus somehow always managed to pull off with what appeared to be a minimum of effort. Every one of us swore that he had eyes in the back of his head and hearing so sensitive that he could hear a gnat fart, and as I was to learn later in order for a Centurion to be good at his job, it is essential that this be as close to the truth as possible. For once I was not going to be one of the first over; instead I would be bracing the ladder, and although I was thankful that I was given a relatively easy duty, I would be lying if I said that I was not also slightly hurt. Until that moment I had not realized it, but I had gotten accustomed to being one of the first into any breach or up a wall, and in the back of my mind, I could not help wondering if I had done something to make the Pilus Prior question my ability, or even worse, my courage. However, as I was about to find out, there was another reason he made the dispositions in this manner.

After telling me I was going to brace the ladder, he turned and pointed his *vitus* directly at Didius and barked, "You there, Achilles," he gave an emphasis to the nickname that did not imply that it was a compliment. "We're going to see what you're made of and if you can live up to the name. You're going up first."

Didius turned as white as I had ever seen him, and before he caught himself started to choke out a protest before stopping immediately when he saw the expression of not just the Pilus Prior, but of all of us. Gulping, he merely nodded and turned away so that his face did not betray his emotions. We all eyed each other, not having to say a word. The horns sounded, the ladders went up, and with another roar the men of the Second Cohort began the climb. Sitting with my back to the wall, I gripped the sides of the ladder to make sure that nobody stepped on my hands, and in this position, I got a front row seat to see Didius mount the ladder. I wish I could say that I felt some sort of pity for him, but I did not; instead, I experienced a great sense of satisfaction seeing the sheer terror on his upturned face as he climbed, his shaky legs nevertheless propelling him upwards. I very clearly felt the tremors of his body as he ascended, and it was with grim pleasure that I thought, now we're going to see how much is talk and how much is deed.

Immediately following him was Rufio, who gave me a quick grin as he followed Didius up and he called out to me, "I think he *cac*ed himself. At least that's what it smells like."

I laughed, as did the others who heard him, though if Didius heard he was too terrified to give one of his normal surly retorts. Scribonius went up behind Rufio and I heard the first clash of metal, followed by a cry as Didius got to the top. Immediately, the progress up the ladder stopped and I frowned in concern, exchanging a look with Vellusius who had just stepped onto the first rung. This was not good; the key to storming a wall is to get as many men on the parapet as quickly as possible, and I wondered if this had happened when I went up the ladder the first time. Being fair, I knew that time was impossible to judge time in moments like this, so it may very well have been the same when I did it, yet it did not seem that way, and judging from the concerned looks on the others' faces I had to believe that there was a problem.

"Achilles, you lazy bastard," Rufio called, "make us some room up there."

Over the clanging of metal, I heard Didius reply desperately, "I'm trying, damn you!"

226

"Well, don't try you stupid bastard, do it!"

Finally, Rufio gave an exasperated growl and forced his way up the ladder, his voice adding to the melee on the wall. In a few heartbeats, whatever had been holding everyone up was taken care of, because the flow of men began again, moving quickly this time. Finally, I was the last one left and I pulled myself to my feet, giving the job of bracing the ladder to the designated man from the Century behind us and followed everyone else up.

The sight that met my eyes was one of chaos, even more than normal in an assault like this, with the Gallaeci flowing down the hill from the town like ants, headed towards the walls, where the men of the First Century were battling the warriors who were still fanatically fighting on the parapet. They were resisting with the desperate courage of men who knew that not only were they the last line of defense protecting their families, they were the last gasps of a rebellion, and defeat would mean the destruction of their people. Caesar's treatment of the Lusitani that he defeated was no secret by this point, and it was this knowledge that kept them fighting long after they should have been exhausted. My heart sank when I saw a number of Roman bodies littering the parapet, and I could only hope that none of them were my tentmates; it was bad enough that they were from my Century. Looking for a place to stick in and help, I saw a small knot of Gallaeci pressing hard against Calienus and Atilius, both of them with their backs to the wall, frantically parrying the blows of the Gallaeci warriors. With a shout, I rushed over to help them, catching the Gallaeci by surprise. One of them turned his attention to me, snapping something to the others, obviously an order to keep up their assault on my two friends while he would handle me. Giving him a savage grin at this sign of his hubris, I beckoned him to come at me. He had a short sword, similar to those that we used and he wielded it with some skill, but in a moment I had his measure; he was too aggressive and prone to over-commit and expose himself. Feigning a retreat after one spirited attack on his part, it gave him the encouragement to press me, which is exactly what I wanted. Once again he made a thrust and overextended himself, so that for a brief instant his throat was exposed because his arm was too far forward. It was enough, and I relished the look of shock in his eyes as my blade punched through, coming out the back of his skull, then twisted the blade to free it, kicking him out of the way as I did so. His comrades had too much faith in his ability because their attention was still turned totally towards Calienus and Atilius, so I dispatched two of them with

227

quick thrusts to the back before the other three realized what was happening. Now they were caught between the proverbial rock and the hard place, and in an instant they were all finished.

"Thanks Pullus," Calienus gasped and I grinned, giving a quick salute before we turned our attention to other targets. Working together, we moved along the wall, trying to link up with the other Century further down, squeezing the Gallaeci into a smaller and smaller space as we did so, giving them less room to work while increasing our chances of hitting someone as they became more densely packed. Things were beginning to swing in our favor and the Gallaeci knew it, prompting some of them to jump off the parapet to retreat up the hill to form another line of defense. Some of our men kept their heads about them and on seeing the Gallaeci warriors jumping down, snatched up their javelins, flinging them into the backs of some of the retreating warriors. As the situation on the parapet began to stabilize, I began looking around for Vibius. When I saw him, a cry of fear escaped my lips before I could stop it.

Vibius was lying on the parapet, his lower body covered in blood as he lay motionless among other bodies, both Roman and Gallaeci. Running to him, I fell to my knees beside him. He was facedown and as I reached for him to turn him over, I saw my hands trembling; I had never been so afraid in all my life about what I might find. Steeling myself, I gently turned him over, a gasp of relief exploding from me as I saw his eyes flutter. He looked up, his eyes fuzzy and unfocused before they finally rested on my face. Seeing that he recognized me, I took this to be a good sign.

"Wha....what happened? Where am I, Titus?"

"You've been wounded," I replied in what I hoped was a comforting tone, but I had my doubts when I saw his eyes widen in alarm. Immediately his hands began to roam over his body, and I grabbed them, saying as gently as I could, "Don't do that. Let me see. I'm sure it's nothing."

I began by examining his lower torso, his tunic caked with blood underneath his armor, not bothering to hide my relief when I determined that he did not have any kind of belly wound. I found the wound when I examined lower down, a huge gash in his thigh, both in front and in back, a sign that it had been a sword thrust that had gone all the way through. The other good news was that the blade had not cut a major blood vessel, since if it had he would have been dead by the time I found him. Telling him the news, I watched his eyes flutter in relief.

"Let me go get a *medici*," I told him, but before I left, I tore off a piece of his tunic to bind the wound, which was still oozing blood, although it was slowing down. I just hoped it was not because he had run out of blood, but he was still conscious, which I took to be a good sign. Jumping up, I looked over the wall to see if the *medici* had made their way this far along yet, then when I spotted one I called out to him. He heard me and promised to come up as soon as he finished with the man he was working on. Despite the fight raging further down the parapet, I sat down with Vibius to wait for the *medici* to arrive and talked to him, staying as cheerful as I could, teasing him that he was going to get out of all the duties for a while, yet I saw he was still worried.

"Vibius, don't worry, you're not going to die. I've seen enough wounds to know this isn't fatal."

"That's not what I'm worried about, Titus," he said quietly. "I'm worried that it won't heal properly and I'll be dismissed from the Legion."

I had not even thought of this, and just the mention of it sent me into a near panic, since I could no more imagine being in the army without Vibius than I could grow wings and flying. Refusing to listen to him, I told him firmly that this was nonsense, and if he continued thinking like this, I was going to give him a good thrashing. After he recovered, of course, I amended hastily, and I think to the relief of both of us the *medici* arrived so I left Vibius with him to continue fighting, promising that I would come see him as soon as I could. Turning back to the sounds of battle, I looked for our Century before hurrying off to join them, leaving Vibius behind for the first time since we had been friends.

Fighting continued to rage, the accursed Gallaeci refusing to recognize the inevitable, and the battle soon degenerated into a series of smaller, more private fights involving at the most dozens of men on both sides. All sense of tactics and cohesion were gone as the situation reduced itself to its simplest denominator, that of men trying to kill each other for reasons that they could no more fathom at this point than they could express them. Finding the Pilus Prior, he was surrounded by a knot of men from my Century, so I hurried over to the group.

Catching sight of me, he called out, "It's about time Pullus. Get over there," he pointed to a spot where some of our men were being hard pressed by a larger group of Gallaeci, "and sort that out."

Sketching a salute I ran over, jumping into a wild melee that resembled a tavern brawl more than any type of set battle. Men were simply bashing each other with both shield and sword, not even bothering to look for an opening or in any other way using their heads, merely trying to batter their opponents into submission. Resolving that I was going to be more logical about this, I waited as I watched two combatants who appeared to be evenly matched, looking for an opening where I could provide some help. After exchanging a series of blows, both the men stepped away from each other, panting from the exertion, their eyes only on each other. Seeing my chance, I stepped in quickly to dispatch the Gallaeci with a quick thrust. The Roman, I believe it was a man named Numerius from our Century, yelled at me in protest.

"I almost had him Pullus, you didn't have to do that."

I looked at him as if he had gone insane; this was not a contest or a training exercise, a point I reminded him of, not mollifying him in the slightest. "Next time, you worry about making your own kill and not wait until I soften someone up so you can just step in and take the glory," he insisted.

I did not know how to respond, just looking at him with my mouth agape. Shaking my head, I turned my attention back to the fight, wondering if I would find someone more appreciative of my help.

Our effort to clear the second wall and move away from it took most of the day. First we would clear a section, with the Gallaeci falling back into the relative safety of the lean-tos and shacks arrayed on the slopes of the hill, but then they would reorganize and rally before we could move out from the wall. They would come rushing back, and more than once we found ourselves with our backs literally to the second wall, fighting desperately to maintain our formation and not get slaughtered piecemeal trying to claw our way back up to the parapet. After a couple of setbacks like this, we kept a reserve force standing on the parapet who would first fling whatever javelins they found to help relieve the pressure, then use the discarded longer spears that the Gallaeci favored, stabbing down at the enemy over our heads as we fought. In this manner we never had to face the prospect of trying to withdraw back over the wall, although it was a close-run thing. During one particularly vicious encounter, I was slashed down my right arm just as I was parrying a thrust from a spear, an opportunistic Gallaeci next to the man I was fighting lashing out with a short blade, scoring my arm from the elbow to just an inch or two above my wrist. While the cut was not particularly deep, it felt like someone poured liquid fire in a line down my arm; even now as I am dictating this I can see the scar clearly, although it has turned white with age. Despite myself I let out a yelp of pain, then gritted my teeth and took savage delight in gutting the man who cut me, laughing brutally into his face as he dropped to his knees, his eyes on me as he died. The blood from the wound ran freely for some time before it clotted; a wave of dizziness struck me after a few moments and I was sure that I was going to collapse on the ground, at the worst possible time. Somehow I found the reserves needed to maintain my footing, once again feeling the rage start to flow through me, giving me a burst of energy. Snarling like a wild animal, I bashed an older warrior with the boss of my shield, shoving him back to give me room to move forward while thrusting and slashing at any patch of bare flesh that I saw. The men around me began roaring their own war cries, feeding off the renewed energy as our group began pushing back away from the wall, moving steadily forward. Other smaller groups saw us and fought their way to us so that after several moments of non-stop fighting, we had gathered perhaps half the Cohort. The Pilus Prior saw our group and made his way to us, using us as a rallying point, and while he had the horns sound the command to form on the standard of our Cohort, I took the time to try binding my wound, taking the neckerchief we wore to keep our armor from chafing our necks off a dead Legionary, Plautius as it turned out, then with some help tied it around my arm. It was a bit restricting, though I was fairly confident that once we started fighting again I would not notice, which is what happened. Meanwhile, the 9th had made their way to a point where they had begun firing the shelters and other combustibles, and the wind, picking up in the day as it is prone to do in that part of the world, had begun to whip its way up the hill, sending a pall of smoke in our direction that was irritating yet not thick enough to obscure our vision. The Gallaeci, seeing us rally and form up, gave their own commands so that a large number of their warriors clustered together, ready to oppose our progress up the hill.

For however many times only the gods knew by this point, the Pilus Prior waved his sword in the air in a circle, before dropping it down and pointing at the men opposite us, bellowing, "Kill those bastards!"

Again, we responded with a roar, rushing forward. Finally, however, we could sense that this was the final push; the last fort, the last bunch of the enemy, the last battle of the campaign before we could rest. For some of us who dreamed of such things, it was also the last chance for glory, meaning that I was at the head of the Second Cohort as we smashed into our enemy.

Once it was all over, it was easily our hardest and bloodiest battle to date, which given the circumstances, was fitting. The Gallaeci fought like lions, and at some point in the final battle to finish off a last pocket of resistance, I found myself feeling very sad that we had to slaughter such worthy opponents as these. It is a feeling that I have had several times since. In fact, there have been times where I found I have more regard for the men I was killing than some of the men I was fighting with, and I know that I am not alone. On that day, we destroyed the Lucenses branch of the Gallaeci as a fighting force, or at least we thought we did, though they have proven to be a most resilient enemy. In the space of 30 years, they regained enough strength to cause the Imperator Augustus troubles that found the Legions marching once again over terrain that I had as a teenager. However, at the time we marched under the command of his adoptive father, we pacified the province, bringing the Lusitani and the Gallaeci to heel and ending the revolt. When all was said and done, the 10th Legion lost more than 200 men killed, with an equal number wounded severely enough to be dismissed from the Legion. In our Century, out of the original 91 men that made it through the final training and marched out of the camp in Scallabis, there were 74 left on active service; 12 men had been killed outright, including Optio Vinicius, and four had to be sent home. None of them were my tentmates, although five of us had been wounded to one degree or another, myself suffering two wounds, though neither of them were serious enough to see me on the sick and injured list. Vibius took a month to recover, and was left with a slight limp that showed up on cold days or at the end of a hard day's marching, but otherwise did not slow him down. The day after we took the last Gallaeci fort, the leaders of the resistance still alive came to camp to surrender to Caesar, throwing themselves on his mercy, at a ceremony where we were paraded to watch the spectacle, which we enjoyed immensely. There are few things more satisfying than seeing an enemy humbled before the eagles of the Legions, and it was an event that never diminished in pleasure for

232

me over the years, except when they were fellow Romans. We, the 9th and 10th, marched back south, to be met by the 7th, who had reduced Portus Cale and pacified the area, before continuing our movement until we met the 8th, still guarding their area of Lusitania for the weeks we were pursuing the end of the rebellion. It was in late September that we marched into Scallabis, to be met by adoring crowds, our standards wreathed in the traditional garlands that denote victorious Legions, with Caesar leading the procession. The 10th was given the place of honor on the march into the city, beginning a long relationship with Caesar as his favorite and most reliable Legion, a fact which we were quick to rub in the faces of the other Legions and was the source of many a brawl in the inns and wine shops of the places we were quartered through the years. We spent a month in Scallabis as the wounded men recovered, before marching to Corduba.

Word shot through the army like lightning that Caesar was being awarded a triumph in Rome, and the rumor was that he would be taking the entire army with him to enter the city. Almost as quickly, the word changed, as it is wont to do in an army, although this rumor had the added weight of turning out to be true, at least partially. We were then told that, rather than taking the army, Caesar would be taking the more senior Legions, meaning the 7th, 8th and 9th, leaving the 10th behind. Supposedly the idea was that, over the next years we of the 10th would have our chances to celebrate triumphs, but I can tell you that it did not set well with us. The day before Caesar and the other Legions left for the march to Rome, near the end of October, we were paraded for one final formation in front of the Praetor, where awards for individual bravery were handed out. It was on this occasion that I won my first decoration, a set of phalarae for my actions on the hill when we had been surrounded.

My only warning was the night before, when the Pilus Prior bashed me with his *vitus* because he judged the coat of varnish on my harness was lacking, and he asked, "What if by some miracle you happened to be chosen to be decorated, eh Pullus? Would you really embarrass the Cohort and the Legion with that sorry job?"

"No, Pilus Prior."

And I applied another coat of varnish to my harness, although I was sure that when I was finished it looked exactly the same as when I started.

233

That formation the next day was a glorious affair, one of the reasons Vibius and I joined the army. All four Legions, arrayed in formation in dress uniforms with the horsehair plumes, those of the army previously earning decorations wearing them, with the Centurions standing in front of their Centuries. The weather was glorious and I wished that my sisters and Gaia and Phocas were here to see what was happening, but I had no time to send word to them. I was one of about 30 men from the 10th Legion to be decorated, including two other men from my Century, Rufio being one of them. Two men were awarded the *corona civicus* for saving fellow Romans from certain death, and while their awards are the simplest, it is the most prized. The award itself is nothing more than grass plaited together to form a simple crown, yet what it represents is the highest honor one individual Roman can win. Pilus Prior Crastinus was awarded the *corona murales* for being the first over the wall in the assault on the first town, his third such award. Although he could have left it to one of the Tribunes in command of the Legion that day, Caesar chose to personally award all the decorations, despite it taking more than a full watch for all of the Legions. Even though he must have talked to more than a hundred men being decorated, he still remembered most of their names, including mine.

"*Gregarius* Pullus, I'm happy to see that you survived your first campaign. From what I heard, that's an exceeding accomplishment, given your habit of always being in the front."

I did not think it appropriate to mention that most of the time I had been at the front, I was ordered there by the Pilus Prior; there are some things that generals do not need to know. Instead, I felt the heat rise to my face and all I could manage was a mumbled thanks, which he was gracious enough to ignore. Despite being at *intente*, I found my eyes moving down to the silver disks that make up the phalarae, each of them emblazoned with a symbol of the Legion, in this case the bull. By the end of my career, the phalarae would bear the likeness of Octavian and his wife, or of Caesar, but at the beginning of my time under the standard it used the symbol that was identified with the Legion that one served with when winning it. At the same time as the individual awards were given, decorations were given to individual Legions and Cohorts for valor of special significance. These awards are discs like the individual phalarae, but they have no special engraving and are larger than the individual awards, and are attached to the Signifer of the Cohort. Second Cohort was awarded two of these decorations, more than the other Cohorts, each of whom received one, a fact that only served to fuel the rivalry and resentment of the other Cohorts, which we did nothing to lessen in any way. The final blessing we received from Caesar came in his closing remarks to the army, where he singled out the 10th for special praise, saying that if he ever had need of a Legion in the future, we would be the first to be called. There is no way to describe the effect of these words among us and I think that day, perhaps more than any of his subsequent actions, Caesar won the loyalty and affection of the 10th Legion, something he would use to the fullest in later days.

The next morning, Caesar left for Rome, followed by the Legions he had selected to march in his Triumph in Rome, who would march at a much slower pace than Caesar did. As fast as Caesar moved with an army, he was even faster when traveling on his own, with only his personal entourage, lictors and bodyguard. He had made it to Corduba from Rome in 24 days, and there was no reason to believe that he would move any slower on the way back. The other three Legions marched off with him, and while we still held some resentment, it turned out that they marched a long way for nothing. Once Caesar arrived in Rome, he was faced with a choice of entering the city in triumph at the cost of running for Consul, the custom being that no general under arms could run for the Consulship. Supposedly the idea behind this was that the voters would be unduly influenced by the presence of armed troops. Therefore, the 7th, 8th and 9th ended up being sent to winter at Aquileia without ever setting foot in Rome, a fact that pleased us to no end. The rest of us were given orders that now that Hispania was pacified, we would be marching east to what would become not only our winter quarters, but our home base for the next two years, Narbo Martius. None of this was known to us at the time; all we knew was that we would be spending the winter somewhere else. Before we left we were allowed a week of leave, staggered over the next month, and so it was around the Ides of November that Vibius and I found ourselves making our way home, a trip that for at least one of us was something to rejoice about, since Vibius was going to see Juno. So was I, but that was more painful than pleasurable; yet, I was looking forward to seeing her as much as Vibius despite the pain.

We came swaggering into Astigi, wearing our full dress uniform, minus our shields and javelins of course, but wearing both of our blades. I took great care to polish the phalarae to a high sheen and truth be known, I was looking forward to showing off to Juno, letting her see for herself who the better man was. Almost as soon as those types of thoughts crossed my mind though, I would feel ashamed, yet at the same time I seemed unable to control my mind from going in that direction. Both of us carried our personal items in our pack slung from our *furca*, loaded with souvenirs and some of the more interesting booty that we had earned in this campaign. Vibius was particularly anxious to give Juno a rather exquisite gold necklace, inlaid with enamel and semi-precious stones, including topaz that Vibius swore would match her eyes. I was dubious; I thought her eyes were more blue than green. However, I was smart enough to know that arguing the point with Vibius might give him an indication that I was paying attention to the color of Juno's eyes, and nothing good could come of that, so I held my peace. For my own part, I brought a couple of bracelets for my sisters, a brooch for Gaia and a gold armband carved with an intricate pattern of leaves and such for Phocas. For Lucius, I brought nothing but myself and my scorn, and the determination that I was going to rub in his face the success I had made of myself, still some months short of my seventeenth birthday. I will say that, even after all these years, the feeling we both got when we walked into Astigi's forum, all eyes suddenly upon these two bronzed and hardened warriors, is a memory that I still savor. Particularly since some of the first people we ran into were our old nemeses Marcus and Aulus, who still spent their days skulking around the town, picking on people weaker than they were. These were the two boys who I once caught dumping Vibius headfirst into a bucket of *cac* that some citizen had neglected to dump out, surrounded by a small group of other boys who they had intimidated and awed into following them about. Using my size and strength, I thrashed Marcus and couple of other boys, while Vibius almost killed Aulus with a rock, and there had been bad blood between them and Vibius and I ever since. Neither of them ever adopted a trade; at least, that is what we were told later by Juno, and yet they always seemed to have enough money to keep them well plied with cheap wine and in the favor of the few whores who lived in Astigi. What I always found strange was that they still managed to attract a small crowd of toadies and minions, weaklings who sought the protection and approval of Marcus and Aulus by being as vicious as they could get away with. Vibius and I stopped to talk with the woman who we had once bought our weekly meat pies from, basking in her adoration and the admiring glances of all the females in the area, not minding that most of them were old enough to be our mothers. As we were chatting I caught sight of the two, standing off to the side, surrounded by their pack, and it was their bad luck that I happened to look up when Marcus was pointing

236

at us and saying something that the others thought to be the funniest thing they had ever heard. Our eyes locked, and I saw the color drain from Marcus' face. That should have been enough for me, but it was not.

I nudged Vibius and when he looked over, I nodded in their direction and said quietly, "Apparently there's something about us that amuses our old friends. I think we should go over to say hello and find out what's so funny. I'm always in the mood for a laugh, aren't you Vibius?"

He grinned at me, and replied cheerfully, "Absolutely! Excuse us ladies, we need to go catch up with some old friends."

As he turned to join me, I saw the looks of alarm on the faces of the women we were talking to and I thought to placate them. "Don't worry, ladies. They're old friends of ours. We just want to catch up."

"Don't take me for an idiot Titus Pullus," sniffed the meat pie vendor, "I know exactly what kind of 'friends' you are with those two, though I can't say that if you killed them anyone here would shed a tear. I just don't need our place of business being torn to shreds, that's all."

Giving her a look of complete innocence, I made my eyes as wide as I could, not fooling her a bit. Walking casually over to the group, none of them seemed to know exactly what to do, choosing to look to Marcus and Aulus for an indication. For their part, we had stared across our shield into the eyes of our enemy enough to read exactly what was going through their minds, and it was not that different than what we had seen in the faces of Lusitani and Gallaeci. Their instinct was screaming at them to make a hasty retreat, while their pride was cementing their feet in place, suiting us just fine.

"*Salve* ladies," Vibius called out, causing both Marcus and Aulus to flush with anger and embarrassment, yet both of them wisely bit back a retort.

Instead, Marcus tried to sound pleasant as he responded. "*Salve* Pullus and Domitius. It's good to see you back safe and sound. We've heard of the licking you applied to those savages up north. I'll bet you both saw plenty of action, neh?"

I felt myself smiling; I can guess that it was not very convincing. "You could say that," I replied coolly. "But at least we faced real men. Better than anyone we've beaten before."

I knew how insulting this was, yet somewhere along the short distance walking over to them, I went from wanting to mildly humiliate them to deciding to provoke them enough to give me an excuse to kill them. All of them if I could find enough of a reason for it.

I saw the look of surprise flit across Vibius' face as well, but he instantly quashed it and like the good friend that he was, waded in by my side. "Yes, Marcus. Titus is telling the truth. The men we killed make everyone we ever faced before that look like their mother's afterbirth."

Both Marcus and Aulus went white with rage and I saw Aulus' hand move to his belt. Underneath his tunic, concealed from sight, I could make out the outline of a dagger of some sort, and the smile on my face widened as I realized that I might be getting my wish. Vibius continued as I watched and waited. "So what have you......*boys* been up to since we've been gone? Been beating up on cripples?"

Finally, Marcus could take no more, though as I look back, I truly wonder if he realized just how much danger he was in the instant he uttered his next words. "Why don't you ask Juno what I've been up to?" he shot back. "She and I have gotten to be very.....close."

I did not even see it happen; as I've said before, Vibius was always much quicker than I was, but even for him this was the fastest I had ever seen anyone move. Before I could blink, Marcus was standing rooted to the ground, eyes open in shock as the point of Vibius' dagger pushed into the soft area just at the base of Marcus' jaw where it met the throat. Vibius pushed hard enough that a trickle of blood began to flow down Marcus' throat, and despite himself, I heard Marcus whimper in fear. If it had ended there, it would have been enough to keep Marcus and Aulus from misbehaving, at least for the whole time we were on leave, but then Aulus had to do something stupid. Seeing his hand closing on the hilt of his dagger, while I was and never would be as quick as Vibius, I was still very fast, so before he had gotten his blade halfway out of his scabbard, I pulled my sword to make a perfect

238

thrust, blade parallel to the ground and aimed at more or less the same spot where Vibius had pinned Marcus, except I did not stop at his throat. The point exited the back of Aulus' skull, striking the side of the building where they were standing, burying itself an inch or two deep into the wood. That mark would remain there for the next several years before the building was torn down and replaced, the blood staining the wood around it, reminding me of that day every time I came home. As my blade struck, there was a collective gasp and a couple of the toadies let out a shout, while Marcus' whimpering became a moan of fear, and the air filled with the smell of fresh urine as he lost control of his bladder. Aulus' eyes remained open, bulging out as they stared at me while I watched his *animus* flee his body, a sight I had seen happen so many times before in the previous months, and his dagger clattered to the ground, making the loudest sound to this point. He remained standing only because I supported him on the end of my blade, and I reveled in the feeling of strength as I maintained my form, my arm out and parallel to the ground, with Aulus more or less dangling from my sword. After a moment, I quickly withdrew my blade and he collapsed in a heap, while I became aware of the heavy silence of the crowd around us, yet I refused to act concerned. Somehow I knew our future rested on how we conducted ourselves in the next few moments; if we behaved like we had done something wrong, then the chances were high that we would have trouble. However, if we acted like we had done nothing more than defend ourselves, and in a sense we had done just that, then I was sure all would be well. Acting deliberately, I wiped my blade off on Aulus' tunic, my nose wrinkling at the smell as his body lost control of its functions and his bowels emptied. Any shock Vibius felt at what I did he instantly covered up, seemingly realizing the same thing, that this was all going to hinge on the next few moments.

Saying loudly enough for everyone to hear as I bent down to pick up Aulus' dagger, I waved it in the air, "Your friend should have been more careful who he tried to kill, Marcus."

Helping our cause was the stark terror, not only on Marcus' part, but on his half-dozen followers, none of whom seemed inclined to point out that we had started the argument. Behind us, we could hear the beginning of talk, followed by the sounds of feet running towards us. I turned, quickly but with deliberation, sheathing my sword while holding onto Aulus' dagger, in time to see three men of the city watch come trotting up, stopping when they saw two Legionaries standing in front of a body. The oldest one, a man of about 40 with a long white scar down the side of his face, approached us, hand on the hilt of his own sword while taking pains to show that he was not inclined to pull it.

"What happened here, Legionary Pullus?"

I remembered his name was Cornuficius and that he had been a member of Pompey's Legions that retired in this area, deciding farming was not to his liking and taking the job as commander of the city watch. We had spoken a few times, but I held no opinion of him one way or another, and he seemed to be of a like mind.

Pointing down to Aulus, I responded calmly, "This man was stupid enough to try pulling a dagger on me. I killed him before he could use it."

Eyes narrowing, he stared at Aulus' body then looked me in the eye, obviously sensing that there was more to the story, but I was not willing to say anything more until I was asked. By this time Vibius had dropped his arm, although he still held his dagger in his hands, never taking his eyes off of Marcus, who was just now seeming to come out of his trance. I realized that for all their bluster and swaggering, neither Marcus nor his gang, and certainly not dead Aulus, possessed any experience in this kind of deadly action, and in fact this was probably the first time they ever faced a sudden death or seen one of their own die violently.

Turning his attention to Vibius, Cornuficius asked him quietly, "And what's your part in this Domitius?"

Vibius shrugged, though he still did not take his eyes off of Marcus. Nodding at Marcus, Vibius replied, "This man insulted my betrothed. I took exception to it, and as we were talking, it's like Titus said. Aulus decided to pull his dagger. Titus was quicker."

His voice was flat, without emotion, a simple recitation of facts given in the manner in which we were trained; no flourishes, no commentary, just a plain and simple action report. It was a method of communicating with which Cornuficius was clearly familiar and he nodded as if it confirmed his suspicions. I thought we were in the clear, when finally Marcus came out of his trance.

"That's a lie! I said no such things. This one," he gestured at Vibius, "just went crazy all of a sudden, right in the middle of a nice

240

conversation. We were catching up on old times, and I was congratulating both of them on the job they did to those rebels up north, when out of nowhere he tried to stab me!"

Seeing Vibius' jaw tighten, I threw up a hasty prayer that he would not lose his temper. Despite his obvious anger, his voice was calm as he retorted, "If I had wanted to stab you citizen, you'd be dead."

Cornuficius nodded. "That's true enough Galba." It was not until that moment that I realized that I had known this boy Marcus, for I could have never have thought of him as a man, for something like seven years yet never knew his last name. "If Domitius wished it, you'd be as dead as your friend there."

Ultimately, Marcus and Aulus' reputation for trouble was the clinching argument that this was not the cold-blooded murder that Marcus claimed it to be. Compounding his problem was the reluctance of his followers to voice support for his side of the story. I have no doubt that there was a part of each of them secretly glad to see them both get their comeuppance in some way; bullies like that do not lead through personal inspiration, they rule through fear, so I was sure that each of the minions had run afoul of either or both of them at some point. For his part, Marcus disappeared a couple of days later, never to be seen again. And for our part, let us just say that although the townsfolk were friendly enough, they gave us a wide berth.

Leaving Vibius behind in town, I left with a promise that we would get back together in a couple of days when we were going to go see Cyclops and my sister. For perhaps the thousandth time in my life, I found myself plodding down the road towards my farm, yet despite the fact that I was now a man wearing the uniform of one of Rome's Legions, I found my heart was still in my throat. In many ways it was still like being a ten year old boy who lost the bag of nails he had been sent to fetch having to go home to face the consequences. Angrily, I shook my head, chastising myself for such silly feelings. I was now over six feet tall, and had added more than ten pounds of muscle just in the few months I was away. The sun had turned my skin even darker brown than it was the day I left, while my hands and feet were encased in calluses so thick they were almost like iron plate. My chest glittered with decorations I had earned and in the purse from my belt dangled more gold in coin and jewelry than I had ever seen in my life. The sword on my hip had seen the death of many men, not to mention women and children, a fact that I preferred not to think of then or to this day. My helmet was polished to a high sheen, as was my armor, oiled and gleaming in perfect repair, with all the damaged or lost links replaced. The horsehair plume was freshly cleaned and re-dyed a perfect shade of black and I was wearing my best tunic. And yet, for all that, I was still a young boy with a knot in my stomach going home to an uncertain fate.

Seeing Phocas before he saw me, I realized with a start that he was old. The moment the thought crossed my mind, I chided myself. I had only been gone for a few months; there was no way that he had aged that much in such a short time. Of course, that meant that he was old when I left, except that I had not seen it until this moment. When I say he was old, he was all of 45 or 46, but when you are a teenager that is truly ancient, and I have no doubt that my perception was also due to the fact that I had been surrounded by mostly young men for the last months; even the Pilus Prior, who I was sure was of a similar age to Phocas, was only 28 years old. Nevertheless, I stopped for a moment to watch him, feeling a tightness in my chest as the unbidden thought came that, slave or not, I wished with all my heart that Phocas were my father, that desire quickly followed by the prickling of tears welling in my eyes. Horrified, I blinked them back, telling myself savagely that I would not shame myself like this. As I regained my composure, Phocas apparently sensed that someone was watching, straightening up and turning to peer at me. He frowned when he saw the Legionary standing in the road, and I could clearly see a look of worry flit across his face, no doubt wondering what troubles could have brought such a man to this farm. This brought a smile to my face, relishing the idea that I had changed so much that I was not recognized. Finally, the frown slipped from his face as recognition of who stood before him dawned, yet even then, he seemed unwilling to trust his eyes.

Taking a step forward, he asked tentatively, "Titus?"

"Who else would be coming to see you, you silly man?"

With that, he ran across the yard to greet me with a proper hug before turning to call to Gaia. She was working in the kitchen as usual, her hands red and raw from her work, and like I had with Phocas, I caught myself worrying at how tired and careworn she looked. Still, she was instantly alongside Phocas, pulling my head

242

down to smother me with kisses, which I made a great show of protesting but secretly loved.

It was hard for her to find a spot on my cheek because of my helmet and finally she said crossly, "Take that thing off Titus so I can give you a proper kiss."

My smile grew broader as I pulled it off, automatically placing it under my left arm as I was trained, while the two of them continued to fuss over me.

"By the gods boy, you look like Mars himself." Phocas grasped me by the arm, looking me up and down with such pride that once again I felt the threat of burning tears.

Instead I forced a laugh as I shot back, "I'm better looking than Mars."

His eyes turned to my phalarae and despite having no real experience of such things, he knew instantly they meant something special. Indicating them, he looked at me with a questioning gaze, and I nodded proudly. "I won those for bravery, during an engagement up north."

If I was expecting a reaction, it certainly was not the one that I got from Gaia, whose smile immediately disappeared at my words. "Bravery? Bravery? What kind of men's nonsense is that? You mean you did something foolish, didn't you?"

I opened my mouth to protest, but Phocas shook his head with a wry smile. "Don't try to argue Titus. That's one battle you won't win."

Almost as quickly, her irritation vanished as her examination of me moved her eyes to the scar down my arm, which was still pink and angry. She let out a cry as she grabbed it, running her hands along the length of the cut. "Titus! What have they done to you? How did this happen?"

Her eyes filled with tears, and now I could not help myself as my vision clouded. I was home with people who loved and cared for me, and there are few finer feelings in the world.

I postponed meeting Lucius for as long as I could, letting him sleep his afternoon drunk off while Phocas, Gaia and I caught up.

From the two of them I learned that Valeria was expecting a child and experienced a strange thrill at the idea that I would be an uncle, something which, to that point at least, had never once crossed my mind. Livia had not become pregnant yet, but was by their account ecstatically happy with her husband. Lost on none of us was that both of my sisters' sense of joy was in no small measure due to their being away from this place but we did not speak of that. Instead, I told them of the adventures I had been having, sanitizing it for both of them, deciding that telling them everything would only make them worry even more. As I talked, I ate some of Gaia's porridge and the memories of happy times came wafting up to me with the scent of her cooking. I gave them the gifts I had chosen for them, along with a fairly large sum of money, telling them quietly to put that someplace where Lucius would never find it. And it was then that I told them my plans concerning them.

"I think that, in a couple more years, I'll have saved enough to buy you your freedom from Lucius." Their look of stunned surprise and happiness made me feel ten feet tall, yet almost immediately it was replaced by one of such extreme sadness on the face of Phocas that I wondered if I had made a serious blunder.

"Titus, there are no words to thank you for what you're trying to do, but your father will never agree to this."

"Why?" I asked indignantly, "I'll give him more than enough money to buy two slaves to replace each of you." When you are young, the world is so simple and problems so easy to solve. Still, Phocas shook his head sadly. "You could give him money to buy ten slaves for each of us Titus, and it wouldn't matter."

Looking to Gaia for support in arguing with Phocas, I saw in her eyes the same sad emptiness. "He's right, my darling boy. It has nothing to do with the money."

"Then what does it have to do with then?" I demanded, although a voice inside me told me that I already knew the answer.

"It has to do with the idea that it's something that you desperately want. You know your father has no love for you, Titus. What you don't know is that his hatred has grown in leaps and bounds since you left. There isn't a day that goes by that he doesn't curse your name."

244

I was stunned, although I do not know why, unless it was because I still entertained some childish fantasy of winning my father's affections by great deeds. The knowledge that his hate for me had only grown in my absence smothered the last spark of hope I nurtured that somehow things could be made right between us, and I felt the coldness return to my heart, seeing in the reflection of Phocas and Gaia's gaze that it was clear to see in my expression.

"Then," I spoke slowly and deliberately, "I'll give you your freedom another way."

At first they did not understand, then a look of horror and...........something else flashed across Phocas' face. "Don't speak of such things Titus."

He said this with an urgency that surprised me. I knew that they would not jump at the idea, at least at first, so I decided to drop it, sure that they would warm to it in time. The fact that I could very coldly contemplate the murder of my own father was not lost on me but I shrugged it off, thinking that what I was just told severed the last thread of obligation I held towards him. If he hated me so, I would return the favor, and I was a much more deadly enemy to have than vice versa, so I dropped the subject for the time being and moved to safer topics.

Lucius finally came staggering out into the main room, his eyes in their usual bloodshot state; as his bleary vision focused on me, he gave a grunt of surprise, and I was gratified to see a look of some fear on his face. Sitting there, I looked at him steadily and when he did not speak, I forced myself to adopt a tone that I hoped sounded pleasant.

"*Salve* father. It's good to see you so........well."

Continuing to stare at me, he said nothing for what seemed like half a watch, before blurting out, "What by Dis are you doing here? I thought we'd seen the last of you." Before I could respond, his face screwed up in suspicion and he continued, "You didn't get thrown out of the Legion, did you? Well, if you did it wouldn't surprise me, but you can't come back here."

Before I could stop myself, I leapt up and stepped toward him, my hand going to my sword. The movement was not lost on him and he gave a yelp of terror as he stumbled back, then immediately lost his balance, crashing into a heap on the floor. He stared up at me, the fear and hatred clear as he made no attempt to disguise his true feelings, and I know that my face reflected the same thing.

"No, old man. See these?" I tapped the phalarae, "I won these. You know how I won these?"

Leaning down, I made sure that our eyes were level before I spoke, more softly this time, my tone only serving to increase the menace, "I won them by killing a lot of men, father. I've shed the blood of more than a dozen men, all of them better than you. You'd do well to remember that."

"You impudent whelp," his lips curled back and I could see that his teeth were rotting out of his mouth, accounting for the stench that emanated from them, "I am the *pater*......."

Before he could finish and before I had any conscious thought, the sword was in my hand, the sight of it causing him to become a cringing dog in the instant it took me to draw it.

"You're a drunken, mean little man," I cut him off, "and you'd do well to remember that. I'm the head of this family now, by the right given to me by this," I brandished the sword, relishing the abject terror that it evoked, "and I'll take that right if you say one.......more.......word."

I gestured with the sword back to his room. "Well, I think we've caught up. You can go back to your room now."

Staggering to his feet, he looked like he was thinking of arguing, a thought that evaporated from his head in the time it took me to point back to him with my blade. He made to leave, but as he stumbled away, I called to him. Turning to look at me, I smiled sweetly at him and finished, "And if you even think for one moment to take your anger out on them," I jerked my head in the direction of Phocas and Gaia, standing as still as statues, "I'll find out from my sisters, and I'll come back and show you one of the tricks I learned about how to flay a man alive. Then I'll tan your hide to use as a cloak and your shriveled ball sac will be my coin purse. Do we understand each other?"

As I said this, I realized with equal parts satisfaction and unease that I meant every word I said. From the expression on

246

Lucius' face, he knew it too. Gulping, he nodded then exited the room.

The confrontation with my father had ruined the mood of homecoming, so I declined the chance to stay the night. Although I was fairly sure that my father would not have the courage to try anything while I slept, I did not feel like sleeping with one eye open. Hugging the both of them and promising that I would write this time, since I had not done so while on campaign, I left them standing at the edge of our property, tears streaming down their face. After waving to them once, I refused to look back, not wanting to risk becoming a blubbering fool in front of them. Deciding then to head for Livia and Cyclop's farm, despite it meaning that Vibius would not come with me, I calculated I would get there after dark, not that I was worried about being alone at night. In fact, I somewhat looked forward to the thought of some bandit or bandits being unlucky or stupid enough to pick me for easy prey in the night. After all, I told myself, it had been more than a month since I last saw any real action, my confrontation with Aulus hardly qualifying in my mind, and I did not want my skills to get rusty. Even as I thought that, though, I knew that I was lying to myself. It had nothing to do with my skills; the feelings one gets during battle can be as crippling a habit as the hold wine had over my father, and like one in the grip of Bacchus, where the lack of the grape causes a violent reaction of the body, so too does the lack of action to a warrior. Such is the feeling one gets when there has been no violent action that your whole being craves that kind of stimulation, like you are starving of some nutrient. I was now infected with the disease, and it would haunt me for the rest of my life. Yet I was only dimly aware of the deeper meaning of all this as I walked down the road, whistling one of our marching tunes. Passing around Astigi, I did so after deciding to give it something of a wide berth because of what had happened earlier. As far as I knew we had escaped any kind of trouble, but I held no desire to find out differently by stumbling into the arms of the city guard. Walking along, I contemplated what I would do if indeed there were some problem with what I did that day, and decided that I would have to take whatever action necessary to ensure that Vibius and I could escape back to camp, then put my faith in the army protecting its own. There had already been several incidents where Legionaries had either severely beaten or killed civilians and to my knowledge, none of them received any punishment. The army's view is that if a civilian is stupid enough to tangle with a Legionary, perhaps they are not meant for this world to begin with, and looking at it rationally, from Rome's point of view, there is more value in a Legionary than there is in the ordinary citizen. As long as one did not go about killing patricians or equestrians, a soldier could be fairly confident that they would be able to avoid the normal consequences associated with murdering someone.

Making it to Cyclops' farm about a third of a watch after dark, I stopped some distance away from the house and hailed it, because in those days walking up in the dark was a risky proposition, particularly with a man like Cyclops. I was pleased to see a light emanating from the window, telling me that they had not yet retired, and after a moment I saw the familiar face of my brother-in-law peer out from the doorway.

"*Salve* brother," I called, and for the second time that day I could see someone's face wrinkle up as they tried to determine who was calling them. Fortunately, it did not take him long, his face creasing in a smile when he recognized me. To get Cyclops to smile was enough of an accomplishment in itself, and it was just another pleasant moment of my return home.

One more time I found myself fussed over, although it was almost completely done by Livia, Cyclops content with a firm handshake and slap on the back. And once again, I sat at their table while Livia rushed about making something to eat, ignoring my protests that I had eaten not long before, as I recounted my tales to Cyclops. While still sanitizing my recounting, I was less circumspect with Cyclops than with Phocas and Gaia, until Livia let out a gasp at one of my anecdotes, whereupon I reined in my tongue once more. Cyclops and I exchanged a look as he rolled his good eye, shaking his head at the squeamishness of women. It is truly a mystery to me how women can go through the toil and bloody business of childbirth, yet the talk of lopping off some barbarian's head gets them all aflutter. I suspect it is one of those things I shall have to ask the ferryman, or some of the wise men with whom I will be spending eternity. When Livia asked me if I had been home yet, I responded as briefly as I thought I could get away with, concentrating on my time with Phocas and Gaia, and only mentioning that I had seen Lucius. I was thankful when she did not press, but I could see by her face that I had not fooled her. Livia went to bed, but Cyclops and I stayed up through the night, and despite being happy to see my sister, I was also thankful for the opportunity to talk more freely about all the things I had seen and done, because I had questions that I felt only Cyclops could answer. I related to him how Gaius Crastinus spoke highly of him, and his face flushed with pleasure.

"Crastinus is a good man," he said as he stared thoughtfully into his cup of wine, "you can learn a lot from him."

"I already have," I replied, "but I sometimes have trouble deciding whether I hate him or love him." Cyclops smiled. "That means he's a great leader, because you respect him out of equal parts love and fear. And in a place like the army, you have to have both."

I could see the sense in this, and I said so. We spent the rest of the night drinking and trying to keep our voices down as we talked, with less and less success, until Livia threatened us with imminent bodily harm if we did not go to sleep.

Waking the next morning with a pounding head, despite the pain, I had to smile. It was good to spend time with Cyclops, this time as a man who finally understood all the things that he had been telling us. I have come to the conclusion that trying to describe battle to someone is much like trying to describe the act of sexual congress; no matter how imaginative one might be, the description pales in comparison to the actual event.

As I bade them farewell, now headed to see Valeria and her husband Porcinus, I thanked Cyclops for all that he had shown me. "It's because of you that not only have I survived, but I've done well," I spoke honestly. I could tell this pleased him, and he surprised me with a bear hug and a kiss on the cheek. "I'm proud of you Titus. I think you have a great destiny in the Legions."

To say I was pleased would be an understatement. Kissing Livia, I waved goodbye as I started down the road, wondering if I could make it to Valeria's farm before dark. It had taken more than a day to escort her to Porcinus' farm on the day I delivered her to her new married life; this time, I wasn't in a wagon with my sister, so I was confident I could make it, and I did, actually arriving well before sundown. For the third time, I went through the ritual of hugs, kisses and concern over my scar, yet I must say that this time was the most enjoyable. Valeria looked radiant, which I heard is how pregnant women were supposed to look, but I was scared to hug her for fear of hurting the baby.

"Titus, you're not going to break me," she laughed, though I was still not convinced.

And for the third time, I was stuffed with food; I ate more in the last two days than I had the previous week, but it was still good to have so much food before me. Porcinus never served in the army, and although I liked him well enough, there was not a lot to talk about with him since I held no interest in farming, but it was the thing in which he was most involved, so not much was said between us after the initial pleasantries. Besides, I was more concerned with talking to Valeria, yet I found for some reason that my reluctance to share details with the other people in my life about all that I had seen fell away with Valeria. I had always been completely honest with her about everything, and this time was no exception. To her everlasting credit, she did not flinch when I told her the things I had done, things like with the woman at the first town we assaulted; she just listened. Once I was done, it was well into the night, and when I bedded down in the main room, she came to kiss me on the forehead, just as she did when I was a boy. I remembered how the last year or two, I had done whatever I could to avoid it. This time I did not mind so much.

The day before we were to return to camp, I went back to Astigi to spend time with Vibius and Juno. It was clear that their feelings for each other were not changed, and in fact, had grown stronger. It was painful for me to watch, but it was also nice to see how happy Vibius and Juno were in each other. Watching them part was more upsetting than I imagined it would be, partly because I wished it were me that Juno was so distraught to see go, but also because I could only hope that one day someone would feel the same way about me. It also made me even more conscious of my obligation to Vibius to keep him alive so that he could return to his true love. I was also envious of the obvious pride that Vibius' father had in his exploits, boasting to his friends about his son the Legionary and his great bravery, yet in this I was happier for Vibius than I was sorry for myself. Saying farewell, we made promises to write that we knew we probably would not keep, although I will say that Vibius certainly made a better attempt than I did. In those days, I had little interest in writing, or reading for that matter, although that would change, partly because once I rose through the ranks it would be required of me. However, another reason for my increased interest, especially in reading, had to do with what we were about to face now that the campaign was over, an enemy that would prove to

250

be one of the most formidable that any soldier faces, no matter how many battles and campaign seasons they face.

When we made it back to camp, we found that the orders to break it down and begin the march to the northeast to our new home had been issued, so there was a swarm of activity. Vibius and I had agreed to say nothing of the trouble we experienced in Astigi, trusting in the Fates that word would not reach the ears of the Pilus Prior or any other officer, and it never did. The chatter of the men catching up on their various adventures during their respective leaves helped make the tasks of breaking the camp down less onerous and within two days we were ready to march, the only difference being that instead of burning down the camp like we normally did when we marched this camp was left intact, manned by a small guard left behind, along with a portion of the *medici* who tended to the sick and the men whose wounds were not yet healed to the point where they could travel. To my mind, and to those of my comrades, the fate of these poor souls was worse than death itself, for they existed between the two worlds. They had survived the initial threat of death but were now lingering on, not getting better or worse as the days crept by. Some of them finally showed up at Narbo, but even fully recovered they were never the same, and I think the idea of suffering this kind of fate scared me more than actually dying did. The march itself took three weeks, with the weather becoming bitter as we moved north along the coast, rapidly growing colder than anything most of us had experienced. This was far different in climate than the Hispania of our birth, despite the fact that we were still in the province for the most part. Neither Vibius nor I had ever been this far north, so we spent every night wrapped in our cloaks and wearing our extra tunics, but still our teeth chattered most of the night. Being as close to the coast as we marched did not make it any warmer because an icy wind blew off the water to further our misery.

Arriving in Narbo at the beginning of Januarius, it was very late under normal conditions, but there were no plans for us in the immediate future, which of course we had no way of knowing. The beginnings of what would start out as a camp had been begun by the advance party and over the next weeks it was transformed into a small city, our tents replaced by wooden huts, still organized around our tent sections, except with wooden floors and a solid roof. The walls were made of planks that we whitewashed then filled in the cracks, making solid little structures that helped keep out the cold. The outer walls of the camp were initially also made of wood, but gradually they were replaced by walls of stone, although that was yet to come. Once the camp was finished and deemed to be suitable to be a permanent base, the lustration ceremonies were held, along with the renewal of our oath of loyalty to Rome. We were led to the camp by one of the Tribunes who would serve with us for this year as the senior Tribune, while a new batch of more boy wonders arrived from Rome. Thankfully the senior Tribune was not Doughboy, who had returned back to Rome to follow the *cursus honorum*; he must have stumbled along the way because we never heard of him again. The Tribune that remained behind to serve as the Senior Tribune was the one that I took notice of earlier who had seemed to have his wits about him, and in the intervening time I learned his name, Gaius Trebonius. Now, it is a name I curse and hope that Cerberus is cracking his bones as he shrieks in agony and torment, because he was one of the slayers of the great man. However, I was happily ignorant then and was content enough to have one of the boy wonders who seemed to know what he was doing lead us, or more importantly accepted what he did not know and allowed the men who did to do what was necessary.

That was when the secret enemy first showed up, an enemy that we had been warned about by the veterans, except until we faced it we did not know exactly how vile a foe it is. In reality it is a combination of two different enemies, working together. They are the twins of despair known as boredom and illness. Once the camp is finished for winter and all the resulting tasks are complete, there is not a whole lot for an army to do, despite the Centurions doing their best to find things to keep us busy. Unfortunately, a substantial number of duties that are considered punishment duties, such as the cleaning of latrines, are reserved for Legionaries who fall afoul of the many rules and regulations needed to ensure the smooth running of the Legions. For those of us who stayed out of trouble, as hard is it might have been to do, that did not give us a lot to occupy our time. A good number of us, by virtue of skills we acquired before joining the Legion, had been given the status of *immunes*; Vibius, for example, worked in the leather factory, making and repairing all the various bits of leather gear, like our harnesses and the tack for the livestock. I had the status of being the weapons instructor after the death of Vinicius, yet there is only so much training one can do in a given day. Therefore, a good number of the men filled their spare time with the pursuit of wine, women and gambling, each man putting the three vices in their own order. Fairly quickly I observed that those pastimes carried their own sets of risks, and more often than not, when a Legionary fell afoul of the regulations, it was a direct result of one or a combination of those three. In our tent section, there were two men who seemed to find themselves on the wrong side of the Pilus Prior's *vitus*, or even worse punishment, on a regular basis. One received more official punishment, while the other's tended to be more unofficial in nature, and more likely than not was at the hands not of the officers, but from his fellow soldiers.

Atilius was a type of soldier that I came to know well during my time in the Legions, and is a fairly common sort in the army, having an extreme fondness for wine and by extension, the joys of revelry and debauchery that tend to come with it. He possessed a talent for finding drink under the most unlikely circumstances and was quick to take advantage of his finds, although I never once saw him drunk when his lack of sobriety meant that it endangered himself, or more importantly one of his tentmates or the Century. However, once the rigors and dangers of a campaign were left behind, Atilius was one of the first over the wall in search of Bacchus. Compounding the problem for Atilius was that he possessed no skill, other than fighting, so he did not have the status of *immunes*, which would have occupied more of his time. He was the type to start out as a happy drunk, but as the night progressed some evil *numen* would inhabit his soul, and anyone participating in revels with him was guaranteed to find themselves in some sort of melee, particularly when there were men from another Legion around, or even worse, civilians. For reasons I never discovered, Atilius hated civilians, which was not a real problem when we were tramping about the countryside. But Narbo, for example, was a well-established town by this point, replete with all the hangers-on that can be found in every town in the Empire that has a Legion present. Pimps were a special problem for Atilius, although in the interest of accuracy, it would be more precise to say that Atilius posed a real problem for pimps. Early on during our time in Narbo I made the mistake of accompanying Atilius, Romulus, Remus and Vellusius on a night on the town. I will not go into detail other than to say I found myself shivering in a ditch that I later found out was used exclusively for the drainage of waste, as I attempted to avoid attentions of the provosts and a party of particularly angry associates of a man that Atilius had thrown headfirst through a wall. Now, I liked a good brawl as much, if not more than any man, particularly because I tended to win. However, I could see fairly quickly that my goal of raising myself up from my current status, both in the sense of promotion in the Legion and the even larger one of improving the lot of myself and my descendants, might be permanently damaged if I continued to attend Atilius' romps. No more than a month had passed at Narbo before Atilius found himself confined to the camp, with a portion of his pay taken, not to mention the thrashing he was given by the Pilus Prior that left him with an especially prominent black eye. However, if any of us hoped that this would serve to warn him off the path he was taking, they were in vain. His second offense happened no more than a week later, when he was caught trying to sneak back into the camp shortly before dawn. Because this was his second offense, the punishment was more severe, and he was given ten lashes, fortunately not with the scourge but the regular lash, and put on latrine detail for a month. This did serve to curtail his activities for a couple of months, and when he finally regained the chance to go back out in town, he was more circumspect, for a while anyway. Regardless, Atilius was destined to never reach above the rank of *Gregarius* and was not even considered for duty as *immunes* because of his problems with wine and debauchery.

The other miscreant in our group did not run afoul of the Centurions, his crime being the type that goes unreported and never appears in his permanent record. By this time, gentle reader, it should not surprise you when I reveal the identity of this individual, and I recognize that at this point you may have suspicions that I am being somewhat unfair to the man. I assure you that if anything, I am being kind. Didius loved to gamble, but more than he loved to gamble, he loved to win, and was not one to scruple much over how he did it. His favorite game was dice, and his gravest crime was that he was too stupid and greedy to know that it did not take long for others to suspect that his winning streak might not be attributed to the many sacrifices he supposedly made to Fortuna as he claimed. Yet he did have a certain amount of skill, because for the greater part the most that he aroused was suspicion since nobody could quite catch him in the act of cheating, as it were. Until one day in early spring, when his run of "luck" expired, courtesy of an "accidental" jostling of his person just as he was making a throw, a bumping that caused the extra pair of dice he was hiding in his other hand to fall to the ground, followed down immediately by Didius himself. It was only because Romulus and Remus were there to intercede that he was not beaten to death; there are few crimes considered more heinous to Legionaries than cheating a fellow soldier, in any fashion, at just about anything. The only exception to that are attempts made to get out of any kind of extra duties of some

254

sort; the ability to do so is universally admired by every soldier I have met, until you gain the *vitus* of course. Even then, I found I held a grudging admiration for the ingenuity that some of the men under my command displayed in their attempts to avoid shoveling manure or some such. And it was due to the fact that, as much as we may have despised Didius ourselves, he was one of our tent section that required Romulus and Remus to come to his rescue. Now one might think that, under the circumstances, a man who found himself rescued under such dire straits would express gratitude to his rescuers, and view himself as forever in their debt. Perhaps the fact that Didius expressed no such gratitude will be an indicator that when I speak of him, I am not judging him too harshly. Not only was Didius ungrateful, to hear him tell it the brothers had stopped Didius from exacting revenge for the unfair accusations made against him by thrashing the half-dozen or so men who had set upon him. The fact that his face was massively swollen, his nose now going in a different direction, with the rest of his body covered in greenish-purple bruises, was a contradiction if one were to listen to his words. Apparently, however, he was simply lulling his antagonists into a false sense of security by allowing them to appear to beat him senseless, and was just about to unleash his master stroke counter-attack when the brothers so rudely interrupted. It took the intercession of Calienus to keep the brothers from finishing the job that the other men had started, with both of them making a solemn oath, swearing on Jupiter's stone that they would never come to his rescue again, no matter what the circumstances. For my part, I must admit that I took some vindictive pleasure in paying particular attention to some of his sorer spots during our weapons drill, in which he had to participate because of an awkward situation, at least for him. Didius could not exactly present himself for the sick and injured list, since the circumstances of his condition would prompt a series of questions that he really had no wish to answer. Despite his protestations of innocence in the matter, Didius was at least smart enough to know that on the face of it the evidence was not in his favor, so there was a relatively good chance that there would be some official punishment. Because the penalty for cheating a fellow Legionary at anything is extremely severe; it is not uncommon for men to be sentenced to death for particularly egregious offenses, Didius' reticence was understandable. Much later in my career there was a case of a Tesseraurius who stole the money of the men he had been charged with banking and the punishment for him was the same as when a unit is decimated, except that nobody had mixed feelings about beating him to death.

255

Therefore, Didius was forced to perform his normal duties, including giving me a chance to beat him senseless with a wooden sword, something I enjoyed immensely.

Every morning, either in winter quarters or in garrison, starts with a formation, where the orders of the day are announced before everyone goes about their business. The winter had passed, the spring had come and gone, and we still performed our normal duties, with no prospects of action. In short, the situation was disgustingly peaceful. We still did our forced marches twice a month so we maintained a certain level of fitness, but to keep Legions honed to a sharp edge for long periods of time is practically impossible. No matter how hard the Centurions tried, those of us stationed at Narbo lost all of the edge that we gained during the campaign in Lusitania. However, one man was prospering; we followed the rise of Caesar's career with great interest, jumping onto every scrap of news about his fortunes. Other officers came and went but the army, particularly the 10th, thought of themselves as Caesar's men, even in those days of inaction. Rarely a day went by where his name was not mentioned, a fact that I imagine the other nobles who were assigned to command us at that time did not particularly care to hear.

It was during our first year at Narbo that Caesar was made Consul, and what is now referred to as the First Triumvirate began ruling Rome, and by extension, my life and those of all of my comrades in the army. Because of the quiet state of affairs, many of the men started relationships with women in the town, and despite marriage not being allowed, they took wives in everything but name. These men were easy to spot, all of them being exceedingly anxious to be secured from duties for the day so that they could rush back to town to be with their women. Naturally, it was not long before the women got pregnant and families began to sprout. These *de facto* families, no matter what their legal status, would be a regular feature of our lives and the officers almost always turned a blind eye, their only requirement being that the small army that followed the larger one as it marched never impeded the progress of the Legions. Many of these women would help their men carry their loads for them, trooping along behind the Legion marching drag, putting in just as many miles as we did, and in many ways enduring more hardships. As much as I cared for Juno, I was hard pressed to see her living like that, and I was glad that Vibius resisted the temptation to send for her, because I knew that she would come without hesitation.

256

The second enemy struck towards the end of our first year in Narbo, in September, during the Consulship of Caesar and Bibulus, although for all intents and purposes Caesar ruled alone, since Bibulus despised Caesar so much that he refused to serve with him, prompting the joke that this was the Consulship of Julius and Caesar. An illness swept through camp, a horrible affliction that saw men dying while spewing the most noxious fluids from almost every orifice of their bodies. Even all these years later, I still find myself questioning the Fates about the justice of allowing men to live through battle, only to be struck down by some invisible phantom, denying all that it strikes from the clean death that a soldier deserves. As I have mentioned before our tent section, while suffering from wounds, had escaped the loss of one of us in battle during the campaign against the Lusitani. We were not to escape unscathed from this enemy, however. Remus contracted the affliction, dying after only a few days, at the end deliriously calling for his mother and telling her that he was done with his chores. Romulus sat next to him, clutching his hand and weeping, begging him not to die, while the rest of us frantically made sacrifices to every deity we could think of, all to no avail. The illness raged for weeks, striking fully a tenth of our numbers, and killing well more than half of those afflicted. The doctors and *medici* did what they could, which was little more than making men as comfortable as possible, with the rest of us searching for anything that would help us ward off the horrible disease. There was a small industry of quacks and false healers who made a small fortune off of all of us, myself included, peddling amulets and potions that they swore would save us. I took to wearing the claw of a hawk around my neck, which a man who claimed to be Greek swore would protect me from the ravages of the disease. While I am of a mind to sneer at this, I am still here many, many years later, so there is a part of me that thinks perhaps it was not such quackery after all.

Although this was the first such outbreak I would witness, it certainly would not be the last, and because I tend to try and observe the world around me as much as possible, by the third or fourth time this type of disease struck I had noticed some similarities in conditions. Even after I witnessed other afflictions, notably the plague, strike armies while out on campaign, this particular disease never seemed to occur while we were on the march. It only happened when we stayed in one place, and it seemed to be only after a period of months in that place before it struck. It also seemed to strike those who were less fastidious in their habits and used the baths or otherwise cleaned themselves less often than the others. I am not inclined to speak ill of the dead, particularly those I consider friends; however, Remus was notorious for not bathing, and even his brother would chastise him severely for it, to no avail. Not once did I speak of these ideas to Romulus, or anyone besides Vibius for that matter, but when I finally made the rank of Centurion, I earned a reputation for forcing my men to bathe more often than most of the other officers, for which I took a fair amount of teasing and ridicule from my fellow Centurions. Until, that is, I pointed out after a sufficient period of time passed that I consistently put less men on the sick list, and suffered far fewer losses when this particular disease would strike, whereupon the others followed suit.

Only now were we down to the more traditional eight men in our tent, or our hut in this case. For a period of several days, there was a sense of tension among us as we waited for another of us to be struck down, but we luckily did not suffer another loss. Despite getting an idea of what caused this affliction, I have never understood what makes it stop, but it does, seemingly leaving as quickly as it arrives. Before long our routine was back to normal, with the life of the Legion in garrison continuing as if nothing had happened, leaving only grieving comrades and brothers behind to wonder at the unfairness of it all. For his part, Romulus was never truly the same after that, like a part of him had been torn out of his soul, which perhaps is not far from the case.

Part 2

Conquest of Gaul

Chapter 5- First Campaign in Gaul

"**C**aesar's sent for us!"

The word shot through the camp like a lightning bolt striking a tree and making its way to ground, with the effect being almost the same. After two years of routine and boredom, we were convinced that the return of Caesar meant that we would be put to use and see action again. At the time, there was no evidence of this other than our belief in Caesar, but it was not long before that faith was justified. After serving as Consul, Caesar was given the governorship of what at that time were two of the Roman provinces in Gaul; Transalpine and Cisalpine, along with the province of Illyricum, for a then-unheard of period of five years. Once it was confirmed that this was no idle rumor as was so often the case, the camp went into an immediate hubbub of activity as we tidied up, repainting the huts, and otherwise showing Caesar that we were still soldiers. The two years in garrison had seen other changes, besides the inevitable softness and slacker discipline that was the opposite of the first campaign season in the Legions. For my part, I had filled out even more, my frame heavily muscled throughout the chest and arms, along with bulk added to my thighs. According to Vibius and the others, I had also grown at least two more inches, standing more than four inches over six feet. As part of my training, I began concentrating more on technique than just brute strength, so that during the Legion games, I was able to avenge my loss in the wrestling match to become Legion champion, and second place in the army, something I was intent on correcting at the earliest opportunity. If anything, I was even more confident than when I joined the Legions, the difference being that I had learned that as talented as I might have been, I was still not invincible. That I had learned the hard way, with the scars to prove it. It was the result of this knowledge that saw me train more than almost any other man in the Legion, using every spare or idle moment not only working on my technique, but watching other more experienced men, looking for moves that I thought might be valuable.

There was also a change that impacted our entire Century, however, coming about as a result of the sickness that had hit the army. Not just ordinary *Gregarii* were struck down, and because of the death of a Centurion in the First Cohort, Pilus Prior Crastinus was promoted to the First Cohort, and was now the Primus Hastatus Posterior, the Centurion of the Sixth Century. In those days, whenever there was a vacancy in other Centuries in a more senior Century or Cohort, the normal procedure was that the Centurion in the next most junior Century moved up one slot. Therefore, the Primus Princeps Posterior, the Centurion of the Fifth Century of the First Cohort, who was the man who died, was replaced by the Primus Hastatus Posterior, with our Pilus Prior moving up to the Sixth Century to replace the Centurion moving up. For us, this meant that the Secundus Pilus Posterior now became our Pilus Prior. His name was Aulus Vetruvius, and he was competent enough, yet I would be lying if I said that we felt the same towards him that we did for Pilus Prior Crastinus. To be fair, Vetruvius was in a very tough situation filling his predecessor's boots, a fact that Rufio kept reminding us about. For his part, Rufio at least was staying put, since he had not been Optio long enough to be considered for one of the junior Centurion spots in the Tenth Cohort. Being selfish, that was fine with all of us, because it was difficult to adjust to the styles of two new officers. Tesseraurius Cordus left us as well, being promoted to Optio of the Sixth Century in the Tenth Cohort, but our Signifer Scaevola also remained with us. Although he technically should have been considered for one of the Centurion slots in the more junior Cohorts, Scaevola was one of those men who, despite being a great fighter and a solid man to have relaying orders, had not developed into the leader that was expected of a Centurion. Even so, I could think of no man besides Vibius who I wanted pressed against my back should things go badly in battle. And courtesy of the Helvetii, Caesar handed us a war that would go down in the annals as one of the greatest feat of arms in the history of Rome.

Caesar ordered the 7th, 8th and 9th to prepare to march from their base in Aquileia, planning on sending them northwest towards the Helvetii. By the time one of Caesar's Tribunes arrived in our camp, we were well into the packing up of all that would be required for the upcoming campaign, Caesar having sent word ahead that we were needed. Interspersed with all the various tasks to be done, the Centurions increased the pace of our training, having us go on twice as many forced marches as normal, with the difference being that the two extra were half-day affairs so that we could still do all of the other things that had to be done to prepare to move. For example, our artillery had to be refitted with new torsion ropes, with every other piece of equipment having to be inspected for wear; even in garrison, equipment suffers wear and tear just through our constant training. And truth be told, there is a huge difference between having everything adequate for training purposes and for going to war. Vibius stayed busy repairing or making new bits of leather gear, while I pushed the men of the Century harder than ever during our weapons training, making sure that nobody left the training field without fresh bruises and cuts, myself included. No matter how hard I pushed them, nobody except Didius and a couple other men like him in other sections complained, since everyone knew by this time that more work put in here meant the better chance of seeing another sunrise after a battle. Once more we prepared to leave camp to go on campaign, except this time was more difficult for a lot of the men. Now that they had set down some roots and were starting families, it was all that much harder to leave them behind, which is why a good number of their women and small children refused to be left. The day we formed up in the forum of the camp to begin the march north to face the Helvetii, there was a second, albeit smaller and worse equipped army waiting immediately outside the gates.

(Diocles: To ensure accuracy, my Master has instructed me to use Caesar's account of the campaigns against the Gauls to provide the relevant facts and dates that are crucial to his account of his experiences with Caesar.)

The whole problem with the Helvetii started because they had decided to move from their homes to find new places to live. One difficulty posed by this idea was that the place they were interested in moving to already had people in it, and they were people that we were told had asked for Roman protection. The Helvetii had already begun the process of migrating, burning their own towns, farms and fields in order to ensure that they would not lose heart and turn back. The other consequence of this decision was that they were not liable to be persuaded, either by reason or force, a fact that we

262

would soon discover when we faced them. First, however, we had some distance to cover to face them; being honest, the first three or four days marching at the pace Caesar had ordered was almost enough to do almost all of us in, and I was just as exhausted at the end of the day as the rest of my comrades, barely having the energy to speculate about what we were marching into as we listlessly chewed our evening meal. One of the more valuable lessons I took from this experience was that, no matter how hard you may train in garrison, there is still a large gap between the type of fitness and endurance that the army tries to maintain in peacetime, and what is needed to survive and thrive during a campaign season. Some of the hardest hit were the *immunes* who were excused from normal training duties, the result being that they were in even poorer condition than the rest of us. Poor Vibius looked more dead than alive at the end of the first day's march, as I literally had to force him to eat his meal, shoving his bread down his throat and commanding him to chew. I am convinced that even as he complied, he was asleep while doing so, and was only marginally improved the next day. Regardless, he did not fall out as a straggler, ending every day's march with the rest of us, for which I was very proud of him.

The country we were introduced to was different than anything I had ever seen in my life. Even in the far north of Hispania, the land is not nearly as lush and green as what we passed through. These provinces were prosperous and peaceful, with everyone giving us a cheerful greeting and a wave as we passed by, the only exception to this being men with daughters, who despite their best efforts would lose some of them to the allure of the Legion tramping by. It never failed that people, not just girls but young boys and some men as well, would attach themselves to our column as we moved, using the Legion in the same manner one would hitch a ride on a bypassing cart to take them somewhere else. For our part, this would engender endless speculation on the motives of these people. Not so much with the boys, it being a foregone conclusion to us that they were lured by the romance of life as a Legionary, a fact at which we all heartily laughed, conveniently ignoring the fact that for many of us, it was the same siren call we had heard. Such is the easy disdain those on the inside show for those on the outside of something like the army. However, for the girls and women who joined the camp followers it was harder to understand, but their actions helped pass many watches spent on the road as we discussed the topic. Not that we were complaining, since almost all of these women either

263

became the women of formerly unattached Legionaries at best, or whores servicing the rest of us at worst.

Fortunately, much of the march was on good Roman roads, so our progress was rapid, although to hear the cursing it was hard to tell. As we had experienced and would learn until it was ingrained as an expectation that we had for ourselves, nothing was fast enough for Caesar. If we marched 28 miles in a day, it should have been 30; if 30 then it should have been 35 miles. Despite learning this was his nature, some of us never grew accustomed to it, and one of them was Vibius.

"There's no pleasing that man," he muttered one day.

The 10th was now a week into our march, and were within two or three day's march of the latest place we had been told to be by Caesar. We were barely into the first watch of the march when Vibius made his comment, but I knew the reaming we had taken from the Primus Pilus that morning was still fresh on his mind, as it was with everyone. Seemingly out of nowhere, with our Cohort waiting our turn to start the march, the Primus Pilus spent that time telling us how disgraced he was at our "sightseeing" pace and how we were letting Caesar down. This was not only shocking to us, it was bewildering, and our confused glances at each other confirmed I was not the only one who felt this way. We could only go as fast as the pace set for us and since our Cohort was not in the lead the day before, we were not sure where this was coming from. As we learned later, the same tongue-lashing was given by the Primus Pilus to every Cohort, along with the cavalry and the men who ran the baggage train. It made us feel somewhat better, at least as far as our feelings, yet the pace set that day was cracking and we instantly knew it was going to be a hard one. Glancing over at Vibius when he made his comment, I could see that even so early he was struggling more than he should have been, and I could only hope that the gains he had made in his fitness over the last few days did not dig so deeply into his reserves that he would have to drop from the march. His face was already red, and the sweat dripped from his nose in a steady stream, despite the coolness of the day. I replied, but even as I did so it was with some surprise, being sure I knew who "he" was referring to, and it was not the Primus Pilus.

"He's just trying to get us there as fast as he can because he wants his best to send into battle", I reasoned.

264

"Fat lot of good it'll do if when we get there, we're too exhausted to pick up a javelin, let alone throw one," he snapped, impatiently swiping at the sweat rolling into his eyes.

For my part, after the first few days of struggle, I adjusted fairly easily back into the campaigning rhythm, which I suspected was another reason for Vibius' irritation. I shrugged, knowing by this time that there were times to argue with Vibius and times not to, and this was the latter. He had made up his mind that Caesar was the cause of his misery, and nothing I could say would change that. It was in this frame of mind that we kept moving, the only sound for many miles the thud of our boots and the jingling of our gear bouncing around. One thankful aspect of this country, I mused, was that it did not kick up as much dust as Hispania, something a Legionary learns to appreciate. Also, the nights were much colder than even in Narbo, so we woke up every morning shivering, and it was not unusual that there was a thin skin of ice on the water buckets that were used to water the livestock. Marching up the valley of the Rhodanus (Rhone), we passed through a number of towns and bypassed the larger ones if possible. Despite the fact the folks in the town, at least in a Roman province, might like the spectacle of an army marching by, towns and cities provided a wealth of temptation for a lot of us. In turn, this inevitably brought trouble in one form or another, so invariably whenever possible we passed them by on an outer road. After a few days, despite the area immediately along the river staying relatively flat, it was still taking a noticeably upward tilt, and the river valley soon was surrounded by hills that grew in height as we moved. The timing of the Primus Pilus' chastisement was unfortunate in that sense; the main reason for our tardiness, if it was indeed real, was more a result of the land over which we marched than any lack of fitness on our part, at least by this point. None of this made an obol's worth of difference to us, of course, and while I was not willing to condemn Caesar to the degree that Vibius had, I will say that even his most ardent supporters were somewhat muted when they discussed him with their comrades. At the end of the day that we received the warning from the Primus Pilus, it was like being on the first day of the march again, at least if one were to judge simply by the obvious level of fatigue. Little did we know, we were relatively as refreshed as it was possible to be, given the circumstances and what Caesar planned for us.

"Dig. Starting where those stakes are marking out. Pile the spoil on that side," Pilus Prior Vetruvius pointed. "The ditch has to be twelve feet deep and fifteen feet wide."

We all nodded, since this was the standard for fortifications we constructed for Caesar, but despite our understanding of the simple requirements, what was escaping all of us was….why? We were not building a camp; we had done that the day before. This was, at least to our eye, in the middle of nowhere. However, this was to be the first of the defensive fortifications for which Caesar would rightly become famous, an 18 mile wall that began at the shores of the huge lake that the locals call Geneva, to the base of the Jura Mountains. Since we never saw maps and were too lowly ranked to be in any of the officers' briefings, we had to wait to learn from the Pilus Prior exactly why we were standing in what was nothing more than a long line of Centuries, half of them fully armed and standing watch, with the other half like us being told to show up with our digging gear. The Helvetii were out of room; this much we knew, and once the Pilus Prior sketched out a rough map in the dirt, it became clearer what their problem was. They lived in a narrow strip of land, with the huge lake to one side, and a range of small but rugged mountains on the other. If facing south, the direction they wanted to march, that lake was to their left, and behind them, hemming them in even further was the Rhenus (Rhine) River, roughly a week's march away. Furthering their problems was that apparently the Helvetii had not been good neighbors to the tribes surrounding them, and I believe it was this knowledge that prompted Caesar to reject their request to pass through the lands to their south. Not trusting them to obey his command, he ordered us to dig a defensive ditch, of the dimensions I previously mentioned, to block the 18 mile gap. Topping the earthen wall were the palisade stakes, for which a large number of trees had to be felled and the stakes fashioned from them. Because we were the first Legion to arrive, it fell to us and a scratch force of Legion strength that was pulled from the garrisons and towns of the province. It is only now that I realize that many times when we were not told the larger reasons for our actions, it was actually in our best interests, although I would have been just as vocal protesting that idea as anyone back then. However, if we knew what we would be expected to accomplish, while we certainly would not have mutinied, there would have been considerable hard feelings. As it was, we were still none too happy, grumbling at the folly of digging a ditch and wall for only the gods knew what here in the middle of nowhere.

266

Originally, we started on the project at a midway point, in what we thought was an attempt to screen our intentions from the Helvetii. It is still astonishing to me, even having seen it happen as many times as I have by now, how quickly an organized, motivated and well-led group of men can achieve something of the scale as the Geneva Wall, as we came to call it. The wall took only two weeks plus a day, despite one or two attempts on the part of the Helvetii to disrupt the work. Once it was finished, Caesar spread all of his available troops along the walls, concentrating most of them at the point closest to the river, whereby we could man the walls to repel any attempts to scale it, not that there was a huge threat of this. Because it was the entire Helvetii tribe moving, what we faced was not a fast-moving, far-ranging group of warriors, so that scaling the wall would only do them limited good. It had to be breached, in a number of places, with each opening having to be at least as wide as their largest wagons. The spot that bore the most watching was where Caesar put us, the section of wall where it made a junction with the confluence of the river and the lake; the scratch troops were distributed along the rest of the way. Our wall was constructed so that part of it actually ran parallel to the Rhodanus, which is fed by the lake, for the length of a mile, giving anyone foolhardy enough to try slipping by and landing on our side of the river exposure to not just our javelins but to the artillery, the bulk of which Caesar ordered to be concentrated in this area. And if anyone was fortunate enough to make it to the point at which the wall stopped, facing them was a camp filled with men with orders to kill whoever made it that far, no matter what their status. Despite all of this, there were such attempts every night the first two or three nights; at least none of them were insane enough to try to go by in the day. Even with the cover of night, however, the passengers who slipped through on the one or two boats that made it past the initial fortifications were quickly dispatched. Fortunately, our Cohort was stationed further up; while I would have obeyed orders the same way I had obeyed such orders in the past, I certainly did not mind missing the opportunity to slaughter women and children.

The blockade achieved the desired effect, though not for long. Since the Helvetii had already taken the drastic step of burning down their homes, farms and anything else of value, they were for all purposes camping out in their own land. Their tribal elders made the decision that instead of trying to force their way past the wall, they would instead lead their people to the opposite end of their lands to the north, then cross to the west through a gap in the mountains there. Since this was much, much larger than an army that they were trying to move, they could not accomplish anything with any real rapidity. Nonetheless, they moved much faster than we would have thought possible before seeing it with our own eyes, when we awakened one morning to a large cloud of dust hanging in the air to our north. During the impasse at the wall, they had camped within our sight as their elders debated what to do, the fires stretching for as far as the eye could see, so despite ourselves, we were impressed by how quickly they were able to move that mass of people, even if it was just a few miles. Caesar immediately spotted the danger, and knowing that one Legion, no matter how good we were, would not be enough, ordered us to move to join the 7th, 8th and 9th, who had marched from Aquileia into a blocking position. I know we felt the same way, because when we were told that Caesar was heading that direction, not only to hurry the other three Legions along, but to raise two more nobody, not even Vibius, complained about it. The Helvetii could make perhaps ten miles a day, if that; this gave us perhaps a little short of three weeks to stop them at the crossing place between the mountains. Militarily speaking, it was important to meet them in the mountains, where the narrowness of the roads and trails could negate the advantage of their huge numbers. We were told they had more than a 100,000 warriors, and that was a daunting number, no matter how confident we were in ourselves or in Caesar. Caesar left us under the command of Titus Labienus, the man who would end up becoming our *de facto* commander for the next few years. While the command is supposed to rotate among all the Legates, Caesar was not one to let tradition get in the way of doing what was best with his army. It would not be fair to say that we liked Labienus, but he had our grudging respect. This was partially because like Caesar, he had shown that he would share our same hardships and living conditions, and also because he demonstrated a good head on his shoulders that did not panic. I believe that more than intelligence, or tactical brilliance, the ability to keep one's head when everyone around you is losing theirs, especially when it is happening literally, is the key to military success. Once our commanders were assured that this was not some attempt on the part of the Helvetii to trick us into prematurely removing us from the wall, we were given the command to march. Caesar left orders that the scratch force would now take our place, taking the reasonable risk that if the Helvetii were to turn tail and come back to the wall, it would not be in the 18 mile stretch between the river and the mountains, but where they might have the greatest chance of success. As was usual for Caesar, he was right;

268

the Helvetii did not give it a backward glance, throwing the dice in the direction they were headed, hoping that they could steal a march on us.

With Caesar going to get help and the Helvetii heading north, Labienus marched us west and south, generally back the way we came. From a soldier's point of view, it is times like this when we reversed our tracks that we really regretted the practice of destroying the camp of the night. It would have saved us some trouble and labor, yet such was our lot that we often found ourselves sometimes within sight of the outlines of the old camp, digging all over again. However, that is just the grumbling of an old soldier. Despite it still being spring, it was early enough, now that we were in the more mountainous areas, for snow to fall, and this was Vibius' and my first real experience with the stuff. We were not alone; most of the men of the 10th had no experience with snow, other than the glimpse of snow-covered peaks in Hispania, so that even the officers could not stop us from becoming a group of boys for a time. We tasted the snowflakes, made snowballs to throw at each other, and in general acted in a manner completely unworthy of Rome's Legionaries. Very rapidly we discovered the cost of such beauty, since none of us had thought to pack our leg coverings or socks, much to our discomfort within a few moments. Our feet had been toughened up by the miles we marched, except they were as susceptible to cold as any other part of the body, and before long I was faced with the unpleasant sensation of being unable to feel my feet. Even as we marched they felt like two big lumps of meat, and it was only because I looked down and watched that I could tell I was wiggling my toes. My only happiness came from the fact that I was not the only one miserable; there is nothing more comforting to a soldier when he suffers than the knowledge that his friends are just as miserable as he is. Vibius was shivering uncontrollably; as we walked I could see his body spasm, fighting the cold. His lips were blue, and I suspected mine were as well, while even the normally patient and long-suffering Calienus was marking each step with a chatter of teeth.

"Not so fun is it now, eh boys?" called Rufio, marching out to the side.

We did not answer; despite the fact we all liked Rufio a good deal, he was still Optio and smarting off to a superior, while a way to get warmed up with a flogging, was not a method we would choose willingly. Truthfully, we did not worry so much about Rufio bringing up a charge, but Pilus Prior Vetruvius was still an unknown quality at this point. Being fair, he had not been markedly different than Crastinus, but we had yet to go into battle with him, and as I was to learn when I reached his place, the men are judging you just as much if not more than you are judging them. I was reminded of that when I left the ranks and faced battle the first time as a Centurion, thinking back to when I was a Legionary watching our new Centurion, trying to figure him out.

Luckily, the weather only lasted one more full day. On the second morning we actually woke to a camp covered in white, the tents blanketed in snow, glowing an eerie white in the pre-dawn darkness. The only marks on the ground were from the men on watch and their relief, although that would change quickly now that the camp was awake. It did not take long for us to discover another problem that snow, despite its beauty, gave in abundance. The leather of our tents had become soaked, making them much heavier than normal, something that may not seem to be an insurmountable problem. However, the amount of weight that every man, animal and wagon carries is calculated down to the pound, making the additional weight of the trapped water a serious problem. Normally the tent section mule carries the tent, the stakes, its own forage and our extra grain, but very quickly we discovered that something had to be removed from the animal's burden, and I will say I was not surprised when all of my tentmates' eyes turned to me. I knew better than to argue, just sighing and accepting the sack of grain, trying to balance it with the rest of my load. My pride would not allow me to act like it was anything but the most trifling of tasks, but I felt my knees shake a bit as I got adjusted to the extra burden. I also knew better than to hope that Labienus or the Centurions would account for all the extra weight we were carrying when calculating the day's march, and in that I was not disappointed in my confidence. Fortunately we were still headed in a downhill direction, back to where we were to meet with Caesar, who would be bringing up the three Legions and whatever troops he raised. Not lost on us was the fact that these new Legions would be close to useless, at least in the first few battles, since they were literally training on the march. The 7th, 8th and 9th would be welcome, however, and those with friends among the other Legions speculated about how much money they could win, or win back as the case may have been. Out of all of us, perhaps Didius looked forward to the reunion more than anyone else, since for the most part he was out of willing opponents for his games of chance, if they could be called such. As I reflect on it,

270

perhaps Didius taking the beating he did was not the best thing, because it made him more determined not to get caught, instead of showing him he needed to change who he was. Perhaps asking him to change was impossible; can we truly alter our nature, or is the best we can hope to do disguise it from the eyes of others? Given the problems he caused for himself and for others, if he had even tried at the least to hide his true colors from others, I cannot help but think how different things could have been.

Reaching the confluence of the Rhodanus and Aras (Saone) rivers on the third day of our march, we turned back north along the Aras; the branches of the Aras and Rhodanus roughly form the letter "V" with the Aras continuing to the north. It is one of the most sluggish rivers I have ever seen, and it is almost impossible to tell which way it is flowing, although it is actually to the south and gradually empties out to Our Sea. At the junction of the two rivers was what is now known as the town of Lugdunum, except at that time it was just a hill fort that commanded the junction of the rivers. If the tribe that held it had been hostile at that time it would have posed a large problem for us to get around, as we could see the men lining the walls clearly watching us go tramping by, but given that we were trying to stop the Helvetii from trespassing into their territory, it is easy to see why they let us pass unmolested. Nevertheless, we were grateful for their lack of hostility and we marched past as quickly as we could. Once we were a safe distance away, yet still within sight of not just the hill fort but the river fork, we made camp to await Caesar and the other Legions, making it large enough to accommodate the rest of the army when it arrived. They marched in a couple of days later, and it was a welcome sight seeing the rest of the army, their eagles and standards marking their progress up the valley to join us, with the obligatory cloud of dust hovering above them. Labienus and the Legion's command group went to meet Caesar, while we were called to formation outside the camp to welcome Caesar and our comrades.

"About time is all I can say," grumbled Vibius, who eyed the hill fort every day, openly worried that our presence would provoke the Gauls inside it to come out to cause us some mischief.

In fact, the opposite was happening, as we would find out shortly, when a Gallic deputation rode out to meet Caesar, not to warn or threaten us but to ask for help. By this time, the Helvetii had passed over the mountains that currently lay to our east and served as the western border of their former lands. Moving through a

271

narrow pass at the northern end of the range, with a detachment of our cavalry trailing to keep an eye on them, the Helvetii were now sweeping back to the south, preparing to cross the Aras River a bit further to our north. They were supposedly a dozen miles away, having commandeered every boat in the area to make a bridge over which they could cross. While Caesar met with his officers and the representatives of the Aedui, Allobroges and Sequani, all of whom had come to us to ask our help with the threat to their lands, we retired back to camp to await further orders. There was an air of excitement crackling through the Legion streets; from our perspective, we were happy to no longer be alone in enemy territory and to be reunited with Caesar, yet we shared the belief with all the other Legions that now that Caesar was here, we would soon be seeing more action.

We were not disappointed. Shortly before dusk, an assembly of the Centurions was called, leaving us to sit by our tents waiting to hear what was going to happen, passing the time in our usual manner of gambling, talking about women and speculating on where we were headed. All of us were sure that we would take off in pursuit of the Helvetii, but what we were not prepared for were the orders the Pilus Prior brought back to break down our tents, pack up and be ready to move by midnight. Caesar was taking ourselves, the 8th and 9th in pursuit of the Helvetii, leaving the other three Legions behind, except he was not content to wait for daybreak, planning instead to steal a march on the Helvetii, making for a hard slog ahead of us. Quickly understanding that the sooner we broke down our gear, packed it up and made ready to move, the more chance we would have of snatching some rest before the appointed time of march, we turned to our tasks with a vengeance. Within two parts of a watch we were done and ready to move, our reward the chance to lie on the now bare ground where our tent had been, using our pack for a pillow, and getting as much sleep as we could. I dropped off immediately, as did almost all of the rest of us; we had all learned by this point the wisdom of sleeping when there was time and eating when there was food because one never knew when the chance for either would come again. Roused shortly before the march was to set out, we were thankful that the sky was clear and the moon, while not completely full, was still bright enough to clearly illuminate the path we were about to take. Even so, when we started out, with the 10th in the lead, we moved with more caution than if it were fully daylight, sending two Centuries ahead instead of the standard one to scout the ground and keep us from falling into ambush. Ahead of the

Centuries even farther were the cavalry *ala*, ranging a mile or two ahead of the advance guard, and it was in this manner that we set out. Caesar ordered strict silence on the march, so we tore strips of spare cloth, wrapping them around the noisier bits of our gear to keep them from clanking together, producing a sound as we marched that none of us had ever really heard before. That night made me realize how one can get accustomed to certain things and accept them as a normal part of their world, but the only time they are noticed is when they are gone. Such was the case with the normal sounds of our march, the only exception being the tramping of our boots, and it was frankly somewhat disturbing, like we were an army of mute spirits marching along. Because of our slower pace, it took us more than a full watch before we pulled close enough to the spot where the Helvetii were crossing that the cavalry *ala* came galloping back to report to Caesar, marching at the front with Labienus and the other Tribunes in command of the other two Legions, that they had spotted them. Dawn was rapidly approaching, so Caesar wasted no time; we were quickly given the order to draw up into formation, ground our gear and leave it with a rear guard before moving about a half mile further to the north, where we were halted once more. There we were arrayed in a *duplex acies*, with the Second Cohort anchoring against the banks of the river, the First forming the other end of the first line, and the Third and Fourth between us. We took off the covers of our shield, and were allowed to kneel and wait for the other two Legions to arrive and form the same formation to our right. By the time all this was done, the sky was lightening rapidly, and I realized with a sinking feeling that our chance of total surprise was diminishing as quickly.

"Hurry up you lazy bastards," I muttered as I peered to my right, barely making out the dark blob of movement that signaled the other Legions hurrying into line.

"Quiet Pullus," hissed Rufio from just behind me, and I started a bit, not realizing that I had said anything out loud.

Finally, a messenger on horseback came galloping across our front to find Labienus, who was standing with the first line further down the formation. Without being told anything, we came to our feet, hoisted our weapons and prepared to advance.

The order was not long in coming, and we began the approach. There was a line of trees across our path of march that, while performing the service of screening us from the sight of Helvetii sentries, was now an obstacle to be negotiated in the semi-darkness as we moved through. Perhaps even worse than the possibility of tripping was the fact that it is practically impossible to keep a large group of men in any type of alignment while moving through such terrain, since being in alignment during an attack of this nature is absolutely essential. Because of this, after we broke through the line of trees, we would have to halt to reorder the lines, taking even more out of the element of surprise than the dawn would. Once I heard the racket we made as we entered the woods, with men tripping over roots and banging into trees, all worries about alignment fled from my head instantly; there was no way that they could not hear us coming, so it would be a miracle if we even got a chance to get properly aligned. Seeing a patch of light ahead that signaled the end of the small forest as we drew closer, I felt the familiar knot in my stomach tighten, fully expecting that the instant we burst through the trees we would be met by a horde of Helvetian warriors alerted by our clumsiness and now waiting for us like butchers wait on lambs brought to the slaughter. Glancing over, even in the gloom I could see Scribonius' face tight with worry, and he met my own for a moment before shrugging then looking away, his expression communicating everything either of us needed to know. He was right; nothing could be done about it now, we just would have to make the best of it no matter what the circumstances. Usually, Legionaries do not like being trapped in places like forests; our style of fighting is not suitable for areas where we are confined in such ways, but this was one time that none of us looked forward to exiting what we now regarded as the safety of the trees, convinced that now that the dawn had arrived, coupled with the noise we were making, we were going to meet trouble.

By the time we inevitably burst out of the woods, the dawn was now fully upon us, but even if we had not been given the order to halt so that we could dress the lines, we probably would have staggered to a stop anyway at the sight that greeted us. Although it was not a battle line of Helvetian warriors like we expected, it was not much better; it was the largest camp any of us had ever seen. As far as the eye could see there were clusters of wagons, each cluster grouped together to form some sort of barrier, except as we were to learn, the Helvetians did not sleep within their protection, however meager. They chose instead to sleep on the ground, huddled together in groups around fires, with only the meanest shelters of skins lain over poles above them to provide protection from the elements. The fires and the smoke from them, as the people designated to restart

274

them in the morning had begun stoking their particular fire, spread so far along the bank of the river that it was impossible to estimate just how large the camp was. Perhaps even more disturbing was not the camp on this side of the river, but the one on the other side, no more than two hundred paces away on the opposite bank.

"By Dis, I think we're in trouble," I heard Calienus gasp, and it was only when I turned in his direction and saw that he was not looking at the scene before us, instead following his gaze that I saw what had caused such a reaction. The camp on the other side was a camp in name only; in area it was a city the size of Corduba at the least.

"There must be a million of 'em," this was from Scribonius, who was not one to normally be so flustered by such things, but then, none of us had ever seen anything like this.

In the moment I took to gaze across the river, I saw a single bridge made of two lines of boats side by side with rough-hewn planks laid across, stretched across the water, allowing perhaps two wagons at a time to cross. This sight at least explained why they had not yet all made it over the river, but that bridge posed a serious problem for us, because it enabled the Helvetians on the other side to come to the aid of their fellow tribesmen. And since we were closest to the river, it also meant that we would bear the brunt of the attack. In the moment it took for all of this to sink in on me, my friends saw the same thing and reached the same conclusion.

"We are all going to die," Rufio said, not bitterly, but as a simple statement of fact.

We should have had more faith in Caesar. Anticipating such a condition, Caesar had expressly put us on the side where he expected the most problem. However, he gave Labienus orders for us that were slightly different from the other two Legions. Once the order to advance sounded, instead of moving on the camp, we were instead led straight to the bridge, forming a box formation with the First and Second Cohorts facing the bridge and the opposite bank, while the Third formed on one side of the bridge and the Fourth on the other. Behind each of our Cohorts was another in support, forming a box two Cohorts deep. Men were designated from both of the Cohorts facing the bridge to gather one javelin apiece from the other Cohorts and bring them to us to use for covering fire, while the two spare Cohorts were given orders to gather combustibles to fire the bridge. Meanwhile, the other two Legions were to assault the camp, sparing no one.

To this day, it is a mystery to me how this all worked out as well as it did; despite the fact that the sun had already started to rise, and the noise we made crashing about in the woods, we still seemed to achieve complete surprise. Afterwards, the men from the other Legions relayed to us how a large number of the people they killed were still lying in their makeshift beds as our men went sweeping through the camp. I can only surmise that the idea of us marching through the night and appearing like some sort of *numens* out of the dawn was so preposterous that the Helvetii never recovered from the shock of being wrong. The Helvetians on the other side were little better; it took them a full sixth part of a watch before a force of a size large enough to threaten us was gathered to try to storm the bridge, but by that time it was too late. Despite the futility, they valiantly made several attempts to get across, even after the fire was lit and went sweeping across the river towards them. For our part, neither the First nor Second Cohorts even pulled our sword, instead wearing our arms out throwing our javelins at anyone who got close enough. The closest the Helvetians on the other side of the river came to getting across was when a small force of horsemen ignored the bridge to swim across. Even they were cut down before they made it to the opposite bank, their horses looking more like porcupines, so full of shafts were they, floating downstream or sinking out of sight, along with their riders. I could hear the sounds of the "battle" if it could be called that, behind me, yet I refused to look around, telling myself that my duty lay in front. The truth was that I heard the mingled screams of women being killed, or worse, accompanied by the shrieks of terror from children and the cries of babies as they were put to death, making it much more than duty that kept my eyes averted. It is the part of soldiering that I hated, and still hate to this day, and as much of it as I have done myself, I have never taken the joy in it that some of my comrades have.

The affair was over in two thirds of a watch, with barely a loss to us, aside from some minor wounds. The bridge went up in flames, leaving the Helvetians on the other side shaking their fists at us, screaming imprecations in their language that we needed no translator to understand. Once it became apparent there was nothing they could do for their fellow tribespeople, they packed up their camp and made preparations to begin the march anew. On our side of the river, once I did finally turn to look, it was a scene of staggering devastation. Bodies lay in large heaps, some of them

276

horribly mutilated, having been cut to pieces fighting, some with a single wound to the throat or chest. Thousands upon thousands of them; men, women, young children, teenagers my age, babies still in swaddling clothes, old crones who gaped with toothless mouths open to the sky, their eyes as wide as their maws, staring in that shocked expression that is common to people who die suddenly. That noxious stench of blood and death was already clearly palpable, and by the end of the day was so overpowering that we began to wear our scarves around our lower face to keep out the foul humors in the air, except it did not help much. The 8th and 9th were swarming over the field, looting the wagons and finishing off the wounded. From underneath piles of bodies people would be found who had escaped harm, and these were rounded up under guard to be sold into slavery, though not before the women among them were sampled by the soldiers who found them. Despite not taking part in the assault on the camp, we were still allotted a section and turned loose to loot it, Vibius and me pairing up as always. It is in times like these that all the camaraderie and good feelings one holds for fellow Legionaries is put under the most severe test; greed has a way of doing that. The customary method is for a tent section to lay claim to one particular house, or wagon in this case, and the others are supposed to respect that, especially this time since there were plenty of wagons to go around. However, it was a matter of who claimed it first, and invariably, there would be two or more groups who would spot an unmolested wagon simultaneously then make claim to it. This is where the Centurions come in, and why they always get a larger share of the spoils from each of us, along with the first pick of the most prized booty. They are the judge and jury of the system and whatever they say is law, which we accepted. Where things get complicated is when the dispute is between Centuries, or even worse, Cohorts, and then seniority is often used, although this is not universally accepted. Worst of all is when it is between Legions, and that is when matters can get violent; I have seen men killed in such disputes, squabbling over a bolt of silk, or in one case, a copper bracelet that perhaps cost a sesterce. That is also when things take a more official turn, with the Centurions involved in the dispute taking their complaints to their respective Tribunes, who then meet and work things out and come to a fair settlement. Of course, that is the theory, but like all things in our system, it comes down to who is willing to give the biggest share of the spoils to the man adjudicating the dispute. Perhaps it is not the most just system, but it works.

After the looting, we turned back to more practical matters, the most pressing being the construction of a new bridge and the burying of the bodies. We hoped that we were going to be given the task of building the bridge, but it was our turn for Fortuna to dump on us when the 10th was assigned the job of digging a mass burial pit. There were more bodies to bury than we had ever experienced before, and while the idea of digging one huge pit was discussed, it was almost immediately discarded as being impractical. Instead, each Cohort was assigned to dig a pit, given a section of the battlefield to clear, and we worked well into the night completing the task. Once we were done we marched back, filthy and exhausted, to the camp built perhaps a mile away from the site and tried to get as much sleep as we could. Meanwhile, the 9th was charged with building another bridge. Although burning the first one had been a practical necessity, it also meant that the materials previously readily available for its construction were destroyed, so the 9th was sent farther upriver to scour the area for more boats. Caesar deemed this the most expeditious manner of getting across, as opposed to building a proper bridge. The other Legions were sent for and would arrive by midday the next day, while hopefully the 9th would find what they needed to help us get across the river. The 8th had constructed the camp we were now occupying, where most of us immediately dropped to our cots, not bothering to take off our armor or eating anything, and dropped off to sleep immediately.

The next day saw the 9th successful in finding the number of boats needed to bridge the Aras although it was going to be narrower than what the Helvetii built. We would find out that this was a huge blow to the Helvetii, not as much by the construction of the bridge itself, but in the damage done to their morale, because it took them 20 days to build the bridge we destroyed, yet it took Caesar only one before we were tramping across in pursuit of the Helvetii. I can only imagine the kind of consternation this caused when they learned this, and as I have since come to understand, one can never underestimate the importance of morale in waging war. By the middle of the day, the other Legions Caesar had sent for reached the crossing, just in time to see the last of our group crossing the bridge, whereupon they joined the tail end of the column, almost as if planned that way, and perhaps it was. A Cohort was left behind to guard the bridge, along with firing the debris left over from the battle the day before, which had been piled into a huge pyre to be set alight. The smoke column that it produced was visible to us the rest of the day as we moved in pursuit of the

Helvetii. For their part, they turned back to the north, seeking a low pass through the mountains that barred their way west, enabling us to quickly come within striking distance, whereupon they sent a deputation to Caesar, led by a chief named Divico who once led a campaign against Cassius, a relative of that bastard who called himself one of "The Liberators." The Helvetii were severely shaken by the easy slaughter of a quarter of their number; once the final count of bodies was finished it numbered almost 100,000 people we buried back at the river. Divico begged Caesar to stop his pursuit of the Helvetii, telling him that they only wanted new lands to settle and would go wherever Caesar wished and do what he asked. Caesar told Divico that the Helvetii must make reparations to those tribes whose lands through which they had already passed and devastated, along with giving up a number of hostages, a perfectly reasonable request given all that occurred. Apparently the old boy did not see it that way and got a bit huffy about it, saying something about how the Helvetii never gave hostages, they took them. Whatever took place, the talks were not successful, so the Helvetii began to march to the north again, this time with an army of six Legions following them.

This was the pattern of almost two full weeks, with the army following the Helvetii procession about five or six miles behind them as they plodded north along the Aras. About the fifth day of the first week, they turned away from the Aras to head west for a pass through the low mountains. The terrain got rougher, yet more importantly their route took us farther away from our supply line, which was the river itself. Caesar had ordered the Aedui to supply us with grain by way of boats sent from their towns along the river, and the farther we marched away from that, the longer our supply line grew. Perhaps it was this that persuaded Dumnorix, one of the chiefs of the Aedui, that it would be more politic of him to withhold the grain from us, a fact that soon became apparent even to us in the ranks. It was made known to Caesar even earlier, who summoned Diviciacus and Liscus, both of them also high officials in the Aedui tribe, to demand an explanation. Diviciacus was a Druid, something called a Vergobret, and previously Caesar had been friendly with Diviciacus, who reciprocated the friendship. Diviciacus more importantly was also Dumnorix's brother, and it was this relationship that Caesar hoped to prevail upon to convince Dumnorix that holding back our food was going to be a bad idea for everyone involved. While this negotiation was going on, Caesar also recruited more cavalry from the surrounding tribes and even from across the Rhenus, fearsome looking men who wore trousers and cultivated long flowing mustaches, though they were reputed to be great horsemen. I will admit they were ready enough for a fight, but they possessed very little discipline. The squadrons now had swelled so that there were some 4,000 horsemen, and aside from the normal outriders and scouts who rode in small groups, they were kept in one body. It was this unit that had the job of keeping in visual contact with the Helvetii column, while the rest of us marched behind. For the first couple of days the marches were very tense affairs, as we were constantly on guard and ready to be summoned into battle. However, it soon became clear that neither the Helvetii nor Caesar had any desire to tangle just yet, a fact that we spent much time in the evening speculating about. After about a week of this we settled into a monotonous routine of marching, then stopping and waiting, then marching again, our pace of travel being much faster than the Helvetii, and Caesar wanting to keep a buffer of several miles between us. It was dreadfully boring, causing the grumbling around the campfire to become more pronounced. One night, as we were talking about it, Calienus said something that finally made some sense to us.

"I wonder if Caesar's lost his nerve," Vibius mused, drawing a chorus of angry remarks, to which he replied defensively, "Then what other reason could we have of not engaging with these bastards? We've passed over good ground that would've made a perfect battlefield, but we do nothing. So what else could it be?"

In this much, Vibius was right and we all knew it. It was not a matter of terrain; even with the hills, there had been plenty of spots where two armies of our size could have deployed then gone about the business of slaughtering each other.

"I don't think it has to do with terrain, I think it has to do with us." This came from Calienus, immediately catching our attention and to be honest, arousing our irritation. Seeing the reaction on our faces that his remark caused, he added quickly, "I'm not talking about us, the 10th, or the other veterans in the 7th 8th and 9th for that matter. But how long have those boys in the 11th and 12th been in the army now? A month?"

Someone calculated quickly and answered, "They've been in one week longer than a month."

"So how well trained could they possibly be?" he asked, rhetorically, since we all knew the answer to that. They had taken a hard course in marching and all that goes with it, we had to give them that, but that left precious little time for weapons training. Their training regimen was composed of snatched bits of time whenever they could grab it. They had undoubtedly been training in the camp when we had attacked the Helvetii at the bridge, yet how much good would that have done? Sitting in silence as we mulled this over, I for one could see the sense of it, and I said so. Caesar was not fighting because he wanted to season the new Legions a bit more before we forced a battle on the Helvetii, so we would continue to march and wait.

The only event of any note that happened during this period was when our cavalry became overeager and attacked the rearguard of the Helvetii, all 4,000 of our men going against what we were told was 500 Helvetian warriors. Our men were bloodily repulsed, a fact that did not do much to instill confidence in our cavalry among the Legions, I can tell you that. This clash only strengthened Caesar's resolve that biding his time was his best option, except that the supply situation soon threatened that, prompting him to try one stratagem before the situation turned desperate. The scouts reported that the enemy had gone into camp at the base of a hill some six miles distant. On questioning the scouts and locals friendly to us, Caesar learned that the hill was sufficiently large enough, with a slope practicable enough that he could send a Legion on a night march to take up position on the crest of the hill, getting there by traversing the reverse slope away from the Helvetii camp. Like we did with the assault on the bridge, the plan was that the dawn would arise to the sight of a Roman Legion, this time commanding the heights above their camp, with Caesar then bringing up the rest of the army to face them, in a pincer movement. The 10th was selected as the Legion to climb the hill, yet another sign of Caesar's confidence in not just us but Labienus as well. Setting out that night once it was dusk, we waved cheerily at the other Legions left behind who were making their usual rude remarks and catcalls at us. The only time we do not hate each other is when we are fighting someone else, I thought as I listened to some of the more inventive and colorful taunts thrown at us as we tramped out of the gate. No matter, all that counts is when the fighting starts, they will be by our side when we need them.

During my career, I have read several books and treatises on the art of warfare, and there is always a phrase that makes me laugh when I read it. The "fortunes of war", or "Bellona's fickle caress", or some such nonsense is how it is usually termed. Although I have no disagreement with the idea behind it, if you are one of those who are subject to these vagaries, it is not quite so easy to dismiss as a sign of the gods' displeasure or indifference. Such was the case with Caesar's night operation against the Helvetii. Oh, we did our part well enough; despite getting lost a couple of times in the dark, we found the enemy camp, skirted around it far enough away to avoid detection, then climbed up the small hill behind the camp, even having time to dig a shallow entrenchment before the sun came up. Then we waited for the rest of Caesar's army to approach from the opposite direction, from the southeast where we had left them. It was enjoyable seeing the consternation of the Helvetii when they became aware of our presence above them, except we got a little nervous as the day wore on. Caesar's progress was clearly marked for all of us to see, the accustomed pall of dust marking his march towards us, and to our eyes, it was painfully slow to watch. Luckily for us, it was clearly visible to the Helvetians as well, which is the only reason I am sure that they did not turn on us. Despite our superior position, they still outnumbered us more than 20 to one in warriors, so that it would not have taken long for them to walk up the hill to crush us. Nevertheless, it was clear that Caesar was up to something and this forced them to hesitate, unwilling to commit to our destruction while leaving the camp either undefended or lightly guarded. So like us, they sat watching that damn dust cloud move gradually in our direction. Then the cloud stopped, the dust slowly settling back to the earth, not more than a couple of miles from us. We could clearly see the army now, although it was still an indistinct mass on the horizon, with the sharper eyes among us reporting a great deal of activity at the front where the command group was normally located.

"What in Dis' name are they waiting on?" fumed Optio Rufio, prompting a snapped reply from Pilus Prior Vetruvius about officers needing to keep their mouths shut.

He was merely voicing our own fears, yet an officer of any sort cannot do that, and the Pilus Prior was right to correct him, no matter how embarrassing it may have been for Rufio. It clearly was on the Pilus Prior's mind as well, because he finally turned and stalked off, looking for the Primus Pilus and Labienus.

We sat for the better of the morning waiting before there was movement, and once it came, it was not what we had expected at all.

282

Instead of advancing on the camp, the army began to march across our front to our left, instead of arraying in battle formation. They maintained a healthy distance away from the camp so that in the event the Helvetians decided to roll the dice, our army would have time to shake out into formation, while we would be poised to strike from their rear. However, the Helvetii were not foolish, at least this day, instead contenting themselves with drawing up into a battle line, then standing there watching as the Legions marched around them. This development caused us a great deal of consternation, since we had no way of knowing what had happened to change the plan. Once Caesar moved a distance away to a much smaller hill, only then did he have the Legions form up for battle, sending all the baggage train to the rear. This new position meant that while we would not be engaged in an assault from their direct rear, we would still be able to swing down the hill onto their flank, and for a bit there was speculation that this might actually be better than from the direct rear. Whatever the case, still nothing happened, the sun rising ever higher in the sky. First we were allowed to kneel, then finally sit down, and we prepared a cold meal while we waited, it being just a matter of moments before the dice came out and the gambling began. It was in this manner that we passed most of the day, with Labienus and the Centurions becoming increasingly frustrated. No word came from Caesar, so our orders still remained in place, but it became clear to all of us that the likelihood of attack was decreasing with every passing moment. The Helvetii sensed this, made their own preparations for breaking camp, and by a bit past midday had moved on again, leaving us to watch them as they withdrew to continue their westward march. After about two parts of a watch, the rear of their column was marching away, and we were soon left alone on the hill, wondering what was going on.

The anticlimactic result came in the form of a mounted courier, bearing orders from Caesar that told us to leave the hill and rejoin the army, which was drawn back up into marching formation to follow the Helvetii. It was not until that night when we made camp that we learned what took place. Caesar had sent a Centurion from the 7th Legion, a man named Considius, to scout ahead and report back to Caesar whether or not he saw us in position on the hill. Considius came galloping back to report that the hill was indeed occupied, not by the 10th Legion, but by Helvetii. He claimed to recognize the helmets and crests of our Legion as being of Gaulish origin, so Caesar took him at his word, and waited for the 10th to dislodge the force from the hill. However, we did not because we were already there, and finally Caesar made the decision to move from his original position to find a defensible location, thinking that the 10th had been wiped out and the Helvetians were of a mind to attack. Consequently, Caesar moved to a smaller hill, where he shook the Legions out for battle, though of course no such battle took place, and instead he watched helplessly as the Helvetii went marching by, intent on making progress, no matter how small. They managed to move less than seven miles that day, so that we only had to march three before making camp. Considius was not formally punished, although he was more or less laughed out of the army; I heard a rumor that he drank himself to death not long after this event. Such are the "fortunes of war" I suppose, except I imagine Considius would call it something else. We rejoined the army without problems, and bedded down for the night, cursing the name of Considius.

By this time, our supply situation was extremely serious. The army was now down to two days' rations for both men and animals, and I imagine that there is nothing quite as unsettling as being the commander of a hungry army. Caesar was forced to turn the army north, to march on the Aeduan town of Bibracte, where he knew there would be supplies in abundance. When the Helvetii scouts saw this, they interpreted it as a sign of desperation, which in a sense it was, so they in turn reversed their march to intercept us. Making camp for the night on the banks of a river, the next morning we broke camp to begin the day's march, none of us in the ranks suspecting what was about to take place. Still headed north, following the river, we had not gotten far when there was a flurry of commotion as horsemen went racing up the side of the column looking for Caesar. The Helvetii had been sighted coming back east down the valley to intercept us, prompting Caesar to make one of those instant decisions for which he is rightly famous. Rather than continuing the march, knowing that we could march faster than the Helvetii and thereby escape them, he ordered an about turn, dispatching a unit of cavalry to go back to harass the Helvetii while he maneuvered the rest of the army into the position that he wanted. For our part, it meant that we had to reverse our course, which is fine if you are the rear Legion in that day's march, but the baggage train is a bit of an obstacle for everyone else. It immediately became clear that we would have to bypass the baggage train in some way, so we cut out over the open ground, foregoing the relative comfort of what passed for a road, marching over rough ground until we were directed by Labienus to turn to the west, where we were

284

shaken from column to line. Forming up so that the 10th was on the right, the other three Legions were arrayed to our left. Marching west, we tramped over the prominent hill that we could see even from the river. Once we crested it, we spotted the vast army of the Helvetii, already in the process of forming up, a few miles across the valley floor. Caesar ordered the two new Legions to stay behind to guard the baggage, using the hill we had just climbed as the rallying point where they would build a barrier of some sort. The rest of us were ordered to march down the slope of the hill a way before we were stopped, then further deployed into the *acies triplex*. While we did this, we watched as Caesar and the command group met at the front of the army to pass his orders.

"There sure are a lot of those bastards." Calienus voiced what we were all thinking.

It is one thing to see a mass of people on the march and realize that a good number of them are warriors, but not until they were actually arrayed before us did we realize just how many there actually were. The Helvetii were in what can only loosely be called a formation; it looked to me more of a grouping of clans or tribes, all of them dressed in whatever armor they could each provide themselves, the metal glinting in the sun. Too far away at this point to make out individuals, it was a silver-black mass that spread out in front of us, on lower ground. In their way was our cavalry, trying to delay their advance while we formed up, and our boys were clearly getting the worst of it.

Our examination was interrupted by an exclamation by Romulus. "Looks like it's win or die, boys," he called out, and we looked where he was pointing. The command group had all dismounted, including Caesar, who donned his helmet and stood, along with the Tribunes and his staff, as the slaves took the horses to the rear.

"That's for us," Calienus commented, just loud enough for us to hear. "He's letting us know that he's not going to cut and run no matter what happens."

My heart thumped more strongly in my chest as the words of Calienus sunk in. Here was a man I could follow, a man we could all follow to the gates of Hades and back if he asked it of us.

Our cavalry was quickly brushed aside, the only obstacle left after that the bodies of men and horses that the Helvetii had to step or climb over as they came at us. They flowed over the dead like a black mass of water, drawing close enough that we could now make out individuals, although we still could not see their faces. Despite the rush, Caesar had managed to place us on superior ground, with the Helvetians forced to climb a fairly steep slope to get to us, where the pitch of the ground would give us more momentum when we began our countercharge. Standing silently, watching them come, the sound of their voices screaming their war cries rolled over us in waves. Suddenly, without any order given, someone began a rhythmic tapping of his javelin against the metal rim of his shield, and it was quickly picked up by the men around him, spreading throughout the ranks, first with our Legion, then with the other three, until the sound went rolling down the slope in a challenge to the roar of the Helvetians. As if running into an invisible wall the Helvetian advance checked, the front ranks crashing to a halt as our response to their cries rolled over them, and now that we could see their faces, there was fear and uncertainty there as they were confronted not by the passionate roar of men consumed in bloodlust but the cold, measured sound of an army of professionals, men who viewed what was to come with a detached sense of duty. These warriors had never seen anything like this; they earned their experience and their scars fighting men like themselves, men who worked themselves into a frenzy, fighting with a passion that, while it ran hot, also spent itself quickly. What stood before them up that hill was unlike anything most of them had ever faced and it stopped them in their tracks, if only for a moment, and they stood there as if uncertain what to do as we waited for them. Then they began to build their courage back up, their voices growing in volume and anger again, the momentary lapse of courage forgotten. At least so they hoped, I thought, as I watched them perform their strange rituals once again. Before they resumed the advance, men would dart out from their lines, brandishing their weapons, screaming at us and despite the fact we could not understand what they were saying, it was clear they were describing what they would do to each and every one of us. As we would learn from prisoners, it was their custom for the men to give their lineage, the feats of their ancestors along with their own, so their enemy could know exactly what fate awaited them, all of which was lost on us.

"They are some excitable bastards, aren't they?

Rufio grinned at my remark, replying, "I just wish they would hurry up and get on with it. I'm getting bored standing here."

Feeble joke it may have been, it was nevertheless appreciated and our laughter, even if somewhat forced, was hearty and loud. The Centuries around us looked over to see what the joke was about, prompting Rufio to repeat it for their ears, and a wave of laughter rippled through the Cohort.

"All right ladies, shut your mouths and save your breath," snapped the Pilus Prior, but we could see a smile on his lips as he said this, and we knew that he was just as proud of us as Crastinus had been. Aside from the slaughter at the bridge, in which we played little part, this was going to be our first major test under the new Pilus Prior, and we were all determined to show him that he could rely on us. Just as importantly, we wanted to see how he measured up when commanding us. The Helvetian advance began again, this time at a slow trot as they approached the base of the hill.

"Prepare Javelins!"

Immediately, the front Centuries assumed the position, as I pulled my arm back with everyone else, feeling the shaft along the length of my arm and aiming the point skyward. I watched the Helvetians now quicken the pace to a run, unleashing a last roar as they charged up the base of the hill. There were so many of them, I remember thinking, that the rear ranks were still more than a half mile away. We would be wading in bodies before the day was through.

"Jupiter Optimus Maximus, protect this Legion, soldiers all!"

I do not know who said it, yet I was glad that someone had. They were close enough now that their charge was not only seen and heard, it was felt, the ground beneath us beginning to shake.

"Release!"

Our first volley knifed through the sky, arcing out and up before turning downwards, picking up speed as the shafts went slicing into the front ranks of the horde. They prepared themselves to receive our javelins, the front rank raising their shields while the men behind them lifted theirs above their head, in something of a crude *testudo*, yet I do not think they were truly ready for what happened when they blocked our volley. Because of the soft metal shafts, although the hardened point of the javelins punched through their shields, even if it did not strike a softer target of someone's flesh the soft metal nevertheless promptly bent. The wooden part of the shafts were now pulled to the ground by their own weight, where the ends stuck, wrenching their shields from their grasp and leaving many of the enemy exposed. I could see there were several men who had interlocked their shields together, and a javelin had pierced both, pinning them to each other. Not all of the volley hit just their shields, as above the roar of the horde came the piercing cries and screams of men who had been skewered. The volley checked the advance for a moment, with bodies tumbling to the ground, causing the men behind who were not quick on their feet to stumble and fall over them, in turn leading to even more of the same. It was like they ran into an invisible wall, and the enemy stopped momentarily while they either dropped their shields or scrambled back to their feet. There was a nice pile of bodies, but it was a drop in a huge bucket and their charge only halted for a matter of heartbeats, long enough for us to receive the second command to throw our next and last javelin.

"Release!"

The process repeated, with another volley lancing into the tightly packed warriors, creating much the same effect as before. Now it looked as if fully a third of the men in the front rank had been forced to drop their shield, and would be meeting us with just their main weapon, which was predominantly the long spear.

"Draw swords!"

The rasping sound of hundreds of blades being drawn filled my ears, and I felt comforted not only by that sound but by the feel of the sword in my hand, using the grip Vinicius had taught me those two years before. Had it really been two years? I caught myself in surprise; it's funny the things that run through your mind right before you go into battle. Standing there, poised to launch the countercharge, the front ranks of the Helvetii now no more than 30 paces away, we looked towards the center where Caesar and his standard stood, waiting for the signal to charge. The blood red standard suddenly dipped, the sounds of the *cornu* blaring out at the same time.

"*Porro!*"

288

I filled my lungs up, and with a roar followed my comrades down the hill and into the enemy.

The momentum that being higher up on the hill gave us was a huge advantage, so that when we hurtled into the Helvetii mass, the crashing of bodies and metal slamming into each other at full speed made all the noise before seem like a whisper. Quickly adding to the initial grunts of men having their breath knocked from them were the screams of men whose opponents' blade found their mark, and it was not long before even in the rear rank where we were, the coppery smell of blood was in our nostrils. Holding onto the harness of the man ahead of me, even this far back in the formation, the vibration and force of the melee in front was clearly communicated into my arm. Peering between the files, I could see the flash of blades as the men in the front rank jabbed at the Helvetii in underhand blows originating from just under our shields, while occasionally a helmet or even a severed limb would fly up into the air, sign that someone had struck home with an overhand blow. Even as I stood there and tried to stay alert, I used my height and position higher up on the hill to see if I could make any sense of what was happening, because there is nothing quite so disconcerting to fighting men as the feeling that one has no idea of the larger picture about what is unfolding. In your area, you may be carrying the day, but if everywhere else your lines are crumbling, you will soon find yourself completely surrounded and your fate is sealed, so it is almost an obsession for men in the ranks to have an idea of what is happening. I could see past the front line to observe that the enemy advance had stalled, the rear ranks of the Helvetii now milling around as they waited for their chance to enter the battle. Farther beyond them, I could make out a huge number of wagons that were being drawn up on a hill, directly across the valley to my right, opposite the Helvetian camp, which was pitched next to a small lake. That camp still had men streaming from it, coming to join the battle, and my heart sank when I saw that even with so many of the enemy heading our way the camp itself was still occupied with a large number of men. I did not know it then, but these were the Boii and Tulingi tribes, allies of the Helvetii who had joined them on their journey. All I knew was there was a good number of the bastards, but to that point they were sitting tight in the camp, for which I was thankful.

Turning my attention back to the matter at hand, I could see with some surprise that we had already gone through two rotations, making my time to fight closer at hand. Glancing over, I saw that

Scribonius had actually moved up a file, indicating that we had lost someone already. In Didius' file, he was even worse off; he was one place ahead of Scribonius, so we had lost two men there. The Century next to me was faring worse; I could see they already lost a half-dozen men, and thinking this through I became concerned. We were going to run out of people if this kept up. I had no idea what kind of casualties we were inflicting on the Helvetii, yet I saw how many there were, and for a moment I cursed my curiosity, thinking it might have been better not to know. Now the tremors I felt while holding onto the man in front increased in intensity to the point that I had to concentrate on holding on and supporting the man immediately in front of me, the shock of the fighting becoming more violent. Twice I almost lost my grip on the man's harness as he staggered back and to the side, moved that way when the man in front of him came hurtling backwards. The third time the man in the front rank staggered back, he fell down and did not get up, and as I stepped forward, I looked down to see that he had taken a spear thrust in the eye that had come out the back of his head, judging from the blood pooling underneath it. His good eye stared up in surprise, and I recognized him as one of the men who gave the beating to Didius. At least he doesn't have to worry about being cheated anymore, I thought, before turning my attention back to business. I was now second in line, and could see that we were making headway as I stepped over some Helvetii dead. This was a good sign, or so I believed, watching more closely to see what kind of skill we were facing. They were certainly courageous, that was clear, but they relied too much on their fury and not enough on technique, although I saw a few men who handled themselves with considerable skill. Their problem was that the skill levels varied widely, and I immediately realized that this was their fatal flaw. If they had taken the time to match men whose skills were roughly equal, then placed them side by side, they would have been formidable indeed and it would not have surprised me if they had carried the day. Instead, one man who was skillful may have a man on either side who was simply flailing about, relying on strength and raw courage instead of technique. When they were facing an enemy like us, where every man is roughly equal in skill, it meant that the mistake of one of the inexperienced men could and would be used in order to exploit the opening available to dispatch the skilled man, who would be engaged with someone else. In other words, they had not learned the value of teamwork; they fought as individual warriors, not as a unit, so that all of the valor in the world would not be enough to stop us. With my time getting closer, I could feel my

290

heartbeat increasing rapidly, and my breathing became quicker as I felt the love of battle start to flow more freely through me, so that by the time my turn came, I was ready to bring destruction to anyone who stood before me.

Feeling the man in front of me tense at the sound of the whistle before uncoiling his body as he heaved the man he was engaged with off of him, he then stepped aside so that I could step in, and I came forward, looking over the rim of my shield into the wild eyes of a warrior who could not have been much older than me. He wore no armor other than a leather jerkin, and if he owned a shield it was gone. His only weapon was a short hunting spear, which he jabbed at me, his face a mask of fear and hatred, but it took no more than a normal heartbeat for me to assess his abilities, and little longer to take his life with a quick thrust. He was immediately replaced by an older man wearing a coat of chain mail similar to my armor except it was fully sleeved and longer. On his head was a helmet in the Helvetian style, adorned with wings of what looked like a raven, and he had both his shield and long spear. This man did not rush me immediately, and I could instantly see the reason why he had lived to see his thirties; he was no wild-eyed youth and this was not his first battle. Additionally, he wielded his spear in an unusual manner, preferring to hold it farther up the shaft than most of the men I faced who used such a weapon. I could not see the value in this until he made his first attack, a lunging blow to my right that I automatically blocked by moving my shield across my body to parry, which is exactly what he wanted me to do. With what appeared to be nothing more than a flick of the wrist, he whipped the other end of the shaft around in a backhand blow that would have smashed into my face, breaking my nose and momentarily blinding me if it had not been for my reflexive action of turning my head so that the hard wood caught me on the ear and cheek guard of my helmet. Stars of a thousand different colors burst in my head as I felt my knees start to buckle, cursing myself for my stupidity, and I believe that it was only my sheer brute strength that saved me from falling, except I now found myself frantically on the defensive, struggling to clear my head as he pressed his attack. Only the many watches of practice and repetition saved me from his onslaught, when as of its own volition, my left arm moved my shield to block his thrusts while my right made half-hearted attempts to find my own opening. Despite myself, I felt myself step back a pace, only stopped by the strong arm of the man behind me bracing me and keeping me from falling over.

"Kill 'im Pullus. Gut that bastard."

Hearing the shout in my ear, I shook my head again to clear it even as my opponent made a thrust that I only partially deflected, the head of the spear glancing off the metal rim of my shield. There was a slicing pain high on my left arm, just below the shoulder as he cut a deep gash into my flesh. Fortunately the pain had the effect of clearing my head, and I let out a roar as I leaped back forward, catching him full in the face with the boss of my shield. I felt his nose crunch under the metal, and he let out a muffled groan, it now being his turn to step back and go on the defensive. But I was in no mood to give him any quarter; he had almost killed me, and for that he would pay. Now he was the one desperately parrying my blows as he sought to clear his own head, except he did not have the support that I had enjoyed. Even with men crowded around him, none of them thought to brace him or help him in any way; apparently it was against some sort of code of battle they had. More fools them, I thought, making a thrust at his gut that caused him to drop his shield before I gave him another taste of his own medicine, taking the pommel of my sword to smash him in the face, hitting him again on his already injured nose. This time the pain was too much for him to bear and a scream came from his lips as he dropped his shield to grab his face with his free hand, whereupon I killed him with a quick thrust to his unprotected chest. He went to his knees then toppled to the ground, still clutching his face, while I was already wading into the next man, moving a step farther down the hill, followed by my comrades.

This was the nature of the fighting for perhaps two thirds of a watch, as we continued to chop our way through the Helvetii horde. Our front line was finally relieved by the second line, attaching their files to the rear so that one longer line was created, just in the manner we drilled it so many times, while we removed ourselves to rest. The butcher's bill for our first shift was a half-dozen men down, although we only knew of two who were killed outright, the others being dragged to the rear. We stood there panting for breath, drinking our canteens dry as we talked about the battle.

"They're not very good, but there's so many of them it almost doesn't matter," gasped Vellusius as he tried to clean the caked blood off his blade so that it would not pit the iron.

"I don't know about that. There was one that almost did Pullus in. He damn near bashed his brains in." I looked in annoyance at the man who said this, then bit my tongue when I saw that it was Rufio. True as it may have been, I did not want to be reminded of it. Pulling my helmet off, I gingerly touched the spot above my ear, wincing despite myself because of the pain.

"Can you tell if your skull is broken by feeling on it?" I wondered.

"The day that skull of yours is broken, I'm packing it in," Vibius said, the lightness of his tone belied by the worried look in his eyes as he came over to examine the spot I indicated.

While he prodded on it, I felt compelled to offer some defense. "It doesn't matter how it starts, it matters how it ends, neh? And I'm still the one standing."

Rufio nodded. "Right enough. But you gave me a good scare there for a moment. I've never seen anyone handle a spear like that, and I thought you were a goner for sure. But you're a stubborn bastard, and you ended up the victor. You're right, that's all that counts."

"I don't think you broke your skull," Vibius announced when he was finished. "You're just going to have a headache for a few days." He was right about that. "You need to worry more about that cut on your arm."

I looked down in surprise; I had forgotten all about it, and I was happy to see that the blood had clotted and despite being a little stiff, the damage was obviously not extensive. To be safe, I wrapped a strip of bandage around it then promptly forgot about it as we used our vantage point higher on the hill to watch what was unfolding.

After stubborn resistance, the Helvetii began a fighting withdrawal back down the hill in the general direction of their camp. I will say this for them, they did not just turn and run, but made a true fighting retreat, leaving the field scattered with both Helvetii and Roman bodies. Once we had rested some, we were ordered back into formation, closing up behind what was now the first line, with the third line staying in place.

"Lucky bastards, we should be in the third line now." Even Didius said something that we agreed with from time to time, and this was one of them and I wondered why Caesar ordered this, but

293

quickly dismissed it as one of those things that a common *Gregarius* did not need to know, instead just shrugging my shoulders as we moved back into position.

In doing so, we also made sure that the Helvetii laying there were not still alive; it would not do to have a group of Helvetians faking their death suddenly rising up from behind us. The battle was gradually moving in the direction of the camp while the sun continued to travel through the sky. It was now well past midday, and the fighting showed no signs of letting up, leading us to speculate what would happen when the sun went down.

"Knowing Caesar, we'll keep on fighting," Vibius sighed, something in his tone telling me that he did not mean it as a compliment, though I held my tongue, not wanting to argue about it. The subject of Caesar was becoming increasingly off limits to us, because in my mind Vibius had developed a totally unwarranted view of Caesar and his motives. Shuffling along behind the first line, we continued speculating on our immediate fate until the horn sounded alerting us that we were about to rotate once more, which was met by muffled groans and curses.

"By Dis, why does it have to be us? It should be those bastards behind us," Didius complained bitterly.

Rufio told him to shut up, but we could tell it was half-hearted at best. Despite our feelings, we hoisted our shields and made ready to go back into the fray.

The Helvetii did not try to get back to their camp, clearly understanding that trying to jam that many men through the camp gates would be a disaster of the first magnitude. Instead, they chose to withdraw to a hill on the far side of the camp, and we followed close behind. As we continued pressing, I heard the Pilus Prior and Rufio conferring about something, so like all good soldiers, I did my best to eavesdrop without obviously doing just that, stopping and pretending instead to work on a loose piece of gear.

"I don't know," the Pilus Prior was saying, "but something about this doesn't strike me as being right."

"What do you mean?"

294

"Look back the way we came," the Pilus Prior pointed, and I darted my eyes in the direction he was indicating. "See the bodies?"

"Yeah, I see them," Rufio replied, clearly puzzled, "so what?"

"There aren't that many," answered the Pilus Prior.

"Aren't that many? What are you talking about? There's hundreds, more than hundreds, there's a couple thousand at least, not counting ours."

"That's exactly what I'm talking about," persisted the Pilus Prior. "You remember what Caesar told us. We're facing something like 100,000 warriors, and they retreat and act like we're beating them for a couple of thousand dead?"

"Maybe they're not as fierce as they're cracked up to be," Rufio said, but I could hear the doubt creeping into his voice while I felt the first icy fingers of dread walking up my spine.

"Does it seem that way to you?" asked the Pilus Prior quietly. "Do they act like they're beaten?"

"No," admitted Rufio. "So what do you think is going on?"

"I think that maybe they're not going back towards their camp for a reason. I think that maybe they're pulling us up that hill so that the camp is to our back."

A lump formed in my stomach as I realized that the Pilus Prior was probably right, and in that moment, my respect for him went up a notch. I finished what I was pretending to do, then hurried on to join the rest of the Century to relay what I had just heard.

"By the gods, I hope he sends word to Caesar," Romulus exclaimed.

"Send word to Caesar? Are you crazy?" Calienus laughed. "Do you think a Pilus Prior is going to stick his neck out to warn Caesar of something that might or might not happen, especially after what happened with Considius?"

He was right; it was too much to expect for a Centurion, no matter if he led a Cohort, to risk his career on a hunch, especially after the fiasco that had occurred shortly before. Nonetheless, that is

295

exactly what Pilus Prior Vetruvius did, sending Rufio off to relay his suspicions, an act that gained him even more respect from the Century and the Cohort. Finishing our move back into the first line, we resumed where we left off, exchanging smoothly with the second line, most of them gasping their thanks as they moved down the files between us. My head was pounding, and my left arm was beginning to stiffen a bit, though I knew that once I was back in the fray I would forget such things. Meanwhile, the Helvetii were slowly moving up the hill, and I could not help noticing that the piles of bodies did not seem to be as deep as one would think they should be for a retreating enemy.

Once the Helvetii made it to the top of the hill, suddenly their retreat stopped and on some unseen signal, the pace of the fighting picked back up as they unleashed the ferocity present in their first assault. For a few moments we found ourselves being pushed, ever so slightly, back down the hill and I was forced to dig my heels in, pushing hard against the man in front of me in an attempt to stop the backward slide. It was right about then that we heard a sudden roar from our right rear, coming from the direction of their camp. Risking a glance back, my heart seemed to stop at what I saw. Boiling out of the camp was another mass of warriors, not as large as what we were facing, though probably in numbers matching the size of the four Legions that were currently engaged. A series of blasts on the *cornu* alerted Caesar and the command group then we saw one of his Tribunes scrambling down the hill towards the third line, the only ones in position to meet the new threat. Even as this was happening, an idea dawned on me that perhaps this was why Caesar had insisted that the third line stay unengaged and fresh, and I was gratified to see how rapidly they reacted to the new attack. There was nothing more that I could do about it, so I turned my attention back to the fight in front, trusting in my comrades and Caesar to make sure that they stopped the advance of this second threat. Soon enough, my turn came again, except this time I was the one moving uphill, and I found myself thanking the gods yet again for my great height, since it helped negate the disadvantage. Also, I was determined not to make any further mistakes, making me more cautious than before, consequently taking longer for me to make a kill, but I contented myself with the thought that I was giving my friends more time to rest. I quickly disposed of three men and had just sliced into the thigh of a fourth when the whistle sounded, and I went back to the back of the line. The intensity of the fighting, if anything, was increasing, with the sight of the Helvetii counterattack heartening the main force while it had the same effect on us, albeit for different reasons. By this time we knew we were now fighting to stave off the destruction of our entire army, placing our trust in our comrades to the rear, and in turn we did not want to betray that trust by letting them down. With the pace becoming more furious, the relief period became shorter, and it was only a matter of a few moments before I was back in front again. Now the bodies were piling up in earnest, making the footing difficult, between the slippery blood on the grass and having to step over corpses. The job of the second man in the line is not only to brace his companion, but to end any foe that has fallen and is not yet dead, and those in the second rank were now busier than ever. Just as I was dispatching my opponent, I heard a cry of pain to my left and looked over to see Scribonius fall to the ground, writhing in agony but still trying to use his shield to protect him from the man who knocked him down. The Helvetii warrior in turn let out a roar of triumph and stood over Scribonius, his arm pulled back for the killing blow with his spear. Without thinking, I leapt sideways, crashing into the man just as he thrust down at Scribonius' unprotected face, the point instead burying itself in the ground several inches deep no more than a hand width away from my friend. In making that move I had helped Scribonius, yet I left myself exposed to a blow from the rear from the man I was facing, and I felt my shoulders involuntarily clench in expectation of a thrust that never landed. Instead, I heard the part-crunching, part-squishing sound of a blade being thrust into the man's chest by my relief, who had lost his grip on my harness when I jumped, but thankfully not his wits. Simultaneously, I made a quick thrust to the throat of the man who had tried to kill Scribonius, his blood spraying all over my arm and face as he made a choking sound and fell to the ground. In almost the same motion, I dropped my shield and with my left hand, grabbed Scribonius by the front of the armor, ignoring his screams of pain, half dragging, half flinging him backwards out of the front line. Once he was out of the way, I picked up my shield and turned back to face the enemy, ready to continue killing.

Fortunately the third line moved quickly, forming up in a single line, angling across our rear partway up the hill to meet the threat posed by the Boii and Tulingi. Fighting in that area was ferocious, the Helvetii knowing this was their one and only chance to overwhelm us and destroy Caesar's army. Understanding that as well, that knowledge kept us going through the day, the sun moving steadily towards its home in the west. Neither side would relent,

297

both knowing the stakes, yet the bravery of the Helvetii was no match for the iron discipline and teamwork of the Legions, as we chewed them up like some huge beast will gnaw on its prey, spitting out heaps of dead and dying men in our wake, relying on the watches of drill that enable us to perform without any conscious thought. First position, bash with the shield, thrust while remembering to turn the hips, withdraw, recover. Over and over, variations on the same theme of killing, not thinking, just doing, ignoring the pain and fatigue in your body, knowing that by giving into it, you will not only shame yourself, you will cause the death of your friends and comrades. So you move forward, your mind empty of every thought that might distract you, and you kill, over and over. We were only vaguely aware of the struggle taking place behind us, while the third line stood firm, battered over and over as if by a huge wave, yet never giving in, never giving ground that might lead to the destruction of the army. Instead, slowly but surely, they began to advance on their foe, who in turn gave ground very grudgingly, at least at first. Then, the second Helvetian attack suddenly disintegrated, and quickly a retreat became a rout, with men running for their lives, heading to their last defense, the hill on which all the wagons gathered. The main force of the Helvetii, the force we were engaged with, having the advantage of being higher on the hill, was able to see the crumbling of the second attack. Seeing now that all was lost, the men in the rear of their formation began to stream away, seeking safety by fleeing the battle, but the men in the front lines had no such luxury. They understood that the instant they turned their back we would cut them down and this knowledge made them fight even harder, something that I did not think was possible until I saw it. They resisted in the manner of men who know that they are doomed, yet are determined to take as many of their enemy with them as they can and indeed, many of us fell, some to never rise again. One of them was Hirtius, our Tesseraurius who replaced Cordus, disemboweled by a spear. Thankfully, I did not see it happen, but it was a painful loss nonetheless. For my part, I do not know how many men I killed that day; I lost track around ten men, worrying me a bit because I had been told that when I sacrificed to the gods, being accurate was very important so one knew the size of the offering to give. We sensed more than saw the thinning of the force in front of us, until finally, there were no more men to kill; only then did we pause to stand there for a moment, chests heaving, standing in a heap of dead and wounded, trying to make some sense of what had happened. As I was catching my breath, I looked up in

298

surprise to see that the sun was hanging low above the hills; this battle had lasted almost two full watches, and it was still not over.

Across the valley, on the other hill, the third line chased the Boii and Tulingi up to the wagon camp, where the Helvetii women and children were gathered in the center, huddled in terror as they awaited the inevitable outcome. Their warriors were on top of the wagons, and were reduced to hurling stones or whatever they could lay their hands on that would make a missile. Meanwhile the men from the third line were now being joined by the Cohorts of the second line, sent to aid their comrades.

"Should we join them?" I wondered aloud, not that I had any desire to. I was exhausted, and killing women and children was never my idea of fun. However, the wagons also meant booty, so that was a temptation.

"We haven't been given any orders to," answered the Pilus Prior, who was standing caked in blood, a long cut running across his cheekbone, the gore having obscured the lower part of his face. "First we need to see to our own wounded. Then if it looks like they need help, we'll head over there."

Immediately we turned to the task; I found Scribonius, who was alive, though he was in grave condition, having taken a spear thrust all the way through his left shoulder, just above the collarbone, the point having passed all the way through. This could be a good thing, as long as none of the material from his tunic, or even worse, none of the links of his armor had been driven into his body and were still in there. If that was the case, he would die a horrible, lingering death, the wound putrefying and poisoning the rest of his body. He was conscious, but just barely, and I knelt beside him, trying to give him a smile.

"I'm sorry if I hurt you when I dragged you out of the way," I told him, drawing a ghost of a smile.

"Pullus, I hate to tell you this, but I don't think a career as a *medici* is in your future. You handle your patients much too roughly."

I laughed at his attempt at a joke then promised to come see him as soon as we were settled in camp and then he was carried down the hill by the *medici*. Calienus was wounded as well,

299

although he could walk with some help, having taken a spear thrust to the thigh. It missed the bone, but when pulled free, it had torn a hunk of the muscle so that it was hanging loose and would have to be sewn back together. I could not help wondering if he would be crippled, but he was too tough for that. Once we were done, we turned our attention back to the far hill. The sun was just sinking below the edge of the horizon, although it would remain light for a couple of more hours, and the order was passed for us to re-form to march over to the hill and help mop up the last resistance, which we did, albeit a little reluctantly. At least, some of us were reluctant; Didius was literally smacking his lips at the prospect of plundering the wagons, and......other things. Part of his character was such that he took no pleasure in coupling with a woman if she were willing, although I guess it is not hard to see why. Even with the whores, he garnered a reputation for enjoying inflicting pain, so soon enough, even women who are paid to be willing were giving him a wide berth, limiting his opportunities for pleasure to moments such as these. Watching him with undisguised loathing as he chattered about what was to come, it made me wonder about the justice of a world where men like Scribonius were struck down while Didius managed to survive without a scratch. I will give him this much; he was a born survivor, and would prove extremely hard to kill.

Arriving at the wagons, it was a scene of desperate fighting. Those Helvetii men left knew they were fighting to save their women and children from slavery and worse, not to mention all their worldly possessions that were contained in the wagons, and this gave them an endurance to match their desperate courage. This was no battle; this was a brawl of the first magnitude, with small groups of men fighting viciously among the wagons, while the women looked on, or in many cases, tried to help the men fight. We were sent around the hill to complete sealing it off, and soon moved up to the wagons, just as the last of the light was fading. Despite our fatigue, we were required to give one last supreme effort as we engaged with the Boii and Tulingi warriors, who were literally throwing themselves off the top of the wagons and down onto us, sometimes knocking us to the ground, where we would roll around and fight like animals. Very quickly I found Vibius and myself embroiled in a desperate struggle with a group of four men, a pair of them teaming up to kill each of us. If they had worked as four against one, or even three against one, with the fourth trying to occupy one of us, they would have made short work of the thing. Instead, they chose this method and paid the price for it with their lives. At one point, I was rolling around on the ground with the last man, trying to avoid his hand as it clawed at my eyes, using my greater weight to pin him while I frantically grabbed for my dagger, having lost the grip on both my sword and shield. Finally pinning him underneath me, I drove the blade up under his ribcage, our faces no more than a couple of inches apart, then watched the life drain from his eyes. This was the closest I had ever been to a man I killed, and found it a profound and somewhat disturbing experience. Finally clearing the wagons, we then moved into the circle to see that the line was now breached in several spots, and Legionaries were rushing about in a frenzy of looting, rape and killing. The screams of women as they were violated began to fill the air, mingled with the cries of despair from young children forced to watch. Not all of the women passively accepted their fate, however. A good number of them fought viciously, clawing, biting and spitting at anyone who came near, and that was how they died, their faces frozen in expressions of hatred, their lips curled back from their teeth like a cornered wolf. The Centurions began trying to restore order, but between the darkness and the manner in which the day's fighting had gone, the Legionaries were wild with bloodlust and the desire to rape, pillage and burn. Vibius and I contented ourselves with looting a couple of wagons, finding hoards of coins and jewelry, along with other odds and ends that we thought would fetch a price when we sold them. Someone set fire to a couple of wagons, probably more to provide light than for anything else, the flickering flames casting an illumination on the scene that fit the nature of what was happening. It did not take long for men like Atilius to sniff out the wine that was part of the cargo on most of the wagons, and soon enough, men were staggering around drunk, making restoring order all the much harder.

The aftermath of the battle was such that we spent the next three days in place. According to Caesar's account, we were tending to our wounded, and while I do not want to dispute the great man, from my viewpoint in the ranks it was less a matter of tending the wounded as it was sobering up the drunk. Apparently the Helvetii liked their drink, and did not confine themselves to just wine, imbibing something fermented from honey they call mead. I despised the taste, yet it is incredibly potent, and for men like Atilius who drink not for the pleasant taste but for the sensation it provides, mead was the perfect answer. Unfortunately, there was a lot of it to be had, and there were a lot of men like Atilius, so in my own humble opinion, it was this more than any other reason why we stayed in place for that time. Regardless of our reason for staying put, there was a massive amount of work to do. As many bodies that were buried at the bridge, this number was dwarfed by what we faced now. In the wagons was found a census roll that stated that the Helvetii, Boii and Tulingi tribes numbered a total of 360,000 people. We buried upwards of 80,000 at the bridge, and now there were some 120,000 to bury here. Additionally, we held some 30,000 prisoners, meaning that about 130,000 of the Helvetii actually escaped from the battle. Despite being a fraction of their earlier number, it was still a formidable force, which I think explains in part why Caesar ordered a halt. Burial of all these bodies took the better part of two days, but luckily, the 10th did not get selected for the duty, since we pulled it at the bridge. Instead, we were to provide security, guard the prisoners who were about to be sold into slavery, and perform routine patrols around the area to make sure that the Helvetii did not circle back and try to take us unaware. They were doing just that, but not for the reasons we feared.

After the three days, we formed back up to march again, the wounded like Scribonius and Calienus being loaded in the spare unburned wagons left by the Helvetii, and we began to follow them again, intent on finishing the job of stopping their migration, one way or another. It was while we were on the march that Caesar was met by a deputation from the tribe who threw themselves at his feet, begging for mercy and promising to do whatever he commanded as long as he did not exterminate them. Caesar gave instructions for them to wait where they were, allowing the entire army to catch up, whereupon he would sit in judgment and decide what to do with them. Reaching the site of the Helvetii camp in two days, we made our own, in a position that was defensible yet provided a good view of the comings and goings of the tribe. Once we were established in a strong defensive posture, Caesar announced his decision concerning the Helvetii, ordering them to return to their homes. Knowing that they destroyed everything, Caesar ordered the neighboring tribes to help supply them with the food that they needed to survive through another planting season and harvest. In addition, he demanded their weapons, along with a certain number of hostages. A group of some 6,000 Helvetii refused to accept this and that night, crept out of camp, headed for the Rhenus and Germany. Caesar sent word that any tribe whose lands they passed through that did not apprehend them would be treated as the enemy, whereupon the tribes faced with this ultimatum promptly rounded them up and returned those Helvetii in fairly short order, where they

302

were all put to death. A total of 110,000 out of the total 368,000 of the Helvetii were left to return to their home territory, and in some ways, their problems were solved. They had originally moved because they did not have enough land for their people, but defying Caesar solved that problem for them, there now being plenty of their land to go around. The Boii were accepted into the lands of the Aedui, who esteemed their courage and desired them to be part of their tribe from then on. All in all, the problem was solved, the surrounding tribes who previously worried about the Helvetii were happy, and deputations from every tribe flocked to the camp to pay their respects to Caesar and win his favor. For our part, we were thankful for the respite from marching and building camps, settling into the routine static camp life very quickly, as we waited for our wounds to heal and for some new crisis to emerge.

There were other changes as well, at least as far as I was concerned. While Calienus healed, I was made acting Sergeant, which I will say I was happy about. So were most of the others, except of course for Didius, who somehow convinced himself that he was best suited for the job. Ignoring his comments like I normally did, I settled quickly into the routine of our duties. There were other spots to fill, the most important being Tesseraurius, since it is a job of enormous trust, if not quite as prestigious as Signifer or Optio. This is an office that is as close to an elected post as any in the Roman army, because the person who is being considered must be regarded as honest and scrupulous by almost everyone in the Century. A few nights were spent by the Optio and Pilus Prior at each of our fires, asking us our opinions about the various men being considered for the job, and it was not long before one name became most commonly mentioned, a name that surprised those of his tent section a great deal, and that was Calienus. It was not that we did not trust him; in fact, he was trusted a great deal, by all of us. It was just that we never really thought about him for the job, and the suggestion did not come from our tent section, but from a number of the others. Not lost on me was the idea that if Calienus were selected, then I might be considered for the job of Sergeant permanently, although it was just as likely that the Pilus Prior would move a more experienced man from another section into his place. Once it was decided, the Pilus Prior went to the hospital to tell Calienus, who was still recovering from his wound, and when he returned, I was told that I was now the permanent Sergeant of the tent section. There was no fanfare, no speech or advice given, the Pilus Prior just said it as a simple fact before going back to his tent and whatever it was that he did in there. As soon as I got the chance, I went to the hospital myself to talk to Calienus and ask him for advice on what I needed to do.

"Do?" he asked, with an arched eyebrow, his leg propped up on a stack of small blocks covered with a folded cloth for padding. He was still pale, yet looked fit enough considering the circumstances, being able to get around on crutches, which were next to the bed, and I could see that he was enjoying my anxiety. "Why, Pullus, you don't do anything. That's the beauty of the job." He laughed, before continuing, "You don't think I would ever take a job where you actually have to work, do you? I thought you knew me better than that."

Clearly enjoying the confused look on my face, he was content to smile and say nothing. Finally I could contain myself no longer. "Pluto's thorny cock, that doesn't help me a bit, now does it?" I demanded, irritated that he looked so smug.

"You've been watching me do my job for two years," he chuckled at my guilty expression. "Titus, I know you've wanted to do the job, and that's half the battle right there. I don't fault you for being ambitious; just because I'm not doesn't mean that I can't appreciate it in someone else. You already know what to do because you've seen me doing it."

I felt slightly better, relieved that he did not find fault with my naked desire for promotion. "So, I just do what you did?" I asked, and he nodded then gave a shrug. "It's really not hard. The only time it was difficult at all was when I had to break you new bastards in, but those days are long gone. Now all you have to do is make sure that nobody tries to take advantage of your friendship and pull things over on you. The only one I can see you've got to worry about is Achilles."

That was no surprise; I had already anticipated that, and I asked Calienus what I should do in the event that he did try something.

His face turned hard and he said simply, "You beat him so badly that he'll never even think of trying it again."

I smiled, thinking that I could do that without any problem. Before I left the hospital I went to see Scribonius, who was lucky in his own right. No foreign matter had gotten pushed into the wound, and it was healing cleanly, although he was not completely out of danger.

"The doctor said that there was a lot of muscle damage, and I'm going to have to build the strength back up. He said it's going to hurt worse than the original wound did."

I simply nodded in sympathy, because I had some idea of what he was talking about from the wound I suffered in the ribs back in Hispania. Telling him the latest news and catching him up on the gossip about what took place with the Helvetii, I promised to come back and visit him in the next few days. He congratulated me on my promotion, then bidding him goodbye, I returned to the tent.

It did not take long for Didius to test me, but I was ready for him, and I gave him a good thrashing that left him with a lot of bruises and a swollen face.

"You know, it would seem that you'd learn after this many beatings," Romulus remarked the night after our confrontation as we sat around the fire, eating our evening meal.

Didius pretended not to hear, yet I could see by the red creeping up his face that the remark had hit home. Despite my loathing of Didius, some inner voice of caution kept me from going too far in humiliating him, and I kept my peace, also pretending not to pay attention as I sewed up a hole in my tunic.

"That's true Romulus," this came from Vellusius, who was sprawled out close to the fire, idly throwing sticks into it. "But Achilles is one of those people who just don't seem to learn from their mistakes. Ain't that right Achilles?"

"Shut your mouths, both of you," Didius snarled. "Or by Dis, I'll......."

I did not allow him to finish, speaking up before anything else could take place. "Didius is right," I said, refusing to look up from my sewing job, "you two need to keep your mouths shut. This is between Didius and me, and nobody else. I don't want to hear you mention it again."

Both men had a look of astonishment on their face at my rebuke, Vellusius flushing then opening his mouth to speak before shutting it and looking away angrily. I knew my words had surprised and hurt them, yet I also realized that I could not even have the appearance of playing favorites, especially since if it were the other way around I would have told Didius to shut his mouth in the same way. My hope was that at least Didius noticed this, and that perhaps it might go a small way to change his attitude towards me and his comrades, though it was a vain hope.

Larger events were taking place that dwarfed our own little contest of wills. At the meeting of all the Gallic chiefs, a number of them asked for a private audience with Caesar, which he granted. Acting as their spokesman, Diviciacus, the Vergobret of the Aedui, told Caesar of the peril that not just the Aedui, but other Gallic tribes such as the Sequani were facing from a German named Ariovistus. It seemed that the Aedui had asked Ariovistus for help in besting their most bitter rival, a tribe called the Arverni, which Ariovistus and his men did. However, when it was time for Ariovistus and his army to go back across the Rhenus, they apparently decided that the fertile farmlands of Gaul were more to their liking, and in short work, subjected the Aedui and their allies the Sequani. This Ariovistus then set himself up as a petty king, demanding tribute and hostages from the tribes, and it was under the fear of death and destruction that Diviciacus came to Caesar asking for help. What complicated matters was that Ariovistus, like the Aedui and Sequani, had been awarded the status of friend of Rome, so it was in this spirit that Caesar first communicated to Ariovistus, politely asking him to meet in order to discuss the dispute.

Apparently, Ariovistus held no such inclination, and although it was not until I read Caesar's account years later that I learned exactly what took place, all we knew at the time was that Ariovistus had been very insulting, not just to Caesar but to Rome, and more importantly to us, the Legions. He made it clear that he did not think much of our army, nor our skills in battle, despite what we did to the Helvetii, and it was not long before word began circulating that we were going to head for a confrontation with this Ariovistus. Orders were given to repair all gear, replenish our stock of javelins and draw marching rations, because we would be on the move in a matter of a couple of days.

Chapter 6- Ariovistus

We were ordered out of the camp and on the march exactly two days after the rumor circulated; it is an interesting thing about the way this gossip circulates throughout an army. Any rumor is considered to be as close to fact as one can get, and when questioned, the man passing it along will always bring up past examples that had come true. However, somehow we all tended to forget the ones that did not turn out the same way and thinking back on it, I realize that for every one that turned out to be the truth, or close to it, there were probably five that were completely off the mark. Yet we always seemed to forget those, instead only remembering the times where someone passed along a piece of information that turned out to be accurate. Accordingly, we had an idea of what was in store, although it would turn out that in this campaign, rumors would almost undo us. Marching northeast, we headed back towards the town of Vesontio, which Caesar learned was in the plans of Ariovistus to appropriate. Since it contained supplies and weapons, it was strategically vital that we not only keep Ariovistus from seizing it but take it for our own needs. All of this we were happily ignorant about, knowing only that we were marching at Caesar's usual cracking pace, while he sent word ahead for the Aedui, Sequani and the Lingones to supply us with food as we marched so that we could travel more lightly, and he had us marching well after dark, forcing us to construct camp under trying conditions. It was in this way that we arrived in Vesontio in the middle of the third day, having covered a hundred miles of open territory in little more than two and a half days. Needless to say, we were all exhausted, but Caesar could not spare us the rest, having a camp to construct, which we built on the outskirts of the town. Vesontio is an eminently defensible position, and it was easy to see why Caesar thought it was so important. Nestled in a loop of the Dubis (Doubs) River, it is surrounded on three sides by water, while the narrow neck of land connecting it to the rest of the area is not much more than 500 paces wide. Guarding the neck is a low hill, where a wall of stone is built protecting the town itself. It was just outside of this wall where our camp was built, situated in such a way that we could easily leave the camp to man the wall in the event of an attack, there not being enough space for our camp in the space between that wall and those of the town. It was thrown up with our usual speed, though also with the same thoroughness and exacting standards that Caesar had come to expect from us. While we were busy with our constructing, he sent a Legion into the town itself to provide a garrison, this being the start of our problems. I will not mention the number of the Legion, since their actions caused us considerable embarrassment, only saying that it was not the 10th. We were part of the force building the camp, and played no part in what was to happen.

It was here where Caesar decided to wait for Ariovistus and during the idle time of the next couple of days we began to learn more about the men we were facing, and with what seemed to be every passing watch, our situation became direr.

"I was talking to my cousin in the 8th," was how it started among our Century, when Romulus relayed what he had learned one evening. "And he was telling me that the townspeople have had a lot of dealing with those Germans of Ariovistus, and they're scared to death of them." This was naturally met with interest, although Romulus needed no prodding. "He said that the townsfolk swear that the small ones are the size of Pullus, and most of them are almost seven feet tall."

"*Gerrae*! I don't believe that for a minute," I snorted, not for any other reason than I refused to believe that there were men taller than I was.

"It's true," he insisted, "that's how they were able to subdue the Gauls so easily." Warming to his subject, he continued, "And he said that their secret weapon is some spell that their witches taught them to cast on their enemies when they line up to do battle. They gaze at their enemies, and if you make eye contact with any of them, it casts a spell on you that paralyzes you so that you can't fight." I laughed at this then quickly realized that nobody was joining in. Looking about at my friends, I saw that they were indeed taking this seriously.

"Well," Atilius said thoughtfully, "given how much of a fight those Helvetii put up, I can't imagine that the Aedui or those other tribes are any less fierce. Look what it took for us to beat them. Maybe that's why Ariovistus was able to take their lands so easily."

I looked at Atilius incredulously. "You're not believing this, surely? This is just talk."

Romulus bristled at the unintended slight. "I know my cousin, Pullus. He's not the type to get worried easily, and he's a good man. If he believes it, I believe it."

Trying to head this off, I apologized to Romulus for the offense, then asked him what else was said, hoping that this would move us to safer subjects. I was wrong.

"He also said that before they can be considered men, each German must kill ten men in single combat, and drink the blood of their enemies. That's why they're so strong; they gather the strength from the men they've killed."

I must admit that even my heart fluttered a little hearing that, although I would like to think that it was due more to the barbarity of drinking your enemy's blood than what it supposedly attained for the Germans. This was the tone of the conversations taking place in every part of the camp, and it did not take long before some sort of panic swept through the army. In my opinion, what made it worse was the reaction of our officers, who not only did not stamp out the rumors, but actually believed them and were in turn infected with the same madness that the common soldiers were suffering. Suddenly, a large number of the fine young men attached to the army as Tribunes suddenly found reasons that they were urgently needed back in Rome. They began rushing about the camp, looking for their high-born friends in other Legions to confer about the best course of action, given that the army was about to be slaughtered by the invincible Germans. Not even the Centurions were immune to this panic, although it was a relatively small number out of the whole. Out of our 60 Centurions, perhaps three of them seemed to be of the same mind as the Tribunes. It must be said that the Tribunes and even the Legates we understood; for the most part they were soldiers in name only, and although there were some of them we respected, Labienus being one, along with young Publius Crassus, they were the minority. Now these puffed up nobles showed all of us their true value, infecting the army at every level with their constant chattering about the impending calamity. But the final blow came when some veterans we respected began voicing fears about our supplies and the forests that we would have to march through. It appeared that we were beaten before Ariovistus even bothered to show up.

Caesar, as he was wont to do, acted swiftly, calling a meeting of the Tribunes and Centurions, where he gave them a severe chastising. Demanding an explanation, he let them know that their actions were not only having a devastating effect on the morale of the army, they were also calling into question Caesar's abilities as a commander, and I suspect of the two, it was the latter that infuriated Caesar more. Reminding them of his uncle Marius, who dealt crushing defeats to the Germans, Caesar minimized the accomplishments of the Germans against the Gauls, pointing out that we had defeated the same men as the Germans, which hardly hinted at their superiority. He was especially harsh with those who, rather than express alarm at the valor of the Germans, disguised their fears as concerns about supplies and terrain, because he viewed these men as questioning his capacity for command. There was even muttering that when he gave the command to march, the Legions would refuse, and it was this rumor that caused Caesar to say something that cemented his place in our heart. If it came to that, he said, he would march with the 10th and the 10th only, since he trusted it implicitly and knew he could count on it to follow him wherever he led. I believe it was this statement more than any that turned the morale of the army around in an instant. Despite the fact that he was speaking only to the Tribunes and Centurions, he had to know that what was said at that meeting would flash through the camp in a matter of moments. For us in the 10th, it made us determined that we would never let Caesar down, because he gave us perhaps the greatest honor a general can give his men, and we made sure to send a message of thanks to him, along with our solemn vow that he would never have reason to regret his words. Many years later, some of the men of the 10th would go back on that promise, but that was far in the future. For the other Legions, they were now shamed by the idea that he felt he could only count on the 10th for support, and they were now determined to show him that their loyalty matched ours. It was a brilliant piece of work, perhaps not what historians will write about, yet is just as important as any maneuver on the battlefield, because it was like a lamp was lit in a previously darkened room, the gloom suddenly banished in the instant it takes for the light to flare to life. Now, instead of worrying about our fates, we were anxious to be put to the test, and the army began clamoring for Caesar to give the orders to march to meet Ariovistus. We were not to be disappointed; on the last day of the month that is now known as August, we marched out of camp, leaving a force of three Cohorts behind to guard the town and the camp. In order to avoid those thick woods that some of the men were worried about the Vergobret Diviciacus, who was acting as our guide, led us in a wide swing to the north before turning towards the east where Ariovistus was located. This added two days to the march which, given the mood of the army before we set out, could have been a problem because it gave men time to think. However, such was Caesar's chastisement of the Tribunes and Centurions that the men were instead chafing at the delay of facing Ariovistus and his Germans. Finally coming within a day's march of where the Germans were camped, we made our own camp on the banks of a river, settling down to wait for further developments. Ariovistus was to the north, and he sent messengers saying that now he was willing to parley with Caesar, with a meeting set for five days' time. Speaking personally, every day's delay was a good thing, since it meant that Scribonius was closer to full strength, thereby bettering his chance for survival in the next battle. His shoulder wound had caused his left arm to shrivel, and he worked extremely hard to restore it to full use, the fear of being found unfit for duty and discharged spurring him to work harder than I had ever seen him. It also meant that I spent extra time with him individually, working on weapons drills, which I was happy to do, despite its meaning that with my other duties as Sergeant, sleep was something with which I only had a passing acquaintance. Calienus had been less than truthful about the duties of a Sergeant, yet when I confronted him about it, he had just laughed.

"You really didn't expect me to tell you the truth did you?"

"If I had known what all was involved, I might have thought differently about it," I retorted.

"Which is exactly why I didn't tell you. I did you a favor Pullus."

Somehow I did not see it that way.

311

In the predawn of the day of the conference, the Primus Pilus paid the Second Cohort a visit.

"Pullus," Primus Pilus Favonius said without any preamble, "Caesar summons you. Get your gear on and meet at the *Praetorium* immediately."

He turned to walk away, but then thought of something.

"And wear your dress uniform, with your decorations."

There was no time to wonder what this was about; I had to dig my phalarae and plume out of my pack, where they were carefully wrapped in cloth to avoid rough treatment. I was just thankful that we had been idle for the last few days, since it gave me time to polish my decorations and clean my armor and helmet. Putting on the tunic I wore for inspections, I donned my gear then stood while the Pilus Prior came to inspect me by the light of the fire. Grunting, he said, "I suppose it'll have to do. Now hurry up and get over there!"

I made my way down the Cohort street and over to the *Via Principalis*, which leads directly to the *Praetorium*. Standing in front of the tent was a small group of men, all from the 10th, but from different Cohorts. With them was the Primus Pilus, who explained what we were doing.

"Each of you has been selected by your Cohort for a very important mission. Today is the day that Caesar is supposed to meet with that bastard Ariovistus." We all nodded, this being common knowledge.

"That smug *cunnus....suggested* to Caesar that they meet only with an escort of ten men each. Caesar doesn't trust him as far as he can throw him, and he thinks he's up to something," Favonius continued. "And we all know how useless our Gallic cavalry proved to be when we whipped the Helvetii," this also was common knowledge and had been one of the reasons some of the men were scared. The Germans were reputed to have excellent cavalry, and ours had not acquitted themselves with any distinction against the Helvetii. "So Caesar is going to trick the trickster. Instead of those useless bastards, he wants boys from the 10th to accompany him.

Each of you was put forward by your senior Centurion as being the best in your Cohort if it comes to fighting, so you're going to be going with Caesar."

Words cannot describe the feeling those words invoked in me, and even after all the awards and decorations I have won, that moment still ranks as one of my proudest. Even as I dictate this, I can feel the shiver of an absolutely delicious sensation of joy recalling these words. Finished with his instructions, the Primus Pilus led us over to the cavalry section, ordering us to pick a horse from the pool of spares, which is when I had my first moment of doubt. As was usual in the army, nobody had bothered to ask me if I even knew how to ride a horse, although in our training we were taught how to vault into the saddle wearing all of our gear. I could count on one hand the number of times I had actually gone for a ride on a horse and have all my fingers left over, and the thought that I would humiliate myself came bursting into my head. My heart started hammering as I gazed at the horses, pretending to consider which beast was best suited for me, and my only hope was that riding a horse was similar to riding a mule, because that I had done many times before I became too large for ours to carry me. With that in mind, I picked out a roan that was larger than the rest, thinking that it would not do to have a horse collapse under me because of my weight. The cavalrymen who had been roused to help us with our selection put my mind at ease a bit when I saw him nod with approval at the mount I chose.

"That's a good strong horse you've chosen *Gregarius*," he commented as he helped me saddle it. "He's got a lot of bottom to him so you won't have to worry about him foundering."

Nodded sagely, as if this were something more than just dumb luck, I leaped into the saddle with all the aplomb I could muster. Fortunately my luck held, the horse accepting me onto his back without rancor, just sidestepping a bit as he adjusted to my weight. Riding from the enclosure back out onto the street and down to the *Praetorium*, we stopped there to wait a few moments for Caesar. Dawn had now come, and the army was awake, with the men gathering to watch the procession leave the camp. Caesar came striding out, bedecked in his best uniform, a muscled cuirass made of silver, inlaid with gold, his helmet made in the same fashion, with a crest made of black feathers. Leaping onto his horse, he disdained the assistance offered to him, then pulled his mount around to inspect those of us who were to be his escort and were aligned in a

313

single row to greet him. Sitting as erect as I could, my eyes were straight ahead as I sensed him moving towards me in the line. He said something encouraging to every man, complimenting them on their awards, or on their fierce countenance. When he pulled up to me, despite myself my gaze broke to look him in the eyes, immediately cursing myself for the breach in discipline, but he did not seem to mind, favoring me with a smile that made my heart soar.

"Sergeant Pullus, it's good to see you again. I'm glad to know you'll be by my side for this adventure." My face must have registered the surprise I felt that he remembered my name, because he laughed and said, "Surely you aren't surprised that I remember you? How could I forget such a giant who marches for me, especially one so valiant who I personally decorated?"

I could feel the heat rising in my face, pleased that he not only remembered my name but was aware I had gotten promoted, and I have no idea what came out of my mouth. Evidently it was nothing forward or disrespectful, because he gave a wave then turned to the front gate, and we formed up behind him in a column of twos, with me in the last rank, trotting out behind him, enjoying the feeling as we waved to our friends who gathered to watch us leave. I do not know who it was that said it, but a voice called out something that would become etched in the history of the Legion, and become one of our first and most famous nicknames.

"Look boys," a voice rang out, "Caesar promised to honor the 10th, but he's going one better. He's making us knights."

There was a roar of laughter and cheering at that remark, which even Caesar thought was witty, since he mentioned the incident in his account of the campaign. So it was with the sounds of approbation ringing in our ears that we left to meet Ariovistus.

The meeting place itself was a small mound of earth that stood in the middle of the surrounding plain, making ambush impossible because there was nowhere that one could conceal a force of any size. We approached the mound from the south, Ariovistus from the north, his escort of ten men with him. As we drew near, I could see that the tales of the great size of the Germans may indeed have not been an exaggeration, with every man in the escort looking to be at least my height, and a couple of men were plainly taller. Ariovistus himself was a powerfully built man of about forty, wearing a helmet decorated with the horns of some wild beast, with engraved images

314

that I could not distinguish from where I was, though it was obviously very fine work. He disdained wearing any armor, preferring to bare his chest, I supposed so that Caesar could see the many scars he bore from battle. His arms were decorated with a series of golden bands, and around his neck was a torq of gold, also engraved, while his hair was jet black, with streaks of grey in the part flowing over his shoulders, and his expression was haughty as he made his formal greeting to Caesar. He made his contempt for us clear by not even looking in our direction, and I could feel the anger rising in my gut as I watched him face Caesar. His bodyguards' demeanor was a mirror image of Ariovistus, and they made comments to each other while pointing at us, laughing harshly at the jokes they made at our expense. Locking eyes with one man in particular, I noticed that he was a contrast to Ariovistus in that his hair was as yellow as gold and his complexion fairer than his chief's. Otherwise, he was dressed in the same manner, carrying a long sword at his side while holding a spear. His lips curled in open contempt when our eyes met, as if to tell me that he had taken my measure already and found me wanting, making it all I could do to keep from charging him right then, except I was smart enough to know that this was exactly what he intended. During our ride to the meeting Caesar had ordered us that under no circumstances were we to respond or retaliate to anything that the Germans said or did, no matter how provocative. That would have been enough information for most commanders, except that Caesar actually took the time to explain why he was giving those orders. Years later, with more experience in leading men, I now believe he knew this would make us even more adamant about following those orders to the letter. Once a common soldier feels that he is trusted enough to be taken into the confidence of his commander, and explained the wider implications of his orders, that man would rather die than see that trust betrayed by violating them. It was rare enough that we were given any reason for what we were doing, so when a man like Caesar took that extra step, it ensured that he could have the utmost confidence that his command would be followed to the letter. He explained to us that the problem lay in the status of Ariovistus; as I mentioned earlier, he was a Friend and Ally of Rome, and that is a legal status that gives the appointed certain rights and privileges under Roman law. Because of that status, Caesar could not be seen in any way to provoke Ariovistus, or make a move that could be deemed offensive in nature. Ariovistus had to be clearly seen as the aggressor in this battle of wills, so that no matter what the provocation, Caesar could not afford to strike the first blow. Our general went on to explain that he was positive that this talk Ariovistus proposed was a pretext for provoking Caesar in some way, and he warned us that it was highly likely that either Ariovistus, or his bodyguard would either say or do something in an attempt to elicit a response that could be turned against us. This warning was in our minds as we sat our horses, watching the men across from us. Despite the mound being relatively small, it was large enough that Caesar and Ariovistus could pull off to a spot several yards away where they could talk privately, leaving the twenty of us to glare at each other and mutter curses under our breath.

"By the gods, they do stink, don't they?"

This came from the man next to me, from the Fifth Cohort, a Signifer named Frontinus. I forced a laugh, anxious to show the Germans that I found them just as amusing as they found us. "They must be afraid of water," I replied, still keeping my eyes on the yellow haired man, who was doing the same.

"Bathing is for women, Roman." Despite the accent, the Latin was intelligible, and I was not altogether surprised that it was the yellow-haired man who spoke.

"Ah, you know our language," said a Sergeant named Rufus from the First Cohort, a man who was close to my size. "Then you'll understand this, won't you, you *cunnus*?"

The yellow-haired man hissed at this epithet, his eyes narrowed in rage, and he moved his horse a few steps towards us, hand on the hilt of his blade, before one of the other Germans gave him a sharp order. He stopped, but was clearly reluctant, spitting on the ground to show his contempt.

"You have a loose tongue, Roman. I think I am going to have to cut it out some day."

Rufus laughed, and pointed to the long blade. "With that thing? You can try, but your guts will be on the ground before you get it out of your scabbard. How long does it take to draw that thing anyway?"

"Fast enough that your head would be at your feet before you could blink, you Roman dog." The German's face was flushed red,

316

his tension clearly being communicated to his mount, which began prancing nervously, its head tossing as it waited for a command from its rider.

Rufus laughed again then looked over his shoulder at the rest of us, winking as he jerked his thumb at the Germans. "They're full of all sorts of tough talk, aren't they boys? Hopefully we'll get to find out how much of it's more than just talk."

We laughed in agreement, more to anger the Germans than anything. With the exchange over, at least for the moment, we continued to sit on our horses as Caesar and Ariovistus talked. A third of a watch passed, then another third, and we began to get bored. None of us dismounted because we were not given leave to, so I was finding that my rear was growing increasingly sore as the time dragged on. Shifting my weight around the best that I could, I fervently wished that this meeting would end. Caesar and Ariovistus had been jawing at each other, politely at first, then growing animated, although Caesar was far more reserved than Ariovistus, who made grand gestures with his hands, even thumping his chest a time or two. We could not hear exactly what was being said, but the tone was clear enough; there did not seem to be an agreement of any sort in the offing.

I am not sure exactly how long into the talk that it happened, but I do know that I was completely caught by surprise when I heard a sharp whinny and looked over just in time to see one our men's horses rearing in the air, almost throwing him off. As I watched the Roman struggling to control his mount, I saw the reason for it; a rock came sailing through the air to smack another horse in the rump, causing it to hop away, its rider furiously trying to control the beast. Looking over I saw the Germans, smiles on their faces, just as one of them hurled yet another rock, this time thrown hard, barely missing the head of one of our men, who jerked back in reflex. Suddenly, a scene of calm transformed as both horses and riders became agitated. By reflex, I found my hand curling around the hilt of my sword, the move not lost on the yellow-haired man who sneered at me and beckoned in a gesture of challenge.

"Hold, men!" This came from Rufus, who was in charge of our detachment, and I remembered Caesar's words, realizing that this was exactly what he had warned about.

These Germans were trying to provoke us, and it was only our discipline that kept the situation from getting out of control. Seeing that they were not succeeding in baiting us, the Germans increased the fury of their provocation, if not the style, continuing to throw rocks at us, while we did our best to dodge them. I heard a grunt of pain as one found its mark, striking a man in the ribs and he reeled in the saddle for a moment before regaining his balance, his horse turning in aimless circles as it looked to the other mounts to see what to do. The air was full of rocks whizzing by as all ten of the Germans now joined in, forcing me to unlash my shield, bringing it up to a protective position. Caesar said not to fight back, but he had said nothing about defending ourselves, and the other men followed suit, using their shields to block most of the rocks thrown at us. A couple more struck our mounts, causing them to jerk in pain, yet even as we were absorbed with this problem, one of our men saw that a fairly large group of Germans had materialized from somewhere and seemed to be headed in our direction. Calling out in alarm, he pointed out their location to the rest of us, increasing our concern about the situation. Rufus turned his mount and trotted to Caesar to report what was happening. Caesar turned to look, saw what was taking place, then turned back to Ariovistus and said something to him in a sharp tone of voice, but he was answered only with a shrug. Clearly angry, Caesar jerked his mount around, cantered to us and called for us to withdraw from the mound, which we did, the jeers and taunts of the Germans ringing in our ears.

The ride back to camp was an angry one, a mood that Caesar shared with us. We had acted in good faith, and the arrogance of the Germans, along with their disdain for the normal protocols of events like this talk rubbed us all very raw indeed. Each of us swore that we would have vengeance, and Caesar assured us that we would have the opportunity, but only when the time was right. When we entered the camp, the men who gathered to greet us could instantly see that things had not gone well, and I had barely returned my mount to the enclosure before I was swarmed by my friends wanting to know what happened. When I relayed what transpired, their anger was soon added to the original ten men who went with Caesar. Before dawn the next day, the whole army was spoiling for a fight, and took every opportunity to let Caesar know that they were ready for battle the moment he commanded it. For two days nothing happened before Ariovistus sent another envoy requesting another talk. This time Caesar was not about to expose himself to their treachery, instead choosing two men, an interpreter named Procilus and a man named Metius who Caesar believed would be safe from harm, since Metius was not high ranking and he knew Ariovistus. I do not know if Caesar calculated that Ariovistus would do something provocative and made his choice accordingly, picking someone whose loss would not do great damage to the army or his prestige, but it still worked out that way. On arriving to speak with Ariovistus both the interpreter and Metius were accused of spying and slapped in chains. That same day, Ariovistus moved his whole army, which as was the custom of their people, included all the women and children, to a spot at the base of some mountains some six miles to our north. The threat could not have been clearer; he was challenging us to come and fight him. Nevertheless, we stayed in camp. On the next day, he moved his host right past us, in plain view of our walls, to a spot about two miles to our south, cutting off our supply route from the Aedui and Sequani, although there were still supplies coming from the west from other tribes. Regardless, it was a threat, not to mention disconcerting, to have such a large host effectively in our rear. Still, we did nothing for five days, short of sending out cavalry patrols that skirmished with the Germans every single day, always coming out the worse for it. One reason for the effectiveness of the German cavalry was that a man on foot was assigned to every rider, this man riding into battle behind the cavalryman, then dismounting and running alongside once they got close to the fighting. Whenever they needed to move rapidly once dismounted, they would grab onto the horse's mane and lift their feet off the ground, being transported in this manner much more quickly than if they were on foot alone. It was effective, and made defeating their cavalry very difficult. Finally on the sixth day, Caesar mustered the army, arraying us outside the camp walls facing south to challenge Ariovistus. He deployed our artillery on the rampart of the camp walls to provide cover and we stood there for the better part of a day, challenging Ariovistus to come and fight, which he refused to do. This boosted our morale even more; as our Centurions pointed out to us, no doubt at Caesar's orders, if the Germans were as invincible as we were told, would they have ignored the chance to destroy us? The logic was irrefutable, although we were also a receptive audience, and it made us all the more eager to face them. For four more days, dawn would find us arrayed for battle, the 10th always on the right, waiting for Ariovistus, yet every day he refused to face us, causing us to lose our last vestiges of fear for the Germans, beginning to think of them with contempt, with each day fueling our resolve to make them suffer not only for the insults that they had borne us, but for the bother of having to stand in formation for five days in a row. It was the sixth day that saw a change, as instead of being arrayed for battle, we were ordered to form three columns in parallel outside the gate, two Legions to a column. We were ordered to be prepared to deploy into line for battle, the idea being to pull the same trick as Ariovistus by marching right past their camp, where Caesar planned on making a new camp a short distance away from the Germans, albeit smaller than the one we currently occupied. Marching south, we passed by Ariovistus' camp to a spot about a half-mile further south, where the *exploratores* had marked out the boundaries for a camp for two Legions. Our new Legions were tasked with constructing the camp, with the rest of us standing in line of battle, daring Ariovistus to try and stop us. This was a challenge that he could not ignore, so he sent a large force out to try disrupting the construction of the camp, but his men were repulsed with heavy losses, and the camp was erected despite their efforts. The 11th and 12th were left at the new camp, while the rest of the army marched back to our original camp. The threat to our supply lines was now answered, so that all that was left was to fight the Germans and send them to Hades.

The next morning, Caesar led the four Legions in the big camp out to challenge Ariovistus, this time venturing farther away from the camp and the protection of our artillery, but despite standing there the whole day, Ariovistus still refused to send his army to meet us. Finally, about mid-afternoon, we were ordered back to the camp, and it was only then that Ariovistus made a move, except this time it was against the small camp. Watching from our rampart, we observed the Germans as they made several attempts to storm the walls, and it was clear that the fighting was fierce as the new Legions fought desperately to hold the fort. They suffered heavy losses, but they gave better than they got, and the heaps of bodies piled around the walls were clear evidence of the price the Germans paid. Ironically it was the living Germans that were taken prisoner who provided the most value, since it was through them that Caesar learned what was keeping Ariovistus in camp. The Germans are a superstitious lot, which is saying much coming from a Roman, and they considered their old women to be the seers and soothsayers of their people. Not surprisingly, Ariovistus and his sub-chiefs went to these old crones for counsel on the best times to wage war. These women told Ariovistus that he had to avoid battle before the next full moon. This was all that Caesar needed to know; it was three days before the full moon, so there was no time to waste.

320

Marching out at dawn the next morning, we repeated our actions of the previous days except that instead of standing in front of our camp, we moved across the plain to join with the 11th and 12th from the small camp, about midway between the two. In order to make our numbers appear larger than they were, Caesar ordered the auxiliary troops marching with us to form up in front of the small camp, giving the impression that we were keeping all six Legions in the big camp instead of sending the 11th and 12th to the small one. Drawing up before the German camp, we did so close enough so that they knew there was no way to avoid battle, with Caesar arraying us in the *acies triplex* and us on the now-customary right wing, where we would be led by Caesar himself. With the sun climbing in the sky, it promised to be a fine day with just a few clouds. It was getting close to autumn, and there were already mornings where we were greeted by frost on the ground, but this day was shaping up to be a fair one, if we lived to see it through. After perhaps a third of a watch, the wagons that served as the main gates of their camp were pushed aside, whereupon the Germans came streaming out. Because the walls of their camp were merely the wagons drawn in a huge circle, their sides served as the ramparts, and was where the women and children of the Germans now crowded, sitting on the top of the wagons, their arms outstretched as they urged their men on to destroy us.

"At least we have an audience," Rufio remarked. "Let's be sure and give 'em a show boys."

This drew a laugh from us, though it was short-lived as we watched the Germans continue coming out of their camp, and coming and coming. There seemed to be no end to them, as they formed up in seven different groups, according to their tribe. They were the Harudes, Marcomanni, Triboces, Vangiones, Nemetes, Sedusii and Suebi, the last wearing their hair in a knot either on the side or the top of their head. Regardless of their tribe, they were all bristling with weapons, mostly spears and long swords, and it appeared that perhaps little more than half wore some sort of armor, while perhaps a third of them were wearing both helmet and armor of some type. During their deployment they were chanting their war cries, the sound rolling over us as they worked themselves up into a frenzy. Just as with the Helvetii, they were fighting for their women and children, who would watch them either win or die, and we all knew that we were going to have to fight our very best this day. I will give them this as well; they were certainly large and well built, most of them looking to be around my height or a bit less, so I certainly would have been no giant the way I was among my own people, and it flustered me a bit to see a whole army of men my size, although I tried to hide it as best I could. There was a brief pause once the Germans finished forming in their groups, and it looked like we were outnumbered by at least six or seven to one. Finally, after what seemed ages, a horn sounded and with a mighty roar, the Germans launched their attack.

It would not be right to say that we were caught by surprise, but what did startle us was the speed at which they advanced, coming at us at a full run, covering the gap between us so quickly that we had no time to throw our javelins.

"Draw swords!"

Immediately dropping our javelins, we were just able to draw our blades before the Germans came slamming into our lines, knocking our front rank back, causing such a shock that I felt it ten rows back, causing my heels to dig in as I pushed hard against the back of the man in front of me. Even so, I felt my feet sliding backwards, while around me I could hear the grunts and gasps of the men as they felt the same strain. Up front, the Germans threw themselves into our lines with such fervor that their back ranks pinned the men in front against our shields so that both lines were standing, shields pressed tightly against the other, neither side giving the other enough room to use their weapons. For several moments, the battle was little more than men looking into the eyes of their enemy, inches away, snarling, spitting and cursing at them in impotent rage. In such a case, it is no longer a contest of skill but of weight and number, meaning it would not be long before our strength failed and our line collapsed under the sheer mass being forced upon us. Even as this thought crossed my mind I could feel my legs beginning to shake from the strain, the sweat dripping freely from my face and I glanced over at Scribonius, whose face was twisted with the effort he was putting into providing support, except he was clearly slipping backwards, then began to churn his feet in an attempt to gain a purchase in the ground.

"Someone better do something quick, or we're all dead!" I am not sure who said this, but it was the truest thing said that day, and my mind began whirling with the idea that we might be finally facing defeat.

322

Then, the deadlock was broken by one man in the second rank, soon joined by others following his example, as these men leapt over the crouched figures of the men straining in the front rank to come crashing down onto the shields belonging to the men in their immediate front. The weight of the first man's body wrenched them from the grasps of both the Germans and the Legionary opposite him, that momentary gap freeing enough space for the man next to the Legionary in the front rank to use his sword. Darting out like the silver tongue of a serpent, he stabbed quickly before retracting a blade covered with blood. The German who had his shield wrenched from him went down in a heap, landing on top of the Legionary who started the whole thing by making his leap and who had not yet scrambled to his feet. In the momentary space that the dead German provided, more Roman blades lashed out, striking two other men before any of the foe could think to plug the gap. Finally, the Legionary on the ground extricated himself, rolling out from under the body of the larger and heavier German, albeit with some difficulty, then on hands and knees crawled back to his place in the second rank, covered in the blood of the dead man. Others who saw his example began to follow suit so that soon there were bodies leaping into the deadlock, crashing into the Germans and forcing gaps in the line that gave us room to use our swords. Within a few moments, bloody holes were opening in the tightly packed mass of Germans and before our very eyes they began changing from the fierce, snarling killers we had been warned about to just a large bunch of scared men who see their doom approaching.

By the time it was my turn in the front, their ranks were considerably thinned by the tactic of leaping onto their shields, giving me plenty of room to work. In the space of just a moment, I was able to dispatch three Germans and I thought with grim satisfaction that they died just as easily as the Helvetii, or even the Gallaeci back in Hispania. My fourth and final opponent this first shift was a man who bested my height by at least two inches, and was perhaps twenty pounds heavier, with a huge barrel chest that was bare and laced with scars. He carried a weapon I had yet to face, a double bladed axe, which he swung wildly above his head as he came at me, his eyes wild with fury, the spittle hanging in long strings from the corners of his mouth. With a beard and yellow hair like the German I saw at the mound, that detached part of my brain wondered if they were related, even as he swung the axe downward in a clear attempt to cut me in half. Jumping to the side, I plainly heard the wind whistling as the blade sliced through the air to land with a thud in the turf. I've got you, I thought, except he was damnably quick, so that before I could make a lunge, he freed the axe and with contemptuous ease, parried my blade with the head. Despite the fact he did it as if swatting a fly, the shock carried up my arm, jarring me so badly that I thought I would lose my sword, but the grip Vinicius had taught me saved me again that day. Before I could recover, he swung the axe again, this time at waist level, in a horizontal stroke that was meant to disembowel me, and I moved my shield just in time to block the blow, but the blade of the axe cut all the way through the wood so that it came protruding through the back, inches from my hand. This time, however, the axe stuck for a moment, except a moment was all I needed, and I gave a quick thrust that he only partially blocked with his own shield, the blade of my weapon glancing off the edge to jab into his upper chest just below the collar bone. It was not a clean blow, but it was enough to cause him to roar in pain, his face contorted with rage as he finally wrenched the axe free from my shield, almost jerking it from my grasp. The German took a step back, then we both stood there for a moment, gasping for breath and staring at each other, completely oblivious to what was going on around us, locked in our own private battle. This man was by far the strongest man I had ever faced, yet I could tell by the look in his eyes that he had been unprepared to meet someone who matched him as equally as I did. Once he began to close with me again, it was with more caution, and I swallowed a glimmer of satisfaction at the sign of respect he was showing, telling myself to save my self-congratulations for later because I was not the victor yet. As he closed, he began weaving the axe back and forth, and despite knowing better I found my eyes following the double-bladed head moving sinuously in front of me. Then he leapt forward with astonishing speed, and I realized that this was exactly what he wanted me to do, my heart sinking with the knowledge that I was bested. In desperation, instead of taking a step back to try opening the gap between us back up, I made my own leap forward, so that now it was his turn to be surprised as our bodies crashed into each other, and I ignored the feeling of the shaft of his axe slamming into my shield. Feeling the breath rush out of my lungs with the impact, I understood that I would have to fight through that and dropping my shield I reached up with my left hand, grabbing the German around the throat to squeeze with all of my might. His eyes widened in shock as in turn he immediately let go of his axe, grabbing me to try wrenching my hand off his throat, so that my wrist felt like it was being crushed by a horse stepping on it, yet I knew that if I lost my grip on his throat he would regain the initiative, and I ignored the pain. His face, inches from mine, turned a bright red, his eyes bulging out as they stared at me wildly, his mouth opening and shutting like a fish out of water, then he began flailing at me with his shield, slamming it into my back and forcing a grunt from me with the pain of every blow, yet I grit my teeth, refusing to give in. His face was purple now, and I could feel his grip on my wrist weakening, then I sensed his knees begin to buckle, facing me with a choice I did not care to make. If he collapsed, I was going to have to either release my grip or go down with him to finish him off, and in battle the absolute worst place to be is off your feet for any reason. But he had almost bested me and I could not afford the risk of letting him go while he still held a breath in his body, so as he began to topple backwards, his eyes rolling back in his head, I fell with him, landing heavily on top of him. Hearing a couple of his ribs crack, he nevertheless gave no reaction and finally his grip on my wrist loosened, his hand falling limply by his side. Regardless, I was not willing to let go until I was sure that he was dead, so I continued to lie on top of him, still squeezing his throat until I smelled his bowels release. Only then did I accept that he was finally gone, except I remained on top of him, gasping for breath, but before I could regain my senses, I felt a hand grab at my harness as someone tried to pull me up. I was much too heavy, so I staggered to my feet to see Vibius standing there, his sword in his sheath while keeping his shield up in a defensive position as he came to my aid.

"You crazy bastard, you should know better than to hit the ground," he yelled at me, but I could just stare at him for a second, his words not really registering.

After a moment, my head began to clear; only then did I realize that there were men streaming past me, and I looked about to see that the entire German left wing had collapsed, with the men of the 10th in hot pursuit. Retrieving my shield, I cursed when I saw that it was ruined, split in half by the German's axe; the cost to replace it would be docked from my pay.

Things went well on our side of the battlefield, but the same was not the case on the left wing, where the men of the 7th and 12th were threatened with being overwhelmed by the German right wing. Caesar writes that it was only due to the sheer weight of numbers, and again, despite the fact I do not like to disagree with the great man, the numbers were not any greater than what we in the 10th faced, but I suppose that's just an old soldier's pride speaking.

Regardless of the reason, the outcome of the overall battle was still very much in doubt, so the horns sounded to call off our pursuit of the Germans we had routed. These men were running for their lives, some of them heading back to the wagons, while most streamed past them heading north. However, it is hard to re-form when the men's blood is up and they are hot on the heels of their enemy, so it took precious moments before we began to gather in some semblance of a formation. Luckily, young Publius Crassus, who was the commander of the cavalry at that point, kept his head about him, and seeing the looming disaster, ordered the entire third line of all six Legions to head to the aid of the 7th and 12th. Moving quickly, they slammed into the flank of the Germans who were now wrapped around the two Legions, almost completely surrounding them. Before our eyes, what was shaping up to be a disaster for us quickly turned around into total victory, and it was not long before the rout was complete, with all of the surviving Germans now fleeing for their lives. Meanwhile, the Legions in the center, the 8th, 9th and 11th, had entered the camp and were eliminating the last shreds of resistance from the German warriors who retreated back there to defend their families. Again we could hear the cries and shrieks of the women watching their men slaughtered before the Legionaries turned their attention to them. By this time, we in the 10th were fully formed up, so Caesar commanded us to move north after the fleeing Germans, in the event that some of them had the presence of mind to regroup into a large formation. At the same time Caesar sent the cavalry to harass and cut down as many stragglers as they could find. Finally the cavalry provided some worth to the army, their pressure keeping Ariovistus or any of his commanders from rallying their warriors. Marching for a third of a watch in a single line of Cohorts, we were ready to confront any group of Germans who decided to stop to make a stand, but it soon became obvious that they were not stopping for anything. Once this was clear, we halted for a brief rest before turning and marching in column back to the battlefield to check for our wounded and dead.

Somehow, Ariovistus managed to escape, getting across the Rhenus in a small boat, but the rest of his family was not so fortunate. He had two wives, both of whom were slain, along with one of his two daughters, the other being captured and sold into slavery. Luckily, both Metius and Procilus were found still alive, although a little worse for wear, having been roughed up a bit by the Germans while being held captive. But the threat posed to the Aedui, Sequani, and other tribes by Ariovistus and his Germans was

326

permanently removed, earning the gratitude of the tribes, at least for a while. Our losses in the 10th had been pleasantly light; in our Century nobody had been killed, with only a couple being seriously wounded and who would return to duty after only a couple of months' recuperation. The 7th and 12th were not so fortunate, suffering heavy losses when they were surrounded by the Germans, but at least now both the 11th and 12th were veteran Legions like us. Despite it still being early to end the campaign season, the fact was that there was nobody left for us to fight. In the space of one abbreviated season, we had crushed the Helvetii and Ariovistus, so Caesar decided to send us to winter quarters early, marching us back to Vesontio, where the camp was awaiting us to make the necessary improvements for winter quarters. When we marched back to the town, the citizens lined the road to cheer us as we went marching by.

"Not as good as marching in a triumph, but it's better than nothing," grumped Vibius, who seemed to be determined to not be impressed or pleased with anything.

This was a trait of his, and I could not decide whether it was becoming more pronounced, or I was just growing weary of it. Despite his sour words, I caught him smiling from ear to ear at the accolades from the people lining our path. The small city had swelled in population; somehow the word that this would be our winter quarters was known by the camp followers long before we heard, so that all the various tradesmen, pimps, wine merchants and whores were there to greet us, along with the proper citizens of Vesontio. Beginnings of a shanty town were already springing up outside the camp gates, and the men started to talk excitedly of finally being released to spend the booty we had earned, some of it on whores, some of it on wine, although most of it would be lost to dice or other games of chance. As for myself, I was still smarting over having my pay docked for my ruined shield, so I had no plans on losing any other part of my money in the same manner as my comrades. It was not that I was a prude, or disapproved in any way the various pleasures of the flesh, and I knew myself well enough to know that despite my best intentions some of my money would end up in the purses of the purveyors of vice. However, I still had ambitions and plans, plans that called for money. Despite my visit home and the admonition from Phocas and Gaia about the folly of trying to buy their freedom from my father, I was determined that I was going to do just that, one way or the other. I also resolved that I was going to make more of an effort to write, although I wish I could say it was for selfless motives. This would be my third winter in garrison and I had learned how boring it was, so I was looking for new ways to pass the time, and for this winter I decided that I was going to pursue learning to read better. Now that I was a Sergeant, I was going to have to start doing paperwork, the bane of every soldier above the rank of *Gregarii's* existence; I knew of several men who would have made fine Optios or Centurions but chose to stay in the ranks just to avoid paperwork.

Before Caesar left for the Province to resume his normal duties as governor, a formation was held where decorations were awarded, and it was here that I earned my first *corona civica*, for saving Scribonius against the Helvetii. It came as a total shock to me; I had not known that I was even being considered, but the evening before the formation, the Primus Pilus once again showed up in front of our tent, bringing the Pilus Prior with him.

"This is becoming a habit Pullus," he joked, which I laughed at dutifully, although I did not find it particularly amusing.

Despite my record and my hunger for glory, I still possessed the ordinary soldier's suspicion of being singled out. Every time I was summoned, even if I was told the reason, I was sure that it would turn out to be for some sort of chastisement or punishment. I think it was this insecurity that made me such a good Legionary; no matter how hard I worked, I never thought I was deserving of any praise, preferring to focus instead on the things I did wrong and convincing myself that I had been found out.

Continuing, he said, "You're being decorated tomorrow morning, so I don't have to tell you that your gear better be perfectly polished. The Pilus Prior will inspect you first thing in the morning, so you better get to it."

Standing there for a moment, I tried to figure out what this was all about. I could not think of anything I had done that was especially noteworthy, so I asked, "Sir, if it's not too much to ask, would the Primus Pilus care to tell me what it is I'm being decorated for?"

He shrugged. "Can't say that I know myself. All I know is that you better be standing tall and ready for inspection an hour after morning call."

I knew better than to argue or keep pressing, so I just said, "Yes sir," and returned to the tent to begin polishing my gear.

That next morning, I and about 40 other men from the 10th Legion were recognized for bravery, while I was one of two from the Legion to be awarded the *corona civica*. Since it is worn on the head, it is necessary to remove your helmet, and it was only when I received the order to do so that I got an inkling of what I was about to receive. My mind raced; we had not assaulted any towns in either campaign, so it could not be a *corona muralis*, and we had not relieved any besieged force. Anyway, I was not of sufficient rank to receive a *corona vallaris*. Caesar stepped forward, Labienus and the Primus Pilus next to him, the Primus Pilus holding a pillow of some rich fabric, on which lay a simple grass crown. My throat tightened; winning this award for saving the life of a fellow Roman citizen is considered the highest honor a man can receive, and here I was barely 20 years old and I was being awarded this honor. Tribune Labienus unrolled a scroll, reading the citation aloud in his braying, parade ground voice, describing the event for which I was being decorated. It was for my rescue of Scribonius that day against the Helvetii, and the instant Labienus spoke the words, I was transported back to that moment, seeing the Helvetii warrior about to plunge his spear into Scribonius' unprotected face. Feeling a warmth flow through me, I thought how happy I was that it was Scribonius that I saved, because I considered him a true friend, a good man and a good Legionary. For another time I found myself looking down at a beaming Caesar, then bowed my head to save him from being forced to stand on tiptoe to place the *corona* on my head. It was very light, the woven grass tickling my closely shaven scalp, and I was barely conscious of the words Caesar spoke to me.

"We meet once again Sergeant Pullus, and once again, you bring honor to the 10th Legion."

"The honor is mine, Caesar," I replied. "I'm just happy that I was able to save one of my friends from death."

He gave me a thoughtful look, then said quietly, "That's really all it's about, isn't it? We do what we do for our friends." His eyes took on a faraway look as he gazed back through his own past. "Did you know I was awarded the same honor, when I was just about your age?" he asked, and I showed my surprise; I had not been aware of it until that moment.

Seeing my face, he laughed, "I know that it was a long time ago, probably before you were born. How old are you now Pullus?"

I almost damned myself to dismissal from the Legions or worse when I opened my mouth, because I was about to blurt out my true age. Thank the gods that I stopped myself in time.

"Twenty-one, sir."

For a moment, my heart plummeted into my feet as his eyes narrowed, giving me a look that I was sure meant that he did not believe me. My relief was almost overwhelming when he replied, "So you were just born then, it took me a moment to add it up. Must be old age," he laughed and I laughed with him, the feeling of escape washing through me.

"Still, it's a remarkable achievement for one of your age, Pullus. I told you once I expected great things from you, and you have not disappointed me. Continue to serve me as you have in these campaigns, and you have a very bright future indeed."

I promised that I would always strive to serve him as I had in the past and that he could always count on me whenever he called, something he accepted with a nod, indicating that such devotion was no more than his due, then our moment was over as he moved to the next man. Once finished, we were dismissed to go back to our place in the formation. Tradition decreed that I would continue to wear the *corona civica* for the rest of the day, which I was happy to do, but I must admit that it felt a little strange to be standing in formation with my friends bareheaded, my helmet under my left arm.

Out of the side of his mouth, Scribonius spoke quietly, "I've never properly thanked you for what you did Titus," using my praenomen, which in itself was rare, at least up to that point. "I'll forever be in your debt, and the only way I can repay you is to let you know that if ever you need me, for anything, all you have to do is ask."

A lump formed in my throat at his words, and I couldn't trust myself to speak, so I merely nodded that I heard him.

Caesar left us behind to build our winter quarters and settle into our garrison routine, which some of the men enjoyed after living under a tent for so many months, but I personally abhorred. I hated the idea of doing nothing, which is what I considered we did in the winter months. Once the gear was mended or replaced, there was nothing but boredom and talk of how drunk we would get that night. This was the farthest north we ever spent a winter to that point, and I for one was not looking forward to the bitter cold. Even in the high summer months, the larger mountains still have snow covering their peaks, so I was sure that we would see more snow and bitter cold than we had ever experienced to that point, and that it would last longer. I was right on both counts; no matter how hard we tried, we could never seem to successfully chink the cracks between the rough boards that made our huts, so that the wind would come whistling through in an icy blast that always seemed to seek me out no matter what part of the hut I was in. Whenever it was our turn to stand guard, we bundled up with every piece of extra clothing we could find, and for the first time I began wearing the *bracae* that is part of everyday dress for Gauls, but was only allowed for our use during the cold winter months. Our *sagum* was all we had to keep out the elements, and it was not long before the tradesmen in town started doing a brisk business in selling regulation *sagum*, waterproofed on the outside in the normal fashion, but lined with animal fur on the inside. It was never allowed for parades or inspections, yet soon every man I knew spent some of their own money on purchasing such a garment. Gloves were not allowed, so we wore socks, which were allowed, on both our feet and our hands. They may not have looked very soldierly, but we had never been in cold like this before. Those townspeople who initially welcomed our presence began to tire of us because of the trouble that invariably followed some Legionaries around, like Atilius who, now that he was off of campaign, began to resort to his old ways of drinking and fighting. It did not help that the army tended to attract a certain class of people that the respectable townsfolk would under any other circumstances have nothing to do with; the fact that they were Roman did not help. While we were originally welcomed as rescuers coming to the aid of the Gauls in this area, once the crisis was averted and we did not leave, the warm feelings that our presence initially generated began to degrade and chill, with much the same speed as the weather outside. It was not long before things became tense, and there were fights between townspeople and soldiers, which was bad enough. Then Atilius killed the son of the headsman of the town in a drunken brawl. This time he was not going to get away with extra duties or shoveling out the latrine; the man he killed was too important politically for such a light punishment. The only thing saving his life were enough

331

witnesses that were not Roman Legionaries who testified that at the very least, it was a situation where it was mutual combat, with more than one townsperson saying that in fact the son of the headsman was the aggressor. No matter what really happened, something had to be done, an example had to be made, which is why we found ourselves standing, shivering in the cold in full dress uniform, with our Century forced to stand in the front rank closest to where the punishment was to be carried out. Atilius was led out by two burly veterans in the provost unit, stripped to the waist, his torso standing out oddly white against the brown of his arms, legs and face. He had been kept under close guard so that none of us could sneak him some wine to dull his senses, and we were thankful that he could at least ascribe the severe shaking of his body to the bitter cold. The snow lay thick on the ground, and we could hear the crunching of their feet on the snow as they half-dragged Atilius to the wooden frame placed in the middle of the forum. Each guard took an arm, pulling him over the frame so that his back was exposed before tying his arms down to the upper part of the frame, then lashing his legs to the poles that supported the frame on the ground. Once in position, one of the provosts offered Atilius a gag made of a stick wrapped in leather for him to bite down on, and Atilius opened his mouth to accept it, his jaws clenching as he bit down. Labienus, serving in his capacity as our Legate since Caesar was elsewhere, then read the charge and sentence aloud for all of us to hear, with Atilius' punishment being ten lashes with the scourge. If it had been 20 or more lashes, it would have killed him; ten would be enough to almost kill him. Also present at the punishment was a group of townspeople, including an older heavyset bearded man, dressed in a rich fur cloak and fine brocaded tunic, his long hair pulled back in the Gallic style. Figuring him to be the father of the dead man, we deduced that he was here fulfilling two purposes, first as the representative of the injured party, and second as the headman of the town. There were a few other folk as well who I took to be members of his council. The Gallic chief's face was set in stone, betraying neither grief nor delight at the sight of Atilius stripped bare and humiliated in this fashion. The man brandishing the scourge was not as tall as me, but he was heavily muscled, and clearly used to administering punishments up to and including execution. Unless, of course, the crime was such that the condemned man's comrades were the ones detailed to carry it out. We had attended a few floggings with the scourge, yet this was the first of anyone we knew, and I could feel the tension vibrating among us as the man with the lash prepared himself to administer the punishment, swinging his

332

arm in a circular motion to loosen his muscles, the strands of the scourge whistling in the air as he did so. The sound of it cutting through the air was a sound we could all plainly hear, and clearly so could Atilius, his shaking becoming more pronounced as his eyes widened in terror. My stomach formed into a hard knot as I watched, knowing that he had to be punished yet not liking it one bit. Now that he was warmed up the punisher turned sideways, his arm bent at the elbow, forearm parallel to the ground and the braids of the scourge trailing in the snow. With a smooth, fluid motion, he brought his now-straightened arm overhand as he stepped forward, bringing the scourge in a full circle in the air to bring the lashes down on Atilius' back with a sickening wet slapping sound. Immediately Atilius let out a scream that was audible even through the gag and despite myself, I winced at the sound and sight of the bloody red stripes on his back, punctuated by deeper indentations where the pieces of metal that are embedded in each lash had dug out small chunks of his flesh from his back.

"One!"

It is the duty of the Legate to announce the count of the punishment lashes and Labienus did so with an impassive face that showed neither pleasure nor distaste at what was taking place. The punisher recovered, returning to his original position, then brought his arm up and over again, striking Atilius another time, the sound of the lashes striking his back, blood now freely flowing as it was, even more pronounced. Again, Atilius let out a muffled scream, his legs beginning to collapse out from under him as he cringed in pain. The knot in my stomach now threatened to burst and I could taste the bile rising up in my throat, yet I was determined not to show any sign of weakness.

"Two."

Eight more to go. There is no way that Atilius will survive this, I thought, he's going to die and there's nothing we can do about it. The blood now dripped off his back, making bright red splotches in the white snow, and I focused my gaze on the ground instead of on Atilius.

Somehow, Atilius did survive the punishment, though just barely. Once he was cut down, we were ordered to drag him off to the *quaestorium*. He lost consciousness about the fifth or sixth lash, and Calienus quietly told us that Labienus had actually done Atilius a favor, because some commanders would have insisted on reviving him before finishing the punishment.

"At least this way he didn't feel those last few," he told us as we walked along.

We were carrying Atilius by the arms and legs, facedown so that we could not avoid seeing the damage done to his back. Dull white of bone along his ribs where the skin and muscle had been flayed from his skeleton were clearly visible, and while I was not sure what purpose the muscles along one's back performs, frankly I did not see how he would be able to get any use out of them whatsoever, as shredded as they were. Nearing the tent, he began to moan, his head moving slowly as he regained consciousness.

"Easy there Atilius," Romulus said in what for him passed as a soothing tone. "You survived and we're taking you to the hospital."

I do not know whether Atilius heard or understood Romulus, for he made no intelligible sounds, just moaning over and over. Getting him into the tent, we placed him on his stomach on the table that the doctor indicated, then he ran us out when we tried to stay and watch the doctor work on him.

Before we left, Scribonius asked the doctor quietly, "Will he live?"

The doctor shrugged. "Only the gods know right now. If he survives the next day, then he has a good chance, but only about half of the men who are scourged do."

"Couldn't you be a little more optimistic?" snapped Vibius.

The doctor's face reddened, and he was clearly about to make a sharp reply, but then he saw our faces and his look softened. "He's your comrade, then?"

"He's our friend," Vibius replied firmly, making sure that the doctor knew that just because Atilius was guilty of a crime did not mean we were willing to minimize our relationship with him. The doctor stifled a smile before continuing, "Well at least he has that going for him. Most of the men who receive this kind of punishment are dragged in here and dumped by their so-called friends, then they get out of here as quick as they can. It's good to see men stick by their friends."

334

His kind words mollified our anger at him for his earlier callousness, and we left it that we would be back to visit the moment the doctor sent word it was possible, which he promised to do. Walking back to our tent, the formation had since been dismissed, but the rack still remained in place, and it would for the rest of the day as a reminder to all of us what awaited those who fell afoul of the rules. Atilius' blood was spattered in a semicircle around the rack, extending a good two or three feet away, yet despite our best efforts, we found our gaze pulled to stare at the rack and its gore as we walked by.

Atilius did make it through the next day, but only just, and he was weak as a newborn babe for several weeks. His back would carry the hideous scars for the rest of his life, a symbol that he had broken the laws of the Roman army and been punished, a fact that he did whatever he could to hide, only very reluctantly taking off his tunic, and only in front of us. As far as his behavior, he was not allowed to leave camp for the rest of the winter, since there were still hard feelings with the townspeople who did not think that his punishment was harsh enough. There were other incidents after that, until Vesontio was made off-limits to all Legionaries, who were then forced restrict themselves to the shacks of the camp followers located outside the walls of the town, a fact that suited the pimps, whores and purveyors of swill that they called wine perfectly well. Of course, the army has many men like Atilius who just seem to have a problem following some of the simplest rules, something that I could never understand. If I was told to stay out of a town or city, I stayed out, yet for some men the lure of the forbidden was just too strong, and it became a regular occurrence for us to be trooped out to witness a punishment almost once a week. What puzzled me was why this was happening so often, when the two years we were at Narbo men obeyed the rules much more readily and we had a punishment formation perhaps once a month, if that.

"You're no longer *tiros*," explained Calienus, and he saw by my expression that I did not understand. "When you first joined as a *tiro* you were scared to death of all the rules and regulations, right?"

I nodded that I understood this.

"But now you know all the rules, and you've seen most of the punishment that the army will dish out to someone who fucks up," he continued. "Add to that now you've faced death dozens of times, so that you've lost your fear of most things, including being punished."

Despite not feeling that way personally, I could see how others might, and I nodded again as I thought about this. Perhaps that was true; after all, we knew death in a way that very few people do, and it had visited men we knew, so that we recognized in a way that most people cannot that death visits us all. Once the fear of death is gone, it removes a major obstacle in one's path, and in some cases, the path that these men were following meant that being caught in town was not of major importance to them.

One person it did impact in a way that surprised us was Didius who, while not changing into a new man exactly, did become much more circumspect in his attempts to find new victims to fleece, even going through a fairly substantial losing streak for a few weeks. That part of his behavior may have changed, but not his hatred of me and the rest of his tentmates, his surliness driving the rest of us to the point where he became an outcast in our hut. I do not know how it started, but I do know that there was no plot; suddenly one night, everyone had enough of his mouth, and while I was at the *Praetorium* turning in some paperwork, the rest of the men bodily dragged him away from our hut to dump him in the Cohort street. When he tried to return, such dire threats were made that he ended up seeking shelter in another hut for several nights, not showing his face for anything other than official duties. Once he returned, he was careful to remain silent and not say anything that would draw our ire, but his silent hatred permeated the hut whenever he was in it, and we just learned to tolerate it.

Nothing else of note happened that winter; our main struggle was coping with the weather, but soon enough we adjusted. Although Gaul, or at least this part in Central Gaul was pacified, we still carried out patrols in the area, once a month doing a three day march, choosing a different direction each time and marching rapidly to a point Labienus chose to investigate. Nothing terribly suspicious was ever found, but we all took notice of the somewhat sullen faces that stared as we would march by. Nobody was overtly hostile, yet it was still a far cry from the welcome we received when we first marched to Vesontio, or when we came back from campaign. It was about mid-winter when we heard the first rumors of secret meetings being held between tribes that were supposedly friendly to Rome and tribes like the Belgae, who had refused to submit in any way. Their lands were farther to the west, the rumors

336

being that they were exchanging oaths of mutual assistance and hostages with tribes in the region we occupied, which unsurprisingly was the topic of all the campfire gossip. Meanwhile, Caesar was busy doing whatever it is that governors do down south in the Province, and when he got a dispatch from Labienus that reported all that was going on, he immediately raised two more Legions, the 13th and 14th. During this period, he sent word back to prepare the army to march, so that once again we went from inactivity and idleness to a flurry of activity where there was not enough time in the day to get things done. This was my first turn as a Sergeant in preparing to break winter camp, and I learned the thousands of details that I had to make sure my tentmates saw to, in addition to taking care of my own gear, all while putting in my time as Century weapons instructor. It was not uncommon that I found myself staggering into our hut a full watch after the rest of my friends were asleep, only to have to rouse myself first so that I could wake them up. There was many a day where I began to wonder if being a plain old Gregarius really was not the best deal around, yet whenever I found myself faltering in my goal, I would remind myself of the life I was trying to make, not just for myself but for my sisters, along with Phocas and Gaia. I was determined that one day, not only would they have their freedom, they would never have to work another day in their life as a reward for all that they had done for me. This is what kept me going when I came close to giving up.

Chapter 7- The Belgae

At the first sign that the snows in the passes had melted enough, Caesar sent the new Legions marching to us, led by a new Tribune, Quintus Pedius. Overall, the situation was rapidly deteriorating, with more news of defections by tribal leaders to the cause of the rebels reaching us every day. By the time March arrived, we felt like we were surrounded by enemies, and while this was the first time, it would not be the last that we were witness to the fickle nature of the Gauls. We had already seen how quickly their passions became inflamed when we faced them in battle; now we also witnessed how quickly their morale and spirit fled at the first sign of adversity. With the passing of time, I finally reached the conclusion that the Gauls are very much like large children; their delight knows no bounds, while their despair knows no depths. They had no discipline, and probably still do not; I often wonder how much we have managed to civilize the Gauls in the years since Caesar conquered them. Despite living among them now, and liking them very much as people, I also have come to realize that I will never understand them. Ultimately I just think that the Gauls have a natural dislike for peace and quiet, preferring noise and chaos because they find it exciting. Truly, I can think of no other real reason for their behavior, especially in those early years when we had not laid waste to much of the countryside and most tribes finally were at peace, not just with Rome but with each other and more importantly, with the tribes across the Rhenus for the first time in living memory. Perhaps that was the problem; things had gotten boring for them. Whatever the cause, not a day went by where a dispatch rider did not come in with news of some new intrigue or development in the ever-changing scene of tribal

338

politics. Alliances were seemingly made and broken in the blink of an eye, and it was not unheard of for one rider to inform Labienus, in the same report, of an alliance made and broken within the space of a watch or two. It was easy to see why Caesar was so alarmed, since he not only raised two more Legions but came as early in the spring as he did, following the arrival of the first Legion he raised by no more than a single week. After his arrival at Vesontio, he quickly gave orders to march, so that within three days the entire army, minus a detachment of auxiliaries and a couple of Cohorts left to guard the camp, went marching out the main gate, headed northwest. By this point we were now an army of eight Legions, the largest force that Caesar had commanded to this point, with the resulting train going on for miles, and no matter how much it chafed at him, our progress was that much slower because of the larger force. While it might not have made Caesar happy, we in the ranks were ecstatic, since it meant that we would not be pushed to our limits the first few days after our time in winter quarters, the way we had the year before. In turn, this kept our spirits up during the march, and when men have good morale, it helps pass the time as we plod along, singing marching songs and swapping stories. Caesar had no such problems staying occupied; indeed, his hands were full dealing with the constant stream of Gallic tribes who came to meet with Caesar, each of them pledging their loyalty to him. The fact that some of these envoys were from the very tribes who were linked to the secret alliance with the Belgae was not lost on any of us, and did not help to raise the Gauls in our esteem any.

"Not one of them can be trusted with a brass obol," Vibius muttered when one such delegation came trotting by, the men decked out in their tribal finery.

I had to agree, since nothing I saw from the Gauls at this point would lead me to argue the point he had made. Things had been somewhat strained between the two of us over the winter, yet I could not quite put my finger on the cause. I did not think he was jealous that I was promoted because he seemed to be just as happy for me as I was myself. Vibius had taken to writing to Juno at least once a week, sometimes more, and he was always overjoyed when he got a letter back from her. She was still remaining true to him, though I knew that he worried about it constantly. Juno was, after all, many, many miles away and was well past the normal age that women marry, yet she remained adamant that she would wait. My feelings for Juno, while not changed, had at least cooled somewhat; my heart no longer beat faster at the thought of her or mention of her name. I still cared for her, but I recognize now that at some point I must have come to a realization that she would always love Vibius more than she could ever love me, and had since we were children. Only recently had I begun to think of the idea of finding a woman like Juno to settle down with, but those thoughts were still intermittent, and whenever they popped into my head I would immediately dismiss them. During that particular conversation, I turned my mind back to the problem with Vibius, even while we continued to chat about some topic long forgotten. Could it be that he was jealous after all? Vibius was as brave as any man in the Legion, and he was a skilled soldier in his own right, but could all the attention I was receiving have rubbed him raw and made him resent my success? Almost opening my mouth to bring it up with him, I then thought better of it. There are just some things that are better left unsaid, I mused, and whatever was wrong between Vibius and I would work itself out over time, I assured myself. We had been friends much too long to let anything ruin that. Or so I hoped at least.

After almost two weeks we arrived at the banks of the river Matrona (Marne), at the edge of the territory of the more hostile branches of the Belgae, in the middle of the territory held by the Remi branch of the tribe. Even as slow as the march seemed to us, at least when compared to past marches with Caesar, we once again arrived so rapidly that the Belgae were caught by surprise at the sight of an army our size sitting in their territory, poised to strike. The Remi in particular, whose territory we were now in, made a quick calculation that their chances were better with Caesar than against him. Consequently, two of their leaders, Iccius and Andebrogius, came to Caesar to offer their assistance, promising to help provide the army with supplies, and most importantly information about the enemy tribes who were aligning to face us. These Remi had originally been part of a two tribe confederation, led by one chief named Galba, who was the chief of the other branch, the Suessiones, and the Remi had tried to persuade the Suessiones that their best interests lay with Caesar. They were not successful; in fact, the primary chief Galba was unanimously named by the other tribes aligned against us to be the overall commander of their host, and quite a host it was. It did not take long before the clerks in the *Praetorium*, who were our chief source of information, even if it was in a roundabout way after it had passed the lips of many other men, told their friends in the Legions that the Remi were able to provide Caesar with an exact count of the warriors that we

340

would have to defeat. The Bellovaci were the largest contingent, promising 50,000 picked men out of an available army of 100,000 men; the Suessiones led by Galba were to provide another 15,000 men. So were the Nervii, while the Atrebates would send 15,000 men; the Ambiani 10,000; the Morini 25,000; the Menapii 7,000; the Caletes, Veliocasses and Viromandui 10,000 men each; the Aduatuci 19,000 men. Finally, the Condrusi, Eburones, Caeroesi, and Paemani would send a combined 40,000 men. All told we would be facing an army numbering a little short of 300,000 men, compared to our strength of around 37,000 Legionaries, 5,000 cavalry and about 10,000 auxiliary troops. If we faced a host this large the year before, I shudder to think how the army would have performed, given how shaky morale was before we faced Ariovistus. However, our confidence now was such that it did not shake us in the least. In fact, hearing these numbers had the opposite effect, the men mentally tallying up how much booty we could expect to gain from defeating an army of this size.

"Let's just say that each of those barbarians has the equal of one gold denarius on him," mused Romulus as we sat by the fire the night we heard the size of the Belgae army. "And you know some of their nobles will be carrying a lot more than that, right?" There was general agreement to this as we sat and listened to Romulus, who was growing enthused the more he talked. "So that's at the very least 300,000 gold denarii just waiting for us to take."

Turning to me, he asked, "What did you say our strength was again, Pullus?" After I told him the number relayed to me, he sat there with his face screwed up as he tried to calculate the sum in his head.

Finally, he just shrugged and finished, "Well, it'll be a lot of gold pieces for each of us is all I know." His face turned red as we laughed at him, while Scribonius supplied the answer.

"It'll be about six gold pieces for each of us, give or take," he said, eliciting looks of astonishment that he was able to work such huge sums in his head.

Romulus' eyes narrowed in suspicion and he blurted, "That can't be right. It's a lot more than that."

"No, I promise you that it's just a little shy of six pieces per man, using your example," Scribonius pronounced this with a confidence that convinced me that he was right, but Romulus was having none of it.

"How is that possible, that you say out of 300,000 gold pieces, each of us would only get six?"

I could tell that Romulus was really getting worked up over this, and I began to have a nagging worry that this might turn into a full-blown quarrel. Scribonius and Romulus got along well enough, yet they had nothing whatsoever in common, and were opposite in temperament as well. Romulus was quick to laugh, although he did much less of that since Remus died, except he was equally quick to take offense. Romulus loved nothing more than to be with his friends getting into all sorts of mischief, whereas Scribonius was much more thoughtful and deliberate, always thinking things through carefully before opening his mouth.

Now, Scribonius was clearly doing his best to be patient, sighing as he tried to explain. "You're worrying about the zeros for nothing, Romulus, that's why you're not working it out right. Look," he squatted in the dirt and drew the number thirty and the number five in the dirt. "All you're really doing is seeing how many times five will go into thirty."

I was confused as well, so I kept my mouth shut, but I instantly saw what he meant. Romulus still was not convinced. "Thirty," he snorted, "where did you get thirty from? We're talking 300,000, not thirty."

Shaking his head, Scribonius replied with a thread of impatience that I hoped only I could detect. "It doesn't matter. All right then, let's try this. Tell me how many times 50 will go into three hundred."

Finally, here was a cipher that Romulus could understand, and I suppressed a smile as I saw his face run the gamut of emotion, going from irritation to the dawning of understanding the correct answer, then quickly back to irritation again as he realized he was in the wrong. He stood there, his lips pressed into a thin line as he scowled at the dirt, arms crossed.

Finally, after what seemed like an eternity, he mumbled, "Six. The answer is six."

342

Scribonius, bless him, did not pursue his victory over Romulus in any way, instead nodding his head enthusiastically as he exclaimed, "Exactly! You got it! The zeros in this problem are meaningless. Good job, Romulus. I knew you'd figure it out."

Romulus' head shot up at Scribonius' last words, eyes narrowing in suspicion as he stared at the other man, clearly trying to determine whether or not Scribonius was mocking him in any way, but that was not in Scribonius' nature. He was truly happy at being able to teach Romulus something, and Romulus obviously saw that, so that he began to smile, beaming with pride just like he was a student in class who had been called on and given the correct answer.

"Yes, I see now. The zeros don't matter," he nodded.

I let out a silent sigh of relief, happy that things had not turned ugly. The instant I had the chance, I pulled Scribonius to the side to thank him for the way he treated Romulus, then made a request of my own.

"Do you think you can show me some of those tricks?" I asked. "It's just that I'm having to do a lot of counting and addition and such, and it takes me forever to do the accounts I'm supposed to turn in."

Scribonius frowned, and for a moment I thought he would refuse me, yet that was the farthest thing from his mind.

"They're not tricks Pullus, they're.....rules. It's just like the army. Once you learn the rules, it's easy."

I immediately saw the sense of that, and I told him so.

"How about this instead?" he asked, catching me a bit by surprise. "Why don't I sit with you and I can do your reports for you, while you watch and learn how I do it? That way, you don't have to worry about writing all that nonsense, and you'll learn how the rules work."

This made eminent sense to me, as well as pleasing me that I would have one less burden on my shoulders, and I thanked him for his offer.

"Pullus, it's the least I can do," he replied quietly. "Remember, if it weren't for you, I wouldn't be here now."

I did not know what to say, trying to laugh it off with some lame joke, but his words touched me. We parted as I went to make my nightly report to the Pilus Prior, and again I was thankful that I had done what I did that day against the Helvetii.

Scouts brought word that the Belgic host was drawing nearer, so Caesar ordered the camp broken down and we went on the march, this time moving north to another river called the Axona (Aisne), crossing over it by the one bridge in the area. Then, with the river to our back to protect us, Caesar directed the camp to be built a short distance away. This was the most elaborate marching camp we ever created up to that point, with Caesar seeking to make the best use of the terrain. There was another small river a short distance to the north that branched off the Axona, the area around its banks a swampy mess. Caesar positioned our camp on a low hill running roughly northwest to southeast, with the southern wall of the camp a short distance from the Axona. Instructing us to make the ditch extra wide, it was 18 feet compared to his normal 15, thereby making the earthen portion of the rampart eight feet, with the stakes for the palisade adding another four in total height. In addition, he had us dig a trench extending along the axis of the *Porta Praetoria* of the camp further north down the hill, extending for almost a half mile beyond the walls, where a small fort was constructed with a scorpion and catapult for protection, manned by a Century. He had another trench dug running along the axis of the *Porta Decumana* to the south down the opposite slope towards the river, the same length and armed in the same manner. The bridge was fortified as well, and was located perhaps a mile and a half from the main gate to our southwest. The orientation of the camp was built so that the Belgae would have to pass directly across our front to get to the bridge, which was the only way across the river for several miles. If the Belgae wanted to attack the camp directly, they would have to negotiate the morass along the smaller river, while under fire from the northernmost fort. It took us most of the day to complete the work, and it was only due to the size of the army that we were able to accomplish all that in a single day. The fort at the bridge was under the command of a Tribune named Sabinus with four Cohorts and a squadron of cavalry. It was within these fortifications that we waited for the Belgae to sweep south.

At around midnight that first night, a messenger arrived with an urgent request for help from Iccius, the Remi leader who had approached Caesar about an alliance. It turned out that the Belgae, having learned of the Remi's choice to side with Rome, changed the direction of their march to the west to besiege the Remi's capital at a town called Bibrax. Iccius begged Caesar to send help, since he was not confident that his small force could withstand a siege by a force of the size that was facing him. Caesar responded by sending a detachment from the auxiliary forces, consisting of Numidian javelineers, Cretan archers and Balearic slingers, all missile troops, who left shortly before dawn. Lightly armed, they were able to quickly travel the seven miles to the town, finding it completely blockaded by the Belgae, whose idea of siegecraft was to surround a town with their warriors then use missiles to scour the parapets of the enemy. Apparently their hope was that the warriors holding the town would finally become discouraged and just give up. The Belgae had no conception of siege engines, and Bibrax was built on a steep hill, with the southern approach being an escarpment, which the Belgae did not think to invest. Consequently, it was short work for our auxiliaries to drive the Belgae away from the town, who instead took out their frustration on the surrounding countryside, putting it to the torch. Satisfied that they made their point, the Belgae resumed their march towards our encampment, arriving after nightfall of the same day that they were repulsed from Bibrax, proceeding to build a camp that was so huge that they were required to use signal fires to communicate from one end to the other. Their campfires extended as far as the eye could see, with the nearest end of their camp perhaps a mile on the other side of the small river and even with the eastern end of our camp. Since the terrain was fairly flat and open and we still could not see the far end of their camp, it had to have been more than three miles in length, a fact that, even with our confidence, unnerved us a bit. It even instilled in Caesar a sense of caution, prompting him to decide to give himself more time to judge the fighting qualities of the huge army before us. To that end, the next morning he sent out a number of cavalry patrols that clashed with similar contingents of Belgae presumably sent out by Galba to do the same thing in testing our ability to fight. We were pleasantly surprised when we saw that our cavalry took the measure of their foes in every skirmish they fought that day, and this outcome convinced Caesar to send us out to challenge the Belgae the next morning.

Six Legions marched out of the camp that morning, with the 13th and 14th staying in the camp to guard it. We were in our place on the right wing, with the camp to our right rear and the other Legions arranged roughly perpendicular to the northwest corner of the camp wall. The moment the Belgae saw us march out, they began to stream out of their own camp to face us, with the small river and the morass between us. In order to attack, they would have to cross the morass, with the southern edge of it just within range of our javelins, while the far bank was in range of our artillery. The Belgae formed up just beyond this, whereupon we stood and stared at each other, our side impassively watching the Belgae work themselves up into a frenzy. However, Galba never gave the order to attack, obviously worried about the problem of crossing the swampy ground under fire. Instead they settled for shaking their weapons at us and bellowing promises of all that they would do to us, as first one individual then another among them worked up the courage to dash up to the bank of the river. Standing there, they would yell some insult at us, usually accompanied by the baring of their backside, before scurrying back to the safety of the horde before our artillerymen decided to poke a hole through them. The Belgic army was arrayed in the traditional three wings, except that because of their numbers each wing, consisting of three lines like our own, dwarfed our entire line of six Legions. Still, despite this huge advantage, they refused to advance.

"This is getting boring," I heard Vibius say, and I had to agree.

It seemed to us that we spent a lot of time standing waiting for Gauls to work up the nerve to attack, and it tended to get monotonous. Because of the immense size of their army, it was difficult for us to keep track of smaller detachments, so it was with some surprise that a courier sent from Sabinus back at the fort at the bridge came galloping up looking for Caesar, who as usual was commanding our wing. He carried a warning that the Belgae had sent scouts about two miles west and found a ford, and were now making for it with a large detachment from the main army, apparently sending men from their third line where we could not see them. Caesar immediately wheeled his horse, and commanding the auxiliary missile troops to follow him, galloped away to head off the danger to our rear, with the cavalry in tow. While this Belgae force crossing the ford was not large enough to defeat us, it was more likely that they would turn to lay waste to the Remi fields that supplied our grain. If that happened we would be forced to move because of lack of food, making stopping them imperative to our

346

overall goal. Caesar and his force reached the ford to find that a small group had indeed made it across, but the bulk of the troops were still on the other side. The water at this spot was waist deep, and Belgae were wading across as quickly as they could, so Caesar ordered the cavalry to deal with the few men who made it to our side as he deployed the auxiliary missile troops, who began firing on the Belgae in the water. There was an immense slaughter at the ford, with our troops standing off at a distance to send a hail of arrows, stones and javelins into the bodies of the warriors trying desperately to get across the river. Bodies began to pile up in the current, the men crossing behind the dead and wounded now having the added difficulty of clambering over the bodies as they tried desperately to close with our missile troops. Soldiers, no matter who they fight for, hate the men who use bows and slings, thinking it a cowardly way of waging war, and no doubt it was this hatred that spurred the Belgae on in their attempt to exact their revenge on our troops. It was less of a skirmish or battle than it was a slaughter, and it was over in less than a third of a watch, ending with the river choked with the bodies of the dead, polluting the water with their blood.

Once the attempt to force a crossing at the ford failed, the Belgae chief Galba obviously made the decision that a battle under these conditions was worse than pointless. We were in a strong position, with artillery support, on terrain that favored us, and that was enough to force the Belgae to begin streaming back into their camp. Waiting until they retired before marching back to our own camp, we were suspicious of some sort of trick. This was no deception, however; the Belgae were done as far as fighting that or the next day. Evidently, there was a council of some sort and a decision was made that we became aware of around midnight, when without warning, the Belgae began streaming out of their camp, except this time not to face us, choosing instead to head in the opposite direction. The racket their withdrawal caused convinced the officer of the watch to sound the alarm, so we scrambled up from our cots, got dressed and donned our gear, forming up ready to march within a few moments. The guards on the walls relayed down to us what was happening, and we were of the same mind that this was some sort of ruse, so we waited quietly for the order to be given to repel an attack on our walls. But it was no ruse; when daybreak came, Caesar sent a patrol out, and they returned shortly to assure Caesar that the camp was indeed empty, the Belgae having fled in the night. Later we learned from prisoners that the chiefs of each of the tribes represented demanded a council be held, with a vote taken that each tribe return to its own lands to wait our approach. A pact was made that the first tribe attacked would sound the alarm, whereupon all the tribes would converge on that point to mass together to crush us. Once Caesar deemed that it was no trick, he immediately ordered the cavalry, the 10th, 11th and 12th out of the camp in pursuit in order to inflict as much damage as we could on the retreating horde. We were assembled and ready to march very quickly, moving out after the enemy, setting a quick pace because we carried nothing but our weapons and a canteen of water. It took much less than a full watch before we spotted the rear of the massive column, and our cavalry went flying off in pursuit, while we shook out into an *acies duplex*, five Cohorts from each Legion in each line, the Centuries lined up side by side to provide the widest coverage instead of our normal three Century front. The cavalry came at the Belgae at an angle, slicing across the fleeing column and effectively cutting off a group of men who were now faced with cavalry pushing them back towards the Legions. If they turned to try and flee, their backs would be to the cavalry, as close to certain death as one can get, but if they stood their backs would be to us as we advanced, just as certain an end. Quick work was made of these men, effectively cutting them down from behind as they fought the cavalry to their front. Once we were finished with them, the cavalry went off in pursuit of more prey, performing the same maneuver, with the same result. Most of the day passed in this manner, carving up small groups of the rearguard, most of them fighting bravely, yet without any sense of cohesion. If the larger body of men had simply turned and attacked us, we would have been in trouble, except they were more intent on using their comrades' death as a means of getting farther away, making killing the members of the rearguard easier. Finally we stopped simply because we were running out of time to return back to camp before dark, and we were definitely aware that being caught out in the dark could be a problem. There was no time to build our own camp and have it ready before it got dark, so Labienus ordered us to turn around, marching at a fast pace back to the camp. I am not sure how many Belgae we killed, but I would guess that it was three or four thousand.

The next morning we broke camp, except instead of pursuing the Belgae army, which was not taking the most direct route back to their homelands but were retracing their steps back to where they left their respective baggage trains, Caesar used this as an opportunity to press the attack on just one of the hostile tribes. To that end, he picked the Suessiones and their stronghold at

348

Noviodunum, to the west of our camp along the Axona. It was a hard day's march away, despite the route being along the river and the trek along level ground, so we were extremely tired by the time we arrived within sight of the walls of the town. Wanting to take advantage of the absence of most of the Suessiones fighting men, since only a few of the older and less bold warriors were left to guard the walls, Caesar had us ground our gear and immediately formed for an assault. Ladders were quickly made, and before perhaps a third of a watch had elapsed from our arrival, we were marching towards the walls, preparing to storm the town. When we drew near, however, it became apparent that ladders would not be enough, because the walls were much higher than they looked from a distance. Compounding the problem was that the ditch was also much wider than we anticipated as well, so we were ordered back to our gear, and despite our fatigue from the march and the hurried preparations for assault, began building a marching camp. Once we finished, we were given just enough time to eat our evening meal before we were given orders to start creating proper siegeworks. Marching to the nearby forest in torchlight, we began felling trees, working for almost a full watch before being allowed to retire for the night. Falling on our cots completely exhausted, most of us did not bother to remove our armor or boots, yet that did not stop any of us from falling asleep immediately.

The next day we arose before dawn to begin in earnest the work of creating the proper equipment to storm the town. Mantlets were created, small huts on wheels that are rolled up to the wall of the besieged town, with sturdy roofs and sides usually covered in wicker or green hides to protect the men working from within, who are either undermining the wall or using a ram to break through. In addition, siege towers were built, and we worked rapidly as the Suessiones could only watch from the walls helplessly. During that first night, the Suessiones war party had returned and since we had not yet encircled the town they were able to enter, so the walls were now crowded with their warriors, yet they were as impotent to stop us as the common citizens of the town. By midday, the towers were nearing completion, built taller than the walls to enable the men who would conduct the assault to effectively run downhill and onto the parapet. There were levels built into the towers where the missile troops and even a scorpion could rake the walls with fire as the tower was pushed into place on huge rollers made out of several of the largest trees that we could find. Another group of men filled the moat up with dirt to provide a path for the towers to be brought to the walls, using large wicker shields called fascines to shelter behind while they worked. The speed at which these preparations were made always astonished even us, but it was no less fearsome and impressive to the Suessiones. Just as we were beginning to roll the two towers into place, and the men working inside the mantlets were dragging their rams to use on the base of the walls, the Suessiones signaled that they wanted to talk, doing so just before the rams actually touched the walls, since that would have been too late. The gates opened and a small group of men, most of them older, with gray in their hair and beards, came out under a flag of truce, asking to speak to Caesar. Our general rode to meet them, dismounting as a courtesy, and listened to their pleas for mercy. Accompanying Caesar was a Remi, who I later learned was Iccius, having come from Bibrax with Caesar when he relieved the town, and the Suessiones begged for him to intercede with Caesar and speak on their behalf, which he did. Caesar agreed to accept their surrender, demanding hostages for security, which they provided immediately, the town surrendering without a single life lost.

"So why did we go to all that trouble if they were just going to piss themselves at the sight of our towers?" grumbled Vibius.

I nodded in agreement; that was a lot of sweat gone to waste, at least from the way we saw it. This might sound strange to one who has never been a soldier, but a town that surrendered meant there was no chance for a Legionary to improve himself, either by feats of bravery or by more coin in his purse. This was how Caesar managed to pull himself out of debt when he was governor of Hispania, when the towns surrendered to him one after the other. It became immediately clear that it was this that bothered Vibius more than anything else.

"Besides, hasn't he made enough money already? Shouldn't we have the chance to get something for ourselves? I bet he planned this all along with that Remi bastard."

I glanced at Vibius in surprise, sure that he was in jest, yet his face was deadly serious. "Do you honestly believe that Caesar orchestrated all this, that he arranged for the Suessiones to surrender but still had us do all that work?" I asked incredulously.

When I put it like that, it made Vibius reluctant to agree, but I could see that I had not really convinced him. He just shrugged and said, "I wouldn't put it past him," then looked away, a clear sign that he was done with the subject. I opened my mouth to argue the point, then thought better of it; there was no reasoning with Vibius once he made up his mind, and it was clear that he had formed an opinion that he regarded as fact. All I could do was shake my head.

Once the hostages were handed over and the Suessiones' weapons were confiscated, we turned west again, this time heading for the territory of the Bellovaci, following the Axona until it ran into the Isara (Isar) River, which the Axona flows into as the former runs in a north/south orientation. Crossing the Isara, we made camp for the night, then set out the next day for the main town of the Bellovaci, called Bratuspantium, arriving there shortly after midday. This time we did not even need to build any siege equipment, the headman of the town opening their gates in submission the moment we marched into view. The Aedui Diviciacus had joined the army by this time, and like Iccius, he pleaded the case for the Bellovaci, guaranteeing their good conduct. Like with the Suessiones, Caesar treated this town with clemency, demanding only hostages, and like the Suessiones, they were disarmed. Spending the night encamped next to the town, we did so with a double shift of guards on the walls of the camp, although I suspect that this was as much about keeping the soldiers from sneaking into the town as it was to guard against a surprise attack. Once again we set out the next morning, still heading west although turning a little more to the north, to the Ambiani town of Samarobriva. Word of our arrival preceded us, and like the Bellovaci, the Ambiani were waiting with a delegation of elders to offer their submission to Rome. The same terms applied, with the exception that Caesar did not disarm the Ambiani, deeming them not enough of a threat to us to worry about. Taking on even more hostages, they joined what had become a part of our train, guarded in the middle of the marching column by whichever Legion happened to be scheduled to be next to them on that day. By this time there were 200 or 300 of them, and since most of the hostages were of noble birth, they of course could not travel without their own retinue, so between servants, slaves, and other sorts of retainers, there were probably 1,000 people in that group, making them hard to manage, as we would learn.

Only a day was spent at Samarobriva before word came about a tribe that not only refused to submit, but were openly preparing for war. They were the Nervii, and were reputed to be the fiercest of all the Belgae tribes, adopting what we thought was a rather peculiar custom.

"I heard from one of those Belgae who speak Latin that the Nervii don't let any traders or merchants of any kind into their lands," reported Scribonius at the end of the first day's march as we headed back to the northeast to confront the Nervii.

"*Gerrae*! Why would they do something stupid like that?" scoffed Vibius.

We were seated in our accustomed spots around the fire, chewing the evening bread and bemoaning that the olive oil was already starting to go rancid.

"I asked the same thing," replied Scribonius as he sat mending a hole in one of his tunics. "The Belgae I was talking to, I think he was a Suessiones, said that they don't let anything into their country that might make them soft. They think that all the other Belgae have rolled over for Rome too quickly, and they claim that they'll show the other tribes that we can be beaten."

"Hmmm, where have I heard that before?" I laughed, and the others joined in, amused by the thought that these Nervii were making the same mistake that a number of other Gallic tribes had already made.

I was surprised when Scribonius did not join in, frowning as he gazed at us. "I don't know," he said in his thoughtful way, "the way this Suessiones talked about the Nervii was......different. It wasn't the usual boasting that these bastards are so good at. He just gave me examples of what make the Nervii different, and feared by the other Belgae."

Dismissing Scribonius' words of caution with another joke, we soon moved onto other more important topics, like the never-ending dice game between Romulus and Atilius, and which whore among the camp followers was the best.

After three days of marching, through the same very gently rolling terrain, skirting the patches of woods whenever we came across them, we stopped for the night on the edge of a scrub forest as Caesar's scouts came to report that the Nervii were camped some nine miles away, having gathered in force at a place where they thought it was likely that we would cross the river Sabis (Sambre). During the night, some of the hostages slipped out of camp, going to the Belgae to warn them of our approach, and to pass on what they

352

thought would be our order of march. Meanwhile, Caesar ordered the pioneers and a group of Centurions, along with an *ala* of cavalry to move ahead to scout a place for the next day's campsite. Word shot around the fires that the Nervii were close, so we began to prepare ourselves for a battle, each of us having developed our own little rituals and ways of doing things that is unique to every Legionary. Some men set up little shrines to worship their household gods and the gods that look over the Legions; I preferred a more practical approach and would spend the time sharpening the blade of both my sword and dagger. Running the blade along the stone that evening, I began to dream of a new sword, using the metal that the Gauls used. Despite their swords being too long and inferior to ours for the type of fighting that we did, the quality of the blades themselves and the workmanship had left all of us impressed. Some of the Centurions had commissioned Gallic craftsmen to make swords for them, and I dreamed of having one made for me, perhaps as early as this winter, since I was saving the money that I had not designated as the funds that would free Gaia and Phocas. But first, I had to live to see the winter, and I sighed as I put my weapons aside to begin the inspection of the arms of my tentmates, thinking to myself that a Sergeant's work was never done.

Breaking camp the next morning, we received our order of march for the day, an everyday occurrence that would prove to be critical on this of all days. Part of the information that the Belgae hostages that fled the previous night gave to the Nervii was that our usual order of march would give them a perfect opportunity for an ambush. Normally, when we were marching with no expectation of contact with the enemy, each Legion's baggage train is behind them. A Legion's baggage train on the march, during Caesar's time, consisted of more than 500 mules, with each animal having a servant or slave to drive it. This was where our tents and extra rations, a mule for each section of men, plus tents for the Centurions, Optios, Tesseraurii, and Signiferi were carried. Then there were the wagons carrying the Legion artillery, along with the other essentials for a Legion on campaign. As you can imagine, gentle reader, all of this takes up quite a bit of space, and while every morning we were aligned in a proper formation with our spacing parade ground-exact, even then the baggage train would extend for almost a furlong, and that was before we started. But on the march, matters get a bit more complicated, since there is a tendency in even the most disciplined army, which we were, to extend that distance a bit, so that the gaps between the animals widened. Although the men of the Legion are orderly and able to maintain the proper distance for the most part, the servants driving the animals, despite being part of the army, are not soldiers and do not value the maintaining of the proper gaps the way we do. Therefore it is not uncommon for a Legion on the march to have a baggage train stretch to almost a quarter mile in length. In Caesar's army, we tried to march nine miles for every watch, except that we were almost always consigned to marching as slow as the baggage train, which at best would average perhaps six miles for every watch, unless we were on a forced march and left the baggage train behind. That distance translates into time, and adding the gap between the baggage train and the next Legion, usually following a furlong behind the one in front of it, this distance translated into an advantage for a huge army like the Nervii. Their plan was simple; once the first Legion marched by and as soon as the baggage train was in sight, they would swoop out of a large forest that they were hiding in to ambush the leading Legion, counting on the delay that would inevitably happen as the trailing Legions scrambled to the aid of their comrades while first having to make their way past the baggage of the Legion being attacked.

All in all, it was a good plan, but it was doomed to fail because Caesar, as always, was thinking one step ahead of them. The Belgae hostages who escaped to warn the Nervii were right; under normal conditions Caesar marched with the Legion baggage train immediately following it, except Caesar did not consider these to be normal conditions. With an enemy known to be lurking less than a half-day's march away, Caesar gave orders that we would march in the manner that we did when contact with the enemy was expected, with all the army's baggage train congregated into one group, which was trailed by the new Legions, the 13th and 14th. When the army finally came into view, masked as we were by a thick stand of trees, the Nervii were confronted by the sight of the Legions, with the 9th in the lead this day and ourselves immediately behind, following each other in close order without any baggage train in between. Our march was delayed by a series of thick hedges, which we were told had been planted by the Nervii as a method of deterring just the type of advance that we were making, and I must say they did an admirable job of it. Being the lead Legion, the boys in the 9th were the ones who had to either find a way around the hedges, or cut through them, making for a considerable amount of work. Most of the time their commander ordered the 9th to cut through them; Roman armies are not much for going around an obstacle. We would much rather just march right through it and will spend the time necessary making the terrain bend to our will so that we can do just that. Once past the hedges, we marched up to the site that the pioneers had selected for the day's camp, a small hill with a gentle slope down to the river, the camp site being on the north side. The river Sabis is a river in name only, not being much more than three feet deep in that area, and we knew that it would not provide much of an obstacle to the Nervii, whose sentries and pickets we could see watching us from across the river. Being the second to arrive, we received orders to begin building the camp immediately while Caesar sent the cavalry, who had been screening our advance, across the river to chase the pickets away. On the opposite side of the river was another hill, with a forest roughly bisecting it running east and west just at the crest, and as our horsemen went charging up the slope it was into this forest that the pickets fled. Every one of us would have been content to stand or sit watching our cavalry charging into the line of trees, then be repulsed before trying over and over again, but we had a job to do so we grounded our packs to begin the routine of building a camp. While we worked, the other Legions began arriving; we were followed by the 11th, with the 8th behind them, the 12th, and then the 7th. The baggage train was still some way off, moving more slowly as usual and guarded by the new Legions who marched behind it. It was perhaps third of a watch after we arrived that the baggage train came plodding into view, and it was this sight that triggered the Nervii attack.

They came swarming out of the forest across the river, sweeping aside our cavalry screen as if it were not there, thousands upon thousands of them running down the slope and across the river, almost before we knew what had happened. From the moment that they burst out of the woods until they hit our lines was less time than it takes a man to run a fast mile, and when an army as large as ours is caught unprepared like we were, it is no simple matter to array for battle. Suddenly the air was split by the sounds of *bucina* and *cornu*, accompanied by the bellowing of the Centurions who ordered us to drop our implements and form a battle line as quickly as we could. The scene was utter chaos, with Legionaries madly scrambling back to their packs to pick up their shields and helmet, grounded with the rest of our marching gear. The standards were quickly grabbed from wherever they were planted in the ground as we worked, forming a rough line parallel to the river. Looking across the river at the onrushing horde, it was clear that we could either form up in our proper Centuries and Cohorts, or we could go grab our gear, but we could not do both. Immediately realizing the gravity of the situation, and knowing that we were in for the fight of our lives, most if not all of us chose to get our gear and hastily don our helmet, although none of us had time to take the cover off of our shields, before looking for the nearest standard. Seeing the standard for the Third Century of the Fourth Cohort nearby, Vibius and I ran to form up the best we could. There was a mess of confusion as each of us instinctively looked for the spot where we normally lined up, yet we were just as likely to find it occupied by a man who had the same spot, but in a different Century. Consequently I found myself with Vibius by my side on the front rank, giving us a grand view of the Nervii horde pounding up the riverbank at us, water streaming from their clothes as they waved their weapons in the air, their war cries filling the air to envelope us with sound.

We could feel the ground shaking beneath our feet as they drew closer and there was just enough time for Vibius to say, "We are truly fucked," before the first ranks slammed into us.

We did not even try to throw our javelins, not only because there was not enough time, but most of us forgot to grab them, instead instantly resorting to the sword, much the same as when we faced the Germans. A man a little older than me, with a full red beard and his hair sticking up in some sort of wild pattern came hurtling at me, his long spear thrusting at my throat. Drawing my shield up to block the thrust before answering it with my own, I delivered my blow under the rim of my shield, the blade angling upwards to drive into his groin. He let out a horrific screech and fell to the ground, but the man behind him did not even break stride as he hurtled the body to slam into me. My shield was driven back into my chest, almost knocking the breath from me as I felt my heels sliding and I waited for the supporting hand grabbing my harness, but none came. Cursing, I strained to push my shield out away from my body, back to the proper position, except the man was now aided by the weight of the other Nervii who had come crashing into him, so I stood there pinned, with no room to use my sword. The stalemate lasted for a few heartbeats before, in an act of desperation, I lowered my shield just a bit while whipping my head forward, driving the rim of my helmet into the man's face. Instantly my head exploded in pain, yet the effect was enough to cause him to recoil backward into his comrades, freeing me up just enough. Lashing out with my shield, I caught him with the boss square in the chest, hearing the breath escape him in a whooshing sound as I whipped my blade over the top edge of the shield this time, the point catching

356

him at the base of his throat. I obviously hit an artery, because I was showered with a spray of bright red blood, and he staggered back, falling against the man behind him, who in turn was covered by the dying man's blood, his heart pumping jets of the sticky fluid into the second Nervii's eyes, causing him to shut them in reflex, giving me the opportunity to take advantage of his temporary blindness. Taking a step forward and regaining the ground that I had lost, I killed the second man with a quick thrust to the chest while he was still struggling to wipe the blood from his eyes. With three kills in perhaps the first thirty normal heartbeats, all around me the fighting was going at the same furious pace. Out of the corner of my eye I saw Vibius ducking a wild swing of a Nervii sword before coming up from his crouch with a powerful blow from his shield that smashed his opponent in the elbow of his sword hand, causing him to drop it, whereupon Vibius instantly dispatched him with a sweeping move of his blade that opened the man's throat. Meanwhile, I heard frantic shouting all around me as Centurions barked out commands, trying desperately to plug holes where there were still gaps, or strengthen lines that were still only one or two men deep. Very quickly I realized that this was the case with us; the reason nobody grabbed my harness was because there was nobody there, yet I could not dare look back to see if any help had come. The Signifer we formed up with was using the staff of his standard as a weapon, swinging it in short, sharp blows, finishing each opponent off with the spiked end. A couple of men came to stand around him, and I could see others running to our formation, but we were still horribly disorganized, except that was all the time I could give to the overall situation as more Nervii came roaring at us. Once again one came slamming into me, and I felt my upper body twisting backwards under the pressure as I grit my teeth, forcing myself to stand back upright to hammer at my foe's face with the pommel of my sword. He had no shield and was using his free hand to try blocking my blows, while with the spear in his other hand, he kept jabbing at me in short, vicious thrusts aimed at my gut. On one of his thrusts, the blade of his spear punctured my shield, and I felt the point bury itself in my left forearm. Despite myself, I let out a cry of pain, while I wrenched the spear out of his hands by jerking my shield down and away from him, ignoring the fact that doing so hurt my arm even more. In an instant, he was disarmed, and I stepped to my left to give him a backhand slash that caught him across the face. Now it was his turn to scream as his hands flew to his face, giving me all the opening I needed to drive my sword deep into his gut, feeling a savage satisfaction.

I do not know for sure how long the fighting went on at this pace, but all along our line, which was a line in name only, every Legion was being pressed to their limit as men fought without any real direction or orders from our Centurions. This was a fight of man against man, or at the most, small groups of two and three men against each other, and this type of fighting brings out the most savage aspect of every one of us. At one point I remember suddenly becoming aware that I was snarling as I hacked away at a Nervii, spewing out sounds that were completely unintelligible, and I could feel my lips curling from my teeth as I waded in the gore of the bodies that we were chopping up. There were no tactics, no maneuvers, just men intent on killing each other, mindless of any higher goal other than the complete destruction of the man across from him. I was vaguely aware that I saw Caesar, holding a shield, calling out to us to continue fighting, exhorting us to greater effort, his own blade bloody.

"Keep calm men! Remember the honor of the 10th! Stand up against these bastards!"

Despite recognizing his voice, none of us even acknowledged that we heard him, so busy were we on maintaining our cohesion. Several times a man would fall in our line, and for a moment the Nervii would force their way into the gap that created, only to be beaten back by the men who had finally joined the back ranks. There were no whistles to signal relief; for the most part, those of us who got stuck on the front line had to stay there until we either fell or the Nervii broke. Luckily, seeing that there was not going to be anything like the normal system of relief, the men who were in the back ranks dashed back to retrieve as many javelins as they could, and finally we heard the whistling sound of them flying over our heads, seeing the missiles cut swaths through the warriors still coming up the bank from the river. One volley, followed by a second, then a third; only after the third did we sense that there was the beginning of a shift. Men were still attacking, just without the same reckless abandon as before. Seeing the chance for a shift in momentum, without any command being given, the men of the first line began pushing forward, slashing and hacking at anyone who stood in our path. The blood was still streaming down my left arm, and I could feel my hand growing sticky from the blood caking on it, but I continued moving forward, Vibius beside me as we cut down several more of the enemy, then somewhere further to our right, we sensed that the flood was beginning to reverse. Looking over in that direction, I saw that the Nervii were not just moving

358

backward one grudging step at a time, but some of them had begun to turn and run.

Once a panic sets in, especially with an undisciplined bunch like most Gauls, it spreads like a flame over dry tinder. Such was the case in front of us; one moment we were locked in a struggle just to stay alive, and the next, men were streaming away from us, running for their lives, completely oblivious to anything but the voice in their head telling them to flee. Whenever there is a great slaughter on the battlefield, most of the casualties come when that moment occurs and the rout begins. The battering force that threatened to overwhelm us just moments before suddenly evaporated, as the Nervii began to turn and run back to the river. Naturally, we pursued them, the entire Legion sweeping after them, catching up to the slower ones as they hit the river to begin wading back across, cutting these men down and striking without mercy at their unprotected backs. We were in a fury, or at least I was, angry that we were caught unprepared, and I was taking my revenge for having to fight for my life. Without any orders, we continued to follow the fleeing enemy, crossing the river and up the opposite hill as the Nervii ran before us, trying desperately to make it to the sanctuary of the woods from which they had appeared. Continuing our pursuit of them up to the edge of the woods, again without any command given, we came to a halt. I was gasping for breath, trying to suck in as much air as I could as I peered into the woods, knowing that charging into that mass of trees and undergrowth was an invitation to disaster. Not only did we not know what lay in those woods; there could easily be another force headed this way, it also made it easier for men to elude us, and once the immediate danger was past, some of them might have the presence of mind to regroup and turn the tables on us. Catching my breath, I looked back over the river and my heart filled with dismay. The area where we were fighting was covered with bodies, and while most of them were the enemy's, there were a disturbingly large number of Roman bodies lying among them. We had taken significant casualties, so I instantly began looking around, trying to locate my friends. Vibius was still beside me, the blade of his sword caked with blood all the way to the pommel, while his armor was liberally splashed with blood as well.

Seeing my concerned look, he glanced down, then shook his head. "Not mine."

Nodding thankfully, I continued scanning the faces of the men around us, as some semblance of order was slowly returning. Like herd animals, we instinctively started looking for our normal spot in the formation, and the Centurions began taking control, except for the Pilus Prior, who I could not see.

"Anyone seen the Pilus Prior?" I asked of the men from my Cohort who were starting to gather in one spot.

"I think he went down over there," said Metellus, the Optio of the Fourth Century, pointing to a spot where there was a large pile of bodies.

I looked where he was pointing, but we were too far away to make out whether any Roman body was wearing the transverse crest of the Centurion. Tribune Labienus came trotting up on his horse, calling for the Primus Pilus, who was on our side of the river. While they were conferring, I heard a commotion and looked over to see some of our men shouting excitedly and pointing back across the river. Following their arms to where they were pointing, I drew a sharp breath. There were two Legions who were being completely surrounded by the Nervii and looked like they would be overrun at any moment.

"Form up, quickly you bastards!"

The Primus Pilus bellowed the order, and the surviving *cornici* began blasting the signal. There was a scramble as men ran to their proper standards, and it was only as we formed up that we could see the gaping holes in our ranks. In our Century, there were at least ten men missing, including the Pilus Prior and in my tent section Romulus and Didius. Since I was Sergeant, it was my responsibility to find out their status then report it to the acting Centurion, Rufio, who had taken a spear thrust high on his shoulder, but quickly bound it up and was standing in the place of the Pilus Prior. Calienus moved into Rufio's spot, the hours of drill paying its dividends now.

"Did anyone see what happened to Romulus or Didius?"

"I saw Achilles take a spear to the chest, but he was alive the last I saw him," Vellusius called out, but on the subject of Romulus, there were only shakes of the head.

360

It was something I would have to find out later, because by this time we were formed up. Labienus dismounted from his horse, and moving to the head of the formation, gave the command to quick time back down the slope, angling over so that we could come to the rescue of the two Legions who even now were being surrounded by Nervii. It was the 12th and the 7th, and what got them in trouble was the success that the other four Legions experienced in stopping the enemy advance, then counterattacking. Like us, the 9th, 8th and 11th crossed the river after repulsing their attack, the 8th and 11th in the center and the 9th and us on the left. They were still engaged with the Belgae forces however, while we drove our opponents into the woods. Labienus, seeing the desperate situation our sister Legions across the river were in, was now marching us rapidly back to their aid. As we advanced down the slope, the new Legions came into view following the baggage train, and they were now rushing forward as well, negotiating their way through the loaded animals and wagons. Meanwhile, the 7th and 12th were fighting for their life, with the 12th in particular having a hard time of it, though they were not helping their own cause. They managed to stay in formation, but because of the press of the Nervii, they had gathered so that they were packed together so tightly that they could not employ their weapons, and we could see Caesar's standard beside them as he exhorted them to open up their ranks to fight. The 7th was surrounded on three sides, the only flank that was protected the one next to the 12th.

"Silly bastards, they're packed together like they're on the march," panted Scribonius.

Coming to the river, we were forced to slow down as we waded across, then stopped briefly to re-form our lines after we got to the opposite bank. Once that was done, Labienus gave the order and the *cornu* blasted the command.

"*Porro!*"

Slamming into the rear of the Nervii, who were completely occupied with trying to destroy the two Legions before them, they were paying no attention to us as we approached their rear, to their own destruction. Almost at the same time, the 13th and 14th added to the weight of the assault, and it was now the turn of the Nervii to be surrounded.

I will give credit to the Nervii; unlike other Gallic tribes that we faced, these men did not turn and run. They stood their ground, the rear ranks facing about to meet us, and they gave as good as they got. The 7th and 12th, the latter being dangerously close to falling apart and routing, saw that help had arrived, so they renewed their own attack with a fresh spirit, even their wounded joining in the fight. The fresh troops of the 13th and 14th, having arrived fully armed, began to shower the Nervii with javelin volleys, and soon there were heaps of bodies lying all around. On our side, we went straight to the sword as we pushed against the Nervii, and for the first time, established a normal rhythm of fighting. The whistles started to blow again, and we began working our way through the rotation, this return to normalcy helping us even further as we cut and thrust at the Nervii. When it was my turn, I fell to with a renewed fervor, letting the anger at the idea of Romulus and the Pilus Prior being struck down fuel my arm as I exacted my own revenge. The sound was deafening as the Nervii roared their hatred for us, or screamed when they were cut down, while on our side, we shouted out the names of fallen comrades as we struck men down for them. The fury of the battle was renewed as well, the Nervii fighting with the courage of the doomed, and it was not long before they were using the bodies of their own dead as platforms on which to stand. Some of them picked up the javelins that landed undamaged to hurl them back at us, and I blocked one with my shield that had been aimed at my chest. Luckily, it was an awkward throw, lacking the proper force behind it so it glanced off the leather cover of my shield, which I should have been happy about but instead got me to cursing afresh. It reminded me that I was going to have to purchase a new leather cover, which once again would be deducted from my pay, and angrily I sought out the man who threw the javelin, marking his face in my mind, thinking I would get to him as soon as I was done sending the man opposite me to the afterlife. We were advancing, slowly but surely as the pocket of Nervii was being reduced on all sides, until there was a pause by the entire army, despite no command given. While not completely silent, there was a noticeable decrease in the noise as we stopped for a moment, completely surrounding the by-now small knot of Nervii standing in an outward facing circle, their weapons in their hands, panting for breath as they stared at us with undisguised hatred. We glared back, and things remained this way for several moments, until the only sounds were the moans of the wounded and dying and the gasping of many thousands of men. There were perhaps 2,000 Nervii left in the last circle, and I wondered if they would be allowed to surrender, but then they answered my question for me when one of them took a step away from the circle, spat on the ground and motioned at us to come on, yelling something in his tongue that needed no translation. He was taunting us, asking what we were waiting for, and with a roar, we descended on the last bunch of Nervii from all sides.

It was over quickly, with not a Nervii surviving unscathed, the wounded soon following their already slain comrades. The next few moments we spent walking among the bodies, quickly dispatching their injured with a quick thrust then finally, the battle was over. Looking up at the sun, I saw to my astonishment that little more than a third of a watch had passed since the Nervii first came streaming out of the woods. Very quickly, order was restored and we began the now familiar task of tidying up after a battle. For our part, we marched back to where our packs were laying, now surrounded by piles of bodies, both Belgae and Roman. One of Labienus' attendants, a Gaul who knew of such things, identified the bodies of some of the enemy not as Nervii, but Atrebates, who had evidently thrown their lot in with the Nervii.

Vibius grunted, "That explains why they broke and ran but those bastards over there," he gestured over to where the 7th and 12th had made their stand, "stood and died to the last man. Not that I'm complaining, mind you," he grinned.

I laughed at this, slapping him on the shoulder before turning to the task I was putting off yet could avoid no longer. Now I had to go examine our own dead and wounded to find my missing tentmates. Even as the battle raged farther downstream, the *medici* assigned to our Legion had already begun tending to the wounded, and a makeshift hospital was already set up, really nothing more than a cleared patch of ground where all the wounded were being gathered. Going there first, that was where I found Didius, who had indeed suffered a real wound high in his chest. The momentum of the spear thrust was slowed enough by his armor that the blade had not penetrated into his chest cavity, instead just slicing through the muscle and stopping there. It was a painful wound, but I had seen men with far worse wounds act less like a woman than Didius, who was moaning rhythmically while clutching the bloody bandage that the *medici* placed over the wound. Seeing me approach, he was sensible enough to at least stop the whining, yet he was uncharacteristically friendly, or what passed as friendly for him.

"*Salve* Pullus. Come to check on me, eh?"

I am not sure why, but I bit back the retort that rose to my lips that I was just doing my job, and instead merely nodded.

"Thank you Pullus," he said and I knew that he could see the shock on my face because his own turned a little red as he gave a self-conscious laugh. "Now I know what all the fuss is about when you almost get killed, neh?" He did not wait for me to answer, "I thought I was a goner for sure. That bastard waited until I was occupied with someone else and nearly did for me."

I was determined to match his pleasant tone, and I tried to sound sympathetic. "Hurts, doesn't it?"

He grimaced and nodded his head, wincing at the pain the motion caused. "More than anything I've ever had before, I can tell you that. Still, it's good to be alive. We gave those *cunni* a good whipping, didn't we?"

I nodded, again biting back a retort about how he was only around for the first few moments and then out of it, so how would he know, but I was honest enough with myself to know I was being unfair.

"That we did, that we did." I cleared my throat. "Well, I'm glad to see you survived."

Now it was his turn to be surprised, and for the briefest of moments, I saw Didius let down his guard as he opened his mouth to say something. But the moment apparently passed, he snapped it shut and merely nodded, not saying anything.

"Did you happen to see what happened to Romulus? He's not here, although I know that the *medici* haven't gathered all the wounded. Do you know anything?"

Again, the mask slipped and I saw what I will swear on Jupiter's stone to my dying day was a look of genuine sadness, though it was gone as quick as it appeared. He looked me in the eye, and without saying a word, shook his head. My blood turned to ice; his meaning was unmistakable.

"Where? Did you actually see it happen?"

He nodded, then with a grimace, lifted his arm to point in the direction where there was a slightly larger group of bodies. "It was after I was wounded. I was down on the ground, but I saw it happen plain as day."

"How do you know he's dead?" I demanded, not caring if my tone was harsh.

Didius' lips thinned in anger, and he opened his mouth, but there was........something different this day for both of us, and I would like to think that at least for this moment, he was just as reluctant to break the fragile truce as I was.

He paused, then replied tightly, "I don't know for sure, but he was gutted, and I saw them fall out on the ground."

My stomach lurched; I would have to face it sooner or later, so I left Didius, still looking as close to sad as I had ever seen him, and walked unsteadily towards the heap of men that he had indicated.

Seeing him while I was still several feet away, I smelled him soon after. Didius was right; Romulus had been gutted, and was laying on his side, with most of his insides in front of him, the flies already starting to swarm. The thrust that did this had sliced through his bowels, and it was this I smelled on my approach. Biting my lip to keep from crying out in despair, I walked up to him slowly, my shadow preceding me and covering his face in darkness. It must have been this change that did it, and I felt my knees almost give out when I saw his eyes flutter, then open as he peered up to see who approached. He squinted as he tried to focus, then recognizing me, opened his mouth to speak. Rushing to his side, I knelt next to him, careful not to touch any of him and quickly tried to hush him.

"Romulus, it's Titus. Don't try to talk; save your strength."

A shadow of a smile crossed his lips as he looked up at me, his eyes telling me that there was no need to lie. "What for? I won't need to be strong for much longer."

Opening my mouth to protest, I instantly realized the pointlessness, so instead merely nodded. Reaching down, I took the hand that was not clutching at his intestines in a vain attempt to pull them back into his body. It was cold already, not surprising given the amount of blood that was pooled around him and already being soaked up by the earth. A thought flashed through my mind as I wondered how much blood this world had soaked up over the years, but I was brought back to the moment by Romulus' voice.

"Titus, will you make sure that I'm put in our family tomb next to Quintus?"

I was puzzled for a moment, since I had forgotten Remus' real name. Seeing my confusion, he smiled again, "We weren't born Romulus and Remus. Remember Titus, when we showed up at camp in Scallabis we were Quintus and Marcus Mallius?"

I nodded, making a mental note to remember to use his proper name so that his ashes would make their way back to the right family. My vision started to blur, and I fought back tears as I began to absorb that both of these brothers were for all purposes now dead, but I was again jerked out of my thoughts by a squeeze of my hand, and I looked down to see Romulus gazing at me, his eyes rapidly dimming.

"Don't mourn for me Titus. I'm happy. Soon I'll see Quintus again, and we'll never be apart."

Again I nodded my head, and I heard my voice choke as I agreed with him. "That's right, Rom....Marcus. You and your brother will be together. Be sure you wait for us, and then we'll all be together, and we can sit by the fire again and lie to each other."

He smiled again, began to reply, then died before he could say anything. Sitting beside him for a moment, I started to weep bitterly, not caring this time if anyone saw me.

Cleanup of the battlefield had to wait while we finished the building of our camp, then the next two days were spent with honoring our dead and cremating them. Once again we had to dig mass pits to bury the Nervii, Atrebates and the other tribe who had joined them, the Viromandui. The air was filled with the remains of our dead as their souls were released by the fire, and I made sure that the urn that contained the ashes we would send back to the Mallius family was correctly addressed, with Romulus' proper name. The mood around our fire was somber for the next several days; Romulus had always been the most animated among us, and was usually the one to start a conversation about some topic that he would seemingly produce from thin air. It was a source of constant

366

amusement to us how he came up with some of his ideas, and now that was missing, nobody really knew what to do. Our tent now had only six men in it, since Calienus had moved out when he was promoted. At that particular moment, it was down to five because Didius was still in the hospital tent, and it is with no little surprise when I say that we missed his presence. As sour and truculent as he may have been, we had become accustomed to having him around, if for nothing else than to serve as the butt of our jokes. We were not the only ones so affected; there was clearly a pall of sorrow and loss hanging over the whole camp, with almost every fire losing someone in such a manner. The 7th and especially the 12th were the hardest hit; in the 12th they lost several Centurions, along with the standard bearer of the Fourth Cohort. Their Cohort standard had even been lost, only for a short time, but to lose a standard for any length of time is a horrible blow to the pride and morale of not just the Cohort, but the entire Legion. I do not wish to be harsh, but of all the Legions, that day the 12th had not acquitted itself well, and a cloud now hung over every man in the Legion, the rest of the army looking at them differently. Until they had the opportunity to redeem themselves, they would be suspect in our eyes. On the matter of Centurions, our Pilus Prior Vetruvius was not killed, but had been wounded so severely that his arm had to be amputated, meaning his career was over. The subject of who would be our new Centurion was not yet decided; again, being the First Century of the Second Cohort meant that whoever was appointed to lead us was also the ranking Centurion in the Cohort, so he had to be senior to all the other Centurions, or there would be bitter resentment on their part. This also meant that Rufio would most probably be promoted to Centurion, but moved to some other Century, or even another Cohort. It was not out of the realm of possibility that we would have a Centurion from another Legion put in command of the Second Cohort, although this was always considered a last resort and did not happen often, at least in those days. These were the topics that occupied what little conversation did take place around our fire as we awaited our new Centurion. Over in the First Cohort, our former Pilus Prior Gaius Crastinus moved up to take command of the Second Century, the First Cohort losing two of their own Centurions. The fact that he was leapfrogged over two Centurions who led the Third and Fourth Centuries was very unusual, but Crastinus' reputation was such that there was little grumbling about the decision, with the exception of the two bypassed Centurions. It was in this manner that the next few days passed, as the army reorganized and rested from what was our toughest battle to date.

While we were in camp along the Sabis, a deputation of Nervii consisting totally of old men who were clearly past their prime as warriors approached the camp, asking Caesar for an audience. It was granted, whereupon they were brought into Caesar's presence, a curule chair on a dais placed in front of the *Praetorium*, with a formation of all the army called to witness what transpired. In front of our hostile eyes, the Nervii elders threw themselves on the ground in front of the dais to beg Caesar for mercy. They claimed that of the 60,000 men we faced, only 500 remained, and had joined the women, children and old people of the tribe in their sanctuary in the middle of a swamp some miles distant. It would turn out the numbers of the slain turned out to be exaggerated, but it seemed credible at the time; we had tallied the dead that we buried, and the number was fifty-three thousand. However, we had not gone into the forest and we made the assumption, mistaken as it turned out to be later, that the remainder were seriously wounded and gone into the woods to die. What we were unable to determine was which of the bodies were Nervii and which were the other tribes. They had been dragged from the areas where they fell into one huge pile before anyone had thought to count by tribes. Therefore it passed that these numbers claimed by the Nervii elders were accepted; later enemies of Caesar would claim that he exaggerated the numbers for his own personal gain. The goal of this narrative of mine is not to defend Caesar, so I would only point out that those who say such things were not there, so to my mind, they are not credible.

Caesar accepted the surrender of the Nervii, choosing not to inflict any punitive punishment on them, deeming that they suffered enough humiliation by the destruction of their huge army. In fact, he allowed the Nervii to return not only to their farms but to their towns, even those that were fortified, and decreed that the tribes surrounding them should not harass them in any way. In fact, he went so far as to declare that their neighbors should provide whatever assistance that was needed. It speaks much to the character of Caesar, and to the respect that he had earned, albeit through our right arms, that his orders were obeyed without protest, even by tribes who were hereditary enemies of the Nervii for many generations. We also were informed that there was another tribe, the Aduatuci, who had been marching to join the Nervii, but on hearing of their defeat turned around and marched back to their lands. This tribe made the decision to abandon all of their other towns and gather their forces in their strongest position, a town on a river that was very similar in nature to Vesontio. On hearing of this, Caesar

368

gave the orders to prepare to march, and it was this command that forced the decision of who would be the Centurion of our Century and Cohort. Consequently, the night that the orders to march were issued, as we sat around our fires, the Primus Pilus came up to us with another Centurion with him, a man two or three inches shorter than me, but with a slender build. He had aquiline features that could have been called handsome except for the scar that ran diagonally across his face, starting at the corner of his right eyebrow, running under his right eye and downwards to the edge of his right nostril, continuing diagonally across his lips and ending at the base of his jaw on the left side. The scar had cut the nerves in the region of his mouth, so his upper lip curled into what appeared to be a permanent sneer. His eyes were somewhat hooded, and were such dark brown that they appeared black, giving his gaze the same fierce countenance as an eagle. He carried his *vitus* in his right hand, and was tapping the end of it in his left as the Primus Pilus spoke to us.

"This is your new Pilus Prior, Centurion Vibius Piso. He's from the 9th Legion and is now in the 10th."

This caused a bit of a stir, and I am afraid our unhappiness was evident, but since this was the last stop in the Century, I was sure that the two Centurions were not surprised, and in truth, probably understood.

When our new Pilus Prior spoke, it was in a deceptively soft voice, and it was on this occasion that we were introduced to a different style of command than we were used to. Centurion Piso rarely raised his voice, but he possessed other ways of getting our attention that were just as effective. "As the Primus Pilus said, my given name is Piso, but I'm more commonly known as Pulcher," he pointed to his face, "because I'm easily the handsomest man in this army."

This brought a laugh from us, and our distrust for him eased a bit as he continued. "I'm extremely proud to have been selected for this post, and I'm equally proud to be in the mighty 10th Legion."

So far, he was hitting all the right notes, but he still had some ground to cover. Oh, we would obey him to the letter like we were trained, except there is a vast difference between forced obedience and willing obedience, and that is the key to good leadership, making your men want to obey because you are the one giving the orders.

The new Pilus Prior finished, "I'm not going to say that I expect every man to do his duty, because the reputation of not just this Cohort but this Century is well known, so I'll close with saying that I'm proud to be your Pilus Prior."

Now, whether or not our reputation was as glorious as he made it out to be, one can never underestimate the importance of flattery to soldiers' egos, and more important than whether it was true or not was the fact that we wanted to believe it. The introductions done, we returned to our work of preparing to march the next day. Rufio was staying put, at least for a while, since he was most familiar with the men of our Century and would be of assistance to the Pilus Prior in learning our ways. Hearing from our friends in the other Centuries that there were some muttered complaints about bringing in a Centurion from another Legion, we also discovered that our new Pilus Prior was something of a legend, not just in his own Legion, but with the older men who had been in Pompey's army that fought Sertorius. With the question of leadership settled, not just in our own Century but throughout the army, we marched out of the camp, leaving behind a mass grave and memories of the toughest battle we had faced yet.

Marching east again, we followed the course of the river Sabis until it met the Mosa (Meuse) River, which continues in the same east-west direction while the Sabis branches off. At the end of our third day of marching, our scouts reported that they spotted the town where the Aduatuci had taken refuge, a few miles ahead. Instead of stopping at our normal time, Caesar ordered us to march closer so that we would be within sight of the town when we made our camp for the night. The next morning, we were marched out in force and arrayed for battle so that the Aduatuci could see what they were facing, while Caesar, his staff and the Tribunes made a reconnaissance of the area surrounding the town. We had been told that this place was much like Vesontio, which was only accurate to a point. If anything, this town was even better situated, the hill that it perched on skirted by steep escarpments of rock almost all the way round its base, making assaulting it from almost any direction terribly difficult. The only vulnerable side was on the northeast, where the slope was gentler, but to counteract this obvious weakness, the Aduatuci had erected not one, but two high walls, there being a space of perhaps a hundred feet between the inner and outer. Once Caesar was satisfied that he had seen everything he needed to, he issued orders and we went to work. He directed several projects to be started, starting with the construction of a

370

rampart a few hundred feet away from the walls of the town, running east and west on the north side of the hill, with the river as the boundary for each end, effectively cutting off the town sitting in the bend of the horseshoe. Meanwhile, he directed the building of an earthen ramp to be built on the northeast slope that would accommodate the rolling of a siege tower up to the wall, along with enabling a series of mantlets to be connected so that a battering ram could be conveyed to the wall to make a breach. Building the ramp was assigned to us, while the construction of the siege tower took place out of the range of the Aduatuci missiles, but within plain sight so that they could see what was coming their way. For their part, the Aduatuci were singularly unimpressed; they ranged along the walls all the way around the town, calling out insults to us, which of course we did not understand at first. It did not take them long to find Latin speakers among them, and it was they who began to mock us.

"What tiny little men you are!"

"Are you all midgets? How could a race so tiny hope to conquer our walls?"

"If any of our children were born as puny as you, we would have exposed them and let the wolves eat them!"

This was the nature of the taunting, to which we were under orders to make no reply, but we smiled grimly at each other as we built the ramp, and wagering began about how long it would take for these arrogant Belgae to change their tune.

Constructing a ramp upon which a siege tower more than 50 feet tall will be rolled is much more involved than simply piling dirt up in a huge heap that ascends gradually to a point next to the wall. If that was all there was to it, we would have been finished much more quickly. Before we could even begin to start piling the earth up, a solid foundation had to be laid, consisting of logs cut down from the nearby forest, which we rolled into place under cover of the mantlets, moving them forward with the logs slung inside. Once there, they had to be put in their proper spot; this we did behind a series of plutei, large wicker shields that were erected side by side at whatever point we were working to protect us from the missiles of the Aduatuci. Further cover was provided by our scorpions and ballistae, emplaced farther back on small wooden towers that were thrown together for that purpose. The building of the ramp was done

371

in layers; first we laid logs down that would serve as the foundation, starting a few feet from the base of the wall all the way out to where the ramp was to begin, before filling the spaces between the logs with earth, sod and rocks. This gap between the wall and the last section of the ramp would be the final part to be filled in, consisting of basically whatever we could get our hands on that we had not already used in the construction of everything else. Once the first layer was done, the process was repeated, with the logs of the next layer being laid in the opposite direction, in order to provide structural stability. It sounds like a lot of work, and it is, but when you have two Legions of about 4,000 men each, our strength by that time, especially when that many men are organized as superbly as we were, even monumental tasks do not take long, so perhaps you will not find it entirely implausible when I tell you that the ramp was completed before the end of the day, with only the last portion to be filled in. While we were completing the ramp, the siege tower was also finished, and apparently it was the sight of this massive tower moving towards their walls that convinced the Aduatuci that perhaps there was more to this race of midgets than met the eye. Suddenly a white flag was waved from the parapet of the wall next to the ramp, with Caesar being asked for a cease fire and an audience, and he granted both requests.

The Aduatuci elders came out, and much like the other tribes did, cried big baby tears about their error, except unlike the other tribes, instead of submitting, they tried to negotiate terms under which they would give hostages but not have to give up their weapons. Caesar refused, demanding only unconditional surrender and the confiscation of all their arms. They agreed, but even from a distance where we stood in formation, ready to begin the attack, it was clear that the elders did not like it. Since we were the closest to the walls, we were commanded to enter the town to confiscate all the weapons. Marching in fully armed and ready for any treachery, we brought several of our wagons that had been emptied to serve as bins for everything we confiscated. The Primus Pilus ordered the men of the town to form into several lines, behind which stood one of the wagons, while several sections from the First Cohort gathered up their weapons and threw them in the wagons. The other Cohorts were sent to search the town, but were under strict orders that there was to be no looting or any other type of activity that could shatter the fragile truce.

"All that work and it goes for nothing......again," Vibius stormed, and I would be lying if I said that I did not agree.

372

Nevertheless, we had orders, and though I did not know it, I was already starting to develop that emotional distance that a leader must have, so I could not appear to agree with Vibius, even if I did. "It's for the best in the long run," I countered. "Yes, we don't have the opportunity to plunder the town, but we save a lot of lives, maybe even our own."

He shot me a sidelong glance, opened his mouth as if to argue, then merely shrugged. "I suppose."

I was not willing to pursue more of a victory than that, and let the matter drop. We made as thorough a search as possible, given the circumstances and the time we were permitted. It was rapidly nearing sundown, and we had been ordered to be out of the town by then, Caesar wanting to avoid the very kind of incidents that Vibius and I were arguing about. Caesar's orders were followed, but I am not so foolish as to think that there were not a few gold pieces, or a necklace or two that found their way into the pouch of one of the Legionaries of the 10th, and while there was no rape, there were a few bottoms and breasts fondled as some of our men "searched" the women for a hidden dagger. But it takes a good amount of time to conduct a proper search, and we were under no illusions that we found everything. As it turned out, neither was Caesar.

Extremely tired from the day's exertions as we were, it was with groans and curses that we were ordered to maintain an alert of 50 percent through the night. "Caesar doesn't trust these bastards, and I don't blame him, seeing the way they reacted when we took their weapons," the Primus Pilus told us as he passed the word to each Cohort.

As a further precaution, Caesar also ordered bundles of sticks and the like, items that were easily ignited, to be left in bunches at various points along the walls of the camp. Therefore, it was not much of a surprise when, during the third watch of the night, the gates burst open and a large armed force came streaming out, heading for the wall built along the neck of the horseshoe.

"To arms! Man the walls!"

Springing up from where I was curled up in my *sagum* in one of the small forts built at strategic points behind the wall cutting off the town, I was thankful that I had kept my armor on and only had to grab my harness and helmet. Running to our assigned place on the wall, I saw that the men standing guard had already lit the bundles then thrown them as far from the wall as they could. It was in the flickering illumination of those bundles that we could see the Aduatuci come hurtling at us, and we were not surprised to see that they were all armed.

"Prepare Javelins!"

This was not going to be a battle, it was going to be a slaughter I thought, pulling my arm back into position. Having the advantage of our walls and towers, giving us the high ground, the Aduatuci were packed into a tight mass, realizing that their only chance was to exploit one small part of the wall. However, that wall was lined with men in three ranks, shoulder to shoulder, for its entire length, and each man had two javelins to throw at a target that was impossible to miss.

"Release!"

There was no need to aim, so we launched our missiles high into the air, letting the momentum spend itself before turning downward to whistle down into the packed men running towards us. There was also no need for the illumination of the bundles to tell us we hit our mark, the screams of men transfixed or pinned together in some cases rolling back to us in the dark. The charge inevitably halted for a moment as men stumbled over the bodies of their dead and wounded comrades, or discarded their shields now that it had a shaft of a javelin dragging and sticking in the ground, before they began running at us again. Another volley knifed through the air, and the effects were just as devastating as the first time. Even above the screams we could hear the twanging of the tension cords of the scorpions as they launched their bolts into the midst of the Aduatuci, with the range close enough that a single bolt could pass through a man's body like it was papyrus to skewer another man behind him, and even another one after that. Although they were being slaughtered, the Aduatuci kept advancing before the third volley finally broke them and they went streaming back towards the gates of the town, our jeers and taunts ringing in their ears.

When the sun came up the next morning, we were greeted by the sight of more than 3,000 bodies, those of the dead mingling with those that would be joining them shortly, once we moved among them and finished them off. The treachery of the Aduatuci sealed their fate, despite the pleas yet again from their elders, although this

374

time they did it from the walls, not daring to show themselves in person after the attempt the night before. They were merely prolonging their fate, however, Caesar giving orders to loot the town and round up the remaining people. The Aduatuci did not resist, surprising me somewhat, although putting myself in their place, I guess they realized that if they resisted, they would all be put to death. Still, they had to know what awaited them in a lifetime of slavery, and it is this point of view that, despite witnessing it many times, I have never understood. For myself, and most of the Romans I have known, the idea of slavery is so horrific that we would prefer to die, preferably with a sword in hand, or at least that is what we say to ourselves and to each other. And when I was young I accepted that as an article of faith, not only about myself but my fellow Romans, yet now that I am at least older, if not wiser, I sometimes wonder if it is only because we never had to face choosing between life, even in an unpleasant form, or the finality of death. Diocles and I have had many debates about this question, and I bow to his gift of persuasion to admit that at least I now will entertain an idea that I once would have rejected out of hand.

(My master and friend does not do himself enough credit. He is correct in saying that we have discussed this at length many times, but I do not think it was due to any persuasive measures on my part that have brought him to this relatively recent viewpoint. I do think that Titus has gained much wisdom over the years, harvested from all of the battlefields and all of his contact with men from all parts of the world. He is very much a man of the world now, although he would threaten to beat me if he heard me describe him so. He is not quite the simple old soldier that he likes to portray himself.)

Nevertheless, we were given the town to sack, making Vibius and admittedly everyone else happy to see that something good came from all their sweat and toil, although I think the Aduatuci did not see it that way. However they had rolled the dice, and they lost, so as far as I was concerned, they had no right to bemoan their fate, although it did not stop them from doing just that. Caesar sold the entire remaining population of the town, some 53,000 people, in one lot, although he did decree that more than one of the slave traders who followed us around execute the sale so that the profits were shared. All the wailing that ensued was tedious, and admittedly somewhat heart wrenching, as we supervised the process of shackling the Aduatuci, their first introduction to their new lives. I was just thankful that I would not be present when they were sold and families were torn apart, each of them going to separate parts of the Empire, or Republic as we thought of it then. Still, it was not a pleasant task, and one that we were thankful when it was over, though once it was done, the campaign was over. The Belgae were subdued, if only for the moment as it turned out.

Chapter 8- The Veneti

All activity did not cease with the fall of the Aduatuci, however. Caesar, with the help of his Legions, had managed to open up a vast new territory for trade, and it was with that in mind that he sent one of the Tribunes, Servius Galba along with the 12th Legion, to open up a new route through the mountains leading to the Province. While we were subduing the Aduatuci, Publius Crassus was sent to the coast of Gaul, along with the 7th, to subdue the tribes of the Veneti, Venelli, Ausuvi and some others I forget, which he did with great success. Galba was not so fortunate, and it is with a soldier's superstition that I say that I often wonder if it had been different if he had taken a Legion other than the 12th. They were already the most under strength Legion of the army to begin with, and while I will not belabor their spotty record, it would be a lie to say that Galba's failure did not give even more credence to the belief that the Legion was cursed. As for the rest of the army, the 7th stayed with Crassus and wintered to the southwest. The rest of us were sent into winter quarters in various parts of the region of the Belgae, in groups of two Legions, and we were sent back to the spot where the Sabis and Mosa intersected. Meanwhile, Caesar left us once more, this time to Illyricum, which was his other province, one he had yet to set foot in, despite it going on the third year of his governorship. What we did to the Belgae was met with widespread rejoicing, and Caesar was awarded a period of 15 days of thanksgiving in Rome, which to that time had never happened before. Most of the army was proud that he was receiving the accolades that he was, though not everyone felt that way of course. When the thanksgiving was announced at one of our morning formations, I mentally counted the heartbeats before Vibius started his grumbling once we were dismissed. I do not believe I got past ten.

"Good for him that he's getting all the glory, but we're the reason he's getting it," Vibius declared as we walked back to our area. "And what do we get for it? Nothing, that's what."

As much as I did not wish to argue with Vibius, I could not let that go unchallenged. "*Gerrae*! What do you call the fact that he's splitting the proceeds of those slaves with the entire army?" I argued. "He didn't have to do that, but he did."

"I'll give you that," Vibius admitted grudgingly, "but there's other ways to show your gratitude, isn't there?"

"Like what?"

"I don't know, but I know there's something he could do," Vibius retorted.

I knew better than to keep arguing about it, so I just sighed and rolled my eyes. Some things would never change, I thought as we continued in silence back to start our workday.

The other event of note was that Caesar, Pompey and Crassus renewed their agreement, which some people called the Three Headed Monster. The Consuls for that year were Gnaeus Marcellinus and Lucius Philippus, and it was now the beginning of the third year of campaigning in Gaul. The winter passed uneventfully, at least as far as we were concerned, although there were elements among the Gallic tribes that were very busy indeed, most notably our friends the Belgae. They had not taken their defeat well, and were even now plotting revenge, yet they knew they could not beat us without help, so one more time Gauls looked across the Rhenus to their more savage cousins for help. The news of their plotting made its way to Caesar's ears down in Illyricum, rightly causing him concern. As if this was not enough trouble, at the same time down to the south, Crassus and the 7th were running into problems with the Veneti, that tribe going so far as to seize two agents sent by Crassus to arrange for grain to supply the Legion. There were whispers of uprisings springing up all over, forcing Caesar to move from Illyricum the instant spring arrived. Deeming the situation in the south to be the most extreme since the Veneti were openly opposing young Crassus and Rome, Caesar hurried to

378

that area, making his headquarters in what is now known as Portus Namnetus, though it was still known as Namneti for the tribe that founded it at that time. Labienus was sent with about half the cavalry up to a spot on the Mosella (Moselle) River, which empties into the Rhenus, doing such an excellent job of picking a spot for a camp that it is now known as the town of Augusta Trevorum. Quintus Sabinus was sent with the 8th, 9th and 14th Legions to the northwest of Portus Namnetus into the territories of the Curiosolites, Venelli, and the Luxovii, with orders to stop them from joining with the Veneti. The rest of the army, with the exception of two Cohorts of the 11th, who were sent to Crassus as reinforcements, stayed with Caesar at Portus Namnetus while he planned the campaign. The future traitor Decimus Brutus was given the task of both building and acquiring a fleet, since the Veneti were a seagoing tribe whose strength was in their ships. Caesar worked with his usual speed, and we were barely arrived in Portus Namnetus from our winter camp when we were given orders to march. The distance to the territory of the Veneti was perhaps 50 miles, a distance that normally could be done in a Caesar-paced two days. However, we quickly discovered that the Veneti possessed a secret ally in the terrain. It was flat enough, but after the first day's march on our move towards the coast, we had to make several halts because our line of travel would have taken us into a tidal marsh, or an estuary of some sort. It became especially bad after we crossed a river that marked the boundary to their territory, where the ground was soft and spongy, the wagons finding the going hard as their heavy load pressed them into the turf. Caesar planned on his usual speed to surprise the Veneti, except it seemed that the earth itself was conspiring against us.

Making matters worse were the Veneti themselves, in the way that they situated their defenses. Constructing a series of forts to protect their harbors and the towns surrounding them, they placed them in such a way that, despite our best attempts, we could not carry them and thereby gain entrance to the towns. The forts were not much to look at; it would take only scaling ladders and a few of our artillery for us to get over the wall to subdue the men inside, but it was where they were built that was the problem. The Veneti would find a spit of land that projected into the water, of which there were countless inlets, coves, estuaries and such in that region to choose from, where it was only accessible during low tide. At high tide the finger of land that connected the fort to the mainland would disappear, and we tried a number of different ways to deal with this. Finally settling on a method, Caesar simply had us throw a foundation of stone dragged from nearby quarries and the like, followed by enough dirt to the point that a mole was built that we could march out on to assault the fort, but this would be where the second advantage of the fort would become apparent, with the garrison simply boarding the Veneti ships and sailing away to the next position. It was in this manner that we began subduing the Veneti, except it was incredibly time consuming, and in our view, tiring and frustrating. Each day would see us caked in mud and filth from the tidal pools, mud flats and marshes that served as our source of raw materials, with not even the most vigorous scrubbing completely removing the stench of salt and decay that oozes from the ground in that part of the world. Very quickly we developed a healthy hatred for this region, and for the Veneti, who continued their tactics of delay, moving from one fort to another. I do not think we killed a hundred men during those weeks, merely playing a kind of a game of chase, moving from one inlet to another. Tempers grew short around the fire as the summer passed, a summer that was the least profitable in every sense since we started campaigning in Gaul.

"No battle, no booty, no women, nothing but this cursed mud and trying to fill in the ocean," griped Vellusius one night, somewhat surprising me since he was not the sort to make comments like this, but it told me that the mood was getting grim.

Vellusius was only saying what the rest of them are thinking, I told myself, while yet again I was confronted by the paradox of command, because essentially I agreed with them. I could not say it, however, because it was my job to keep this kind of talk confined to the interior of our tent or around our fire, as long as it was not too loud or too sharp. All soldiers complain; we consider it a right given to us by both Mars and Bellona, although I have heard some soldiers laughingly suggest that the right to carp and complain has to come from the female god of war and not the male. In that moment, I could see the heads nodding at Vellusius' comment, so automatically I looked at Vibius, waiting for him to speak, but I was surprised because he said nothing, instead contenting himself with looking vacantly at the fire while gnawing a piece of bread, spitting out the kernels of grain that had escaped being ground down. By this time we had just "taken" our fifth fort, if by taking one means that we occupied its vacant space once the Veneti had embarked on their ships, and all we knew at the time was that the orders were to march the next morning.

380

Apparently Caesar had endured enough of what we were doing also, for which we were thankful, because our general decided to wait on the fleet that Brutus was building, where we would then take the battle to the sea. This meant only one thing for us in the ranks; we would be sitting this fight out, which after the frustrating and futile effort we had been putting forth, was fine with us. We were marched to a spot overlooking a bay that would serve as the marshaling point for the fleet, awaiting the arrival of Brutus and his ships, making a camp on that spot. It was a matter of a few days before the word was shouted that ships were sighted; as usual Caesar had chosen his ground well, our camp being situated on a point much higher than the bay below us, giving us a perfect view of not only the bay but the immediately surrounding area. It was into the bay that our fleet sailed, and I stopped counting at a hundred ships of varying sizes. I was not a sailor, nor did I have any knowledge of nautical affairs, but I was hard pressed to see how any fleet of Gallic ships could stand up to the onslaught facing them. My opinion immediately changed when, standing with all of my friends on the ramparts of our camp to watch the show, we saw the Veneti fleet come into view.

"By the gods, they're huge," gasped Calienus, and coming from the normally imperturbable Tesseraurius, this alone was enough to make us worry.

The Gallic fleet was not just huge in the size of their ships, dwarfing our triremes as if they were rowboats, there were substantially more of them than was contained in the fleet Brutus was leading.

"You know what this means," Atilius said glumly. "We're back in that cursed swamp, filling in the ocean just to chase these bastards off."

This was our frame of mind as we watched, expecting defeat, instead witnessing a miracle.

It was a miracle only in the sense that once again, our *praefecti fabrorum* showed their true genius. Unable to ram the larger ships since the timbers of ours were not built to withstand the rougher water of the open ocean, our engineers contrived a way to rob the Gallic ships of their most precious asset, mobility. Unlike our ships, which used both a sail and oars, the Gallic craft were powered by sails alone, so the engineers created an implement that was little more than a long pole with an iron hook on it. Although the Gallic ships were bigger and stronger, they were also slower, especially when the wind was not in their favor, thereby allowing our oar-driven vessels to maneuver alongside. Once in position men on deck, holding the pole, would grab at the wooden horizontal crossbeam that held the sail in place, then while they were holding tight, the captain of the Roman ship would give the order to begin pulling away. The strain was such that the ropes holding the wooden cross-piece would snap, and before our very eyes, the sails on the Gallic ships began to tumble down, each craft slowing to a stop to lie dead in the water.

"That's not good," commented Calienus dryly, "if you're a Veneti at least."

We laughed at this, and in delight we watched as one by one the Gallic craft were immobilized, whereupon they were swarmed by the smaller Roman ships, the men on our vessels then clambering over the side. From our vantage point, we could not see the action on the decks because it was too far away, and were barely able to make out the figures of our men climbing up the side of the Gallic ships, but it was clear enough what was happening. One by one, the Gallic vessels were overcome in this way, until it became clear to those Veneti who were left that their cause was hopeless, whereupon they turned to flee out to the open water. That is when the gods intervened, once again showing the Romans their favor, as the wind, a stiff breeze that had been blowing the whole day, suddenly stopped for no reason. While the Gallic ships were just beginning to pull away into the distance to the point where we could no longer tell what was happening, we could at least see that suddenly our own craft caught up to them, and the remaining Gallic ships were quickly subdued. Just before dark, the wind freshened, enabling some of the Veneti craft to slip away, but the vast majority of them were taken, with the damage done. Before the day was out, the Veneti had been conquered.

As an example to the other tribes in the region, Caesar had the entire Veneti council of elders put to death. During the time we were slogging away in the marshes to the south, Sabinus and his Legions had been busy as well. The tribes that threw their lot in with the Veneti; the Lexovii, Aulerci and Eburovices, led by a man named Viridorix, were the tribes that Sabinus was sent to chastise. And chastise them he did, indeed. Using a stratagem of guile by appearing to be weak, Sabinus induced Viridorix to attack a fortified

Roman camp with a mile of clear ground around it. When we heard the circumstances of the Sabinus victory, we had a good laugh at that, knowing that it was the height of folly for a Gallic tribe of any kind, having such disdain for the science of siegework as they did, to attempt an assault of a Roman camp. The battle was more of a slaughter than anything, prompting the confederation of those three tribes to immediately fall apart with our victory, so that three more tribes of Gaul found themselves at the mercy of Rome. It made one wonder when they would learn; at least that is how I looked at it.

Young Crassus was not being idle either, down in Aquitania. Sweeping all before him, he punished the recalcitrant tribes for the folly of resistance. Crassus did not use guile, instead taking a page from Caesar's book, relying on audacity and surprise when attacking a Gallic camp. As we heard it, the issue was actually in doubt, with the Gauls asking for help from some of the tribes a little further south in Lusitania. Some of the men who answered that call and came to assist had fought under Sertorius, meaning they had learned their craft well. Because of that influence, the Gallic camp had been built in the usual Roman style, so the 7th was having a hard time of it in the beginning, until a cavalry scouting party saw that the Gauls had thrown all their troops into protecting the front wall but left the rear gate unattended. Once this was discovered, the outcome was inevitable, despite the Gauls putting up a good fight. Even with all of these successes, as this campaign season drew to a close there were still some questions hanging in the air. Two tribes on the northern coast, the Menapii and the Morini, that had entered into the alliance with the Veneti, despite being separated by hundreds of miles, still refused to submit to Rome. As far as we were concerned, that meant that there was unfinished business, and we would still have some fighting to do the next season. However, Caesar was not willing to wait until the next season, so almost before we knew it, we found ourselves again on the march. This time, we would cross more than 400 miles, marching past where we fought the Nervii, doing without the customary rest day, which Caesar could only have done with an army as seasoned as ours. Despite the fact we could take it physically, it did not make some people love Caesar any more, and even I, a man with complete faith in his judgment and abilities as a general, found myself questioning the wisdom of this move. Yes, we would reach the lands of the Morini much more quickly than they anticipated, but what shape would we be in, and how much of a season would be left? The further north we moved, the more frigid the climate, and the earlier winter comes. When we got there, it would be at the end of the month we now call August, meaning we would have at best another three weeks of true campaign season left, and that was only if the winter did not come early.

Sabinus and his Legions joined us on the march, and it was indeed in late August that we arrived on the fringes of the lands of the Morini, who were warned of our coming. Instead of facing us, they immediately retreated into the refuge of a great forest, larger than anything I had ever seen before. Trees were so thick that once we entered it, there was never truly anything that could be called day, the light from the sun barely making its way through the branches and all the way down to the ground. It was an eerie place, where we could feel the eyes of the Morini watching us while we marched, relying on the pioneers and advance party to fell trees in order to tell us which way to go. One afternoon, perhaps four days after we entered the forest, we stopped and were building the camp when the *bucina* sounded. The Morini had launched a surprise attack, the area they chose being the part of the camp that the 13th Legion was charged with constructing. Although the Morini were beaten back with ease, some of the Legionaries, overzealous in their pursuit, were subsequently cut off and killed, some 50 men being cut down. In response to this, Caesar was determined not to be surprised again, so as we marched, he sent out flanking parties who cut down the trees some 200 paces on either side of the marching column, stacking the logs as they went. Naturally, this slowed down the advance, but Caesar was determined, confident that the effort to subdue this tribe would not take long, and in this he was probably right. However, the gods are fickle, even with Caesar, and it does not take much for them to turn on you. We had penetrated a fair way into Morini territory when the rains started. It was not unusual for this time of year, and normally would not have been a problem, except that the rains never stopped. Day after day after day, for a full week the rain came down, until the leather of our tents was saturated to the point where in some cases, the roof gave way, dousing its unlucky inhabitants with icy cold water. The camps we made quickly became a morass of mud, and before long, the mud on the march was so thick that if we made five miles in a day, it was a good day's march. Finally, even Caesar could not ignore the signs, so with great reluctance, he gave the order to reverse our march to head back south, where the weather was more hospitable. Before we left, however, we set every village, town or lonely farm to the torch, razing everything we found.

384

Our losses in this season had been astonishingly light, and in fact, we lost more from illness than deaths in battle. My tent section was still intact, at least as far as it was constituted starting that year, and for this my friends and I paid for a bountiful sacrifice to Fortuna, Mars and Bellona. It set us back a few hundred sesterces, but we felt it well worth it.

Caesar marched us south to Mediolanum, where he left us for the winter before continuing his own progress south. This winter he elected stay at least on the other side of the Alps, having a number of political issues with which he had to contend. The 10th spent the winter at Mediolanum Aulercorum, along the banks of a smaller river that feeds into the Sequana (Seine) River and where Lugdunensis stands today. Once again, we found ourselves part of a game played between the Gauls and Caesar, the Gauls conspiring with each other to somehow usurp Rome's authority over them. As part of his renewal of the Triumvirate, Pompey Magnus and Publius Crassus' father Marcus were named Consuls for the year, a fact which had no bearing on our fortunes, save for the discussion around the fire of the political situation. At that age and time, I had absolutely no interest in politics, and even now, despite possessing a deeper understanding of its nature and importance, I engage in political discussions reluctantly. It is not so much from ignorance as it is a belief that, when all is said and done, it does not matter. Legions march, Rome conquers, and Rome endures because it is so. Accordingly, I had no interest in much beyond any activity that directly impacted whether or not I would find myself standing shoulder to shoulder with a comrade. Even now, in my dotage I have this attitude and it has served me well enough these last years. Oftentimes men mistake disinterest for ignorance; I am not ignorant of what is going on, but ultimately it does not matter what I think and therefore I am not particularly interested in wasting time on subjects over which I ultimately have no control. And that, gentle reader, is one thing that has not changed about me, so when Vibius, Scribonius or any of our friends from within the Legion began to discuss politics of an evening after dinner, I was always one of the first to excuse myself to attend to other duties. I would make the excuse that as Sergeant, I had a number of details that demanded my attention, which was true enough, but it was just not the main reason for my disengagement. What was of more immediate interest to me were the activities of the Usipetes and Tencteri, two German tribes from across the Rhenus that were being forced out of their territory by the more warlike Suebi, who we had occasion to meet when they fought under Ariovistus. The Suebi pressed the Usipetes and Tencteri hard, crossing into their lands to savage the fields of the two tribes, until in desperation, for surely that could be the only real motive they could have had to defy Caesar, they crossed the Rhenus.

Because of their spotty performance, Caesar had released the cavalry force that he used for the last two seasons and ordered a fresh levy to be drawn, a decision that was fine with us since the group that had been with us had proven to be little better than useless, though that may be the normal disdain a soldier has for a cavalryman. Regardless, while the *dilectus* for the cavalry was being performed, Caesar sent emissaries to secure the necessary forage for our livestock and grain for ourselves. Once these two tasks were completed, we began our march to the north, traveling farther to the east than we ever penetrated before. The distance was such that the march took up almost a month of the season, meaning that we arrived at the edge of the disputed territory having marched off all the flab that we accumulated over the winter. Passing the site of our battle with the Nervii to the south, we crossed the Mosa River at the point where it runs parallel to the Rhenus. Not long after we crossed the river, perhaps a day, we were met by a delegation representing the Usipetes and Tencteri, who had heard that Caesar and his army approached. Despite coming as supplicants, they refused to retreat across the Rhenus when Caesar demanded it, claiming that certain death at the hands of the Suebi awaited them, instead asking him to designate some land in Gaul where they could settle. Caesar made a counterproposal that offered the two tribes some land back across the Rhenus where the Ubii lived, who just a few months before had submitted to Rome and become a vassal state. The envoys of the Usipetes and Tencteri agreed to take this offer back to their tribe, asking Caesar to keep his army in place while they went to confer with their elders. Caesar smelled a trap and refused, instead keeping us moving towards the German camp that was at the junction of the Mosa and Rhenus. At the end of that day, as we were preparing camp, the envoys of the tribes came hurrying back, begging Caesar not to continue his advance. Our scouts told us that we were no more than a half-day's march away from the German camp, so Caesar knew that the Germans were stalling for time. While refusing to stop us from advancing, he did agree to move another few miles to the banks of another river, whose name I do not remember, so that we could replenish our water supply and wait for the decision of the tribes' elders. Our new cavalry was 5,000 strong, and they reported that the Germans' own cavalry was not in the immediate

386

area, apparently having ranged far and wide to find forage and food for the tribes. When Caesar was made aware of this, he drew the conclusion that the request for a delay was so that the German cavalry could come back to rejoin the main body. Still, he would not go back on his word, so we were under strict orders not to engage any of the Germans in battle and thereby violate the truce.

We did not have to, because the Germans did it for us. Caesar ordered our cavalry to scout the area between our two camps and while doing so, in a direct violation of the truce, our host of 5,000 was attacked by no more than 800 German cavalry. The surprise was total because of this treachery, so despite being no admirer of cavalry, I will admit that the element of surprise in war cannot be overestimated. Whatever the circumstances, there was fierce fighting, during which many of our men were slain, with the remainder taking flight back to our column, at that point still a mile short of where we said we would stop. That made Caesar's decision for him, and I know that this decision has brought much censure, especially because of the events that transpired. I think, gentle reader, you know by now that I am a great admirer of Caesar, so that if he were to miraculously come back to life, I would find the strength in these old bones to don my armor and helmet and pick up my shield and sword to follow wherever he directed. But even I, one of his most ardent supporters, cannot truly justify the actions that he undertook once the truce was violated. When I was younger, I pretended that I not only understood but supported his decision, but the years have stripped even that shell of a pretense away. Some of the dreams that rob me of my sleep are from what took place there with the Usipetes and Tencteri, and Diocles can be witness to the nights that I jerk awake screaming in horror, sweat soaking my nightclothes like I had just gone for a swim. Those are the ramblings of an old man, however, and have no bearing here, so I will direct my mind back to the specifics of what took place. Caesar's concern was twofold; first was the act of treachery itself, because it gave a clear indication that the Germans could not be trusted. The wider implication was the example it would set with those tribes in Gaul still harboring dreams of overthrowing Rome, so it was with these two motives he acted, no matter how they are seen in the light of history. Making camp at the appointed spot on the banks of the river, it was the next morning that a deputation of chiefs from the two tribes came to apologize for the actions of their cavalry. Their claim was that they had been returning from foraging and therefore had no knowledge of the truce. Being completely honest, I can see the truth of this statement. However, the fact was that the truce was broken and Caesar, having reached his conclusion that these Germans could not be trusted under any account, refused to grant them an audience. Instead, he deduced that their supposed humility was a ruse designed to gain the tribes' time to organize an attack, which may or may not have been the case. Regardless, whether it was true or not did not matter to Caesar, or so it seemed, because he immediately ordered us to form up to march on the German camp, while having the German chiefs thrown into chains.

Even now, after all these years, I cannot bring myself to speak of what happened when we attacked their camp, at least in any detail. With the absence of their leaders, even if they were prepared to meet us, I believe the outcome was inevitable. However, they were not prepared; the surprise was total, the result what one could expect of a battle-hardened army that had been campaigning for three years. No mercy was given, the Legions putting all they found to the sword, no matter their age or their disposition. Men, women, children, babies, old people, it made no difference to us. Those few who survived the initial onslaught we scattered, pursuing them with our cavalry who were forced to march in the rear of the column as a mark of their shame, and were therefore eager to exact their own revenge on the Usipetes and Tencteri. Remember those names well, gentle reader, because they no longer exist, so total was our victory and so thorough our punishment. Those precious few who fled the camp were chased all the way back to the Rhenus, where they threw themselves into the swift current and were swept away, in the same way we swept away the rest of their people. I will not pretend that I am blameless; my sword was as bloody as any of my comrades when the day was done, and I was as indiscriminate in who I killed as the next man. My only excuse is that I took no pleasure in it; in fact, I found myself vomiting up all the contents of my breakfast, and I will say that I was not alone, a small comfort, knowing that there were others who felt like I did. In fact, I believe it was only because of my size and reputation that some of my comrades did not mock and ridicule me for being soft, especially since I saw many other men who had the same reaction as I did unmercifully teased. The Legions are a hard place, where any sensitivity is viewed as a weakness, and is immediately pounced upon by one's very own friends. I might have escaped the ridicule of my fellow Legionaries, but I did not escape the faces of the many I slew that day as they chased me through my dreams.

The reaction in Rome was one of total shock. There was even talk of holding Caesar accountable for supposed crimes against the Germans, there being much made of his violation of the truce, which we in the ranks did not understand. We found it hard to believe that Caesar had neglected to report that it was the Germans who violated the truce, but we soon saw what was happening in Rome for what it was, an opportunity seized by his political enemies to smear Caesar's name. It was at this time that I first became acquainted with the name of the man who I hope even now is like Sisyphus, Marcus Porcius Cato. Vibius was a great admirer of Cato, and it was his admiration of the man that I believe eventually contributed to the rift that existed between Vibius and myself for many years. I had not paid much attention to the actions of the great men in Rome, for reasons that I mentioned earlier, but many of my comrades, Vibius among them, were avid followers of the political dramas that were taking place in Rome. Like all things, these men turned it into a gambling opportunity, wagering each other on the outcome of legislation or whether a particular man's position on a topic would carry the day.

"Cato is a great Roman, maybe the greatest of all time," Vibius enthused one evening by the fire.

Despite knowing that I should not indulge him, I found myself asking, "How so?"

It was not more than a handful of moments later that I found myself sorry that I had asked.

"Because he not only believes in the values of the true Republic, he lives them in his everyday life." Without waiting for prompting, Vibius continued, "He refuses to wear a tunic under his toga, because our ancestors didn't, and he claims that it's a sign of the weakness that has infected Rome."

I rather saw it as a sign that men had finally figured out a way to be more comfortable, though I knew better than to argue.

"His toga is black," Vibius finished, which did raise a question, passing my lips before I knew what had possessed me.

"Why in the name of Dis is that?" I demanded, "So he can wear it after it gets dirty?"

Vibius indignantly shook his head.

"Not at all. He wears it as a sign of mourning, for the loss of the true Republic and the *mos maiorum*."

Shaking my head, I knew by this point that I was going to regret asking the next logical question, "And why, pray tell me dear Vibius, does he believe that the true Republic is dead?"

"Because it is!" Vibius was emphatic on this point, "Look at how elections are rigged. Candidates who are just straw men, while only the richest men can afford to hold office."

To my mind, this was always the way things had gone, but I held my tongue.

"And now the rabble has all the control, because whoever courts the mob and wins their favor will have the true power, not the Senate and the Tribunes of the plebs as it should be," Vibius finished, sitting back down at his spot, looking very pleased with himself.

"Vibius," I reminded him gently, "if the truth be known, we," I indicated all the men sitting at the fire, "are part of that rabble that you speak so badly about."

While I saw the heads of most of my friends nodding, I will admit that I was not surprised when I saw Vibius was unmoved.

"Rabble we may be," he countered, "but we're citizens, and we have the right to vote. Rome has been invaded by foreigners, and they're a large part of the mob now," he was really warmed up now, "and their influence is equal to that of freeborn Roman citizens like me," to which he hastily added, "and you, Titus. Surely you see that."

In fact I did not see, and even if I did, I did not care. What I cared about was the same thing that I had cared about when I had lied about my age to join the Legions; the opportunity to improve myself and my family's standing in our society. That and the chance to win glory, for the sake of glory alone. The rest of it, at least as far as I was concerned, was unimportant, and I could not conceal that indifference from my best friend, who found it infuriating.

390

"Don't you see?" he cried out in frustration, "This isn't what our ancestors wanted for us when they drove the kings from Rome. The Republic, as it was first formulated, is the perfect form of government! There's none better anywhere in the known world. If we continue the way we are, we might as well be Greeks!"

He finished his last statement by spitting into the fire to show his contempt. There are few insults worse for a Roman than being called a Greek, something I always found somewhat puzzling, given that most of the nobles considered their education to be incomplete until they had spent time in Athens or Delphi. As Vibius finished, I remember making a mental note that one day, I would like to visit Greece. Little did I know that I would get my wish, just not in the way I hoped.

However brutal Caesar's actions may have been, they did serve to quell the appetite of the Germans to cross the Rhenus, since they now knew that the days of easy plunder were over. To emphasize the point, Caesar marched us to the banks of the great river, whereupon he performed perhaps his greatest feat of engineering. To be fair, his *praefecti fabrorum* were the ones who did the brunt of the work, but Caesar possessed a keen mind for problems involving engineering, and it was on crossing the Rhenus to which he turned his attention. On the opposite side lay the hordes of Germania, from where the incursions into Gaul that so disrupted the peace emanated. Caesar made the decision to give the Germans an example of what Rome could do if it chose, commanding the building of a bridge. The spot chosen was at a point in between two islands, the river being about two furlongs wide at this point, and despite being a good distance, was still the narrowest point where the ground on both sides was suitable. Immediately put to work, the entire army, save the 14th which served as a guard, chopped down the trees necessary to construct a bridge sufficiently large to allow the passage of the army and all its baggage. We were lucky that this area was heavily forested; indeed, the trees were so thick that there was a permanent gloom that was present no matter the time of the day within the confines of the forest, just like the lands of the Morini. Such trifles are not enough to stop an army of Rome and we were set to the work, which we performed with a will, knowing that we were part of history in the making. There had never been a bridge across the Rhenus, and this was yet another demonstration of the superiority of Rome that we were only too happy to demonstrate to the Germans across the river, their scouts watching in dismay from the opposite bank at the work being done. One day more than a week later, the bridge was completed, stretching the distance over the river, originating about 50 paces on our side, and terminating about 50 paces on the opposite bank. Being Caesar's favorite Legion, we were given the honor, after Caesar himself and his cavalry bodyguard of course, of being the first to march across, and all of us, Vibius included, did so with a large amount of pride. This bridge was living proof of the might of Rome, the tromping of our boots only serving to emphasize that point. The next two weeks were spent burning the crops in the fields that were just beginning to ripen, and putting every farm we found to the torch, while killing every Sugambri, the tribe that lived in that region, within our reach. We did not follow the stream of Germans that we saw fleeing into the great forest at our approach, for the same reason as always. Once Caesar deemed we set enough of an example, we marched back to the bridge, crossing back to our side of the Rhenus, whereupon Caesar ordered the bridge to be partially destroyed, leaving the approach and piers supporting them on our side of the river intact as a warning that we would not hesitate to come back.

With the end of the campaign season not far away, it led to speculation among us that Caesar would deem our subjugation of the Usipetes and Tencteri, along with our foray across the Rhenus enough, but he still had things for us to do. For yet another time we found ourselves marching back west, but the farther we marched the more rampant the rumors grew about where we were headed, and as seasoned as we may have been by this time, as confident in ourselves and our leader as we were, it was not without some trepidation on our part with which we faced our immediate future. Crossing back across the Mosa, the river by now seeming like an old friend, we continued marching west, making our way through the rough hills and forests of our old enemies the Nervii, for the second time that season marching past the battleground at the river. Once through the hills, the land grew flatter and flatter, though there were still huge stands of forests that this time we negotiated a path around rather than through, making our progress even slower. After it appeared that we put the forests behind us, we began passing through land that seemed to have a river or stream of some sort every mile, with much of the terrain in between being marshy, which of course we had to steer clear of because of our wagons. None of the Centurions said anything, yet there was a clear sense of urgency that made every delay, no matter how short, an occasion that brought out the best cursing that our officers had to offer. This did not help the mood of the army any, the speculation and rumors becoming more and more pointed and focused on one, and only one possibility. One night, Vibius finally spoke out loud what we were all secretly thinking, and dreading.

"Caesar wants to sail to Britannia," Vibius announced at the evening meal.

We had just finished a particularly trying day that saw us move into an area of ground that, on the surface, looked normal yet was incredibly soft and spongy. By the time the decision was made to change direction to find firmer ground, two Legions, including the 10th, found ourselves ankle deep in some sort of muck that proved incredibly difficult to clean off. The moment Vibius said it, it was as if we all let out a collective breath at the same time, like some invisible dam just burst, with all of our thoughts and concerns pouring out. There was a babble of voices as all of my tentmates sought to contribute whatever nugget of information they had heard at some time in their lives about Britannia.

"It's a myth; there's no such thing," Atilius was adamant about this. "It's a tale put out by a band of pirates who prey on anyone stupid enough to believe it exists and go looking for it."

"If that's true, where exactly are these pirates hiding? They're not anywhere on the coast of Gaul or we'd have heard about it." Scribonius could always be counted on to think things through.

This flummoxed Atilius for a moment, then he shrugged and retorted, "I don't know, but it doesn't matter. It's still a myth."

We mercilessly hooted at this, but Atilius was nothing if he was not stubborn; it was not often that he ventured an idea of his own, so when he did he was not going to let something as trivial as logic get in the way.

"It exists all right, but the reason nobody has ever set foot on it and lived to tell the tale is because of the huge monsters that are between the coast of Gaul and Britannia. If they don't get you going over, they get you coming back." Vellusius was no less certain than Atilius, and this idea had the merit of not being overtly ridiculous. We all knew as a matter of course that there are huge monsters that roam the waves, preying on those unfortunate souls who wander too far from the sight of shore. That is why so few who venture far out to sea return.

393

"That's all nonsense," this was Calienus, who had dropped by our tent to chat with his old friends. He still carried a slight limp from the wound he had suffered, but it did not slow him down and if it pained him, he kept it to himself. "There're no monsters at sea. It's on the island itself. The men of Britannia are giants, the shortest is more than ten feet tall."

"And how could you possibly know this?" demanded Vibius, who apparently was none too pleased that the thunder of his announcement was taken over by speculation about the fate that awaited us. The fact was that we absolutely believed him. All of us were convinced that Caesar was intent on going to Britannia, so we had moved onto the next logical subject, and that was what awaited us when we got there.

"From Gisela," Calienus said seriously.

Gisela was a girl who had joined the camp followers in the last year. She was a Suessiones, and was much different than most of the other women who were part of the contingent of people following the army. Where they were dark, she was extremely fair, with hair the color of copper and freckles sprinkled across her nose, which unlike our proud Roman noses was more snubbed, although for some strange reason it enhanced her beauty rather than detracted from it. She had a wondrous figure, but her most striking feature were her eyes, a green that was almost as rich and deep as the grass that grew in her country. She was a sensation, and could have had her choice of any man in the Legion, Tribunes included, except for some reasons that none of us could understand, she chose to be Calienus' woman. We regularly cursed his luck.

"She had a kinsman who married a woman from the Menapii tribe, and they do business with the people on the island. He told her, and she told me. She said that he told her that they're all huge, and they practice a religion that requires them to sacrifice a human being on special days." That struck us to silence; although we had heard of peoples who practiced such rituals, we had not heard of what he described next. "After the person is sacrificed, every one of the tribe has to eat a piece of the flesh of the person."

There were exclamations of disgust at that, and I searched Calienus' face intently for a clue that he was trying to put one over on us, but his face was deadly serious. With that piece of good news, he bade us goodnight to ponder our fates.

394

Reaching the coast at a point far to the north of Samarobriva, the army took notice that we were the farthest west and north than we had been in the three almost full years of campaigning in Gaul to that point. I mentioned some time ago that our principal observation was that winter comes earlier the farther north you get, though for what reason I cannot say, and now we had the added element of the wind coming off of the ocean. We were told that this spot we were at was the point closest to Britannia, and we waited there a few days as Caesar sent word to find every available transport ship. At the same time he sent one of his Tribunes, Gaius Volusenus, to reconnoiter the coast of Britannia to find a suitable landing area. Caesar's fame always preceded him wherever he went, and this time was no exception. The camp was abuzz with the news that a ship arrived, carrying emissaries from the tribes that lived on the island, and we all sought excuses to be near the *Praetorium* when they were presented to Caesar. It should not surprise anyone to know that, with men dropping all pretense of work to come running to examine our guests, there was spirited wagering going on about their appearance. That story of the ten foot tall men was about to be put to the test; surely, men argued, that if there were such specimens of manhood to be found on the island the Britons would send these men as the emissaries to Caesar. There was the usual announcement at the gate that there were visitors on official business, requesting an audience with Caesar, which was promptly granted. The gates swung open, with the men standing on the tips of their toes to be one of the first to glimpse the delegation. After all, there was now money at stake and such is the nature of man that each of us feel we must be the first to know which way the dice falls when we have coin riding on it. The delegation was mounted, if one could call it that, on some of the smallest horses we had ever seen, with great shaggy coats and long unkempt tails. In dress, I could see the similarities between themselves and their Gallic cousins, but that is where the resemblance ended. Meanwhile, the crowd of men alternately let out groans of disappointment or yells of exultation, depending on which way they bet, because they were by all appearances normal-sized men, not a giant in the lot. This racket clearly confused our guests, who peered at us with what looked like mild concern at our behavior. Primus Pilus Favonius started bellowing out orders to disperse, and we quickly returned to our normal duties. What struck me and my friends the most was not so much what they wore in the way of clothes but the way in which they decorated their faces. We would come to know this style very well over the course of the next two seasons, but this was the first time we saw any men who put designs on their face and chests using some sort of blue paint.

The emissaries had gotten wind of Caesar's intentions, via traders and I suspect spies among the Gallic tribes along the coast who had developed a lucrative partnership with the Britons on the island and did not want to see it disrupted. These Britons offered their obedience to Rome, which Caesar accepted, while in order to assure their good faith, he sent back with them to Britannia a Gaul named Commius. Caesar had selected Commius as king of the Atrebates and considered the man a friend who supposedly carried some influence with the tribes of Britannia. Also working in our favor was the submission of the Morini, the tribe in whose lands we were camped, and who fought us the year before. They were now coming as supplicants begging forgiveness, claiming that they were led astray by the firebrands and hotheads in their tribe. This was a welcome development, since it did not make any of us sleep easier knowing that we were surrounded by a tribe that had been our bitter enemy not so long ago. While these diplomatic events were taking place, the shipping that Caesar needed to accomplish his goal was being assembled, except it was not of sufficient numbers to carry the whole army, in one trip anyway. Five days after he departed, Volusenus' ship sailed back up the estuary and into the harbor that our camp overlooked, reporting to Caesar that he had found a suitable landing for the Legions that Caesar would bring with him. There was much speculation, and much wagering, on which Legions would be asked to accompany Caesar on this momentous event, and it is fair to say that the 10th considered their inclusion to be as close to certain as possible. This did not make us any more popular with the rest of the army, yet they were forced to accept, however grudgingly, that Caesar trusted us above all others in his army, a fact that we were always quick to point out whenever we had the opportunity. Many a brawl was started in this manner during the winter months.

The most Caesar could muster was 80 transports for a total of two Legions, with ourselves and the 7th being selected. The 7th had acquitted themselves with distinction under young Crassus down south, so their reward for their valor was to be included in this historic event. I cannot lie; there were considerably mixed feelings about being selected to accompany Caesar. On the one hand, we were aware it was a tremendous honor. On the other, our fear and superstitions were given free rein, and I believe it was with some malice that the men of the other Legions did what they could to fan

396

the flames of our doubt. As was his habit, Caesar did not tarry; Volusenus was back in port less than a full day when he gave the order that we would be embarking during the next night. We were told not to pack like we were going to be gone long, and it was with some trepidation that we left non-essential items behind with the invalids and shirkers who would be staying behind to guard our gear. What the army deemed non-essential items tended to be things that we valued and cherished the most, for a variety of reasons, thereby making them more valuable to our fellow Legionaries. Packed up, we marched down to the harbor to begin the process of loading onto the transports. Caesar was also bringing a few hundred cavalry, although they were destined to never show up on the island, thanks to storms that drove them further down the coast to seek shelter. Loading the transports was an irksome and boring process, with each transport only carrying at the most two Centuries. Each Century had to troop up the gangplank onto the ship then arrange themselves according to the wishes of the master of the ship before it moved out into the harbor to await the others. Fortunately, or so we thought at the time, we loaded by Cohort, so that the Second was early in the loading process. What we did not take into account was the fact that until everyone was aboard we would have to wait, the only difference being whether it was onboard ship or not, and we gave the men who crewed our vessel great cause for amusement as most of us began to get sick almost immediately.

"If your stomach can't handle the harbor, we're going to have our hands full when we put out into the channel," laughed the senior man of the ship, whose title I do not know.

His jest we did not find amusing in the slightest, although he was right. Once we reached the open sea, which the crew of the ship took great delight in telling us was really just a relatively protected channel, we were even sicker than in the harbor, something I did not think possible. This was far worse than our experience on the barges during the campaign in Lusitania, we unanimously agreed, with men continually running to the side to empty the contents of their stomach. It was in this state that we began our great adventure.

The ships carrying us sailed through the night, while some of the warships holding not only Caesar but the contingent of archers and the artillery that we were taking pulled far ahead. These artillery pieces carried by the warships were mounted so that they could fire from the ships. To the galleys went the honor of being the first to sight the isle of which we had heard so much yet knew so little.

Meanwhile, behind them sloshed the transports, bucking and pitching as they fought through the current that seemed to be conspiring against us. With the dawn approaching, we roused ourselves from our stupor to gather along the sides of the boat to peer anxiously towards the west, wagers being made about who would be the first to sight land. Finally, about the first part of the watch after dawn, a shout arose as the sharpest eye among us pointed to his find, and money or markers changed hands. Naturally, we all strained our eyes and could just make out what appeared to be a.......white line? In our limited experience, land would show up as a black or perhaps green line on the horizon, except Britannia was different. We could make out a white line that we were sure were not the whitecaps of waves and immediately wagering began on whether what we were seeing was snow. While we could not credit the idea that snow would be falling this early in the year, there was no denying what we were seeing, and I was among those who were sure that this Britannia was a land that was perhaps encased in perpetual ice and snow. How else could one explain why so few people had visited?

Ever so slowly, the truth was revealed to us and perhaps a third of a watch or so after we got our first view of land, we drew close enough to determine what we were looking at with such eagerness. An almost universal groan escaped from the two Centuries on the boat; very few men, if any, had wagered that we were seeing some form of white rock, yet that is exactly what it was. Sheer white cliffs as it turned out, once we finally caught up with the galleys. By the time we actually joined them, because of the tide running against us, a good part of the day had passed by, and we anxiously watched the sun dropping inexorably towards the horizon. Although the dangers ashore concerned us, what was of more pressing urgency was the idea that we would have to spend another night on this boat, so we were happy to see when Caesar summoned all the officers to his flagship. As they were rowed across to meet with the general, it was right about then that someone noticed something was amiss.

"How do we get off this damned thing?" Vibius mused as he stared down at the solid wooden side of the boat that came up to above his waist.

At first I did not understand what he was saying, thinking of course we would get off the same way we got on. That is when the realization of what he was saying hit me. I began looking around at the boat; no, the sides of the boat were smooth and of one piece, and

398

there was no obvious place where somehow the side would magically lower so we could walk down a gangplank. Instantly after this idea hit me was the understanding that there would be no gangplank, since I thought it highly unlikely that the Britons, who we could now see standing on the cliffs watching us, would offer us assistance of any kind. Despite the diplomatic words of their envoys, what we saw arrayed on the cliff looked anything but peaceful.

"Are those....chariots?" This was gasped by Scribonius, and a moan of apprehension rippled through the rest of the men, a feeling that I must say I shared. We had never faced chariots before, although every Roman child has grown up on stories about their use in war. Our experience with chariots was confined to the races in Rome between the various teams, the Reds, Greens, Blues and whatnot. Even as we watched, with almost contemptuous ease, the men driving the chariots wheeled them back and forth along the cliff, in the same manner as a restless beast of prey paces when put in a cage. This would be what was waiting for us when we got ashore, I thought, as soon as we figure out how to get off the damned boat.

Sometimes the answer to a problem lies in its simplest form and such was the case here. Once the fleet gathered in the shadow of the white cliffs, shortly after the officers were rowed back to their respective ships from Caesar's flagship, the current suddenly and mysteriously, at least to us, changed direction to begin pushing us farther north along the coast. The Britons on the cliff saw us leaving, and wheeling their chariots around, darted out of sight, the men on foot with them trailing behind, presumably to move to a different vantage point. Sailing for about another third of a watch before there was a signal that a suitable landing place was spotted, without hesitation the signal to land came from Caesar's ship, with the transports immediately turning to head straight for the shore. The sight of the island drawing inexorably closer brought us all to our feet, as orders were shouted to make ready. Looking nervously about for some sort of indication that might give us an idea of what was about to happen, to our inexperienced eyes it looked very much as if the plan was just to run these ships straight onto the beach. One of the men in the other Century walked over to ask the man steering the ship, and we could see his face turn white at the answer he was given, although it was drowned out by the sound of the wind whistling past the sail and the water slapping the sides of the boat.

The Legionary walked back in our direction, saying loudly enough for us to hear, "This crazy bastard is just going to run us up onto the beach at full speed."

I can tell you that this caused a bit of a reaction among the lot of us, the men talking excitedly, grabbing at whatever they thought would be solid in preparation for the landing. Clutching the side of the ship, with Vibius next to me, we both leaned out over the side to peer at the beach we were heading towards, and I heard Vibius mumbling to himself.

Thinking he was talking to me, I leaned closer to hear him. "I still don't know how we're supposed to get off this damned thing."

I will say the shock was not nearly as bad as we expected, mainly because the bottom of the ship scraped against the seabed before the bow actually made it out of the water, yet while this may have softened the shock, it presented another problem. Once it was clear that we had stopped we ran forward to the front of the ship, where I caught my first glimpse of what was waiting for us. Our first difficulty was that the ship had scraped bottom while the bulk of it was still in the water, so jumping out of it even at the point closest to shore meant we would be jumping into water where we could not see the bottom. Additionally, it was what was waiting for us on the beach that made the prospect of jumping into the water even less appealing, as a multitude of Briton warriors, most of them bare-chested with long flowing mustaches, were standing there. All of them as far as I could see were wearing the same blue paint that the envoys had worn, except this time not just on their faces but chests and arms as well. They stood just a short distance away from the beach, which was not sand but of smoothly rounded stones of varying sizes, and the combination of these two obstacles meant that nobody was willing to jump down into the water. In my case, I was not as worried about the depth as the others because of my height, but for men like Vibius, I imagine that in their minds there was a very real fear of going under the surface and not coming back up again. Now the Britons were roaring their defiance at us, shaking their weapons and their fists, taunting us as the transports all came to a stop along the beach. From what I could see, every other ship was in the same predicament; nobody would be jumping onto dry land, so like our ship, none of the men aboard the other vessels wanted to be the first over the side. We all knew that whoever leaped first would be the center of attention, paid to them by men who looked eager to skewer them. Such was the state of affairs for several moments, as we all glanced sidelong at each other, waiting for someone else to throw caution to the winds and earn eternal glory for themselves and for Rome. I was as hungry for that as the next man, yet I was just as rooted to the spot where I stood as everyone else, and it was growing increasingly clear that we were at a stalemate.

The impasse was broken when we heard a huge splash, and looking to our left, saw the *aquilifer* of our Legion, holding the eagle standard, which was silver in those days, over his head as he struggled to stay above water. Fighting the surf, he moved towards the shore as he looked not at the enemy, but back over his shoulder as he shouted something we could not hear. We did not need to hear him; we knew exactly what was being said, and the sight of our most prized possession, the symbol of the 10th that we solemnly made a vow to every Januarius, being carried towards an eagerly awaiting enemy was enough for us.

"Over the sides boys, we can't let any of those blue bastards take our eagle," a man shouted.

Turning just in time to see him disappear over the bow as he threw himself, shield and javelin in hand, over the side, a column of water splashed up an instant later. Men began climbing over the side, while one man, either overeager or having lost his head, threw himself over the side farther back towards the rear of the ship, sinking like a rock, never to be seen again. Pushing Vibius forward as the men in front disappeared from sight and we waited our turn, we could see that our actions were stirring the enemy into activity. For the first time, we saw how these tribes made use of their chariots. As our men struggled to get out of the water, the missile troops among the Britons began flinging javelins at them, and we could see the men in the water were having a hard time blocking them. With the men on foot flinging missiles, the chariots were doing the same, albeit in a different manner. They turned to run parallel to the shoreline, passing in front of us, with one man driving and another man hurling javelins at us. They made several passes; since there were several chariots, they were heading in both directions and it looked like chaos to our eyes, yet it was something they obviously practiced before because none of the chariots heading in opposite directions collided. The air grew thick with the Briton javelins, and I saw a number of men struck, some of them sinking below the waves and not reappearing, the water where they had been stained red as they slipped from sight.

401

Our landing was in serious jeopardy of being repulsed, even as we continued pouring over the sides of our ships to join the men struggling their way up to the beach. The shower of missiles continued, the Britons slowly gaining the courage to pull ever closer to us, until some of their javelins actually struck the sides of the ships. At first they bounced off, but with the enemy moving closer, the missiles began to bury themselves in the timbers of the ships, if we were lucky. Vibius was just ahead of me and as he moved to a now-open spot on the rail, the Legionary next to him, a man from our Century named Ahenobarbus, took a javelin directly in the chest, penetrating his armor to drive several inches deep into his body. The dull thud of the missile striking home was clearly audible, and I was standing at a point where I could see the expression on his face as it turned to a look of surprise, then puzzlement as he tried to climb down off the rail while his body refused to obey his commands, finally being replaced at the last by a look of resignation as he toppled into the surf, despite Vibius' attempt to catch him. Swallowing hard, my heart in my throat, I stepped into the open spot, just in time to hear Vibius.

"Death by drowning, death by javelin, some choice," he muttered as he closed his eyes, took a deep breath and stepped off into the water.

Hitting the surf with a great splash, he immediately sank from sight, then before I had a conscious thought, I threw myself in after him, intent on saving him from drowning. I went under too, the shock of the cold water almost causing me to open my mouth in a gasp, but I just managed to keep my wits about me. My feet found the bottom and I thrust upwards, my head breaking the surface, the water streaming down my face and temporarily blinding me. Even so, I could clearly hear Vibius spluttering and thrashing about as he surfaced on his own without my help.

"By Dis this water's cold!"

Whereas I was standing in water up to the middle of my chest, Vibius' head was barely above the surface, a fact that actually turned out to be a blessing in disguise since he made a smaller target. Despite trying to keep my shield above my head to keep it from being waterlogged, I was only partly successful, and I could feel the wood soaking up the water as it got heavier with every heartbeat. Now that we had our bearings, we both began to struggle ashore and it seemed that the entire Briton army gathered on the beach selected me as the target for their javelins. One after another they came whistling past my head, some of them close enough that I could feel the breath of them on my face as they hurtled by, seeking my death. Initially holding my shield slightly above my head for protection, it robbed me of my ability to see what was happening, forcing me to drop it low enough that I could see over the rim. My gut twisted; the beach was now packed with Legionaries who were unable to make any headway off the shingle because of the continuing storm of missiles. We were being strictly defensive, which is not only against our nature, but also is in some ways even more tiring than attacking because of the need to constantly move your shield to block a blow as your eyes dart back and forth, looking for another attack. Our men were gathered into small groups, trying desperately to get into some form of cohesive formation from which we could fight, and the Briton cavalry now came into play as men on horseback charged in trying to scatter our small groups. Out of the corner of my eye, I caught movement of a large object and looked over to see Caesar's galley, along with a pair of other warships, come rowing up as close to shore as they dared before turning broadside to the Britons so the archers and artillery on board could do their work.

Now it was the turn of the Britons to be put on their heel, as our own missile troops, from Crete as I recall, along with the artillery on board began to return the favor of what we were receiving. Letting out a cheer as the first volley sliced into the tightly packed Britons, I saw several dropping to the ground either dead or wounded. Perhaps now we will get some breathing space I thought, as we plunged forward through the surf, now knee deep. Despite the scene still looking chaotic, order was slowly being restored, men gradually finding their own standards to fall into their accustomed places, finding comfort and a semblance of security in the familiar. I had yet to draw my sword and both of my javelins were either floating somewhere behind me or sunk to the bottom, I did not know which. Our Century formed up quickly, yet as I looked down the length of the beach I could see that this was not the case in the other Cohorts and Centuries. Men were still being assailed, usually from the weak side where they had no comrade to cover them with their own shield, with individual battles breaking out among small groups of fiercely fighting men, one side protecting their homeland, the other side trying to avoid drowning. Since we had received the advantage of Caesar's galley we were the first to have some of the pressure relieved, so fairly quickly, orders were given for the other galleys to move quickly within range of the fighting going on further down the beach. Across from us the blue-painted men saw that we were organizing and on some command yelled in a language I had never heard before, they came thundering towards us, intent on breaking up our unit cohesion, weak as it may have been. There was no time to throw javelins, which most of us had discarded or lost anyway, so the order went out to draw our blades, followed immediately by a countercharge at the rapidly closing enemy. The impact was ferocious, the Britons throwing themselves at us in much the same way that the tribes of Gaul did, except with even more abandon and savagery than their cousins across the channel. Scrabbling for traction as the mass of men pushed against us, we were further hampered by the water that had soaked up into our shields, making it harder to whip them about to deflect blows with the needed speed. Their increased weight did have one advantage, however; when we did manage to use them offensively, they carried a much greater impact, causing considerable damage when used in this manner. It reminded me of when we used our training weapons and that thought cheered me a bit as we continued battling the Britons.

The first Briton I ever slew was an average sized man for a Gaul, certainly not ten feet tall, but I must say that the effect of the blue patterns he had painted all over his bare skin was a bit unsettling. Throwing himself against me, he smashed into my shield, yet I did not move backwards an inch, my weight and size giving me a solid footing. In his right hand he was waving the long sword that the Gauls favored, whipping it forward in an overhand stroke, which I deflected with my own blade, the two clanging together with a tiny shower of sparks as I felt my arm take the shock of the impact, immediately starting to turn numb. In training ground fashion I bent my knees, then using my superior size I put my shoulder into my shield to heave him away from it, following up with a punch of the boss to the face, a blow he just managed to duck. My blade sliced out at the same time as he twisted to avoid the shield and I felt the blade plunge deep into his gut, forcing a shrill scream of pain out of him that quite startled me.

Falling to the ground, his hands dropped his own weapon to clutch his belly, and I heard Vibius. "Did you just kill a woman?"

404

Despite the circumstances I let out a spontaneous laugh; Vibius was always likely to say something at the oddest times that would force a chuckle or laugh out of me, and this was one of those times.

"I'm not sure, he didn't look like one but he sure sounded like a girl," I shot back, the part of me that is always detached enjoying the banter, while the other part again performed the moves taught to us those years ago. Another Briton took his place, as it slowly dawned on me that because we were seemingly the best organized group on the beach, we were drawing the most attention from the enemy. Sneaking a quick peek over the head of the man standing opposite me, I saw that we were fighting a group several ranks deep. It is somewhat hard to convey in this manner the speed in which all these things happen. We were probably on the beach no more than a tenth part of a watch, but we still had not made any significant headway off of it. Transports continued being run up on shore and unloaded, while the ones carrying the first wave pulled away from the beach to anchor a distance away. I could hear the welcome sound of our tongue being spoken behind me as more men came to join us, but at that moment we were still horribly outnumbered. A considerable pile of bodies had fallen now that we had come to grips, and they were becoming a bit of an obstacle as we continued to thrust and hack away at the Britons. As far as the Britons went, their ardor had yet to cool, another way in which they are different than the Gauls of the mainland, since by this point in a battle one could usually count on a quick breather as the Gauls broke off the attack to regroup and work their courage back up. Not so with these men, and they kept hammering away at our very, very thin line, almost penetrating a couple of times when one of us went down and one of the blue devils would leap into the gap. Fortunately our men were just as quick to react, and there would be a sharp but brief struggle as the two fought for the space. When I compare this battle to all the others, the only odd counterpoint was the sounds of the surf, that and the fact that we could not understand a word they were saying. Although none of us spoke any of the Gallic or German languages fluently, we had been in the region long enough to have picked up enough to at least know when we were being cursed at, yet this was a tongue that while sounding somewhat familiar, was different enough that I could not recognize a word of what was being shouted at us.

Slowly but surely our two Legions became more organized, and it was at this point that the chariot troops began entering the battle, or at least the ones who did not drive. Their drivers would pull the chariot up near the fighting, whereupon the warrior with him would jump off to throw himself into the fray. Then the chariot would pull a short distance off to wait for their man to be victorious or be forced to flee. My arms were beginning to grow tired as we battled; I do not know how many rotations we went through, but it was several. Gradually, the training and discipline began to reassert itself, and the Britons seemed to sense that their chance was rapidly slipping away. The bodies, most of them Britons, though there were a fair number of Romans, were now piling up, making the water just next to the shore almost completely red from the blood spilled. Hearing a roar of pain, I glanced over to see Scribonius had received a good stick to his sword arm, one of the Britons taking the opportunity to strike while Scribonius was engaged with another man. Blood was streaming down his arm, his face a mask of pain and fury as he thrust his sword into the throat of a man, and I remember offering a brief prayer hoping that Scribonius had just dispatched the man who stabbed him. Odd, the things one remembers from battles that happened many years ago. Vibius was beside me, none of us having time to get completely into our normal formation, and I covered his unprotected side with my shield as we both advanced, stepping over the bodies around us, pushing a little deeper into the mass of the Britons. Both of us knew that there was a point at which, by some unseen signal, Gallic warriors will in an instant lose heart, turning to flee so quickly that one is left somewhat bewildered by what just happened. Such was our goal in continuing to press; after a few battles, one learns to sense when that moment is nearing, and both Vibius and I could feel it coming. I do not mean to imply that it was just Vibius and I who had this sense about them; all along our line, men were doing the same thing. Instead of waiting for the enemy to step forward, we were taking it ourselves to press the Britons harder and harder. Despite my fatigue, I continued fighting, even picking up the intensity as I sensed that victory was in our grasp.

As with the other Gallic tribes, it happened just as I have described it; seemingly one moment you are engaged in a life or death struggle with the outcome very much in doubt, then suddenly you see the back of your enemy as they let out a great howl of despair before turning to flee for their lives. Immediately the scramble began, and no matter how tired we may have been, we knew not to let this moment pass, so we went running after them. The swifter among us caught the slower men, cutting them down with a quick thrust to the back without missing a step. Those men

406

who climbed off their chariots had the advantage, most of them getting away by clambering back aboard. Not all of them, however. Vibius caught a man who, while dressed the same as the other Britons, wore clothes of a much higher quality than the other men around him, along with a gold torq around his neck. Sensing Vibius almost upon him, he turned in desperation, throwing his hands in front of him in a gesture of supplication, but we had no such orders and chances are we would have cut him down even if there were. Once a man gets to a certain level of excitement, and his blood is boiling in his veins, it is no easy matter to suddenly just remove the heat, so to speak and return to a calm and disciplined state of mind. Well-trained we may have been, but once the bloodlust surged through us, the only thing that would satisfy it was sacrifice. Vibius cut him down with a quick thrust, the despair plain to see in the man's face as he toppled to the ground, Vibius pausing just long enough to relieve the now-dead man of his torq, along with a quick and practiced search through his clothes.

Flashing a grin at me, he held up the torq. "Not bad for a day's work, eh?"

I did not answer, instead turning to resume the pursuit of the fleeing Britons, partly because it was my duty, but an equal measure being that I did not want to sit at the fire that night empty-handed. Nevertheless, I was to be disappointed; my momentary stop cost me any chance of profit, so I was in a sour state of mind when the *cornu* sounded the recall, signaling a halt to the pursuit. It was at this moment that the cavalry being caught in the storm exacted a price, because Caesar was not willing to continue the pursuit with just his Legions. This was the main thing that cavalry did anyway as far as we were concerned, come swooping in after the hard fighting to take the easy pickings, grabbing all the glory. They might have their uses, yet even now, I would not give an amphora of my piss for a cavalryman.

By this time it was almost sunset and there was still much to do. Once a semblance of order was restored, we began working on the camp, and Fortuna smiled on my section, designating our Cohort to stand watch while the others dug. This was the best assignment one could get; the first watch meant that you would not be called again during the night, and you avoided the drudgery of digging and building the camp. It is a good thing that this duty is always rotated, because I could easily see it costing a great deal of trouble if one Cohort was always selected for the first watch guard. This would be different than other times; having just fought a battle, it kept us exceptionally alert, since it was not out of the realm of possibility that the Britons would see us making camp, reorganize and launch another attack. Thankfully it was not to be, and the camp was built without incident. Although he did so from offshore, Volusenus had chosen well; this was the only high ground for some distance, it was in a clear area, although forests were near enough that it was not an onerous task to chop the wood we would need for the camp and for our fires. It was close enough to the beach to provide protection to the fleet, which we were all very aware was the starting point of our lifeline back to the mainland. Caesar ordered the galleys to be beached, while the tubby round ships that carried us were set out a way and anchored for the night. Our camp, like always, was rapidly erected, so it was shortly after dark when we were relieved and allowed to take care of ourselves.

Nobody in our section was hurt besides Scribonius, who required a few stitches, his arm now neatly bound up. The Century suffered a couple dead, including Ahenobarbus, and a few wounded, though only one seriously enough that his life was in danger. Pilus Prior Pulcher, who we had become accustomed to and admired despite his much different ways than our previous Pili Priores, stopped by the fire to check on us. The scar on his face caused the light of the fire to make it appear even more sinister, yet the moment he smiled, any thought of him being evil in any way instantly vanished.

"So you boys dry yet?" he asked as he squatted by the fire. Laughing dutifully, we talked about the day. "I'll give them this, those *cunni* certainly know their way around a chariot," he remarked, the response to this more enthusiastic.

While I had not seen it personally, several men were talking about these Britons and their chariots.

"I saw one of those bastards leap over the body of the chariot and onto the yoke, from a spot where there is no way he could have seen where to land, but he did it just like we hop up and down on the ground." This came from Vellusius, with Atilius nodding vigorously, and even Didius gave a grunt that we had learned was his form of agreeing with us.

"I saw that too Vellusius. Just as quick as you please, but then he walks out between the horses." Atilius' tone emphasized his incredulity. "And these horses were at a full gallop, mind you. I've never seen the like."

He ended with a shake his head, still trying to understand what he had seen. Perhaps it was because I had not witnessed it, but I was not so easily impressed.

"Didn't help them fight any better though, did it?"

Expecting wholehearted agreement, I was chagrined to see my question, which in fact was more of a statement, met with nothing more vigorous than shrugs and a chorus of quiet comment that could have been either agreement or disagreement. Feeling the heat rising to my face, I was very conscious that the Pilus Prior was present, and here I was their Sergeant, unable to muster any kind of real support. Then I was saved, or at least that was how I looked at it, but not by whom I would have expected.

"You're right Pullus. It doesn't matter if those bastards had done somersaults, we whipped them good." I looked in surprise at Didius, and I was not the only one.

He refused to make eye contact, but instead was staring into the fire, and a thought struck me. Could this be Didius' way of trying to make peace, I wondered? His obligations done to us, the Pilus Prior bid us goodnight, making his way over to another tent, and truth be told, we were not excessively sorry to see him go. We were uncomfortable around Centurions, especially our own.

The next day was occupied by disposing of the enemy dead while taking care of our own, along with maintaining a strong presence along the ramparts to let the Britons know what waited them if they dared to attack a fortified camp. Early in the day, under the flag of truce, a delegation of the Britons approached the gate, accompanied by the man Commius who Caesar had sent ahead of us. They were allowed in, and the usual silliness occurred; they were sorry, they said. It was the work of young hotheads and firebrands, and not done with the approval of the tribal elders. Caesar, once again demonstrating his clemency, accepted this bald-faced lie of an excuse, making the usual demand of hostages, some of which were handed over right then, the rest promised to be gathered and sent to us by the surrounding tribes. Those warriors that we fought on the beach were ordered to go home, and we sent out Cohort-sized patrols to ensure that this happened. Our vigil we maintained however, knowing full well the treacherous nature of any tribe of Gauls, island or not. Staying more or less in camp for the next four days, until the last day of August, it was then that disaster struck.

Starting with a gale that blew in from the ocean, a violent rainstorm driven by high winds lashed at our tents, reviving memories of that dreadful point the year before when our tents were rendered more or less useless. It was especially miserable on guard duty, since the day the storm struck it was our luck that we were the guard Cohort. For those men in the towers at the corners of the walls, there was at least a bit of shelter, but those of us stuck out on the ramparts huddled beneath our *sagum*, bitterly cursing the Fates that let this happen. What we did not know was that it just so happened that the lost cavalry transports had chosen that very day to try their luck in crossing the channel again. Once more they were swept away by the storm, although they managed to get back to the mainland without losing a ship, man, or beast for that matter. But what we did know was the catastrophe that befell our fleet, the fleet that carried us over and was supposed to carry us back home. I believe I mentioned that while we were trying to flush out the Veneti from their forts, they relied on some trick of the gods that regulates when the oceans rise and the oceans fall. Well, it was this same trick that struck us an almost mortal blow as suddenly, for no reason at all, the level of the sea rose several feet, reaching well past the point where we beached our galleys, thinking that we had dragged them past the highest level that the sea would rise. However, the gods had other things in mind, as the seas, driven by the storm we were sure, rose to a point where the beached galleys now floated and because of the violence of the storm, were flung against the stone beach and broken into pieces. The gods were not through with us however; the storm was violent enough that the cables holding the transport ships at anchor were snapped, and these too were hurtled towards the shore, driven onto the shingle much more violently than when we had landed, so much so that most of the transports were damaged in some way. The day dawned to the sight of the beach, cleaned of bodies yet now littered with wreckage and the damaged ships of our fleet. The fleet that we relied upon to get home.

This sight of our wrecked fleet sent an immediate panic through the camp, so to my dying breath I will believe that it was our own reaction, along with the damage done to the ships that caused the British chiefs who were "guests" in the camp to follow the course of action that they did. There was a constant stream of

410

traffic into and out of the camp by the various tribes on the island, so it was not of sufficient moment to remark on the passage of some of the chiefs who left the camp. It was what they were doing that would cause the mischief. Seeing the wreck of our fleet, and deciding from the size of our camp that we were a relatively small force, the chiefs summoned all the warriors who were dispersed in the days before, telling them to assemble at a site some distance away from our camp. This in and of itself would have been trouble enough, yet the bigger challenge facing us was due to the fact that we were told to travel light, meaning that the heavy tools, of the type needed to work on ships for example, got left behind on the mainland. There was a feeling of desperation that swept through the camp, the prospect of being stranded here on this strange island gripping the imagination of every man, including me. True, we had seen no men ten feet tall, but I was just as convinced as my comrades that there were things on this island of a fantastic and evil nature that we had yet to confront. I held no doubt that were we forced to spend the winter here, we would be faced with these horrors soon enough. There is only one thing that thrives on gossip more than a collection of women and that is an army, and I am too ashamed to recount some of the more fantastic tales that made the rounds during that time. This sense of impending doom was palpable, throughout the camp and both Legions. Two of the most veteran and hard-bitten of Caesar's Legions were almost paralyzed with the fear of what would befall us on this island.

Luckily for all of us, not least himself, Caesar alone kept his head. A call went out for the *immunes* with skills in carpentry and working with metals, their duties now to repair the fleet. Because we were stranded here longer than Caesar originally planned, our food supplies were running low, and it was this fact that the chiefs of the island tribes planned to capitalize on, as their warriors answered the summons. Our men were eagerly volunteering for *immunes* duty, many of them fabricating their experience in carpentry and metalworking, just for the opportunity to help work on our fleet, understandable since it was our only way home. For those of us too unimaginative to turn the time we spent chopping trees into a full-fledged career as a carpenter, we were left to perform the normal duties of camp life. Gear always needs mending and whenever there is a spare moment we train, which is where my time was spent, despite the lack of training weapons. Meanwhile, the food situation was becoming dire and despite only having a total of 30 cavalry who shipped over with Commius, Caesar put them to good use, sending them far and wide looking for consumables. They came back to report several fields of grain just waiting to be reaped some two miles to the west of the camp, near some woods. Most of the other fields had already been harvested so Caesar, not wanting to waste an opportunity to feed us, sent the 7th out to gather up the grain, ordering them to march with only their weapons, sickles and wicker baskets. That day I was involved in weapons training, using our normal swords in their sheaths since we did not bring our training weapons, the men of the Century cursing me and wishing all manner of horrible things to befall me, a fact that I took as a sign that I was making progress. The 7th was gone for perhaps two thirds of a watch when, seemingly out of nowhere, the horns sounded the call for assembly under arms. Luckily, we were all wearing our armor and helmet and since we were using our regular weapons for training, we were one of the first Centuries to make it to the forum. Caesar had mounted Toes, while the Tribunes and Legates of both Legions, the ones from the 7th staying behind undoubtedly to catch up on their rest or to bugger one of the young slaves, were running about in a high state of alarm.

"What by Pluto's thorny cock is happening, you wonder?" I heard Rufio ask the Pilus Prior, who merely shrugged.

"Don't know, but I imagine it's got something to do with the 7th out there getting grain."

Within moments the Legion was assembled, with our 8th and 10th Cohorts ordered to relieve the two Cohorts on guard. The instant they ran to their posts the guard Cohorts that were relieved came to join us without waiting to be properly dismissed, and shortly after we were trotting out of the main gate. Clearing the gate, we could clearly see what caused the alarm; there was a huge dust cloud, much larger than would be normal for a Legion on the march, hanging in the air some distance away. This did not stop Caesar from ordering us to double time, and there were audible groans as we began trotting towards the dust cloud, heading to help the 7th.

Within less than a sixth part of the watch, we drew within sight of the 7th and could immediately see the problem. This was our first indication that the Briton chiefs were plotting, because the 7th was surrounded by a large mass of warriors, with a much larger number of chariots than met us on the beach. This could only mean that some mischief had been in the works for some time, since it would take several days to assemble such a large host.

412

"Those bastards saw our ships wrecked and decided to throw the dice," gasped Scribonius as we ran towards the melee in front of us.

Only grunting an acknowledgement, my mind was occupied with the details of what was about to happen next. I did not think that Caesar would order us to charge pell-mell, in column, directly into the battle, so I was thinking about what the next command was going to be, guessing that it would first be an order to quick time, our normal marching pace, in order to allow us to catch our breath, followed a moment later by the command to deploy from column into line. When the *cornu* did indeed sound the call to begin marching, it was followed a moment later by the command to form into a line of Cohorts, which we executed with the practiced precision of veterans, while I mentally congratulated myself for being smart enough to recognize the obvious thing to do. Seeing the Britons alerted by the sound of our horns wheel about to watch us approaching, the sight of the 10th arriving on the scene served two purposes. The 7th was being hard pressed, having actually formed into an orbis, which is only used in the direst of emergencies. With our approach, it gave the 7th sufficient heart to order the redeployment into a more standard *acies duplex* as they awaited our arrival and link up with them. For the Britons, this was the signal to break off the engagement, their own strange horns now blowing what was obviously their signal to withdraw. They retreated in good order I must say, leaving the battlefield behind to disappear into the nearby woods, from where they had initiated the ambush. As we were to gather from the events, this was an elaborate trap; the fields that the 7th were sent to reap were not harvested in order to act as bait. The 7th fell into the trap, which was no shame, but apparently their orders were to ground their shields and javelins, doff their helmet, with no guard set, especially in the nearby forest, thereby allowing a surprise attack. We would have jeered them for such laxity, but they carried enough bodies with them back to the camp that we felt they learned their lesson.

With the fleet rapidly being repaired, we still had one more surprise waiting for us. According to Caesar, only a total of twelve ships were totally destroyed and their salvaged parts used to repair the rest of the fleet. Again, I do not wish to dispute the great man, but perhaps my skills at counting are not quite as developed as his were; I counted no less than 20 ships wrecked beyond repair. No matter really, in the end both Legions were transported back to the mainland, but not before the Britons made one last attempt to inflict enough damage upon us to convince us never to return. For several days after the ambush of the 7th the weather was similar, just not as violent, to the great storm that wrecked the fleet, confining us to our tents as the elements lashed us with what seemed to be a never-ending rainstorm. Between the weather and our lack of cavalry, Caesar deemed it prudent to refrain from trying to chastise the enemy for their violation of their oaths of submission, and we sat huddled together, listening to the wind howl and the rain throw itself against our tents. Once again we were reminded of the year before, except thankfully this year our tents held up. Even with the violent weather, the men who volunteered to help repair the fleet, many of them now repenting their choice much to our glee, continued on. Through the wind and rain, they continued to work on those ships that could be salvaged, and we were heartened by their progress to be sure. But the Britons were not quite done with us, giving us one last test before we left this accursed island.

Even as the work progressed despite the weather, the Britons were not idle either. Their summons to battle was only partially answered when they attempted to ambush the 7th during our grain harvesting. However, by this point they had sufficient time to gather in their true strength, and it was with this strength that they appeared on the horizon one day after the spell of weather broke.

"To arms!"

With that command ringing out, the *bucina* carrying the call throughout the entire camp, for perhaps the hundredth time I found myself thanking Calienus for the early lesson he had given us in the value of placing our gear in the same place, every time, every camp. Automatically pulling on my armor and helmet, then grabbing my harness and quickly strapping it on, I exited the tent to grab my shield, stacked outside along with my javelin. It is in such a manner that a Legion can assemble and be ready for battle in a matter of moments, no mean feat for several thousand men. On the horizon, spreading before us, was the Briton host; chariots, cavalry and foot, all determined to make us pay such a heavy price that we would never venture to set another foot on their island again. It was here that they made their biggest mistake, in daring to fight us in a set-piece battle. Compounding their error, they gave us not only the time to form up, then march out of our camp, but to array ourselves in Caesar's favorite formation, the *acies triplex*, arranging our lines in front of our camp. Seeing the vast horde before us, perhaps it is

414

hubris, but I will tell you that there was not a man among us who held any doubt about the outcome.

"Stupid bastards, aren't they?" This was asked by Scribonius as we moved into our accustomed position.

Unlike other battles we fought in, there were not three wings but two; even so, we did not have to be told on which side to form up, and we moved into our place on the right, looking out at the Briton host impassively. I had to agree; they were stupid indeed to try besting us by using the tactics that were our strongest. I merely nodded, not saying anything, preparing myself for the slaughter that was about to come.

This battle is almost too inconsequential to write about. The Britons charged us, their chariots churning up clouds of dust as they sped towards our formation, heading straight into our lines as if they planned on running headlong into the front ranks. Suddenly, they turned sharply to parallel our front, with each warrior aboard throwing javelins as fast at us as he could manage. One noteworthy thing was that I finally saw with my own eyes the feats that the others were talking about, when one of the warriors leaped over the front of the chariot, landing nimbly on the wooden yoke attached to the horses. Not done, he took a couple of sure steps farther along the yoke before hopping up to plant each of his feet on the backs of the horses, who obviously had been through this before since they did not falter. Standing thus, he bellowed something I am sure was abusive at the top of his lungs, glaring at us while his driver guided the chariot along our front. His display earned him an ironic cheer from us, seemingly startling him, his face turning a dark red, obviously furious at what he perceived as an insult. It was not really meant that way; enemy or no, what he did was impressive and we Romans always appreciate a demonstration of excellence. Once the chariots expended their missiles, this apparently was the signal for the Britons to begin their pre-battle ritual of foaming at the mouth and hopping about while they screamed their insults at us. A few of them bared their backsides to us, drawing a laugh. Someone in our ranks began to reciprocate the gesture but was immediately persuaded against it by the threat of a flogging. Our men were shifting about, moving from one foot to another, growing bored, and all through our midst could be heard muttered imprecations and exhortations to get on with it.

"Pluto's thorny cock, what's taking them so long?" Vibius groaned, and I smiled at his impatience, though I felt it too.

Finally, they seemed to be ready at last, and with the undulating wail from what they call a horn blasting three notes, the mass of men on foot began running towards us, their weapons held high, their shouts ringing in our ears. Immediately after our last volley of javelins was done, the order to counter-charge was given, and we began running ourselves, colliding into the Briton horde at a dead run. No more than several moments later, before I even got a turn at the front, the Britons broke and ran, with both Legions in hot pursuit. Running as fast as I dared while carrying my naked sword over the broken ground, my long legs helped me close the gap, enabling me to wet my blade before sheathing it again. Our small group of cavalry pursued the fleeing men, and despite their small numbers, managed to account for a large number of enemy dead. All told, we killed about 4,000 Britons in the space of perhaps a sixth part of a watch from the time we lined up until we stopped the pursuit, and we did not lose a single man. During our return to the camp, we put to the torch a small village, along with a few small farms and the surrounding fields.

Back in camp, the word went out that the repairs to the fleet were finished and we were told to break down the camp, prompting great jubilation. We had experienced enough of this island, although there was little doubt in our minds that we would be back.

"Caesar's not going to be satisfied with burning some crops. He's got to find some villages to plunder and people to enslave to make himself richer than he already is," Vibius declared as we were packing.

Biting back a sharp reply, partly because I did not want to quarrel, it was also because I knew that Vibius was probably right, and I did not want to give him the satisfaction of reminding me of it when we found ourselves on these shores again. Even as we were striking our tents, another delegation of Britons came to the camp, yet again begging forgiveness for their mistake in attacking us for the third time. And yet again, Caesar gave them pardon, although he doubled the number of hostages he demanded this time around. This was one decision that we did not agree with, but looking at it now, I can see that Caesar really had no other choice. We were packing up to leave and would not be back for several months. If he refused to accept their apology and peaceful overtures, this would warn them

416

that war was coming, whereupon they would spend the winter months in preparation. They may have done that anyway, but with Caesar refusing them, this was a certainty. Accordingly, Caesar made the choice to allow the pretense of peace between us. By the time the delegation left, the camp was stricken, except for the ramparts, which are always last, and we put all the other parts of the camp that used wood to the torch. That done, we pulled up the stakes along the rampart then filled in the ditch before marching down to the beach to load up on the ships and sail back to the mainland.

Leaving the shores of Britannia in the same way we left to get there, we finally shoved off at midnight, heading back to land at the same place where we embarked. Our trip was uneventful, except for the heaving of our stomachs, the prospect of which we simply accepted with resignation as the cost for getting back to Gaul, and we were happy enough when about mid-morning, land was sighted. There before us was the thin green strip that we had expected to see when we first saw Britannia, and as we approached, we began talking about what we hoped to do when were finally safe on dry land. Since the end of campaign season was almost on us; it was now the second week in September, and we would be marching to winter quarters soon, not surprisingly much of the talk and the inevitable wagering centered on where we would be quartered. Nobody thought that we would be staying this far west, in the event there was trouble farther east, but there was much speculation about how far north or how far south. Also, going into our fourth winter, we had developed favorite spots where we wintered before, along with not so favorite spots to which we held no desire to go back. This was how we passed the remaining time before entering the harbor, the men from the other Legions lining the hill of the camp to watch us disembark. Men looked for friends they had made, or sometimes even relatives, in the faces of the 7th and 10th as we went marching past, sharing jokes and insults with us. Unfortunately, I could see the faces of some of the men who did not find who they were looking for, and I knew that there would be mourning around some of the fires in the camp that night.

Not all of us arrived at the same harbor. Two ships, with about 300 men from the 10th, landed further south in Morini territory and the natives got carried away with the idea of attacking the Legionaries and taking their weapons. Luckily for our men they were immediately missed, scouts were sent out looking for them and one of the mounted men saw the Legionaries formed in a square,

417

surrounded by a few thousand men. Galloping back, the camp was alerted, with all of our available cavalry mounted and out of the gate in moments, racing to the rescue of the stranded men. Because we had just arrived and were still in full uniform, we were ordered to follow behind, and since these were men of the 10th we needed no urging, moving at double time down the road behind the cavalry. By the time we arrived at the scene, the cavalry had already driven the Morini off, the Gauls fleeing so hastily that some of them actually dropped their weapons, leaving them scattered on the ground around the Legionaries. Marching back to camp, reunited with our missing men, we arrived only to find out the moment we entered camp that we were going to be leaving the next morning to punish the Morini for their transgression. This order was met by curses and groans, the feeling being that we had done enough, there being other Legions in camp who had been doing nothing all season. Nevertheless, we marched out the next morning as ordered, the 7th also being selected, commanded by Labienus. Marching south, the gods smiled on us in one sense; there had been a drought in that area and the marshes, which the Morini used as refuge before, were now dried up, so we did not have to march in knee deep, slimy muck. It also meant that the Morini had nowhere to hide, and after one very minor skirmish where we lost nobody and they lost a few dozen, they submitted. Again.

Chapter 9- Second Invasion of Britain

D espite our campaigning being done, any hopes we held for a soft winter were quickly shattered. Caesar did not leave us at his normal time, staying with us until mid-November, once we were distributed in our winter camps, the locations of which were another source of complaining. None of us got our wish to be further south; instead, the Legions were distributed throughout Belgae territory, the feeling being, correct as it turned out, that they were still not completely pacified. This winter, however, was not going to be one of our usual routine, because Caesar had plans, ambitious ones at that. He ordered a fleet built, numbering more than 600 ships, requiring each of our camps to be on a river and relatively close to the sea, at a point where the river was wide and deep enough to float the finished ships down. Our particular camp was on the Sequana River, a few miles inland, in the territory of the Veliocasses, who lived on a narrow strip of land inland along the river for several miles. For this project, we all worked as shipbuilders, with Gauls skilled in these matters being brought in to teach us what we needed to do, although they directed the work. I will say that, despite moaning and complaining about performing this kind of labor, it did make the time pass by more quickly, and I for one enjoyed the physical exertion. The ships we built were different than the ones that took us to Britannia and were of Caesar's design; having seen the difficulties we experienced in going over the side, he ordered that our new fleet be constructed with much lower gunwales to enable easier unloading. They were also wider, with flatter bottoms that enabled them to get closer to shore, improvements we all appreciated, and which I pointed out to Vibius as an example that Caesar truly cared for our well-being, to which he said nothing. When Caesar left us, he went once again to Illyricum, this time because there was trouble brewing. Also leaving the army was young Publius Crassus, not only one of the most liked of the Tribunes and Legates, but also one of the most respected, a rare feat. Labienus we respected yet did not particularly like because of his sour disposition and the fact that he could be excessively harsh in his discipline, but he could fight, and for that we at least respected him. When we heard of young Crassus' death at Carrhae, from all accounts due to his own father's incompetence and arrogance, there was true sorrow in the army.

Januarius of the year of the Consulship of Lucius Domitius Ahenobarbus and Appius Claudius Pulcher, 456 years after the founding of the Republic marked the beginning of our fifth year in Gaul. I was turning 24 that year, 25 as far as the army was concerned, and I was still happy that I had joined the Legions. Vibius I was not so sure about; he loved being a Legionary as much as I did, but oh, how he pined for Juno. These years apart had not changed their love for each other as far as I could tell; they still wrote each other constantly, and I believe that it was only this enforced separation that marred Vibius' time in the army. He never let it interfere with his duties, yet there were times at night around the fire that I would glance at him to see him staring at but not seeing the flames, with a melancholy look on his face. Whenever I saw him like this I did my best to cheer him up, although I do not know whether I was any help or not. As for the rest of my friends, much was the same as before. We had adjusted to the death of Romulus, but we never forgot him, and many a night one of his antics was a topic of discussion around the fire, all of us laughing as hard as if it had happened yesterday. The change in Didius turned out to be temporary; soon enough he was back to his games and his surliness. His presence and attitude became something like a spot on your boots that rubs you wrong that never goes away no matter how hard you try to remove it, until you give up and a callous develops that keeps from rubbing you raw. Having grown accustomed to his ways, while we did not like them we accepted them, mainly because we had no choice. For his part, he learned how far he could push the rest of us and did not cross that line, at least not very often. Atilius' flogging had scared him straight, if only for a time, although I will say that he was much slyer about his forays out of the camp, and they did happen less often. Vellusius remained unchanged, although he did laugh less than before, something I attributed more to the absence of Romulus than I did to any change in him. Scribonius was, next to Vibius, my closest friend, partly because of our proximity to each other in formations and on marches. Also, I respected his intelligence and his way of thinking things through before weighing in on a subject. Calienus we did not see as much of as we had when he was in our tent, partly due to his duties, but mostly due to Gisela, with whom he spent every possible moment and for which none of us blamed him. He trusted her well enough, but he had no trust in his fellow soldiers, quite rightly I might add. We may kill for each other, and we may die for each other, but I quickly saw that on the subject of women, there were no rules of conduct. If a man wanted a woman and she belonged to another Legionary, the only consideration was whether or not one could defeat the spurned lover in a fight of some sort. Only in the case of very close friends, and sometimes not even then, did the bonds of friendship matter at all. Another happy consequence of doing the work that we did building ships meant that we had less time to get in trouble, with that winter seeing fewer trips to the forum to witness punishments than any other year before this.

Caesar sorted things out in Illyricum then headed back to the army, arriving in late spring, a bit later than usual for him because of the troubles in his other province. Working feverishly to finish work on the new fleet, this was followed by the preparations always necessary at the start of campaign season. The men of the army were heartened to hear that this time, we were going to do things in a manner that we in the ranks considered the proper way; we were bringing all of our heavy gear, along with a force of 2,000 cavalry. With the fleet finished, we took our first boat ride of the season, this time down the Sequana to the mouth of the river then the short distance up the coast to Portus Itius, designated as the place from which the fleet would sail. Perhaps we were getting used to it, or perhaps it was just because we were on the river, then in sight of the coast the whole way, but the seasickness was much less widespread this time. Arriving at the camp erected by the other Legions who spent their winter at Portus Itius building their part of the fleet, we all settled in to wait for Caesar. He arrived, but was in camp no more than a day or two when word of trouble with the Treveri was reported to him. After assessing the situation, Caesar deemed that it was too dangerous to leave until after we returned from Britannia, so taking his most veteran Legions, the 7th through the 10th, we found ourselves once again marching to the east. The Treveri chief was named Indutiomarus, and apparently he had been loudly claiming that he pissed on Rome and owed no allegiance to us. The march took almost two weeks, long enough to make us angry that once more we were forced to deal with recalcitrant Gauls. It was a funny thing; when we thought of Gauls as a race, we hated them with a passion because of what we considered to be their treachery and deceitful ways. Yet when we dealt with them individually, it was hard to find a Gaul that we did not like. They are a strange race, and even now after three decades under Roman rule and having lived among them all this time, I still do not feel that I truly know or understand them. In some things I would trust them with my life, while in others I would not be shocked if they tried to cut my throat. That spring, we found ourselves marching once again because of some faithless petty chief who thought he alone could withstand the might of Rome. There was one happy note; for the first time we did not suffer through the first true marching of the spring, the work we did on the ships keeping us more fit than we would have thought possible. Consequently, we retired each night without the aches, soreness and total fatigue that was always present in the past, and this marked something of a turning point, because we no longer complained as loudly when we were ordered to perform exertions during the winter.

Our confrontation with the Treveri was anticlimactic to say the least. Approaching their main town, just the sight of us in battle array was enough to send Indutiomarus scurrying out to claim that Caesar must have heard wrong, he made no such claims. To be sure of his good faith, Caesar took an unusually large number of hostages, including the son of Indutiomarus, whereupon we immediately turned around to march back to the coast. We were not happy, but neither were we surprised at this point, having learned that Gauls are capable of any type of behavior. Making a few stops on the way back, Caesar took the opportunity to adjudicate local disputes and give the locals a glimpse of the Roman army as a reminder of who had defeated them once, and would do so again if need be. Whenever he met a local delegation, he made sure that we were there in the forum in formation, requiring the Gauls to pass between our silent ranks and it was clear to all of us that they were intimidated, exactly the effect for which Caesar hoped.

Getting back to the main camp, we began our final preparations to sail to the island. Caesar selected five of the eight Legions to sail with him; of course we were selected, yet we were a bit surprised when we heard that Labienus, who had almost always been our commander on detached operations, was going to be left behind to baby-sit the 11th, 13th and 14th. I have always wondered if this was the real reason that in the difficulties that ensued years later, Labienus chose to turn on his old general. We were also a bit surprised by the inclusion of the 12th, for the reasons I have previously mentioned, and we speculated that Caesar was giving them one last chance to redeem themselves. Also sailing with us was a large number of Gallic chieftains and their personal escorts. It was Caesar's way of keeping an eye on them, especially since he had already seen more than sufficient evidence to convince him that if he left these rascals behind, they would in all likelihood make a good deal of trouble for him. Included in this group was one Dumnorix, one of the more powerful chiefs of the Aedui, even having coins with his name and likeness struck to act as the currency of his people. He was reputed to be the leader of the anti-Roman faction of the Aedui, who as a tribe still bore the title of Friend and Ally of Rome, so of all the chieftains, Dumnorix was the one whom Caesar wanted to keep an eye on most. Once the chiefs were summoned and arrived at Portus Itius, all was ready to depart. Then we sat to wait for a more favorable wind.

We ended up waiting three weeks, the wind continually blowing from the northwest and making sailing in that general direction impossible. Being prepared to embark at a moment's notice, since the wind in this region is notoriously fickle, we were more or less confined to our Cohort area for days. Naturally the waiting got very tiresome, the army more than ready to depart, so it was not long before we were at each other's throats. I had to break up more fights than I can remember, despite the fact that I was just as raw as everyone else and wanted to leave just as badly. I think this marked the point when I finally accepted the burden of keeping my personal feelings completely hidden and separate from the actions I was taking, because I secretly agreed with the malcontents; I was just as ready to go as they were, although I could not act in such a manner. In the past I struggled with this feeling but now, finally, I fully accepted it. I made sacrifices to the gods in control of such things as wind and tides almost daily, yet neither my supplications nor those of the rest of the men were answered for almost a month.

The waiting was not just hard on us; the delay obviously wore on the Gallic chiefs who were accompanying us to the point Dumnorix of the Aedui finally decided that he had enough waiting. Just a day before we ended up embarking, he left the camp, despite Caesar's express orders to the contrary. Caesar could not allow this kind of flagrant disobedience, so he sent a detachment of cavalry to catch up with Dumnorix and bring him back to the camp but he refused to cooperate, choosing instead to fight, whereupon he was cut down by our cavalry. The other Gauls in the camp were enraged by Caesar's action, yet could do nothing about it, although their sullen expressions and hostile attitude was a clear enough message for all of us that we had to watch them closely the entire expedition. Commius was coming with us again, along with a Trinova named Mandubracius. Perhaps the potential unrest was the reason that Caesar chose Labienus to stay behind, since he was considered Caesar's most able Legate. Whatever the case, it was on the sixth day of the month now named for Caesar that we began the loading of the army, and it was during the loading process that I had my first brush with a new Tribune accompanying the expedition. His name was Marcus Antonius, and even now, all these years after his death I still have mixed feelings about the man. When I first laid eyes on him, I saw he was just a couple of years older than I was; he was an incredibly handsome man, and despite the fact he was not nearly as tall as I was, his physique closely matched mine. Heavily muscled in the chest and arms, tapering down to a narrow waist, with strong thighs and huge calves, he radiated an animal magnetism that was clear to see even then. He had curly dark hair, and his facial features were strong, with a thoroughly Roman nose, thick full lips, strong jaw and somewhat dimpled chin. Hearing him before I saw him, he was roaring in laughter at a joke that I did not hear, and I first saw him standing on the docks, waiting to board with the 10th. Surrounded by rankers like me and my friends, their faces were split in wide grins at whatever jest he found so hilarious. Antonius was a man's man; carelessly thoughtful, extremely generous to his friends, and preferring the company of the common soldier than to those of his class, at least in those days. He could also be petty and extremely vindictive; just ask poor Cicero with his hands nailed to the door of the Senate house. Antonius was also extremely unpredictable, yet even with his faults I found it extremely hard to dislike him, even many years later, after he changed so drastically, but I am getting ahead of myself. In that moment on the docks, Vibius was taken with him immediately, having left our section to wander over to see what the fun was about. Also accompanying us on this voyage was the younger brother of the aforementioned Cicero, along with Gaius Trebonius, yet another feckless, faithless bastard who owed his rise to the man he later helped slaughter. But all these events I was happily unaware of; instead I was just relieved that we were finally about to sail back to Britannia to do the job properly.

424

It was not until the late afternoon of that day that we were finally ready to set sail for the island, turning to the northwest to begin our journey. Just like our trip the year before, it was not going to be easy, with the currents and wind once again seeming to conspire against our best efforts and we began drifting farther north than where we were supposed to land, roughly the same beach where we landed at the year before. Another of the refinements to the transports that Caesar ordered was that we were not completely powered by sail; holes were drilled in the sides of the boats to allow the use of oars, and the signal was given for us to break them out to begin rowing back to the southwest toward the beach. There was the usual cursing and groans, punctuated by muttered comments that we had not signed on in the army to be sailors, but the Centurions and Optios quickly put a stop to this, and we set to the task. Fairly quickly, the spirit of competition began to set in amongst us as, without any order given, we began rowing at a pace that allowed us to keep pace with the war galleys. Before long the galleys noticed us catching up with them, so they began to quicken their rhythm. It was not a few moments later that we were in an all-out race for the landing beach, putting everything we had into at the least keeping up with the galleys, if not overtaking them.

Because of the tricks of wind and current, we did not begin the landing process until around midday of the seventh. With our disembarking, the changes to the design of the transport made unloading go much quicker and more smoothly, while the advance party went out to find a spot to camp. One pleasant surprise was the absence of any Britons waiting for us, although we were sure that they knew we were coming; it is impossible to keep secret a fleet of almost 800 ships, between the newly constructed vessels and the ones that we used the year before. Whatever the cause, we were thankful that we did not have to fight our way off the beach again, this landing going much more smoothly than the year before. Part of the advance party came back to guide us to the spot chosen for the camp, a little more than three miles to the northwest from the beach. Even as we were marching to the campsite, cavalry scouts went out ranging through the area, capturing some prisoners. From them it was learned that we were indeed seen and expected, the Britons actually forming up to fight us on the beach. Then, upon seeing the huge size of our army, they decided that discretion was the better part of valor, retreating instead to some high ground nearby. Caesar was determined to press the attack immediately, so leaving about ten Cohorts chosen from each Legion behind to guard the fleet, which was brought up onto the beach, he ordered us to throw the camp up as quickly as we could, since he was determined to march that night to meet the Britons.

"We're supposed to put up a camp, then immediately start marching again? What kind of madness is that? We'll be so tired by the time we find those bastards we won't be able to do anything more than curse their ancestors," Vibius complained, supported by the others, who all agreed vociferously.

"You've gotten pretty soft, Vibius," I countered, "Are you scared of a little hard work?"

Because I used the tone of voice that told him that this was not his friend but his Sergeant speaking, Vibius refrained from retorting, yet I could see that my barb found its mark, his face turning red. Instead of speaking, he turned back to the digging of the trench, attacking the sod in front of him like it was one of those blue devils we would be facing shortly. The others followed suit, but it was with a sullen silence that told me that their sentiments were with Vibius, not me. Our camp was on what passed for a hill in this area, barely 20 feet high, while the ground around us was wide open, with the nearest cover in the form of a small forest more than a mile away. Finishing about a full watch before the time we would be departing, it gave us some time to rest before we were to set out at midnight, so we gobbled down our meal to give us as much time as possible to catch some sleep. That is, the others did; I had a number of duties to attend to, so by the time I was finished, I decided that the amount of sleep I might get would actually make me feel worse. Instead I sat outside the tent, staring up at the sky, lost in thought. It is a strange thing, but the farther north one goes the longer the days, so at this time of year there is really never a true night. It is still somewhat light at midnight, fading away to what we think of as dusk for perhaps two thirds of a watch, before the sky begins to get light again. It was this phenomenon that allowed us to start the march at midnight without stumbling around in the dark.

Promptly on time, we marched out of the camp, leaving behind the ten Cohorts to guard it and the fleet, heading almost due west towards the higher ground where the Britons were supposedly gathered and waiting for us. Marching for perhaps ten or eleven miles, our scouts came galloping back to report that they spotted a force of cavalry and chariots that had chosen to occupy a line of high ground overlooking a river running from the southwest to the

426

northeast, with the intent of contesting our crossing. However, Caesar sent our cavalry force around their right flank to force them from that position, making the Britons retreat to a line of even higher ground, protected by thick woods, where they threw up some hasty earthworks, felling trees to form a series of abatis to block our advance. Their position was a strong one, and because of the abatis, a funnel was created through which only one Legion at a time could have a chance of success. Therefore, because they were in the vanguard of the advance and able to deploy the quickest, Caesar ordered the 7th to assault the position. Immediately they went in, formed up in a series of *testudo*, with the Britons sending a shower of missiles and rocks at them as they advanced. The 7th carried bundles of sticks with them to throw into the ditch that the Britons dug, piling them up until the ditch was filled. Once it was, the men of the 7th came out of their *testudo*s to unleash their own volleys of javelins before rushing across the bundles and over the rampart, sweeping away the Briton defenders. Despite the Britons putting up a brief fight, they quickly saw that their cause was lost and began melting into the woods, with the 7th in hot pursuit. Caesar was worried about unleashing his men into terrain which he knew very little about, so the recall was sounded and since it was late afternoon already, orders were given to build a camp in a cleared area on the edge of the woods. We were told that we would pick our pursuit back up in the morning, but with all of our stakes, tents and other equipment back at the main camp, we had to make do with deeper ditches than was normal even for Caesar. Spending the night under the stars, we were wrapped only in our *sagum*, though thankfully the weather held.

That next morning, Caesar divided us into three columns, with a contingent of cavalry assigned to each one, the idea being that the cavalry would either pin the fleeing enemy down while we hurried up to finish them off, or they would circle around the enemy and drive them back into us. He chose to stay behind with the Cohort left guarding our temporary camp to wait for the situation to develop. Marching out of the camp, we picked our pursuit back up, hurrying along, carrying just our weapons and a canteen. Fairly quickly, we spotted the rearguard of a group of the enemy and were just beginning to double time when we were alerted by the shouts of the men in the rear of the formation that there was a courier approaching. Finding the Tribune in nominal command of our column, the courier relayed the order to turn around and head back to the coast, stopping at our camp only long enough to pick up our gear. Once again, Neptune had been harsh with us; another great storm had arisen, wreaking havoc on our fleet one more time. Because of this development Caesar ordered that we head back to the beach with all haste, taking care to maintain security and giving us the permission to defend ourselves if attacked. All three columns received this order, so we reversed our march to head back to the camp of the night before. Grabbing our gear, we did not even stop to destroy the camp in our normal manner, beginning the trek back to the beach, wondering if the gods were trying to give us a message that we could no longer ignore.

The sight of the ravaged fleet, the ships laying in various stages of damage, with debris scattered among them as witness to the severity of the storm, was a sobering sight. There was a feeling that we were once again being tormented by the gods and there were mutterings among us that perhaps at least one legend about this island, that it was cursed, was true. Those Cohorts left behind were already clearly busy, the Centurions organizing them into working parties to begin the operation of repairing the fleet. We were Caesar's men, meaning if there was one thing we learned under his command it was that of all the enemies we faced, the greatest one was time. It was well into summer, so there could be no delay in repairing the fleet because we had already witnessed the severity of the weather in this channel once it got later in the year. Caesar had no choice but to put offensive operations on hold, not only from the viewpoint that it was the strategically sound thing to do, but also because we in the ranks would constantly worry about how we were going to leave the island. It would have dominated the conversations around the fire every night, as well as the watches of marching, so it was wise of Caesar to put these fears to rest. Of course, nothing was said openly on this topic, since it would give an indicator that we did not have faith in our general. Nevertheless, there was a silent sigh of relief when our orders were confirmed that we would be working on the fleet until further notice. The men designated to perform certain tasks the winter before now went back to them, and very quickly, work began to repair the fleet.

The *immunes* labored through every watch, doing their jobs by the light of oil lamps during that brief period of time where it was dark enough to justify the extra light. They were set up in shifts, so that they could snatch some sleep and feed themselves, yet they worked extremely hard nonetheless. Caesar also sent for more skilled workmen, via his fastest galley, and they were soon added to the workforce. In order to prevent a catastrophe of this nature

428

happening a third time, Caesar ordered the construction of an enclosed area, much in the nature of a fort, placed at a point where neither the highest tide nor the most severe storm could wreak any damage. Because of the space needed to contain all of the ships, it was by far the largest project of this type we ever worked on, and even with the labor of 20,000 experienced and willing men, construction of the enclosure took more than three days. Once it was completed, we began the process of moving the ships up off the beach and across the ground, thankfully flat, through one of the gates of the enclosure, of which there were four in the normal manner, except that they were all large enough to accommodate the width of our largest transports. Using huge amounts of grease brought over from Gaul that we applied to a number of logs, we pulled the ships across the rollers into the enclosure, where the men skilled as shipwrights began their work. Day and night, the activity was incessant, and it was of the type that had all of us praying to be selected for guard duty. Normally we abhorred it because it was so boring yet also so easy to find oneself in some sort of trouble. Even so, we felt it was better than the alternative. We were not one of the lucky Cohorts until almost the very end of the project, where we stood on the ramparts gazing out at a large group of Britons who we were told had made it a habit to come watch us work, seemingly fascinated at our activities.

"They think we're completely crazy," Vibius commented.

I nodded my head, since this was the same thought running through my mind as Vibius and I stood, watching them watch us, either on horseback or sitting on the platform of a chariot, ready to bolt at the first sign that we would order the cavalry out to pursue them. They were not painted for war, yet we did see something that either escaped our notice the year before, or was evidence of a new tribe entering the picture, because some of the men had done something very interesting to their hair. Using what we would find out later was a mixture of lime and water, they made their hair stand on end in great spiked tufts. Apparently this was designed to strike fear into their enemies, but I am afraid that at least as far as we were concerned, the effect was more of some amusement than anything else. We had long since learned that men adorning themselves in a certain way, or wearing certain clothes did not make them any more or less hard to kill; the only exception to this of course was whether what they were wearing was designed to protect them in a practical manner, like armor. Otherwise, we were singularly unimpressed with the lengths that men went to in order to try and give themselves an extra edge in battle.

Work on the damaged ships continued until the end of the month; finally, we had affected the necessary repairs, and ensured the security of the fleet to an extent approved by the Legions with the construction of the enclosure. Turning our attention back to the Britons, we saw they were not idle either, as it turned out. Like most of the tribes on the mainland, the tribes of Briton have their own internal political struggles and rivalries, their hatred of each other only set aside because their hatred of us was greater. During the time we spent repairing the fleet, they were working on the political front, with an alliance formed between the tribe initially facing us, the Trinovantes, and one of the most powerful tribes, led by a man named Cassivellaunus. It was his warriors with the spiked hair that we saw watching us a couple of days before. Picking up where we left off, a force was left behind to guard the camp and enclosure, with the rest of the army retracing our steps back in the direction of the camp we made earlier in the month. There was one difference this time; the Britons were not going to be content to wait for us to come to them.

Marching in column with our cavalry as a screen around us, the first attacks began, predictably with their chariots and some cavalry. Our horsemen successfully repulsed the attacks, though as was usual with our Gallic cavalry, their passions ran high. When things went well, they were incredibly fierce and aggressive. This time was no exception and they pursued the Briton chariots into some nearby woods, which was their mistake. Almost immediately their shouts of triumph turned to cries of alarm when they were set upon by warriors waiting in the woods. Not more than a handful of moments later, our cavalry came streaming out of the woods, many of the horses without men riding on them. Pressing on, we watched for further attacks, yet the Britons seemed to be content to trail along on our flanks, much like wolves do when they are stalking a herd of animals, waiting for the one that cannot keep up to provide them with their evening meal. Moving over the open ground, we approached the same river as before, to find that for the most part our camp was left largely undisturbed. All that needed to be done was to place the stakes of the palisade and repair some of the ditch that had fallen in, and we immediately set to work, confident that the Britons would refrain from attacking us.

430

We were wrong, very wrong. While we were repairing on our portion of the camp, close to the *Porta Decumana*, a great shout arose from the guard Cohorts placed a short distance out from the main gate. Because of the nearby enemy Caesar doubled the guard to two Cohorts, but these were men from the 8th, and despite being veterans, they were not part of the expedition the year before and consequently had not faced the chariots before this. Also, the Britons were more committed this time, and under better leadership by the Briton Cassivellaunus, resulting in the two Cohorts being quickly surrounded by the fast-moving chariots, their warriors leaping off them to run quickly up to the Legionaries to slash and thrust at their selected target, only to dash away back to the chariot when pursued by our men. Along with the chariots came a large number of men on foot using the same tactics, not packed together like they usually were, but in loose order, rushing in and out in a similar manner as the chariots. Caesar quickly ordered two more Cohorts to the aid of the guard, except they were of the 8th as well and did not go out together as one unit, but with an interval of perhaps 200 paces between them. This was enough of a gap to allow the Britons to surround each Cohort in turn, the chariots speeding in between the two, the warriors hurling their javelins at the hurrying Legionaries, some of them inevitably finding their mark, felling several of our men. The battle was barely visible because of all the dust created by the chariots crisscrossing back and forth in front of and around the Cohorts, so it was only in brief snatches when the whirling dust parted for just a moment that we could see our men fighting for their lives. All work had virtually ceased as we all tried to see what was happening, shading our eyes and speculating among ourselves what was happening.

"Those boys in the 8th have their hands full. I wonder how long before Caesar calls on us."

Hearing the familiar voice of the Pilus Prior, who had joined us as we watched, I was somewhat surprised that he was not yelling at us for stopping work, but he seemed just as interested in the fighting as we were. The scar on his face gave him a normally grim expression, but his countenance was even graver as he watched our comrades fighting for their lives beyond the front gates. Moving to a spot just on the other side of the ditch we were preparing where we had a better view, such as it was, we were standing there in a small cluster. I was wondering the same thing, yet Caesar had other ideas, probably thinking that the other Cohorts of the 8th would fight harder because it was their closest friends in trouble, with the

431

command going out for the remaining Cohorts to leave the camp and go to the aid of the men fighting. Along with them went a contingent of our cavalry, their pride already stung and eager to avenge their earlier setback. Finally, after an entire Legion deployed in front of the camp the Britons withdrew, but not after inflicting a fair number of casualties, including one of the new Tribunes who had joined us for this campaign, a young man named Quintus Durus. We drew blood as well, the bodies and the wrecks of a couple chariots attesting to that fact out in front of our camp. Settling in for the night, we watched as the 8th mourned their dead and built their funeral pyres.

Next morning, we sent out our normal cavalry patrols, with the Britons falling back on the same entrenched hill we assaulted, before coming down in their chariots and on horseback to engage our cavalry. The results were much the same as the day before, in that neither side inflicted the damage it desired on the other. All morning our patrols engaged with small groups of their mounted troops, and we could track each skirmish by the sudden column of dust rising in the air, borne upward by the small whirlwinds produced by hooves and wheels. Every so often a courier would come galloping in to give Caesar a report of what was taking place, but it did not take a master strategist on either side to know that the tactics currently at play would not produce a decisive engagement. With that in mind, Caesar raised the stakes, ordering out a foraging party, perhaps the most heavily armed in the history of warfare, consisting of the entire cavalry and the 7th, 9th and 10th Legions. Oh, to be sure we did march out of the gates carrying our sickles and baskets, except we marched with the covers of our shields off, ready to change from farmers to soldiers at the first opportunity. Caesar selected Trebonius to command the detachment, still something of an unknown quantity to us. However, we possessed enough confidence in our own Centurions and the experience we had won these years of campaigning. Truth be told, none of us thought that this idea was going to have the results Caesar desired, believing instead that we would come marching back with baskets full of forage for the cavalry, but that was all. And it is just one more reason why he was the general and we were marching in the ranks.

To this day, I still do not easily understand how the Britons decided that this was the opportune time to attack us. Reaching a series of meadows, Trebonius set just the 7th to reaping the grass that would serve as feed for our livestock, while he kept ourselves and the 9th in full battle order, as if we were ready to cross the fields

432

and attack an enemy. Our cavalry was split into two sections, one on either flank, and we were arrayed thus when the Britons came thundering down out of their position on the low hills to throw themselves at us. If they carried the element of surprise with them perhaps it could be understood, but we were positioned far enough away from the nearest line of trees or hills that we had advance warning of their attack. Unlike the day before, when they used a formation spread far enough apart where their speed and mobility was a decided advantage, they chose this day to come in a closely packed mob, in the same manner as almost every other Gallic tribes we fought. Their close formation also gave us a Legionary's dream of a target for the javelins, with no way to miss. Our one regret was that we had not carried two out with us, only hurling one before we went to the sword. Just yards away from us we received the order to countercharge and the two lines went slamming into each other. Metal on metal, flesh on flesh, bone on bone we met, yet it was only a matter of moments before our precision and experience began tipping the scale in our favor. Another factor in our favor was the desire to pay the bastards back for the men they cut down in our ranks, and along with it giving us extra fervor on our part, it also meant that we would give no quarter. Bodies began to pile up along the front line of fighting, and we continued to apply the pressure on their warriors. For a moment, neither side is moving; men are locked in their own private battles, not giving an inch. Then, something happens, and I do not know what it is, but something inside a man tells him to take a step backwards, just one step and no more. Perhaps he tells himself that it is only to open more space in which to fight, it is not really the beginnings of a retreat, and as long as it is just that one man, the outcome is still in doubt, victory is still possible. It is when the man next to him, out of the corner of his eye, sees the man next to him taking that step backwards, leaving him exposed that triggers what is to come. This is especially true if it is the man to his right who is supposed to be shielding him. Perhaps this man wavers for an instant, thinking to himself that he will be accused of giving ground, but there is the nagging worry that if he does not act immediately, he will very quickly find himself surrounded. Then, almost as if acting with its' own mind, his rear foot takes a step backward, his leading foot immediately closing his stance back up so he does not lose his balance. Now there are two men giving ground, and a small pocket is beginning to form in their front line, which experienced soldiers like we Legionaries of Rome will immediately spot and take full advantage of, pressing our own bodies into the now vacated spot. Now there are two men, on either side of the pocket who are flanked, and it would be nothing short of suicide if they were to stay there without anyone rallying to come to stand by their side to try to dislodge the enemy. This is when training and discipline are their most valuable, and it was obvious that the Britons possessed none of either quality. So the moment when a draw changes to a retreat, then to a rout, happens almost before one can draw more than two or three breaths. Such was the case here, when I could feel the sudden relaxing of the pressure I was putting on the man in front of me, followed by his lunge jerking his harness out of my hand as he began the pursuit of the now-fleeing Britons. Because they chose to attack in such a tight formation the one weapon that was troublesome for us, the chariot, was practically useless in their short-lived assault. Even worse for them now was that men, out of habit I suppose, ran and jumped onto the back of their own chariots, only to be unable to move anywhere because the mass of men fleeing around the horses was so tightly packed that the beasts were standing motionless. Their warriors were screaming at the drivers as we ran by, cutting them both down with a quick thrust to the body. Our cavalry, seeing their own chance for revenge, came pounding into the mass of men, slicing through bodies with their longer swords called the spatha, their faces twisted into savage grins of exultation at this cavalryman's dream.

Despite the chaos, we maintained our cohesion, running after the Britons in as tight a formation as can be managed running over open ground, cutting down any man who stumbled or faltered. Some of them suddenly seemed to make the decision it was better to die fighting than running and turned to face us, screaming their hatred, their blue faces and spiked white hair making them appear like some sort of dolls all painted up. Again, if they had any discipline and maintained the presence of mind to gather into small groups to make a final stand, although it would not have changed the outcome, it could have made it more costly. Not that I am complaining in any way for that lack in their character, except that perhaps it would have made killing them more meaningful. There is no particular skill, or joy for that matter, in cutting down fleeing men, at least for me. I would much prefer the honor of killing a man face to face, each of us giving our best, rather than the simple task of sinking your blade into a man's back, especially when he is not prepared for it. But I also knew that any man I let live today could be a man with a score to settle the next battle, so I did not shirk my duty, cutting down my fair share of Britons, adding just another mass of men for which I must offer sacrifice to the gods to appease them.

434

This was the last time that the Britons tried to face us in open battle, their defeat being so resounding that the alliance of the tribes collapsed immediately, with men who traveled long distances to fight now simply turning about and going home. Those who survived, at any rate, since we slew a few thousand to be sure, yet we were most pleased to see we did a great deal of damage to the ranks of their charioteers, the shattered hulks of them scattered about serving as witness to our victory. Wasting no time burying the dead, we instead left them for the carrion birds and beasts to continue the march west, since Caesar did not want to lose the momentum our victory won for us. Our own losses were laughingly light; no more than a dozen dead among the two Legions, and a handful wounded. My section was never even put into rotation, so naturally we suffered no losses, although Atilius twisted an ankle on our pursuit stepping in a hole or something. He was much too embarrassed to go to have it looked at by the *medici*, since that meant he would have to be entered on the sick list, and I suppose he knew that the amount of teasing he would take far outweighed the benefit of any treatment the *medici* could provide. Passing through the killing fields from the first day, the only other sign of life besides the army were the birds circling overhead, waiting for us to leave. Not one solitary Briton was seen that day, or the next; it was not until our third day after the last battle that our patrols spied a small group of horsemen. What we did not know at the time was the political situation among the tribes, as Cassivellaunus fell back on the hit and run tactics that gave us so much trouble the first times we faced the Britons. The chariot reemerged as his preferred method of attack, but never again would we see hundreds of them like we did that day. Instead, there would be perhaps two or three in a group that suddenly burst out from the cover of the plentiful small forests and glades, darting in close so the warrior could hurl as many missiles as he carried with him, before dashing off with our cavalry in hot pursuit. Sometimes we caught them, but more often than not they would reach the cover of the woods, where our cavalry had already paid such a heavy price and only dared to enter in full force, penetrating less than a furlong into its depths. The ground was very flat, with what passed for hills only being perhaps a hundred feet or so high, meaning that progress was easily made, yet this was one time speed was not foremost in Caesar's mind.

As we moved, we were given orders to send flanking parties ranging out farther than their normal mile or two, going three and four miles in either direction, perpendicular to our line of march. His intent was to find all sign of life, particularly in the form of flock and fields, Caesar's purpose being twofold. One was to feed us, since an army of our size takes massive amounts of food and water to power, while the other, more strategic purpose, was to wreak havoc on the island and demonstrate the might of Rome, which we did with a vengeance. By this time we had developed a healthy dislike for the island and the people on it, partly due to the nature of our enemy, with their blue paint and chariots, but also because we came to believe that this island was truly cursed. How else to explain the storms that caught us not once, but twice and so devastated the fleet that we were forced to devote a good portion of the season just to repair the damage? Never before had we faced chariots, nor seen men with blue faces or white, spiked hair. However, perhaps the most compelling reason for such hatred among the ranks was due to those men we call the Druids, of whom I have not spoken of for a reason, nor do I intend to devote much time to now. It is enough to say that the entire army, myself included, saw the powerful magic that these men possessed. Setting aside their foul practices and despicable rites, to most of the men in the army they were considered the prime reason that this island of Britannia was, and is cursed even today. This is another reason why we took to our task of ravaging the land with such enthusiasm, thinking that anything we could do to hurt the Druids was a good thing for us in the long run. Our progress on each day's march could be followed by the columns of black smoke marking the farmsteads and fields that we found, while our quartermasters were kept busy slaughtering all the livestock that we gathered up, though to be sure there was grumbling about the prevalence of meat in our diet compared to our daily bread. I was one of the few who did not complain, it being reminiscent of my childhood when Lucius had been such a sorry excuse for a farmer that he could not provide much for us other than what grazed on our farm. Still, I sat and pretended to be sympathetic as we sat around the fire, listening to the rest of my friends bemoaning the fact that not only was our bread in short supply, but our supply of olive oil was running low.

"Look at me, I'm wasting away," Vellusius complained, pulling up his tunic to pinch the skin around his waist.

It was true that there was not very much there to grab, if there was any at all, yet he did not look to me like he was any lighter than he had ever been. But I was learning by this time that it is better to allow the men to complain about the small things such as this because if you put too much effort in trying to stop it, when they are complaining about really important or sensitive matters, your arsenal of tricks has been used up. So I contented myself by smiling sympathetically as the others picked up his complaint.

"I swear to Dis if I have to eat cow, or sheep, or anything else that was running around the day before, I'm going to......to....well, I don't know what I'm going to do exactly, but it's not going to be good," Atilius pronounced, provoking more laughter than agreement.

"So, if it's been dead more than a day, then it's all right?" Vibius teased, prompting a rock to be thrown at him by Atilius, which instead bounced and hit Didius in the shin. "By the gods......"

"We know, Achilles, you're going to gut us, and make us sorry," Atilius cut him off, causing an eruption of laughter, which even Didius, while not exactly joining in, did not see fit to argue about, giving us a grimace that I guess passed as a smile for him.

This was about the fourth day of our march to the west, while we relaxed around the fire, knowing that the next day promised little more than much of the same. A sudden blaring of horns somewhere along the column, a burst of activity as the cavalry was summoned to the spot from where the ambush was launched, followed by the briefest of clashes before the Britons dissolved back into the woods to wait for another moment. The best we could hope for was that one of the chariots would be slow, either from one of the horses going lame, or the driver letting his mind wander. Only then would the men on foot have a chance to strike back, and it did happen occasionally, but more often than not all we had to show for our efforts was a Century or so of panting Legionaries and a couple of men wounded, or worse. We understood why Cassivellaunus adopted the tactics that he did, and I have no doubt that in his place most of us would have done the same. That did not mean we respected it however, and I have often wondered if he did what he did actually believing that he could wear us down in such a manner, or was it simply because he did not know what else to do?

On the sixth day of the march, we reached a river that is now called the Tamesis (Thames), and is one of the main waterways that the Britons use to carry the goods they acquire from the mainland deeper into the island. This river also marks the southern boundary of the territory of the tribe of Cassivellaunus, so it probably should not have surprised us to find him once again arrayed on the opposite bank, at the only fordable spot for several miles in each direction. Our cavalry had managed to round up a small number of prisoners who claimed to be deserters trying to go back to their own lands, having their fill of life with their army. They told our scouts that not only was this the only ford but submerged just below the water were a series of sharpened stakes, pointing outwards toward the middle of the river, designed to stop our assault across it. Since we were not the vanguard Legion this day, the task fell to the 9th to storm across the river, while we were ordered to ground our gear in place and draw up in formation in case our support was needed. Before we even made it to the riverbank to our designated spot, however, the affair was over. Caesar ordered the cavalry to dash across first, but the men of the 9th acted so swiftly in forming up for the assault that the effect was that a combined force of horse and men entered the river at the same time, despite the water being up to some of the men's necks. Whatever courage they had mustered up that caused them to make this stand immediately deserted the Britons, all of them turning to flee, with the cavalry pursuing a short distance and inflicting some casualties. After retrieving our gear, both the 9th and 10th re-crossed the river and continued the pursuit.

Cassivellaunus, falling back on his old tactics, harassed us every step of the way as we entered the land of the Trinovantes, who came ahead to meet with Caesar to submit to him, giving up not only hostages but enough grain to supply the army with a day's ration. Despite relentlessly following Cassivellaunus, he managed to send word back to some of the tribes in our rear to assault our naval enclosure, gambling that the Legion left behind would not be enough to stop a determined assault, especially given its size. Not for the first, nor last time, was he wrong. That assault was handily repulsed, not without loss, yet not only did it secure the fleet that would take us home, it also raised the standing of the 12th in our eyes. Consequently, the submission of the Trinovantes triggered the surrender of a number of other tribes, and just like the snows in the Alps, Cassivellaunus' support was melting away before his eyes. Nevertheless, he himself refused to give up, still ambushing us when he could, shadowing our army on the march. We became quite accustomed to the sight of a few dozen chariots, their horses slowly walking at the same pace as the army, the Britons onboard watching us just out of range of our cavalry or missile troops. They gave up trying to taunt us and for that at least we were thankful; mainly, we found it irritating, although it certainly did not unnerve us like they

438

hoped, which I believe they came to realize. Either that or their voices finally gave out. Whatever the case, we welcomed the relative silence, the sounds of the march back to the more accustomed tramping of feet, jingling of metal bits clinking together and constant buzz of conversation as we passed the miles away talking.

Envoys from the surrendering tribes soon brought news of the location about the whereabouts of the stronghold of Cassivellaunus, and deeming the information credible, Caesar gave the orders to make the slight change of direction necessary to close on it. By now, Cassivellaunus had lost the support of all but his own tribes and some hotheads from the others, although it still totaled around 10,000 men, and about 4,000 chariots. However, by choosing to make a stand Cassivellaunus negated his most useful weapon, the chariots themselves, because they would be of no use in the defense of a stronghold of any kind. Personally, I believe that he simply came to the realization that he was not going to do enough damage using his tactics to make us go away, and most likely out of desperation, determined that he would make a final stand. His stronghold was barely a day's march away from the spot where we forded the Tamesis, despite his leading us on a merry chase before turning and heading for his fort. Reaching a spot perhaps two miles from the stronghold on a small plateau, we could see that it was protected by marshy ground along the banks of a river that followed the contours of the base of the height. The southeastern approaches was covered in thick woods, ground that did not favor us because of the dense growth, besides which the enemy would know every inch of the land. Walking into those woods meant certain death, and on the two remaining sides that were not protected by natural defenses, the Britons had erected a rampart, before which was a wide and deep trench, filled with sharpened stakes. It was made of earth, obviously dug up from the ditch, much in the nature of our own marching camps, and would not require the use of any siege equipment except for scaling ladders. Arriving at the spot designated as the site for our camp at the end of the day, we went through the normal process of preparing it, then settled in to get some rest before we began the assault the next day.

The plan for the assault was simple; we would not even unlimber the artillery, relying instead on the Cretan archers to keep the heads of the Britons down while we rushed the two approachable sides with assault ladders. The 9th, because of their resolute action crossing the river, was selected along with the 10th

439

to be in the first wave of the assault, with the 7th and 8th in support and the 11th in reserve. Forming up before first light, Caesar and the rest of us had learned never to underestimate the impact on your enemy's psyche of being greeted with the rising sun and the sight of a veteran army standing there silently, ready to begin the day's work. That was what met the eyes of the Britons, and I believe that more than any battle we ever fought, this one was won by that very tactic. Even from a distance, the howls of despair and fear were clearly carried over the otherwise still morning air, and we could see the women of the tribe join their men on the ramparts, as if to see for themselves the doom that approached. Despite their obvious distress, Cassivellaunus was stubborn and there was no offer of surrender at that point, so the *cornu* sounded the advance and we marched in silence towards the walls. Following closely behind were our archers, who began loosing arrows at the men on the walls the instant they were in range, and we heard the whizzing of the missiles flying over our head, streaking towards the defenders and making a comforting sound. They may not have struck many men down, especially after the first volley or two, the Britons quickly learning the value of keeping their head below the parapet, yet that was almost as good because it prevented their own men from using slings and javelins. Almost completely unopposed, we went through the now-familiar steps of placing the ladder and I was one of the first up, just being beaten by a man in the Fourth Cohort farther down the wall. Instead of taking the first step onto the rampart, I vaulted over while kicking one of the men with the white spiky hair in the head, sending him flying off the parapet, howling in pain and rage all the way down. Now with a spot to land I wasted no time, lashing out with my shield even as my feet touched the earthen ramp, catching another blue demon square in the jaw, dropping him unconscious at my feet. I recall thinking to myself that I needed to remember finishing him off at the first opportunity so that he did not rouse himself while my back was to him as I stepped away from the ladder to allow Vibius, who was right behind me, to join me on the rampart, but he did the job for me. Cutting and hacking a space away for the rest of our comrades, we began spreading quickly along the ramparts, the Britons falling before us like we were cutting wheat. The din of the battle was of its usual deafening quality, and we made quick work of the few men who dared to stand before us and fight. It was no more than a few moments' effort before we cleared the rampart and jumped down to work our way through the fort. This was not a town, despite having several buildings, most of them serving as a combination of barracks and

440

stables, while there was a large cleared area where the unhitched chariots were left, arranged in a neat pattern that I did not take the time to appreciate. Despite the fact it was not a proper town it was obviously meant as a refuge, the muddy strips that passed for streets between the low-slung buildings choked with women and children, all of them now screaming in panic as they fled to the opposite side of the fort, their goal making it to the relative safety of either the woods or marsh. Many did, but a large number did not, the lucky ones being cut down, the others taken prisoner to be sold as slaves. There was the usual mayhem when taking any fortified position, be it town or stronghold like this, and the screams of the women who did not escape rang out through the air as we began to round up all the livestock, bitterly cursing the sight of the storehouses empty of any grain. Putting everything to the torch, the column of black smoke was clearly visible for miles away as we crushed the last spark of fight that Cassivellaunus and his people had in them.

Retiring to our camp, before the next day was out Cassivellaunus sent emissaries to negotiate a surrender, one that was very brief. Caesar offered the same terms that he did to every vanquished foe; unconditional surrender and the mercy of Caesar, since his clemency by this time was well known. I believe that more than one cunning native chief made the calculation that it was better to resist Caesar, even if for a short time, then receive his mercy, rather than just capitulating without putting up any resistance, because it seemed that the vanquished profited more with Caesar than some of his allies. Whatever the case, the Briton surrendered, giving up the usual hostages, which by this time had swelled to form a small army in itself and was an increasing burden on the army to support. This was particularly true since most of the hostages were nobles who demanded to be treated and fed in the style to which they were accustomed, and to be fair, which Caesar took great pains to accommodate. This large host of prisoners also meant another problem; even with as much of the fleet being repaired as possible, we still lost a fair number of ships. Because we were packed to the brim on the trip over, and had not suffered many losses, it was now impossible to carry the army and the hostages over in one trip. It took a few days for us to march back to the coast, taking the same route by which we came inland, the land still in smoking ruin from our initial passage, and it was at the end of the month of August that we found ourselves reunited with the 12th, ready to make the voyage home. I cannot say that it was a profitable trip, as far as booty and loot were concerned, except that we made history and

441

most of us were content with that. The first trip back to the mainland contained all of the prisoners, along with the 11th and 12th to guard them, and they made it back to Gaul with no incidents, the entire fleet intact and landing at Portus Itius. However, the gods were not through with us just yet, having one last trick to play, the beginning of the winter weather earlier than usual, with the wind turning contrary and keeping the fleet from making it back to us. For the next several days we stayed on the beach, passing the time in the same manner as when we left for the island, confined to our areas in camp waiting for a break in the weather. It was very much beginning to look like we would be stuck wintering on the island; in fact, that very day, Caesar called a meeting of Centurions to announce that it was time to start planning on spending the winter here, when the weather broke and the winds turned favorable once again. However, not all of the fleet made it back to the island, but instead of making yet another trip, Caesar determined to get us all across, packing us as tightly as salted fish to make it back. Thank the gods the weather was mild, so the crossing was not particularly rough, but being cheek to jowl in this manner guaranteed that if one man got seasick, everyone around him was going to suffer because of it, and as I learned the hard way, it only takes one to start an outbreak that spreads like the plague. I fervently believe that the sound of our retching could be heard all the way back to Britannia. Nevertheless, we made it back safely, and it was with not a little surprise when we considered that even with the fickle weather on both years, and the damage wreaked by the storms we were in, we still suffered not one man lost in any crossing. As we pulled away, some of us roused ourselves from our misery long enough to take notice of those strange white cliffs, which I have not seen now for the rest of my life. And I do not miss them a bit.

442

Chapter 10- Revolt in Gaul

Returning to Gaul, we found it in a high state of unrest. Despite Caesar quelling one possible source of revolt with the death of Dumnorix, there were still many Gallic chieftains harboring similar designs. They were chafing under Roman rule, and Caesar's absence in Britannia only gave them the encouragement and opportunity to resume plotting. Another factor leading to the discontent was the fact that the harvest that year was exceptionally poor, so from a Gallic point of view, it was going to be hard enough to sustain their own people, let alone feed eight hungry Legions with all the attending mouths attached to it. Understanding this, Caesar ordered that for the first time, the army be widely dispersed around the whole of Gaul. Adding to Caesar's own troubles was news of the death of his daughter Julia, an event that the army observed with great sorrow, such was the affection we held for our general. She had been married to Pompey, and while we did not know it at the time, this was the beginning of the end of the friendship that had sustained Caesar and Pompey against all their political enemies. At that moment, it was just another tragic event in a life full of such tragedies, and soldiers, hard as they may be, are not without feeling. Also, some of the men had begun having children of their own, so they felt the loss more acutely than callow youths like myself. More pressing, from our perspective at least, was the prospect of a hard winter, yet before we could worry about that, the Gauls had other plans for us.

It was late autumn when we were dispersed; the 10th marching with Labienus once again, this time to a camp about 60 miles northeast of Duroctorum, setting up on a substantial island in the middle of our old friend the Axona River. Gaius Fabius took the 8th to winter in the lands of the Morini, Cicero took the 7th to watch the Nervii, setting up camp on the Sabis. Three Legions, the 9th, 11th and 12th, were stationed in the area of Samarobriva, along with five Cohorts of the 13th. The remaining Cohorts of the 13th and the 14th, under the combined commands of the former Tribune, now Legate Sabinus and another Legate Cotta were sent to Atuatuca, in Eburone territory. It was this dispersion whereby Caesar unwittingly helped fan the flames of rebellion, giving the Gauls their first opportunity to strike a blow at Rome that would not instantly lead to their annihilation. First to feel the wrath of the Gauls was the 13th and 14th, where Ambiorix, the chief of the Eburones, waited just long enough for the Legions to build their winter camp, get settled in and begin to believe all was well before he attacked, laying siege to the camp. As we would learn later, this was no random move by a single chief eager to win notoriety with his people; Ambiorix was urged to the attack by none other than Indutiomarus, the chief of the Treveri, who promised to rise in revolt at the same time. Caesar had dealt with Ambiorix before, so he sent two men that served as his emissaries in his past dealings with the chief, Gaius Arpineius and Quintus Junius, and they accompanied Sabinus and Cotta in the event that there needed to be some form of dealings with Ambiorix. Ambiorix used this familiarity, first by asking for a truce whereby he could parley with our commanders, then once the truce was granted, Ambiorix relied on this relationship with these two men to offer an honorable way to end the siege, swearing that if the troops surrendered, they would be allowed to leave unharmed. Apparently, there was a heated argument between Sabinus and Cotta on whether to accept the terms; Ambiorix also claimed that within two days, a large force of hired Germans would be at the camp and once they arrived Ambiorix would be unable to forestall the inevitable slaughter. He further claimed that he was being forced to lead this attack by his people, at the risk of death if he did not agree. Ambiorix insisted that was the only reason he did so, recognizing how much he owed to Caesar for his position and for the return of his own son from bondage by another tribe, which Caesar had arranged. One thing in which all the Roman commanders apparently agreed was the fact that a tribe like the Eburones, who had never been considered one of the more belligerent tribes, were unlikely to do this on their own. With this offer from Ambiorix in hand, Sabinus and Cotta ordered a council of war, which the Tribunes and Centurions attended. One Tribune, Arunculeius by name, was obviously made of sterner stuff than some of his comrades, arguing

444

against accepting terms and pointing out the security of their position, along with the fact that they already repulsed the first assault on the camp with heavy losses to the enemy. On the opposing side was one Quintus Titurius, a friend of the emissary Arpineius who countered that, as all agreed, Ambiorix would not take such an action unless he was sure of the outcome. One of the reasons he could be sure, Titurius argued, was his belief that Caesar had already left the country and returned to the Province. Besides, if they chose to stay, the only way to find out who was right and who was wrong would be to fight and probably die at the hands of Germans, who were still angry about the thrashing given to Ariovistus a few years before. Finally, he asked, if we do not leave here under the terms promised by Ambiorix, what was the plan of the Legates? What stratagem did they have in their bag of tricks to get them out of this mess? The result was that Sabinus landed on the side of Titurius, much to the fury of Cotta, and supposedly the argument raged for multiple watches. It must be said here, for the sake of truth, that the troops loathed Sabinus, who was a political appointee and a Legate in name only. The earlier successes of Sabinus, it was said around the fires, were more despite his presence than because of it. Unfortunately, of the two he was senior, and if there is one thing that is ingrained in a *tiro* from the first day, it is obedience to orders, instantly and without any hesitation. Therefore, word was sent that the terms offered by Ambiorix were accepted, and arrangements were made for the 14th Legion, along with their unlucky comrades of the 13th, to march out of the camp the next day.

What happened is well documented, and is an unfortunate blot on the honor, not just of Caesar but the whole army. I can only imagine the glee with which Ambiorix heard about the acceptance of his terms, while I also think there might have been some disbelief that his trap was entered so easily. Now all that remained was for it to be sprung, and it was, in the form of an ambush in the first wooded area into which the Legion marched. About two miles from the camp, just as the Legion descended into a ravine, the jaws of the trap snapped shut in the form of a very large force that appeared not only on both flanks, but at the rear of the formation once the baggage train entered. From what was extracted under torture from Eburones there at the time, apparently the only senior officer that acquitted himself with any honor was Cotta, who had apparently resigned himself to this happening. Titurius, by every prisoner's account, yielded to panic, running every which way trying to put

Cohorts into position, all to no avail. Finally, Sabinus ordered the abandonment of the baggage train and the Legion formed into the orbis, as sure a signal to a ranker that all is essentially lost as waving a white flag. For some men, this gives them the courage of the damned, and they fight like heroes of Troy; for other men, they meekly await what they believe to be the inevitable in their death. Such resignation can infect a Legion quickly, and I am as sure as an old soldier can be that this was part of the problem. Enough of the men of the 14th reacted in the former manner to not only impose a high cost on the enemy, but to force the Eburones to adopt a new tactic. Ambiorix ordered his men to move a safe distance away before continuing the assault by missiles, using both javelins and slings. It was in this manner that the second phase of the battle, if such can be called began, with men continuing to fall. Making things even more difficult were some of the greedier Legionaries dashing from the formation to run to the baggage train in an attempt to retrieve their valuables, only to be inevitably cut down. Finally, Titurius spotted Ambiorix in the formation and asked for a parley, which was granted. Ambiorix proceeded to tell him that he had no objections, but the Romans would have to approach where Ambiorix was standing, instead of meeting halfway as was normal. Titurius went to ask Cotta if he wanted to go along to parley with Ambiorix, yet Cotta, despite already being wounded, resolutely refused to place himself at the mercy of Ambiorix. He was the smart one; Titurius convinced Sabinus, and most shamefully to those of us in the ranks, some of the senior Centurions to go along with him. When they approached Ambiorix, they were ordered to drop their weapons, which they did, whereupon Ambiorix had them slaughtered where they stood. Now without many of the senior leaders, the Legion was doomed, and I have little doubt that they knew it.

Despite their desperate situation, the remaining Centurions ordered a fighting withdrawal back to the camp, which they performed, battling every step of the way. I can only imagine the agony of those two miles, yet somehow, a small number of men, perhaps 300 in all, made it back to the walls of the camp. The *aquilifer* of the 14th Legion, a man named Lucius Petrosidius was trapped against the wall of the camp, unable to break free of the press of the Eburones, who knew how highly we value the symbol of our Legion and were as equally determined to take it as he was to keep it. Even with him putting up a ferocious fight, he clearly saw that he was doomed, so rather than let the eagle fall into the hands of

446

the enemy, he threw it over the wall before being cut down. The remainder of the men managed to make it into the camp, yet despite the temporary respite, they knew that their overall situation was hopeless. That night, rather than fall into enemy hands, they made a pact, killing themselves to a man. Some men, perhaps 50 all told, made a break for the woods beyond the camp rather than entering it, at least that was their story when they finally made their way to our camp some 50 miles away. I do not doubt that many of these men were truthful, that they fought their way out of the ambush back to the camp, whereupon they decided to throw the dice, betting on the uncertain safety of the forest, but which also provided the only chance of living past the next few watches. Their wounds, the condition of their clothing and most importantly, the look in their eyes told us that they were speaking the truth. There were others, however, whose condition was suspiciously good for what they had supposedly been through, and these men were treated with suspicion and hostility. Every Legion, no matter how stalwart, has its share of men who are the first to break and run when things get dangerous, even though it is a risky thing to do, since the punishment for such behavior is death by beating from your comrades. But in our army, where even the newer Legions had served for a couple of years, the most obviously cowardly of the lot had long since disappeared, one way or another. Those men left who were of a similar mind were much more cunning, having learned how to disguise their flight as something other than cowardice. Even in my own tent section, we had a man who was of such a nature, but as much as I hate to be fair to Didius, he was not a complete coward. Whatever the cause, these men who escaped brought us tidings of the greatest disaster to befall our army, and Caesar, since we were in Gaul.

This disaster was just the beginning of the troubles. Ambiorix, flushed with success, headed into the territory of the Aduatuci, persuading them to join his cause. Following that, he moved into the lands of the Nervii, our old enemies, who we had been told were slaughtered at the river that day. Despite the fact that they were greatly diminished in numbers, they were not the 500 warriors that the old men claimed; it was during this time we learned definitively that more than 7,000 had escaped into the woods. They needed little prodding to throw their lot in with Ambiorix and the Eburones, and it was to the younger Cicero's camp that they headed next. Ambiorix had set out almost immediately after the bodies of the remaining men in the camp of the 14th that slew themselves were discovered, with he and a group of horsemen riding hard to reach first the Aduatuci, then the Nervii. Because of the speed of his advance, word of the disaster had not yet reached Cicero's camp; piecing things together later, we calculated that the first of the survivors of the massacre were just arriving at our camp when the combined host of Gauls swooped down onto Cicero and the 7th. They first surprised a group of men out on woodcutting detail, slaughtering a full Century to a man, before surrounding the camp and beginning the assault. It was only the courage and steadfastness of the men of the 7th that kept the enemy at bay that first day, and from all accounts, it was a close-run, desperate thing, yet when night fell our boys still held the camp. Cicero possessed the presence of mind to send not just one but several messengers to Caesar telling him of his predicament, although he and his men held little hope that they would be able to hold out long enough for relief, even if any of the messengers got through to Caesar. During that first night, all the men of the 7th, even those on the sick list because of a bloody flux that was sweeping through the camp, along with men wounded in that first day, pitched in to strengthen their defenses and repair the damage to the camp suffered during the first assault.

Such was the nature of the siege of Cicero's camp; during the day the Gauls would do everything in their power to create a breach in the wall but never succeed, with the men of the 7th spending the night patching up holes and repairing damage. Cicero knew that every day he held out was one day closer to Caesar coming to the relief. Regardless, he continued to send messages out with volunteers, giving Caesar an almost watch by watch account of what was taking place. Fortunately, Cicero had another ally, although he probably was not aware of it at the time, and that was the impatient nature of the Gauls themselves. Ambiorix's men were becoming bored, and he knew that time was no longer on his side because he faced either the appearance of Caesar, who by this time would undoubtedly have learned of the fate of the men of the 13th and 14th, or the disappearance of his own army as winter began to settle in. It was this that spurred him to ask for a parley with Cicero, determined to use the same ruse that had worked with Sabinus. Cicero, despite being something of a dandy who loved to spend his time spouting philosophy of the Epicurean school and writing tragic plays, was still made of much better stuff than Sabinus, so that when Ambiorix made his proposition, Cicero calmly replied that the only way he could intercede with Caesar on behalf of Ambiorix was if the Gauls immediately threw down their weapons and begged for mercy. By all accounts, Ambiorix was thunderstruck; here he was

448

with a vastly superior force, besieging an enemy with little hope of relief, yet the commander of the besieged army is blithely advising Ambiorix to surrender immediately! I can tell you that when word of this spread through the army, our opinion of Cicero rose to the heavens. His generous offer turned down, Ambiorix left the parley in a fury, deciding another change of tactics was in order. As I have mentioned, the Gauls have no experience, and for the most part no interest in the science of siege warfare, except this occasion was different. Knowing his time was running out, Ambiorix decided to adopt our own tactics and began, in the Gallic way of course, to build siege engines, mantlets and towers to assault the camp.

Under the eyes of the dismayed Legionaries, the Gauls prepared to conduct a Roman-style assault on the camp. On the seventh day of the siege, a great windstorm blew up that the Gauls decided to take advantage of, despite the fact all of their preparations were not completed. Using small pots of burning pitch, flaming arrows and other such devices, they showered the camp with these fiery missiles, relying on the wind to whip the flames and spread them quickly onto anything flammable. However, despite succeeding in destroying most of the buildings in the camp, and almost all of the men's personal property, they did not succeed in diverting the attention of the men of the 7th away from the walls. Without as much as a glance back at all of their possessions going up in flames, they stood at the walls, waiting for the onslaught. The Gauls had only managed to build one tower, although they had numerous mantlets which they planned on pushing up to the walls, so that the men could shelter within while carrying poles with large hooks designed to pull down the palisade stakes. Despite the enemy coming at them from all sides of the camp at once, the men of the 7th stood firm, and even taking heavy losses, dealt much more punishment to the Gauls. The Gallic tower was rolled to the wall in the area of the Third Cohort, where they managed to destroy it before it could be put to use, whereupon our men stood on the ramparts daring the Gauls to try their luck again. While it was a victory, it was a costly one, and Cicero knew the overall situation was even more desperate. Luckily, a Nervian noble named Vertico had deserted Ambiorix and come to our side at the very beginning of the siege; using his slave, he managed to send a message out that finally reached Caesar. When the slave arrived, he learned that none of the other messengers, perhaps 20 or 30 men in total, had made it to Samarobriva. Such was the sympathy of the native tribes for the cause of Ambiorix that when the slave of Vertico finally entered the headquarters with the message tied to a javelin, it was the first word Caesar had received of the siege. No more than a sixth part of a watch later, Caesar was sending messengers out to the various camps, giving orders. Marcus Crassus, elder brother of Publius, was in command of one of the three Legions nearby and was ordered to leave immediately from his camp to come take Caesar's place at Samarobriva, while a courier was sent to our camp, ordering Labienus to march to Cicero's camp, with Caesar planning on meeting us along the way. Plancus was ordered to bring a Legion from where he was camped in the territory of the Morini as well, and not long after the first couriers went galloping out of Caesar's headquarters, Caesar himself was on the way. Little did Caesar know that we already had our own hands full.

The Treveri first showed up outside our camp the day after we learned of the massacre of the 13th and 14th. Although they did not formally lay siege, they arrayed themselves on the northern side of the river, interposing their army between us and Cicero, in sufficiently large numbers that cutting our way through them was no sure thing. There were perhaps 12,000 or more men that we could see, yet what worried Labienus, and us, was what we did not know. There was no way to tell what lay beyond the Treveri; would we fight our way through them, only to find another tribe waiting for us? Would we be fighting every inch of the 60 miles to Cicero's camp? Subsequently, it was with a heavy heart that Labienus sent word back to Caesar that we could not take the risk of leaving our camp, a decision that Caesar later approved as prudent. Caesar would have to make do with what he could scrape together, and it was with a great deal of anxiety that we sat waiting for further developments, while keeping a close eye on the Treveri. For their part, they seemed content to wait and let whatever was taking place with the Eburones and Nervii to play out. Later we determined what the Treveri were waiting on was the destruction of the 7th, after which they planned on being joined by Ambiorix and his army. Meanwhile, Caesar was moving with his usual speed, having beefed up his Legion with the remaining five Cohorts of the 13th, and it was on his march to the east where the courier sent by Labienus found him, giving him the first word of the massacre of the 13th and 14th. His reaction was one of immense grief, making a vow then and there not to shave his beard nor cut his hair until the loss was avenged. Perhaps it was luck, although I believe it was the work of the gods to include the remaining men of the 13th in the relief column, because they were now filled with a terrible resolve to

450

avenge the death of their friends. Caesar continued the march towards Cicero's camp, with a very angry army at his back.

Caesar sent Vertico's slave ahead to try getting word to Cicero, which the slave did, although in such a manner that it was not noticed for a couple of days. Tying Caesar's dispatch around the shaft of a javelin, the slave hurled it while taking part in a Gallic attack on the walls, where it buried itself in one of the stakes of the palisade, remaining lodged there until a Centurion noticed it. That was the official story; more likely one of the rankers found it but his Centurion took the credit. Whatever the case, the men behind the walls were heartened by this news, yet were still pessimistic that Caesar would arrive in time. Nevertheless, Caesar moved with his usual speed, and in fact the signs of his approach could be marked by the columns of smoke rising in the air as he laid waste to every farm and village on the way in punishment. It was the signs of this punishment that actually raised the siege of Cicero's camp, the Gauls seeing what was happening behind them and thereby turning to stop Caesar. Caesar's scouts warned him of this new movement, so he gave orders to immediately stop the march and make camp. He had some 7,000 men and 300 cavalry that he had thrown together against perhaps 60,000 men, so he knew that he could not face them in pitched battle. His only hope lay in the strength of our camps and the discipline of the Legions, both of which he used to their fullest extent. Ambiorix and his allies stopped on the other side of a small river when they saw Caesar's camp, which he sited so that from a small knoll the enemy could look down into the camp, far enough away where they could not deploy missile troops with any effect, yet close enough that what was taking place in the camp was clear to see. Caesar then instructed his men to act like they were in a state of panic as they hurried about the camp, apparently trying to improve the defenses. His cavalry screen went out and on his orders, fled when the enemy tried to engage with them, as if reluctant to do battle. The combination of these ruses served its purpose and the enemy rode across the river to surround the camp. Judging the gate too sturdy to attack, they began to fill in the ditch at a couple of points in preparation for their assault. So confident of victory were they that they did not worry about any kind of attack from within the camp, exactly what Caesar was planning on. Instantly, from both side gates our men came boiling out, led by the cavalry, immediately striking deep into the flanks of the Gauls, who were completely unprepared for an attack of any sort so it did not take long to rout the whole force, with our men inflicting heavy

451

losses before Caesar called off the pursuit. Now with the enemy scattered to the winds, Caesar left his camp and completed the march to relieve Cicero, arriving at the gates of the 7th's camp in the middle of the afternoon where he was understandably met with much jubilation. Caesar had broken out of his camp and inflicted heavy casualties without the loss of a single man; the same was not true for Cicero, where only ten percent of his men had no wound of any kind. Word of Caesar's victory reached our own camp at midnight of that day as a dispatch rider used the darkness to slip past the Treveri watching our camp. Indutiomarus, at the head of the army of the Treveri, decided that the time to strike had not yet come, and ordered the army around our camp to disperse for the time being. But he was not through yet.

Because of all the turmoil in Gaul, Caesar abandoned his usual custom of leaving the area and going back to the Province or elsewhere, deciding it was best if he kept an eye on things. There was also the matter of punishing the tribes involved in the massacre of the 13th and 14th Legions, which had given the Gauls the first sign that we were not invincible. I believe it was this knowledge more than anything else that set in motion the events that were to transpire, and even we rankers knew that this winter was going to be unlike any we had ever spent since we had been in the army. Remaining at our spot, Labienus ordered us to spend more time than was usual in erecting proper fortifications to protect us, an order we cheerfully obeyed despite the extra work. Meanwhile, Caesar decided to winter at Samarobriva, summoning all of the Gallic chiefs, many of whom were involved to one degree or another in all the plotting, to come to Caesar to explain themselves. Most complied; some did not, Ambiorix being the most notable, although I cannot say that I blamed him. Neither did Indutiomarus, for the same reasons. The chiefs who did show up were thoroughly cowed, as Caesar gave them detailed accounts that showed them the extent of his knowledge of all of their intrigues with each other. They were allowed to leave, but only after renewing their oaths of loyalty and providing even more hostages as surety of their word. While Caesar was working on strengthening the bonds of the tribes of Gaul to Rome, Indutiomarus was working to solidify his own power within the Treveri. He was co-ruling at that time with his son-in-law Cingetorix, but Cingetorix was too friendly with Rome for his tastes and family or not, Indutiomarus decided that Cingetorix had to be replaced. He also was working on strengthening ties with the other tribes who had not answered Caesar's summons, particularly the

Sennones, who sentenced to death the chief that Caesar had appointed to lead them. Unfortunately for Indutiomarus, Rome had plans of her own concerning him and his future, plans that he would not like very much.

Indutiomarus was rebuffed by the Germans when he sent for aid at the beginning of the uprising, reminding him of the fate of Ariovistus, and I would like to believe that the identity of the Legion he was facing was part of that warning. However, Gauls and reason do not go in the same sentence together comfortably, if at all, and perhaps it was in fact our identity that spurred him to his next move. When Caesar relieved Cicero, at the same time he ordered the Treveri to disperse, yet now Indutiomarus summoned them again, so that late one morning the *bucina* sounded the alarm that an armed force was in sight of the camp. Dropping what we were doing, we rushed to our tents to gather up our gear and were in formation on the forum very quickly. Meanwhile, the sentries reported that it was Indutiomarus again, except instead of being content to watch us like the last time, he moved his army across the river to surround our camp. Before the Gauls managed to encircle us, however, Labienus sent couriers riding to the neighboring tribes who had submitted to Rome, demanding that a force of cavalry ride to our camp. Labienus also gave us strict orders not to retaliate or respond in any way to the insults that were being hurled at us by warriors who would gallop near the wall to perform their usual ritual. By this time, both sides had learned enough of the others' language that we could at least tell when we were being insulted and what was said. As an aside, I find it amusing and somewhat interesting that whenever a soldier enters new lands, the first words of the other people's language he picks up are invariably either curse words or words that one needs when negotiating for a whore. In our case, we simply guarded our area around the wall, watching impassively as each of the Treveri tried to outdo the man before in the inventiveness of his invective. Far from making us angry, some of their barbs brought much amusement, yet our orders had been interpreted that we were to betray no emotion, no matter what it was. The day was spent in this manner, us watching them as they gradually got bored with hurling insults at us, finally understanding that we would not be answering back.

Labienus was very specific in his instructions to the cavalry that would be coming to the camp, and in giving them, demonstrated a knowledge of the Gallic mind that only comes from fighting them for almost five years. He understood that unless you were very specific in your orders, the Gauls would give them only the loosest interpretation, so he told them that they had to arrive at our camp one third of a watch after midnight. If they arrived any sooner, or later for that matter, he would not let them in the camp, meaning they would be on their own to face Indutiomarus. This would never have worked with a Roman Legion outside the camp, since the penalty for letting an enemy slip by undetected while on watch is death, so no matter how tedious or boring, Roman sentries stay alert. Not so with the Gauls; they would watch us and be alert for a while, then those assigned to guard duty would hear their comrades by the fire, drinking and boasting of their various exploits. Unable to resist the lure, they would slowly edge closer until they could usually be found sitting amongst their friends, laughing and talking. If any chief had bothered to execute one or two of the miscreants, they would not suffer surprises like the one Labienus planned to spring on them. For once, the Gallic cavalry proved to be prompt, riding quietly through the Treveri sentries to appear at our front gate precisely at the appointed time. They were let in, whereupon Labienus immediately had them dismount, keeping their horses as quiet as possible, ordering both men and beasts stabled in the same quarters. Additionally, they were given express instructions that none of them were to leave the buildings they were housed in until Labienus himself gave them permission to do so. They were not even allowed out to answer calls of nature, so thankfully the period of time they were to stay hidden was brief. Dawn came to find that, to the eyes of the Treveri, things were exactly the same as the day before, with a fifty percent alert on guard through the night. My Century was one of them, standing on the wall, bleary-eyed and quietly cursing the lack of sleep. To our eyes, things also appeared the same; the force of Indutiomarus had not increased appreciably in size, but it was still large enough that it was a sobering sight to greet the day.

"You think they'll try today?" Scribonius and I were standing on the parapet, gazing out at the array before us, the Treveri beginning their pre-battle rituals.

Nodding at what they were doing, I replied, "Looks like it." I turned and grinned at Scribonius. "At least we won't be bored, neh?"

He laughed and nodded at that. Similar conversations were taking place up and down the walls, as we quietly waited for the Treveri to get down to business.

454

"When do you suppose Labienus will let the cavalry out?" Vibius wondered.

I shrugged; nothing had trickled down to our level that might give us a good indication one way or another. Despite our dislike of Labienus we did respect his fighting ability and I said as much, reminding my comrades that we could be sure that it would be at the best possible moment. Finally we were relieved off the wall, retiring to our tents for a meal and some sleep when we were told of Labienus' intentions. The Pilus Prior came by, tapping his *vitus* against his leg as he relayed what he knew.

"After it gets dark, we're to form up in battle order at the *Porta Decumana*," he told us. "We're to prepare as quietly as possible, and move by Century to the gate. That's when the cavalry will come out, and once we see those bastards relaxing like they did last night, we're out of the gate quick as Pan."

He motioned in the direction of the other Cohort areas.

"We'll be part of five Cohorts that's going out in support of the cavalry, and we're going to be moving fast. We only have one goal, and that's to find and kill that *cunnus* Indutiomarus. Labienus has offered a thousand sesterces reward for the man who brings back his head."

This was naturally met with approval, and he left us to talk excitedly about who among us would be the man to take the prize. Within moments, Didius was taking odds, and the betting was spirited. We ate our meal then retired in a good mood at the prospect of action and a reward on top of it.

At the appointed time, we moved quietly into position by the rear gate, smelling our cavalry escort before we saw them, looming black shadows in the night, speaking quietly to each other in their own tongue. Seeing Vibius grin, his teeth showing faintly in the gloom, I smiled back. Normally, when such a situation arises where speed is of the essence, it is smart money to bet on the men riding horses, but for once we thanked Didius' underhandedness. As hard as it was for me to understand, he did have friends in other Centuries, and not just in our Cohort. One of those friends was part of the guard Cohort that night, and had managed to be stationed in the tower next to the *Porta Decumana*. It was from this vantage point that he could look out and watch the movements of

Indutiomarus; even in the night he was distinguishable by the large contingent of bodyguards who followed him. Once it got dark, some of them carried torches as he moved from one fire to the other, and it was in such a manner that our comrade in the tower could track him. He was ordered to give everyone the direction in which to head, but at the same time, claiming that there were a number of possibilities, give the cavalry one direction and his friend Didius the true direction where Indutiomarus actually was. Of course this was not given for free; Didius had to offer him 20 percent of the amount in case we won it, to which we grudgingly agreed, knowing that without that head start and tipoff, our chances were next to nothing. Knowing that the fix was in, it was all we could do to contain ourselves and keep from babbling to each other about it, though we just managed. The Gauls were ready, and we all strained to look upward at the tower, waiting for the signal. At the last moment, there was a bit of a commotion at the rear of the Gallic column, and it was only when I heard Atilius give a slight groan that I got an idea about the scope of the calamity. Whenever an officer is present, the mood in the air instantly changes among the rankers, and now that I had been in long enough to recognize that change, my heart sank. Nevertheless, I held out a small hope as I turned my head in the direction of the sound, then bit back a curse when I recognized the ruffled feather helmet that signaled the presence of Labienus himself. There was no way that our man in the tower could risk sending us in two different directions now, with Labienus on horseback riding with the Gauls, and we all knew it. Still, I thought, miracles can happen; maybe we would still be able to claim the prize.

There was no miracle; Indutiomarus was indeed caught as he tried to get back across the river, his head removed from his shoulders by a Gallic cavalryman, a particularly smelly, nasty brute who should have used part of his reward to buy new clothes since his were so filthy that burning them was the only right thing to do. Consequently, the coalition of tribes that Indutiomarus was trying to form instantly collapsed, and it was not a complete loss, especially for me. During our pursuit of Indutiomarus, we were trailing just behind the cavalry and came across what had to be the chief's own marching camp. Our Gauls, or most of them anyway, were too hot on the heels of Indutiomarus to stop and properly loot the camp, yet we were under no such orders, so in the confusion we took the camp, killing everyone who had not fled before going through the wagons and tents of those we had just slain. I came across a small treasure trove, and even after splitting it with my tentmates, I had about 5,000 sesterces worth of gold and jewels. At that time this was almost six years' pay, and given what I won in the years before, I now had more than enough to pay for the freedom of Gaia and Phocas a few times over, no matter how much my father wanted to force me to pay. I also decided that I would buy one thing for myself, something that many of the men were doing, and that was a Gallic sword. The Gauls were, and are today, the finest craftsmen of just about every type of metal, but their work with bladed weapons is unparalleled. Accordingly, a good sword, one of perhaps not the same quality that a Caesar would carry, but close to it, would cost me at least two years' pay, yet I viewed it more as an investment in my life than an expense. It would prove to be one of the best and smartest things I ever bought, and I am looking at it hanging above my fireplace even now as I dictate. My first seven years in the Legion, I ruined a good dozen blades, and even had two snap on me, although fortunately it was not in combat but in using it to hack down small brush and the like. This Gallic blade would never once fail me, and although I did not know it, I had much more fighting to come.

While the death of Indutiomarus stopped the immediate threat that we faced, this winter proved to be no winter at all in the sense of our normal routine. Instead we were marched and counter-marched all over the country, as first one tribe then another began making noises about rebelling against Rome. The one event of any moment, at least for me, was my promotion to Optio of the First Century, Second Cohort of the 10th Legion. A Centurion in the Tenth Cohort had died and Rufio was promoted, which was expected since he was of the right seniority and qualifications. However, my promotion was a surprise to many people, myself included. By rights, Calienus should have been promoted, and I was more than a little apprehensive about the first time I faced him after my elevation, despite the fact that I outranked him. For a couple of days I tried to avoid him, then quickly realized it was pointless, since in the course of our duties we would have contact several times a day. Finally, I went to his hut, stood outside and drew a breath, about to ask permission to enter before I caught myself. I now outranked him, and I think more than anything that idea bothered me the most, because I looked up to Calienus like we all did and it was a hard adjustment to make. Still, I cleared my throat then made enough of a scuffle outside to let him know that I was coming in, and while I should not have been, I was still surprised when I found the hut empty. It was in the evening after our daily duties, and I instantly knew where he was, cursing myself for not thinking about it sooner. Calienus would be with Gisela; she lived in a small house behind the wineshop where she worked as a barmaid, a place called Pride of Bacchus or some such, a wineshop no better or worse than any of the other cesspits where soldiers on their off-duty time went to drink. These places, and the buildings where the people who ran and worked in them lived, always sprang up outside of a winter camp and the construction of them, if that was what it could be called, was so slipshod that there was always a considerable amount of wagering done about when the first one would fall down, which one it would be, and how many people would be killed. Because she was Calienus' woman, Gisela had a much better constructed house than almost everyone else in the camp town, primarily because he helped build it and some of the Legion's own building supplies went into the job. This was such widespread practice that I have to believe that it was like the unofficial marriages; our officers chose to turn a blind eye, as long as it was not too flagrant or egregious. Walking down the mud-churned street to the wineshop, I remember wishing that I had thought to stop and get something to drink somewhere else before talking to Calienus and was about to do that, except just then he emerged from Gisela's house, walking to the door of the wineshop. He looked up and saw me, then stared at me for a moment, making my heart sink as I thought, he is angry with me. But then a smile crept across his face and instead of walking into the bar he turned to greet me with his hand outstretched.

"*Salve* Pullus! I haven't had a chance to congratulate you on your promotion!"

Startled, I took his hand and without thinking I blurted, "Thank the gods! I thought you'd be angry with me."

His smile disappeared as he looked at me for a moment, then realization flooded his face and he laughed. "So that's why you're outside the camp. That's why I gave you such a look when you first approached; I couldn't believe my eyes. You never leave camp to come crawl in the gutter with us."

I flushed; what he said was true enough, but no man likes to be thought of as a prude, and I opened my mouth to protest.

458

Before I could he slapped me on the back and said "Come on, if this isn't an occasion for a drink, I don't know what is. You can say hello to Gisela." Without waiting for a reply, he entered the bar.

We found a table, and Gisela came over, smiling at us as she brought two cups of wine. "*Salve* Titus Pullus," she spoke in heavily accented but understandable Latin. "Congratulations on your promotion. Calienus told me all about it."

I thanked her, suppressing a chuckle at how she had picked up the army habit of calling everyone by their last name, even her man.

"So," Calienus lifted his cup in toast, which I answered, "why would I be angry with you for being promoted?"

"Because by rights it's yours," I replied, somewhat surprised by his attitude. When you are young it is hard, if not impossible, to look at the world through another man's eyes, so I attributed to Calienus the same reaction that I would have had, if the situation were reversed. However, I was not Calienus, and it would be a few more years before I understood this. In answer to my response, he shook his head.

"Not if you don't want it," he said, taking a drink.

I was still puzzled. "Why wouldn't you want to be promoted?" I asked, truly mystified at the idea that someone could be content with their lot in life.

"Because I'm not you, Pullus," his tone was quiet, telling me he meant no offense. Gesturing with his head to Gisela, he continued, "I have all that I'll ever want or need. Being made Optio means even more responsibility, and after my enlistment is done, I plan on getting out. You," he tapped my arm, "are different. You were made for this, Pullus. You were born to be in the Legions, whether you know it or not. For me, it's just what I do for now."

He shrugged then finished his cup of wine, leaving me to ponder what he said. Calienus was right, at least in the sense this was something I had been born to do. I took to the Legions in the same way that a young duckling will know how to swim, or a young horse to gallop. Although I had not known it, my childhood and teenage years were merely preparation for this, and in the army I experienced a sense of belonging that I never had before. Oh, I was

459

close to my sisters and loved them dearly, yet because of the hostility my father held towards me, he never imbued in me any sense that I was part of a family, clan or tribe. Perhaps that was because he was an outcast too, and as I have grown older I am forced to acknowledge, however grudgingly, that perhaps Lucius was merely passing on to me the only way he knew how to treat a child. I had obviously let my thoughts meander, prompting another laugh from Calienus as he signaled Gisela to bring another round, "By the gods, don't tell me that one cup of wine robs you of your senses. I expect more out of an Optio of the 10th Legion!"

I really do not remember much more of that evening, since it was one of those relatively rare occasions where I got gloriously, roaring drunk. It was only because Calienus possessed a better head for wine than I that I did not hold the record for the shortest promotion in the Roman army, helping me get back to camp and on my cot in time for me to be counted as present for roll call. As Optio, I rated my own tent and servant, although it was a good deal smaller than the Pilus Prior's, but it was still more room than I ever had to myself the whole time I was in the army. The servant's name was Zeno, and Rufio warned me before he left for the 10th Cohort to watch Zeno since he had light fingers, though otherwise was competent enough.

"Just beat him every so often," Rufio told me, "to remind him who's the slave and who's the master, because he has a tendency to forget."

I nodded agreement, not wanting to betray the fact that I had never beaten a slave in my life, yet I quickly learned that Rufio was right; Zeno was an uppity little bastard, and it was not long before I had to smack him. There was a world outside mine, however, and there were events transpiring that soon enough would impinge on it, with the situation in Gaul becoming more volatile, seemingly by the day. In answer to the mounting threat, Caesar commissioned raising a new Legion, along with a *dilectus* to fill the ranks of the wiped out14th, as well as a special levy to help fill out the ravaged 13th, having lost half their men because of Sabinus. He also asked Pompey to surrender the Legion that he was raising as Proconsul, so that Caesar now commanded ten Legions. The new Legions would be rendered as the 15th and 16th, although there was some sentiment that it was bad luck to resurrect the 14th, that it should be named the 17th and given a fresh start. But Caesar was never much for such superstitions; the more I watched him, the more I saw that

460

he was quick to use such beliefs when it was to his advantage, and to ignore them when it was not.

The beginning of the year in the Consulships of Gnaeus Domitius Calvinus and Valerius Massalla Rufus saw the situation in Gaul in a very serious state. The Nervii, Aduatuci, Menapii and Eburones were all in open revolt; the Senones and Carnutes were little better, although not openly rebelling. Caesar being Caesar, he decided not to wait for winter to relinquish its icy grip, and marching from Samarobriva with four Legions, quickly crossed into Nervii territory, achieving total surprise and taking many prisoners before the startled tribe members could flee for their lives, so yet again the Nervii capitulated. Spring came, with Caesar convening his now-annual meeting of the tribal chiefs, and all tribes but the Senones, Carnutes and Treveri answered the summons. Once the council was over, Caesar struck again, marching rapidly south to face the Senones, whose chief Acco was caught completely by surprise, and through the Aedui, was forced to beg Caesar for terms. Again Caesar showed his clemency, demanding that 100 hostages be delivered into the hands of the Aedui, the only Gallic tribe that to this time remained more or less constant in their faithfulness. The Carnutes soon followed in the same manner as the Senones, asking Caesar for clemency, which he granted. With these local revolts back under control, Caesar now turned his full attention to avenging the loss of our Legions on Ambiorix and the Treveri.

Even with the death of Indutiomarus, the Treveri did not stop harboring their delusions of overthrowing Rome, and they finally managed to entice some of the tribes across the Rhenus, those much farther away than any we had punished earlier, to join them in their quest. Such were the tidings from our spies and scouts, and in response, Caesar sent reinforcements to us, in the form of the 7th and 9th, along with the heavy baggage of the whole army, while Caesar took the remainder of the army up into the country of the Menapii, who still had yet to submit to Rome. The last time we tried, we were forced to turn back because of a combination of bad weather and heavy forests, but Caesar was not to be turned back twice. Once again the Menapii chose to retreat into the depths of their forest, so Caesar laid waste to every sign of inhabitation that he found, sending his army in three columns deep into their countryside, ravaging everything. When the Menapii retreated into the marshy part of their land, Caesar simply built causeways, bridging the deeper parts, all in an overwhelming show of superiority, until the Menapii were finally forced to submit. Caesar

461

left Commius, the Gaul that came with us to Britain, behind with a force of cavalry and strict instructions that when Ambiorix came running their way, they were not to allow the Menapii to give him refuge, or else they would face the wrath of Rome in all its terrible might.

Caesar was not the only one who was busy. Once the 7th and 9th arrived, Labienus contrived a stratagem of a similar nature that we used when we killed Indutiomarus, luring the Treveri into a battle of his choosing. Leaving five Cohorts of the 7th behind, Labienus and the rest of us marched out of our winter quarters, heading north as if to confront the Treveri. They were keen to attack the 10th when we were still alone, but the two Legions arrived before they could get organized, so the warriors withdrew to the north about 15 miles, in order to await the tribes from across the Rhenus that had agreed to come to their aid. Labienus marched us within a mile of their camp, our respective positions separated only by a tributary of the Mosa River that was steep-banked and difficult to cross. Labienus then held a council of war, to which the commanders of our Gallic cavalry were invited, where he announced that he had underestimated the strength of the enemy, was not going to risk losing two Legions and the half of another, and gave orders to march back to winter quarters the next morning. Once the meeting was over, Labienus then immediately held another meeting, with just the military Tribunes and the most senior Centurions from each Cohort, giving another set of instructions. Afterwards, the Pilus Prior subsequently called a meeting of all Centurions and Optios, to be held away from our Legion area in the vicinity of the forum. This was the first meeting of this type I was to attend, and I was extremely nervous as I approached, seeing the Pilus Prior standing in the torchlight. Keep your mouth shut Titus, I remember thinking to myself, you're much too new to be anything but furniture at a meeting like this. I could see that there were other gatherings of a similar nature being held in the forum, small knots of men talking quietly. Standing there, I decided to move a little to the back of the small crowd, thankful that with my height I could see no matter where I was as I surveyed the faces of the men standing around the Pilus Prior. Hard men, all of them, some of them bearing scars similar to the Pilus Prior, yet all of them looking exactly what they were, professionals about to be given a job to do. I could feel a lump form in my throat as I looked with pride at the men around me, thankful at least that here in the back they could not see my moonstruck expression.

462

"Here's what's going on," the Pilus Prior said once we were all present. "Labienus had a council of war with all of us, including the Gallic cavalry commanders."

We nodded; this was common knowledge and was standard for operating in the vicinity of an enemy. "But he held another meeting, with just the Centurions. The Legate's counting on there being sympathizers among the Gallic cavalry, and that what he said is going to reach the ears of those Treveri *cunni* across the river."

He had our full attention now, and he knew it. Smiling grimly, the scar on his face made the corner of his mouth twist downward, giving it an appropriately sinister look, "But we have a surprise waiting for them. We're going to break camp in about a watch, except we're going to make it look like we're doing it in a panic. He wants to give them the impression that the only thing we have in our minds is getting out of here and back to our winter camp."

I could see the grins of appreciation and anticipation on the other Centurions and Optios as the Pilus Prior spoke. When we learned just what the Treveri had in store for them, I could feel a smile pulling the corners of my mouth upward as well.

The next pre-dawn saw all of us rushing around, making preparations to march at first light. Because there was little more than a mile between the two camps, Labienus was banking that the word of our hasty departure was going to be relayed almost immediately by one of the Gallic cavalrymen, and he was proven right. First Cohort of the 10th was selected as rearguard, and it was barely finished with the customary torching of the camp when the Treveri came thrashing across the river, where our boys were waiting, ready for the enemy. In further preparation for this, yet completely unnoticed by the Treveri, Labienus sent the baggage train out first, with only an *ala* of cavalry to guard it, while our order of march was carefully arranged so that when the *cornu* sounded, we could quickly move from our column into line and be in our proper battle order. The banks of the river were very steep, then past that the ground sloped upwards in the direction of our camp, thereby giving us the high ground. Waiting just long enough to make sure the Treveri were fully committed, Labienus had the order sounded to deploy in line, which we were expecting, although we still had to move quickly. I think it was fortunate that things had

463

to move so quickly that I did not have time to worry about the fact that this was my first time not actually in the ranks but as an Optio.

The job of the Optio in battle is to patrol the back of the formation, where he has three main responsibilities. In a raw Legion that has never tasted battle, the Optio is sometimes the busiest man on the battlefield as he makes sure that none of the men in his Century lose heart and turn to run. His duties are very clear; do whatever he has to in order to ensure the cohesion of his Century, whether by threats, encouragement, or beating. If none of these work, and a man still turns to run, the Optio is under orders to cut the man down and kill him before his panic infects the rest of the unit. I was thankful that I was made Optio in my own Century and Legion, where I knew all of the men and that Cerberus himself could not make one of us turn our backs to the enemy. Therefore, in this first battle I concentrated on the second job of the Optio, which is to watch the formation carefully, making sure any holes in the front line are quickly plugged. Even that was not much of a chore with a Legion as experienced as we were by that time. Finally, the last job of the Optio is to keep an eye on the Centurion, and take his place as rapidly as possible should he fall. Being a Centurion is a risky business; that has not changed since the days of Cincinnatus, and it is the only reason why any of us with more ambition have a reasonable hope that we might one day attain that prestigious rank. Of course, while it was not something that I dwelled on, it was not lost on me that I was aspiring to attain the very post that was only open to me because so many men in that position were cut down. However, I think all of us who strive to attain the rank of Centurion harbor the secret belief that we are the only one out of all the people in the history of the world who might truly be immortal, being one of those lucky few who actually make it to the rank of Centurion and live to be my age. I now know that I am most certainly not immortal, as I also know just how much luck played a role in my story. However, I like to think that my skill in battle, and my love of the army life had something to do with it as well.

On cue, the *cornu* blast sounded the signal that we were waiting for, whereupon we immediately moved from column into line, facing the river near the top of the slope. The surprise was complete; almost before any of the Treveri could react, we went from an army marching away with our tail tucked between our legs to a solid line of veterans, staring out over our shield into the astonished faces of the enemy. A prudent commander would have realized that he had been duped, but the passion of the Gauls was

464

strong enough to overrule any sense of caution, so instead of beating a retreat across the river, they chose to come on. It was understandable in a sense; because of the steepness of the banks along the river, even on foot we would have been on the rear of their army as they struggled back up them. They would incur heavy losses most probably, but still the Treveri would have an army at the end of the day. Once all but a few stragglers were across to our side river, with the main force coming into range, the orders rang out to launch our javelins. Our first volley flew into the front rank of horsemen, felling dozens of them, both man and beast and causing havoc. Immediately after the second volley, the command for the countercharge was sounded, and with a roar we bounded down the slope to slam into the now thoroughly disorganized and demoralized Treveri. I went bounding along with the rest of the Century, and because I was unencumbered by a shield, before I knew it my long legs outstripped the rest of my friends, the fact of which I was completely oblivious to until I heard the Pilus Prior's voice.

"Pullus, you idiot! You're too far in front! Get back where you belong!"

It was only then that I realized that I was well out in front of my Century, and glancing quickly around, saw that I was in effect leading our whole Legion. We were just a couple dozen paces away from the enemy when I came to a skidding halt, my face more red from embarrassment than any exertion. The Century went rolling past me, and I heard more than one remark thrown over my friends' shoulders as they slammed into the enemy. The Pilus Prior went by me without a word, his eyes fixed on the impending collision, though I knew that there would be a talk after this was over. Shaking off my embarrassment, I turned to concentrate on what I was supposed to be doing.

This battle was very short, with not a man on our side lost, while the same cannot be said for the Treveri. They were cut down like wheat in the field, most of them as they were finishing their scramble up the banks of the river, and the slaughter was so great that one could almost literally walk across the river on the bodies of the dead without ever touching water. The river, both at the site of the killing and for a few hundred paces downstream was solid red, as if that were its natural color. We did not pursue the Treveri very deeply into the woods on the other side of the water, still wary of the dangers posed to an army that fought in our fashion in the close confines of a forest, yet even without that pursuit, we killed several

465

thousand of the enemy. Labienus sounded the recall, we re-formed to march back to our former places in the column, picked up our gear and began the march back to our winter quarters, our spirits buoyant at the easy victory.

It was less than a week later when the surviving leaders of the Treveri showed up at the gates under a flag of truce to offer their submission. They claimed that the family of Indutiomarus were the instigators of this latest revolt, and once we defeated them at the river, the Treveri banished them from their tribe, sending them packing across the Rhenus. The German tribes coming to the aid of the Treveri heard about their defeat and submission, turning back without ever crossing the great river. Labienus, under orders from Caesar, accepted the submission of the Treveri, although such things became something of a running joke in the camp since they happened so often and lasted such a short period of time. The submission of the Gauls among us rankers was compared to the sworn fidelity of a whore; it only lasted as long as the money did, or until a better offer came along. Cingetorix was reappointed chief of the Treveri, while Caesar came to join us at what could no longer be accurately described as our winter quarters, since it was now rapidly approaching late spring. Bringing three Legions with him, including our compatriots from Hispania, Caesar gave orders to make preparations for another trip across the Rhenus, and work began immediately. It was at that time I took delivery of my Gallic sword, and my comrades did not even bother trying to poke fun, instead just looking at it reverently. The only man I would let touch it was Vibius, and the Pilus Prior of course, who asked to see it. All of my friends were aware of how much it cost, and some of them talked about getting one for their own. Only Vibius, who had been thrifty like me but for different reasons, saved enough money to buy one for himself, except he had other plans for his money. We were halfway through our enlistment, with every day bringing him closer to Juno, who was still waiting for him. As for myself, I was beginning to get the itch that only a wife and family can scratch, surprising to myself not a little bit, and I began to have thoughts about things like settling down for the first time in my life. I do not know what scared me the most; the idea of settling down, or the fact that I was considering it, yet it was a subject that occupied my thoughts a great deal of the time.

Marching to the Rhenus, back to the site of the bridge, we found the pilings we had not pulled up still standing exactly as we left them a couple of years before, and began the process of building

466

another one. This was more difficult in the sense that we had to range somewhat farther for materials, the forest immediately surrounding the area already being denuded. I remember having a thought one day, as I was working at chopping one of the larger trees down that would serve to replace the destroyed pilings. How long would it take for these forests to return back to the state in which we found them, and if some people in the future would be able to follow the track of every Legion of Rome by the destroyed forests that marked their passage? I must admit that I thought of all manner of strange things to help pass the time, something that I have never divulged until I blurted it out just now. Still, these were the types of things I sometimes contemplated, and I would not be surprised to find that I was not alone among my comrades. The work building the bridge did not take ten days like the time before, mainly because the design was already created and the pilings on our side of the river still stood. It was on the morning of the eighth day, Caesar giving us a day of rest after we finished, that we marched once more across the Rhenus and into the territory of the Ubii. They were there to greet Caesar to make sure he knew that they were not the tribe that the Treveri had summoned, and never broke faith with him. This was true enough; the Ubii's name was never part of the rumor mill that produced the true food of the Legions, but the same could not be said for the Suebi. They were working with some of the other tribes to gather an alliance of German tribes to oppose us and it was the Ubii who informed us of this fact. Using this tribe as scouts, Caesar sent them into the lands of the Suebi to ascertain their intentions, and they returned to inform him that the Suebi had in fact gathered in force in the heart of their largest forest, where they were waiting to confront us. Word of where they were waiting for us was met with some trepidation on the part of the army, truth be known. It was not just that the types of forests that are endemic in this part of the world are so thickly treed, with heavy underbrush that makes fighting in our manner extremely difficult; it is well known that the forest contains more than its fair share of *numen* that haunt every nook and cranny. Anyone who fell in its fastness was almost sure to be confronted by the *numen* of the forest, angry at the intrusion. While I cannot speak for my comrades, I know that one of the things that bothered me most about the idea of being killed in a forest was the knowledge of all the trees that I felled over the years, and I could not help but believe there would be a reckoning. Sacrifices to the gods of the area became more commonplace, as we did everything we could think of to appease them at what we knew was about to happen. As I have said,

467

Caesar was not one to be ruled by superstition, and despite his title as Pontifex Maximus, I never got the sense that he was overly religious, but the same could not be said for the men in the ranks. No matter how many offerings we made, we knew that we would be heading into that forest, no matter what was in it.

Caesar was always a man for surprises and he had one in store, not just for his enemy but mainly for us. Despite our conviction that we would be heading into a deep, dark forest to confront not just the Suebi but any other creature, real or supernatural, that dwelled within, Caesar determined that he instead would force the Suebi from their position. Instructing the Ubii to bring in all the Suebi cattle and harvest whatever grain had ripened, he denuded the land of anything edible, depriving the Suebi of their food supply, except it did not have the intended results. Instead, it drove the Suebi further into the fastness of their forests, where their skills at hunting kept them well-fed, or so insisted the Ubii. Whatever the cause, there were many prayers of thanks when the orders were given that, instead of pursuing them, we would be retreating back across the Rhenus. However, to remind both the Suebi and the Ubii of our might, Caesar instructed that our entire side of the bridge, not just the pilings this time, be left intact, so that it would only be a matter of a couple of days whereby we could re-cross the river and be back in their lands, should Caesar desire it to be so. It was now passing into the later part of the summer, so Caesar decided to turn his attention to a man who had occupied our thoughts for this whole year. It was time to settle the score with Ambiorix.

Putting the cavalry under the command of one of the fine young men by the name of Minucius Basilus, Caesar sent this force ahead on our march to the west. Meanwhile, we returned to our winter quarters, almost momentarily it seemed, spending perhaps a night there to pick up the other Legions he ordered to meet us. Among them were the raw *tirones* of the 14th, and when we saw them, we almost pissed ourselves with laughter at how young and green they were, until Calienus pointed out that it was not that long ago that we looked exactly the same. This sobered us instantly, causing us to look at each other, realizing the truth of his words. Additionally, there was no hiding the fact that there were men missing from our midst. It is moments like this, when you stop to think about what you have truly lost, that make your time in the army difficult and it was a sober bunch of us that marched past the youths of the 14th, each of us saying a quiet word to whatever young boy was nearest us, giving them a word of encouragement. I

468

met eyes with a young lad, something astonishing in itself; there are not many men I can meet eye to eye without looking down, and I looked into a pair of blue eyes that widened at the sight of me, undoubtedly thinking the same thing I was. In the instant our eyes met, I smiled, throwing him a wink, the canny veteran letting the young *tiro* know that everything would be all right. He smiled back, and as we marched by I could see, with some relief if the gods must know, that while he was my height he did not have my build. He was quite stringy, really, his armor hanging from his frame as if it were on the wooden stand instead of on a man, and I remember thinking to myself, he'll have time to fill it out.

Young Basilus, although even as I characterize him so I am forced to chuckle, since I was at best a year or two older than he, rode rapidly through the vast forests that stretch to the west from the Rhenus. Under Caesar's orders, they made cold camp every night, not lighting a fire and eating their rations cold. Following behind, the entire army was now united, and such a massive amount of men and animals takes an almost unimaginable amount of food and forage, yet thanks to our organization, we were almost always well-fed and well-watered. Because of all of the artillery our baggage train was excessively heavy, and with the army intact we could not march with our usual speed, Caesar or no, so we trudged along, walking down now-familiar paths heading back towards the west to find Ambiorix. Along the way, we came across the old camp of Sabinus and Cotta, and despite what we believed to be the ill omens attached, Caesar gave the order to resurrect it, instructing that the baggage slowing us down be left behind, along with the boys of the 14th Legion to guard it. This order would not have been met with much enthusiasm normally, but Caesar gave this command to young Cicero. He had acquitted himself with much honor and glory in the siege of his camp some time before, although the 7th Legion was now seriously understrength because of that ordeal, so we felt better at the idea of leaving our valuables behind with the boys of the 14th. Because that is essentially what we were doing; when a commander refers to "heavy baggage", he is referring not only to his own personal luxuries, and as much as I loved, and still love Caesar, he was not one to travel without his comforts. In our case, heavy baggage meant that every valuable that we could not conveniently carry in our pack, or tuck away on the Century mules, or even the Legion's wagons had to be left behind. One of the benefits of marching with Caesar's army was the plunder; although many men did not finish that way, at one point, particularly by the fifth year,

469

we were all rich men. While I was frugal, immediately selling anything of value that I could not carry and depositing it with one of the plutocrats that dealt with the army, many men had other ideas. The most common form of plunder were the statues of the various Gallic gods rendered in some sort of precious metal, usually gold or silver. If one of them came into my hands, I would immediately sell it or have it melted down, yet many men refused to do so, partially because they thought it more valuable in its original form or they banked that some rich citizen would buy it so that he could brag about being involved in the conquest of Gaul. However, I believe it was mostly due to their fear of drawing the ire of the god that the statue represented. Regardless, they were essentially stuck, and it was items such as these that were part of "heavy baggage."

Now, since we were leaving that baggage in the hands of the 14th as we continued to march, we were able to move more rapidly. During our movement, we received word that young Basilus had indeed managed to ambush Ambiorix with our cavalry, affecting such complete surprise that it was only by his own bodyguard sacrificing themselves that Ambiorix was allowed to get away, but he did manage to escape. With the bulk of the army following close behind, Caesar divided us into three smaller forces, sending each column into an area where there was a possibility of Ambiorix hiding. Into the land of the Eburones was where Labienus and 10th were sent, along with the 9th and 15th, the latter one of the new Legions, where we began a methodical search of the countryside. Every building, every hamlet, no matter how small or mean, was not only searched, but put to the torch. Because Ambiorix was one of their tribe, it made us just as determined to punish them as we were to avenge ourselves on Ambiorix himself. Yet the deeper and deeper we went into Eburones territory, it was clear that finding not only him, but any Eburones to punish would become more difficult with every passing day. Their lands are riddled with marshes, forests and glades where any resourceful people can hide, and this had been their home for generations, so they knew every inch. Realizing this, instead of putting us at risk, Caesar sent word to all the surrounding tribes, including those across the Rhenus, that the possessions of the Eburones, having been forfeited as a result of their rebellion, were now available for any tribe willing to send a large enough force to take them. As far as we were concerned, we were turned around and marched back in the direction of our baggage, sure that the surrounding Gauls and Germans would pick up ravaging the countryside where we had left off.

It was during this period and because of Caesar's order that another tragedy befell our army, again hitting the ill-starred 14th Legion. Caesar had chosen an experienced hand in Cicero, or so we all thought at the time, although to be fair it is hard to fault him personally for what happened. When we left the baggage, he told Cicero that he would be gone no more than a week, so there would be no need for him to leave the camp to forage. If Caesar was not delayed, there would have been no tragedy, yet Cicero, having heard no word from our commander for the entire week and now out of food, made a command decision. Ordering five Cohorts, along with about 300 men from all the other Legions who were convalescing to go forage for food, Cicero dispatched a cavalry escort for good measure. What he did not know, and truthfully what Caesar did not know, was that our general's offer for other tribes to maraud the Eburones would end up being the cause of the trouble. One of the tribes across the Rhenus, the Sugambri, had indeed been on the march to plunder Eburones territory, except their scouts spied our camp first, taking the measure of the 14th instantly. The foraging party was not gone more than a mile away when the Sugambri descended on the camp, completely encircling it then throwing themselves at the gates, trying to force a breach. It was only through the efforts of one of the convalescing Centurions, Sextus Baculus of the 12th, who was too weak to accompany the foraging party and rose from his sick bed at the sound of the commotion, that the enemy was repulsed from the gates, despite inflicting heavy losses. Meanwhile, the foraging party, alerted to the danger, began marching back to the camp to come to the aid of their comrades. I do not know exactly what happened then; there was talk in the army that some of the men who were made Centurions in the new Legion were not ready for such responsibility, so when the moment came to be tested, their nerve failed them. Whatever happened, the result was that there was a splitting of the Cohorts, with the experienced men banding together, along with the convalescing men, to march their way back to the camp, cutting their way through the Sugambri. The *tiros*, either refusing to move or being so scared that they were unable to do so, instead stood huddled on a small knoll, watching their more experienced comrades fight their way back to the camp. From all accounts it was a scene of utter chaos, making it easy to see how young, inexperienced men lost their heads. Unfortunately, either because they refused to listen to their Centurions, which is what the surviving Centurions and Optios claimed, or because they were abandoned when they did not instantly obey orders while under attack, which is what was more commonly accepted as fact, the loss of their heads went from the figurative to the literal. A total of a little more than two Cohorts were lost that day, further reinforcing in our minds that not only the site of the camp, but the 14th Legion itself was damned.

The aftermath of this battle was not yet cleaned up when we arrived back at the camp, the word spreading quickly through the column about what happened. I was saddened but not surprised when I saw the stiffening corpse of the young boy I had locked eyes with that day when we marched past, and I offered a short prayer to the gods to speak for him, although I never really knew him. This was the last operation of the season as winter was setting in. Although Ambiorix escaped, his people would very likely not survive the winter, because we not only laid waste to their lands, but also forbade any other tribe giving them aid, on pain of being considered in rebellion with them. We were going to be sent to new camps for the winter, distributed according to Caesar's wishes, with ourselves and five other Legions going into winter quarters at Agedincum, where we made camp on an island in the middle of the river. Meanwhile, Caesar held a tribunal at Duroctorum, where the chief who we learned was the power behind the scenes that initiated all this business, Acco, was tried and found guilty of fomenting insurrection, and sentenced to death. With the army settling into its winter routine, most of us wondered if we would have another one as active as the last.

Chapter 11- Rebellion of Vercingetorix

The fact that Caesar went to the trouble of actually subjecting Acco to the formality of a trial had an unforeseen consequence because it prompted the chiefs of the various Gallic tribes to discuss this event among themselves. They came to the conclusion that Caesar subjecting Acco to such a punishment could only mean that Caesar was intent on subjugating Gaul to the point where it would be named a Senatorial province of Rome. I cannot say what was in Caesar's mind, yet speaking from the ranks, it never occurred to us that Caesar held any other goal but making all of Gaul a Roman province. I for one found it puzzling that here, six years into Caesar's campaigns in Gaul, these Gallic chiefs were just coming to a conclusion that we had assumed as fact for so long. Whatever the case, the discontent and resentment were about to boil over yet again, with the chiefs beginning to plot the overthrow of Caesar and Rome. In their earlier attempts what crippled them was that they still thought of themselves as separate tribes, so that they were either unwilling or unable to put aside old hatred for one tribe or another in order to work together. Then later, once they learned that they would have to cooperate if they were to have any chance of overthrowing us, they were faced with the problem of not having a leader with the vision and charisma needed to unite such a fractious lot. They were saddled with the likes of Ambiorix, who for whatever reason did not excite the other tribes to rally to his cause in sufficient numbers to be troublesome. Indutiomarus had his hands full trying to solidify his power within his own tribe, and replacing his son-in-law alienated as many of his people as it won to his banner. But now, there came the kind of man who was able to unite the tribes, a man who was the first real threat to our control of Gaul. His name was Vercingetorix.

While Vercingetorix was an able enough man in his own right, it did not help that the political situation in Rome was so unstable that word of the upheaval in the city reached the ears of the faraway Gauls. Caesar's man Clodius, running for Praetor, was murdered by one of his opponents Milo and it was said the streets ran red with blood as the city went mad. Temples were burned, and there was daily rioting in the Forum, inevitably spilling out into the rest of the city. Martial law was declared by Pompey; decent citizens dared not show their face outside, which of course meant that commerce, the lifeblood not just of the city but of the Republic, came to a standstill, causing shortages of staples like bread that ignited fresh rioting. Also, word of the disaster at Carrhae reached us, and even as all of the veterans of the Legion mourned the loss of young Crassus, this event, coupled with what happened to the 14th not once now but twice, ignited a celebration in Gaul. The firebrands and rabble-rousers used these examples as further proof that Rome was not invincible after all. It reached a point that we were not allowed to leave the camp alone, being required to have at least one companion with us at all times, and it was during this period that Vibius and I began to spend more time with Calienus and Gisela. If I had been Calienus I would not have been particularly happy to have us hanging around, yet I sensed a change between him and Gisela. Despite not wanting to pry, I was intensely curious about what was happening, and I also looked forward to these times spent outside of camp because it was only under these circumstances that Vibius and I could be friends. My promotion to Optio had widened the gap between us in terms of our friendship, although Vibius was named Sergeant to replace me, so I looked at the order to not go unaccompanied as a gift from the gods that would allow me to help close what I saw as the growing distance between us. As I was to learn, there was such a rift, except it had nothing to do with our different ranks, but with Caesar, and it was during these off-duty times after a couple cups of wine that I learned just how big a gap was growing between us because of our commander. However, being honest, I will have to say that spending time with Calienus, and by extension Gisela, was at least as important to me, if not more important as trying to repair my friendship with Vibius. I thought I concealed that motive very well, except looking back, I cannot help wonder if I was transparent enough that Vibius was aware of my motives and that this was as big a problem as Caesar was. Perhaps

474

he was remembering how I had felt about Juno, and was upset to see that I was essentially doing the same thing with Calienus and Gisela; I was falling in love with another man's woman. Sitting there watching the interplay between Calienus and Gisela, as inexperienced as I may have been with women, it was plain to see that things were not right between them. Yet it was several nights, along with several cups of wine before I got up the courage to bring it up. After an especially tedious and trying day, in my exasperation, I decided not to limit myself like I normally did to my standard two cups of watered wine. We were sitting at our accustomed table near the bar, where Gisela came to pick up cups of wine to serve to the other men and their women, some of the latter rented for the evening. Bringing our drinks, Gisela had just slammed down our three cups, shooting Calienus a look that needed no translation.

"By Dis, Calienus," I remarked in what I hoped was a playful tone, "I can see the frost forming on your eyebrows from the look Gisela gave you."

For an instant, I thought I overstepped, his head shooting up from staring moodily into his cup, his eyes narrowed as he searched my face. Gisela had always been a touchy subject, as well she should have been, yet when Calienus looked in my eyes I guess I must have disguised my true feelings well enough, because his face softened and he gave a rueful smile. "She's...........upset with me," he shrugged, "not that that's any different than any other day lately."

I was about to open my mouth, but Vibius beat me to it. He was just as curious as I was about the relationship between Calienus and Gisela, albeit for entirely different reasons. His hope was that he could learn the intricacies of how to manage a relationship with one you loved by watching the mistakes and missteps of others.

"So what did you do this time?" Vibius asked the question as if the cause was a foregone conclusion, and Calienus looked about to protest before sighing then shrugging his shoulders again. Looking at Gisela as she walked to the other side of the bar to serve other customers, he lowered his voice and replied, "It's not so much what I did do as what I didn't."

We waited for more, but nothing was forthcoming, and I was about to open my mouth to urge him to keep speaking when Calienus shot me a warning glance, shaking his head as he nodded over my shoulder. Sneaking a peek I saw that Gisela was grabbing

475

another round of wine, so we remained silent until she walked away. Once he saw her engaged in conversation with one of the other patrons, Calienus continued, watching Gisela furtively to make sure she stayed out of earshot. "I didn't tell you boys this, but Gisela was pregnant."

Our initial reaction was to burst out in congratulations before the full meaning of his words cut through the fog of wine building in my brain. "Was? You mean," I wasn't sure what the right word was, never having reason to use the word miscarriage before, "she…lost it?"

He nodded, looking more miserable than I had ever seen him, as Vibius and I exchanged a glance, totally unsure what the right thing to say to such news was.

Finally, Vibius spoke hesitantly, "I'm sorry Calienus. That must have been very hard for both of you." Trying to look on the bright side, he continued cheerfully, "But that doesn't mean you can't try again, and that's half the fun, neh?"

Calienus smiled wanly, but his voice betrayed his sadness as he replied, "That's just the thing. Gisela is convinced that somehow I'm cursed, and any child borne by her that's mine is destined to die."

Vibius and I looked at each other in shock. "Where did she get that nonsense?" I demanded this a bit too loudly, causing Calienus to wince while shooting a nervous glance over at Gisela, who thankfully was still engaged in her conversation. I could see how disturbed Calienus was, because he normally would never have tolerated her talking to another man he did not know for such a long time, but that seemed to be the farthest thing from his mind. "She went to one of her people's soothsayers, and the bitch told Gisela that any child of mine was destined to die."

"But why?" Vibius asked. "She had to have some reason for saying that."

Calienus looked away, and I could not tell if he was embarrassed, or if there was something else bothering him. Keeping his face turned away so that he was not looking at us, he replied, speaking so softly that we almost did not hear him. "She said that the reason our children would die is so they wouldn't have to live without a father. The soothsayer said that I'm going to be dying.....soon."

We sat there for a moment, stunned. Both of us had heard tales of men who received divinations of one sort or another that foretold their deaths, but none of these men were anyone we knew until this moment. As we sat there absorbing this, there was something that bothered me, and I asked Calienus, "But why is Gisela mad at you? You have no control over what the soothsayer told her, and it's not your fault you lost the baby."

Now Calienus looked both embarrassed and pained. "It's just that......" he stopped, staring down into his wine cup. We sat there for what seemed like several moments before he finally finished his sentence, blurting out, "It's just that after she lost the baby and she went to the soothsayer, I signed on for another enlistment. That's why she's mad at me. She thinks I'm openly defying the gods."

I probably should have left well enough alone, yet the thought that Gisela was punishing Calienus for re-enlisting bothered me to the point that one night, with Calienus deciding that perhaps it was best that he stay in camp for a few days, I violated the rules and went to see Gisela alone. Making my way to the bar, when I entered by myself Gisela looked at me in surprise then walked up to me, giving me a quick hug like she always did, while I felt a thrill of excitement like I always did.

"*Salve* Titus Pullus," she said in her accented camp Latin, waving me to our normal table.

Without asking, she brought me a cup of wine, then remained standing there, staring at me with those green eyes. I could swear that she was looking into my soul and seeing my true feelings. I felt the heat rising to my face, making me thankful when she cut the silence that was growing between us by asking, "And what are you doing here all by yourself? Where is Domitius?"

I was surprised that she did not mention Calienus, although I probably should not have been. Not sure how to approach the subject, I decided to handle it in the same manner I did with all things in my life, head on and swinging away. "Why are you angry at Calienus?" I asked bluntly.

If I had thought to take her by surprise, I was to be disappointed. Her eyes showed nothing but a hint of anger. "Did he send you here for him?" she demanded, putting her hands on her hips, cocking her head to one side as she waited for an answer.

I struggled to keep my focus on the topic and not get lost in my inspection of the freckles sprinkled across her nose. A part of me continued the conversation, as I protested, "No! He knows nothing about me being here."

Her expression softened, but just a little. "Then why are you here?"

There was no way that I could give her the real reason, so the best I could do was a lame, "Well, because I'm worried about him."

She laughed, and I saw how impossibly white her teeth were, making me feel positively dingy in comparison. "Calienus? You're worried about Calienus?"

She shook her head, but all the humor left her face when I responded. "I know about the soothsayer," I said quietly.

Her face flushed red, except I could not tell whether it was anger or embarrassment or both. "He had no right to tell you such things," she hissed.

"He's our friend Gisela," I shot back. "He had to talk to someone about it."

"And did he tell you what he did after I told him?"

I nodded. "Yes, he told us. But you're consulting one of your soothsayers, correct?"

"Yes, but what does that have to do with it?" she demanded, and in truth, I did not know myself. I just said that because I did not know what else to say. However, I had blazed the path in this direction, so I must see it through, I thought to myself, even if it makes her even angrier. "It has to do with the fact that you and your soothsayer have your own gods. They're not our gods."

Even as I said it, I suspected that this would make her angrier, and I was right.

478

"So, you are saying that your gods are more powerful," she spat.

I shrugged, not saying anything for a moment, seeing that she was in no mood to make this easy on me. "Isn't it obvious?" I asked, and in truth I thought it was, and still do. "We've conquered your people, no matter how much of a struggle you put up. Isn't that proof that our gods are more powerful than yours?"

The blow caught me completely by surprise, her tiny white fist lashing out with surprising speed to strike me square in the chest, and I say with no shame that she almost knocked the wind out of me. I was stunned, but when she drew her fist back to strike me again, I was not about to let her hit me again, catching her wrist as she lashed out instead. She was surprisingly strong, but she was no match for me and I came to my feet to tower over her. Thinking that the strength of my grip would dissuade her from any more violence, it turned out I was wrong, because she lashed out with her left hand, with an open palm this time as she slapped me across the face, hard. My head rocked back and I felt the fire where her hand had hit me on my right cheek, the first stirring of real anger coming over me, anger and.........something else. Drawing her hand back to hit me again, I caught that one as well, so that I now held both her arms, but she was not through yet. Standing there for a moment, the only sound was our breathing as she struggled and thrashed wildly, the barman and the two other patrons in the place shocked into silence. I stood there, immobile and unyielding, watching her fight wildly to escape my grip, her red hair whipping about like liquid flame, her cheeks flushed red and her lips parted as she gasped for breath, so that whatever reservations I was feeling up to that moment vanished, deciding then and there that she would be my woman, one way or another, whether I had to fight Calienus for her, or if her gods turned out to be right after all. The instant that thought crossed my mind it was like being dashed with a bucket of cold water and I came to my senses, shocked at myself. To that point I was standing there passively as she struggled, but now I shook her, hard.

"Stop this nonsense," I roared in my best command voice, and to her credit, she did stop.

Her hair was in her eyes, but I could see them blazing through at me, her breasts heaving and despite my horror at what I was thinking, I could not help noticing a trickle of sweat running down between them, and I felt the heat coming back. Before it could take hold, I said in what I hoped was a soothing tone, "Gisela, I meant no disrespect to your gods. I was just trying to explain why Calienus re-enlisted. He feels that our gods are strong enough to protect him."

"Well, more fool him," she snapped. "Our gods are much more ancient than yours, and they are just as powerful."

I was smart enough at least not to argue the point anymore. Instead, I took a conciliatory approach. "All right, fair enough. I just wanted to come talk to you because he's one of my best friends, and I know how much he loves you."

Her face softened, and her body went limp, so I released my grip on her arms, trying to ignore the angry red marks I had left, yet she seemed not to notice. Her expression saddened, and she replied softly, "Calienus is a good man. I know that. I could have had any man I chose, even the Centurions and Tribunes, but I chose him."

I was about to open my mouth and ask exactly how that happened, then decided to keep my mouth shut, not wanting to ruin the fragile peace. She looked up at me, and I could see the beginning of tears shining in her eyes. "That is why I do not want to lose him. But he chose his path, even after I told him what it meant. I cannot spend any more time loving someone who I know I will lose. I already lost everyone else I ever cared about. It's better that I stop caring about Calienus now, while he is still alive, then suffer again."

This was the first time I had ever heard her make any mention of her family's fate; Calienus once told me that it was a subject that they never discussed. Listening to her, I realized that I could not fault her for feeling this way. She obviously had already suffered great loss, something I do not believe that we Legionaries every really understand, nor particularly care about. It is not because we are that callous, although in many ways we are, but to dwell on such matters make the people we fight and conquer more like us. Once your enemy starts being human, it is not long before you hesitate when facing one of them, and that is when you become food for the carrion birds. Consequently, it is better to harden one's heart and survive; at least that is what we tell ourselves. Leaving Gisela, I walked back to the camp deep in thought. A seed was planted in my mind, and it would take root and grow. I would make Gisela mine, somehow. I just hoped that it was not going to be over the body of my friend.

While our own little drama was being played out, the larger events around us were picking up momentum. After the trial and execution of Acco, Caesar left us to go to the Province to hold the assizes, and the Gallic chiefs worked quickly to strike while Caesar was away. Two of the chiefs of the Carnutes, Cotuatus and Coconnetodumnus started the revolt by descending on the town of Cenabum, by now an important grain depot for the army, subsequently attracting a fair number of Roman citizens, all of whom were put to the sword. It was still winter, but late in the season, yet despite the snow laying on the ground and the overall difficulty of traveling at such a time, word of the massacre at Cenabum spread like wildfire in a drought. News of the slaughter reached the ears of Vercingetorix before a full day passed, in his hometown of Gergovia, some 150 miles to the south of Cenabum. Vercingetorix was the scion of the Arverni tribe, his father having at one time been considered the most powerful chief in Gaul. Vercingetorix was a young man, about my age I believe, and he immediately began pressing for war. His uncle, a man named Gobannito, along with other tribal elders were not willing to countenance such talk, so Vercingetorix was banished from Gergovia. Undaunted, he began raising an army, first starting with fellow outcasts and bandits of every description. Soon after, his powerful personality and name drew the young men of not just his tribe, but those surrounding Arverni territory. In a matter of weeks his power grew to such proportions that he was unanimously named commander in chief by all the tribes involved, no mean feat.

Vercingetorix was not only charismatic, he was smart. Knowing that his best opportunity was to strike while Caesar was not in command, he wasted no time in doing so. Dividing his army into two, he appointed a Cadurcan named Lucterus to march rapidly south to the border of the Province, into the lands of the Ruteni, with the goal of creating a situation where Caesar could not safely travel north to unite with us. Meanwhile, Vercingetorix headed north to pressure the Bituriges, their lands bordering the Aedui, the only tribe in Gaul who had constantly kept faith with Rome these now-six years, into making a choice. The Bituriges sent for aid to the Aedui, prompting the Aedui to ask Labienus for advice, and he ordered them to send aid to the Bituriges. Being fair, they did raise a force that actually marched to the banks of the Liger (Loire) River, the boundary between the two tribes. However, that is as far as they went; they sat on the banks of the river for a few days before turning around, returning to their homes without striking a blow. The reason they gave was that they worried that by crossing the river, they would be at the mercy of both the Arverni, their traditional enemies, and the Bituriges who might take this opportunity to throw in with the Arverni in the hopes of gaining territory. Whether this was true or just an excuse, the result was the same; the moment the Aedui left the banks of the river to return to their homes, the Bituriges indeed allied themselves with Vercingetorix. Vercingetorix's first goal was to keep Caesar from joining his army, and he was initially very successful. By this point in mid-Februarius, the Gaul had managed to form a coalition of Arverni, Bituriges, Senones, Parisii, Pictones, Cadurci, Turoni, Aulerci, Lemovices, Andi and the maritime tribes along the southern coast. Lucterus succeeded in subverting the Ruteni and was now marching on the Nitiobriges and Gabali tribes. Within days Vercingetorix' lieutenant managed to gather a huge army.

Caesar, and by extension, the army was in a difficult situation, to put it mildly. If he ordered his army to come to him, we would have to march south while facing a vastly numerically superior force without him at our head. This was a prospect that none of us looked forward to, even men like Vibius. I know that the conduct of Labienus during this period was called into question by some, and despite the fact I think that he is a catamite who will be dining on his own blood along with all the other traitors to Caesar, I happen to know that his inactivity was enforced by Caesar himself. Events were happening much more rapidly than anyone could safely keep track of, and as much as Caesar trusted Labienus, he did not want to expose even a part of his army to such a fluid situation. One day we would march out of the gates thinking that we were going to subdue one tribe, only to face five that had decided to join together. Compounding our own difficulties was the fact that Drappes, a chief of the Senones, managed to muster a sizable band of cutthroats and bandits who preyed on the convoys that kept us in Agedincum fed. He was not always successful, yet he caused enough of a disruption to threaten the supply line should we go on the march. Therefore, we sat tight, watching events unfold, knowing that the eagles would be marching soon enough. Of course, the detractors of Caesar did not hesitate to grumble about his seeming inaction, and Vibius was one of the loudest, at least in my circle of friends.

"What's he waiting for?" Vibius complained one evening when I came to spend time at their fire.

These were the times I missed most of all, but I could not be seen to favor one tent section over another, even if it was the one I came from. To counter any accusations of favoritism I worked out a system where I rotated spending time with each section a few moments every evening before trudging back to my tent and Zeno, who was always waiting to hand me reports to be filled out.

"He's waiting until he can safely rejoin us," I was a bit surprised that it was not I who uttered these words but Scribonius. Soon enough it became clear that Scribonius had taken on the role of defender of Caesar now that I was gone.

"More likely he's waiting so that their army is so huge that when we beat them, he gets more glory," Vibius grumbled, poking at the fire with a stick, causing sparks to fly in every direction and drawing the curses of his friends as they frantically beat out the embers before they caught something flammable. Ignoring this, Vibius continued, "It just doesn't make any sense, keeping us in camp while all around us the world is falling to *cac*."

I watched as Scribonius thought a moment and replied, "While I agree that it doesn't seem to make sense, I also know that there are things going on that we don't know anything about. I think that of all men, Caesar has earned our trust."

There was a chorus of agreement from everyone, with one exception, who scowled at everyone in turn. "You're a bunch of old women," Vibius fumed, "Caesar isn't a god, he's a mortal man, and mortal men make mistakes."

"Mortal he may be," Scribonius shot back, "but mistakes? He doesn't make many, and the few that he does make he turns to our advantage quick enough that we've never suffered permanent damage." This was met by another round of agreement, but Vibius was still not convinced. Sighing as I turned and left, I remember thinking wryly to myself that there were worse things than paperwork.

To increase the pressure on us, Lucterus took his new army and began to advance in the direction of Narbo, the city that was our home for two years. To counteract this move, Caesar traveled quickly to the city, drawing levies of troops from the retired Legionaries in the region and placing them at strategic points in the surrounding area, while also ordering a *dilectus* for fresh auxiliary troops. That arm of the army had gradually grown over the years in Gaul so that they alone numbered some 10,000 men. Leading about 2,000 such men, Caesar once more demonstrated why he was so respected and feared. Without waiting for the snows to fully melt from the passes, he marched through the mountains to descend into the lands of the Arverni, even as Vercingetorix and his army were more than 100 miles away consolidating their gains and training his army in the lands of the Bituriges. Now the tables were turned, with Vercingetorix the one who was threatened, prompting the Arverni among his army to beg him to turn around and head back to their homelands, knowing that Caesar would lay waste to it. This was exactly what Caesar wanted him to do, because it would clear the way for Caesar to circle around and join the Legions. Having his own spies letting it be known that he was not leaving the army but going to perform another *dilectus* to raise more cavalry forces, Caesar left Decimus Brutus in charge of the auxiliary force as they burned and pillaged everything within sight, while Caesar made great haste to Vienne, where the 7th and 12th were stationed for the winter. Vercingetorix was caught flatfooted by Caesar's strike, but to his credit, he knew that he could not afford to worry about mistakes made in the past, so immediately he began to move his army again, this time choosing to fall on the town of Gorgobina.

Vercingetorix was now moving north to Gorgobina from his home territory, scattering our auxiliary forces and cavalry under Brutus, who escaped destruction by retreating back into the Province proper, where they were now guarding Narbo. Meanwhile, Caesar was moving from Vienne to where we were quartered at Agedincum. Picking up all of us in the Spanish Legions and leaving the 15th and 16th behind in Agedincum, we began to march south to confront Vercingetorix. By besieging Gorgobina, the young Gaul put us in a bit of a dilemma; with passions running so high and open rebellion happening all around us, Caesar could not afford to let Vercingetorix have at Gorgobina unchallenged. Early in the first year of the campaign I believe it was, Caesar ceded control of Gorgobina to the Aedui, and it was the Aedui more than any other tribe that we relied on for our supply of grain. To leave Gorgobina to its fate would send a message that being an ally of Rome and of Caesar did not mean much. On the other hand, the people of Rome, and more to the point, the Roman citizens who lived in the region were demanding vengeance for the massacre at Cenabum. In typical fashion, Caesar contrived to kill two birds with one stone. Marching on Gorgobina, we went first by way of Vellaunodunum, a Senones stronghold a hard day's march to the west of Agedincum, where we reduced the fortress in three days with a quick assault once we prepared our siegeworks and affected a breach. Caesar's purpose in taking Vellaunodunum was to ensure there was no enemy in our rear to threaten our supply line. After taking this town and leaving it in the hands of Gaius Trebonius and Cohorts of the 14th Legion, we turned to continue the march west to Cenabum, still in the hands of the enemy. Making it to the city walls in another two hard days of marching, despite having to travel through the huge forest that lies between the two towns, we nevertheless arrived too late to begin preparing a siege. The major feature of Cenabum is the bridge that spans the Liger River, the northern end of which is directly against the city walls, the town being built right up to the river. Catching the Carnutes by surprise, it was obvious that they expected Vellaunodunum to hold out longer than it did. Despite a show of defiance from the men lining the walls, the Carnutes decided that the best course of action was to try sneaking out over the bridge at night to flee south to join with Vercingetorix at Gorgobina. Caesar was ready for this, placing ourselves and the 8th on alert, holding us actually outside the camp, with only our *sagum* to protect us from the night chill. However, we were rewarded for our hardship.

Around the beginning of the third watch, close to midnight, our sentries reported that the gates to the town were opened, with people beginning to stream across the bridge. Instantly, the *bucina* sounded and the 8th, positioned on the far side of the bridge along with ourselves, leapt up and with a great roar went pounding across the bridge towards the gates. Before the Carnutes knew what was on them, we seized the gateway, then to make sure that the huge doors could not be shut, set fire to them. The flames caught rapidly, providing a lurid light as we slaughtered anyone trying to escape across the bridge. Within moments, our cavalry ran down those who were the first across the bridge and had managed to cover a little distance, while Caesar appeared among us to issue further orders.

I saw him standing there in front of us, framed by the light of the burning gates, announcing in his parade ground voice as he gestured to the town, "Comrades! I told you that you would not suffer the hardships of a cold night outside in vain. The town is yours!"

He may have said something more, but I could not hear it, his voice drowned out by the roar of approval from the two Legions. At this point in our time with Caesar, we were nowhere near the full strength of almost 6,000 men who answered the call for *dilectus* all those years before in Hispania. Both the 8th and 10th were Spanish Legions, as we were called, and the more than eight years of service and the campaigning had whittled our numbers down. The 10th was at a score shy of 4,000 effectives at this point, with my Century down to 63 men. But we were hard men, and it was these hard men that Caesar loosed on the town. I will not go into details about what transpired, gentle reader, as I have not in earlier chapters, yet it is sufficient to say that we showed the Carnutes in the town no mercy. To begin with, we had a debt to pay for the slaughter of the innocent Roman families that lived in Cenabum, and that night we more than took our revenge. All I will say is that as Optio, I was now entitled to a larger share of booty, not just of my tent section like in the past, but from the whole Century. Men like the Pilus Prior, if they survived, were entitled to a cut from the whole Cohort, and we lucky few who lived were able to retire as rich men because of it. That night went a good way towards enriching myself, and the future was bright for men like me. All I had to do was to survive long enough to make good.

We were only given that night to take our revenge; the next morning the army was crossing the bridge, heading south to relieve Gorgobina, hangovers of some of our men notwithstanding.

"By the gods, Caesar is an inhuman beast, making us march like this after a night like that," groaned Atilius as we tramped along.

By this time I had grown accustomed to my spot on the march alongside the Century, marching with the Pilus Prior and Scaevola, but I did miss being in the ranks and being able to talk to pass the time. For his part, Atilius was less interested in the material gains to be made, or gains of the flesh for that matter, than in bowing to Bacchus, for which he was now paying with a monstrous hangover. Didius was describing in detail the attributes of one of the maidens he ravished, to the disgust of the other men marching with him. In other words, it was a normal day on campaign, and despite thinking Didius' detailed description of events the night before distasteful, I found myself smiling. Could there be any finer thing, I thought, than to be part of a triumphant army on the march? I could not think of anything then, and even now I still cannot. The reason that my comrades found Didius' recounting as repugnant as I did is that, or at least I like to believe, there is an unwritten rule demanding we not speak of such things. Deep down, each of us knew that there was

486

something inherently wrong with some of the things we did, yet a man's flesh has needs, and those needs must be satisfied. For some reason, as long as I was in the army and according to veterans who were in longer than I to that point, while it is perfectly acceptable and in fact expected to boast to your friends about sexual exploits, events like the one that transpired the night before were frowned upon, although I do not know why. Regardless of any rule, Didius was oblivious, giving graphic descriptions of the maidens he deflowered, plunging on in his tales despite the jeering of his comrades. I do not want to portray Didius as being an exception, because in fact he was not; there were a large number of men who felt no shame at what they did when taking a town, but I will say that they were not the majority. Now, in the fullness of my old age, I have to wonder if Didius at least was honest enough to admit who he was and what he did; the gods know that none of us, myself included, had done any differently than he. It was just that we did not boast about it.

Continuing to move south towards Gorgobina, once again Caesar did not want to leave an enemy in his rear, so we besieged the town of Noviodunum. More accurately, we began the siege, then very quickly a group of men came scurrying out to beg for mercy. Yet again, Caesar granted it, but only on the condition that the men of the town were disarmed, to which the elders agreed. A contingent of Centurions was designated to handle the confiscation of the weapons, and it was while this was happening that some of Vercingetorix's cavalry appeared from the south, their appearance giving the Bituriges, the people occupying the town, the delusion that they might yet win their freedom. Suddenly, there was a mad scramble as men tried to retrieve the weapons they had already discarded in one of the designated wagons, but of all the people that a Gaul wants to trifle with, a Centurion of Caesar's army should accordingly be the last on their list. Drawing their swords, the Centurions held the townsmen at bay, managing to withdraw safely without losing a man. The same cannot be said for Caesar's cavalry contingent, unfortunately, consisting mostly of Gauls from the few tribes that were not in revolt, and they took heavy casualties from Vercingetorix. However, after seeing the valor of them in action against the Usipetes and Tencteri, Caesar called for some 400 Germans and it was these men he sent forth. They came sweeping onto the field, brushing aside Vercingetorix's cavalry with contemptuous ease and minimal loss. With the situation now in hand, the Bituriges came back out of the town to finish their

487

surrender. I can tell you that it did not set well with Caesar's veterans that we did not put the town to the sword for their treachery, and I am one of those who disagreed with Caesar's decision to show clemency. However, orders are orders, so they were left unmolested for the most part.

Still marching further south, we stopped to besiege the town of Avaricum, and this marked a turning point in the tactics of the Gallic chieftain. Admittedly, after a series of setbacks Vercingetorix reacted quickly to try to forestall what we believed to be the inevitable, the submission of all of Gaul to Rome. Recognizing that he could never hope to match our might, Vercingetorix instead decreed that the entire countryside must be laid to waste. The young Arverni was powerful enough of a leader that his people followed his orders, despite knowing it meant that their families would starve. Accordingly, he also decreed that even the towns must be put to the torch, and none of them defended by the warriors in his army. He was determined to make the countryside a desert, and by doing so, force Caesar to turn his immense army southward to the Province for supply, giving the Gauls their freedom. As I have said, the Gauls are an argumentative lot, so it was not an inconsequential feat to get the vast majority to follow orders to lay waste to the land. Yet there were bound to be dissenters, and in this case it was the Bituriges, who had already lost one town, while we were laying siege to another. They did not openly disobey Vercingetorix as much as ask that an exception be made, pointing to the overall wealth of Avaricum, and more importantly, its defensibility. In this at least, they were correct; the town is almost completely surrounded by extremely marshy ground, with only a narrow strip of land where the one road leading into the town is the only practicable approach. Supposedly there was a great argument, the Bituriges more or less throwing themselves on the mercy of their fellow Gauls, begging that Avaricum be the one spared. I will give them this much, it was a wealthy town, and while I normally did not much take notice of such things, Avaricum possessed a certain air of beauty about it that marked it as different from all the other towns we either marched past or destroyed. Even as this matter was being debated, the other Gallic tribes were following the orders of Vercingetorix, putting to the torch not only their fields, but their towns and homes as well. One could make one full revolution of the horizon without a pall of smoke ever leaving their line of sight, the Gauls putting more than 20 towns to the torch. However, the Bituriges prevailed, with

488

Vercingetorix reluctantly bowing to the will of the majority, deeming that Avaricum should be defended.

Because of the nature of the ground around Avaricum, we could not effect a circumvallation in our normal manner. Setting up our camp directly on the opposite side of the strip of solid ground leading into the city, we began the work of preparing the ground for the siege. Because the lay of the land, it was not feasible for us to concentrate our efforts to take the town just using this narrow strip of land, since it was barely wide enough for one Legion to march across at a time, thereby negatin our superiority in numbers. This is what kept Avaricum safe from investment by any of the Gallic tribes, yet they were not the engineers we were. Caesar looked at the marshy ground, and instead of throwing up his hands then hurling us one at a time across the dry ground in a bloody assault, he simply decided to fill in the marsh at certain points. At selected spots directly across from every wall, we began the process of filling in the marsh, not just throwing dirt in, but constructing a terrace similar in construction to the ramp I described previously so that our heavy artillery and the towers we were constructing could roll safely, moving up a ramp about 80 feet high where it touched the wall. Avaricum's walls loomed some 20 feet above that, these easily being the highest and strongest that we were ever up against. The height was partly because the city sat on the top of a small hill, with very steeply sloping sides, but the walls themselves were exceptionally high. What was astonishing to us was how the Gauls could build a wall that high without it toppling over; Caesar gives a detailed description in his Commentaries, so I will not go into it in any detail other than to say that despite ourselves, we were impressed.

"If they ever learned how to conduct a proper siege, we'd be in trouble," the Pilus Prior observed after we got a look at their walls up close. This time we did not face any of the same derision or ridicule that we had in the past when building our siegeworks. Our reputation was well known, so it was nothing but anxious faces looking down on us from the walls of the city as we worked.

This was going to be the largest, most involved siege to date, and it was clear that we would be here for the next few weeks, which actually played into our enemy's hands. The tactics of Vercingetorix were beginning to be felt, with our foraging parties forced to go farther afield than normal, only to be ambushed by the Gallic forces. To combat this, we had to send out larger foraging parties in order to bring back anything at all. Then, they began to return empty-handed, as well as in smaller numbers than when they went out, causing our supply situation to become very serious. We began subsisting on the livestock that the foraging parties came back with, in lieu of bread. Once again I quietly thanked the gods that such a diet did not disagree with me the way it did with many of my comrades. It seemed that whenever our diet switched to mostly meat, men began suffering all types of intestinal problems, and it was not unheard of for men to fall seriously ill and die because their systems could not tolerate it for whatever reason. One thing I remembered from my childhood was Gaia's absolute insistence that the meat be thoroughly cooked, and I did notice that the men who seemed to have the most problems were the ones that were the most impatient, snatching their share off the fire before it was fully roasted. Now that I was Optio, I could enforce on the whole Century the practice of thoroughly cooking their meat, and while this was met with some resistance at first, once it was clear that we had less men ill than the other Centuries, I no longer had to order the men to do so, they happily did it on their own. Still, there was much grumbling about the absence of bread, yet it was the dim prospects of fixing that problem that worried us the most.

"What happens when we run out of cattle?" Calienus mused as we sat by the officer's fire one night.

I shrugged; to me, the answer was simple. Either the siege would have to be lifted, or we would stick it out and take the town so we could eat the food within. From everything our spies told us, the people of Avaricum were still well supplied, yet who knew how accurate that was? Whatever the case, we continued working on the two large terraces. Once we constructed enough of a foundation to support the requisite weight, towers were built that housed our artillery, particularly the scorpions, and it was with these that we kept the Bituriges from stopping us as we moved closer to the wall. This ramp was different from the other we built previously because it was designed to allow not only the rolling of the tower, but on either side several series of mantlets, joined end to end that led to the base of the wall, where men would then work to dig under the wall and undermine it, causing it to collapse. Working day and night, in shifts, it was still a huge amount of work, meaning that our progress was slow, and our supply situation did not help. After a week of nothing but meat, morale and the overall health of the army began to flag, and I confess that I felt as discouraged as my friends. But I was an Optio, so I had to maintain a professional detachment,

490

and it was during the siege at Avaricum that I was forced to discipline one of my tentmates for the first time.

Being Optio for a year now, I had been forced to discipline several men in the Century, yet somehow I managed to avoid being forced to confront what faced me now. When I speak of discipline, I am not referring to the unofficial sort, the type that was administered to us as *tiros*; I broke more than one *vitus* over the backs of many of the men in my Century, including my tentmates and on one occasion Vibius, who did not like it but understood. However this was the first time that one of my tentmates did something serious enough to be punished in a formal manner, and in the context of what we were facing, it was an extremely grave offense. Atilius was caught offering his food ration for wine to one of the camp followers, the exchange being witnessed by a Centurion in the Fourth Cohort, who dragged Atilius to our area in the camp to deposit him at my feet.

"I caught this bastard trading his ration for some wine," growled the Centurion, a squat Campanian whose name I forget, as he died at Alesia not long after this.

Atilius' expression was as much of an admission of guilt as I needed, though it did not really matter. Whenever a Legionary of a senior rank, particularly of Centurionate status, makes an accusation, that is enough to presume guilt, especially in the absence of any other witnesses. Because the other man with Atilius fled into the labyrinth of thrown together huts and hovels that followed us wherever we went, it was therefore essentially decided already. The punishment was equally clear in such a matter; instead of the usual bread ration, the offender was put on a diet of bread made from barley, which is usually reserved for the livestock, horses in particular. What made this so serious was that we did not even have barley at this point, meaning that in this case, the man was essentially cut off from food of any type, for a period of five days. If we were in winter quarters, with only slack duties, it was probable that Atilius would have survived, not easily, but he would live to see another campaign season. But here, already weakened by the short rations, with the kind of brutal labor that we were performing, this was as close to an outright death sentence as one could receive. And when a Legionary is on punishment, then falls ill because of that punishment, he is not considered eligible for reporting on the sick list, and in fact would face a flogging if he missed a day of duty. Such are the rules, and harsh as they may be, they are well known throughout the Legions, so Atilius knew the risk he was running for a flask of wine. Still, I felt my throat tighten as I looked into his face, knowing his probable fate, though I kept my face a cold hard mask and ordered him to his feet. Telling Atilius to follow me, I went to find the Pilus Prior to inform him of what had transpired. I found him supervising the rest of the Century, just starting their shift working on the ramp. Pulcher sized up the situation at a glance; me walking towards him, my back stiff, *vitus* under my arm, face hard, with Atilius following behind, shoulders slumped and head down, not willing to look up at his comrades, all of whom had stopped working when they saw us. Doing my best to avoid meeting the eyes of any of my tentmates, despite my intentions Vibius caught my eye, his face clearly asking the question. I could only shake my head gravely as I kept walking.

Saluting the Pilus Prior, I spoke in my official voice, "Pilus Prior, I bring you *Gregarius* Atilius, who was caught by Quartus Princeps Prior So-and-So trying to trade his ration for wine. I haven't yet written up the charge to enter into the Legion diary, since I thought it best to bring him to you first."

The Pilus Prior's face turned grim, his lips turned down into a frown as he stared at Atilius, tapping his *vitus* into his other palm. He did not say anything for several moments, but once he did, his voice was as cold and hard as the glaciers in the Alps.

"Very well, Optio. Take *Gregarius* Atilius to the orderly tent and have his punishment entered in the Legion diary, then escort him back here."

I saluted again, turned about and with a curt nod of my head, motioned Atilius to follow me. Once we were out of earshot, Atilius cleared his throat, speaking for the first time since this sorry business had begun. "Pullus, I'm..." I let him get no farther.

"Shut your mouth," I snapped. "I don't want to hear anything you have to say. You know the rules, and you knew what would happen if you were caught."

Atilius said no more.

The business of entering his crime in the Legion diary done, I returned Atilius to begin work, my anger at him still far outweighing any pity I felt for him, because now it was my job to make sure the

492

punishment was carried out in the proper manner. That meant that I had to watch Atilius at all times during our off duty time to make sure his tentmates, my closest friends, did not sneak him any of their rations. If they did and were caught they would have to join Atilius, and if that happened, it would be because I was the one who caught them. It was this thought that occupied my mind as I watched Atilius shamble over to his comrades, Vellusius handing him a spade and saying a quiet word. As he did so he glanced over his shoulder, saw me staring at him, so he looked quickly away, guilt written plainly on his face. I could only hope that my catching him stopped him from doing something stupid.

"Are you all right?" The quiet voice of the Pilus Prior startled me, and I turned to see him looking at me, his concern plain to see. I was somewhat taken aback, not sure what to say.

"This is your first time to punish one of your tentmates, isn't it?"

I nodded, still not speaking. This did not seem to bother the Pilus Prior, who continued talking quietly so the rest of the men could not hear. "Unfortunately, it doesn't get any easier," I was not sure if he was trying to make me feel better, but he was not doing a good job. "But hopefully, what'll happen is that the rest of them will know that you'll do what's necessary, and they'll watch themselves and each other more closely."

I could only hope this to be true, yet I was glad the Pilus Prior had at least said something.

Work continued despite the hardships, with our situation now exceedingly desperate, and it was because of these straits we were in that Atilius was saved. He did well enough the first day; the second day he was in morning formation and made it through a full day of work, but all of us could plainly see that if he was able to rise out of his cot the next morning, it would be a miracle, a short-lived one at that. His face was pinched, his eyes hollow, burning holes in his face as he stared out at the world and despite my anger with him, I found my stomach turning in knots at the sight. Then there was a miracle of sorts, formed out of our desperate situation. At the end of the second day of Atilius' punishment, as Vellusius and Scribonius walked on either side of him to help him stay erect, technically a violation of the rules regarding his punishment but one I overlooked, the Pilus Prior and the other Centurions were ordered to the forum for a meeting with Caesar. When Pulcher came back, I was puzzled by his expression. While he looked grim, there was a look in his eye that told me that not all the news was bad.

"We're going on half-rations in the morning," he told me. I nodded, this having been expected. What was not expected was what he said next. "And Caesar has decreed that all men on punishment are hereby forgiven, and their punishment is rescinded. Atilius can begin eating again."

He smiled as I grinned back, genuinely pleased at this development, despite what some might view as the slackening of discipline. Do not mistake me; I am a firm believer in the need for discipline in the army, and I have accepted the rules and regulations as the manner in which I live my life, yet none of us want to watch men we consider friends suffer, and this was one of those occasions where the gods smiled on Atilius, despite the fact that the rest of us would have to tighten our belts, literally.

Three days later, we were put on quarter rations. Things had never been this bad, as now even the strongest men, myself included, began feeling the effects of slow starvation. Accordingly, the pace of our work slowed; it was now the eighteenth day of the siege, and it was during that day, about noon, when Caesar appeared among us, moving from one Legion to another. Before we knew what was happening, he joined us, a quick formation being ordered a short distance away from our worksite. Despite moving as quickly as we could, even under the eyes of Caesar our weakness was apparent in the lethargy of our movement. We were sluggish in everything but our minds; in the moment we thought we were moving as quickly as we always did, but it was clear that this was an illusion. Once we were settled and at *intente*, we were ordered to stand at ease, and for a moment Caesar said nothing, just gazing at us sadly.

"Comrades," he finally began, "I cannot bear to see you suffering in this manner any longer. You have made my heart swell with pride at the way you have continued in your duties, despite the incredible hardships you are facing. But you are as my children are to me, and I can no longer bear the sight of your suffering."

We began to stir uneasily, stealing glances at one another. Catching the eye of the Pilus Prior, he just shrugged, shaking his head to tell me that he had no idea of what was happening.

494

"Therefore," Caesar continued after a pause, "I have decided that we are going to lift the siege. We will march back to Agedincum, where we will resupply and regain our strength."

For a moment, there was complete silence as our benumbed brains tried to comprehend what he had just said. Then, somewhere towards the rear of the formation, then quickly sweeping forward, began what started out as a low moan but just as quickly grew into a roar of protest. Looking around, I was slightly bewildered, thinking that this news would be greeted with much joy and approbation, but I was wrong. Over the mumbling roar, a voice rang out, again from the rear of the formation.

"No, Caesar! Please don't give that order! We won't let you down, we swear it!"

This triggered a flood of similar shouts, and now the scene was one of utter chaos, men beginning to openly beseech Caesar to change his mind. At that moment, I was watching Caesar closely and with more exposure to him than most of my comrades, I was more familiar with his countenance, so I swear even to this day that I saw the ghost of a smile flash across his face, as if he was actually getting what he wanted. Instantly, it was replaced by a look of astonishment, then he held his hands out to the formation, signaling them to quiet down, which took a few moments. Finally, when he could be heard again, Caesar gave a great sigh, shaking his head as he announced, "Very well, comrades. I fear that I am making a grave mistake, but your valor and fortitude have humbled me. I am ashamed that I made such a suggestion."

Immediately after these words, his head shot back up erect, and we were once again faced with the commander who led us to so many victories, his face a study in cold determination as he finished, "We will stay here and finish what we started, and as always, I will count on the 10th to lead the way."

He said something else, which was completely drowned out by the cheers. Glancing up as the noise swelled and rolled over us to see Gauls standing on the wall watching what was taking place, even from this distance, I could see their bodies slump in defeat at the sounds of our cheering. It was not until later that night when we were back in camp that we learned that Caesar had made the same speech to every Legion, and gotten the same response. I could not help but shake my head in admiration for the man; he knew how to play us like a Greek plays the flute.

The tactics of Vercingetorix were not having an effect on just us; even the enemy was feeling the pinch of hunger. As we were nearing the completion of our work at Avaricum, Vercingetorix moved his army closer to us, and according to some prisoners, then left the infantry behind in his camp while bringing his cavalry closer to try to inflict more damage on our foraging parties, along with finding forage for his own army. Caesar decided to seize the opportunity and risk ending the rebellion in one stroke by stealing a march to attack the bulk of the Gallic army while their leader was absent. The location of the camp was about ten miles to the northeast, and the 10th, 9th and 8th were given orders to prepare to march at midnight. In order to keep from alerting the Gauls in Avaricum that something was in the air, we were kept at our job of constructing the ramp, so that we were especially tired when we marched quietly out of camp. I suspect that is why Caesar chose his Spanish Legions, knowing that we were hardened enough to be able to handle this added strain, albeit not without difficulty. Traveling light, without artillery or other baggage, it enabled us to close the distance rapidly, despite having to stop numerous times either to rest or when we ran into Vercingetorix's patrols. Our German cavalry accompanied us, and even in our limited time with them, we respected them more than we ever did our normal Gallic cavalry. Arriving just short of the enemy camp immediately after first light, we saw that it was on a small hill, surrounded on all sides by extremely swampy ground, with what looked like two causeways that gave access to the hill through the morass. In the growing light, we could see that the enemy had destroyed the causeways, making the only way of assaulting the hill by wading through the swamp while under fire from their missile troops. This was one of the few times I saw Caesar in a state of seeming indecision, as we stood there for almost a third of a watch while he seemingly was making up his mind on what to do. Presently, a meeting was called for all the officers, Optios included, and we moved to Caesar's standard. He was standing there, waiting for us to assemble, and once we were all present, he spoke.

"Comrades, after seeing the tactical problems that we would have to overcome in attacking this position, I have decided that we will not hazard an assault."

He barely finished before we let out an instinctive howl of protest. To this point in our campaigning, we had never failed at anything we set out to do, making this the first time we would be forced to turn back without accomplishing our goal. Crying out to Caesar to let us take the risk of the assault, we told him that we were willing to suffer however many casualties we needed rather than turn back. He stood for a moment, not speaking, letting us voice our protest, before putting up a hand to quiet us, bringing instant silence.

"Comrades, do not worry about your reputation for valor, it will remain as untarnished as always. The failure here is mine, not yours."

If he thought that this would quell our importuning, he was mistaken. If anything, our protests became more vehement, all of us trying to make our voices heard. The din caused by our display reached back to the ranks, and I could see the men in formation becoming restive as they began talking openly to one another, speculating about the cause of this disturbance.

"*Silete!*"

I recognized the voice of Primus Pilus Favonius, and we did quiet down, although it took a few moments before it was quiet enough for him to be heard. Once we were still again, the Primus Pilus turned to Caesar, saying loudly enough for all to hear.

"Caesar, don't you realize that any damage to your dignitas is just as damaging to the men of your army who have followed you all these years?"

We roared our agreement with the statement of the Primus Pilus; once more, Caesar put his hand up for silence, and it did not take nearly as long for us to shut our mouths when Caesar demanded it.

"Primus Pilus, your words move me, they truly do. But as important as my dignitas may be to me, and I will not deny that it is, the lives of my soldiers, who are like sons to me, is of exceedingly more importance."

There was really no response to this, and we were smart enough not to try to argue with him. As kind as Caesar could be, he had a nasty temper when provoked, no matter who it was trying his patience. Seeing that there would be no more argument, Caesar dismissed us to pass the word back to the rest of our comrades.

It was with some grumbling, but we turned back around quickly enough to march back to Avaricum, the sounds of the jeering from the enemy on the hill ringing in our ears not making the march back any more pleasant. What we were not aware of was that this bloodless victory actually caused Vercingetorix almost more problems than if we actually carried out the assault. Upon Vercingetorix's return to his camp, he was confronted by members of his army who accused him of treason. Their reasoning was that his absence from the camp was because he planned on betraying his army to Caesar; why else would he be gone when Caesar and his army showed up? But Vercingetorix was a canny bastard, I have to give him that. While out foraging he captured some of our camp followers and put them on starvation rations, and now he dragged them out to perform for his accusers. They were prompted to say they were Legionaries who had deserted because they were starving, and that Caesar had informed the army that if the siege was not resolved within three days it would be lifted. Vercingetorix finished by pointing out that it was his tactics of attrition that was on the verge of achieving this result, just like it was his leadership that united the tribes. This show of unity had brought the Romans to the point that, should Caesar be forced to lift the siege, it would not be the end of his problems, since all the tribes in the region pledged to Vercingetorix that they would offer no aid to Caesar or his army. True to their fickle nature, those Gauls who were just clamoring for the head of Vercingetorix were so won over by his words that they now reaffirmed his status as commander in chief, proclaiming him to be the greatest general in their history. Another development from that meeting was the decision to try getting another 10,000 men into the town of Avaricum, although nothing ultimately came of that.

At the site of the siege, work was progressing, albeit with great difficulty. Because of the cut in our rations, we were ordered to abandon work on one of the ramps, instead concentrating all of our efforts on the remaining one. The Bituriges did everything in their power to stop us, so that as much of the work that we did in those final days was to repair the damage done in their counter-siege efforts as it was in advancing the siege itself. Compounding our misery, the weather turned nasty, forcing us to spend most of our time wet and cold which, when added to our hunger, made for the worst conditions we had faced to date during our time in Gaul. We looked and acted like we were already dead; stumbling around, our

498

eyes hollow with hunger and fatigue, and as lean as we may have been starting the siege, we were now beginning to look like walking skeletons. The Bituriges showed a lot of ingenuity and energy in their attempts to destroy the ramp. Using their experience in mining, they tried to undermine it, forcing us to dig our own counter-mines to intercept them. The fights inside those close, dark spaces under the earth were by all accounts vicious, nasty affairs, taking place in almost total darkness. This was another time I was thankful for my size, although it was the first time I was glad because it kept me out of a fight. I have no love for enclosed spaces, finding it hard to breathe and to keep a calm head. Vibius was not so lucky, his diminutive size making him a perfect candidate to go down into the dark holes in the ground to kill other men. Every time he went down into the ground I was almost beside myself with worry until I saw him emerge, grimy and often spattered with blood, none of it his thank the gods. The efforts of the enemy were not confined to subterranean methods; it became commonplace for the gates to be thrown open, whereupon a band of men armed with torches and small flaming pots of pitch would come pouring out, heading for the ramp and tower to hurl the pots at anything they thought flammable. Their success was limited; nothing was damaged to the point where we had to start over, but they were certainly successful in delaying us. As the ramp raised in height, so would our towers where the artillery was stationed. To further combat our efforts, the enemy erected a series of turrets, similar in construction to our towers, covering them with green hides that made burning them almost impossible, and was where their missile troops were stationed. Whenever we raised our towers, they would correspondingly raise the level of their turrets, building another level on top of the original one. By this point in the siege, all of the usual interaction between the two sides; the Bituriges jeering down at us from their spot on the walls, our rejoinders to them which I believe most of us on both sides enjoyed and looked at as a diversion, had long since ceased. Between our weakness from hunger, the weather, and the actions of the Bituriges, all sources of levity were gone. Conversations were almost non-existent, being seen as useless expenditures of energy, so that all over the camp and the siegeworks a pall of grim silence hung in the air like the mist that greeted us every morning.

It was on the twenty-fifth day of the siege, or night more accurately, when the Bituriges made their final and most determined bid to destroy the ramp. We had reached the most difficult part; the bridging of the last section which, as I have mentioned before, is filled in with basically whatever we can get our hands on just before the assault. The mantlets that we used for this last part had to be of the strongest construction, because they would literally be directly beneath the walls, where the largest stones could simply be rolled off the parapet to fall onto their roofs. They also had to be fireproof, and usually the roofs were covered with either clay shingles or green hides. It was at the beginning of the third watch when the alarm was sounded and I rolled out of my cot, our Century just relieved perhaps a third of a watch before, grabbing my gear and running out to see what the problem was. Our camp was perhaps two furlongs from the beginning of the ramp, so in the gloom it was impossible to see what was happening, yet men were running past heading in that direction, calling out to each other as we all tried to determine what was going on. Finding the Pilus Prior, he grabbed Scaevola and was bellowing for the Century to rally on the standard, a call that I picked up so within a couple of moments, we were gathered and could begin trotting towards the wall.

"Do you know what's going on?" I gasped to the Pilus Prior as we ran along. I was cursing myself for my weakness; there was no way under normal circumstances that I should be out of breath after a run of less than a furlong, yet it showed me just how much a toll the reduced rations and the work had taken out of me. My next thought was that if it were this bad for me, how bad must it have been for the others?

I was snapped out of my head by the Pilus Prior. "Look!" He pointed and I followed his finger, cursing at what I saw.

The ramp was on fire, not smoldering like before in the earlier attempts by the Bituriges, but well and fully aflame. In the light of the growing blaze, we saw the silhouettes of men running in every direction, and just a few paces later we began to hear the cries and sounds of fighting. In accordance with our usual practice, two Legions were standing guard during the night, and they were fully engaged with the sortie that the Bituriges sent out. It was a well-planned and well-coordinated attack; the firing of the ramp accomplished by a mine that finally got through to the underlying timber and taking hold, while the sortie was timed so that it did not begin until the fire was well and truly started. Now, we were faced with a choice; do we fight off the attack, or do we put out the flames? Compounding the problem, the walls were lined with Bituriges hurling down their own flaming pots of pitch. Some of the pots hit men instead of the ramp, turning them into blazing,

500

screaming human torches until one of their comrades took mercy on them and killed them with a quick thrust, their corpses adding to the lurid light of the flames. Reaching the base of the ramp, we found Caesar there giving orders as Centurions came reporting in with their respective units, the general pointing them to where he wanted them to take their men followed by what he wanted them to do. Our Century came running up, slowing to a halt, the Pilus Prior saluting Caesar and asking for our orders, just like we were on the parade ground and not in the middle of chaos. Caesar was clearly illuminated by the flames, which were now beginning to climb through the first layers of logs on the ramp, and I could not help giving a worried glance up at the walls, thinking that rarely had our enemies had such a clear shot at our general. Just as calmly, Caesar pointed to the ramp, ordering us to go help deal with the flames, so I gave the order to ground shields and javelins, then trotted over to the ramp to help put out the fire.

The battle raged through the night, both against the Bituriges and the fire threatening to engulf the ramp. Our towers were dragged safely out of the way, so that now the real work was trying to quell the flames, which we did with a combination of water and dirt thrown into the spaces between the logs in an attempt to rob the fire of air to breathe. Scorpions in the small towers kept up a steady fire, trying to keep the Bituriges from raining their flaming missiles and bombs down on our heads. For the most part they were successful, yet there were inevitably casualties. A Sergeant in the fourth section of the Century, a man from Gades named Fabius was one of the unfortunates who took a direct hit from one of those savage weapons, going up in flames like a dry field from a lightning strike, and he screamed in agony as he ran crazily in circles before the Pilus Prior could get to him and put him out of his misery. His shrieks stopped abruptly, enabling us to hear the cheering of the Bituriges raining down on us, building a terrible hatred in us and a thirst for vengeance. Nearly as difficult to deal with as the flames was the smoke, billowing thick and choking from whatever holes in the ramp that it could find, blinding us and making us gag as we gasped for clean air. The smoke also served to obscure our vision in a wider sense; it was only with our ears whereby we could track the progress of the battle. One moment it sounded like the Gauls succeeded in pushing up to the edge of the ramp, then it would recede as our men fought back, driving them in the direction of the gate. I remember thinking at one point that if there is truly a Hades, it must be very much like the scene that night; the cacophony of screams from pain and fear, the clashing of metal on metal, the roaring sound the flames made, the fire creating a dancing, lurid light that the smoke diffused in such a way that made for a world of more shadow than substance. It was only because of the toughness and experience gained over the years that we did not falter that night, managing instead to put out the flames and beat the enemy back inside their walls by first light the next morning.

Most of the next day was spent repairing the damage done from the night before, mainly in shoring up the spots on the ramp where the fire did enough damage that there was a risk of collapse. On the other side, Vercingetorix apparently recognized the hopelessness of the situation, and smuggled in orders by way of the swamp to evacuate all the fighting men from the city that very night, under cover of darkness. It would have been a challenge, even if we were not alerted to the plan. Although it was not particularly unusual that we found out, the way that we discovered the plot was, because it came from their very own women. When the order was given that only fighting men would be evacuated, the women of the town began pleading and wailing for their men not to leave them to our mercy. This siege had gone on long enough, the last few days seeing enough bitter fighting that they were under no illusions about the fate that awaited them. They ran after their men as they gathered in the streets of the town to organize their escape, begging them to stay, while the men were equally determined to break out. Seeing that they were not having any success, some of the women ran to the walls to begin yelling at us, waving their arms and crying out to us in their tongue. Those women raised a racket to be sure; once their words were translated, the alert was sounded throughout the camp, and the cavalry was ordered out to surround the sides of the town at the edge of the marsh to warn us when the breakout began. I have often wondered whether or not these women were truly trying to save themselves and their children or, having recognized that their fate was decided, were determined that if they had to suffer the men should as well. After all, if you listen to women talk, all of the wars and killing since the dawn of time have been started by men, not women, and I suppose that there is some truth in that. Whatever their motives, they ensured that the men defending the town would not make good an escape from Avaricum, thereby suffering the same fate as everyone else in the town.

The order for the assault came during third watch that night, after the threat of the breakout was quelled and the damage repaired, the attack to be launched shortly after first light. Given the nature of

502

the siege, Caesar deemed that some subterfuge was in order, so shortly before dawn, those men of the 10th and the 7th taking part in the first wave of the assault were given the order to quietly assemble, then under cover of darkness and aided by a heavy downpour, move into the mantlets that lined the ramp. However, when the light finally grew strong enough for the defenders to see the immediate area, they were greeted by the sight of what appeared to be nothing but our normal routine. Legionaries from our Cohorts not participating in the attack and the other Legions began the day in the same way we had for the previous three weeks, trudging out in the rain to continue the work of filling in the last section of the ramp. The ramp was now built to a height where the wall could be scaled not just with the towers, but with ladders as well. These we dragged into the mantlets with us where we waited, crouching in discomfort, the sound of the rain beating down on the roof drowning out our heavy breathing and attempts at muttered conversation. The Pilus Prior had asked for our Century to be in the lead group and we were a bit surprised when the request was granted, until we discovered that he promised his personal share of the spoils to the Primus Pilus for the privilege, a fact that raised him in our esteem all the more when we found out about it. So now here we were, waiting for the signal to come out from under the cover of the mantlets and begin scaling the wall. The ramp was more than a hundred paces in width, giving us several points where we could scale the walls, and we had previously decided the spot where we would place the ladder, just a few dozen feet from the mantlet itself. The rain continued, yet even over the din we could hear the rumbling that signaled the advance of the tower and the beginning of the assault.

Seeing us burst out from the mantlets, our artillerymen in the towers immediately began a furious barrage, sweeping defenders from the wall. In quick order, the ladders were thrown up, and without waiting, I took my place as the first man up, with the Pilus Prior climbing the other ladder. The tower was rolling into place, even as men began climbing to the top level to wait for the ramp to drop, while the cries of alarm and panic rang out from the defenders on the wall now that they understood that the assault was finally beginning in earnest. Climbing the ladder, I was intent on what was happening at the top so that I would have some warning if one of the Bituriges pushed the ladder away to send me tumbling down. Seeing a set of hands grasp the top of the ladder, I felt it begin to move when a blur of motion streaked by at the edge of my vision, the hands disappearing as a bolt from a scorpion found its mark. Reminding myself to thank the men on the scorpions, I continued climbing, leaping over the parapet in the manner that had become my preferred method of mounting a wall. My sword was out and ready, but I felt naked without a shield, although it would have been a real impediment with the climb in the rain. A Bituriges warrior, perhaps in his thirty's, came roaring at me with a lunge of a spear from which I just managed to twist away. When he withdrew for another thrust, I struck downward with all my strength, the Gallic blade of the sword slicing through the heavy wooden shaft like it was a twig. My opponent's eyes widened in astonishment, and even I was a bit taken aback at the ease with which the blade cut through the wood, yet I recovered more quickly, making a quick thrust to the throat. The man who tried to push the ladder was already dead on the rampart, the bolt having gone clean through him. Hearing someone land behind me, I moved a step over to make room as we consolidated our position on the rampart. Another man came at me with an axe that he wielded overhand, drawing it back to deliver a blow that would have cut me in two lengthwise, except I took a quick step forward, punching my blade into his body right underneath his sternum. Letting out a gurgling shriek, he staggered backward, colliding with another man who was running to the attack, knocking him off balance and giving me the opportunity to cut him down as well. Within the first few moments, the area around us was cleared of Bituriges, at least of the kind who were still breathing. Looking around, I could see that this seemed to be the case all along the wall, which surprised me, given the bitterness with which they were battling to stop the siege these past days. Nevertheless, they had not completely given up yet as we saw what they were attempting to do. Deeming the loss of the walls a foregone conclusion, the Bituriges apparently decided to try to make an organized stand in the streets of the town, where they gathered in small, compact groups, their shields forming a barrier akin to our *testudo*. Every main street in the town soon had such formations, and we all stood on the parapet, looking down while there was a discussion among the senior Centurions about the best course of action. With more and more men joining us on the walls, we began to spread further along its circumference, with Legionaries moving to encircle the town. Seeing that we would not come down, but also seeing the spread of our army along the top of the wall the Bituriges panicked, obviously worried that we would cut off their last line of escape into the swampy area. Without any warning, their formations suddenly dissolved, men throwing their weapons down to begin

504

fleeing back towards the center of the town. With a roar, and with no command given, we leaped down into the muddy streets and gave chase. The slaughter was on.

The sacking of Avaricum was one of complete and total destruction, as we exacted further vengeance for the massacre at Cenabum, as well as for the trials and travails that the siege put us through. Out of the 40,000 people, men, women and children, only some 800 survived to escape through the swamp to make it to the camp of Vercingetorix. Our supply problem was temporarily assuaged, since the people of Avaricum had been living very well indeed, and we spent the next few days living off the town, eating like rich merchants. We were billeted in the town as well, staying in the houses of the people we had just slaughtered and if it were not for the misery that we endured during the siege, I believe that most of us would have elected to stay under the leather, as we said, because the thought of the restless spirits of the newly dead did not make us sleep easier. However, it was technically still winter, the weather still raw; there was often a skin of ice in our buckets in the morning, making us overlook our feelings of unease, so we settled in while we regrouped. Over the course of the siege, we lost perhaps 500 men throughout the army; in our Century, we had three more dead, bringing our strength down to 60, with perhaps another half dozen temporarily out of action with wounds. Once again, my tentmates managed to escape without injury or death, yet in my heart of hearts, I knew that it could not last forever. What worried me most was who it might be. When the Avaricum survivors arrived at the camp of Vercingetorix it triggered another crisis, with some of the allied tribes beginning to openly express misgivings about the prospects of fending off Rome. As he had before, Vercingetorix relied on his oratorical skills to avert the emergency, pointing out to his audience that he had been against the defense of Avaricum in the first place and that one could not expect to win every battle. This is a point we would have openly mocked, since we had been doing just that, but we were not there, and his rhetoric revived their flagging enthusiasm once more. He also announced that he would issue instructions for a fresh levy of troops to replace the losses suffered at Avaricum, while renewing his oath to drive us from Gaul. Sending out emissaries, he made good on at least his first promise of raising more troops, along with gaining oaths from the tribes who remained aloof to this point. Other events were taking place as well in other parts of Gaul, most worryingly among the Aedui. Some sort of disagreement erupted between two men, both contending for one office, resulting in a threat of civil war. Not wanting such unrest in our rear just when we were going to begin our campaign in earnest, Caesar kept us at Avaricum while he traveled to the lands of the Aedui to adjudicate the dispute. For us, there was a few days with nothing much to do; the bodies of the Bituriges were disposed of, the siege equipment either dismantled or destroyed, and our broken bits of gear mended or replaced. Consequently, for all intents and purposes, that period of time we spent while Caesar was off with the Aedui was our winter. The only change from the normal winter routine, besides its brevity, was that living arrangements were different, without the regularity found in our normal winter camp. Despite the Tribune in charge of billeting trying his best to group us in the same vicinity by putting all the men of one Century on the same street for example, it was not always possible. This had one unforeseen and not altogether unpleasant consequence, because it exposed us to more of our comrades in the army, so that fairly quickly what had been passing acquaintance became something closer to real friendship among some of us. There was another consequence, but this one did not surprise anyone all that much. For every new friendship formed, there were at least one or more disagreements, each of them almost invariably leading to fighting, keeping all the Centurions and Optios busy breaking up fights, yet despite our best attempts at preventing it, a few men lost their lives. Some were the losers in whatever fracas had broken out, but there were a few who were the killers and were then executed themselves. In these cases, the punishment is especially brutal, as a means of discouraging such behavior. The condemned man is required to run through a gauntlet consisting of the Century to which the murdered man belonged, each armed with axe handles or staves, and before the condemned can be put out of his misery, every bone in his body must be broken. It is a particularly painful and ignoble way to die, yet even with such penalties, men's passions would still get the better of them and in a moment of the same kind of madness that sometimes swept through us in battle, they would seal their own fate. I am somewhat ashamed to say that one of the men of the Second Cohort was condemned and executed in this manner, and I know that like all the other men of all the other Centuries who escaped punishment, we offered a prayer of thanks to the gods that the victim had not been in our Century. To avoid that, I kept a particularly close eye on both Atilius and Didius; Atilius for his joy of fighting men from other Legions, and Didius because of his shady dice. Fortunately, neither of them gave me any problems, although Didius took my extra attention with his usual grace. The only thing that really changed between Didius and myself was that he no longer uttered the same kind of threats that he did to the rest of his tentmates, knowing full well that such words, spoken even in jest, could be punished by death. I do not think he trusted me enough not to use one of his outbursts as an excuse to be rid of him, and I cannot say that the thought did not cross my mind, but whether I hated him or not, Didius was one of the men for whom I was responsible, and part of that responsibility meant trying to keep him alive. With all of these events taking place, it was with some relief that we viewed Caesar's return, since the discipline in the army was getting more and more difficult to enforce. It was not that we were any more lax in our enforcement of the rules, but in many ways an army is like a large pack of wolves. Once they scent blood, they will not be satisfied until their bloodlust is fully sated, and ours had just been aroused with the fall of Avaricum. The season was about to begin; we were anxious to pick up where we left off, so it was with much excitement and not a little relief on the part of the Centurions and Optios when we were given the orders to march. We were headed to a place called Gergovia.

Chapter 12: Gergovia

C aesar split the army in two parts, one under the command of Labienus, with the other under his own. Along with Labienus went the 7th, 12th, 15th and 16th, and the rest of us went with Caesar. Labienus went off to quell the tribes along the Sequana River, while Caesar's army marched first to Noviodunum, where he installed some of the 10,000 auxiliaries that he requisitioned from the Aedui as a garrison. This put us on the east bank of the Elaver (Allier) River, from where we turned south in pursuit of Vercingetorix. Once he detected our pursuit Vercingetorix, who was on the west, or opposite side of the river, hurried to burn the bridges, although he left the pilings intact. The result was that we marched side by side for three or four days, with Vercingetorix's advance patrols burning the bridges they found but keeping an armed force of sufficient size at the site of each bridge, telling Caesar that any attempt to repair them would be bloody and risky affairs. Yet Caesar came up with what can only be described as a brilliant solution to the problem. On the march one day, we entered a sizable forest, of sufficient size so that the whole column was hidden from sight from even the most alert of Vercingetorix's cavalry scouts. Once the whole army was within the screening safety of the woods, the command was given to halt, then very quickly, the 9th and 10th Cohorts from each Legion were ordered out of the formation and told to stand to the side. Once that was done, we reduced the width of our column and put the extra men in the spots where the removed Cohorts had been, to give the appearance that we were the same length as when we entered the woods, knowing that a shorter column would be easier to spot from the vantage point across the river than the width, and before much time elapsed, we were on the march again. Despite there being a slight delay, such stops are very common, and just as Caesar hoped, Vercingetorix suspected nothing. Staying behind with the 12 Cohorts, Caesar ordered the army to resume its march, stop at the normal time and make camp in the usual way. Once he calculated that we had reached the end of our march for that day, Caesar ordered the 12 Cohorts into action, marching the half mile back north to the site of the latest burned bridge. With the pilings still intact, it was not much work to repair the bridge, so by midnight that night, a rider came to camp and ordered us to backtrack and cross the bridge. Leaving the camp more or less intact, we just took our stakes with us but did not burn the towers or fill in the ditch because that would alert the enemy something unusual was happening. Catching Vercingetorix completely by surprise, by the time he recovered, we already had the detached Cohorts on the other side of the river, ready to defend the bridge before anything could be done. To his credit, he reacted quickly; realizing that he could not stop us, he instead decided to put distance on us by marching towards Gergovia at a quicker pace.

Now that we were on the right side of the river, we did not try to close the distance back to the enemy, not wanting to make haste and thereby stumble into an ambush. Despite the fact we had always prevailed to this point, we did have a grudging respect for Vercingetorix, because he was proving to be the one Gallic chieftain who demonstrated that he at least knew the types of tactics that gave his army the best chance of success, even if his men were too undisciplined and untrained to execute them. In fact, that was an ongoing topic of conversation around the fires at night; whether the Gauls were capable of instilling in themselves the kind of discipline that it would take to put their people on a more equal footing with us. From what I could tell, opinion seemed to be almost equally divided.

"Look at how they've picked up our siegecraft," argued Scribonius one night while I was visiting the fire of my old comrades. "And that *cunnus* Vercingetorix almost starved us out at Avaricum. Those are Roman tactics, so how long do you think it'll be before we're facing a *testudo*?"

"You can teach a bear to dance, but that doesn't mean he'll be able to sing," Vibius shot back, provoking a hoot of laughter from all of us, even Scribonius.

"True enough, but they're not bears, they're men. And they're smart men," Scribonius countered. Vibius, and truth be told, Vellusius and Atilius, along with a couple men from another section in the Century who had taken to sitting at our fire, voiced their disagreement.

"They're not as smart as us," Vibius said scornfully. "Look at how they fight, Scribonius. Even since Vercingetorix has been in command, they still line up and come running at us, flailing about and howling like Cerberus, even after we cut them down like wheat before the scythe. And that hasn't changed one bit in the years we've been out here."

"I'm not saying that it won't take them time to change," Scribonius replied, and I could tell he knew how weak that sounded.

"It's been five years Scribonius," this from Atilius, his comment being met with a chorus of agreement.

There was a pause; I was staring into the fire, only gradually becoming aware that the silence was drawing out, and when I looked up, I saw all eyes were on me.

"So what do you think, Tit......I mean Optio?" I glared at Vibius; we had talked several times about his habit of forgetting to address me by my rank in the presence of others.

It is not that I cared particularly, but addressing a superior above the rank of Sergeant by their praenomen is technically an offense, and I was worried that someone like Didius would report this to the Pilus Prior if he ever got mad at Vibius, which in turn might force Pulcher to act. Feeling I made my point with a look, I considered the question carefully before answering, realizing that as Optio, no matter what my relationship had been with these men, I was still their superior, and rankers tend to take what their superiors tell them as if it came from the lips of Caesar himself.

"I don't think the Gauls are as stupid as you think Vibius," I began, and I could see his eyes narrow a bit, a sure sign that he was close to being angry, so before he could say anything that would put us both in difficulty, I hurriedly continued, "but you can't deny that no matter what the reason, they're not picking up our tactics. So maybe it's not intelligence but some other fault in their character."

510

Even as I mentally congratulated myself on such a diplomatic answer, Vibius pressed me further. "So what's this character flaw, if it's not that they aren't as intelligent as we are?"

Now I was on the spot, because truth be told, I had just made this up as a way to avoid an argument, since the truth was that I agreed with Scribonius. My mind raced for an answer as I looked at Vibius, sitting across the fire, his arms folded, giving me what I knew to be his triumphant look at outwitting me. He knows me too well, I thought wryly; he saw through my ruse and was putting me on the spot now.

"Constancy," I blurted out.

"Constancy? What by Pluto's thorny cock does that even mean? Is that an officer's word?" Vibius laughed, pleased at his own wit, and I felt my ears beginning to burn as blood rushed to my face.

"No Vibius, it's not an officer's word. Everyone knows what it means."

"So what does it mean?"

Despite having only a very vague idea, I had long since learned that sounding confident in your answer was half the battle to being believed, so I plunged in.

"It's the aspect of your character that'll see you through tough and dangerous times."

"That's just bravery," Vibius countered, and I shook my head, the idea of what I meant taking more substantial form.

"It's not just bravery though. It's the part of your character that gets you through difficult but not dangerous tasks as well, like........our training."

That was it, I thought, and I could see heads that had been still or even shaking back and forth at what I was saying start to stop. Now to get them to nod up and down, I thought, as I finished my thought.

"The training is tough, but it doesn't require all that much courage, or bravery, whatever you want to call it. It's just like at

511

Avaricum. Caesar gave us the opportunity to call off the siege, but to a man, we all refused. It wasn't bravery, because we're all veterans and we know that if we aren't going to fight that day, we'll be fighting on the next, so bravery played no part in our decision. At least it didn't in mine. No, it was more about seeing a job through, no matter how hard or unpleasant. That's constancy."

Now the heads were nodding, and I saw with some relief that even Vibius seemed to accept that my response made sense. Not wanting to lose the advantage, I finished.

"And that's what I think is missing from the Gauls. It's not bravery; we've seen enough examples to know that it's not through a lack of bravery that we defeat them. It's just when things get tough, or they require a lot of hard work, with little immediate payoff, the Gauls aren't capable of seeing things through."

And that is what I believe to this day.

At the end of our fifth day on the march, we came within sight of Gergovia. Hardened veterans we may have been, but the sight of that hilltop town still gave us pause. Like most Gallic forts that grow into towns, it was perched on a hill, except this one was higher and more massive than any we faced before. Approaching from the north, it was easy to see that the slope on that side was almost vertical, immediately telling us that there would be no assault from that direction. Despite it being at the end of our marching day, Caesar pushed us on to swing around to the east, while he and his bodyguard rode around the base of the hill looking for a weak point. It turned out that the east side was just as bad as the north, although we did find a good spot for a camp, southeast of the hill, beginning the process while Caesar continued exploring. The site for our camp was on a low hill, giving a clear view of the town to our northwest, with a small valley perhaps two miles wide between the two points. Caesar returned shortly before dark, calling a meeting of his staff and the Primi Pili of the Legions, leaving the rest of us to sit and speculate about what would happen next.

"No doubt he'll want to invest the place, but by the gods, that's one big hill," the Pilus Prior mused as we stared up at its dark bulk, now crowned with lights from the torches the Gauls had placed along the walls of the town.

Sitting around our own fire that night was the Pilus Prior, Scaevola, Calienus and I, while Zeno and the Pilus Prior's slave, a Thracian named Patroclus I believe, were preparing our meal for the evening. I will say that one of the things I did like about being Optio was not having to worry about cooking meals, the one part of soldiering I always disliked the most, although I have no idea why.

"I wonder how big around that bastard is," Calienus mused. "Because no doubt Caesar's going to want a circumvallation of it, and that's going to be a lot of work."

I could only nod in agreement with his sentiment; we had marched too long with Caesar not to know at least some of his habits, and the one thing the man believed in was the engineering aspect of warfare. This is not to say that we did not complain all the same, but deep down we all knew the truth of the soldier's saying that was most often repeated while engaged in the use of a pick or shovel.

"The more you sweat now, the less you'll bleed later."

But it is a soldier's right, given to us by Mars and Bellona themselves, to complain, and we took full advantage of that gift. Sitting there that night, I was struck by a thought.

"Do you suppose that there's some Gauls up there, looking down at us, and they're complaining about all the work they're going to have to do to keep us out of that town?"

This drew a hearty laugh from my companions, and I was secretly pleased that they liked my wit.

Once our Primus Pilus was briefed by Caesar, he summoned all of the Centurions and Optios to a meeting in the forum. Gathering around, I found myself standing next to Crastinus, our old Pilus Prior and now the Primus Princeps, the Centurion in charge of the Third Century. Seeing me, he grinned cheerfully, giving me a slap on the back.

"*Salve* Pullus, it looks like this is going to be a right bastard of a job. Did you see the size of that hill? And how many of the bastards that are up there on it that want to keep us from taking it? It's going to be bloody, that much is sure."

Before I could respond, the Primus Pilus called for our attention.

"Men, this is going to be a right bastard of a job."

Both Crastinus and I had trouble suppressing a snicker at his unintentional echo of Crastinus' words. Fortunately we were quiet enough in our mirth that the Primus Pilus did not hear. Continuing, he jerked his thumb over his shoulder in the direction of the hill.

"But you can see that for yourselves. Caesar's done a reconnaissance of the hill, and there's only one place that we have a chance of cracking this nut. But in order to do that," now he turned to point at a smaller hill directly south of Gergovia, squatting like a small guardian over the narrow dip between the two hills, "we have to take that first."

About halfway up the slope of the hill of Gergovia stood an outer wall, constructed as a buffer between it and the walls of the town proper. In the cleared area between the two walls on the slopes was the camp of Vercingetorix's army. The strategic value of the small hill is that it overlooked the stream that fed the river to the south of us that was our water supply. However, that stream was also the water supply for the Gauls in Gergovia, along with their army encampment, so if we could command the heights above the stream we could cut off their water supply, or at least a major source. But Vercingetorix was no fool, and he saw that as well, so in the time he had before we arrived, he put his army to work fortifying the small hill and manning it with warriors. Even from this distance we could see that a wall of some size had been thrown up; our best hope was that it was done hastily, and not constructed like the wall at Avaricum, or we would indeed have our hands full.

"Caesar hasn't decided when and who'll assault that hill, but that's the first step. So stand ready, because we don't know when, and we don't know who he'll send to take that hill. All we do know is that it'll happen."

"I'll bet 500 sesterces that I know who it'll be," called the Hastatus Posterior, Centurion of the Sixth Century, a squat little turd named Felix, reputed to be one of the worst gamblers in the army despite his nickname, a fact that did not dissuade him from wagering on just about anything. Despite his reputation for being unlucky, at gambling at least, he was supposed to be one of the most

514

fearsome fighters in the Legion, and he immediately had several takers on his wager.

"Good thing we just got paid at Avaricum," laughed Crastinus, "or poor Felix would be so far in debt that he'd be busted back to the ranks."

For that is yet another regulation in the army; if a Centurion falls into debt over a certain amount and is unable to pay it off, he is subject to discipline. If the money he owes is to his own men, it is even more egregious, and a flogging with the scourge could be ordered. Luckily for Felix, his men loved him too much to do something like report him, which was just as well for his sake, because when the time came, he lost yet another bet.

For several days, we did nothing but watch our cavalry force skirmish with the Gauls. It was decided that a night assault on the hill had the best chance for success, and the moon was waxing full those first nights. Taking this opportunity, we improved the fortifications of our camp, since all indications were that we were in for a long siege, longer than Avaricum by far, and we accepted as an article of faith that we would try to completely encircle the hill, despite it being many miles around. Early in our first year on campaign in Gaul, had we not dug a ditch and built a wall 18 miles long, we reasoned? It seemed to be the only way to contain such a large army here, but still no orders were given to begin the entrenching work. Finally, the first moonless night was about to arrive, and word was sent that it would be the men of the 8th and 9th making the assault, much to the chagrin of Felix and to the joy of all the men who counted on his famous luck, or lack thereof, on holding for at least one more wager. That night we were ordered to stay in our Legion areas, it being customary for the men left behind to gather at the gates to wish the men going on whatever mission luck as they left. On this occasion, however, Caesar did not want to give the slightest hint that anything was different, so instead we sat by the fire, listening to the tramping of boots and clinking of gear as they marched out of the gate. Since there was no way to see how the assault was going, the distance from camp to the hill being a little more than two miles, it was only possible to hear that there was a battle but not how it was going. Therefore, we decided to retire for the night, trusting to our comrades and Caesar that when we awoke, the hill would be ours.

And it was; Caesar and the two Legions were in possession of the hill. Under the cover of darkness they threw up their own fortifications, these facing the opposite direction than the original ones. Immediately on his return to camp, Caesar ordered the digging of two parallel trenches linking the two camps, allowing men to move between the two undetected and protected from any missile or artillery fire. By making two trenches, placed about ten feet apart, we could also allow two-way traffic, or in the event of an emergency, send men up both trenches. It was one thing to dig a simple trench, even if it was really two trenches two miles long apiece, but we soon learned of the calculations that Caesar had made for a complete investment of Gergovia, and it was disheartening to say the least. In order to completely encircle the town and camp of Vercingetorix's army, we would not only have to surround the hill that the town sat on, but another promontory to the west that Vercingetorix turned into a stronghold, including the saddle between the two heights where part of his army was camped. This translated to the creation of about 12 miles of fortifications, much more complex work than a simple trench, since in Caesar's army the dimensions of fortifications were different than what other commanders of the recent and historic past had deemed sufficient, which may have added to the strength of the fortification but also meant more work for the men. A ditch three feet wider and five feet deeper may not seem like a lot, but it is just that much more work that has to be done. Add to that the necessity of creating a palisade far in excess of even the largest camp, not to mention that the stakes we used were already part of our marching camp, required more trees to be cut down and stakes fashioned from them, all of a uniform size. Then there were the towers that had to be built and positioned at intervals along the distance of the entrenchments, all within sight of the towers on either side, to allow signals to be passed quickly, along with providing mutual support. Finally, smaller camps for housing the men not standing watch on the walls at any given moment had to be constructed as well, so that they were not forced to spend a significant amount of their time off duty actually moving back and forth between their posts and the main camp. And all this was to be done with just us, the Legionaries; auxiliaries and cavalry are never allowed to perform any of the labor, nor are the slaves who are assigned to the Legion, nor any civilians, slave or free. From a labor standpoint, this meant that Caesar had six Legions; at that time our combined strength was perhaps 25,000 men, give or take a hundred, down from our original strength of more than 35,000 when all of the Legions were at full strength. Years of fighting had been cruel, but so were the illnesses and diseases, along with the injuries and the drunken brawls, whittling us down bit by bit. This was what Caesar had at hand to not only conduct an operation of investment, but also to keep at least one, if not two Legions constantly on alert to a counterattack by the enemy. In short, it was a seemingly impossible task, even for the army of Caesar.

Compounding this problem came what I believe was perhaps the biggest shock that Caesar, and by extension the rest of us, ever received. While Caesar believed, with good cause I might add, that he had resolved the dispute among the Aedui and secured the stability of the tribe that was our staunchest ally, it was not to be. The Aedui rose in revolt, led by none other than the *cunnus* Convictolitavus, the very man who Caesar had negotiated with the opposing faction to put into the post of Vergobret. But Gauls are Gauls, and if there was ever proof needed, this betrayal is the best example, because Convictolitavus owed the very influence he used to incite a rebellion against the man who gave it to him in the first place. As we would find out later, the faithlessness of Convictolitavus did not come cheaply; Vercingetorix offered him a bribe massive enough that the *cunnus* could buy off a good number of sub-chiefs to join the cause. It was not all money that persuaded them, however. Apparently a feeling had been growing that perhaps Vercingetorix was indeed the man who could bring Caesar down, and the Aedui were starting to grow concerned that the Arverni, traditional rivals, would then become the most powerful tribe in Gaul, should they be victorious. Convinced that throwing their weight behind Vercingetorix would tip the scales in the favor of the Gauls, the Aedui reasoned, not without some logic, that since they could then claim to be the decisive factor in the defeat of Caesar and Rome, they could at the very least claim equal partnership as dominant tribe with the Arverni. Such was the mindset at least of the man who sounded a call to arms among the Aedui that some 10,000 men answered, and it was the news of this column now approaching from the east that spurred Caesar into sounding an emergency assembly, late in the morning.

"Comrades," he cried, once we were assembled in the forum, the Centurions in the rear Cohorts relaying his words for all to hear, "we have been betrayed!"

Despite having already gotten wind of this, his confirmation produced a stir, and he waited for a moment for the men to subside.

517

"Even now, a force of the faithless Aedui are marching to join Vercingetorix, and we will find ourselves trapped between two armies."

One aspect of Caesar's leadership was that, rather than try to minimize the danger, he was more likely to confront what we would consider bad news head on, and indeed sometimes I think he may have exaggerated it a bit, given how things always seemed to turn out in our favor. Nonetheless, this was one time that he seemed to be genuinely, if not alarmed, at the least surprised. "What I am about to ask you to do will not be easy, given the labors that we have been undergoing," he continued, "so I will not order, but I will ask you to do this for your commander. We must not waste time; we must march, now. I will leave two Legions here, one in the big camp, and the 8th manning the small camp. The four remaining Legions I ask to march with me, to confront the Aedui. Together, we will make them pay for their treachery!"

Now, we would have gone no matter what, except if he ordered it, we would have done so grumbling every step of the way. However, by couching it as he did, a humble favor begged of us by their commander, it made us not only willing, but eager to grant it to him. As the men began to cheer and shout their agreement to march, I was swept up in my admiration for the man before us. Once again, he struck the perfect notes, making such a beautiful melody that we could not help wanting to dance to it. Breaking the formation, we ran to get our gear to form up to march, and it was almost like we were going to some sort of games or festival, so lighthearted was the mood. I even caught Vibius smiling and talking animatedly to Scribonius, although when he saw me looking at him, he tried to put on a scowl, as if he were displeased, but even he could not pull it off and we both burst out laughing as we got ready to march.

The Aedui host was commanded by a sub-chief named Litaviccus, and along with his 10,000 men on foot, he had about 500 cavalry. Marching with the 9th, 11th and 13th, along with all of our cavalry, our force included a contingent of Aeduan cavalry, at least the ones who did not flee to join the rebels. When Caesar learned that it was Litaviccus leading the advancing column he ordered the arrest of the sub-chief's two brothers who were serving in our cavalry, but they had already fled to join him. We did not much blame them for that; blood is blood, and it is only right that family stand together. It did not mean that we would not kill them just as quickly and unmercifully as anyone else, it would just not be with the rancor we felt for men who chose to rebel on their own, without the inducement of family ties. On their own march, at the end of the day, we later learned that Litaviccus held an assembly of his army, whereupon he informed them that Caesar had already treacherously murdered all of the Aedui cavalry, then producing the same two brothers, made them swear that they managed to escape and the story was true. This understandably roused the Aedui into a great fury, so that they resumed the march the next day in a state of great wrath. Meanwhile, we marched through the day and into the night, covering more than 20 miles before it got dark. To be sure we were tired, but we were still in great spirits, with Caesar marching on foot with us every step of the way, one of his slaves leading Toes, his horse that was almost as famous as Caesar by this time. As far as whether or not his steed had toes, as the name implies and for which he earned his fame, I will make no comment on that matter because I do not wish to dispute more learned men who claim that the horse's hooves were of this nature. Our scouts spotted the enemy's camp just as they were beginning to start on their day's march, prompting Caesar to order us to deploy in a *triplex acies*, as if we were about to go into battle, which very well may have been the case. Taking our spot on the far right, with the 9th to our left, we waited while Caesar and his bodyguard rode ahead under a flag of truce. Accompanying him were two Aedui who had not defected, Eporedorix and Viridomarus, two young noblemen, who ended up being the unwitting cause for the collapse of the Aedui army, and rebellion. It turned out that Litaviccus had mentioned these two men by name as two of those slaughtered, since both of them came from powerful families and were well-respected by the rest of the Aedui. Seeing them alive and unharmed, the Aedui instantly knew they were duped, but before they could drag him off his horse, Litaviccus and his retainers escaped back to Aedui territory. The entire force of 10,000 men then swore another oath of loyalty to Caesar, claiming that they were misled. Caesar accepted their oaths and they went unpunished; in fact, he considered these to be the 10,000 men that the Aedui swore to provide when he adjudicated the dispute between them. Subsequently, we were told to stand down, although no camp was made, just being given a total of a full watch to rest before we turned around to head back to camp at Gergovia.

It was during this rest interval that a courier came galloping up to Caesar on a lathered horse, leapt off and cried, "Caesar, the camp's under heavy attack! It's about to fall!"

Vercingetorix saw an opportunity, and he seized it. Mounting a full scale assault on the big camp, the Legate Caesar left behind, Fabius, with us for a couple of years at this point, was barely managing to maintain the integrity of the camp defenses. It was our artillery that saved the men of the 14th and half of the 8th from destruction, wreaking havoc in the ranks of the Gauls while, despite our fatigue, we marched through the night, hurrying not just to the aid of our comrades, but to rescue our valuables left back in camp. Doubtless, we wanted to save other Romans, just do not mistake our motives for being completely selfless. Many, if not most of us, were at least as concerned with the camp being plundered as we were the fate of fellow Legionaries. Whatever it was that pushed each of us, we marched through the night, coming within sight of the camp shortly before dawn. The Arverni, now that they faced the bulk of the army, immediately retreated back up the hill, yet they inflicted a fair amount of damage, mostly on our men, and mostly the result of slings and arrows. This had one somewhat happy effect; the number of killed in the Cohorts was not nearly as high as it could have been, but even so, the 8th and 14th suffered a good number of men out of action for a while. And Gergovia still remained unconquered.

While we rested, Caesar made his way to the small camp to check on the situation there, and it was when he was there he saw that finally, Vercingetorix made a mistake. Like Caesar, the Gaul recognized that the saddle between the plateau on which the town sat and another set of hills to the west was of strategic importance, because it offered the only route that could safely be traveled by mules, thereby making it the main avenue for supplies. However, because he recognized its importance, Vercingetorix chose to concentrate his forces, and to do so, he abandoned the hill nearest the second camp that overlooked the beginning of the area of the saddle. Vercingetorix pulled his men and positioned them to defend the most practicable approach, located on the west side of the clump of hills across the saddle from Gergovia. If we could gain the height of the hill they abandoned, we would in effect be on the flank of the Gauls, almost directly behind the defenses that they were erecting to block the expected line of attack. It was from this that Caesar formed his plan, and he hurried back to the main camp to put it into action. We were about to assault Gergovia, and suffer the first taste of defeat that most of us had experienced.

The plan was to convince Vercingetorix that he had made the right choice, that it was indeed the western slope of the hills that we were going to attack. To that end, at the beginning of third watch at

520

midnight, Caesar sent the cavalry out, not with any stealth but with the exact opposite affect, ordering them to make a great show of leaving the camp. The move was designed to be so obvious that even in the gloom, Vercingetorix's sentries would spot the movements and alert him. Once dawn broke, another mounted contingent left the camp, and despite looking like cavalry, they were anything but mounted troops. Using the mule drivers and giving them helmets from stores as well as from the dead, and accompanied by some real cavalry, this group made another great show of leaving camp, following the path of the river west, acting like they were going to swing around to support the expected assault from that direction. Reaching a spot about four miles downriver where there was a large forest that reached to the banks of the river, they hid there. Following shortly were the men of the 14th, again making no attempt to hide their intentions and traversing the same route that the false cavalry took a short time before, coming to a halt in the same woods. The original cavalry force that was dispatched at midnight had by this time ridden even further to the west than the spot where the other two units were hiding. During this activity, we were ordered to make for the small camp, by way of the trench, with strict orders to keep the standards or eagles below the lip of the trench, and to move in complete silence. This we did, covering the ground quickly but then we stopped just short of the camp, not wanting our numbers in the small camp to suddenly and mysteriously increase. Caesar had by this time returned to the small camp himself, from where he would direct operations. The 10,000 Aedui were left in the large camp, but they had a part to play in this drama as well. This was by far the most complex operation we had ever attempted, with much depending on everyone doing their part, and most importantly, everything going right. I believe it was only because Caesar put so much faith in our abilities that he was willing to gamble in this manner in the first place.

Once the army was assembled, minus the 14th down in the woods, we were given our final orders and instructions. Much to our initial chagrin, Caesar ordered the 10th to stay in reserve, although it turned out to be a move blessed by the gods. Command of what would be the assault element was by Caesar, who would stay for the time being with the reserves, and his orders were clear; the primary goal of the operation was to separate the army of Vercingetorix from the town proper. Only if the opportunity presented itself in an open gate or some other favor of the gods was the assault to continue into the town. I very distinctly remember that Caesar placed an emphasis on the Legions not stopping to plunder the camps of the Arverni army, but instead sweep them from the area between the two walls before maneuvering into position behind the enemy army, who by now looked like they were completely convinced that an assault from the west was imminent. Supporting our belief was the fact that Vercingetorix shifted the remainder of his troops to the expected main line of resistance, urging them to improve the fortifications in anticipation of our assault. In other words, the ruse worked perfectly, and all was ready for us to spring the trap to stop that bastard here and now.

In my mind, the only thing more fickle than Gauls are the gods themselves, which is why I have severed all ties with them now. In the beginning, Caesar's plan worked brilliantly; on a blast from the *cornu*, along with the waving of Caesar's standard that was relayed back to the main camp, the assault began just as planned. Springing from the gates of the small camp, four Legions quickly assembled in the relatively open and flat ground to the east, or to the right of the front gate as we were facing Gergovia, quickly and efficiently, a move that was practiced both in training and in battle hundreds of times. We of the 10th exited the camp as well, and were standing on the slope of the hill watching our comrades begin their march up the opposite incline. The slope rose northward before bending slightly west to form the saddle between the plateau and the hills where Vercingetorix was waiting for an assault that would never come, at least from the direction he was expecting it. Quickly, the Legions marched up the hill and with almost contemptuous ease, quickly crossed over the outer wall, knocking it over in many places as the Legionaries discovered that it was just loosely piled rock, with no mortar to hold it together. Attacking three separate camps of the enemy, the only men they found defending them were the sick, lame or lazy as we said in the army. Or in one case, the bodyguard of one of the kings of the Nitiobriges, who was forced to flee naked on his horse while his bodyguard stayed and died to buy him time. The sight of his white, puny body astride his horse galloping away gave us much cause for mirth, and I had tears streaming from my eyes as I watched him flee. Little did I know that before this day was through I would be crying again, if for different reasons.

I cannot say exactly what went wrong, or where it went wrong, although I have my suspicions. Oh, the reason things went sour in a hurry was clear enough; once they swept through the camps, Caesar ordered the *cornu* to sound the recall, apparently so that the Legions would re-form back up to face the inevitable counterattack from

522

Vercingetorix once he was aware that there was a Roman army in his rear, except I do not think that is where things went bad. To my dying breath, I believe that the men in the assault element heard the recall, but chose to ignore it. Instead, they were pushed on by Centurions like a man named Lucius Favius, who apparently was on the sick list when Avaricum was sacked and therefore did not receive any share of the spoils. This day, the initial success was so easy and so overwhelming that he convinced the men of his Century to continue to the walls of the town proper, his goal being getting into the town first to grab his share of loot. Once a Century moved in that direction, the others, not wanting to miss out on the chance of spoils, were quick to follow. Before any orders could be given or relayed, the whole army was charging toward the walls of the town. The first Century to arrive naturally was that of Favius, who was boosted onto the walls by his men, whereupon he immediately pulled some of them up to the parapet. Elsewhere along the walls of the town, we could see women beseeching the Romans not to enter, some of them even throwing themselves down to the men to be ravished by them in a vain attempt to assuage their lust. I cannot speak of their fates, but I think it sufficient to say that I hope that any man left alive who was part of what happened suffers nights of tormented sleep because of it. Initially, everything was going our way, while the sight of Romans at the walls of the town created a panic among the townspeople and the garrison of the town. Even the Legion designated to fortify the hill vacated by Vercingetorix, the main objective of this operation, now looked and saw what appeared to be a town falling under our arms. Dropping what they were doing, they hurried to join their comrades, who were now at the base of the town wall trying to help each other get up and over it. Then, the tide began to turn as the people within the town started to realize that as formidable as our army was, what faced them was only a fraction of it, and besides that, our men were still vastly outnumbered by the Gauls on the other side of the wall. Within moments, the fighting became fierce, with more defenders appearing in answer to the cries of the women and children, while some of the women were brandishing their babies in front of their defenders in an obvious attempt to convince them to repel our men at the walls.

I will say that the Gallic warriors did not take much convincing, and almost before we could realize exactly what was happening, our army was in trouble. Caesar sent orders for the Tribune Sextius, left behind in the second camp with five Cohorts of the 13th on guard, to bring the men out to form a line farther down the slope than where we were presently standing. Their directions were to wait and pounce on the right flank of the enemy if they began to pursue our army at the walls, who at that very moment were beginning to take steps backward. Following Caesar, the 10th moved down the slope to perhaps 100 paces from the outer wall, while he waited further developments. One Century was at one of the town gates, their Centurion leading an attempt to tear it down when he was overwhelmed by a counterattack of the enemy. Surrounded by Gauls the Centurion, Petronius was his name, fought savagely to keep the enemy at bay while ordering his Century to retreat. At first they refused, but finally they withdrew down the hill, leaving Petronius behind to die a glorious death, taking as many of the Gauls with him as he could. As this was going on, Caesar moved us into a position that was almost perpendicular to the outer wall, in the anticipation of being able to descend on the flank of the enemy should our men turn back, and the Gauls decided to pursue. Our men at the wall were engaged in a ferocious battle, as now the final trick the gods held in store for us came into play. Looking to their right, to the east, our men saw the Aedui column ascending the hill in their own diversionary attack. I believe with all of my heart that, had the men at the wall not been so hard pressed, they would have had the presence of mind to remember that this could only be the Aedui launching their assault and were in fact part of our force. Unfortunately, in their embattled state, with every man fighting for his life, what they saw was another Gallic army heading more or less in their direction, and this was enough to break the dam and release the flood.

Our men, beginning with those on the right nearest to the advance of the misidentified Aedui, turned and began running down the slope, triggering an effect much like a cascade, with each successive Century either sensing or seeing the Century to their right suddenly turning and running. Caesar was rapidly marching us east now, to a small rise that served as the outer edge of the rest of the army's retreat. Using faultless logic, he quickly determined that fleeing men will automatically take the easiest escape route available, and would therefore not bother with running up the side of a hill, however small, if there was a way to avoid it. The configuration of the slope was such that it served to act as a funnel between two small rises, just bumps really, but it was between those bumps that the vast majority of our army headed. The 10th was on the small hill on the eastern side, still facing perpendicular to the outer wall, with Sextius and his five Cohorts opposite us on the other. The Gauls, seeing the backs of a Roman army for the first time in their lives were in hot pursuit, the troops of Vercingetorix, by this point alerted to what was happening in their rear, now leading the chase. Like an avalanche, our army went streaming down the slope, heading for a clear and level area where they could form up again, except if we and the men of the 13th did not stop the pursuit of Vercingetorix's men, they would have no chance to regroup. It was of the utmost importance that we stop the enemy's headlong pursuit, so to that end, we arrayed ourselves in a single line of Centuries to give all of us a chance to assault them as they went running by. The enemy came closer and closer, not seeming to notice us standing on the slopes of the small hill, so intent were they on the destruction of the other Legions.

"Prepare Javelins!"

The familiar command rang out and as one, we pulled our arms back.

"Release!"

Like an invisible hand, our first volley knocked men down, those being struck crashing into the man next to them, slowing the headlong pursuit for a moment. However, the momentum built up by some 30,000 men running downhill, trying to finish the first victory against Rome which any of them had ever been part of, was more than enough to restart them almost immediately. A second volley followed, but while the momentum slowed again, it did not stop.

"Draw swords!"

Then a heartbeat later, "*Porro!*"

Then we were on them, using the advantage of the slope to help build our own momentum, and I went roaring down the hill to smash into a Gaul who wore a look of extreme surprise on his face, reveling in the feel of my blade sinking deep into his gut. Giving a twist before I withdrew, I left the man screaming in agony from being disemboweled in my wake. Wading into the mass of Gauls, they were just beginning to realize the threat to their flank and stopping their pursuit to face us, but not before I killed two more men. Completely forgetting my responsibilities as Optio, I was once more a *Gregarius* concerned with nothing more than killing the man in front of me, and I roared my delight and joy at being set free to do what I knew best. My Gallic blade made a distinctively different sound when it clashed against another blade, one that seemed to me to be a note of the most wonderful music, and I reveled in the song as I thrust, parried and hacked my way through the enemy. It did not matter to me whether or not they carried sword or spear, whether they held a shield or had mail armor like mine. All it meant was that the manner in which I killed each of them was slightly different. What mattered was that they faced death, and that I was victorious. There is something intoxicating about imposing your will on another man, to the point where you take their lives from them at your whim. Perhaps it is evil, or wrong, but I would merely ask, how could something that is evil feel so wonderful? Everywhere around me similar contests raged, and the Gauls started to reel back from our onslaught. I was vaguely aware that barely 200 or 300 paces away, our comrades of the 13th were meting out the same type of destruction, and it was between these two inexorable forces that the Gauls found themselves. Under such intense pressure, it was not long before the first Gaul, a man once flushed with victory, bursting with the idea that at long last they had defeated a Roman army, now found himself taking that first, inevitable step backwards. What I knew at that point, and it was all that I knew, was that my blade was singing a song, and I wanted it to continue. Step forward, wait for them to make the first move, parry it, then strike quickly. First position, despite it being awkward without a shield and feeling slightly ridiculous offering nothing in defense but my left arm, yet it never ceased to amaze me how one's opponent would always lunge to make that first strike, even if it was only my left arm. Twice a Gaul hit their mark, albeit with glancing blows, so my arm was now covered in blood as I held it out like an offering to the gods, daring my next opponent to strike it. Then, as suddenly as it began, it was all over. One instant I was surrounded by snarling Gauls, the next they were moving back up the hill, with a considerable number of bodies heaped in front of us. Standing there for a moment, panting for breath, my right arm began shaking from the effort and my left started to burn, the by now-familiar feeling that liquid fire had been poured in a couple of lines along my forearm. I remember thinking to myself after inspecting my left arm that I was going to need stitches and that my arm was getting increasingly scarred, yet before I could spend too much time on such notions, the Pilus Prior's voice penetrated through my fog.

"Pullus! Get me a butcher's bill immediately." Automatically I answered, my mind struggling with what needed to be done next.

Ah yes, I thought, the butcher's bill, the list of casualties, dead and wounded. I remember thinking to myself that it should not be a very long list; I had fought in enough battles to sense how hard the fighting was on our side, and this one was going to be fairly light. And it was, in a manner of speaking. In other ways, however, it was one of the most costly battles we ever fought.

Moving among the Century, I asked each Sergeant for their list of dead and wounded, and as I thought, the list was very short. It was only as we were forming up that I noticed a spot missing in the formation, my heart resuming its hammering in my chest at the sight of the empty place. Our wounded were already carried off, and I was sure I had an accurate count of them; only four men were wounded severely enough to need a litter. I began moving along the line where our Century had been fighting, but it was only after I moved some bodies of Gallic dead, along with one wounded Gaul who I finished off, that I found him. Calienus was already dead; his eyes staring openly at the sky, a gash across his throat making it look like he had an extra mouth. I have mentioned before the problem with the Gallic long sword, that it is a slashing weapon, not a stabbing weapon, and being such it means that there are relatively few spots where a slash can kill instantly. Somehow, an either incredibly skilled or incredibly lucky Gaul found his mark, and now Calienus was dead. Beloved Calienus, my first Sergeant and a good friend, a man who had been through so many battles and skirmishes that I could not count, had somehow been slain. Without thinking, and in truth without much caring, I let out a cry of anguish while falling to my knees. My tentmates, hearing me, broke formation to come rushing to my side and when they saw who was lying there, joined me in our moment of anguish. I felt tears running down my face, except for some reason I was unashamed of them at this moment, perhaps because I was not alone, as I looked up to see both Scribonius and Vibius across from me, their faces marked by the anguish I felt. Even Didius knelt beside us, his tears mingling with the rest of ours in our grief at the loss of this man, this veteran who was our first and best friend when we were *tirones*, raw youth with nothing more than a dream of being a Legionary. It was Calienus who took the time to explain the reasons for some of the things we were forced to do, who commiserated with us when we needed commiseration, and had been harsh with us when we needed that.

527

Now, he was dead, and I was stunned to find how much it actually hurt.

Despite running from the wall, the men from the other Legions stopped on their own once they reached the point the ground got level to re-form and were now standing there, waiting for the charge of the Gauls. However, the enemy had experienced enough and were already streaming back up the hill, stopping only long enough to shake their weapons at us, shouting cries of exultation that rang bitterly in our ears. The men of the 13th and the 10th were ordered to march back down the hill once it was clear that the Gauls were done for the day, and it was an incredibly quiet and somber army that returned to the main camp via the double trench. It was no surprise; while the 10th's casualties were extremely light, no matter how painful they may have been to some of us, the Legions that took place in the assault could not say the same. An incredible number of Centurions, 46 total, along with some 700 *Gregarii* were killed. The rest of that day and all that night were spent in sending our slain brothers to the afterlife, followed by the inevitable reorganization that came from having so many officers slain. Some Optios from our Legion were promoted and transferred to the junior Cohorts of the other Legions who had suffered, in order to fill the slots for each Century. I was not considered, having been Optio barely two years, yet it still stung a little that I was not selected, such was my hubris. The remains of our dead were consigned to the flames, a heavy pall of black smoke hanging over the camp, which was fitting because it matched our mood. This was the first time we had ever tasted defeat, and even we in the 10th retched from its bitterness. The Gauls were openly celebrating; even from a distance we could see large fires lit as they feasted and congratulated each other for doing what had always been deemed impossible, especially by us. In our area, we held our own ceremony for Calienus, making offerings to the gods of a white lamb as a sign of how highly we thought of him. I do not know why, but by some unspoken consent the rest of the Century designated that I would be the one to tell Gisela, and it triggered in me a most confusing flood of feelings. I was genuinely heartbroken at the loss of Calienus; it was the death that hit me the hardest up to that point out of all the men we lost. Yet I cannot deny that there was a sudden thrill of excitement when I was told that it should be me telling Gisela the news. It was in this state of confusion that I left the camp on a pass signed by the Primus Pilus, late that night. Our work was done; Calienus' ashes were interred in the burial urn, along with the four other men who died

528

from our Legion that day, but the other Legions were still going on with their rites, the night sky lit by their funeral pyres, creating dancing shadows as I walked, lost in thought. I was not sure what I was going to say, even less sure where exactly to find her. The shantytowns that spring up outside a marching camp are never as neatly arranged or organized as the camp itself, although people did tend to place themselves more or less in the same area from one camp to the next. There were even streets of sorts between the tents and makeshift shelters attached to the wagon of someone or another. Gisela was traveling as a barmaid for the same wine shop that she had been working for the last couple of years; her cousin was the owner, as I recall. During a siege, or any protracted stay in one place, the more permanent the structures used for shelter and which did double duty as shops during business hours became. It mattered not; within a watch of the word that camp was being broken, the village would disappear, a line of wagons, mules, men, women and children then materializing, ready to march. All of this was virtually ignored by Caesar, along with every other commander of a Roman army, if he knew what was good for him. Not only did these people provide valuable services; the mending and replacing of lost items that would otherwise be drawn from army stores, the washing and mending of clothes that gave us the time for other duties, while relationships formed between the men in the army and the women who were part of this group that the Legionaries viewed as solid a bond as any official marriage. All that was asked of the camp followers was that they stay out of the way and not impede us on the march, neither of which they ever did. Now, I was walking along on my way to tell one of those women that her man was dead and passing through the gates, I realized that I was hardly alone. An unusually large number of men, most of them Optios like me, were walking towards the civilian encampment. I could tell by their grim expressions that they were on the same errand as I was. Without anyone saying anything, we all banded together so that we were walking in a group, almost like we were in formation. Approaching the camp, I thought to myself that the finding her part might be easier anyway, because just like we banded together, there was a large gathering of women standing at the edge of their camp, watching us approach. It was then that I realized that this must be old routine for them by now. Just because it was my first time to make this trip, it did not mean it was theirs. I will never forget the different expressions the women wore on their face as they watched us approach. Some were fearful, clutching their hands tightly together, their mouths clearly trembling. Others stood there as if

529

they were waiting for confirmation of something they already knew, with a look of resignation that screamed out "Let's just get this over with, shall we?" But what surprised me was that more than one woman stood there looking angry, their hands on their hips, glaring at us as if daring us to be headed to them.

Once we drew closer, one of the other Optios muttered, "I hate this *cac*. And I've got three women to tell tonight."

We gave him a look of sympathy; that was an unusually high number. Without any order being given, the whole group stopped, still several paces away from the women, and for a moment both sides stood there, staring at each other, neither side wanting to do what had to be done.

"Let's get this over with."

It was the same Optio who had spoken first, just before he broke from the group, calling out a woman's name, followed by the name of the man with whom she was associated. This triggered the rest of us and we waded into the group, as I used my height to see if I could see the red head of hair that belonged to Gisela. It was not long before there was a shriek of unspeakable grief, followed by sobbing, and that was just the beginning. By the time I searched through the crowd of women to see that she was not there, I was surrounded by women wracked with grief, some falling to their knees, some offering support to others, all of them crying.

Grimly making my way through the group, I tried to get my bearings and remember what part of the encampment the wine shop usually occupied. While most of the other merchants, once they had established a clientele, more or less picked the same spot so that their customers could find them easily, the same was not true for wine shops. Experience taught them that off-duty men are not particularly loyal to one shop or another, preferring to just drop into the first one that is suitable for their tastes and budget. That meant that there was always a scramble among the wine shop merchants for the most lucrative locations, so I was not particularly optimistic that Gisela would be in the last place I saw her in the last camp spot I visited. Nevertheless, I had to start somewhere, so I headed in that general direction. Behind me, the wailing and mourning was picking up in intensity, as more women were informed of the fate of their men. Not all the women were there; like me, I spied a few other men prowling the streets, calling out a woman's name. Deciding that I would only start yelling Gisela's name if I did not have initial luck in finding her, I continued walking, arriving at where I thought she might be. Coming to a stop, I heaved a sigh of relief; hanging above one tent was the sign for the wine shop. Apparently they weren't worried about their location, I thought, walking towards what served as the front door of the shop. Before I got there, however, a figure stepped out and while I recognized that it was a woman, it took me a moment before it registered that it was Gisela. Once I recognized her, I stopped abruptly, my call to her dying in my throat before it left my mouth. What was I going to say? It did not matter; coming out for a breath of fresh air, as she was giving a casual glance up the street before she walked back in she turned and saw me. Holding the flap back, she was illuminated by the lamps within, so I saw her standing there staring at me, and I watched the progression of emotion play across her face. Looking puzzled for a brief instant, she started to smile when she recognized me, then just as quickly, the smile vanished as she realized why I was there. I had yet to say a word but she already knew, her hand dropping the flap as she took a staggering step backward before some inner voice got her back in hand. Stopping where I was, I watched even as she received and understood my message before I began walking towards her. Despite my resolve, I heard my voice shake, as I began what I had prepared in my mind to say.

"Gisela, I've come to tell you........"

I got no further, because I could not keep my composure, once again feeling hot tears running down my face. The shame of crying in front of a woman washed over me, only making things worse and I lost sight of her as my tears blinded me, so I jumped a bit when I felt her hand on my arm, touching the bandages lightly as she stepped closer towards me.

"He's gone, Gisela," I blurted out, shaking my head in sadness, my vision clearing a bit so I saw that while her eyes were liquid and shiny, the tears had not started running yet, and she had not yet said a word.

Finally, she spoke and her voice, while composed, betrayed the effort she was making to keep it so. "Thank you Titus Pullus, for coming here to tell me this news. I....."

She got no further, the dam suddenly bursting and she began sobbing, collapsing into my arms. By reflex, I put my arms around her, savagely trying to repress the thought that this was the most natural thing in the world, that it was as if she were made to fit in my arms. Self-loathing filled my soul, yet it only made me cry more, and there we stood, for how long I know not, emptying our grief into each other.

After we regained possession of ourselves, we entered the wine shop and I found myself repeating the news to the owner, who burst into tears himself. Calienus was well loved, his death a cause of grief to many people. I sat at a table, with Gisela automatically bringing wine and two cups. Then to my surprise, she sat down with me, pouring herself a cupful.

Once our cups were full, we paused for a moment, and then I said quietly, "To Calienus. One of the best friends I ever had."

Even as we clinked our cups together in salute, I felt the tears coming again, but I just managed to blink them back. It was bad enough that I unmanned myself in front of Gisela, I was not about to do it in front of anyone else. Instead, I cleared my throat and continued, perhaps a bit too gruffly, "Well, I suppose you'll be going back to your people then."

She did not say anything for a moment, just regarding me quietly before shaking her head. I could not help noticing a teardrop falling to land perfectly in the middle of her wine cup. Appropriate, I thought. Waiting for another moment, I then opened my mouth to speak but she broke the silence first.

"I cannot go back to my people, Pullus. They will not have me."

I was surprised at this, but pleasantly so, I am ashamed to say. I made no attempt to hide it, either, at least the surprised part. "Really?" I asked. "Why's that? You've done nothing wrong."

"I gave myself to my people's enemy, Titus," she replied softly, with more than a tinge of bitterness.

"Surely they've accepted Rome by now, haven't they?" I know now how naïve a question it was.

What could be described as scorn flitted across her face, but since she could tell I meant no harm, her expression softened. "No Titus, they have not accepted it. Nor, I fear, will they ever accept it."

"Then, why did you join up with us? Why do you follow us?"

She shrugged, still staring at the table. Finally, she answered simply, "I fell in love." I was confused, and seeing it, she continued. "I came to see the Romans for myself because I had heard so much about them. At first, I thought you were puny little men," she laughed, "not you of course Titus. But you are almost a giant among your people. So I will admit that at first I was not impressed. Then, my cousin opened this shop, and I decided to spend some time working here so that I could understand Romans better."

This was nothing short of astonishing to me, and I could not resist blurting out, "But how did you get to do this? Surely your father didn't approve."

She laughed again, and I felt better that I was at least making her laugh at this time.

"Titus, Gallic women are much different from Roman women. We can choose who we marry, for example."

While I had heard this, I never credited it as true, yet here was a Gallic woman telling me so!

"And I was always my father's favorite. Besides, I told him that I was only working here to learn the habits of our enemy, and that one day that information would be put to good use. Then," the laughter in her ceased, sadness descending once more, "this man named Calienus came into the shop. And he talked to me like no other man had ever talked to me."

Despite myself, I leaned forward in order to glean any information that might help me win her heart. It is hard to describe the conflicting emotions that were running through me. Calienus' ashes were barely cool, yet here I was, trying to find a way to win her for myself. Immediately another part of my mind answered, why not? Why not you, because you know that there will be men sniffing around her first thing tomorrow. You at least know her and treasure her for who she is, and not just because of how she looks. Or so I told myself anyway. Completely oblivious to my inner turmoil, she continued.

"He did not talk to me the way a man talks to a woman he wants to sleep with."

To my horror, I could feel a flush creeping up my face at these words. She either ignored or did not see it.

"No, he talked to me as if I were an equal, a person whose opinion he valued, not just as some trophy that he could brag to his friends about."

As she said this, I realized it was true. In fact, it was how we learned that Calienus had a woman, not because of what he said, but what he refused to talk about. And when someone, even in jest, spoke too lewdly about her Calienus would be all over them in an instant. This is good to remember, I thought to myself as I listened, although it puzzled me. There is nothing a man likes more than for his woman to brag about him to other women, yet apparently this is not so with women.

"So, he would come in, and we would just talk."

"Talk about what?" I was intensely curious about this.

"Anything. Everything. The campaign," I felt my eyebrows raise in surprise at this, "the political situation, poetry, music. Farming, even. Everything."

She finished with a shrug, suddenly picking her cup up to drink deeply from it, leaving me to watch her throat moving up and down as she swallowed. I had never seen anything so lovely in my life, I was sure. Setting the cup down she caught me staring, and smiled self-consciously as she wiped her lips with the back of her hand. It was the type of thing men do, yet it was both mannish and more feminine than anything I had ever seen before, and in that moment I saw past her beauty, realizing why Calienus loved her so much.

"He was a very lucky man," I said quietly.

Now it was her turn to be surprised, at first, then her eyes started to fill again.

"You know Titus, he thought very highly of you," she responded. "He told me once that you had the potential to be the finest Legionary in the army."

I felt my chest swell with pride, and I could not help smiling.

"He also said that you had a huge ego, and if anything destroyed your chances, it would be that."

Like a bucket of cold water thrown in the face of a drunk, her words dashed against me, whatever pride I felt instantly evaporating. I think it hurt more because I knew she was right; I was reaching a point in my life where I was able to look at myself as if through another's eyes, and I could see that my vanity was perhaps my greatest flaw. Every soldier needs pride, along with the conviction that they are good at what they do, but there is a point at which there is too much of that quality and I was having trouble recognizing that point. I must have let it show that she wounded me, because she leaned forward and placed a gentle hand on my arm.

"Do not be hurt Titus. He wanted to see you succeed, and that was his one worry."

I sat looking at her hand, how white and small it was, draped on my sun-dark, scarred forearm.

I sighed, and nodded. "I know. He was right. Sometimes I know that I go too far with my boasting, but I want to be the best Legionary that's ever lived. It's all I think about, day and night."

While this was not exactly true, it was near enough, and I was surprised at myself that I was willing to utter something that I had told no one before, not even Vibius, at least since we joined the army. I looked down at the table, unwilling to meet her eyes.

"I know," I whispered, "it's stupid. It's just the bragging of a boy."

"Titus, there are a lot of things I think of when I think of you, but boy has never been one of them."

Her words hit me like I had been struck by lightning. Did this mean that she viewed me as.......something else? I looked up to see her looking me square in the eye, and she gave my forearm a squeeze.

"There is nothing wrong with ambition, Titus. And it's one of the things that makes you so......attractive."

I gulped, hard. Her eyes never left mine, and I could feel the heat that started in my face sweep through my body. I felt myself leaning forward, just as a voice in my head shouted STOP!

Jerking my arm out from under her hand and standing quickly, I stammered, "Well, it was nice talking to you, Gisela." Then a feeling of horror flashed through me and I tried to correct myself. "I mean.....it was nice, but under the circumstances, I mean, it was not nice. I........" Being completely flummoxed, I finally burst out with, "I'm sorry for your loss, Gisela."

She sat, just looking at me, and I could not tell whether she wanted to laugh, or cry. I got up, stumbling out into the night, heading back to the camp with my mind whirling.

The next morning, a formation was ordered for the entire army and we assembled in the forum to await Caesar. After settling down and being brought to *intente*, Caesar appeared from the command tent, mounting the rostra made of shields. He was dressed in his full armor, and his face was grim as he stood surveying us for several moments before he began speaking.

"Comrades," he began, and we could tell by the sound of his voice that this was not going to be one of his talks that left us feeling like we could conquer the world, "I must tell you how disappointed I am in your conduct yesterday."

His words struck the army like a massive fist, hitting us all in the gut. There was a stir in our ranks, with a low buzz of disbelief that he was including us in what happened; it was our actions that saved the rest of the army from destruction! I do not know if he was already planning what he said next, or he saw our reaction and moved quickly to disarm us. Regardless, he did so, turning towards us to hold out a placating hand.

"In my censure, I naturally do not include you men of the 10th," then he turned in the direction of the 13th, "or you Cohorts of the 13th who were under the command of Sextius."

The relief was palpable; you could see it in the posture of the men as they slumped in relief, at least as much as one can slump when standing at *intente*.

536

"Your conduct and your actions were exemplary, and your comrades in the other Legions owe you a debt of gratitude for protecting them when they turned their backs to the enemy."

His last words were like the lash of a whip, whatever smug triumph we felt immediately smothered by the stricken looks on the faces of our comrades in the other Legions. There is no greater shame to a Roman Legionary than the idea of turning ones' back to the enemy to flee, yet that is exactly what happened, and the shame was clearly written in the faces of the accused Legions.

"However," Caesar's voice lightened a bit, and it was almost pathetic seeing the look of hope cross the face of these hard men, "your dishonor was not due to any lack of valor. It was due to a lack of discipline perhaps, and indeed, to an excess of fighting spirit."

Men's heads lifted a bit as they listened intently to our commander's words. It was like watching drowning men being thrown a lifeline.

"It was never my intent to press the attack on the walls of the town," he continued, "but in your zeal, and in your dedication to the idea of victory, you overstepped my orders. I cannot fault your courage, my comrades."

Just as the men sensed that perhaps this was as bad as it was going to get, the puppet master pulled one more string. His voice to that point had been what one could call soothing, but now it turned to icy, controlled anger.

"But I can fault you for disobeying me, your general. By rights, I could order the offending Legions to be *decimated*," he roared this last word, instantly followed by an audible gasp from the entire army, ourselves included, despite the fact we would not have been subject to that horrible punishment. Just as quickly, his voice returned to that of a kindly, loving but firm parent and he finished, "But that is not my wish, nor will it happen, now or ever because I am confident that my words today are enough chastisement, and that you will never disobey me again."

Again, a palpable sense of relief swept through the army. I heard a voice cry out from one of the offending Legions.

"We'll never fail you again Caesar, or you can order us all to put ourselves to the sword!"

The rest of the men roared their agreement, with Caesar allowing the demonstration to continue for a moment before he held up his hand. As if to prove their commitment to their words, the camp fell silent instantly, faster than I could ever remember when Caesar called for silence. I was close enough that I could see that ghost of a smile cross his lips, but his voice remained steady, betraying no emotion.

"I know that you will not fail me again. And now comrades, I am going to give you a chance to redeem your honor!"

Another roar of approbation, another gesture followed by complete silence as we all strained to hear what he was planning.

"We are going to go out today and show Vercingetorix and his army that they have done nothing more than arouse our anger! We are going to offer them battle, and let us see if they have the courage to respond to our challenge!"

This time, he let our roaring continue, the sound rolling out over the walls of the camp. I have no doubt that Vercingetorix and his mob heard us, and knew that we were coming for them.

Marching out of the camp, we arrayed ourselves in our normal *acies triplex* with the 10th on the right, and the 13th anchoring the far left. Caesar positioned us along a roughly north/south axis, facing the gigantic hill, in the small valley between the hill on which our camp was located and Gergovia, perhaps a mile from the base of the plateau that the town sat on. And it was there we waited, through almost two full watches, daring Vercingetorix to come down and fight us, but he must have possessed some Roman blood because he did not act in the normal Gallic fashion. Indeed, he refused to face us not only that day, but the following day when we performed the same maneuver. While this action may have restored our pride to a degree, the larger situation was still deteriorating rapidly, the word of our setback at Gergovia sweeping through Gaul. In response to these developments, and truthfully, recognizing that the army at his command was not large enough to invest Gergovia, we were ordered on the march, moving back to the north. Vercingetorix, for reasons that can only be guessed at, chose not to pursue us, probably wise given the openness of the terrain we were marching over, and our mood. Moving along the Elaver River, on the third day of the march we repaired one of the damaged bridges, crossing back over to the eastern side. It was here that Caesar learned that the *cunnus* Litaviccus, who somehow made it to Gergovia after he fled his fellow Aedui that day, was heading back to them, leading most of the Gallic cavalry in another attempt to convince them to switch to the side of Vercingetorix. The difference this time was that it was almost a certainty that he would be successful; after all, did Vercingetorix not just prove that we were not invincible? The two men Eporedorix and Viridomarus, who helped us turned the tide that day with Litaviccus and been marching with us ever since, now begged Caesar leave so that they could try to reason with their fellow tribesmen and convince them to remain faithful to Caesar. Who knows, perhaps they were sincere at that moment; all I know is that the next time we heard their names, they were now riding with Litaviccus instead of against him. In other words, the usual faithless Gauls.

It was about three days after the two traitors left that the most catastrophic news to date reached the army. What one must realize is that, despite the best intentions of the officers, there are no secrets in an army. It matters not what size it is, there is no way that any piece of intelligence, orders, or especially gossip, the more salacious the better, will not be common knowledge by the lowest *Gregarii* less than a day later. Therefore, when word that Noviodunum was taken and sacked, the garrison of auxiliaries massacred, and all of our grain either carried off or destroyed, something close to a panic whipped through the army. Our situation had never been so grim, and we all knew it. Even men like me with the utmost faith in Caesar held serious doubts that he would be able to get us out of the dire straits in which we found ourselves. All around us, Gallic cavalry patrols were scouring the countryside, locating any supplies and either taking them or destroying them. Behind us to the south were the Arverni and the main army of Vercingetorix, still at Gergovia, at least as far as we knew. We were heading to cross the Liger River in order to reunite with Labienus and his four Legions, but the mountain snows were exceptionally heavy, making the river a torrent so that crossing it was an exercise that would take more time than we could afford. To our west, the Bituriges were thirsting for revenge for Avaricum while the Aedui, now in full revolt, had as their object pinning us between the Liger and the Elaver, then starving us into submission. Our choices were extremely limited, to put it mildly. If we were to try retreating south back to the Province, not only would it be a dangerous move because of crossing the snow-covered mountains that serve as the boundary between the Province and Gaul, we would also be essentially leaving Labienus and the four other Legions alone, cut off and surrounded by a massively numerically superior enemy. But then, Caesar received a piece of intelligence, and in that one bit of information, saw a way not only out of our present predicament, but also a way to turn the tables on the enemy once more.

As part of Vercingetorix's grand strategy, he gave orders that every tribe must destroy their own supplies of food, both in grain and cattle. He understood that the key to beating us was only by weakening us and the best way to do so was by starvation. Personally, I think it is something to be admired about him that he was able to convince such a fractious people as the tribes of Gaul to obey, and they all did as he commanded, despite it meaning a long, hard winter for them. All but one tribe, however, and it was this piece of news that Caesar seized upon, that the Aedui, so confident of success now that they were with Vercingetorix, saw no need to starve themselves. And as usual, he wasted no time; we were ordered to break camp within the watch that he received the news, despite the fact that it was shortly after dark and we just finished building the camp in the first place. However, we all knew that our fates were hanging in the balance, so there was no complaining at the order. Not more than a third of a watch after it was given we began to march. This was another of the very few times marching with Caesar where we did not destroy the camp, as I believe that he did not want to give the Gallic cavalry assigned to watch us any idea that something was happening. Marching through the night, we stopped for a rest only lasting two parts of the watch shortly after dawn, before picking back up and resuming our movement. Pressing on the next day, we stopped once again in the afternoon to rest, making it just around sunset when we reached the banks of the Liger, a few miles south of what remained of Noviodunum, the smoke from the town visible for the last full watch of our approach. There was no time to build a bridge, so Caesar sent his cavalry to look for a fordable part of the river, and they found one, if it could be called a ford. The only way we could get across was by the cavalry moving upstream to block the flow of water, with another line of cavalrymen downstream serving to stop any man who lost his footing from being swept away. The water was neck deep for most of the men, forcing them to hold their shield in one hand above their head, along with their pack and javelins in the other. Although I was

540

not immersed as deeply, I was just as subject to the frigid temperature of the water, courtesy of the melted snow. Because we were one of the first Legions across, we were forced to stand, shivering and waiting for the rest of the army to cross before we resumed the march.

The Aedui were caught so completely by surprise that they made no attempt to neither try contesting our crossing, nor try to stop us from raiding their granaries and rounding up their cattle. Spending two days restocking our supply wagons, every man was issued marching rations of almost two weeks, which we had to divide between ourselves and our section's mule. It is amazing how something as simple as knowing that there will be food to eat can so completely restore an army's morale, and we were in a much better frame of mind when we turned to the next task, going to the aid of Labienus. He had been sent to subdue the Parisii, a tribe mainly congregated in the island town of Lutetia, yet like our part of the army, the fever of rebellion fired the ardor not just of the Parisii, but the imaginations of the non-warrior class of Gauls, and it was usually these people on whom we relied for information. So it was not a surprise when we later learned that the peasants told Labienus not only of the defeat at Gergovia, but that Caesar's army had tried to cross the Liger and failed, so for want of supplies was now marching back to the Province, leaving Labienus and his army to worry about their own fate. Additionally, the word of Gergovia emboldened the Bellovaci, living to the northeast of Lutetia, to rise in rebellion as well, so that now Labienus had an enemy at his front and his rear. His only hope, as he saw it with the information that he possessed, was to somehow make it back to Agedincum, where there were two Legions and his supply base. However, he was on the wrong side of the river. Seeing that no matter where he tried to cross, there would be an enemy force opposing him, he decided that he might as well cross right then and there. Since I was not present at this battle, I cannot provide much detail, and Caesar has described it in his Commentaries, but it is sufficient to say that Labienus was victorious, his army fighting its way out of the trap. They marched to Agedincum, resupplied and picked up the other two Legions, then began heading south in our direction because Labienus learned the truth about Caesar and his army at Agedincum. Our two armies linked up about two days' march south of Agedincum, where we made camp, with the word being that we would be staying put for a bit.

Even with the joining of our armies, the situation was still extremely serious. I cannot help but think that if it were not for that flaw of character I spoke about at the fire those weeks before, we still may have been well and truly fucked. All of Gaul was now in rebellion; every tribe threw their support behind Vercingetorix, although much to our great fortune some of those tribes' support consisted of gold and not men. All the hostages that Caesar had gathered were at Noviodunum when it fell, so we did not even have that hold on them anymore, but true to their nature, the Gauls experienced just as much trouble dealing with prosperity as they did adversity. It was through the actions of our friends the Aedui that the trouble began. The Aedui and Arverni had been rivals for a long time, much longer than they held any animosity towards Rome, or even knew of our existence for that matter. And now the Aedui sought to reassert what they saw as their true place of dominance among the Gauls, making the claim that now they were involved, the leadership of the army should go to a man of the Aedui. This caused a huge uproar, to the point where an assembly of all the tribes of Gaul was called at Bibracte. According to our spies, every tribe in Gaul sent representatives, with the exception of the Remi, Lingones and Treveri, the latter because they were dealing with incursions from the Germans from across the Rhenus. The former two tribes chose to remain aloof because they both had firsthand knowledge of Roman power, and were gambling that Caesar would be successful. This assembly must have been quite a sight, lasting several days, yet when the matter was finally brought to a vote, not one Gaul voted against Vercingetorix. He alone, they cried, had brought them victory against the Romans, and he alone would be their leader. The Aedui were outraged at what they perceived to be a slight and I often wondered if at that point they experienced second thoughts about turning on us, except they could not risk open disagreement in front of every other tribe. I can imagine it was with great reluctance that their representatives, none other than those two rats Eporedorix and Viridomarus, swore allegiance to Vercingetorix. As far as Vercingetorix was concerned, he was committed to continuing the strategy of attrition, using the error made by the Aedui as an example of why it was important to destroy their own supplies. Despite having more than 120,000 men at his disposal, Vercingetorix knew that it would be impossible to feed such a large host, their very size meaning that his greatest asset, his maneuverability, would be compromised. To help correct this problem, he sent 40,000 home, keeping a host of 80,000 men on foot, and 15,000 cavalry. This was the force that he would use to destroy Caesar, and us.

Vercingetorix had other plans as well, which he quickly put into motion. As a sop to Eporedorix and Viridomarus, he gave them an independent command of 10,000 Aedui, bidding them to march south to the territory of the Allobroges. He authorized them to offer bribes to the Allobroges to throw in with the rest of the Gauls, the army that was with them to take the territory by force if necessary. The land of the Allobroges constituted the northernmost part of the Province, technically making them Roman subjects, but I will say that the last governors before Caesar treated them ill, so it took no stretch of the imagination to believe that they would play us false and join the rest of the tribes in revolt. Fortunately, Caesar had treated them well, saving them from the Helvetii those years ago, while conferring honors upon their leaders. As a result of Caesar's policies, they were now satisfied with Roman rule. A kinsman of Caesar, Lucius was his name, upon receiving word from Caesar, raised 10,000 men, with forts erected at all the likely crossing points of the Rhodanus, which marked their boundary, to resist any attempt at forcing a crossing. There was one attempt made to cross the river, repulsed with heavy losses, so for the time being our rear was safe from the Gauls but it was only a temporary reprieve. One thing that concerned all of us was the number of cavalry that Vercingetorix had at his disposal; indeed, it was this force that saw the most use implementing his strategy of attrition. Roaming around the countryside in search of any rumored caches of food, our own much smaller force raced to beat them and return to our camp with those supplies, if they in fact existed. But while our force of German cavalry had proven themselves, and did so to the point that starting in this campaign that was all Caesar ever used for his personal bodyguard, they were still far less than the 400 he originally levied, whittled down in the countless skirmishes to a number a little more than two hundred. Sending across the Rhenus, Caesar requisitioned more mounted troops, but despite their fighting ability, the one weakness of the German cavalry when going against their Gallic enemies was in the quality of the horseflesh they rode. Therefore, Caesar ordered that all Tribunes, still six to a Legion, and members of the Evocati, the group of retired Centurions and Legionaries that Caesar deemed to be valuable additions to the army, and who as a signal of their status were given mounts, relinquish them to the Germans who joined the army. There was a lot of complaining about that order, I can promise you; I just think that the fine young men were born that way while the Evocati had grown soft and too accustomed to the comfort of riding. Whatever the case, we increased and augmented our cavalry in this way, along with adding some German auxiliaries of foot of questionable value. It was with this force that Caesar now turned his attention back to the Province.

Despite the Allobroges being successful in turning back one attempt to invade their territory, the chances that they would hold out indefinitely were not such that Caesar was willing to risk it, so we left the camp we occupied for several weeks to begin marching south. During this period of time we were in camp, Vercingetorix had decided that his best base of operations was the town of Alesia, like Gergovia a fortified town sitting on the top of a plateau. Once we started to move, and once Vercingetorix determined our intent, he ordered his massive army to leave Alesia and march in a direction that would meet us before we were able to cross the Rhodanus into the Province. About four days into the march, scouts alerted us to the presence of the enemy nearby, just a few miles from our own camp. I do not know why, but the orders were given to proceed with the next day's march as planned, and in the morning we left the ruin of the night's camp behind, continuing our march south. Our orders were that each baggage train followed their Legion, which I must say was a grave error on our part. Vercingetorix's attack consisted of cavalry only, and in this I believe he made his first huge mistake. His cavalry host was of sufficient size that he disposed of it in three columns, sending one to harass the vanguard Legion and advance party at the head of the column, with the other two attacking the main body from either side along the column. Because we were still in Lingones territory, who remained solidly in our camp, Caesar did not send out his usual far-ranging patrols and we paid for it. All along the column, the sounds of the *cornu* and the cries of the Centurions rang out, each section of the massive body of men spotting the attack of the Gallic cavalry at roughly the same time.

"Form square!"

The command echoed down the line, but we needed no extra instruction on where we were to form square, each Cohort from each Legion running quickly to their preassigned spots around their baggage train, forming a square around our most precious possessions. Despite the fact it takes a while for a single command to a column consisting of ten Legions to be passed along, we were experienced enough to know what needed to be done without

544

waiting for orders, making the move more or less simultaneously all up and down the long column once the initial command was given. Standing in my spot, just behind the last rank in the Century, I used my height to survey the ground, trying to see through the dust that swirled around the hooves of the Gallic cavalrymen. Never before had I seen so many horsemen in one place, the dust they churned up soon obliterating my view of anything other than the few feet in front of the first rank. Suddenly out of the haze a number horsemen came bursting into view, riding directly towards our front line. Men immediately behind the front row grabbed onto the man in front to brace them for the impact, as the men in front, instead of throwing their javelin like they normally would, thrust them out as lances to spear the onrushing horses. The beasts, seeing what was in front of them, tried desperately to skid to a halt, yet between their own momentum and the savage whipping they were being given by their riders, the poor things had no chance. Screams of animals in agony rent the air as the impact of the combined weight of men and horses slammed into the Century, and I could feel the shudder through the very ground on which I stood. For a moment the men in front leaned backward, struggling under the weight pressed against them while the Gauls, still astride their mounts struggling to free themselves from the points imbedded in their flesh, whipped their long swords down onto the heads of the front men. The men in the second rank were using their javelin to stab upwards at the Gauls and it looked for the slightest time as if the force of the Gallic horsemen was going to overwhelm us. However, we all knew that any break in our formation meant death, not just to the men around the hole but to all of us, since the Gauls would whip their horses into the gap to exploit it. We had seen it happen enough to know what fate awaited us, so despite the intense pressure, we held. Finally our javelins hit their marks, stabbing the Gallic riders. In a matter of a few heartbeats from when they first appeared, there were several dead men at our feet, along with a horse that only managed to walk a few unsteady paces before collapsing. The other animals, less seriously wounded, went galloping away with blood streaming down their hides, driven by the mindless instinct to flee from what had hurt them. The remaining horsemen sheared away to disappear into the haze of dust. I always felt badly for the horses in war; they had no say in the matter and they suffered some of the most horrible deaths. It was something I never spoke of, because I would have been teased unmercifully, but it did bother me nonetheless.

All around us, similar small skirmishes were taking place, before our own cavalry came thundering past us to confront the Gauls. In the same manner as our enemy, Caesar split our horsemen into three columns, each one assigned to one of the enemy formations. Once the Gauls tried to break through our lines a couple of times, only to be bloodily repulsed each time, we became spectators to the action. With the battle wearing on, our Germans began carrying the day, much to our delight, and we heartily cheered them whenever they would go hurtling past as we caught just a glimpse of them.

"This is like watching the chariot races in Rome," remarked Scribonius, and I looked at him in some surprise. As close as we were, Scribonius talked very little about his past, where he had come from or where he had lived for that matter. And normally, this was not a thing that we talked about in the army; if a man did not want to discuss his past, we assumed it was for good reason and did not pry, but I was so surprised, I blurted out, "You've been to Rome?"

Giving me a sidelong glance, he hesitated, then nodded. Keeping his eyes on the action, he said, "I lived there."

I will confess that I was astounded. Here was one of my two or three closest friends, boon companion since being *tiros* together, and this was the first I heard that he had lived in Rome! Suddenly, the battle was completely forgotten as I asked eagerly, "Pluto's thorny cock! What's it like? Is it as wonderful as they say?"

I could see him make a face, his reluctance clear to see, but then he glanced at my own face and laughed. "You're not going to let this be until I tell you, are you?"

I shook my head emphatically, and he sighed. "All right, I'll tell you all about Rome. But not now. Later."

"When later?" I demanded.

Rolling his eyes he replied, "Tonight, by Dis. Is that good enough for you?"

Nodding, we turned our attention back to the fight and watched as our cavalry carried the day from the Gauls.

Our German horse swept the Gallic cavalry from the field with heavy losses, yet one of the great mysteries of the day, and the

546

mistake that I referred to earlier was why Vercingetorix did not order his infantry into the battle. They were formed up, outside of their camp with a view of our column as it approached, yet never left that spot. Once it was clear how the day was going, they broke down their camp and marched hurriedly away. Their army was much too large for our cavalry to try to engage while we shook ourselves out into battle formation, so we watched the dust cloud that signaled their marching away to Alesia. Vercingetorix, with the remnants of his cavalry, followed behind the rest of their army, leaving almost 3,000 horsemen dead on the field. All that Vercingetorix worked so hard to achieve in the last six months was lost in a day when he kept his infantry back from the battle, because the truth on Jupiter's stone is that we were surprised, just like we were by the Nervii when making camp that day. Now, however, Vercingetorix was running, and the place he was running to would be his last stand at Alesia, so it was there that we now marched. That night around the fire, Scribonius had a rapt audience as he described Rome, but even with his attempts to make it sound squalid, dirty and dangerous, by the time he was through telling us of the sights to be seen, all of us were afire to see the city for which we marched to glory.

Chapter 13- Alesia

We came within sight of the hill that Alesia sits on at the end of the next day. The enemy army managed to retreat in good order and had invested the town. Since Vercingetorix decided to make Alesia his base of operations and his final redoubt some time before, the fortifications at Alesia were well developed, and the Gallic army was working on improving them even as we marched up. Our approach was from the east, and while the hill is not as high as Gergovia, it is at least as steep if not steeper. Unlike Gergovia, there was not a string of hills immediately surrounding the town where we could entrench. Perhaps a mile to the east are two hills, side by side with a narrow valley in between that leads straight to the foot of the hill on which Alesia stands. At the foot of the hill on either side lay two small streams, one on the northern side and one on the southern side. On the other side of Alesia, to the west, lay a relatively flat plain, extending for about three or four miles, and it was on this western side where the Gauls were putting the most effort in improving the defenses by building a stone wall that ran north and south between the two streams. Caesar stopped the army on the northernmost hill on the east side of the town, while he and his staff conducted a reconnaissance as we made camp. The *bucina* sounded Caesar's return shortly before dark, and less than a third of a watch later it sounded the signal for all Centurions to report to the *Praetorium*. Since it was only Scaevola and I left sitting by the officer's fire, and he was not very good company, I got up to wander around our area, stopping at every fire to chat for a while as we waited to hear what was in our immediate future. The wagering was

548

already started of course, and the best odds were a complete investment of the town.

"It only makes sense," one of the men of the third section, a swarthy veteran of Pompey's army named Valens was holding forth at his fire. "Now that Labienus and his four Legions are here, we're going to be digging like moles in a great big circle all the way around that fucking town."

"I don't see it," argued Crispus, who had been a *tiro* the same time as us. "I think he's just going to order us to assault the damn thing and be done with it. It's been dragging on too long, and Caesar is going to want to end it."

Naturally, my presence meant that my opinion would be solicited, and Valens turned towards me, confident that I would agree. "Well Optio? What do you say? Are we going to invest the place, or are we going to do what this dunderhead thinks and go charging in like amateurs?"

I had to fight a smile at the way he put it, but the truth was I agreed with him.

"I think you're right Valens," I replied, to his cry of glee and Crispus' moan of disgust.

The way I looked at it, either way I went, I was going to make somebody mad, so I may as well tell them what I thought. But I did not want to sound unreasonable; I was green enough back then that I worried that the men understood where I was coming from. "I think Valens is right, we have four more Legions, and just by eyeballing the place, it's not as big around as Gergovia was," I explained, but Crispus was having none of it.

"Then that means that Caesar is willing to stay here through the winter, Optio? I don't believe that; he wants to get out of here just as much as we all do."

I nodded. "That may be, but I also think Caesar is going to do what he thinks gives us the best chance to win, and that's using our engineering skills."

"You mean our strong backs," Crispus said miserably.

In that he was right at least; whatever the work, it would be done with our sweat. "Just remember Crispus," I tried to put a cheerful face on it, "the more you sweat now..."

Before I could finish, the whole section chimed in, "....the less you bleed later."

"We get it Optio," concluded Crispus, "but we don't have to like it."

I smiled. "I'd be more worried if you did."

Pilus Prior Pulcher returned and took a seat at our fire, not saying anything for a moment. He chose instead to stare into the flames, the line of his scar in the shadows cast by the fire making him look older. Finally, he looked up and announced, "Well, we're going to invest the place."

I was not surprised, so I merely nodded while Scaevola gave a grunt. Over the years I had learned that Scaevola was a simple soul; not very intelligent, but smart enough to know what needed to be done, and absolutely ferocious in a fight, to the point that sometimes it was hazardous being near him, because when he got carried away, he tried to kill anyone within reach.

"That'll make Valens happy at least," I finally replied, and Pulcher looked at me with a raised eyebrow. I related the conversation we had, and he laughed. "These bastards will bet on anything, won't they? That's really why Crispus is mad, not because he has work to do, but because he bet the wrong way."

His smile disappeared as he continued soberly, "And we're going to have work to do, right enough. Caesar's decided on a double envelopment, with one set of fortifications turned inwards and another turned out. He's betting that this is the last stand, so that the Gauls'll do everything they can to keep Alesia from falling, so we need to be ready for an attack from both sides."

We sat absorbing this, then Scaevola grunted again, this time loudly enough that we knew it was the signal that he was about to say something, a rare enough occasion that we looked at him in some surprise.

"Well, if we finish these bastards here, maybe we can go home."

550

Our mild surprise turned to shock; this was the first time I ever heard Scaevola say anything that indicated he had a home other than the army. I glanced at the Pilus Prior, who returned it with a raised eyebrow and slight shrug. "Scaevola, where would such a heartless bastard like you call home other than the army?" the Pilus Prior teased.

"Rome," Scaevola said quietly, staring into the fire. "The Subura, to be precise. It's where I was born."

You could have knocked both of us over with a feather; I had been marching with Scaevola since the Legion was formed, the Pilus Prior a few years less, but still a good stretch of time, and this was the first we ever heard that our standard bearer was born in Rome. First Scribonius, now Scaevola, I thought; will wonders never cease? I knew that he was one of the veterans from Pompey's Legions salted into our ranks, and once I thought of it, it made sense. It was still a shock, however, but my questions about Rome would have to wait.

I rose and looked to the Pilus Prior. "Shall I tell the men, or do you want to?"

He waved me along, "You do it Pullus. I have some questions for Scaevola about whether all the things I've heard about the whores of Rome are true."

With a laugh, I left to go tell our comrades what awaited them.

"A double investment? Pluto's thorny cock, that'll take.....I don't know, but a long time," Vibius swore, and I bit back a retort.

Forcing myself to be patient, I replied, "I know it's a lot of work, but ultimately it's for our protection."

Warming to the topic, I tried to light some sort of fire of enthusiasm for what was going to be a brutal amount of work, no matter what. "Boys, this is it! We have that bastard bottled up, with the bulk of his army. We finish him here, and we're done. Nobody is left for us to fight!"

"I don't know," Vibius repeated doubtfully, "the way these Gauls breed, there's still a lot of 'em running around that aren't part of that lot up on the hill."

"*Gerrae*! By Dis Vibius, must you find a turd in the porridge in everything Caesar does?" I stormed. I had lost my temper, and even as I swore at myself for losing control, I continued to rage. "I've listened to you moan and complain about every order you've been given by Caesar since.....since I can remember, and by the gods I'm sick of it! I've put up with it because you're my best friend since we were kids, but enough is enough!" My voice hardened into the tone I used when giving commands or officially chastising one of the men. "You forget yourself, Sergeant. Your place is not to question our commander's orders, your place is to obey them and carry them out to the best of your ability. This is the last time I'll tolerate such a display, do you understand me?"

The shock was clear on Vibius' face, as it was on everyone else around the fire; never before had they heard me speak to Vibius in this manner, but I had reached my limit.

"Titus, I meant no........."

"*Tacete*!" I surprised even myself at the volume of my voice. "And stand at *intente* when I'm addressing you, Sergeant!"

As shocked and angry as he may have been, discipline in the Legions runs deep, and he snapped immediately to the position, eyes locked straight ahead.

"You're not addressing your friend Titus Pullus, you're addressing your Optio right now, Sergeant," my voice was a bit softer, but only by a fraction.

"Yes, Optio," Vibius replied, and to anyone else his tone sounded perfectly correct, but I could detect the barely controlled fury. We stood there for a moment; he could not speak unless I gave him leave, and I was suddenly at a loss at what to say. Things had gotten out of hand and I knew that, except I did not know what to do. In my defense, it was not just a matter of youth. I knew that to back down in any way at this point was to undermine my authority; a leader cannot be seen to be indecisive and weak, and backing down now would cause me problems down the road. Nevertheless, I also knew that my friendship with Vibius had just suffered a tremendous blow that might not ever be repaired.

"Very well, carry on. We've got a big day tomorrow so I want everyone in the tent early tonight."

552

Without saying another word, I turned and walked to the next section to pass the word, thinking that at least I would not have to deal with Vibius.

Beginning work the next morning, nine Legions worked while one Legion, the cavalry and the auxiliary troops kept a vigil on the town and camp of Vercingetorix. The camp covered the eastern slope, where they had dug their own ditch and erected a wall six feet tall, covering the distance between the two streams in the same manner as on the western side. The result was a rough rectangular shape, which we needed to completely encircle. Dirt flew as thousands of spades dug; axes rang out as the wood needed for the forts was chopped down and dressed appropriately. Within the day, we built a number of camps to spread the Legions out, with two camps on the north side, and two camps on the south side. Arranged around the western side of the town, camps were built specifically for the cavalry and the auxiliaries. The inner trench and wall was dotted with smaller forts, 23 of them, ranging in size from just large enough for a Century, with one or two artillery pieces, to a couple large enough for a Cohort, with several artillery pieces, the latter being placed in areas where Caesar deemed it more likely that there would be an attempt to break out. The camps were completed, along with perhaps half of the inner trench and wall, by the time it got dark the first day. Work continued in shifts through the next day and into the night, in the same manner as at Avaricum. The major difference is that we were not hurting for food at Alesia, and I think this along with the belief that we were in the final stages of crushing the rebellion spurred us to work at a furious pace. Our Cohort worked through the day shift, retiring to one of the camps on the southern perimeter just erected, tired and filthy. Listlessly eating our meal, too tired even for a bath, once finished the men collapsed on their cots, while I plodded to my tent, where a report on our supply situation and the daily report were waiting for me.

By the third day, about half of the forts were completed, the inner trench and wall was finished and we were beginning work on the outer wall when Vercingetorix sent his entire cavalry force out in an attempt to destroy our cavalry, his intent to cripple our ability to forage, the main job of the cavalry during a siege. The *bucina* sounded the call to assembly and we dropped our tools to run to where our gear was gathered, forming up in battle order as we watched the cloud of dust to our left grow in size, the sounds of the clash carrying to us. We had no real idea what was happening, only glimpsing the blurred forms of horsemen hurtling in one direction or another in random moments when the dust clouds would briefly dissipate, before a fresh spate of action dropped a curtain back down on the scene. All we knew was what we could glean from the sounds of the various horns, giving signals that were relayed from one fort to another. Despite being naturally absorbed in what was taking place to our left, we actually were assembled to keep an eye on the town and camp in the event that the Gallic infantry were ordered from their positions to support the cavalry. The battle raged for the better part of a third of a watch, then seemingly for no reason, we saw the Gauls turn about and begin whipping their mounts back towards their camp. Surging back towards their position, they finally broke clear of the dust cloud and in a few heartbeats, we could see what started the rout.

"It's the Germans," someone cried, and in a moment it was clear that it was indeed the Germans, their camp being on the northernmost point of the ring of cavalry camps. This distance caused them to arrive to the battle late, but the impact of their charge was enough to shatter the Gallic attack. Gauls were now galloping headlong for the single gate, and even from where we stood it was clear that there would be a massive crush at the entrance, there being more men and horses trying to jam through a relatively small opening than could reasonably fit. Caesar saw this as well, giving us the order to advance closer to the Gallic position, in the event that in the panic that was about to result there would be an opportunity for us to rush the gate and force entry. The sight of our advance did indeed cause a panic among the defenders in the camp between their outer walls and the walls of the town, so what started outside the walls was now transferred to the men in the camp as they began to run wildly towards the town gates. Meanwhile, the Gallic cavalry reached the gates, with chaos ensuing as men tried to escape the onrushing Germans, who rode in cutting and hacking at the enemy trying desperately to jam themselves through the gate. Some men leaped from their mounts onto the wall, scrambling to get away from the certain death that awaited them. The screams of men being slaughtered carried across the field, mingling with the triumphant shouts of the Germans and the panicked neighing of the horses trapped against the wall and the mounts of the Germans. Just as the first of the men trying to flee into the town reached the gates, they were shut on them, causing even more of a panic as the locked out Gauls began hammering at the wood while looking up at the warriors along the wall, gesturing to them in a clear attempt to convince them to open the gate and let their comrades in. The men

554

on the wall obviously refused, and now there were two scenes of mayhem and chaos, one by the outer gate, with the Germans finishing their slaughter of the Gauls who had not managed to squeeze through, and the other by the inner gate as the infantry milled about, waiting for us to come across the outer wall. Despite the obvious confusion, no order was given to advance and assault the wall, so once the slaughter was over at the outer gate, our cavalry retired back to their camps, leaving a field piled with the bodies of men and horses as we returned back to our tasks.

Work continued; now that the inner trench was finished, completing a circle some 11 miles around the town, we began work on the outer trench and finishing the forts. Before the forts could be completed, Vercingetorix ordered the remainder of his cavalry to break out at night, with each man going back to his own respective country carrying orders to raise whatever force they could to come to the rescue of the army trapped within the walls of Alesia. They broke out with the help of a contingent of infantry who stormed out of their camp, some armed with hooks on long poles that they used to pull part of the turf wall down, with others carrying bundles of wood thrown into the ditch then covered with the dirt that they pulled down to allow the horses to pass over. The whole operation took no more than the time it takes to march a mile, so by the time the alarm sounded and enough troops were rallied to the point of the breakout, the horsemen had long gone, heading in so many directions that any pursuit was pointless. However, it did serve to instill a greater sense of urgency in our work to build the outer trench. On the western side, with about a quarter mile between the inner defense and outer, we began work on the second trench, but this one was large, even by Caesar's standards, some 20 feet wide and 12 feet deep, and most unusually, made with perpendicular sides to provide the most difficult obstacle. This hopefully would protect us while we fortified properly, with Caesar's love of engineering fully expressing itself here at Alesia, albeit from the sweat off our brow. These extra works required more wood and since we had denuded the surrounding area of any tree large enough to suit our purpose, working parties had to range farther than before to bring back wood for the extra palisades and towers. Even so, Caesar had even more surprises in mind for the Gauls than our standard fortifications. Once the trench was completed, it was filled with water diverted from the flow of the streams, with yet another trench dug behind the outer one, this one only about five feet deep but lined with green branches, one end sharpened to a point before being hardened in the fire, with the other end buried on the opposite side of the ditch so it was pointed in the direction of attack. A few yards beyond the second trench, small pits were dug where smaller sharpened stakes were placed, then covered over; we called these things "Caesar's lilies", though I do not know where the name came from, since they looked nothing like lilies to me. There were eight rows of these. Even further along was another set of small pits, where we placed blocks of wood imbedded with iron hooks sticking up. All in all, these were the most formidable fortifications that we ever constructed, and they would need to be for the coming trial.

The Gauls were busy as well; the cavalry that escaped the town scattered to the four winds going to their respective people to sound the call for reinforcements to hurry to Alesia. In preparation for this, Caesar stepped up the foraging effort, ordering that a reserve of 30 days' supply be laid on, in the anticipation that we would be cut off from food when the inevitable relief column arrived. Work continued on improving the fortifications, through all watches, towers being erected every 120 yards, while smaller turrets that could house a single scorpion and serve as a shelter for the sentries were set every 80 feet. Several deserters informed us that all the Gallic food was brought into one place, to be rationed by Vercingetorix, and there were barely 30 days' rations left. This told us that we could expect some sort of relief effort almost any day; everything depended on how quickly the Gauls could gather their forces and set out on the march. Every day we worked on the fortifications, strengthening them in preparation for the coming onslaught, while almost every night the Gauls sent out a sortie from their camp in an attempt to disrupt our work and to affect a breach at some point in our fortifications. It was clear to all of us that Vercingetorix was determined to attempt a breakout of some sort, whether it was on his own or with the assistance of the relieving army. The forces coming to the relief of the Gauls were gathering in the lands of the Aedui, and such was the valor and notoriety of Vercingetorix by this point that of the 45 different tribes that inhabited Gaul, 44 sent contingents of men of varying size, so that the army that gathered numbered 250,000 infantry and 8,000 cavalry. Only the Bellovaci refused to send a contingent of any size, claiming that they preferred to deal with Caesar and his army on their own. But it was who was at the head of this vast army that angered us. Because of the tribal jealousies, the Gallic army had to be led by four different generals, and when we learned their identities it only strengthened our resolve. One of them was

Commius, who traveled with us to Britannia; another two were the faithless bastards Eporedorix and Viridomarus. The fourth was the only one that we understood and held no malice towards, and that was the cousin of Vercingetorix, Vercassivellaunus, who was only marching to the aid of his kin, something that we understood and accepted. Despite managing to gather relatively quickly, moving such a vast host takes not only a fair amount of time but a huge amount of food and water, and to administer such a force the Gauls selected tribal elders to oversee the administration of the feeding and care of the army. It was this council with which the generals had to contend on a daily basis, meaning there were disputes almost every day, according to the deserters and scouts we managed to capture. Whatever disputes there may have been, the Gallic army was still approaching.

For once, the situation inside the walls was more desperate than outside; while we were forced to range farther and farther for food, the people stuck in Alesia had no way to resupply and with every day that went by, their plight became more serious. The relief force was moving towards us, their whereabouts easy to track because of the huge size of the army, and it was the topic of conversation around every fire.

"So there's about 80,000 men on that side," Atilius mused, looking in the direction of the town. "And there's, what, 250,000 heading towards us from that direction," he pointed in what was essentially the opposite direction. "So, that would be........." his face wrinkled up as he tried to work the sum out in his head.

Because Scribonius had helped me learn how to calculate sums I wanted to show off a bit, so before he could answer, I replied, "That's 330,000 men that we have to kill."

We sat silent for a moment, I think all of us stunned at the thought of facing an army of such momentous size.

"And what's our strength, Pullus?"

For a moment I considered the idea of adding to the sum of our forces, but immediately dismissed it. There was no sense lying to my own men, so I replied, "We have ten Legions, but we're all understrength to one point or another. I can tell you that the 10th can field about 3,800 men; we have more than a hundred out of action for one reason or another. I haven't heard but I'm guessing that most

557

of the other Legions are in the same shape, so we can probably field about 40,000 Legionaries. We have about 8,000 auxiliaries, and about 3,000 cavalry. So that's about 51,000 men."

"To face 330,000?"

Vellusius sat glumly, throwing twigs into the fire as he asked his questions.

"So, that means we have to kill how many of those bastards apiece?"

"About seven," I said quietly, for I had done the figuring on this the day we heard about the size of the relief column.

"Well, that's a whole lot of killing to do. I think I'm going to turn in early," I tried to sound cheerful, waving goodnight to my comrades, eager to be away and free to think my own thoughts.

The day before the relief army arrived, an event took place that was difficult to watch, even for hardened Legionaries like ourselves. Early in the morning, the gates of the town were flung open; amid a cacophony of howls and cries of protest, a pathetic group of people, obviously civilians and either too old or too young to fight were forcibly ejected from the town. It turned out that this poor lot was none other than the Mandubii, the tribe to which the town of Alesia belonged, and their guests were expelling them by force. This was the most concrete sign of the state of Gallic supply; there was no other reason for these people to be ejected other than to save what little food was left. The mass of people, about 20,000 in all, were pushed along towards our lines, causing the alarm to be sounded and a scramble to man the walls. When they reached the first ditch, they stopped and cried out to our men on the wall, with those civilians who could speak Latin asking to be allowed to leave, saying that they had no part in this and were just innocent victims. Word was sent to Caesar, asking for instructions, but he refused to allow them to depart, not wanting to relieve the pressure on the Gauls in any way. The cries and lamentations of the Mandubii carried all the way to our positions, where we stood watching as the mass of people milled about, not able to leave the siege, but not able to go back into the town. A few tried to force their way back in, and were cut down by their own warriors, dissuading the rest from trying the same thing. They were not allowed to remain in the camps of the Gallic army either, so they wandered to the far eastern side of the siege, sitting down to await their fate.

"That Vercingetorix is a · hard bastard," the Pilus Prior commented. "Those are his own people he's doing that to."

I nodded; while Caesar was essentially doing the same thing, the Gauls were not our people. Their crying and shouting lessened to the point that there was only a dull moan, sounding more or less continuously as the women and children cried softly, bewailing their fate. It was hard to listen to, making nerves already stretched and raw even worse, so it was not long before a number of quarrels broke out among the men. I found myself running from one fight to the next, bashing men about the back and head with my *vitus*. The only way things calmed down was by the *bucina* sounding the signal to let us know that an army approached. Instantly, all petty squabbles were forgotten as we ran to the ramparts to get a glimpse of the relief column.

It was the biggest army we had ever seen by far, looking like a black swarm of ants that completely covered the hills to the west, a pall of dust hanging over them like dirty brown rain clouds hovering on the horizon. I was struck by the thought how apt that was, since a storm of sorts was certainly brewing. Once we got a good look at the approaching host, I sent the men back to our area to begin preparations for battle. I did not know exactly when we would hear the call to assemble but it would have to be soon, because we were now effectively cut off and surrounded, with no chance of supply. Back in our area, the men began making themselves ready, as did I, each of us performing by-now familiar rituals. Some of us once again set up our personal shrines with our household gods, making sacrifices to them. Others went to visit the augurs, paying a little extra for a clean liver and good omens. Not being particularly religious, I preferred instead to rely on the things that I could control, like making sure that the blade of my sword was razor sharp, along with that of my dagger, although I had only used it once in battle. I also polished my helmet, along with my phalarae, since it was the practice in Caesar's army to wear all decorations when we marched into battle. Combing the horsehair plume, oiling my armor and varnishing my leathers, I was lost in thought as I performed what was by now a comforting routine. Once done, I passed the word of a full inspection in a third of a watch, smiling when I heard the sound of cursing move from one tent to another as Zeno relayed the order. Some things will never change, I thought.

559

Fighting started not long after the Pilus Prior and I held inspection, with the cavalry engaging on the western plain again. In order to support the cavalry, Vercingetorix sent a large contingent of his infantry hauling bundles of wood to throw into the ditch, with other men again carrying the long poles with hooks to pull down the wall to create gaps through which they could send armed infantry and bowmen to provide support for the cavalry force of the relieving army. For another time we were relegated to being spectators as Caesar ordered the 10th to man both inner and outer wall. With our Century arrayed on the inner wall, we did not have a clear view of the ensuing battle, forcing us to try and determine what was happening by the behavior of the Gauls inside the walls that we were watching. From their reaction things were looking grim, the battle raging first for a third, then two parts, then a full watch. Standing on the parapet of the town, the Gauls trapped within soon went hoarse from cheering the efforts of their comrades, while our men began getting more nervous. I was standing by the Pilus Prior for a bit, chatting quietly about what we thought was going on, then after some time passed he sent me to the outer wall to see what was happening. Staying for a few moments, by this point the dust clouds completely obscured the plain, making it impossible to tell exactly what was going on, so I turned to an Optio of the Sixth Cohort, stationed on the outer wall since the beginning, asking him what he knew.

Shrugging, he said, "About as much as you do. I will say that before the dust got too thick, it looked like our boys were taking a good drubbing. Their archers were picking 'em off pretty good, but that was a watch ago now. Now, your guess is as good as mine."

I stifled a curse; it was not his fault that we could not see, so I thanked him and returned to the Pilus Prior to tell him what little I knew.

"Pluto's cock," he swore bitterly. Then, shrugging, he said, "Well, we'll find out one way or another."

It was just about sundown when something happened, a change that we could hear, as the fury and pace of the battle suddenly increased. Even as we watched the Gauls in the camps and town their animation and cries suddenly became alarmed, their tone quickly turning to despair, and shortly after, we saw the beginnings of a general retreat of the infantry back up the hill, in much smaller numbers than had headed down.

560

"Looks like we finally broke them. I bet it was the Germans again," the Pilus Prior mused.

He turned out to be right. As usual for them, they arrived late, yet when they arrived it was with devastating effect, turning the tide of the battle. Once the dust settled, we could see the plain littered with the dead and dying and despite the majority being Gauls from the relieving army, there was a fair number of Gallic cavalry who fought for us laying there as well. We stood on the walls through the night, but there was no more action, the Gauls in both camps content to lick their wounds and prepare for another assault.

The whole of the next day was quiet, for which we were thankful since it gave us a chance to get some rest. Then in the middle of the third watch, the *bucina* blasted again and we scrambled up, donning our gear before heading to the walls, to be greeted by a huge racket and the sight of the Gallic army in Alesia streaming towards us in the dark. They were alerted by their brethren on the outside of the walls that the relieving army was assaulting with the sound of horns, their own blaring the signal to advance in response. Running forward with the hurdles of wood, the Gauls began to throw them into the outer ditch. The relieving army brought with them a fair number of missile troops, especially archers, the first time that we faced such troops in large numbers, and they fired at the men on the outer wall, forcing them to seek shelter behind the palisade. The main thrust of the assault on the outer walls was occurring behind us to our left, so it was in this general direction that we could see the bulk of Vercingetorix's troops heading. They were crossing the expanse in front of us, exposing their flank to our artillery, and the twanging sound of the torsion ropes of the ballistae, scorpions and catapults began singing in the night, followed by the screams of men being alternately impaled, or struck by the one pound rocks thrown by our artillery. Because the Gauls were out of range of our javelins, we used slings, which each of us carried and practiced with whenever we had time. Despite the darkness, the Gauls were tightly packed enough that it was easy to hit someone and the night air filled with the thudding of our missiles, most of them made of lead, striking flesh or bone, followed by shouts of pain and curses of rage that needed no translation. Our arms soon grew weary from whirling the sling overhead, releasing one end of it to send another missile crashing into the mass of men that reached the inner wall and were now trying to pull it down in the same manner that the men on the other side had the day before. All along our walls, we could hear the blasts of *cornu* and the shriller sounds of the *bucina*, alerting men in the area that there was danger of a breach, while the Tribunes were busy sending men hither and thither to defend a threatened area. Time passed, and despite suffering no direct assault on our area of the wall we were still busy, helping carry ammunition to the artillery pieces that constantly needed to be fed like some beast, or using our slings until our lead shot was gone, whereupon we stumbled around, trying to find stones of a sufficient size and smoothness that would work as ammunition. The Gauls fought with the desperation of trapped animals, yet their raw courage was not enough; Vercingetorix's men were unsuccessful in creating a breach of a sufficient size to affect a breakout, despite it being a close-run thing. Before the sun rose, and obviously in fear of a counterattack on their flanks by those of us who remained unengaged, the besieged Gauls retreated back up the hill, their own horns signaling to the men on the other side trying to break in, who in turn retreated from the walls, leaving heaps of dead and moaning wounded laying before our works.

Daylight illuminated a scene of gruesome carnage; Caesar's lilies, along with the other obstacles were highly effective, leaving men impaled and unable to gird themselves sufficiently to pull their bodies off of the stakes. The men who stumbled into Caesar's lilies had gotten hooked like fish, either in their feet or through their calves, and despite their wounds, still were dangerous to approach. Accordingly, they had to be finished off from a distance, giving men the opportunity to practice their javelin work, wagering on who could kill one of the poor bastards with one throw and the like. Once they were bored with trying to affect single shot kills the wagering then turned to how many throws a man could survive, and shortly, the screams of the Gauls who were the object of this game could be heard ringing up and down the walls. Despite ordering our Century to not participate, of course a few men managed to sneak off to have their fun, Didius among them. My one consolation was that he came back broke, having bet everything on one Gaul who managed to survive three javelins longer than Didius wagered. Finally, the betting stopped as the last Gaul died, some of them looking like blood-soaked porcupines before they were finally finished off. Once it was safe, burial details were sent out to try to clean up the area, and since we were not one of the Cohorts hard pressed the night before but were close to the action, we were one of the lucky ones. It was times like these I was thankful I was Optio, convincing myself that this was the one small reward for all the other onerous duties I had to perform, since I did not have to dig the mass grave, or drag the bodies to throw them in. What I did have to do was walk around to make sure that no Gaul was thrown into the pit still alive; many of my comrades were not very scrupulous about such matters, but because of my fear of enclosed spaces, I could not bring myself to let someone, even an enemy, suffer such a fate. Thinking about it now, it is somewhat peculiar that I tried to avoid digging or dragging, but viewed killing essentially defenseless men as a less onerous task. That is what army life does to you I suppose, hardening your heart. And truth be told, most of the men I dispatched were alive only in the sense that they were still breathing, while those few who still had their wits about them were in such pain that when I stood over them, they looked up at me with thankful eyes, knowing that I was about to end their suffering. That is what I tell myself at least; it helps me sleep better at night, although it does not keep the faces from appearing in my dreams.

The Gauls were down to their last throw of the dice, deciding to try their luck at another spot in our defenses, on the north side of the town. It was on the north side where the terrain was arranged in such a way that there was a hill that we could not completely enclose within our works, so that one of the camps was actually located on the downward slope of the hill, with the bulk of the hill above them. It was at this point that the relieving Gauls would make one final attempt to assault, break through and link up with the besieged force. Vercingetorix's kinsman Vercassivellaunus would lead 60,000 men in the assault. Realizing that the element of surprise was essential, they crept out of their camp on the hill to the southwest of the town at night, taking a circuitous route, consuming all of the remaining night and part of the next morning before they reached their attack position. At a prearranged time, or signal, we never learned which, the remainder of the Gallic cavalry came thundering out of the internal camp, heading for the western wall once again, with the remaining infantry in the relief camp arraying themselves on the slopes of their hill, preparing to move forward. Simultaneously, Vercingetorix's army came out of the town, heading for the same spot where they first attempted to cross and some of the ditch was indeed filled in, which we were unable to clear out. Their intent was obvious; they were going to breach the inner wall at the most vulnerable spot, and then in the space between the two, swing up to the northern part of our works, where the assault element of the relieving army was attacking. Their goal was to hit the two Legions, the 8th and 13th, in the left flank while they were engaged to their front. Every redoubt was given a number, with the numbers moving from left to right if one was facing north; the redoubts under assault from the outside force, along with the camp were 21, 22 and 23. My Cohort occupied redoubts Seven, Eight and Nine, with my Century and the Fifth Century manning redoubt number Seven. The spot they chose was relatively close to our redoubt, directly to our left, and it was to this spot that Caesar came to direct the defense of our works, his presence signaled by his red standard, and his *paludamentum*. We were close enough to see the desperate struggle of Vercingetorix's men frantically flinging their long hooks up at the wooden palisade, trying to pull it down, the first step in breaching a wall. Our men were just as vigorously knocking them aside, striking down Gauls who were too impatient to wait for the wall to come down and instead were trying to clamber up by hand and foot. The main thrust of the attack of Vercingetorix was focused between redoubts One and Two, yet for the moment our men were holding. A rider came galloping up to Caesar and despite being too far away to hear, by his gestures and posture it was clear that the northern camp was in serious trouble. Labienus was sitting his horse next to Caesar, and we could see Caesar turn to say something to him. Labienus gave a quick salute, then came galloping in our direction but did not stop. A few moments later, men came double timing past us and we saw that the size of the detachment was a number of Cohorts. As they ran by we shouted to them, wishing them good luck, while they called back to us with the usual good-natured taunts about being left behind. A total of six Cohorts, led by Labienus, went running to relieve the camp; three Cohorts from the 10th and three from the 9th, which was positioned next to us and with whom we shared our camp. After they left, we turned our attention back to the fighting, wondering if we would be called to move to where the battle was raging. As it turned out, we did not need to, because the fighting came to us.

I do not know what prompted it, if there was a decision made, or if it just happened. Whatever the case, on some sort of unseen and unheard signal, Vercingetorix's force broke off their attempted assault then headed straight for us. Perhaps it was the sight of Caesar's standard, but suddenly there was a large group of very angry Gauls pounding down the gentle slope to our position.

"By the gods, they're going to overrun us," I heard someone shout, and I snapped back, "If one of you bastards takes one step back, I'll cut you down where you stand."

564

Then the first of them reached the ditch to begin throwing in their bundles of wood and clumps of turf as we began hurling our javelins, mowing men down, most of whom seemed to either fall, or knowing they were dying, throw themselves into the ditch in order to help fill it up. Within a matter of moments, it was filled and the Gauls came pouring across, waving their long hooks about in an attempt to grab one of the stakes of the palisade. Moving close to the edge, I slashed down at one of the poles, my blade slicing through one as big as a man's wrist like it was a twig. However, there were hundreds of poles and despite our frantic attempts, some of them managed to find their mark, with first one, then another stake tumbling down. Some of the Gauls used their hooks as weapons, and out of the corner of my eye I saw one grab a man by the neck. The Gaul gave a mighty heave, sending our man's head tumbling into the air, blood spurting from the stump of his neck a few inches into the air before his body tumbled over the parapet. The noise was deafening, the Gauls roaring out their anger and desperation, as we roared out our own back at them. Soon there were gaping holes in the parapet where several stakes were pulled out, whereupon the Gauls turned their attention to the turf wall, men using the hooks or their bare hands to try bringing the wall down. Our men were standing above them, slashing and thrusting down so that whenever they landed a blow it was usually to the head and face of the Gaul in front of him, who would tumble back, howling in pain, hands covering the horrible wounds. Yet the instant one man fell away, it seemed there were two more to take his place, and in several spots the wall began tumbling down. Running to the nearest area under threat, I was just in time to see the main part of the wall tumble away, a man in the first section named Sido falling screaming onto the spears and swords of the Gauls below, his shrieking cut mercifully short. Into the gap clambered two Gauls, scrambling as quickly as they could to their feet on the undamaged part of the parapet. Without hesitating they threw themselves at me, screaming their war cries. One carried a spear, the other a sword, and I found myself desperately parrying first one blow, then another, backpedaling away and praying that I did not trip over a body behind me. I did not have an opening for an offensive move as they continuously pushed at me. Then, the man with the spear, eyes wild with bloodlust and fear, managed a solid blow that pierced my armor, breaking several of the links. When he lunged, I desperately twisted to one side, yet even as I did, it felt like I was being struck along the ribs with a stave, the wind bursting from my lungs from the force of the blow. A searing pain shot along the length of my ribs and it was only instinct that caused me to reach out with my left hand to grasp the shaft of the spear with all my strength. Trying to withdraw the weapon, he was jerked off balance when it did not budge from my grasp, and I used his momentum to fling him to the side off the parapet, where he fell, losing his grasp of the spear to land heavily on the ground in the space between the two walls. With him out of the way at least temporarily, I gritted my teeth against the pain, using the butt end of the spear, swinging it quickly at the second man, who took a glancing blow on his right elbow, causing him to gasp and drop his sword. Before he could recover I was on him, and he frantically parried my thrusts with his own shield. However, now that I possessed a second weapon I quickly reversed the spear to begin jabbing with it, while thrusting with my sword. Now it was his turn to back up and in a matter of a few heartbeats I forced him to the edge of where the wall had been pulled down. He obviously felt the edge with the back of his heel because the panic on his face was clear to see. Despite himself, his eyes darted down to see how close he was to tumbling off, and that was all the opening I needed, my blade making a quick thrust to catch him directly in the throat, feeling the grate of bone as it exited the back of his neck. His eyes widened then rolled back in his head as I used my foot to kick him off my blade, sending him tumbling down onto the heads of some of the other Gauls who were just then scrambling up into the breach. The pain in my side was excruciating and I could feel the warmth of my blood spreading down my side, yet I could not spare a moment, the Gauls still swarming out from the nearest breach, making it look very much like our position would fall.

The fighting continued with this intensity, as I found myself running from one spot to the next along the parapet wherever I saw Gauls get a foothold and our men hard pressed. The Gauls fought with the intensity of wild animals trying to escape a trap, which in a sense was exactly what they were, and we quickly discovered that the only way to give ourselves a chance of survival was to match them in their fury. My arm was heavy from constantly using my sword, but it was my side that bothered me most, the blood continuing to seep and now running down my leg. Our wall was breached in several areas by this point, with the Gauls still climbing up onto the parapet and there were a number of small skirmishes all along the wall between the redoubts. The *bucina* sounded the call for reinforcements, yet I was not optimistic that they would arrive in time. Immediately after the call I looked over to see a couple of our men leap down from the parapet, retreating from the Gauls. They were men from my Century, and I was overcome with a sudden fury, even as the Gauls gave a triumphant roar. One of them turned back to his comrades down below, indicating that the breach had widened where he stood, and was quickly joined by another man. Before I could stop to think about the folly of what I was doing, I let out a bellow of my own, rushing at the men who forced my comrades to retreat for the first time ever, determined to redeem our reputation. I must have looked like I was coming from the gates of Hades, covered both in my blood and the blood of the men I had slain up to this point. Feeling my lips pulling back in a savage grin, I saw my enemy's eyes widen in fear at the sight of my approach. Even before they could bring their shields up I slammed into both of them, using a shield I had picked up from a man who no longer needed it despite having no memory of doing so, sending them both reeling backwards. The two men bounced into the Gauls behind them that were just climbing to stand on the parapet, causing several of them to tumble in a heap at my feet. There was a mess of arms and legs as they tried to scramble back upright, with the men on top looking up at me in terror, trying their best to protect themselves. I thrust and slashed with my blade, along with using the edge of the shield as another weapon, so that the cries of triumph that they were sounding a heartbeat before turned into screams of pain as my blade found its mark over and over. I could feel the razor sharp blade cutting into flesh and bone as I severed a man's arm above the elbow when he held it up in a futile attempt to protect himself, while in the same instant I chopped down with the metal edge of my shield to cleave into another Gaul's skull. Blood splashed all over my legs and torso while the men on the ground flailed at me with their own weapons, all of which I easily blocked with my shield or parried with my blade. In a matter of moments, what was just a threat an instant before was nothing more than quivering, steaming chopped meat, and I could feel their blood on my face and arms, my chest heaving and legs trembling from the exertion.

Turning to the two men who were still standing below the parapet, their faces blank with shock as they watched what I had done, I pointed at them with my sword and snarled, "You two bastards are on a charge. You better hope you die because I'm going to flay the both of you." Without waiting for any reply, I ran off, looking for the next danger point.

Hearing the clanking and pounding of boots approaching before I actually saw reinforcements arriving, a total of seven Cohorts were sent to help, and they turned the tide of the battle

567

fairly quickly. Once Vercingetorix saw that there was little chance of creating a breakout at our positions, the Gallic horns sounded again, the remainder of his force hurrying away, this time heading to the northern edge of the works, where the relief force was still furiously attacking the camp and redoubts Twenty-Two and Twenty-Three. As suddenly as it started, the fighting ceased in our sector, the sounds of battle disappearing to be replaced by the moans of the wounded and dying. Standing for a moment, I fought the dizziness that threatened to overwhelm me, brought on by the combination of my exertions and loss of blood. Luckily, the bleeding finally stopped, but it had dried, caking my armor all down my side, making movement difficult and I knew that any violent movement would tear the clots free and the bleeding would start again. Regaining my breath, I surveyed the damage, feeling my stomach tighten at what I saw. Every inch of the parapet in both directions was covered with bodies, and although most of them were Gauls, it was not by much of a majority. Even as I stared at the sight, the earth of the parapet seemed to move, with wounded men either struggling to pull themselves upright, or going through their death throes before they succumbed to their wounds. For a moment I did not know what to do or what direction to head, instead trying to decide the best place to start finding all the men of my Century, since I did not see the Pilus Prior anywhere about. Finally determining that it was best, and easier on me to stay where I was and call the men of the Century to rally on me, I tried to use my command voice, yet found the effort made me extremely lightheaded. Instead, I called for our *cornicen* to sound the assembly, but he did not answer. Cursing, I took a few breaths then bellowed out the call to assemble, almost keeling over in the process and only then men began to gather. I was relieved to see Vibius, covered in blood not his own, along with Scribonius, Vellusius and even Didius. Atilius did not show up, nor did almost a third of the Century, and it took a moment for the import of this to register. Yet the biggest shock was yet to come; the Pilus Prior was nowhere to be found, even after I sent men to search through the bodies. We had come to respect and admire Pulcher a great deal, despite the differences between our two previous Centurions, and I hoped that he was alive. Whatever his condition, we did not have time to dwell on it, because once more the *cornu* sounded, this time giving the signal to advance. Looking over, I saw Caesar jump up to the parapet from Toes, and he called out to us.

"Comrades, this is the moment we have been waiting for! I know that you are tired, I know that you are hurting from your wounds and the friends you have lost, but now is the moment when we can end this! Vercingetorix has turned his back on us, and he will pay for that mistake, I swear it to Jupiter Optimus Maximus!"

Pulling his own sword, he lowered it in the direction of the enemy and called out, "*Porro!*"

Making our way across the ditch, we formed up quickly, trying to ignore our fatigue and our diminished numbers, because we knew that Caesar was right. It was a mark of the desperation of Vercingetorix that he turned his back on us; perhaps he thought that he had inflicted enough damage on us that we would not be willing or able to take any offensive action, and it was this idea that inflamed our anger even higher than the loss of so many men. Beginning the advance at the quick step, as I was stumbling along behind the Century, Scaevola stopped and turned, calling to me.

"Pullus, get up here! You're the Pilus Prior now. Take your place!"

Despite being startled, I realized that he was right, so it was somewhat sheepishly that I moved up to the spot that Pulcher normally occupied. Once we closed the distance, the *cornu* sounded the command to begin double time, and I was concerned that the Gauls would hear it, yet they were so absorbed in their attack on the men of the 8th that they did not notice. Trotting closer, we drew within the range where we normally stopped to launch our javelins, but since most of us did not have any left and Caesar did not want to ruin the element of surprise, the command to charge with the sword was given immediately. With a roar composed of equal parts rage and triumph, we broke into a run. It was only then that the men in the rear ranks of the Gauls realized the danger that was upon them, but before they could turn to face us we slammed into them. Breaking out into a run ripped the clots in my side loose, so despite myself I let out a cry of pain, feeling warm liquid begin to run down my side again. Regardless, I gritted my teeth and started to hack and thrust my way through the now panicked Gauls.

The rout was total, and it did not take long to make happen. Within a matter of moments, the Gauls were running around the end of our lines, fleeing back to the town, most of them throwing down their weapons and shields so they could run faster. We only pursued a short distance because we were exhausted, although they needed no pursuit to keep them fleeing for their lives. While we were pressing the attack on the besieged army, our cavalry, circling around behind the relieving army, launched an attack on the rear of the Gauls on the outside of the walls. Labienus and the reinforcements he brought with him kept up the pressure in the front at the same time, so it was not surprising that the Gauls could not withstand it. The relieving army disintegrated, men being cut down by the cavalry, and Vercassivellaunus was captured, along with 74 enemy standards. Only the cavalry was in any shape to pursue the fleeing remnants of the Gallic army, the chase continuing well past midnight. The battle was over; all that was left was the aftermath of finding our wounded, burning our dead, and burying theirs. I could barely stand, my legs shaking so badly that I was worried that I was going to collapse in front of the men. Somehow, I found the reserves of strength to order them to form up, thankful that at least this last phase of the battle caused us no casualties. Marching back to our original positions, we saw that the men who worked as stretcher bearers were still busy, the *medici* for the Legion performing a quick assessment on our fallen men. The dead were already being laid out, waiting for their comrades to identify and claim the bodies to take them back to camp to prepare for their funeral rites. We were missing 15 men from our Century; I found six of them already laid out waiting for us, though none of them was Atilius. He was found being attended to by a *medici* as he sat, blood-spattered, with the faraway look one often sees in wounded men. The *medici* was working on his right hand and when I approached, I saw that he was missing two fingers, the little and third finger, the stumps protruding perhaps an inch from the base of his palm, the bone gleaming through the blood and torn flesh. While it may not seem like it, he was lucky; if it had been three fingers, or even his first two fingers instead of his last two, he would be discharged because of his inability to hold his sword. I called to him and for a moment he did not respond, then turning his head he saw me, a look of vague surprise on his face.

"*Salve* Pullus," he called out woodenly, and I responded, trying to sound lighthearted.

"Well, you lucky bastard. You won't be pulling any duty for a while," I told him, and a flicker of a tired smile crossed his face.

570

"I suppose not, now that you mention it. But Pluto's cock, I can think of other ways I'd rather get out of duties. This hurts like Dis," he replied.

"I can imagine," and even as I said this, I became aware of the pain in my side again, suddenly not feeling very well myself.

Regardless of how I felt, I still had to find the Pilus Prior, and I asked Atilius if he saw him go down. For a moment, Atilius acted like he had not heard me, staring off in the distance, and I was about to repeat myself when he raised his left hand, pointing to a place where the wall was breached.

"I saw him fall into the ditch over there," he said quietly, then met my inquiring gaze with a shake of his head. "I don't think you're going to like what you find over there, Optio. He fell right in the middle of a pack of Gauls, and they tore him to pieces."

Gulping, I tried to keep my face impassive, nodding my thanks. Telling him that I would see him soon, I stumbled over to where Atilius indicated, steeling myself for what I would find. Mounting the rampart, I gazed into the ditch, and as much death and killing as I had seen, I still felt my stomach lurch. There was a heap of bodies, yet I could see scattered among them bits and pieces of what obviously had been a Roman Centurion and I felt my jaw clench as I stepped down into the ditch, trying to keep the contents of my stomach down. Atilius was completely accurate; the Pilus Prior had indeed been hacked into pieces, and even today, the thought of what I saw makes my stomach lurch as I break out into a cold sweat. Fighting against my revulsion, I forced myself to gather his remains, placing each piece of him that I found up on the rampart, despite being forced to leave some of him behind because those parts were so badly mangled I could not tell exactly whether or not it was him or a Gaul. Nonetheless, I managed to recover most of his body, and calling the stretcher bearers over, I ordered them to place him on a stretcher to carry him over to where the dead lay. At first they balked, before I convinced them that their fate was going to be very close to his if they refused, so they sullenly piled him onto a stretcher and carried him over, depositing his remains alongside those of our dead who had not yet been moved. Only then, did I sit down, or more accurately fall down, and a *medici*, seeing my distress came over to examine me. I do not remember much more than this, as I fell backwards, my last memory looking up at the sky.

Waking up in the field hospital, my sudden movement into consciousness almost caused me to faint again. Waiting for my head to stop spinning, I sat up slowly, looking around as I tried to determine what time it was. Through a flap in the tent I could see it had turned dark; I must have been out almost a full watch. My side felt like it was enclosed in some sort of vice, and I looked down to see a bandage tightly wound around my torso, although it was stained red. Someone had made a half-hearted attempt to clean my blood off of me, but I still looked like half of me was dipped in it. My next thought was about my sword; it would be worth a small fortune for anyone sly or stupid enough to steal it. Feeling underneath my cot, I found to my relief that it, along with my blood-encrusted armor, helmet, and harness were there. Giving a short prayer of thanks to the gods, I carefully swung my legs over the edge of the cot, bringing myself to a sitting position. Despite my care, my head began to swim and I was sure that I would pass out in a dead faint, grimly holding onto the sides of the cot with my hands until my head cleared. Then I stood up, feeling my legs shaking but immediately ignored the tremors, telling myself that they were shaking earlier as well. Then with a bit of effort, I dragged my gear out from under the cot, where I almost pitched over again from bending over. That is when it hit me that my Century was without a leader, the memory of what happened to the Pilus Prior flooding back into my head, and I was forced to close my eyes to fight the nausea that threatened to overwhelm me.

"Here now, Optio," an accented voice called out, and I turned to see one of the Greeks who worked as a *medici* hurrying towards me, a worried look on his face. "You're not well enough to be out of bed just yet," he said, snapping his fingers and pointing to my cot, his meaning clear. If only he had not snapped his fingers at me, I probably would have listened and obeyed him, but his officious manner made me angry, and I was damned if I would let some civilian give me orders.

"Go fuck yourself, freedman," I snapped, causing him to stop dead in his tracks, his face a study in surprise and not a little fear, making me feel better. "I'm going back to my Century, and if you try to stop me, I'll cut your fucking throat," I tried to growl in my best impersonation of Pilus Prior Crastinus. Despite it sounding false to me, it clearly gave him enough of a pause that he reluctantly nodded his head. However, while he would not stop me, he would also not expose himself to some sort of punishment. "Very well, Optio," he replied reluctantly, "but if you insist, I must demand that

572

you sign yourself out. Wait here and I'll bring the necessary paperwork."

I could not help but groan out loud, and I saw a shadow of a malicious smile cross his face at my consternation. Was there no escaping paperwork, I thought to myself, even when all I want is to go back to duty? One would think that the army would like to see such dedication in their officers, but apparently not. Nevertheless, I signed out and carrying my gear, walked slowly back to our area, having to stop several times when the dizziness threatened to overwhelm me, one time being forced to sit on a barrel to catch my breath. Clearly I had lost more blood than I thought, but I was still completely focused on getting back to the Century to help prepare our dead for cremation. It is hard to describe how important it is to a Legionary to properly honor our dead, and I imagine that part of it is from a desire that if and when the time comes and it is your turn, that your comrades will give you the same attention and respect. Except it is deeper than that; it is the last way we can honor our friends and comrades, and it is also our chance to say goodbye, so it is extremely important that we do so in the proper manner. The final butcher's bill for the Century was a total of seven dead, including the Pilus Prior, and eight wounded, three of them so severely that they would either die before dawn, or if they did survive, their days of marching under the standard were over. Once the rest of the men recovered, we would be marching with 50 effectives; just a bit more than half strength from what took the final oath out of the original *dilectus* in Hispania, and about two-thirds strength of what started the campaign in Gaul. Now I was acting Pilus Prior, although I did not even consider that the position would be made permanent. The men were gathered around the dead in small groups, each tent section working on their own dead comrade, carefully, indeed one could say lovingly cleaning the body, wiping the blood from the corpse, and doing what they could to close the wounds that killed them. Somehow, by some miracle, the men of my original tent section had again escaped death, the only serious wounds being that of Atilius, and I guess if I counted, myself as well. Vibius saw me approach and in that moment, all the difficulties and disagreements dropped away, his eyes filling with tears at the sight of me. He came running to me and we embraced, holding each other, squeezing tightly despite the pain in my side.

"It's over, thank the gods," he whispered, then kissed me on both cheeks.

573

I returned the gesture, although I had to bend down to do so, which hurt a bit. The rest of my comrades came to surround me, even Didius among them, and without a word we stood huddled together, the tears flowing freely among all of us now. We had survived.

The funeral pyres burned throughout the night and into the next morning, all over the camp. Our casualties were heavy, particularly in the 10th and the 8th Legions, and my Century, First of the Second Cohort, along with the First and Second of the First Cohort, suffered the most. Primus Pilus Favonius had been killed, along with a total of nine Centurions of the 10th, meaning that there would be promotions. By mid-morning, our dead were burned, their ashes interred in the urns that would be sent to each of their families, their designated comrades taking care of their wills and disposing of property as the deceased deemed fit. Before noon, the *bucina* sounded the signal that a party of Gauls was approaching the camp; it was emissaries of Vercingetorix, offering his surrender. Despite this being expected, the reality of it created a huge amount of excitement and joy, the men congratulating each other, happy in the victory and that they survived it. Soon after, word was passed to assemble in the forum in two thirds of a watch, in full dress uniform, in order to witness the surrender of the leader of the Gauls. This presented a bit of a quandary for me since my armor was pierced and there was no time to have it repaired, nor to clean it, so I sent Vibius over to the quartermaster and although I had to pay a premium, he returned with new armor, already oiled and ready for inspection. He helped me to don it since I was so stiff it was almost impossible to lift my arms over my head. In fact, all of my comrades came to help me, polishing my leathers, shining my phalarae, and combing out my horsehair plume. I had to turn away to hide the tears I felt welling in my eyes at the sight of my friends helping me.

"You know," Vellusius commented, "you're probably going to get decorated again."

I was surprised at this, and asked why he thought so.

"Because you're such a big bastard, whenever you do anything everyone notices. If you fart you get decorated for it," Didius declared, yet for some reason, I knew that he was not insulting me, as did the rest of my friends. In fact, this caused a roar of laughter, Vibius slapping Didius on the back in recognition of his jest. I do not know who was grinning more broadly, me or Didius.

"Seriously," Vellusius continued once the laughter died down, "you were everywhere. You fought like Achilles, and we all saw it."

There was a chorus of agreement, and if I never got another decoration the rest of my life, I thought, this would be enough. Medals and awards are fine things, but the recognition of one's friends and comrades is so much finer, it is beyond comparison.

I did not know what to say, and finally all I could manage was a lame, "Well, someone had to do it. You flat-footed bastards were standing around with your thumbs up your asses."

There was a round of mock jeers at this, and in high spirits, we went to form up for the ceremony.

All in all, it was something of an anti-climax, at least until the very end. Caesar commanded that every chief of the Gallic tribes that took part of the rebellion present themselves to him, while he sat on a raised dais in the forum, surrounded by his Tribunes and Legates, Labienus and Antonius most prominent. I have spoken much of Labienus, but Antonius, over the last two years distinguished himself as well, and the early impression of him as a man's man and a friend of the *Gregarii* was reinforced during that time, so we were glad to see him in a place of honor. One by one, the Gallic chiefs approached, riding their horse and dressed in their finest armor, then dismounted and dropped to their knees before Caesar.

Then one of his staff, Hirtius I believe, would announce the name of the chief and the tribe of which he was chief, then ask Caesar, "What would you have of him?"

Most of them were stripped of their chieftainship, although a surprising number were allowed to retain their freedom, causing a bit of muttering in the ranks. At first, it was all very interesting, but once we saw how things were to go, it became quite boring, quite quickly. Finally then, there was only Vercingetorix left, and any boredom we suffered evaporated as he came riding into view. Everyone strained to get a look and once again I found reason to thank the gods not only for my height, but for my place in the First Century, especially since now that I was acting Pilus Prior, my place was in front of the men. I must say that he was an impressive looking man, wearing a helmet of the Gallic style, from which sprouted the wings of a raven. His armor glittered, inlaid with gold and silver, and he wore the long mustaches common to the Gauls, yet even so, it did not conceal his youth. He's not much older than me, I thought in astonishment, but despite his age, he bore a look of regal command that was clear even from a distance. Mingling with my hatred of him for what he put us through I found myself admiring him as well, because even as he dismounted his horse, a beautiful white stallion, to surrender to Caesar, his bearing carried a dignity that told us all that even though he was surrendering his body, his spirit remained unconquered. Every eye followed him as he walked slowly, with ponderous dignity, towards Caesar, before ever so slowly sinking to his knees, then offering up his sword with both hands, bowing his head as he did.

"Vercingetorix, of the Arverni, self-styled king of the Gauls," Hirtius intoned with what I felt was unwarranted malicious glee, putting special emphasis on the words "self-styled".

He was king of all the Gauls, I thought, there was no self-styling about it. Only he was able to unite all but one of the tribes, and nobody before him had done that. As these thoughts went through my mind, I heard angry mutters at my back and I could tell that I was not the only man who felt this way. Despite our anger towards him for causing the death of so many friends, we recognized his greatness, and indeed, by belittling him our victory over him was being diminished. The muttering quickly became mumbling, sweeping through the ranks, and I could see Hirtius' eyes widen in surprise, our anger and displeasure clear for him to hear. Caesar remained impassive, though I swear I could see the corners of his mouth turn up a bit, as if in approval at our displeasure, which made some sense because it was diminishing his own victory by applying such demeaning terms.

Hirtius hurriedly finished with the "What would you have of him?" and we quieted down.

Caesar did not answer for a moment, and when he did, he spoke so softly that we could not hear, but instantly Caesar's personal standard bearer dipped it down in front of Vercingetorix, forcing him to kiss it in a symbol of obeisance. Hirtius stepped forward, taking Vercingetorix's sword from his outstretched hands, then handed it to Caesar, who immediately passed it to another member of his staff.

576

Standing from his chair, Caesar looked down at Vercingetorix, and announced in his oratorical voice, "Vercingetorix, king of all the Gauls," his omission of Hirtius' term was a clear rebuke, and I could see his aide's face turn bright red, "you have risen in rebellion against Rome. Your rebellion failed, and under the rules of war, you and all of those who followed you into rebellion are now subject to disposition as we, the conquerors see fit. You, Vercingetorix, will accompany me to Rome, to be part of my triumph for the conquest of Gaul. As for your followers, I give your common soldiers, and any wives and children with them to my army, at the rate of one slave per *Gregarius*, to do with as they please, two for all Optios, and four for all Centurions. The remainder of the common people will be sold in a lot, with the money disbursed among myself and my fellow officers. The noblemen and their families will be allowed to return to their lands, but only after giving oaths of loyalty and surrendering of hostages. That is my judgment."

Nodding to the two Centurions standing on either side of Vercingetorix, he finished, "Take him away to confinement."

The two Centurions, both from the 8th, grabbed Vercingetorix roughly, pulling him to his feet, then proceeded to strip him of all his armor and his clothes, leaving him completely naked. Then, they placed a rope around his neck as a symbol of his bondage, leading him away to the jeers of the assembled army. Once he disappeared, an excited buzz swept through the formation, the import of what Caesar had just done hitting us. A slave is perhaps the single most valuable commodity that one can own, and would bring a lot of money, if their new owners decided to sell them. I would have two of them and I began to think excitedly about the possibilities. Would I sell both, or keep one for myself, as a status symbol? Of course, that meant that I must feed and clothe them, so perhaps that was not the best thing to do. I shook my head; it was all too much to take in at once. We were dismissed, and we headed back to our areas to talk about the sudden increase in our prospects.

With that piece of business out of the way, the next thing to be taken care of was filling the positions of Centurions, Optios, and the lesser ranks that were vacated because of death or serious wounds. It was with some trepidation that I waited to be informed who would be our new Pilus Prior, but nothing happened for some time, which in itself was extremely unusual. I thought that it must have to do with the fact that such a large number of Centurions and Optios were slain and that made deciding who was going to fill what spot more difficult, yet as the first day passed and announcements were made in other Cohorts, it became more and more of a puzzle. However, I was happy to learn that our new Primus Pilus was none other than Gaius Crastinus, replacing the slain Favonius. Despite this, still no word arrived of who our new Pilus Prior would be, and with the day dragging on, the speculation among the men of the Century became more urgent. Not once did I hear, nor did I myself consider my name as a possible candidate, so that when Primus Pilus Crastinus appeared and summoned me to follow him, I was completely confused about what was happening. Despite my best attempts, Crastinus, even in light our former relationship, refused to give me any kind of hint about what was going on, so the closer we got to the *Praetorium*, the more my heart raced as I tried to think of what reasons there could be to discipline me in some way. Again, despite being an Optio for a few years now, I still sometimes thought like a *Gregarius*, and that is always the first thing that goes through a ranker's mind when they are summoned to stand tall before the general. By the time we reached the flap of the tent, I was as close to panic-stricken as I think I had ever been. Stone-faced, Crastinus stopped and with a jerk of his head, indicated that I should enter.

"You're expected," was the only thing he said as I passed, and it was all I could do to keep from fainting dead away.

Stepping inside, I immediately stopped, not only to let myself adjust to the dim light, but to compose myself. Then, approaching the orderly's desk that stood guard outside the door into Caesar's office, I saluted the bored looking Tribune.

"Optio Titus Pullus, First Century, Second Cohort of the 10th, reporting to Caesar as ordered," I rapped out in what I hoped was my most official voice.

The Tribune was busy chewing on an apple, apparently thinking that the study of it was of the utmost importance as he studiously ignored me, fascinated by the piece of fruit. However, I had been in too long to be thrown by such tricks, knowing that this was the only way a pup like the boy in front of me could feel like he had any control over a wolf like me, so I stood impassively at *intente*, waiting him out. Once he determined that I was not going to fidget, he sighed, exasperated at being bested at his little game and got up, waving at me to wait. He stepped inside and I heard him announce me, then he reappeared, and said curtly, "Caesar will see you now."

Taking a deep breath, I squared my shoulders and stepped inside, unsure of what fate awaited me.

Caesar was seated at his desk, examining some papers in front of him. Nearby, sitting on the corner of a table was none other than Marcus Antonius, also chewing on an apple while he conversed idly with Labienus, who was sitting on the other side of the table with his feet propped on it. Hirtius was there as well, sitting at a smaller desk off to the side, along with the usual contingent of slaves and scribes busily scribbling away at the mountain of paperwork composing most of Caesar's day. Ignoring them, I marched to Caesar, stopped and saluted, intoning the same salutation I offered the orderly outside. Unlike the Tribune, however, Caesar stopped writing to acknowledge my salute, then leaned back in his chair, fingertips pressed together with his index fingers against his chin as he looked at me, saying nothing. Whatever composure I had managed to gather was rapidly melting away, and I felt my knees beginning the faintest tremor, my mind racing with the portents of this meeting. Finally, Caesar spoke, in a neutral tone that told me that he was neither happy to see me, nor displeased. I was simply a matter of business, which was even more unsettling, since my contact with Caesar had always been an occasion for happiness and pride.

"Your Pilus Prior was killed in action, as you know."

I was not sure what response was expected, so I merely nodded and responded, "Yes sir."

"And we have yet to name a replacement. I'm sure you've noticed that almost every other Century and Cohort that needs a replacement has already been seen to, correct?"

"Yes sir."

"So why do you suppose we have been waiting to name a replacement for your Century?"

I was flummoxed; I had no idea, and it indeed was the topic of speculation, yet I was not about to blurt out the various theories that my comrades had thrown out. "I....I really have no idea, Caesar,"

579

was the best I could manage, a faint look of surprise coming across his face.

"Really?" his mouth quirked at the corners, as if he was fighting a smile, deepening my confusion, "You don't know that there has been a huge debate raging about the suitability of one of the names being considered for the billet?"

Just the faintest hint of a dawning began to register in my brain, but I immediately put the thought out of my mind, dismissing it as hubris. There was no chance I was going to utter the name that popped in my head, so I decided to continue playing dumb, which fortunately was not very hard. In answer, I instead just shook my head this time, not verbally responding.

Caesar turned to Labienus, asking conversationally, "Labienus, would you care to utter that name?"

It was immediately clear that whoever it was, Labienus was against him, because his hawkish face turned dark, his irritation clearly visible and I marveled at the impunity of such a thing in front of his commanding officer. However, as I was to learn, Caesar was not much for formality behind closed doors, actually encouraging his Legates, Tribunes and even senior Centurions to voice their opinion without fear of repercussion.

Finally, Labienus muttered the name, but so softly I could not hear it, evoking a hearty laugh from Antonius, who poked at Labienus with a finger, "Come on man. The boy can't hear you."

I bridled at that a bit, since he was no more than a year or two older than me, yet that was how officers viewed us. A raw Tribune no more than 25 regularly called a *Gregarius* twenty years older "boy"; at least the dumb ones did. Antonius was not dumb, he was just nobly born and apparently that gives you 20 extra years' experience the day you are born.

"Optio Pullus."

You could have heard a gnat fart in the silence that followed, and there was a roaring in my ears as for a horrified moment I thought I was going to faint. Immediately following this was the stirring of anger; I was sure that these fine gentlemen decided to have some fun at my expense. Of course, why they would pick me

580

out of the 35,000 people in the army to choose from was not something I put any thought into, all I was sure of was that I was the butt of their joke. My surprise was evident to all, yet only Caesar seemed able to tell what I suspected.

"No, he's not joking Pullus. I know that this is somewhat unusual, that normally if you were promoted to Centurionate rank that you would be made a Junior Centurion and serve in the Tenth Cohort, or perhaps the Ninth. But it's not unheard of, and given the high casualty rate among the Centurions, when we looked at a list of candidates, your name was at the top of the list."

Before I could respond, Caesar added, "That's not to say that everyone," and he looked over at Labienus, who was still fuming, "agreed. But I saw what you did when Vercingetorix's men tried to breach the wall. You fought like ten men, and that's what convinced me that I'm making the right choice."

Because I was not sure what the proper response should be, the best I could manage was, "Thank you sir, I won't let you down."

"You'd better not, or I'll never hear the end of it from Labienus," Caesar replied mildly. He stood then, and offered his hand.

"Congratulations, Pilus Prior Pullus."

Leaving the *Praetorium* in a daze, I found Crastinus standing there waiting for me, his earlier reserve gone, a broad smile on his leathery face.

He slapped me on the back, exclaiming, "Congratulations you big bastard."

"You knew?"

"Of course I knew," he shot back somewhat huffily, "I was asked my opinion on the matter. I saw the list of candidates they had drawn up."

"And you thought I was the best one?" I asked half in astonishment, half in hope.

"Nah. I just figured that you couldn't fuck it up any worse than the other *cunni* on the list."

581

I had to laugh at that, but a pit was forming in my stomach. I was now the senior Centurion of the Second Cohort, and although I knew I was respected, having been in the army almost ten years, I was still only twenty-five. There were men much more senior than I who had just been passed over. The thought of their reaction dampened my enthusiasm like a sudden rainstorm, and Crastinus saw my glum face.

Growing serious, he said quietly, "I won't lie, Pullus. It's not going to be easy. This is going to piss a lot of the boys off, particularly the other men on the list. That's one reason it was so hush-hush; I think Caesar always planned on picking you but didn't want to create a storm of *cac* flying and get men riled up enough that he couldn't promote you without it being a big problem. Now," he mused, "he's dodged a javelin by just doing it. You're the one who's going to have to deal with it."

"Thanks, I feel better already," I replied sarcastically, drawing a barking laugh.

"I'm not here to provide sympathy boy. But I'll do what I can to help. Mostly though, it's going to be up to you. You're going to have to prove to everyone that you're worthy of the promotion."

We were walking to the quartermaster's tent to draw the crest I would need to affix to my helmet, along with some of the other extra gear that the rank provides. The first the Century would know I was now their Pilus Prior would be when I showed up wearing the crest; I already carried a *vitus*, although that was later abolished for Optios. There would be a formal promotion ceremony, but that was done all at once, in front of the whole army. Before that happened, I first had to call a meeting of the Centurions of the Cohort, followed by a meeting of the Cohort itself. My mind was racing with all the things there were to do, so I missed what Crastinus said, prompting him to call me by name. I looked at him, and he shook his head in mock seriousness.

"Not a very good start, ignoring your Primus Pilus."

"Sorry, Primus Pilus Crastinus," I admit to a bit of apple-polishing in addressing him by his full rank, since I knew that he had not heard himself called by that much as of yet, and I could tell it pleased him.

582

"I was saying, for whatever it's worth, I know you can do it Pullus. And I'll help you any way I can."

I looked at him in gratitude, then unbidden my mind raced back almost ten years before when I hated this man to the soles of his boots, marveling at how far I had come.

Approaching the Century area, the men were lounging by the fire, and they looked up as one of them automatically called out that senior Centurions were approaching. They all immediately popped up to stand at *intente* before any of them noticed that something was different, and I am sure their first thought was something like, "Here comes the new Pilus Prior. By the gods, he's as big as Pullus."

It was a few heartbeats after that before there was a registering of the fact that not only did the new Pilus Prior look like me, it was indeed me in the flesh. Even at their position of *intente*, I was heartened to see smiles creeping across the men's face as they realized what it meant.

A knot in my throat started to form, then the Primus Pilus' voice cracked out, stopping the moment. "What are you *cunni* smiling at like drooling idiots? Haven't you ever seen a Pilus Prior before?"

He looked at me and said sternly, "I apologize Pilus Prior Pullus," giving my new title and name a boost in volume so that everyone not in eyesight could hear the news, "your new command seems to be composed of imbeciles and lunatics. I don't know who trained this lot, but they should be dismissed from the eagles immediately."

Of course, this was all in jest, since it was Crastinus himself who trained this very Century and was our first Pilus Prior. Now they were on their fourth, and if I was not so happy it would have been a sobering thought. Only one was promoted, and he stood before us. One was forced to retire while the other died, not exactly reassuring odds. But there was a saying; if you wanted to live a long life, why did you join the Legions? Live hard, die young and leave a good looking corpse behind for cremation was how most of us looked at things. Very few of my comrades thought seriously about the future the way I did, and I have often wondered what role this played in my survival through so many battles. My side was aching, meaning I was still not quite up to doing anything strenuous, but I had survived yet again and I made a mental note to find some way to properly thank the gods with an appropriate offering. The Primus Pilus left me with the men, and immediately after I gave them the command to return to their prior attitudes, they came bounding to me, offering their congratulations. I wanted to think that most of them were sincere, but I was smart enough to know that a fair number of them were merely trying to grease the wheels in the event that they fell afoul of me at some point down the road. Just when I was about to get upset, I thought wryly, why should I, it's exactly what I would have done, and I think one of the keys to my success in many areas was that I never lost sight of what it meant to be a *Gregarius*. During my career, I saw too many Centurions who underwent some sort of transformation, thinking that suddenly because they were no longer in the ranks and had their own latrine, their *cac* did not smell the same as the rest of the men. The men whose reaction I was most anxious to gauge were of course my former tentmates, particularly Vibius, because I was now two ranks ahead of him. Then I realized with a sudden thrill that now that the spot of Optio was open I could appoint who I wanted, provided they were sufficiently senior, which Vibius certainly was, and of the appropriate rank, which he was as well. Just as suddenly, however, my stomach twisted as I was hit by the recognition that because I was already operating at a disadvantage, with the Centurions under me watching every move I made like a hawk, there was no real way I could make Vibius my Optio. It would not matter whether he was qualified or not, his promotion would cause jealousy, making it as close to guaranteed as possible that whispers of favoritism passed from one fire to another. I felt like I was dashed by cold water, even as I went through the motions of accepting the congratulations from the men, agonizing over how to tell Vibius. The fact that I had not even brought the subject up with him but was already worried about how he would react at being passed over shows how entrenched in my own viewpoint I was back in those days. It never occurred to me that perhaps Vibius did not want to be Optio; because of my own ambitions, I naturally assumed that others shared the same goals. Luckily, for both of us I think, once I did broach the subject with Vibius, he instantly threw up his hands in horror at the thought of being considered for Optio.

"Titus," he said once we walked away to chat in private, "I've got no desire to be an Optio. This is as far as I want to go. I've got a little more than six more years to go, and then I'm going home to start my life. This isn't my career like it is yours. I may have thought so at one time, but I know that although I love the army, I'll be ready to go home when my time is up."

There was no way to adequately express my relief at his resolution of this one dilemma, yet I still faced others ahead of me, and we both knew it. I have sometimes thought that the main reason Vibius said he did not want to become Optio is to help spare me at least one of the trials that lay ahead.

My meeting with the other Centurions did not start auspiciously, since I was late to my own conference, although I do not remember the reason for my tardiness. The five other Centurions were gathered in my tent, all of them rising to *intente* as I entered, startling me. My reaction caused a couple of smirks, and my heart sank at this sign that I was already making a hash of things. It is probably a good idea now to give the names, along with the Centuries they commanded, of the first Cohort I was to command. Gaius Domitius Celer was the Pilus Posterior of the Second Century; a squat, ugly little man with a nose broken so many times it was just a misshapen lump protruding from his face. Normally, he would have been the leading candidate for the position I now held, but Celer possessed a tendency to drink a bit too much, and I guessed that this was the main reason he was passed over. He clearly did not see it that way and would prove to be the most obstinate of the Centurions in the Cohort when it came to accepting my authority gracefully. Titus Flavius Priscus was the Princeps Prior, leader of the Third Century. Priscus was a good man, even if just to look at him he did not present the sight of what one would think of as a Legionary, let alone a Centurion, but this was deceiving. He was of average height, several inches shorter than I, of medium build, with plain regular features and a strong jaw that slightly jutted out his only distinguishing characteristic. The Centurion in charge of the Fourth Century was Princeps Posterior Marcus Arrius Niger, a dark swarthy Capuan who got his start in Pompey's army and was a crony of Celer's, to the point where he mimicked the other's attitude in everything, including how he viewed me. He bore a long scar down the length of his arm that he earned in our battle with the Nervii, but he was a brave enough man and a decent leader. Marcus Julius Longus was the Hastatus Prior, the Centurion in charge of the Fifth Century, and was a man to watch because of his apparent fondness for finding reasons to punish his men. There were plenty enough men like Longus in the Legions who completely forgot what it was like to be a *Gregarius* and therefore decided to rule by fear. While I have no problem with using fear in itself, there had long been whispers that Longus was using these punishments to enrich himself. Once I got settled in and reviewed the Cohort diary, in which every activity and punishment is recorded every day, I was struck by the fact that, despite leading the Cohort in writing his men up, the rate of those accused of charges serious enough to earn some sort of corporal punishment, like a flogging, was the lowest in the Cohort. The vast majority of the infractions for which he wrote his Legionaries up were of the variety that called for monetary fines and it was this I found disturbing, although discovering the problem would have to wait for a while. First, I had to get the idea in their head that I was leading the Cohort, whether they liked it or not. Finally, there was Marcus Antonius Crispus, the Hastatus Posterior, Centurion of the Sixth and final Century. At that time I did not know much about him; what I did know amounted to the mutterings of his men that I overheard. He was the oldest of all of us, and I believe he had either accepted or resigned himself to the idea that this was as high as he would go and no higher. Here they all were, standing before me, technically subordinates to me, but I could already tell that there were a couple of them who were going to pose a problem. Clearing my throat, I began by offering them some wine, an offer which they all accepted. Zeno, who was actually more experienced in matters of this type than I was had already prepared for this meeting, presenting a tray with six cups. In his will, Pulcher left me a number of amphorae of Falernian wine, though at the time I did know why, but I suspect now that he had a hunch that I would be his replacement. Because I had no real interest in wine, he probably figured that I would not worry about using it in a profligate manner. In fact it was Zeno who casually informed them that what they were being offered was Falernian, and I saw a number of different reactions, ranging from surprise on the face of Priscus, a hint of anger that was in a clear struggle with desire on the face of Celer, to a look of concern on the face of Niger, who kept glancing at Celer to gauge what reaction he should be having. Unfortunately, Celer was torn between the idea of refusing the drink, which I suspected was part of the plan he hatched with Niger, thereby drawing a clear line of battle, yet was taunted by the spirit of Bacchus that resides in every wine lover's soul, and in the end Bacchus won. Giving Niger a slight shrug, he licked his lips thirstily as he reached for the cup. Once their cups were charged, I offered a salute.

"To the Tenth, and to the best Cohort in the Legion, led by the best Centurions. Second Cohort!"

"Second Cohort!"

They echoed my toast, and we all tossed back the cup of wine.

"Congratulations on your promotion, Pilus Prior," said Longus, in a tone and manner that oozed insincerity. However, I made no comment, choosing to accept his words at face value for which I thanked him politely. Now that the formalities were out of the way, I motioned for the Centurions to take a seat on the stools. Since Pulcher held many meetings in his tent, there were more than enough stools to go around, and I took one, although I faced them. They sat, hands on knees, none of them speaking, all waiting to hear how I would approach this. The truth was that despite agonizing over it, I still had no idea what would come out of my mouth; the only thing I could control at this point was the manner in which I spoke, so I tried to remain as calm and unemotional as I could.

"Gentlemen," I began, "thank you for your kind wishes. I'm extraordinarily proud and more importantly, humbled by the trust that Caesar has placed in me."

These were not idle words; I wanted to introduce Caesar's name as quickly as possible, to reinforce the point that it was he who promoted me and nobody else.

"I can only hope that I live up to the high honor he's given me, but with you helping me, I know that the Second Cohort will acquit themselves with as much glory and devotion to duty as we have in the past. I look to the example you've already set, and I'll do my utmost to meet that standard."

Heads nodded; I was not saying anything particularly surprising at this point and it has never ceased to amaze me how susceptible to flattery Legionaries of all ranks are, and I include myself in that group. We love to be praised, and I could see my honeyed words were striking home with at least a couple of them.

Forging ahead, I continued, "As you all know, we're in the process of reorganizing the army, and then we'll be dispersed to winter quarters."

This was common knowledge, yet what I hoped to do was to impress them with something they did not know.

587

"Perhaps you'd be interested to know where the 10th is going to be stationed this winter." My words created the desired effect, because to a man they sat forward on their chairs. Waiting for a moment, I savored the undivided attention I was being paid, before I told them, "Narbo. We're going to be going back to Narbo."

This was met with a round of cheers; Narbo had been our home for two years and we carried fond memories of the town. Perhaps it was because of the milder climate than the other places we stayed in, although I think it had more to do with the friendly townsfolk, particularly the females.

"Now that you know, we can begin the work of getting the Cohort ready to receive the orders. Whether the men know where we're going or not, we're going somewhere, since it's close to the end of the season and for all intents and purposes the war is over."

My last sentence raised some eyebrows. Raising his hand, Crispus asked warily, "Excuse me Pilus Prior, but what do you mean 'for all intents and purposes'? The war's over, we all know that. Are you saying that something's afoot?"

I hesitated, because the truth was that I had heard no such rumors; my feeling that there would be more fighting was mine and mine alone, putting me in a bit of a dilemma with this question. If I tried to add to the veracity of my beliefs by fabricating some sort of information I was supposedly privy to, then nothing else happened, I would be seen as someone who at the very least exaggerated, if not outright lied. However, if I were to tell the complete truth, that this was merely a feeling I had, how would it be received by these men who, in their eyes at least, were more senior than me, if not by rank than at least by virtue of time in service? My mind raced as I tried to decide the best tactic.

Suddenly, I was inspired. "What I'm saying Crispus is that how many times have Gauls done the stupid thing? What I'm saying is that as long as there's a Gaul alive, given their unpredictability it's only prudent that we be prepared for another attack at any moment."

I saw Crispus digest this, and as I would learn about him, despite not being a particularly quick thinker, he inevitably would arrive at the most logical conclusion if given time. Celer and Niger were not willing to even go that far, however, with Celer choosing this moment to make his first overt stab at me. "So, Pilus Prior,

588

you're not saying this because you.....know anything specific, correct?"

While I did not like the way he inflected the word 'know', I could not really argue the point, so I merely nodded. Celer smiled, but it was not a friendly smile as he continued "While your reasoning is certainly sound, Pilus Prior, if I could be so bold to suggest, as a man who's been a Centurion for some time, that it would be a good idea to refrain from that kind of speculation where there are ears that can hear. You know how the *Gregarii* are; washerwomen have nothing on them when it comes to gossip."

He finished with a laugh, and I saw Niger try to smother a smirk, but I was not going to be cowed that easily. "Of course, Pilus Posterior, but I'm speaking to my Centurions, not to the men. Are you suggesting that I need to be wary of what I say in front of my officers?"

Looking about in mock surprise, I stared at each of them in turn as if I were trying to determine to whom Celer could possibly be referring. His face turned a satisfying shade of red, and he spluttered, "Of course not! I'd never dare to suggest something like that. I've served with these men for a long time, and I trust each of them with my life."

"As do I," I replied evenly. "But I'm glad that we settled that question early on. Thank you very much for your insight, Pilus Posterior." I managed to keep my face completely blank, but it was a struggle.

Before we were marched off to our respective winter camps, the army was assembled one last time, for the final decoration ceremony. My friends were correct; once again I was singled out for decoration, another set of phalarae, causing them to joke that it was lucky I was as big as I was or I would not have room for the decorations. I was one of 20 men of the 10th who were decorated, while there were probably a total of more than 200 decorations given out to the Legions and auxiliaries, particularly the cavalry, the German cavalry most especially. Awarding so many decorations meant that we were standing there for a very long time, and my legs were still very shaky because I was not totally recovered from my wound. In fact, I would never fully recover, at least in the sense that I was never again as limber in some ways, unable to twist my body like I was able to before it happened. Finally I went to the Legion doctors who told me that scars of this nature form a tough tissue with no flexibility that covers the torn muscle, and that I would just have to live with it. Therefore, I stood as still as I could as each Legion received their awards, then each eagle was garlanded with the traditional ivy as a sign of our triumph. Once all that was done, we hailed Caesar as *imperator* three times, and he was presented with the ivy crown as symbol of his status. I know that a few years later his thinning hair got to the point that he wore it all the time, but he still had enough hair then that he did not feel the need. He did wear it the rest of the day, then put it away.

In the wider world, while the rebellion was essentially crushed, there were still embers of resentment smoldering among the tribes. The 10th was indeed sent to Narbo, the farthest south of any of the Legions. Because of that, we experienced a quiet winter, and somewhat depressingly a quiet next year. The other Legions were not so lucky; before the end of that year Caesar was on the march again, first against the Bituriges, taking the 11th and 13th into the field. It was not much of a rebellion, Caesar realizing that it was more out of desperation than for any other reason because their lands had been ravaged, making them desperately short of food. It took little more than Caesar marching into their lands for the rebellion to collapse where, in order to keep the peace, Caesar did not exact any punitive punishment. Instead of the normal custom of taking hostages and allowing the Legions to enrich themselves by plunder, he paid the troops a bounty out of his own pocket of 200 sesterces per *Gregarius*, and 2,000 per Centurion as compensation, leaving the Bituriges unmolested. Less than a month later, the Carnutes did the same thing, so Caesar called for the 14th to join him, along with one of Pompey's Legions that Pompey lent Caesar almost a year before that was in garrison and had not marched with us much, the 6th Legion. I would come to know the men of the 6th very well indeed, but that was still in my future. Caesar forced the Carnutes to flee from the town of Cenabum, as once again the Legions occupied the homes in the town, with the Carnutes forced to live off the land, hiding in the woods and foraging for food in the middle of winter, meaning it was not long before they submitted like the Bituriges. Then, just a couple of weeks later, it was the turn of the Bellovaci, except this was a larger threat than either the Bituriges or Carnutes presented, because the Bellovaci was one of the two tribes that held back from joining with Vercingetorix, so they did not suffer in the same manner as the other Gauls. Now, Caesar called the 7th, 8th and 9th, and despite the fact we knew it

590

was only because we were so far away, this did not sit well with the Legion. We were accustomed to being the Legion that Caesar relied on and now sitting in camp far away, we could not help feeling like this was a slight on our honor. Consequently, I will believe to my dying day that this was when the seed was planted that blossomed a few years later, when the 10th mutinied during the civil war. The one benefit of all this activity was that I was proven right in my prediction, which quieted down Celer and Niger, if only for a bit.

This was the pattern for the next whole year; a local rebellion would flare up, and Caesar would go rushing off with first one group of Legions then another stamping it out. In almost every case he acted with his usual clemency, but only on one occasion did he make an example of the rebels and I believe that it was a sign of his frustration and growing anger at the intransigence of the Gallic tribes that he did so. It was at the town of Uxellodonum, and as you no doubt know, gentle reader, Caesar ordered the hands of the entire garrison chopped off then thrown in a pile outside the town walls as a sign to all of Gaul that Caesar's patience and mercy had its limits. Meanwhile, the 10th sat in garrison throughout all of these small campaigns, and I have already mentioned what I believe the end result was, but it had an impact on a more personal level, in a number of ways. Professionally, the lack of opportunity for combat was problematic in asserting my authority over the Cohort, since it was on the battlefield that I truly felt in my element, and where I bowed my head to no man. Whenever I was fighting, I suffered no doubts, no hesitation, and never questioned myself about whether I was doing the right thing. Handling a Cohort in garrison presented a different set of challenges than commanding them in battle, but were just as difficult, perhaps more so, at least in their own way. Celer always looked for subtle ways to try to undermine my authority, usually focusing on things that emphasized my youth, which as I discovered seemed to be the main source of contention. My battle record during my time in the Legions was perhaps not the most notable in the entire army, yet I do not think it is hubris when I say that my name would be among those mentioned as contenders, so those Centurions giving me problems were wise enough not to comment on that aspect of my leadership, since above all things, rankers respect fighting ability. They instead concentrated on my overall life experience, or lack thereof, word of which filtered back to me through my friends.

"I have more gray hairs on my head than the days that Pullus has been shaving," was one of the more memorable comments.

What they did not realize was that although it was irritating, it was equally as amusing to me, just as it was to Vibius, because we were the only two who knew that I was in fact only 26, not the 27 that was my official age. Still, these attempts were just one more thing I had to worry about, along with keeping my men out of trouble, a full-time occupation in itself. Legionaries are funny creatures; as much as we grumble about the constant marching, the back-breaking work of making a camp and the dangers posed in battle, we quickly become bored by peace, and Caesar's army more than any other in Roman history, I believe, suffered most acutely from this malady. We were constantly in action for eight years, as a result losing our taste for a peaceful life. Although in some ways it was similar to when we were new *Gregarii*, young and full of energy, eager to show the outside world how tough we were, now it was a much more dangerous proposition. Before, it was as much boyish exuberance that fueled our confrontations with the civilians in the surrounding area; now it was simply that we were so inured to killing that it seemed to be just as suitable a solution to a dispute as settling things peacefully, or even with one's fists. We had killed so much that now it held all the emotional impact on us of making a fire, or cooking a meal. In short, the ability to inflict violence on another man was simply a skill, in the same manner as being a carpenter, or being a good orator. Naturally, this attitude was a guaranteed way of causing problems with the civilians in the town, so that I found myself heading into Narbo every few days, carrying a purse heavy with coin, my mission to buy off an enraged father whose son was stabbed to death over a dicing dispute, or a family left destitute by the killing of the husband and father of the family. What I always found interesting was how quickly most people's rage turned to calculation when they heard the jingle of the coins, to the point that within a few moments the weeping invariably stopped and the haggling began, with a man's life reduced to a number of coins, the only point of contention now being the relative value that the life held to the injured party. All of the money that I spent was my own, although it did not make much of a dent in my fortunes, since I decided to sell both of the slaves I was awarded. But not every situation could be salvaged with gold, and I will never forget the day that I heard Vibius call for me outside of my room. The tone of his voice immediately told me that something serious was afoot, so I did not bother to make myself look more official by belting my tunic the way I was supposed to, bidding him enter instead.

The look on his face was almost grief-stricken, and his voice choked as he said, "Titus, you're needed in town. It's Atilius. He's in a lot of trouble."

Vibius was not exaggerating, and I knew the moment I heard the circumstances that I did not possess enough gold to buy him out of trouble this time. The months of peace were hard on all of us, but were the most wearing on men like Atilius who required the absolute discipline of an army on campaign to keep him from falling into his old habits. Every day of peace eroded the hold the army had on Atilius, and while all of my old tentmates did whatever they could to keep him from destroying himself, after a time it became clear to them all that if a man is intent on doing something, no matter how stupid and dangerous it is, he will find a way to do it. And truthfully, one's patience only goes so far when dealing with men like Atilius, at least it did in my case and I suspect I was not alone. Still, now that the inevitable had happened, we were all horrified and upset that it finally came to pass. This time, Atilius somehow convinced himself that a local girl was giving him signals of encouragement that any amorous advance he made would be welcome, then one night decided that the time was right, following her from the market where she bought bread for the evening meal, back to her home. If what he did was not bad enough, the fact that she belonged to the local nobility was more than enough to tip the scales and seal his fate. Waiting for dark, he climbed up to the second story, somehow picking the right window to crawl into the girl's room. He was still in the room when I arrived, held there by three very angry men, the only other occupants being three bodies, the blood pooled and congealed around them. As angry as they were, these men knew that if they killed Atilius before alerting us and giving us the opportunity to administer justice on our own terms there would be a lot more deaths, and they would not be Romans. Stepping into the room, being brought there by Vibius and the rest of my old section, my nose wrinkled at the smell of death and I was struck by the fleeting thought that I was getting soft. There were three men, each of them holding a Gallic sword, but Atilius was not giving them any reason to worry that he would resist as he sat slumped on the floor a short distance away from the body of the girl lying on the pallet that had served as her bed. She had been pretty, and young, not looking a day over fifteen. Her face was pale, and there was a gaping hole under her chin where her throat was cut as she lay on her back, eyes staring wide up at the roof of her house. Her nightclothes were ripped open, so she was essentially naked and as I saw my men, Didius most overtly, gazing at her naked body, I felt a surge of anger.

"Cover her up, you Gallic bastards," I spoke savagely, two of them blanching in fear, while the third man became visibly angry, his face turning red, hand tightening on the hilt of his sword as he took a step towards me. Immediately, my men drew their own weapons, surrounding me, pointing them at the angry Gaul, his hostility immediately deflating to become as obsequious as the other two.

"I apologize for my anger, Centurion," he spoke in heavily accented Latin, "but the only reason we have not covered her up was because we wanted you to see the scene exactly as it was found."

I was mollified by this response; it made sense, so not wanting to make things worse, I adopted a civil tone as well. "Very well. I have seen her, so please cover her up."

My command was obeyed immediately, one of the men taking a blanket lying on the floor and covering her whole body. The other two bodies I was not concerned with; they were men and while wearing their nightclothes, were decently covered. They lay in a small heap, one on top of the other, and a quick examination told me that they were killed by what was clearly a Roman blade, both with thrusts to the chest. Satisfied, I turned to where Atilius was sitting, seemingly oblivious to the world around him, his knees drawn up with his arms wrapped around them, mumbling something unintelligible. Stepping towards him, I saw the sword sitting on the floor next to his hand, covered in blood, as was he, although a quick examination told me that none of it was his. Well, I thought to myself, he always could fight. That was never his problem. Moving closer, once my feet came within his view, his head slowly rose as he focused and recognized the Roman boots on my feet. Almost comically slow, his gaze traveled up my body, as if he was trying to take in exactly what was standing before him, but the moment his eyes got to my face he broke into a smile. Despite my anger and disgust I felt my heart twinge, watching as he pulled himself unsteadily to *intente*, and I could smell the wine emanating from every pore of his body, my nose again wrinkling from the sour smell.

"Pul....I mean, Pilus Prior Pullus, sir. It's good to see you sir! There's been some sort of misunderstanding, but now that you're here, I know it'll be taken care of, and we can go home, right sir?"

I kept my face hard, except I did not want to put him on his guard, so I asked him in the same tone I would as if we were sitting around the fire. "First we have to find out what happened here, Atilius. Once we get that straightened out, then we'll see what happens next."

I knew I had to be careful not to give the Gallic men the impression that we were just going to escort Atilius back to camp then free him, and I felt their hard eyes on me as I talked to Atilius, measuring my intent.

"Sir, I didn't do anything wrong," protested Atilius, prompting growls of rage from the Gauls, along with gasps of disbelief from Atilius' comrades.

Before I could say anything, Vibius burst out, "You didn't do anything wrong? Atilius, look around you. This place looks like a butcher's shop."

"I was just defending myself," Atilius exclaimed, his eyes never leaving my face, knowing that ultimately it was what I believed that would determine his fate. "Me and the young lady were having a nice quiet time, when those two," for the first time, he looked away from me, indicating the two corpses with a contemptuous nod, "came busting in, waving their blades about and roaring their gibberish at me. I tried to explain, but then she started screaming like a *numen* with her ass on fire, and started clawing at me. See," he pointed to his face, and indeed he did have scratches along his cheeks, not particularly deep but clear for all of us to see. I had to shake my head; he actually thought that pointing out the scratches that the girl inflicted on him was going to help him corroborate his story, not condemn him further.

"Atilius," I tried to be patient with him, though it was difficult, "those scratches don't help back up your story that you and the girl were having 'a nice time' as you put it. In fact, it does just the opposite."

A glimmer of dawning crossed his face, but he was not going to cut his losses and keep his mouth shut. "You know how women are sir, especially these noble-born *cunni*," the use of that word caused one of the men to howl in outrage and he took a step forward, the only way he was stopped was by the point of the sword Vellusius held to his chest. The Gaul glared at Atilius, then spat on the floor, muttering something about Roman dogs under his breath. This situation was growing worse by the moment and I knew I had to draw matters to a conclusion as quickly as I could.

Atilius, however, was oblivious as he continued. "They want to have a roll with us low-born trash because they're just like all women, they love warriors, neh? But the moment those two kicked in the door, she had to pretend that I was doing something she didn't want, but that ain't true sir. She wanted me sir, that's all there is to it. We've been seeing each other almost every day, and today in the market, she let me know she wanted some of ol' Atilius and she couldn't wait for it."

That was the first glimmer of hope that Atilius might have a chance to escape with his life, and I pounced on it. "Atilius, this is very important. Did anyone else see you two together talking in the market?"

For a moment, Atilius looked puzzled at my question, then just as quickly my hopes, and his, were dashed. "Talking sir? I wouldn't say that we were talking. We didn't exactly have a conversation, sir. She just let me know by.......you know how women are sir. It's not what they say, it's the way they look at you."

There was a chorus of groans from his comrades; they knew then that Atilius was doomed, except he still seemed to be oblivious to his rapidly approaching demise. He responded to the reaction of his friends by protesting, "You boys know I'm right, you just don't want to say so in front of the Pilus Prior. A woman doesn't have to tell you she wants you for you to get the message, you boys know that."

"Atilius, if what you say is true, why are her clothes ripped off?"

I watched him closely as I asked the question; seeing the flicker of guilt flash across his face, my heart hardened towards Atilius in that instant. If I were convinced that he honestly thought that he was invited into the girl's room, no matter what transpired, while it might not have changed his fate, it would at the very least

596

make me more sympathetic and more inclined to seek some sort of alternative to what would probably be his punishment. But in that moment I saw that Atilius knew that what he was doing was wrong, if not morally then at the least against the law, and my sympathy for him vanished like a drop of water thrown into a sizzling pan. Regardless, Atilius was stubborn, although I imagine that by this point he realized he was fighting for his life and was not about to give up without putting up some sort of defense.

"Sir, you know that some women like it……rough. They like to play at being afraid, and like to put up a struggle. It just spices things up a bit. That's all that happened here, there wasn't no harm meant. We were just having fun."

"It doesn't look to me like she would agree, Atilius, I replied coldly. "So I guess you have a good reason why her throat's cut?"

Atilius at least possessed enough humanity at this point to look ashamed. "That was a mistake sir. The two men came busting through, and she began fighting me…."

"Wait," I interrupted, "I thought you just said she was already fighting you. Playing around, as you say, but still putting up a struggle."

He reluctantly nodded. "That's true sir, but she really started putting on a show when those two came in. Before, she was bucking around and trying to throw me off of her, but that was just playing around, like I said. But the instant they came in, she had to make it look real, sir."

I was beginning to put this together, and I was struck by another thought. "Atilius, when exactly did she scratch you?"

If he knew where I was going, he was either too frightened or too resigned to try to lie. "After I put paid to those two bastards sir." He brightened for a moment. "It was a neat piece of work, if I do say so myself sir. You'd have been proud. I didn't even get off her; I held her down with one hand, and I ran those bastards through with the other, neat as you please."

Immediately after the words left his mouth, he realized that he was not helping himself, a look of helplessness and resignation coming back to his face, settling there and ultimately never leaving.

"So, once she saw you kill her father and brother, she started fighting back harder? Is that about the size of it?"

I was making no attempt to hide my contempt and anger now, seeing out of the corner of my eye the head of one of the Gauls turn towards me to study me, obviously trying to divine whether or not my outrage was real, or was a show for them. Atilius did not answer; there was need to, but I was not done.

"So she scratched you, and you cut her throat for it?"

He stared at the floor, refusing to meet my eyes, now fully understanding what awaited him. There was no question in anyone's mind that Atilius' fate was sealed, at least among his comrades. I am sure the Gauls still believed that we would pull some sort of trick and Atilius would escape the punishment he deserved. Oh, we might flog him, but there was only one real punishment that was worthy of his crime, and we all knew it. The question in their minds was if we Romans would carry it out.

With the interrogation done, I ordered Vibius, since he was the ranking Legionary, to bind Atilius, who submitted without protest. His tentmates surrounded him as we exited the house, followed by the three Gauls, and they immediately began calling for their friends and neighbors to surround us. In moments, before we could move halfway down the muddy street, we were completely encircled by a mob of very angry people. One of the three men, an older, scarred warrior with ginger colored hair and the long mustaches that was their mark of manhood, stood in front of me.

"Give him to us, Roman."

It was a simple statement, not a request but a demand, and I felt my chest tighten. I knew we would give a good account of ourselves; I congratulated myself for making sure that the men donned their armor, weapons and shields, except there were only five of us, not counting Atilius, who I would only cut loose and arm as a last resort. No, I was going to have to use my brain for once. Stepping forward to stand directly in front of the Gaul, I positioned myself so that my men were directly behind me.

"No."

I said it quietly, except my body language obviously sent a clear signal of my answer, causing the crowd to growl like it was some huge animal, which in a sense it was. Rome had disarmed all of the native townspeople except for the nobles and their household warriors some years before, but staves and axe handles are formidable weapons by themselves, and when there are a hundred or so people waving them about, someone is liable to get hurt.

The Gaul smiled grimly, then with a nod of his head, indicated the mob around us. "Perhaps you do not understand the situation Roman. That was not a request. We can take him. All I have to do is give the word. Now, give him to us."

I stood looking him in the eye, not answering for a moment, then spoke quietly enough so that only he could hear. "He's going to die. And I can promise you that the manner of his death won't be pretty. In fact, it's going to be very much what would happen to him here, now, if we gave him to you and this mob. But this I will not do. He's a Roman Legionary, and he's subject to Roman military justice."

He snorted, his lip curling up in a sneer. "So you say, Roman. But you know as well as I do that these things have happened before, and the men involved were never properly punished. You may have conquered us, but we will show you that just because you have a boot on our neck, it does not mean we will lick it."

I could hear the bitterness, anger and frustration oozing through every word as he talked; I also knew that what he said was true, at least as far as Legionaries escaping punishment in the past. But the circumstances were different now; Gaul was conquered and we were ordered to ease up on the Gauls in order to try to win them over. The political situation dictated a change in the way we managed our relations with these people, and now that I was a Centurion, I was a representative of that new policy. However, I also knew that, just like Uxellodonum, there was a limit to how far we would allow ourselves to bend.

"Consider this," I said, in the same tone as before, conscious that my next words could tip us off the sword edge we were balanced on, "you could probably take our man," he snorted again at my use of the word probably, but like Rome I was only going to bend so far. I leaned forward a little and repeated, "You could probably take our man, but at what cost? How many bodies would

599

we leave behind? There are only five of us, that's true, but we're Caesar's men, and from Caesar's most favored and feared Legion."

I could see the beginning of doubt creep into his eyes, so I pressed harder.

"And the one thing I can promise and you know that it's no idle boast, that you may win a victory here, but this whole part of Narbo, and all the people who survived this initial fight would cease to exist. Do you want to be the man who'll be known by his people from now until the end of time as the one who destroyed the Gallic quarter and everyone in it?"

He pursed his lips, then I saw his eyes dart around to the crowd, and I realized then that he was in as difficult a predicament as I was. True, he was the one to create this situation, yet now he was prone to being carried away by the flood just like we were. His status as a leader hung by a thread; if he was seen as weak, the mob was just as likely to turn on him as it was on us. Such is the changeable nature of the Gauls, as ever.

"What's your name, by the way?" I asked, startling him back to reality.

"Vetorodumnus," he replied, clearly puzzled by my question.

"Well, Vetorodumnus, my name is Titus Pullus. I'm the Pilus Prior of the Second Cohort of the 10th Legion. I'm going to give you my word as a Roman Centurion that this man will be punished in a manner that you'll find suitable. Do you know what the punishment for rape and murder in the Roman army is?"

He nodded; it was well known throughout all of Gaul by this time the various punishments that we employed.

"If that's not the punishment rendered for *Gregarius* Atilius, then I'll return, and offer myself in his place for whatever punishment you deem fit as a substitute. Will you accept this?"

In truth, I was asking if the mob would accept this, except it served no purpose to make this fact obvious, because as tenuous a grip as he may have had on the mob, he still could call it down on our heads if I pushed him too far. The look of relief was momentary, but it was enough to tell me that I had given us both a way out of the immediate situation. He nodded, so I offered my hand, which he

600

took solemnly. This quieted the crowd, sensing that something important had just happened. After we shook, he turned to address the crowd in his tongue, of which I knew just enough to determine that he was relaying the essence of our agreement. As he explained, I turned to Vibius and motioned for him to come to me. Quietly I told him what was happening, and I saw the warring emotions cross his face, all at once. We were friends too long for me not to know exactly what he was thinking. He understood that having made such a bargain, I ensured that Atilius would be executed, and that he and his comrades would have to be the ones to do it, beating Atilius to death, but not before breaking every bone in his body.

I will not describe in any detail the execution of Atilius, except to say that the sentence was carried out and that the men of his Century, including his oldest friends, as well as mine, did their duty. The one incident that I will describe happened the night before the sentence was carried out, when Vibius came to see me.

"We're going to bust Atilius out and help him get back to Hispania," he announced without waiting to finish the cup of wine I had offered.

Thunderstruck, I sat for a moment, unable to reply. I know why he told me; he was relying on our friendship and the years spent slogging about with Atilius, except Vibius underestimated the pull of my own ambition. When I was younger, I would be dictating to Diocles some high-flown drivel about how once I was promoted to Centurion, I had to become more politically astute since I was directly responsible for carrying out the policies not just of Caesar, but of Rome. But I am old now, and near the end of my string, so I no longer feel the burning passion within to put myself in the best possible light that I once did. The simple truth is that I would not allow this to happen because it would be a probably irreparable blot on my career. It was bad enough that it was one of my men, although sooner or later every Centurion is put in the same position. However, having a condemned man escape is a career killer. The fact that the would-be escapee was a long-time comrade, and was aided and abetted by my closest friend could very well mean that I would be walking the gauntlet in place of Atilius and that was simply not happening. That was not how I put it to Vibius, at least as far as my career was concerned, but I certainly did point out that a possible consequence of their actions was in me replacing Atilius. Once I put it like that the plan was quickly dropped, and we spent the rest of the evening in glum silence, drinking ourselves into a stupor to gird ourselves for the coming day.

The execution of Atilius did have one positive effect; I no longer found myself plodding into town to pay off townspeople, since my men were on their best behavior from that point forward. There is nothing like witnessing the brutal death of another Legionary at the hands of his own comrades to sober a man up and convince him that good behavior is a wise course. None of my old tentmates were ever really the same after that, at least as far as I was concerned. The laughter around the fire was more muted; despite the fact that the boisterousness and cruel humor that is as much a staple of camp life as the bread we eat was not completely gone, it was not something that happened every day as in the past. The one benefit, if it can be called that, at least to me, was that it distracted Celer from his constant picking at me and I believe it was because the men felt some sympathy for what I was forced to do to Atilius. We had all been together a long time, almost every man in the Legion part of the *dilectus* now ten years ago, so all knew that Atilius had been a tentmate of mine. Despite thinking that I carried out my duties with a grim detachment, clearly those around me could see through the mask I wore and how much watching one of my oldest friends beaten to death by my other oldest friends tormented me. Celer was a lot of things but he was not stupid, and he evidently saw that his continual attacks on me had a high probability of backfiring at this point. He was patient as well; he would wait until the execution of Atilius was a more distant memory before picking up the offensive once again. For my part, I did not care what the reason was, I was just happy for the respite from having to pay attention to the whispers around the fire.

Not everything in my life was bad; my professional trials aside, my life off duty became more interesting. It probably will not surprise you gentle reader, when I recount that it was during this period at Narbo that I took a woman, and that woman was Gisela. I could say that it was an accident, that it was just something that happened but that would be a lie, because I had been determined to make her mine a long time before, and I was happy to learn that she was as interested in me as I in her. I am not now, nor was I then, completely blind to the fact that there was a fair amount of self-interest in her receptiveness to my advances; I was climbing rapidly through the ranks, and as one of Caesar's hand-picked men, I could provide for her comfort in a better manner than Calienus ever had. We never spoke of him, although I do not know why. Perhaps it had to do with the idea of arousing his spirit and not wanting to anger him if he saw that I had taken his woman, but I think that was more in Gisela's mind than mine; she was always more superstitious than I was, and am. To help woo her, I bought a house that belonged to a Roman merchant that gambled his business away and was forced to return back to Rome, yet when I tried to present her with her very own slave, I thought she was going to scratch my eyes out. She absolutely refused to have any slave in the house, forcing me to hire a freedwoman and her husband, although the extra expense was worth the peace in the house. I spent perhaps three nights a week at the house; I was still too insecure in my control of the Cohort to spend more than that outside the camp. It was apparently enough, however; about four months after Gisela became my woman, she got pregnant, as my life suddenly changed in so many ways it was hard for me to comprehend. I was a Centurion, with a wife in all but name, I was about to be a father, and I was a still month shy of turning 27 years old. Vibius, while happy for the news that he was going to become a quasi-uncle, was clearly stung by the fact that I was now at the place in life that he longed to be, and had longed to be for almost ten years. One evening, sitting in my tent and playing idly at *alea*, I saw how melancholy he was, so I set down my wine cup and cleared my throat, which I have been told is the sure sign that I am about to broach a subject that I consider to be important, or potentially contentious. Vibius looked up from the board, one eyebrow arched as he clearly perceived something was afoot.

As I sat trying to compose what I wanted to say, he said impatiently, "By the gods, Titus. Quit chewing on what you want to say like it's a piece of gristle. I've known you too long, so out with it."

Very well, I thought. "Have you thought that it might be time to send for Juno, and go ahead and make her your woman?"

I saw his face darken; this was a topic we had been over so many times that I could not count, and I held my hand up in a placating gesture. "Wait a moment, Vibius. Hear me out."

He gave a curt nod, but I could tell by the set of his mouth that I would have to summon an argument worthy of Cicero if I wanted to persuade him of what I was thinking. "I know why you don't want to do so, Vibius and believe me, I understand and respect it. And you know how much I care for Juno; she's been a friend of mine nearly as long as you have. But that's what grieves me, because when you read me her letters, or at least the parts you don't want to keep to yourself," I grinned, and I was heartened to see that despite his initial displeasure, he grinned back, "she longs for you just as much as you long for her. What kind of friend would I be if that didn't hurt me, for both of you?"

I could see that he at least was listening, so I plunged ahead.

"Do you really think that any of your comrades are going to think less of Juno if you bring her here and begin to live like you've both always wanted? They know how much you love her, and they know what a good woman she is. She's waited for you for ten years, Vibius. Her virtue is unquestioned, and all of our friends have the utmost respect for her. The fact that you wouldn't be legally married isn't going to diminish their respect for her."

Vibius sighed; it was clear that this was a subject that he thought about more than anything else in his life. "Titus," he replied slowly, "I hear what you say, and in truth, I've been considering it more lately than I ever have before. I don't know why; I think it has something to do with seeing you and Gisela."

He was not telling me anything I did not know, and I fought the urge to impatiently assure him that I knew exactly why he was feeling this way. I had to let Vibius go about this in his own way, or nothing would be accomplished. By the gods, I thought to myself, I must be growing up.

"And I know that our friends wouldn't look down at her in any way, but it's not them that I worry about. It's the men in the other Cohorts, and the officers. You hear how the Tribs and Legates talk about our women, and you know how some of them will go out of their way to take a *Gregarius'* woman just to show that he can. If one of those slimy little bastards tried that with Juno, I'd end up just like Atilius."

Vibius was right, or at least partially so. The nobles, and indeed even some of the rankers, looked down their noses at women who joined themselves to a Legionary as little better than a whore, and while other *Gregarii* who might feel that way were wise enough to keep their mouths shut about it, officers had no such compunctions. At least, bad officers did not; I noticed over the years that the Tribunes and Legates who we respected the most returned it back, the one possible exception being Labienus, but he won and much is forgiven with a man like that. Nevertheless, I did not think that this would be the same for Juno, part of the reason being what I relayed to Vibius, but another part of it was because he was my friend. I must admit that it is a mark of my hubris that I believed that my reputation and authority would shield Vibius, but more importantly Juno, from any of the scorn and risk posed by predatory officers.

Besides, I had formed a half-cooked plan that I was sure would solve more than one problem, and I sat forward, eager to launch my attack. "I understand all that Vibius, but I've got an idea that I think will put your mind at ease. What if," I paused for a moment, for no other reason than to make him wait, his earlier expression of consternation replaced by an almost pathetic hope "you bring Juno, and she can move in with Gisela? They can live together, and look out for each other."

I am not sure what reaction I was expecting, but it was not what I got. Instead of showing any enthusiasm, Vibius' eyebrow raised again, and I knew this expression intimately. It was the same look I got when I proposed that to save time we cut across a neighbor's field that we always avoided because of the very large, very angry bull that claimed it as his domain. We were around eleven and twelve, so I felt that we had grown sufficiently strong and fast enough that getting past some tired old bull would not be much of a challenge, a sentiment that Vibius did not share. I only convinced him by taunting him to the point where his anger overruled his caution, and despite the fact we made it across unscathed, it was not without a mad dash and a dive over the stone wall, the bull's breath literally blasting our heels as we dived over. A fact that he never let me forget, and I was half-expecting that damn bull to be brought up now. Thankfully, he remained back in that field in Hispania.

"Have you talked to Gisela about this? I mean, is she all right with this idea?"

Of course I had not talked to Gisela, so while I waved the question off and gave a snort of manly contempt, Vibius' question ignited a little nagging fire in the back of my brain. "What does she have to do with it?" I demanded, and for a moment I was sure that Vibius' eyebrow was going to reach new heights that neither of us had ever seen before. His open skepticism stung me, and I continued a bit more hotly than needed, "Gisela will do what I tell her to do.

She's my woman, and she lives in my house. Besides, she'll love Juno the same way we do. How could she not?"

I think that idea had more impact than anything else I said. As far as Vibius was concerned, Juno was as close to perfection as a mortal could be, and indeed, who could not grow to love her the way he did?

"Well," I could tell he was weakening, and I thought hurriedly for something to tip the scale, as he said slowly, "if she lived with Gisela, I think that's the only way I could see this working. Still, I just don't know."

It was then I was struck with the inspiration. "What if you could go back home to get her, visit your family and bring her back?"

I knew I had convinced him, his other eyebrow shooting up to join the first in a look of surprise and joy. "You'd sign me a pass for that long? I mean Titus, it'd take at least a month." "More like two," I responded. "But you've earned it, and we're sending men home on leave now anyway. In fact," I tried to sound casual, "I was thinking that I might take some leave as well."

I had been thinking no such thing, and in truth, I was not sure that when it came down to it, I could afford to take the time away from the Cohort, what with Celer lurking around. However, if it convinced Vibius, I would at least consider it. I was pleased to see that my last remark tipped the scale, and Vibius and I spent the rest of the evening, the *alea* board forgotten, talking excitedly about finally going home.

I planned on spending the next night at the house in town, except that I found that certain urgent matters suddenly cropped up that demanded my presence in camp, so I sent Zeno to let Gisela know that I would not be coming home that night. She took it well enough, as she did the next night, when other matters came up. On the third night, Zeno came back clearly flustered, apprehensive about relaying the message that Gisela gave him to deliver to me. On the fourth night, he staggered back, the blood barely dried from the cut on his head where a cup bounced off of it. It was then I realized two things; I was putting off talking to Gisela about the whole Juno idea, and that pregnant women are at least temporarily insane. This did not make going home any more attractive a proposition, yet I knew further delay would make things worse, and I will confess right here and now, walking up the street towards the house my heart was hammering in much the same manner as it did before I went smashing into a line of Gauls. The lamp was burning outside the door as always, but it was not the warming, welcoming sight to me that it was meant to be. In my state, it marked the entrance to Hades, and I spent several moments pacing outside the door, working up the nerve to go in.

"Oh-oh, someone must be in some trouble. What did you do, Centurion?"

Snapping my head around, I saw an older man, a Roman merchant from the look of him, grinning at me. For a moment, I felt an angry retort rise up, then it disappeared in a wave of sheepishness, and I found myself giving him a rueful grin. "I've been staying away a few nights."

"Ah, found another bed to warm, did you? Well, that may be a man's right, but in my experience, women don't tend to see it that way." His reference to another woman was the first time it even occurred to me that this was a possibility that Gisela might consider, and if my heart were racing before, it was a mild trot compared to what it was doing now, my stomach now threatening to join in the mad dash. My dismay was plain for him to see, so he wrongly assumed that he had guessed right. "Well, in my experience Centurion, a gift is always the best way to smooth these things over. The shinier the better."

"She's pregnant," I said miserably, his face instantly changing to one of open sympathy, and even worse, pity.

"*Gerrae*! Well, then I'm afraid that you're in for it, Centurion. At least you wore your sword, but you might want to go back and get into full battle gear for this. Good luck." He turned to continue on his way, but I plainly heard him mutter, "You're going to need it."

It did not go well that night. Not only was I denied the right of the conjugal bed, I was denied the physical bed as well, banished instead to spend the night in the servants' quarters, making them a bit nervous as you can imagine. I could have simply gone back to camp, yet for some reason, an instinct that I never felt before told me that it was important that I stay the night. I was right; in fact, I sent the freedman back to camp to inform the Primus Pilus and the Centurions of my Cohort that I was delayed by urgent business in town, and that Celer, as the next ranking Centurion, would take command of the Cohort until I returned. Although I was not happy with the idea of Celer running things, I reasoned that the amount of damage he could do in a day would be far less than the damage done to my relationship with the mother of my unborn child if I left the house. My instinct proved to be correct; in fact, the act of staying and not returning to camp had more impact on Gisela than any of my words did, since she knew not only of my devotion to the army, but my ongoing battle with Celer. The fact that I stayed to talk to her smoothed the waters more than any gift, and it was an important lesson for me in how to keep peace in my home. I decided that it was not a good idea to bring up the whole Juno question, given that I just made the peace, so when I did return to camp shortly before midday I now was faced with either avoiding Vibius, who was eagerly waiting to hear how things had gone, or lying to him. Fortunately, Celer did not get a chance to inflict much mischief in my absence, and I took over the Cohort to resume our day.

My ongoing quandary about taking leave was also weighing on my mind, to the point that I did something that I very rarely did, even before going into battle, and consulted the camp priests, paying for a healthy white kid goat to be sacrificed in order to help me find a way that I could fulfill my promise to Vibius without having to worry about Celer undermining me behind my back. Vibius kept pressuring me to sign the pass; I had already submitted the proper paperwork to both the Primus Pilus and the duty Tribune, and his leave was approved at both levels. All that remained was for me to sign the pass, but Vibius was also expecting that I would be going with him. This was yet another subject I had not brought up with Gisela, so every passing day made me more anxious about the looming talk with my woman, who in my mind grew more and more insane, almost by the day. She was well into her fourth month of pregnancy, and I could not imagine what things would be like in another few months. Physically, she seemed to be thriving; I paid handsomely for the best midwife and practitioners I could find, not wanting the same fate that befell Calienus' child to happen to mine. I will confess that it was not only concern for the baby; despite the fact I am not very superstitious, it just seemed to be a bad omen if she lost the baby, given Calienus' fate. I suppose it is a good thing that we were such a veteran Legion at this point that much of the day-to-day routine ran itself, the habits of ten years being so ingrained to the point that the lowest ranking *Gregarius* knew what needed to be done. Training continued as always, the forced marches being cut to twice a month, although every so often the Primus Pilus would throw in another one on a day's notice just to keep everyone on their toes. The discipline was the same, except that the pall of Atilius' execution still hung over at least our Cohort, so the only problem Century I had was that of Longus, but I was beginning to figure out exactly what the real story was with his Century. He was using it as his very own source of income, and the way he exerted pressure on his men to pay him was in the use of punishments. Longus was always careful to send men up for punishment for offenses that only cost money or extra duties and not a flogging or worse, and I suspected that what he was doing was threatening his men with writing them up for a greater offense. Then, in exchange for a few coins, he would instead turn in a report that detailed a crime that was minor enough that we did not have to form up in punishment square to watch someone be flayed. He was smart, I will give him that; he was not flagrant about it. If one were to casually glance at the reports turned in by each Centurion, he was only one or two men above the average per month, but it was consistently so. After being in charge of the Cohort for a year, I was able to actually spot a pattern, yet at that moment it was just a matter of a nagging feeling that something was not right. All in all however, things were running smoothly, which was a good thing since I was very distracted with my personal troubles. With every passing day the worry I felt increased, as of course every day guaranteed that Vibius grew more impatient, while Gisela was likely to throw more than a cup at me.

The gods answered my prayers in an unlikely way, by arranging the death of Celer's father, who was summoned home to arrange his affairs. This meant that I could leave the Cohort in the hands of Priscus, and despite it taking a bribe to the Legate that made me wince, I was given leave to go home with Vibius, for a period of 60 days. Now all that was left was to tell Gisela, and once again I stood outside my house with a pounding heart, except this time I did not stand outside for any extended time, knowing that it was no use postponing any longer. I entered, and despite trying to act like it was a normal day, I made it no more than two or three paces past the front door when I was confronted by Gisela.

"What's wrong?"

I froze; for a moment, I thought about bluffing and insisting that nothing was wrong, yet as I stood there trying to decide what to do, I actually saw her for the first time in a long time, and if it were possible, I fell in love with her even more. She was wearing a simple gown cut to accommodate her growing figure, a rich green in color that accentuated the green in her eyes. Her red hair was unbound, in the Gallic fashion, which I liked more than our Roman style, and her cheeks were flushed, something I noticed seemed to happen more often now that she was pregnant. Her head was up, her chin tilted outward in a defiant manner, but behind the mask I saw the worry in her eyes and I felt about as low as I could remember at the idea of causing her such concern.

"Nothing," I began, but she cut me off with an oath in her native tongue that she was fond of using.

"Why do you think I'm a fool Titus Pullus? I know you better than you think. And I know what is bothering you."

For a moment I thought she had presented me with a good way to introduce what I wanted to talk about. I could not have been more wrong. Before I could answer, she spat, "You have found another woman, and you're about to put me out and move her in here."

I was struck speechless, which unfortunately she took as a sign that she guessed correctly. We had just moved into the dining area, where the table was set for our supper. From it she picked up a plate and in a blur of motion hurled it at me, and it was only the reflex gained over years of battle that allowed me to twist my body out of the way just as the plate went whizzing by my head to smash against the wall.

"You bastard! You son of a whore! I knew you would do this!"

I was still rooted to the spot, completely shocked into immobility and speechlessness as she raged, her hands grabbing at another plate to throw. That finally spurred me into action and I crossed the room in two quick strides, catching her arm as it came forward. She struggled like a wildcat caught in a bag, yet I was careful not to grab her arms too strongly, being worried about the baby. She had no such concerns, so I did not see the foot come up to strike me violently in the groin, sending a lightning bolt of pain through my body, the breath leaving me in a great whoosh. For the first time since I could remember, I was knocked to the ground; the fact that it was at the hands of a pregnant woman did not even register, so great was my agony. I lay gasping for breath, and I was looking at her feet as she stood over me.

"At least you won't be able to use that for a while," she said with satisfaction as I cupped the part of my body she was referring to, groaning in pain.

"I......I'm not throwing you out for another woman, Gisela. I haven't been with another woman since we've been together," I gasped. I heard her snort in disbelief.

"It's true," I insisted, "I was going to ask you to accompany me back home to meet my family. I've been given leave, and I wanted you to come."

Now, this is not exactly the truth, though at that point I did not see any reason why she needed to know that. I barely finished my sentence when she dropped to the ground to grab my head, smothering it with kisses and asking forgiveness. There are some times, I reflected as I lay there, where the truth is not necessarily the best idea.

Leaving for home the next week, we set out in a hired wagon so Gisela could be comfortable, and to bring Juno and her belongings back. I still had not told Gisela the complete truth, swearing to do Vibius great bodily harm if he let it slip out before I was ready to tell her the rest of the story. All I knew at the time was that she was happy, and if she was happy, I was happy, so that meant I was content to let it stay that way for as long as I could manage it, no matter how much it pained Vibius. When I told Vibius that Gisela was coming, at first he was not thrilled, saying it would slow us down. Then he realized that the plan to have Juno live with Gisela would most likely go more smoothly if both were given the chance to get used to the idea, and a journey together would be the best way to accomplish that. Since we could not do a return journey with the two of them without bringing Gisela along on the first leg, he quickly got used to the idea. I was not quite so quick to agree with his conclusion, for a couple of reasons. First was the inconvenient fact that I still had not told Gisela, and every passing mile heightened my anxiety, my imagination running wild thinking of her possible reaction. Would she demand that we turn around and go back? And if I refused, would she get out of the wagon and start walking back? If so, what would I do then? The second part of all this that bothered me was my worry about the baby; I did not know much at all about women and pregnancy, yet I was fairly sure that sitting in a bouncing wagon was not a good thing for it. However, when I brought this up to Gisela, she scoffed at the notion.

"Pullus, I marched with Caesar's army every day, up until a week before I gave birth. This is more luxury than I know what to do with." I was smart enough to know that pointing out that she lost that baby was not a good idea, so I simply kept my mouth shut. The way matters turned out, I finally broke the news to Gisela on the third day of our journey, over breakfast as we sat at an outdoor table at an inn along the way. She was munching on a piece of bread to go with the boiled bacon we had purchased to supplement our rations, a wisp of hair straying down across her forehead, which she distractedly kept trying to put back in place as she watched the people around us. She was always fascinated by everything going on around her, and it was this curiosity about the world that I found so appealing, probably because it matched my own.

Clearing my throat, I began, "Gisela, there's something I want to talk to you about."

Her head whipped around, eyes narrowed suspiciously as she waited for me to blurt out whatever it was I had to say, and I felt an icy finger trip up my back. I can laugh about it now, the fact that I felt as much or more fear facing my woman than I did facing another man in battle, but back then it was no laughing matter. There was a healthy dose of fear of Gisela's anger, although to be fair it is not as if I had not been warned; Calienus regaled us with stories of her rages and tantrums, yet they were much more amusing if you were not the subject of one of them. Vibius immediately got up from the table, mumbling something about answering a call of nature, and inwardly I cursed him for his cowardice.

"What? Well, come on, out with it. Don't stammer about."

This of course was a guarantee that I was going to do the exact thing she told me not to, so I stumbled and fumbled, trying to phrase things in such a way that there was less likelihood of the cup she had snatched off the table as I was talking being hurled at me.

"Well, Vibius asked me something, and I wanted to talk to you about it before I give him my, I mean our, decision."

612

There, I thought, I might as well drop Vibius in the *cac* if I were going to be swimming in it too. She did not reply, just lifting that damn eyebrow that told me to press on.

"He's decided that he's going to ask Juno to come back with us."

Before I could finish, her face split into a smile, her rosy cheeks lifting as she clapped her hands together.

"Oh Titus, that's wonderful! I've been hoping that he would finally get up the nerve to do the right thing instead of mooning about." This was a good sign, so I decided to just get the real nut of the matter out and done with, yet before I could, she said something that is just further proof that I will never understand women.

"Of course, she will stay with us," she announced, and I felt my jaw drop.

Seeing my expression, she completely misread it, saying crossly, "Now, you do NOT think that she is going to live by herself, away from home for the first time and never having been around the army? Don't you even think about arguing about this, Pullus. I will not stand for it. Besides," her face took on that practical expression that I knew so well, "she will be a help when my time approaches and I can barely waddle about."

She looked me directly in the eye and said with a sweet smile that was as much a direct order as any that came from Caesar, "You agree of course, don't you my love?"

I gulped, and nodded.

It took a week and a day for us to reach Hispania, thanks to the roads that Caesar had the Legions build during our winter years in Gaul; without them it would have taken more than two to get there and leave us barely a month at home. I sent word ahead as soon as I knew that both Vibius and I would be coming, and I am ashamed to say that the letter was the first in several months. More accurately it was a couple months short of a year since I last wrote, but I told myself that it was only because I was so busy as Pilus Prior, which had the benefit of being partially true. The bigger reason was that I had changed, and no longer really had anything in common with my family. I felt that I left them behind, becoming something they could never understand, especially since their world consisted of the ground they could cover in a day's walk, whereas I had seen so much of the world the idea of going back to that way of life was unthinkable. And being brutally honest, I had long outgrown my homesickness and stopped missing my sisters, as well as Phocas and Gaia, some time ago. I still planned on fulfilling my promise, and in fact carried with me a large amount of money, more than twice what I thought I would need to free Gaia and Phocas from my father. Despite my ambivalence about going home initially, I will say that the closer we got the more excited I became, as Vibius and I bored Gisela to tears regaling her with stories of our childhood, not that she showed it. My worries about the trials of a long journey and the toll it would take on her proved to be unfounded; if anything she seemed to flourish being out in the open air. Vibius and I did not completely dominate the conversation, however; I learned more about Gisela, her childhood and her people than I did in the previous years I knew her. She had seven brothers and sisters; that I knew, but I did not know that she was especially close to one sister who died when Gisela was twelve and her sister fourteen. Her eyes filled with tears as she spoke of her, and it was the first and last time she ever spoke of it. As she talked I thought of Livia and Valeria, and resolved to let them know how much I did care about them, even if I had not done a good job of showing it. But as I was about to find out, I was too late for one of my sisters.

Rolling into Astigi, both Vibius and I were struck by how small the town was compared to our memories. Neither of us had made it to Rome at this point, yet we had seen places like Narbo and even Vesontio that made our town look positively shabby. The scene in the forum was much the same, with the same people doing the same business. Although people recognized and seemed to be happy to see us, I could tell there was a certain apprehension in their attitude towards us, reminding me of our last homecoming. Vibius noticed it as well, turning to me as we rode through the street towards his house.

"Try not to kill anyone this time, will you Titus?"

Needless to say this got Gisela's attention, but I ignored her questions to retort, "Try not to get yourself into trouble you can't get out of, and I won't have to."

We laughed as Vibius climbed down from the wagon and grabbed his gear. Making arrangements that we would return in a few days so that Gisela and Juno could meet, I headed the wagon towards my farm, telling Gisela what happened the last time we came home.

Topping the low rise and seeing the farm, I felt my stomach lurch as I wondered if there would ever be a time in my life where the sight of my boyhood home would not make me feel like I was ten years old, coming home without a bag of nails because I lost them. Gisela sensed my mood; without saying anything she reached over to put her hand on my arm, and I felt my face flush as I slapped the reins, turning the wagon off the road and bumping up the path to the farm. Despite it looking much the same as I remembered I saw some slight changes, things that had fallen into disrepair, like the holes in the path that normally would have been filled. I did not see Phocas at first, but the rattling of our wagon caused the door to open, then I saw his familiar figure emerge, peering at us from the gloom of the house. Having experienced the sensation of how he aged the last time I was home, I prepared myself for the change an even longer interval of time had wrought on him, or at least I thought I did. Nevertheless, I was shocked, because Phocas had become an old man, this time for real. The slight stoop I noticed the last time I visited was much more pronounced, and what was left of his hair had gone completely gray. The wrinkles around his eyes had deepened and moved down the length of his face, leaving crevices around his cheeks. With some people this is a sign that they have spent a lot of their time laughing, but I could see that was not the case with Phocas. Waiting for him to recognize us, I finally realized that his squinting at us was not due to just the bright light; his vision was obviously degraded as well, so it was not until we were no more than a dozen paces away that his face dawned with recognition. Staggering a step, his hands went out towards me as if I were some sort of apparition that he was trying to ward off.

"Titus, is that truly you?" it was his voice that caused the tears to flood my eyes.

Gone was the soothing, mellifluous deep voice that still carried the accent of his native land, replaced instead by the quavering croak of an old man. I tried to speak, yet could not, and I was ashamed of myself, but as I glanced over I saw Gisela's eyes filled with tears as well. Instead of saying anything, I jumped down from the wagon and strode over to him, engulfing him in an embrace, my shock deepening at the feel of his fragility. Still, his grip around my neck was just as strong as I remembered it, and we both stood there weeping for I do not know how long before, wiping our eyes and sniffling, we broke our embrace, both laughing embarrassedly.

Finally, I spoke, "Yes, it's me Phocas. I've come home to visit. And to fulfill a promise I made to you."

I am not sure what reaction I was expecting, but it was not what I got. Phocas' face took on an expression of extreme sadness, with a fresh spate of tears immediately flowing down his cheeks, bewildering me, and I was about to press him on the cause of his grief when he stepped around me, peering up at Gisela in the wagon.

"And who is this then? And what are you doing dragging a pregnant woman all about the country?"

Embarrassed that I had completely forgotten her, I mumbled the introductions, but Gisela did not seem to take offense. Without waiting for either of us to help, she climbed down from the wagon by herself. Walking over to Phocas, to his surprise, and some discomfort I suspect, she swept him into her embrace.

"I am Gisela, Phocas. I'm Titus' woman, and I'm carrying his child. He has told me so much about you, and I'm happy to finally have the chance to meet you."

To my irritation, Phocas looked surprised. What, am I so unable to attract a fine woman that it should provide such a shock, I thought sourly? However, I said nothing. Turning to me, Phocas beamed.

"Well done, boy. She is truly a jewel."

"Where's Gaia?" I asked, looking over his shoulder, puzzled that the commotion did not bring her to the door. I was not expecting such from my father, but I was sure that Gaia would have been all over me by now. There was no answer, and my heart skipped a beat, so I turned to face Phocas, his face telling me everything I needed to know, and it was my turn for more fresh tears to run down my face.

"She died almost a year ago," Phocas told us as we sat at the table, and looking about, I could see that things were hard for Phocas and my father. Phocas had done his best, but there is just a difference between the way a woman keeps a house and the way a man does it, especially one the age of Phocas. I was still unable to

616

speak, so great was my shock, and Gisela was sitting next to me, trying to comfort me, as was Phocas. He poured us some wine and I noticed that he did not add water to his, as was his normal habit. Staring into his cup, he continued.

"She had been complaining about being tired," he smiled sadly, "at least more than she normally complained. You remember Titus, how she was always sure that she was coming down with some malady."

I smiled back. It was true; rarely a month went by where Gaia did not dramatically pronounce that she was sure she had come down with some ailment that was likely to take her life. Phocas and I teased her unmercifully, with Phocas even joking that it would give him the excuse to find another woman, which she always answered with a tart retort that he did not have to wait for her to die, he was more than welcome to go find some foolish woman who was stupid enough to fall for his blandishments. Despite the words, the tone was always loving between the both of them, and that teasing was a part of my childhood I remembered with great fondness.

"Well, she complained as usual. And as usual, I didn't listen," suddenly his composure broke, and he was racked with sobbing. It took him a few moments to compose himself, as I sat there helplessly, not sure what to do. I had never seen Phocas like this, and being in the army ten years such tender feelings were signs of weakness, so I just sat there waiting for him to regain his composure. Gisela glared at me before pulling herself to her feet to place her arms around Phocas, and as he lay against her arms and continued to sob, I realized that this was probably the first time he had a chance to grieve. After all, I could hardly imagine Lucius being any comfort. Finally composing himself, he continued.

"But then she started losing weight, and you know Titus that she didn't have much to lose. I went into town to consult the priests and even hired a doctor. I tried everything, but nothing worked. She just........faded away."

I sat there, unable to speak, partly because I did not know what to say, but also because my sense of shame was so overpowering that I did not trust myself to speak. I had been selfish and completely absorbed in my own career and my own life, turning my back on the people most important to me. Now, all my promises about freeing them were empty since Gaia was dead. I could not

617

even cry anymore; I was past being worried what Gisela would think, so deep was my shock and sadness. Instead we sat there in silence, gulping our wine as I imagined I felt Gaia's *numen* hovering above us.

"Phocas!"

Even all these years later, the sound of his voice sent a thrill of hatred and fear up my spine. My head shot up, catching Phocas' eye, and he answered my unspoken question.

"He's worse than ever. Truthfully, I don't know what keeps him alive."

Smiling meanly, I stood up and said, "Well, maybe a visit from his long lost son will do the trick and send him to Hades where he belongs."

Heading to my father's room, I left Gisela sitting open-mouthed, and Phocas looking grim.

"Hello, Father."

My greeting had exactly the effect I desired; laying in a filthy bed, unshaven, smelling worse than any German, my father let out a shriek of fear at the sight of me, and when I stepped towards the bed my nose wrinkled at the smell as his bladder lost control, his fresh piss mixing with the stale smell. When Gaia was alive, she at least forced him to bathe at somewhat regular intervals, but now that she was gone, Phocas had neither the inclination nor the energy.

"What....what are you doing here?"

The hatred and fear in his voice was both satisfying and unsettling, yet I was not about to let him see that he had rattled me.

"Father, is that any way to greet a beloved son, your only son?" I asked smoothly. Taking another step towards him, Lucius jerked and fell off the bed, landing in a filthy heap at my feet. I looked down at him with contempt as he scuttled like a crab into the corner, whimpering in naked fear.

"Why are you afraid, Father? What do you think I'm going to do?"

"You're here to kill me! I know why you're here! You want all that I have, and you're here to take it from me by killing me!"

I am not sure how long I laughed, but I was soon gasping for breath and forced to sit on the corner of his bed as he stared at me in gape-mouthed astonishment, unsure if I had gone mad. Catching my breath, I pulled the purse tied to my belt. In it were freshly minted gold denarii, and although it represented perhaps a third of my wealth at that time, just what I carried could have bought my father's farm and everything on it several times over. Contemptuously, I dropped the purse on the floor in front of him, the sound of the coins clashing together making a heavy, metallic sound.

"Lucius," I sneered, "I could buy this place, and a dozen like it just in what I carry on my belt. Believe me; you have nothing I want, except one thing."

A look of naked avarice filled my father's face as his addled mind tried to calculate how much wine could be bought with what I carried, and in front of my eyes he actually began salivating at the thought, a thin line of drool falling from his chin like the silver thread of a spider's web. My disgust for him could not have been any higher than it was at that moment, yet I forced myself to remain as businesslike as I could.

"Well, what is it, boy?"

Standing up, I walked closer to him, then squatted so I could look him directly in the eyes, causing him to push himself hard against the wall.

"You know what I want, Lucius. I'm here to buy Phocas' freedom."

I was sure that my father could no longer hurt me, and I was right at least physically, but he still could draw blood with a few words. His voice was filled with a malicious glee when he shot back, "Too bad you didn't come a few months sooner. I'd have made more money selling the both of them."

Fighting the urge to reach out and strike him, I settled instead for simply saying, "Yes, that would have been nice. More money means you could have drunk yourself to death more quickly. Name a price, old man."

I had to satisfy myself with the look on his face as I left the room.

I wish I could say that there were no more shocks or surprises waiting for me, but when I returned to the main room, I could tell by the way Gisela and Phocas quickly stopped talking, and the way that Gisela avoided my gaze that more bad news awaited.

Sighing, I sat down and asked Phocas, "What else?"

He gulped a swallow of wine before speaking, deepening my anxiety. "It's about Livia," he began, and just the way he said it told me everything.

My throat tightened, and I managed only a strangled, "How? When?"

Looking at me with great sympathy, Phocas put his hand on my shoulder, his grip still strong from years of hard work. "She died in childbirth, Titus. Three months ago."

I had not thought it possible that I could feel worse just a few moments before, but I was wrong. And I am ashamed to say that almost as quickly as fresh sorrow hit me, it was followed by the thought that the same fate could befall Gisela. Phocas knew me, and he knew my mind, which is why his hand on my shoulder was such a comfort. Looking over at Gisela, I saw she was gazing at me with an expression I had never really seen before.

"How's Cyclops?"

My question caused another hesitation, so I prepared for more bad news, though it was not quite what I expected. "I don't know," Phocas replied, "he disappeared just a few days after she died. Nobody has heard from him since."

I absorbed this, feeling the weight of gloom and guilt settling on me. Phocas decided I needed some good news. "Valeria thrives," my head came up at this, and seeing my interest, he smiled. "She has two children."

"Two?" I said in surprise.

620

I knew about Gaius, her son who would be about eight years old, but I did not know about the second child.

"Yes, she had a girl a while back. I expect the baby is about six months old now. Her name is........" he searched his memory, looking at the ceiling for a moment, before he brightened, "....Julia, yes that's it. Her name is Julia."

"Well, I plan on going to see her the day after tomorrow. I suppose there's no sense in going to Cyclops' farm."

Phocas shrugged. Gisela, who was silent the whole time, excused herself from the table to relieve herself.

Once she was gone, Phocas asked quietly, "You really love her, don't you?"

I was startled by the question; honestly I had never really thought about it much.

"Yes, I do. Very much."

I tried to keep the surprise out of my voice, but Phocas had known me too long. He grinned and said, "It sneaks up on you, doesn't it?"

I could not help but grin back. As usual, he was right; it had sneaked up on me.

We left for Valeria's farm two days later, shortly before dawn. I finished the transaction with my father giving Phocas his freedom, taking the necessary documents into town after Lucius grudgingly signed them. The look on his toothless face when I contemptuously tossed the agreed amount, contained in a leather bag, into his hands made my stomach turn. He was oblivious to my disgust, licking his lips and peering into the bag, mumbling to himself in glee.

"That should keep you good and drunk for the rest of your life," I said as I walked out of his room, but he made no retort. The morning we left for Valeria's, I asked Phocas to come with us, and my father thought to stop him, demanding that he stay to take care of him.

"I'm sorry sir, but I'm no longer your slave," Phocas told him quietly, and the look on my father's face as he realized exactly what that meant was worth ten purses of the size I paid. With great dignity, Phocas climbed into the wagon, and we rolled out of the yard of the house, leaving my father spluttering in impotent rage and not a little fear. He never had to take care of himself, ever. Now he was all alone, and I could not have been happier. We laughed about that exchange for at least a third of a watch on the road to my sister's, until tears streamed from our eyes. I could not remember a time where I felt as good about myself as I did that day, just watching Phocas' face as the realization that he was truly free finally sunk in. Valeria was as lovely as ever, at least in my eyes. Being a mother agreed with her, and I was quite taken with little Gaius, who followed me everywhere, peppering me with questions about the number of Gauls I had killed.

"He's been completely obsessed by the exploits of his Uncle Titus," Valeria explained, and I shot a quick glance at her husband, but he did not seem to mind. Valeria caught my glance, and after he left to work in the fields, she assured me that he was not jealous. "He never had dreams of glory the way you did," she said, and Gisela interrupted with, "He still does," making Valeria laugh.

Much to my relief, Valeria and Gisela hit it off immediately, and in fact seemed to enter into some sort of silent conspiracy aimed at me, where knowing looks were exchanged between them when I said something. I found it extremely irritating, and it finally forced me to go seek out Valeria's husband Porcinus outside. However, he was really only interested in talking about his crops and his animals, reminding me of why I was so anxious to get off my farm in the first place. The moment I could extricate myself politely, I went and found Gaius. We sat talking for quite a while, and despite myself, I was amused at the idea that I would find the company of an eight year old more desirable than that of other adults. Yet I was fascinated by the way his mind worked, and despite his age he asked some very intelligent questions.

When I commented about this to Valeria, she looked at him with maternal pride and simply said, "Oh yes, he's very smart. In many ways he's like you; I don't think the farm is going to be enough for him."

As she finished that statement an expression of worry clouded her face, and realizing that I had seen that look before when she looked at me, I tried to think of something comforting to tell her, but the truth was there was really nothing to say because I completely understood. I think that is when the idea first formed in my head that somewhere down the road, I would be playing a larger role in Gaius' life.

Spending four days with Valeria and her family, as much as I enjoyed myself, by the end of the third day I was bored out of my mind. Valeria knew me too well for me to hide it from her, but if she was disappointed, she did not show it. The most notable thing that happened occurred on the morning we left to return to Astigi; I was surprised to see Phocas showing no signs of being ready to leave. I was about to talk to him when Valeria caught me and pulled me aside, telling me quietly, "I've asked Phocas to stay here, and he's agreed."

I am not sure why I was surprised, but I was. "Why would he want to do that? He's free now; he can go wherever he wants."

Valeria shook her head, and replied, "Look at him Titus. He's an old man now, and he's worked hard his whole life. He was as much a father to me as he was to you, and I think the least I can do, after what you've done for him, is give him a place where he can live in peace."

I saw the sense in this, but I wanted to make sure that Phocas had indeed agreed to this and was not just going along with Valeria to appease her. I knew how strong-willed she was, so I could imagine that Phocas might have figured that the easiest way of dealing with her was to pretend to go along, then just sneak off in the night, but he was as adamant as she was.

"I'm completely capable of making up my own mind Titus," he sniffed, seeing through my stated reason for asking him. "Your sister may be formidable, but remember I lived with Gaia for 30 years, so I know how to handle a strong woman. No, I'm happy to stay here. Besides, it will do me good to be around Gaius and the baby. Children keep you young, you know."

I knew no such thing, but I was convinced that he was sincere in his desire to stay behind.

"Look at it this way," he finished, "think how angry your father will be when he learns I chose to live with your sister."

That thought indeed brightened my day, and it was in a happy frame of mind that I kissed my sister, picked up Gaius and tossed him laughing in the air one last time, then shook her husband's hand before climbing in the wagon. Gisela and Valeria clung to each other for what seemed to me an inappropriately long time, and through their tears they whispered things to each other that made them both laugh, all the while cutting their eyes towards me. Perhaps, I thought, leaving was not such a bad idea after all. At least they wouldn't be together to hatch plots aimed at me.

Heading for Astigi that morning, being honest, I was more nervous now than at any other point on the trip, because Juno and Gisela were about to meet. It made me anxious on a number of levels; what if they did not get along? What if Gisela was able to tell that at one point I had feelings for Juno? And perhaps more importantly, what would happen if the moment I laid eyes on Juno I realized that those feelings had not completely died, and worst of all, Gisela could tell? Such was my state of mind as we plodded along the road, the wagon kicking up dust, marking our slow progress towards town, and I tried my best to hide my thoughts but Gisela was always able to see through any such attempts on my part.

"What's wrong?" she asked, and I was sure I could detect a note of impatience in her voice, not helping my frame of mind.

"Nothing," I replied a little too quickly, only serving to confirm her suspicions.

She harrumphed, making it clear that she was not buying any such nonsense, though I was thankful that she did not press the issue. However, after a couple of miles of silence, I found myself turning to her.

"It's just that I'm worried that you and Juno won't get along."

I was thankful that, even if she saw through this, she did not choose to make an issue of it. "I'm sure we will get along fine," she announced confidently.

I just hoped she was right, for all of our sakes, or else it would be a long trip back.

Arriving at Vibius' house, I banged on the door. After what seemed like a full watch, it cracked open, and an old crone that had been part of Vibius' household since we were children peered out suspiciously. Her eyes took in the sight of me and Gisela, and despite seeing she recognized me, her reaction was not exactly welcoming. She was never the cheerful sort, but she would at least grunt in recognition and open the door. However, this time she just stood there, not budging. Stifling my impatience, I tried to assume a reasonable tone of voice; I had learned that being a Centurion did not awe civilians nearly as much as Legionaries.

"Is Vibius in? He's expecting us."

Still, she said nothing, but I saw a look of indecision cross her face and I was about to just push the door open to enter when she finally spoke.

"Master Vibius is not receiving any guests today."

She made a move like she was going to close the door, but I stuck my foot out and stopped her.

"We're not guests. You do recognize me, don't you?"

She nodded, but she still stood her ground, although she was looking more and more nervous.

"I know who you are Master Titus, but my orders are very specific, that Master Vibius is not receiving any visitors. Mistress" meaning Vibius' mother "was very specific on that point."

I bit back a curse, feeling my temper rise. "Will you just run and tell Vibius that we're here and see what he says?"

She thought about this for a moment before grudgingly nodding her head, but before I could cross into the vestibule, the normal place for visitors to wait, the door was slammed shut in my face. The look of shock on my face caused Gisela to giggle, which she tried to stifle with limited success, only serving to increase my irritation. When I scowled at her, it only caused the laughter to tumble from her and despite myself, I started laughing too. We were still in this state when the door creaked open and the crone reappeared, this time making no attempt to hide her discomfort.

"I am sorry Master Titus, but my orders remain the same. Master Vibius is not receiving visitors."

"I'm not a visitor, damn you," I barked, causing her to visibly shrink in fear, only making me angrier, but at myself. Standing there for a moment without any idea what to do, I was then struck by an inspiration and reached into my pouch, withdrawing a gold denarius and waving it in front of her. "Old Mater, I understand that you can't let me in. But you know who I am, you know I'm not only Vibius' oldest friend, but I'm also his commanding officer. So you can at least tell me what in Hades is going on, can't you?"

She stared at the denarius, the battle within her showing clearly on her face, and as usual, greed won out. With a speed that would make a Legionary proud, her hand snatched the coin from mine.

"There will be no wedding," she announced, and she could not have shocked us more if she had set herself afire in front of our eyes. I glanced over at Gisela, who looked just as surprised and speechless as I felt. Finally, I managed to splutter out, "What kind of joke is this? This has been arranged for years! What happened?"

The crone shrugged. "The lady," and her emphasis on that term conveyed her feeling that Juno was anything but, "has married another man."

My shock deepened, as did my confusion. "How could that be? Vibius and she had been communicating for years, and believe me, I would have known of such a thing because he would have told me."

"He would have told you," the crone agreed, "if he'd known the truth."

Gisela moved next to me, as rapt in her attention to the woman as I was. Seeing that she had a spellbound audience the crone warmed to the task, first taking a fearful glance over her shoulder then stepping outside, pulling the door closed behind her.

"The lady never told Master Vibius the truth that about a year ago she fell in love with another. They kept their love a secret; nobody knew about it or we would have let Master Vibius know."

"But how could Juno do that to Vibius?" I demanded, my own anger at what she had done surprising me. And Gisela did not miss it either, her eyes narrowing in suspicion, though I was too far gone at that moment to care much.

"Because she's a weakling and a fool," the crone spat, and for a moment we stood silently, sharing in our mutual loathing for someone who betrayed someone we cared about.

"When did Vibius find out?" Gisela asked.

"Not until three days ago," the crone replied.

"Three days ago! We've been home for more than a week! How did she avoid telling him for so long?" I was completely mystified.

"Oh, the usual ways a woman uses when she doesn't want to see a man. She claimed to be ill, to be having female troubles, but it wasn't until Master Vibius finally went to her house and more or less broke down the door and confronted her that the truth came out."

"What happened?" I asked. "He didn't hurt anybody, did he?"

She shook her head. "No, it was even worse than that. Paulus, one of the house servants who went with him said it was like all the life went out of him. He didn't do anything, he didn't say anything. He just turned and left. He came back to the house, locked himself in his room, and he's been there ever since."

"He didn't........." I almost could not bring myself to say it aloud, but I still had to know, ".....cry, did he? I mean," I said hastily when I heard Gisela's snort of anger, "in front of her?"

She shook her head again. "No, he kept his *dignitas*; at least until he got home. Then he howled like Cerberus gone mad all night long and into the next day before the poor thing finally lost his voice."

I did not know what to say; selfishly, this had as much of an impact on my life in some ways as it did Vibius. Gisela would not have a companion to help her when her time came, yet I could not begin to imagine how Vibius was feeling, and in turn I felt totally helpless. I thanked the crone, who disappeared back inside the house. Turning to Gisela, I said, "We need to go get a room at the inn. I don't think we're going to be staying here."

The gods have a sense of humor, I have always believed that, but I have also learned that it is usually a cruel one, and it was at this moment they chose to play a little prank on Gisela and me as we walked to the inn. We were just approaching the forum, with Gisela and I completely engrossed in conversation about what we had just learned, so that when we turned the corner and almost bumped into two people, it was not particularly surprising that we did not notice them. But when I turned away from Gisela to excuse ourselves, I found myself staring into a familiar pair of eyes, open wide in what was clearly as much fear as surprise, eyes that I first gazed into on a dusty day long ago after rescuing my best friend from a bucket of *cac*. Both of us stood stock still, and while my eyes never left her face, my mind registered a figure standing next to her, a man a few inches shorter than me, which was not unusual, but of almost as muscular a build as me, which was. Nevertheless, my eyes never left Juno's, so I do not know how long we stood there before her mouth actually produced an intelligible sound.

"*Sa..sa..salve*, Titus," she stammered, then before she could say another word, I felt my own come tumbling out.

"How could you do this to Vibius, you.......whore?"

I did not even know I was going to say it, and the instant the word came out she looked like I slapped her, and I heard Gisela gasp behind me. However, it was the man with her, who I assumed was the bastard who had stolen her, that took a menacing step towards me, his hand moving to a civilian dagger at his belt. Before either of us knew what was happening my hand, as if possessing a mind of its own, grasped the hilt of my sword, pulling it in one smooth motion and placing the tip of the blade against the man's throat, my arm held straight out. All it would take was not much more than a twitch of my shoulder and the blade would punch through his throat. A part of me was grimly amused at the idea that here I was on only my second visit home, and I was already about to kill someone else. For his part, the man did the right thing, standing completely motionless, all hint of aggression gone from his face and body.

"Titus, please, I beg you don't kill Quintus. He's my husband! I can't tell you how horrible I feel....." I must say that the fear I heard in Juno's voice was quite satisfying.

"Shut up," I told her quietly. "Let the men talk."

628

Locking my gaze with Quintus, I took his measure, while he took mine, and I saw with some sadness that there was not much there that I thought worthy. Oh, he was strong enough physically; I learned that he was a smith, actually running a very successful business with several apprentices and journeymen under him. But there was no spark there, no anger at having a blade at his throat, no hint of defiance that told me that while I may have gotten the best of him that moment, he would not forget and I would have to look over my shoulder the rest of my life. Instead, there was just the naked fear that a civilian has for a trained soldier, and I would be lying if I said I did not savor the moment.

"So, Quintus is it? Tell me why I shouldn't kill you, Quintus. You stole the woman of my best friend, you ruined his life." I sighed, shaking my head in mock sorrow, "I must be getting old and soft because by rights your head should be rolling at my feet right now. So give me a reason why I shouldn't avenge him this very moment."

"Please sir," he possessed what I thought was a whining quality to his voice, but was actually a bit lower pitched than mine, though it may have been due to the circumstances of the moment, "I didn't mean your friend any harm. I only recently came to Astigi to start my own smithy, so I didn't know beforehand that she had ever been involved with someone else. In truth, I didn't even know she was betrothed for some time after we met, and by the time I knew, well," he ended with a shrug.

I turned to look at Juno, surprised by what I had just heard. "Is that true, Juno? You didn't tell Quintus here that you had sworn an oath to be true to Vibius?"

Juno refused to meet my gaze, looking at the ground, her shoulders hunched in misery as tears started flowing down her cheeks. For a moment she did not speak, then spoke in a small voice, "I was confused Titus. I didn't know what to do. I had waited so long, and I was so lonely........."

Now I felt real anger stirring in me. "You were lonely?" I spat. "And you think Vibius wasn't? Do you know he never took a woman, even for a night, because he loved you so much?"

Despite this not being the exact truth, it was near enough as far as I was concerned, because Vibius certainly never had a lasting

629

relationship with any woman. Now Juno broke out into open sobs, and despite not wanting it to I felt my anger soften a bit; it was clear that Juno was feeling some sort of pain and remorse. Nevertheless, I still felt like I had not done enough for Vibius.

"So how many other men have you been with, whore? How will Quintus ever be able to trust you knowing what you did to Vibius?" I said this both for Quintus and for Juno, although it was more to hurt Juno than anything, but I saw that my words scored a hit on Quintus, his expression immediately changing. It was clear he had never thought about this, yet now that I planted the seed, I knew it would take root and grow, and he would never look the same at Juno again. It did not feel as good as I thought it would, but I had already uttered the words, so it was too late to bring them back now. Juno, if it were possible, looked even more hurt and wounded than she had a moment before. Despite the look on her face, I am a professional, and have learned to finish the job even if I find it distasteful, so while I found I was losing the taste for this, I was determined to deliver the killing blow.

"Know this, Juno. I'm not a religious man but I'm going to make an offering to Dis to curse this marriage, and to your namesake Juno, as well as to Lucina that you're barren and bear no children. I wish on you nothing but pain and sorrow for what you did to Vibius, who was more true and faithful to you than you obviously deserved. As of this moment, you're dead to me."

I turned to Quintus. "Quintus, I bear you no real malice, but know this. The next time I see you, you better run the other way, because I'll kill you where you stand."

Without another word, I grabbed Gisela's hand and pushed past them, leaving Juno standing white-faced and trembling in fear, with Quintus in much the same condition.

For a few moments, neither of us spoke as my temper cooled, before Gisela finally said quietly, "Remind me never to make you truly angry."

Gisela and I spent several more days in the inn, and every day I would go to the house, only to be told that Vibius was not accepting visitors. Finally, I had enough, waiting only long enough for the crone to intone the by-now familiar words before I roughly pushed past her to enter the house. On this day I decided to wear my uniform, so that Vibius' family would know that I was here on official business as Vibius' commanding officer and not as his friend. I did not take this action lightly, because I knew that it was going to cause perhaps an irreparable rift, if not with Vibius himself, then his family. His mother was standing in the main room, alerted to my intrusion by the sound of the crone's calls for help that someone had broken into the house. She was clutching a kitchen knife, a defiant yet fearful look on her face, but when she recognized me she sagged in relief.

"Titus Pullus, you nearly scared me to death," she gasped, clutching her heart.

However, I did not smile, or try to give her any comfort in any way; I had hardened my heart to do what I needed to do. "I'm here on official business, Domitia," I was using what I thought of as my professional voice, which had the desired effect.

The smile froze on her face, the impact of my words sinking in. "Wha…what does that mean, Titus?"

"It means I'm here to fetch Sergeant Domitius back to return to the Legions. Our leave is almost up, and we'll have to hurry to get back to the Legion on time. We can delay no longer."

"But he's not ready to travel, Titus," she protested, making a move to block my way when I began to move towards Vibius' room.

Staring down at her, I held my gaze until her defiance withered under my glare. "Don't try and stop me, Domitia. I'm doing what's best for Vibius."

"You're doing what's best for yourself, Titus," she hissed, her anger and mother's instinct getting the better of her composure. "You don't care a rotten fig for Vibius, it's your precious career that means more to you, and that's the only reason why you're here."

My surprise at her words evidently was written on my face, because it clearly gave her courage. "Oh yes, don't think I don't know. Vibius has been writing for years, and he told us how you turned your back on him to pursue your precious career, so don't pretend that you care what happens to him now."

I felt like I was struck in the gut, but falling back on the discipline instilled by my years in the Legion, I kept my face a cold mask. "If what you say is true, then you know that I'll stop at nothing to bring Vibius back," I replied coolly, stepping past her to walk to Vibius' room. Without bothering to knock, I kicked the door open, causing a satisfying crash as it flew against the wall. The room was dark and stank to high heaven, and I could just make out a lump lying in a bed in the corner that scarcely stirred at the noise.

"Sergeant Domitius, on your feet," I roared, but I was rewarded only with a slight movement. Once my eyes adjusted to the gloom, I walked over to the bed, seeing just the top of Vibius' head poking out from underneath the covers. Kicking the foot of the bed with my boot, I was rewarded with a low groan.

"Go away Titus, I don't want to talk to you."

"There's no Titus here," I told him coldly, "and you'll get on your feet when addressing your senior Centurion."

I had hoped that this would be enough to give Vibius the needed impetus to get up, but he had always been stubborn. "Don't pull rank on me," his voice was muffled by the covers, yet I could hear plainly enough the beginnings of anger in his voice. Good, I thought, that's a start. Instead of kicking the bed again, I reached down, grabbing one corner to give it a good yank, turning the mattress over and dumping Vibius out on the floor. His nightclothes were stained with wine and I did not want to speculate what else, yet he got to his feet quickly enough, letting out a huge roar of anger as he turned on me. Before he could get any closer, I lashed out with my *vitus*, striking him hard in the ribs, causing him to gasp with pain. Despite the blow he kept his feet. Any other man would have buckled under that, I thought with some pride, but not Vibius. For his part, it just made him angrier and he charged at me headlong, his speed once again catching me by surprise. Even as I fell backwards, I thought with some chagrin that I always forgot how fast he really was. Tumbling into a heap on the floor, the combination of my armor and the weight of his body forced the air from my lungs in an explosive gasp. Encouraged by this sound, Vibius began to thrash at me, but I was able to block most of the blows with my arms, although a couple landed along my body, sending shafts of pain shooting through me. I was content to let him tire himself out and was glad to see that at least the slack living and moping about had sapped his conditioning, because it was only a few moments before

632

I felt his strength flagging. Once he paused, I heaved him off of me, throwing him across the room while leaping to my feet, crossing to him before he could recover. I did not use my fists, because that would have been personal, instead thrashing him with my *vitus*, using it like he was a *tiro* in his first month of training and I did not stop until he was curled up in a ball, trying to protect himself. Finally finished I stood panting over him, and said harshly, "I won't enter this into the official record Sergeant, since you know the penalty for striking a superior officer is running the gauntlet, followed by crucifixion," I heard his mother gasp at this, "but I'm not going to tell you again. We're leaving to return back to the Legion in a third of a watch. I expect you to be standing outside this house, fully packed and in full uniform, ready to go. Do you understand me?"

It seemed like forever, but was probably only a few heartbeats before he answered, "Yes, Pilus Prior. I understand. And I will obey."

I grunted. "Very good. Now," I turned to leave, "clean yourself up and say goodbye to your family. The 10th is waiting for us."

Ignoring his mother's poisonous stare as I left his room, I exited the house. I knew that there was a good chance that our friendship was now ruined beyond repair. But Vibius' mother was right; I would not jeopardize my career for anything, or anyone.

It would be a lie if I said that I was not a little surprised to see Vibius standing outside his house, pale and looking haggard, but in an immaculate uniform. The servants must have been jumping through their own assholes, I thought wryly when Gisela and I pulled up in the wagon. This was the first that Gisela had seen Vibius since we learned of Juno's betrayal, and I was glad that only I heard her sharp intake of breath at the sight of him.

The moment we pulled up, Vibius snapped to *intente,* giving his best parade ground salute, intoning in the expressionless voice that all rankers use to let their superiors know what they truly thought of them, "Good morning Pilus Prior."

Then, with a shade more warmth he turned and said, "Good morning Gisela."

"Good morning, Vibius," Gisela replied in a cheerful tone that I recognized was forced, although Vibius did not seem to notice. "Lovely day to start back, don't you think?"

Vibius shrugged as he threw his gear in the back before climbing into the back of the wagon. "Good as any, I suppose. Ready when you are, Pilus Prior."

I do not know why I was hoping for anything other than what I was getting, yet I was disappointed nonetheless. I only hoped that things would return to a semblance of normality at some point in the near future. Once he was settled in, I slapped the reins, beginning our journey back to the base as I idly wondered whether or not my nemesis Celer had returned and been making trouble for me after arranging his father's affairs. Suddenly, it did not seem to be so important now.

The trip back was a misery. Vibius was determined to make me feel as guilty as possible. While in the beginning he at least made a pretense of communicating with me, albeit always in an official tone, he finally dropped even that. By the end of the second day, we were reduced to using Gisela as our medium; I would ask Vibius a question, except it would be asked of Gisela. In turn Vibius would respond to Gisela, who would roll her eyes, but thankfully played along with the game. By the third day I grew tired of this and just stopped talking, at Vibius or to Gisela for that matter, my mood becoming so pervasive that they rarely spoke either. Consequently, it was a silent, sullen lot that traveled the roads back to the base. Our only relief came when we would stop for the night at some inn, where we could freely engage in conversation with strangers, and it was on the road back that we heard the first bits about what was happening in the wider world since we had been gone.

"Caesar's a plucked and boiled chicken, that's what I say," we overheard an olive oil merchant from Campania telling a younger man dressed as a knight, at an inn still a few days away from Narbo. "Cato has him by the short hairs, that's for sure," he continued, and both Vibius and I, our differences temporarily forgotten, exchanged a glance. I raised an eyebrow in a silent signal and Vibius nodded, getting up from our table to walk over to sit next to the merchant. This was something we had long since perfected; Vibius being a much less imposing figure than I was, people warmed up to him more easily.

"Say you, friend. I couldn't help but overhear," he said genially, "what's this business you speak of? What about Caesar?"

The merchant looked Vibius up and down, both of us having changed into our only civilian outfits for the journey, but we were still wearing our boots and our belts, telling everyone that we were from the Legions.

"Soldier, eh?"

There was no malice in the merchant's tone like we sometimes ran into, and Vibius, picking up on the lack of hostility, nodded. "Home on leave down to Astigi," he told the man, "now returning to our base."

"What Legion are you with?" the young knight asked.

"The 10th," Vibius responded, and even from across the room I could hear the pride in his voice. The effect on the others was palpable; the 10th's fame was now well-known throughout the Republic and the provinces.

"Caesar's favorites," the merchant's tone was admiring. Then, he turned cautious, "Say, if I tell you what's happening, you're not going to take out Caesar's troubles on us, are you? I mean, we're just the messengers here."

Vibius laughed, "No chance of that, friend. What happens to Caesar is his trouble, not mine. I'm just curious, that's all."

That was not exactly true, but it satisfied the two men at the table, and they filled Vibius in, either not knowing or not caring that there were two other sets of ears listening avidly to the news. The merchant was not exaggerating; Caesar was indeed in a tight spot. His old nemesis Cato had been a constant thorn in Caesar's side for years, yet now the situation was becoming dangerous. Cato was working tirelessly to see that once Caesar's term as governor of Gaul expired, he would be tried for a variety of crimes, most of them actions that we were involved in to one degree or another. Most troubling to the Legions was the charge of massacring the Usipetes and Tencteri those years ago, and despite not understanding exactly why we did it, I did not think it just to try to punish Caesar for it. There was a war going on for gods' sakes, what did the fine gentlemen of the Senate expect? To forestall the prosecution, Caesar decided to run for Consul, and was working the system to ensure his election. The problem lay in the fact that the only way he could run for Consul was to give up command of his army to enter the city, yet the moment he did that he lost his imperium, and with it the immunity from prosecution. He attempted to have a measure passed in the Senate exempting him from this rule, but Cato and his allies blocked it. Now, just a few months away from the end of Caesar's governorship, this was the situation he faced. A complicating factor was Pompey, the old war horse and the man who had been the First Man since Vibius and I were born, but whose primacy was being eclipsed by Caesar. Despite being bound by oath, and by the marriage of Pompey to Caesar's daughter Julia, her death in childbirth cut the last real tie that bound the two together. Cato was continuously in Pompey's ear, dripping all sorts of poison about Caesar into it, meaning the rift between the two was ever widening. This was the situation to which we were returning, and needless to say, it gave us a sense of urgency as we increased our pace back to the base the next morning.

Arriving back at Narbo with a day to spare on our leave I put it to good use by finding a midwife for Gisela, and making other arrangements that she deemed necessary. She tolerated the trip very well, but I could see that she was tired and needed rest by the time we got back to base. The situation with Caesar had one salutary effect; Vibius and I began talking again, albeit only on political matters, but I hoped that it was a start to repairing our relationship. Even better for me was that Celer had only gotten back a couple days before us, giving him no time to make much mischief, and his toady Niger was useless without him. The Cohort ran smoothly under Priscus; I was happy to see that the punishment list was very short, Priscus having given his report in my quarters the moment he knew I had returned.

"Excellent job, Priscus. Thank you." He was standing in front of my desk in my quarters in camp.

He shrugged, yet I could tell he was pleased. "Just doing my job Pilus Prior," he said modestly.

"That's true, but it's still good to know I don't have to look over my shoulder when I leave you in charge." We both laughed; he knew exactly what I meant.

The Legion was buzzing with activity and gossip and we were assailed on a daily basis with news from Rome. One of the most difficult aspects was trying to separate fact from fiction; one day, the word spread through the camp that Caesar was arrested, and thrown from the Tarpeian Rock, causing a near-riot before the culprit who spread the rumor was found and flogged until he confessed that he made it up out of boredom. Then there was the word that Pompey had gathered his Legions and was marching on Caesar at Ravenna, where he decided to spend the winter, quickly followed by a counter-rumor that it was Caesar who was marching on Rome. That, as it turned out, was the truth. Caesar crossed the Rubicon with the 13th Legion, and was moving on Rome. And Gisela went into labor a week early.

Chapter 14- Rubicon

L ooking back, it is difficult for me to clearly separate the events that took place over those next weeks. What I remember are bits and pieces of memories, flashes of conversations, so once again I will be relying on the Commentaries to provide a chronological order to the events that had such a huge impact, not only on me but on the fate of Rome itself. Essentially, as I mentioned before, Caesar was on the horns of a dilemma. Despite having managed, through Pompey's efforts, to have a law enacted that allowed him to stand for a second Consulship in absentia, making it so that he did not have to surrender the imperium that came with his governorship, his enemies were not defeated, staying very busy hatching plots to destroy him. Also, Pompey changed the law concerning the interval between which a candidate could hold a city office such as Consul or Urban Praetor, and the beginning of a governorship of a province. What this meant in effect was that a man other than a Consul of the previous year could hold a governorship. In theory this could help Caesar, except that two of his bitter opponents, Aemilius Paullus and Claudius Marcellus were elected Consul, whereupon they immediately put forward a motion to recall Caesar immediately, months before he could run for Consul. This would make Caesar a private citizen and strip him of his imperium and immunity, making it clear that his enemies, Cato being principal among them, would use that status to destroy Caesar. However, Caesar was not standing idly by, buying one of the Tribunes of the Plebs, a young rake named Curio who used the Tribunician veto to forestall Caesar's recall. Meanwhile, negotiations were taking place to attempt a peaceful solution between Pompey and Caesar, with intermediaries coming and going between the two with proposals and counterproposals. Curio, whose alliance with Caesar was a secret at the time, put forward a proposal that garnered a great deal of support with the moderates; namely, that both Pompey and Caesar lay down the command of their respective armies at the same time. As promising as this may have been for a peaceful resolution, there were powerful men who wanted no such thing. Unsurprisingly Cato was the primary force behind those who opposed Curio's proposal, and I place most of the blame for what happened on his shoulders. Even Vibius was uncomfortable with the developments engineered by Cato, although it was his actions that actually got Vibius and I talking again in a manner that was almost back to normal. I was visiting my old tentmates, where naturally the topic of conversation was the events in Rome, and more importantly to us, when Caesar would be calling us. To that point, only the 13th was with him, but orders had come to begin preparations to march, so I had been inspecting the Cohort's readiness before stopping by.

"So Pullus, what's the latest? When do we move?" Scribonius asked as he worked on polishing his helmet.

I shrugged. "I haven't heard anything more than what I've already passed on, other than all the crazy rumors."

I remembered something. "Oh, I did hear that Pompey has summoned the Legions from Spain."

The 6th had been recalled from their service with Caesar some time before, an act that was certainly within Pompey's rights, but it was also an ominous sign, along with Caesar surrendering the 15th, thereby reducing the forces at his disposal. Both Legions were now sitting in Italy, waiting for orders. Supposedly they were bound for an expedition to Parthia, but nobody believed that.

"Well, I hope that prick Cato ends up on a cross, that's all I can say," declared Vellusius.

Almost immediately all eyes darted over to Vibius, who was sitting silently in the corner, stuffing items into the pack that would be loaded on the Cohort baggage wagon. He did not answer at first, then seemed to notice the silence, and looking up to see all eyes on him, he shrugged. "Well, I wouldn't go that far, but I definitely think that he's put Caesar into a no-win position, and I think he's brought about the ruin of the Republic, even though I know that was the exact opposite he intended."

You could have heard a mouse fart; this was certainly not what we expected to hear from Vibius of all people, who had been a strong Catonian for years.

"Hopefully a peaceful solution will still win out," Scribonius said; he was always the peacemaker among my tentmates. He was a fierce fighter, yet he hated to see any kind of conflict between his friends. This time, his attempt was met with open disagreement from all of us.

"Not likely," Vibius shook his head. "I think things have gone too far, and honestly, I don't think those boys in the Senate, Cato leading the way," with that he glanced meaningfully at me, "want a peaceful solution. Between what Marcellus did in flogging that official from Novum Comum, and them spitting on the proposal for both sides to disarm, I say we're marching in a month, maybe sooner. What do you say, Titus?"

This was the first non-official exchange between Vibius and me since I kicked him out of bed back home, and I was smart enough to recognize the peace offering for what it was. I also knew it was no time to quibble about him calling me by my first name in front of others, no matter how old friends they may have been, also recognizing that this was his way of testing the waters. If I corrected him, our friendship would more than likely never be repaired. Still, even knowing that I hesitated for a fraction of a heartbeat, a part of my brain screaming at me to upbraid him for his lapse. I am glad I did not listen.

"I think you're right, Vibius," I said quietly. "I think we're going to war, sooner rather than later."

"I wonder what it's like fighting our own?" Scribonius asked, and while at that point it was somewhat of a rhetorical question, I know that it was a topic that filled my mind. It comforted me to know that I was not the only one who was thinking such thoughts.

"We'll at least know what they're going to do, not like those fucking Gauls," Didius spoke for the first time from his spot, lounging on his bed closest to the fire. I still did not like Didius much, and I had my doubts about how reliable he would be in a really hard fight, but like it or not, he was one of us, my longest and best companions, no matter how high up the ranks I climbed.

640

Besides, what he said was true, and there was a chorus of agreement from the rest of us.

"Still," Scribonius insisted, "it's going to be strange looking over the shield and seeing another Roman doing the same thing."

"I just hope it's nobody we know," Vellusius replied, and that sentiment touched the nub of what was bothering us all. It was bad enough that we would most likely be facing our own kind, but the thought that we might have to fight and kill someone with whom we sweat and bled was what kept us up at night. With that last comment, I excused myself and left their quarters. I had gone only a few paces when I heard Vibius call my name, so I turned and waited for him to come to me, where we stood for a moment, neither of us speaking. I was not sure what was on his mind and did not feel right saying anything first, mainly out of foolish pride, which was probably what kept him rooted there.

Finally, he blurted, "Look, Titus. I just wanted to thank you for giving me the boot in the ass back home. I was........."

I stopped him there. "No apology necessary, Vibius. You'd have done the same for me. And," I added with a grin, "I'd have been mightily pissed at you for probably longer than you've been at me." I gave him a friendly push, and laughed, "Although I would have kicked your ass."

"In your dreams," he snorted. "You're strong, but you're slow as an ox. I," he drew himself up to his full height of five feet four inches, "am lightning. You never know where I'll strike."

Now it was my turn to snort in derision. "I seem to remember catching that lightning a time or two."

"A blind dog'll find a bone every now and then," he retorted, and our bickering continued all the way back to my quarters, lasting through a jug of wine.

Events were gaining momentum; after crossing the Rubicon, Caesar invested Ariminum, Pisarum and a number of other towns, all without any violence. Despite, or perhaps because the Senate was against Caesar, the people were solidly behind him, and it was the citizens of the towns who forced the Senatorial garrisons to surrender. Some of the fine gentlemen commanding the garrisons remained true to the cause of the Senate, but an equally large, if not larger number came over to Caesar's side at the first opportunity. The 12th was summoned, joining Caesar when he moved into what was supposedly the heart of Pompeian territory, his home province of Picenum. Even there, the people were either solidly behind Caesar, or so half-hearted in their support of Pompey that Caesar encountered no real opposition. It was not until Caesar, with some Cohorts of the 13th, and reinforced by the 12th, reached Corfinium that he met anything that could be called resistance. Domitius Ahenobarbus, one of his bitterest opponents commanded what amounted to three full Legions, 30 Cohorts of men, but they were all raw *tirones*, and there was no doubt that our boys would slaughter them. However, Ahenobarbus' hatred of Caesar blinded him to this military reality, so he made preparations to defend Corfinium. By this time the 8th, along with a total of 22 Cohorts of the levies that Caesar raised to protect The Province to defend from Lucterius' thrust during the rebellion of Vercingetorix, also joined Caesar and the army, and with this force he invested Corfinium. Before the encirclement was complete, a final message from Pompey reached Ahenobarbus that let him know that he was on his own, that Pompey considered what he was doing foolish in the extreme and that he had no intention of risking the two veteran Legions closest to hand, the 1st and 3rd in a risky gambit to relieve the town. Ahenobarbus, now that he was forced to face the fact that his cause was futile, apparently began planning for his own escape, despite telling the boys in his army that all was well and help was on the way. His men got wind of the truth, consequently sending their own envoys to Caesar so that just seven days after Caesar arrived, Corfinium fell without a fight. It was at Corfinium that I believe Caesar made one of his greatest errors, although I say this with the unerring accuracy of vision supplied by hindsight. There were more than 50 men of the Senate and equestrian order who were in Corfinium, almost all of them staunch Pompeians, yet Caesar not only let them all go free, he also did nothing to Ahenobarbus, a man who was one of his bitterest enemies for more than ten years. Caesar also returned the pay chest of 6,000,000 sesterces that was there to pay the troops, in a sign that he was not after pursuing wealth but only wanted to assert his rights as a Roman citizen. His clemency certainly helped to win the populace over to his side, although I can tell you that it was not very popular with the Legions, particular his very strict orders against looting, even if I for one could see the sense of that. Caesar might be able to beat the combined forces of the "good men", but he could not beat both them and the ill-will of the people. There is nothing

642

quite like having all your possessions taken then seeing your wife and daughter raped to give a man a bitter feeling towards someone. Nevertheless, his generosity and clemency was a case of casting pearls before swine, particularly with the likes of Ahenobarbus, who swore an oath that he would not oppose Caesar, but immediately broke it the moment he was a mile down the road. I cannot help but wonder if Caesar had been a little more bloody-minded, particularly with the men like Ahenobarbus, if things would have turned out differently.

I do not want to paint a picture that Caesar suffered no setbacks of any kind, because that is not the case, and one of those setbacks was more of personal betrayal, at least as far as we were concerned. Labienus, who commanded the 10th most of our time in Gaul and was the Legate in charge of our camp at Narbo, defected to Pompey. I cannot speak for Caesar, especially given his public reaction, yet to a man the 10th took this as one of the bitterest blows of the whole civil war. From our viewpoint, Labienus owed all that he was to Caesar but he obviously did not see it that way. In fact, as we were to learn over the next several months, according to Labienus it was the other way around; he had made Caesar the man he was. I will grant that Labienus was a good general; he knew how, and more importantly when to fight and when not to, but he was not even a full shadow of the leader that Caesar was. We respected him, but we did not love him the way we loved Caesar and there was more than one man in the army who would have slit his gullet wide open if he thought he could get away with it. However, Caesar made no public, or private as far as I know, comment against Labienus and indeed, ordered that all of his baggage, including all the loot that he was awarded by Caesar, be sent after him. For his part, Labienus never made any kind of sign of gratitude for that gesture, but the gods always have a way of evening the scales, and Labienus' day of reckoning was waiting down the road. At the time, however, his actions brought a stain of dishonor to the 10th, at least as far as we saw it. Thankfully, Caesar did not feel the same way.

Caesar's move through Italy was so rapid and his conquest, albeit bloodless, so complete that Pompey, the Senate and all of those aligned with them, having first abandoned Rome, now made to abandon Italy, with Pompey marshaling his army at Brundisium for shipment to Greece. Caesar set off in hot pursuit with the 8th, 12th, 13th, and a new Legion he formed out of the Cohorts from Transalpine Gaul that he named the 5th Larks. Whether they were so named because he authorized them to wear those feathers as crests for their helmets, or they wore the feathers in their crests because of what he named them, I never knew. Pompey may not have been the boldest general, at least now that he was older, but he was a master of logistics, and I do not think it is insulting to Caesar or his memory to acknowledge that Pompey's organization and skill at moving large numbers of men was unparalleled. These qualities enabled him to withdraw his entire force almost completely intact, despite the fact that Caesar and the army arrived at Brundisium several days before the evacuation, making several attempts to stop the crossing. Only two ships were lost, run aground on booms that Caesar ordered constructed in an attempt at cutting off the harbor while Pompey, his supporters and the rest of his army made it away safely. More importantly, Pompey took the entire merchant and military shipping with him, leaving Caesar nothing with which to pursue. He would have to buy and build a fleet of his own, and that task would take months. During the week that Caesar and Pompey were in close proximity to each other, Caesar made several attempts to arrange a face-to-face meeting with Pompey, in a last-ditch attempt to avoid a full-blown and bloody civil war, but Pompey steadfastly refused. Therefore, Caesar was left standing on the shore, watching Pompey run away. There was nothing left to do at that time but go to Rome.

As interesting and as much of an impact on my, and the Republic's, future all these events were having, I still found it hard to devote my full attention to matters. Gisela tolerated the hard journey, along with the tension between Vibius and me on the way back, about as well as one could reasonably expect and she gave no signs of distress in the days leading up to the birth of our child. Nevertheless, a full week before the midwife, the soothsayers and the medicine men from Gisela's people had said, she woke me one night by punching me full in the chest. Jerking awake, I found her sitting up, gasping in pain, her knees up. My heart started hammering; I had no idea what to do. We had arranged for the midwife to begin her vigil, staying at our house, but she would not start that for a couple more days. Fumbling around, I managed to get a lamp lit, then just sat there dumbly at the edge of the bed, looking at her. There was a stain of something wet spreading on the mattress from between her legs and I felt my stomach lurch, the sight of it rooting me to the spot, paralyzed.

"Titus, you idiot! Don't sit there like a useless lump. Go get Thuria! Then have the boy go get the midwife. My time has come!"

I still did not move; I do not know whether I did not want to believe that the moment had arrived or what, but there I sat. "But...but it's not your time! It's not supposed to be another week!"

"Well, apparently," she said through clenched teeth, "he has other ideas!"

Even through my panic, that one word penetrated through. "He? What do you mean he? How do you know?"

"Because only a man would cause me this much pain," she howled before slapping me, hard, across the face.

That got me moving, I can tell you. Everything after that is a blur; Thuria did her best to calm the both of us while we waited for the midwife, but finally my anxiety was too much and I was banished to the outer room, for which I was eternally thankful. The midwife arrived, and she was the only one of us who did not appear to think this was unusual. I remember confronting her about what it meant that the baby was early, which she shrugged off.

"It might not be," she replied. "Maybe there was a miscalculation of the date. Or," she said over her shoulder as she walked into our bedroom, "it's early."

That was not a great help. The labor lasted gods only know how long; afterwards Gisela told me very surely that it lasted more than four full watches, and I imagine she would know. What I remember most vividly of that night and day was the fear, a fear that I never mentioned to Gisela, but one that she learned from Valeria, that my baby would do the same thing to Gisela that I did to my mother. After all, I killed my mother because of my size, so I had to believe there was a chance of the same thing happening again. I sent for Vibius, who sat with me, doing all he could to take my mind off of my worry, and he was a great help. Even so, the waiting was an agony, but finally in the middle of the afternoon we were rewarded with what sounded to my ears, at least at that moment, like a cat that just had its tail cut off. Vibius and I looked at each other before leaping to our feet and rushing over to the bedroom door, almost bowling over a tired but happy looking midwife who was coming to get me.

"*Salve*, Centurion. Come meet your new son."

There are moments in one's life that are frozen in memory, vivid pictures that can be recalled simply by closing your eyes, summoning that day to be savored, all over again. The moment I held my son is one of those. He was like any other newborn, I suppose, yet at the same time, was something I had never seen before. Even as inexperienced as I was, I could tell that he was a large baby, his weight both heavy and unbearably light at the same time. Heavy with the implication of what I was holding, a new life, one that Gisela and I created, yet less than a shield, barely more than a sword, and more fragile in some ways than either. Looking up at Gisela, shimmering there, resting against the headboard, my tears made her dance in front of me, yet even through the tears I could see her smiling at me, and I have never loved a moment, or any other human beings, as much as I loved my family at that moment.

"His name is Vibius," I said hoarsely, and she did not look surprised in the slightest. I walked over to her, bent down, kissed her forehead and told her, "Thank you."

She laughed, "You're welcome. Now, go show Vibius his namesake."

I was surprised. "How did you know he was here?"

She favored me with that half-amused, half-scornful look that it seems only women can give men they love, and retorted, "Where else would he be? I knew you couldn't do this by yourself."

I did not reply; as usual, she was right. Carrying my son out of the room, I studied him, as he did the same to me. He was very pink, and very wrinkled, and he smelled horribly, but I thought he was the most beautiful thing I had ever seen. Pushing the door open, I saw Vibius standing there, his face a mixture of happiness and what I realized was regret; by rights, this should have been he and Juno, and I should have been the one waiting. It's funny, and cruel, how life works at times.

"Vibius, meet your namesake. Vibius, meet your godfather."

And I handed him over.

Life as a father of a newborn babe was strange, wonderful and extremely trying all at the same time. I think my relationship with my own father in an odd way played a huge role in how much I was involved in the life of young Vibius more than most fathers are, because I was bound and determined that my son would never have the kind of doubt about his father's love that I had suffered and that I would play a part in his life and make him a man in whom I could be proud. Quite naturally, I took a fair bit of ribbing about this attitude from my friends, yet I bore it with as much good humor as I could muster. One thing that helped was that Vibius was just as doting on the babe as I was, and every day, the moment our duties permitted we would find ourselves walking quickly back to my home to listen to Gisela brag about the boy's latest achievements. Frankly, at that point his only accomplishments concerned the prodigious amount of *cac* that he generated on what seemed to be a constant basis. He was a greedy little piglet as well, always hungry, a trait that Gisela laid squarely on my shoulders, which I could not deny. As pleasant as this time was, we all knew that it was just a brief pause in the gathering storm, and young Vibius was just a few weeks old when we were finally given the orders to march, joining up with the bulk of the army. The word was that we would be heading back home to Hispania, where the Pompeians Petreius and Afranius held the province with what we were told was a large and veteran army consisting of some of Pompey's toughest Legions. To prepare ourselves, we picked up the intensity of our training, beginning with forced marches of increasing length and frequency, trying to shake off the rust of the almost two years of relative inactivity. Now that I was Pilus Prior, I had been forced to relinquish my post as training officer, but I kept up my own personal training regimen. What I could do was to make sure that the men in my Cohort were pushed as hard as they could go, and I heard many muttered imprecations aimed at me, which I took as a sign that I was doing what needed to be done. Of course, I had to deal with Celer at every turn, as he did what he could to stir up trouble among the men. He was smart about it, I will give him that; he never openly questioned my orders, instead taking on the role of the sympathetic Centurion, willing to listen to the griping and moaning of some of the men, promising them that he would do what he could to stop the excesses of my training program. Naturally, he did not speak to me once, something that only served to raise the antagonism of the men because they believed that I was refusing to alter my approach. In fairness, I doubt that I would have softened at all, but it would have been good to know that men were complaining. Meanwhile, other preparations intensified as equipment was readied. The artillery was refitted, the axles of all the wagons greased, supplies of grain and chickpeas came rumbling into the camp in a never-ending train.

Caesar would eventually join us, but not until we had already moved across the Pyrenees into the eastern part of Hispania. In command of our march was Fabius, stepping into the role previously played by the traitor Labienus as Caesar's second in command. The army was together almost two weeks before all the Centurions were called to the forum to receive orders, and they were what we had been expecting for days.

"We march tomorrow for Hispania," Fabius announced once we were all quiet.

Despite knowing what was coming, a ripple of excitement still passed through the group of hard-bitten veterans. Fabius waited for the buzz of conversation to die down before continuing, but we only listened with passing attention, since it was the normal drivel that officers tell men in the ranks about glory, honor, duty and the like, and we were much too veteran a group to be taken in by such nonsense. Fortunately, Fabius was a good officer and knew to keep such blather to a minimum, understanding that we were more concerned with the practical considerations of getting our respective Cohorts prepared for movement than anything he could say. Therefore, quickly enough we were dismissed to go about our business.

There is one event that happened before our orders to move out that I feel important to relate, and that was the retirement of the group of men who had formed the backbone of the 10th when we first enlisted. Included in this group was none other than the Primus Pilus Gaius Crastinus, their decision prompting the resulting shuffle in the ranks as men were promoted. I for one was sorry to see Crastinus go, and frankly was a bit surprised that he opted to retire, but when I talked to him, he was adamant.

"I've had enough Pullus," he insisted. "I'm ready for a little peace and quiet. Besides, I don't feel like fighting our own."

I laughed at the idea, but he was serious. Still, when we parted I predicted that our paths would cross again, and I was right.

So this was the situation in those hectic days, just before the storm descended that would wrack the Republic and all its citizens for the next several years. We were marching into an uncertain future, but most of us were resigned to the idea that there would be no solution to Caesar's dilemma without blood being shed. Where some of us differed was how much of it would soak into the soil before matters were resolved, one way or the other. Men that I respected a great deal, Scribonius chiefly among them, were optimistic that perhaps after one or two battles, where the great men saw the terrible cost their ambitions would incur on the Republic and the Legions, some sort of accommodation would be reached. But as much as I respected Scribonius, I was not so inclined; I believed that only after rivers of blood were shed would either side acquiesce, and my only real hope was that it would be Caesar who prevailed. Because now it was not just myself I had to worry about; I had a family who looked to me to protect and provide for them, and it was a worrying feeling that twisted my stomach. Even as we marched away, I could feel that burden with every step I took, moving us farther away from my new family, and down a road with too many twists and turns ahead for me to easily see the end of the journey.

Now I must stop to rest, for which poor Diocles is favoring me with a look of almost pathetic gratefulness. There is still much to relate; more marching, fighting, killing and dying to be done, and more history to be made. However, I am now an old man whose energy fades and I need my sleep so I beg your indulgence, gentle reader. Once refreshed, I will pick up my tale again, for old I may be, but I am still Titus Pullus, Legionary of Rome, and I still have a duty to perform.

Commonly Used Terms

Bracae- Essentially a pair of trousers, favored by Gauls and adopted by the Romans for use in cold weather.

Cac- Unsurprisingly, this is the slang term for shit.

Conquisitore- A minor official charged with the raising of a Legion, once a *dilectus* was called by a Praetor, Consul or ProConsul. In the Imperial period, these positions were much sought-after because of the opportunity for enriching oneself through bribery. During Caesar's time, when the raising of Legions was much less formalized and haphazard, the position was temporary and not as lucrative.

Dilectus- The actual call for enlistment of a Legion. During the early Republican period, Legions were enrolled for single campaign seasons, a practice that soon fell by the wayside as Rome's expansion became more aggressive. Very quickly, the term of enlistment expanded from four, to six, then ten and finally, sixteen years. Although there is no definitive evidence for when this actually began, in Marching With Caesar, the assumption is made that it starts with the first Legion raised by Gaius Julius Caesar, and that was the 10th Legion. This is because the subsequent Legions raised by Caesar, starting with the 11th Legion, were enlisted for a term of sixteen years. Also, it was almost exactly sixteen years after their formation that the 10th mutinied because their discharges were due.

Edepol- An exclamation of surprise, used by Roman males.

Gerrae- Similar to *Edepol*, but was not commonly used by the upper classes. This term is similar to the American Northeast "Get the fuck outta here".

Gregarius- This is the shortened version of the rank *Miles Gregarius*, the first and lowest rank in the Roman Legion. It is akin to the modern day Private.

650

Immune- An *immune* was a Roman Legionary with a particular skill that was deemed vital to the running of a Legion. Unlike their modern counterparts, a Roman Legion was required to be self-sufficient as much as possible, needing only the raw materials to make the implements and weaponry needed to wage war in the Roman fashion. An example of an *immune* would be an armorer, or a leather worker. This was a rank immediately above that of *Gregarius*.

Intente- The Latin command for "Attention", the military command to assume a position of alert readiness for the following command.

Numen- A disembodied spirit or force, *numen* were perhaps the most ancient supernatural form, and as such were much more simplistic and primeval.

Paludamentum- The scarlet cloak worn by Roman commanders of at least Legate rank.

Porro- The Latin command that signals a Legion to begin the assault.

Praetorium- Both the headquarters tent in a Roman military camp, and the residence of the Praetor of a province. In camp, the *Praetorium* is the first tent erected, in the center of the camp, and all the dimensions of the camp were measured from the *Praetorium*.

Probatio- The status for those who have enlisted but not yet started the training in the Legion. While a minor distinction, it was an important one, and represents the need for some sort of hold over a recruit during the period of time it took them to travel to wherever the Legion was being trained, then waiting for the training to begin. This is supposition on my part, but is based on my experience as a recruiter in the Marine Corps. Fundamentally, the reason is pretty simple; while needing to retain some sort of hold over new recruits, it wasn't very likely that they would be subjected to the harsh discipline of the Legions right away, when they were being escorted to their training camp.

Quaestorium- Next to the *Praetorium*, the most important location of a Roman military camp, as it held the quartermaster. It was located next to the *Praetorium*.

Salve- Common form of (formal) greeting. Equivalent of "Hello".

Silete- Latin for silence, this is the more polite way to ask someone to be quiet.

Tacete- The Latin equivalent of "Shut the fuck up".

Tirones- This is the term used for recruits enlisted in the Legions who have actually begun training. This is a distinctly different class than *probatio*, and assumes that the recruit has actually begun the training that was required to become a member of the Legion.

Vitus- The twisted length of vine stick that was a symbol of the Roman Centurion. Even out of uniform, Centurions would carry the *vitus* to let others know their status.